REBECCA SHAW
Three Great Novels

Also by Rebecca Shaw

TALES FROM TURNHAM MALPAS

The Village Show

Village Secrets

Scandal in the Village

Village Gossip

Trouble in the Village

A Village Dilemma

TALES FROM BARLEYBRIDGE

A Country Affair

Country Wives

REBECCA SHAW

Three Great Novels

The New Rector
Talk of the Village
Village Matters

This omnibus edition first published in Great Britain
in 2002 by Orion,
an imprint of the Orion Publishing Group Ltd.

A CIP catalogue record for this book
is available from the British Library.

ISBN 0 75285 286 8

Typeset in Minion at The Spartan Press Ltd,
Lymington, Hants

Printed in Great Britain by Clays Ltd, St Ives plc

The Orion Publishing Group Ltd
Orion House
5 Upper Saint Martin's Lane
London, WC2H 9EA

Contents

The New Rector
Tales from Turnham Malpas

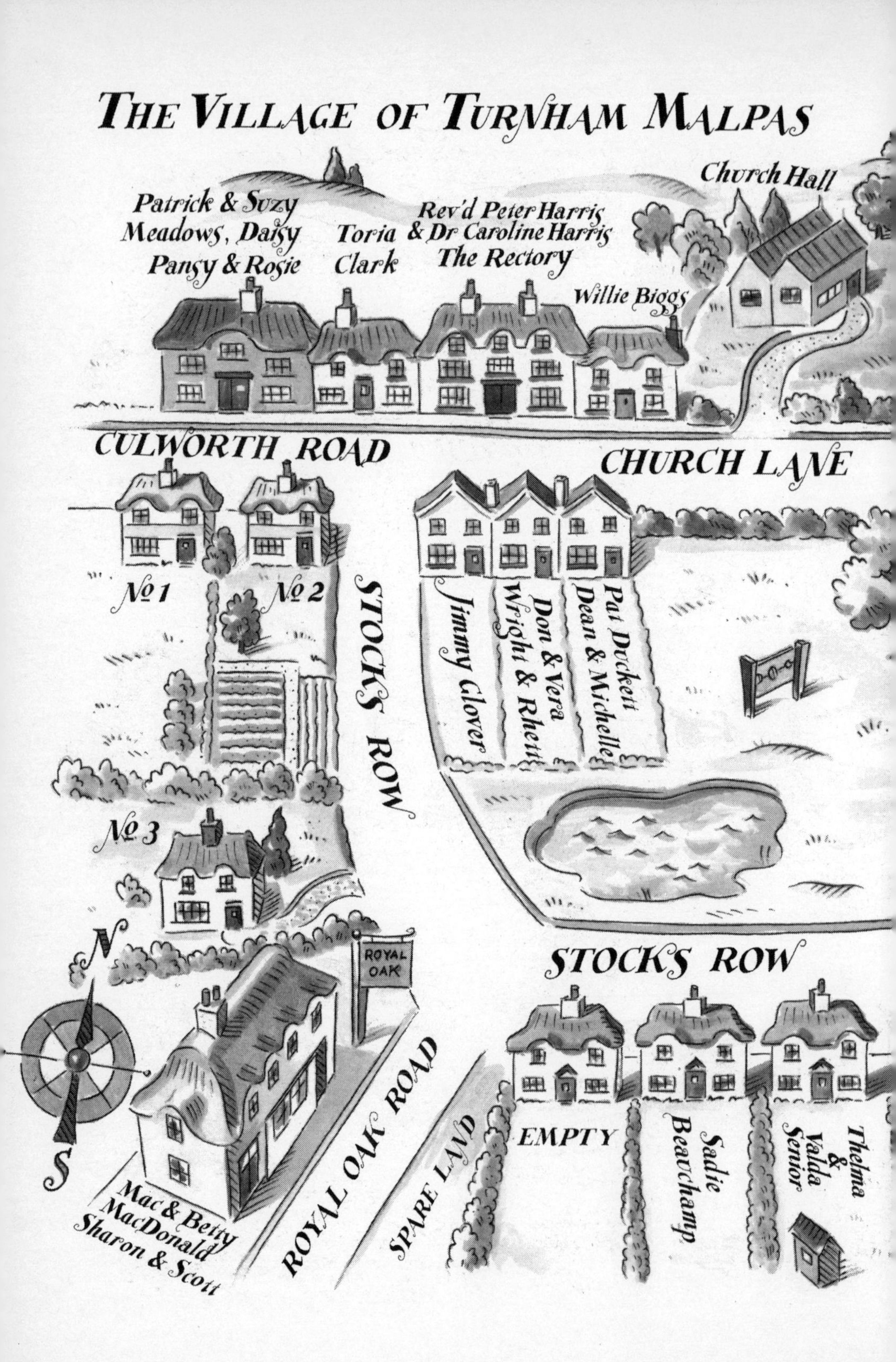

THE VILLAGE OF TURNHAM MALPAS
Church Hall
Patrick & Suzy Meadows, Daisy Pansy & Rosie
Toria Clark
Rev'd Peter Harris & Dr Caroline Harris The Rectory
Willie Biggs
CULWORTH ROAD
CHURCH LANE
№ 1
№ 2
STOCKS ROW
Jimmy Glover
Don & Vera Wright & Rhett
Pat Duckett Dean & Michelle
№ 3
N
S
ROYAL OAK
STOCKS ROW
ROYAL OAK ROAD
SPARE LAND
EMPTY
Sadie Beauchamp
Thelma & Valda Senior
Mac & Betty MacDonald Sharon & Scott

St Thomas à Becket
Muriel Hipkin
FOR SALE
Liz & Neville Neal Guy & Hugh
GLEBE COTTAGES
GLEBE HOUSE
CHURCH LANE
School House Michael Palmer
Jimbo & Harriet Charter-Plackett Fergus, Finlay & Flick Village Store
STOCKS ROW
JACKS LANE
Swimming Pool
Turnham Malpas School
SHEPHERDS HILL
Methodist Chapel
FD'01
Sir Ronald & Lady Bissett
pond
SPARE LAND
BECK
TURNHAM
footbridge

Inhabitants of Turnham Malpas

Sadie Beauchamp	Retired widow and mother of Harriet Charter-Plackett.
Willie Biggs	Verger at St Thomas à Becket.
Sir Ronald Bissett	Retired trades union leader.
Lady Sheila Bissett	His wife.
James Charter-Plackett	Owner of the village store.
Harriet Charter-Plackett	His wife.
Fergus, Finlay and Flick	Their children.
Toria Clark	Village schoolteacher.
Pat Duckett	Village school caretaker.
Dean and Michelle	Her children.
Jimmy Glover	Poacher and ne'er-do-well.
Revd Peter Harris MA (Oxon)	Rector of the parish.
Dr Caroline Harris	His wife.
Muriel Hipkin	Retired solicitor's secretary. Spinster of the parish.
Betty McDonald	Licensee of The Royal Oak.
'Mac' McDonald	Her husband.
Sharon and Scott	Their children.
Patrick Meadows	Nuclear scientist.
Suzy Meadows	His wife.
Daisy, Pansy and Rosie	Their children.
Neville Neal	Accountant.
Liz Neal	His wife.
Guy and Hugh	Their children.
Michael Palmer	Village school headmaster.
Sir Ralph Templeton	Retired from the Diplomatic Service.
Vera Wright	Cleaner at nursing home in Penny Fawcett.
Rhett Wright	Her grandson.

1

Muriel Hipkin turned over in bed to look at her floral china bedside clock. It said a quarter to eight – another fifteen minutes before she needed to rise. It was Easter Sunday today, such a special day in the Christian calendar, and this particular Easter Sunday was extra special, for the new Rector would be taking his first service. The Reverend Peter Alexander Harris MA (Oxon) was young and full of vigour, so different from dear Mr Furbank. She'd always had hopes of dear Mr Furbank, but now he'd died and so suddenly, too, and it was too late. Too late for lots of things.

Her tiny bedroom caught the first shafts of sun each morning and she lay revelling in its warmth. The neat floral curtains with their tiny pattern matched the neat floral bedspread. The carpet was cream with a tiny pattern on it, too. This was the first house she'd ever lived in where the choice of colours and furniture had been her own, her very own. Before, it had always been Mother's choice – nice, sensible dark reds and browns, lifeless and 'practical'. That particular bondage had been laid to rest four years ago. Muriel had been a willing slave but it wasn't until her mother passed over Jordan that she realised how she had been bound hand and foot. Her money kept the house and fed them, her money paid the bills for the special foods and the extra warmth, but she'd made none of the decisions.

Released from her chains, she'd returned to the village of Turnham Malpas where she had been born, and bought this 'starter home' – except that for her, it would be the starter *and* the finisher. No moving up to better things. This was it – till she needed constant care in a home, heaven forbid. The house was tiny. It had one living room out of which a square was taken to provide a minute kitchen. In the back corner of the living room was a spiral staircase which led to the small landing, hardly bigger than a doormat. Upstairs was one bedroom, and one miniscule bathroom. Not even a space for the vacuum cleaner, which had to live under the spiral stairs. Its compensation was that it was built alongside the churchyard. Glebe Cottages, the little row was called. No one else wanted Muriel's house, with its view of the ancient graves and the lych gate and the church, but it had a large garden which curved comfortably around the churchyard wall. Muriel loved gardening, and hers was the pride of the village. She'd won so many prizes at the annual Village Show the two years she'd been entering, it was becoming embarrassing. Maybe this year she wouldn't enter anything at all and give everyone else a chance.

Eight o'clock. As the church clock chimed the last stroke, Pericles came tip-tapping up the stairs. His bright brown eyes sparkled with delight as he flung himself on Muriel's bed. His snow-white fur contrasted sharply with his bright black nose.

'Off the bed, Perry, you naughty dog! Get off.' He leapt down and sprang about the bedroom, looking for slippers or shoes to race off downstairs with. Muriel got up and chased him out. Looking through her bedroom window, she could just see the back garden of the village store. Eight o'clock on Sundays, James Charter-Plackett – new owner of what was the village shop, but which now gave the appearance of being a miniature Harrods Food Hall – stood naked on the side of his brand-new pool and dived in, shallowly, for the pool was not really deep enough but it was the only way he could force himself to take his morning exercise.

Harriet Charter-Plackett, also naked, followed him in. Muriel could just glimpse them as they stood side by side on the pool edge. She'd once seen her father undressed when she was nursing him through his last illness and had been somewhat surprised, but James, or 'Jimbo' as he preferred to be called, was the first man she'd actually had a chance to take a good look at. This cavorting naked in the garden had caused a minor scandal when the couple first started doing it, but the locals now accepted it as one of the idiosyncrasies of a townie. Besides, they liked the revival of their village shop. Mrs Thornton's fly-blown cakes and tired lettuces and the cigarette ash dusting everything was no longer acceptable in 1990. After all, you had to move with the times, hadn't you? It was time for a change.

Muriel glanced at her slim figure shrouded in its long cotton nightgown – white, of course. In school photographs Mother had only to look for the palest blob of a face to find it was Muriel. She was still a pale blob. Pale skin, pale blue eyes, pale fair hair, and that was going paler still now it had white streaks in it. In strong sun she was almost obliterated. At boarding school (only a minor one – her parents couldn't afford one of the better ones) she had been taught to undress without the necessity of revealing any part of her anatomy. It was unseemly to expose oneself, the Anglican nuns had declared. Muriel often wondered how much their teaching had influenced her relationships in later years. They'd taught her embarrassment and shyness and modesty to such an extent that she had never been able to communicate properly with the opposite sex – except for dear Mr Furbank, of course. Some people might have sniggered that maybe he wasn't of the opposite sex, anyway, and that was why she got on with him so well. She straightened her shoulders; she must correct her habit of stooping.

Her bathroom was dedicated to cleanliness. Crisp clean towels, snow-white, lay in regimented rows interspersed with fresh face cloths. They were all crisp to the touch for they'd been blowing on the line for the best part of a day getting dried and 'freshened up'. She actually had seven face cloths, one for each day of the week. All white. That way you knew when they were clean. The walls were white, the bath, basin and lavatory were white; the floor had white tiles, the curtains were white, the ceiling, the taps, the towel rail . . . all virginal, like Muriel. She had an all-over wash first thing in the morning, after having been in bed all night.

Baths she kept for evenings. She would lie in the scented water with the bathroom light turned off, and just the moonlight creeping into the corners of the room. She would dwell on life and its meaning, though she never had many answers. Sometimes she pondered what her life would have been like if she had married. Children, perhaps four. All nice clean little girls with pretty faces and nice blonde curly hair. Clever at school and well-mannered, not like that young Sharon McDonald from The Royal Oak, all boldness and flashing hips and eyes. Her girls would be sweet and well-behaved. She would prepare lovely meals for her husband each evening when he came home from the office. He would have a military moustache and fair hair, he'd be tall and fresh-complexioned, and he would be gentle and amusing to be with. Occasionally, though, when soaking in the bath she would see her life endlessly unfolding before her and would weep at its barrenness and isolation. Then, like the good Christian that she was, she would count her blessings and begin to scrub herself vigorously so she would go to bed immaculately clean.

Everything clean, as on every day in the week, Muriel descended the spiral stairs with care. Another ten years and she could have problems with those stairs. Perry dashed to the door to be let into the garden. She'd taught him to relieve himself in one particular spot so that she could disinfect the area each day. He was usually very good. She warmed her blue and white teapot, which matched her breakfast set, with boiling water, preparing it lovingly for brewing her tea. Muriel loved the delicate blue flowers which danced up the spout and around the lid. The handle of her cup had flowers climbing up it, too. She'd chosen the set with a picture in her mind's eye of her little dining table, hardly bigger than a card table, in the window of her living room. The small silver toast-rack awaited its load, the honey pot, matching, gleamed alongside the silver sugar bowl with its air of Georgian gentility, also matching. A bowl of All Bran followed by toast and honey – her breakfast unchanged since her chains fell off – was augmented by a banana this Sunday morning. A little treat to mark the special day.

When the kitchen was tidy again Muriel glanced at the clock. Time for Pericles' walk. The back door locked, she took his lead from the hook behind it – a hook shared with her neat white and blue flowered apron which matched the tea cosy and the oven gloves. Hearing the rattle of the lead, Pericles began chasing round in circles, yapping. Poodles did yap a lot, but she didn't mind. The gardens at the front of Glebe Cottages were open plan so she had to watch that Pericles didn't forget his manners.

Straight ahead was Jacks Lane, which ran between the school and the back garden of the village store. On school days she chatted to the children on their way to school and they loved to pat Pericles and ask her why he had such a funny name. Today being Sunday, the school was silent, resting from its labours. Over the wall she could see poor Mr Palmer sitting reading his newspaper on the garden bench. His school-house came with the job. Muriel always pitied him – a widower in such tragic circumstances. Of course the village had stood by him, but there were murmurs which wouldn't be stilled. He'd stayed on with the stuffing knocked out of him, but for all that the children loved him and he was an excellent head teacher.

There must be nearly forty children in the school now. It had dwindled to five at one time and the County said they would close it. Then in moved these townies with their families, fancying a country life, and then the Big House had been turned into a home for children at risk, so they, too, had helped to fill up the school. What they were at risk from, Muriel wasn't quite sure. That tale Willie Biggs the verger had told her simply didn't make sense. She read things in the papers which she couldn't make head nor tail of, but there you were, they still needed loving like all children.

'Morning, Miss Hipkin. I got four eggs this morning.' Finlay Charter-Plackett was sitting astride the stone wall surrounding his parents' garden.

'Oh, good morning and a Happy Easter to you, Finlay!'

'Did you get an egg, Miss Hipkin?'

'No, dear, I've no one to give me one.'

'Here – have this Cadbury's creme egg. Mummy's got plenty in the shop.'

'I couldn't, dear, really I couldn't. Your mother wouldn't like it.'

Harriet Charter-Plackett, now fully clothed, emerged from between the conifers and looked over the wall into the lane. 'That's all right, Miss Hipkin, of course you must have it. I like my children to be generous. Happy Easter to you.'

'Oh, thank you very much. I shall eat it this afternoon with my cup of tea. Bye bye.'

Pericles was in a hurry to be let off the lead. She crossed Shepherd's Hill and went into the opening onto the spare land behind the tiny Methodist Chapel. There she undid the little dog's lead and he raced off to his favourite spots. It seemed ridiculous that he could find such enjoyment every day from sniffing the same clumps of grass. The new coat of paint on the chapel walls had helped to improve it but, oh dear, it *was* so bleak and austere. Muriel much preferred the gentle beauty of her St Thomas à Becket, with its stained-glass windows, the banners, the altar and the flowers. There would be Easter lilies from the glasshouses at the Big House this week. A bit severe, but a delightful change from the usual fussy arrangements done by Lady Bissett. How could anyone be knighted for being a trades union official and be called Sir Ron? Sir Ronald and Lady Bissett. Before the knighthood he'd always been known as Ron Bissett. Now it was Sir Ronald. How could he justify accepting a knighthood? It went against everything he had ever stood for, surely? Lady Sheila Bissett believed she had assumed the mantle of the squire's wife, but only in her own mind; everyone else knew she'd been serving behind the bar in The Case Is Altered in Culworth before she married, and unfortunately had never left it behind. She carried the aura of it with her wherever she went.

'Good morning, Miss Hipkin. Happy Easter to you.'

Muriel blushed bright red. Lady Bissett's Pomeranian sniffed at Pericles.

'Good morning, Lady Bissett, and a Happy Easter to you, too.'

'See you in church later on. Bye bye.'

It was so embarrassing. Of course Lady Bissett couldn't read her mind but she felt as if she could.

Muriel glanced at her watch and decided to take the short cut across the green as time was running short. No ducklings yet on the pond. The oak, well the Royal Oak, was coming into bud again. Two years ago, it had looked as if it were dying but it had perked up again. When the Royal Oak died, the village would die, too – that was what everyone believed. But the village was beginning to throb with life again, with new people, new ideas.

As she waited to cross Church Lane, the new rector – Peter, he asked everyone to call him – crossed from the Rectory into the churchyard. He waved to her and called a cheery 'Happy Easter!' She waved back and for a moment wished it was dear Mr Furbank; she could have made him very happy. The two of them there in the Rectory tending the Lord's garden and watching His little flowers grow. In our dear Lord's garden. Ah well, you couldn't put back the clock.

The morning service began at ten o'clock. The children were already in their places when Muriel entered. Willie Biggs gave her a wink. That man would never improve. Dear Mr Furbank should never have given him the job; he was misguided there. Muriel wore her navy suit with the Sunray pleated skirt and a buttercup-yellow blouse. Her navy straw had buttercup-yellow flowers decorating the brim; she only ever wore it on Easter Sundays. One of her navy gloves had developed a hole but they would have to do. No one would notice if she carried it and wore the other. Organ music flooded the church. Just as Mrs Peel the organist arrived at a particularly triumphant bit, Sir Ron and Lady Bissett came down the aisle to take their places. In less polite circles his stomach would have been described as a beer belly. He had grown his white hair quite long and wore it brushed back without a parting, while his florid face and heavy jowls implied good living, which earlier stalwarts of the trade union movement would have scorned. Muriel found his hale and hearty personality overwhelming.

The church was filled this morning, partly because it was Easter and partly because the whole village wanted to hear the new rector.

The processional hymn began and they all stood. Peter wore a beautiful surplice decorated with heavy antique lace. He made an impressive figure with his thick hair forming a bronze halo around his head. His broad shoulders seemed designed to carry any burden asked of them, and at six feet five he towered above the verger and the choirmen as well as the boys. He ought to be a bishop, Muriel thought. Suzy Meadows, mother of three and new to the village, thought he was sizzlingly attractive. Daisy, Pansy and Rosie sat beside her in front of Muriel wriggling and giggling. Muriel wished they hadn't decided to sit near her, they were so distracting in their loveliness. So sweet and so alike, except for their size. Daisy was five and round, Pansy four and very thin and Rosie three and just right. All pretty and blonde like their mother. Patrick Meadows never came to church. He worked somewhere in one of those secret nuclear places and never joined in family life at all.

After the hymn had been sung and the congregation was settling down, in came the rector's wife, looking harassed and breathless. She was so feminine and pretty. Her dark curly hair was cut short in a no-nonsense style, but the curls still made themselves evident. She had a clear ivory skin and bright blue eyes. She rushed down the aisle, sat in the rectory pew and hastily knelt on the specially embroidered kneeler with symbols appropriate to a rector's wife. It hadn't had any use while dear Mr Furbank had been there, for he'd lacked a wife all the thirty years he'd been the incumbent. Muriel had been delighted that at last there was to be a rector's wife, but her hopes had been dashed when she'd learned that Caroline Harris was a hospital doctor in Culworth. Full time, too. No babies or Mothers' Union for her – she belonged to the new breed.

An inspirational sermon followed by uplifting singing and a new modern anthem from the choir made a beautiful Easter morning service. Muriel realised that dear Mr Furbank's sermons had become very dull. She had only enjoyed them because she loved his beautiful enunciation and the gentle aspect of his face.

Peter shook hands enthusiastically with the entire congregation as they left, saying that next Sunday he hoped they would all stay for coffee afterwards in the church hall and he would do his best to get round to see every member during the next few weeks. Willie Biggs winked at Muriel and said out of the corner of his mouth, 'Not quite like the old rector, is he? Got a bit more go, like. You won't be coming with your jars of lemon cheese for this one. He plays squash and runs, he does. Smarten us all up, he will. Bashing tambourines and kissing and hugging we shall be before long, mark my words.'

Lady Bissett came pouring out of the church, hand outstretched.

'My dear Peter, welcome to Turnham Malpas! We're so glad to see you – you're like a blast of fresh air. You've met my husband, of course, but I haven't yet met your dear wife. Ah, here she is. My dear Mrs Harris . . .'

'*Dr* Harris, actually.'

'I'm sorry, Dr Harris. I'm Lady Bissett and this is my husband Sir Ronald.'

Caroline Harris turned to look at Sir Ronald, and Muriel saw a mischievous light come into her eyes.

'I seem to recognise you from the television. Aren't you a TUC person?'

'Oh, he's often on the telly, er – television, aren't you, Ron . . . ald?'

'Frequently. When you've held public office it's hard to keep your face off it.'

'Surely you must be the one who orchestrated that massive strike at the engineering works in Bradley?'

'In all truth I actually tried to stop it, Mrs . . . Dr Harris.'

'Oh, it didn't come across like that on our television,' Caroline said, then she turned to Muriel, still smiling and said: 'You must be Miss Hipkin. Willie Biggs tells me that your family has been in this village since the Conquest.'

'Well, I wouldn't say quite as far back as that, but my ancestors worked in the gardens and the park for generations at the Big House, then when Lady Templeton had to sell up after the war my family moved away and now I've come back to live here again.'

'You must come and have tea with me one day and tell me all about the village. I'll call in and let you know which day I shall be at home and we'll get together.'

Before Muriel could thank her for her kindness, Lady Bissett had edged her way between them and thanked the rector's wife for the invitation. Short of being extremely rude, Dr Harris had to concede the point and include Lady Bissett in her invitation. It quite took the pleasure out of it for Muriel, but then she remembered her Christian duty and smiled her delight.

Pericles was standing behind the door when she got back from morning service. He'd been terribly sick on the mat. She rushed him out into the back garden, where he was incredibly sick again. Considering what a small dog he was, it was amazing how much he'd had in his stomach. Cleaning the mat put her off her dinner so she put her thick cardigan on and sat in the back garden with him instead. He lay all afternoon looking extremely sorry for himself. About three o'clock, she made herself a cup of tea, put her Cadbury's creme egg on a plate and carried the tray into the garden. She had a small table out there which she used for potting up but with a scrub it served as a tea table in the warmer weather. The creme egg did taste lovely – very rich and rather sickly and very indulgent. But she didn't have many pleasures. From her chair, Muriel could just see over the wall into the churchyard. Sunday afternoon was the time when most people who cared took fresh flowers to the graves. The churchyard tap was alongside the gardener's shed near the wall. It was far enough away not to block Muriel's view but near enough for her to see what was going on.

Michael Palmer the headmaster was putting fresh water in the vase from his wife's grave. He came every Sunday, winter and summer. You'd never think he was only forty-five – he looked a good ten years older. Up the path came Sharon McDonald from The Royal Oak. A right little madam, thought Muriel. That skirt couldn't be any shorter nor tighter, and that T-shirt was surely meant to sit equally on her shoulders, not be dragged over to one side so that her whole shoulder was exposed. A man would have to be blind not to notice the flagrant exhibition of her feminine charms. Sharon stood provocatively in front of Mr Palmer, her shrill voice carrying on the wind.

'Hello, Mr Palmer. Remember me?'

'Why, of course, Sharon.' He straightened up, holding the vase full of water in one hand and the flowers in the other. 'It's some time since you were in school but I remember you quite clearly. I don't see you around nowadays.'

'No, I work in Culworth, in Tesco's. Boring, but there's not much else. How are you? Still teaching in this godforsaken little dump?'

'Still teaching, Sharon, yes I am. I like it here.' He set off to walk to the grave. Sharon followed, teetering along the rough path in her stilettos. As he crouched down to arrange the flowers, Sharon bent over and rested her hand on his back. Muriel couldn't hear what she said but she saw Michael stand up quickly and move out of her reach. He was shaking his head and protesting. Their conversation lasted a few more moments, with Michael Palmer still backing away and shaking his head. Sharon seemed to find their conversation a huge joke, and her laughter carried across the churchyard towards Muriel. It sounded cruel. Mr Palmer turned on his heel and marched away with the wrapping paper from the flowers still in his hand. Muriel knew he always put it screwed up into a ball in the bin provided by Willie Biggs. He must be upset. A man of meticulously regular habits, was Mr Palmer. She knew because she played the piano for the singing in the school on Monday and Thursday mornings.

Sharon wandered aimlessly across the churchyard. She saw Muriel watching so she put her thumb to her nose and waggled her outstretched fingers in Muriel's direction. Muriel turned away. How rude that girl was. Her parents ought to teach her better manners. Still, what could you expect? Running The Royal Oak left Mr and Mrs McDonald little time to spare for Sharon and her brother Scott. He was a rude, arrogant young boy. Mr Palmer said he was very clever but Scott didn't care enough to bother.

Pericles took a turn for the better so Muriel walked him out and then went inside to make a substantial tea for herself. She didn't usually go to church in the evening unless it was something special; instead, she watched the religious programmes on TV, and then perhaps a good play afterwards. TV was her life-saver. Mother wouldn't have it, even though Muriel had offered to pay. Old people can be very tyrannical.

Easter Monday dawned clear and bright but there was nothing of interest planned by Muriel for this day of leisure. Just after she got back from walking Pericles there was a knock at the door. Muriel tucked Pericles under her arm and opened it. Caroline Harris stood there smiling.

'I know you probably have a very busy day booked, with it being a Bank Holiday, but could you possibly fit in afternoon tea with me?'

'Why, good morning, Dr Harris. How nice of you, I'd love to do that! Thank you.'

'Good – come about three. If it's warm we'll sit in the garden. Peter is away today so I shall be glad of your company. See you later, then. Your daffodils do look lovely. I shall be glad of your advice regarding our garden: I'm afraid it's very overgrown.'

For her outing, Muriel chose her pale cream blouse with a brown tweed skirt and a toning brown cardigan – well, rust really. She brushed her hair and tortured it into a French pleat – the style she'd adopted when it was the height of fashion and had never troubled to change since. In honour of the invitation she put on a tiny amount of orangey-brown lipstick. She stepped gently along Church Lane, past the lych gate and Willie Biggs', where she noticed the curtain twitching as she went by, and rang the Rectory bell.

The door was opened by Caroline Harris, her three Siamese cats standing by her feet, their long tails winding around her legs.

'Come in do,' she said warmly. 'I've got some scones in the oven and they're nearly ready. Let's go in the kitchen while they finish cooking.'

Dear Mr Furbank had not been good at housekeeping and Muriel was dreading the embarrassment of his unkempt kitchen; however, Caroline Harris had worked wonders in the few days since they had moved in. The walls had already been painted – a bright melon colour – copper pans gleamed in racks, the old cooker had been burnished to within an inch of its life and a large pine table had replaced the nasty gateleg thing that dear Mr Furbank had used for dining. A huge fridge freezer stood where there had once been a grubby mesh food cupboard. The floor had been sanded and stained, and Indian rugs covered it in a deliberately haphazard manner.

'Why this is beautiful!' Muriel said, looking around with pleasure. 'You've worked miracles in here, and in such a short space of time, too. I love the curtains. Are they Indian?'

'Yes, they are. I went there for six months, working with the down and outs in Calcutta, and brought loads of things back. It's what Peter refers to as my Indian period. Milk and sugar?'

'Just milk, thank you.'

Caroline carried the tray into the garden. It was laid for two.

'Lady Bissett isn't coming, then?' Muriel asked tentatively.

She answered, 'No,' in a manner which rejected any further queries, and then added: 'Will you call me Caroline? I much prefer it. Now, tell me all about your family and what you do in the village, Miss Hipkin.'

Muriel launched herself on a potted family history and then on a brief history of the village. She'd only been back three years but she'd caught up on forty years of happenings in a very short time. Finally, she remembered herself and exclaimed, blushing: 'Oh dear, I've gone rambling on and you've told me nothing about yourself.'

'Miss Hipkin, there isn't much to tell,' Caroline laughed. 'Peter and I have been married five years. I've thrown myself into my work to compensate for the fact that I can't have children. We're both very disappointed but there you are. It's my fault and nothing can alter it.'

A door slammed in the Rectory and Peter himself came into the garden, bearing a mug. He leant over Caroline and kissed her, cupping her chin with his spare hand. 'Mind if I join you?' he said, addressing them both.

'You're back early,' his wife remarked.

'Yes, I am. How are you, Miss Hipkin?'

'Very well, thank you. I should like it very much if you would both call me Muriel. It seems more friendly.'

'Certainly we shall.' Peter took a huge bite out of a scone as he said this, then, with his mouth full: 'I thought Lady Bissett was coming today as well?'

'No.' Caroline offered no further enlightenment regarding Lady Bissett so Peter turned to Muriel.

'I shall tread very carefully about making changes here,' he told her, 'but changes there will have to be. We need to do more to encourage the local children. Do you have any ideas?'

'I have often thought that there are a lot of little ones on the farms and in the more isolated houses who could well do with one of those nursery schools. That way they get used to mixing with other children before they actually start school. I play the piano for the singing on Mondays and Thursdays for Mr Palmer and I do notice that the new ones have great difficulty learning to join in.'

'What a perfectly splendid idea. We could use the church hall, couldn't we?'

Muriel considered this and then said, 'It would take some manoeuvring, because there is a yoga class and a ladies' quilting group which meet regularly in the mornings – and Lady Bissett has a flower-arranging group there, too. But I'm sure the timetable could be adjusted.'

'I shall see to that immediately. All we need is someone willing to organise it. I'll talk to some of the mothers with small children, as they might do it as a group rather than having just one person in charge. What do you think, Caroline?'

'The Council will have something to say about facilities. Perhaps it could start as a mother and toddler group until proper permission has been obtained.'

Peter stood up and went to kiss his wife on the top of her head. 'What would we do without your common sense?'

Shortly after this, Muriel left. Pericles would be getting restless, she said, and thanked them for a lovely afternoon. Peter accompanied her to the door.

What a charming young man he was. Just what the village needed.

2

Peter Alexander Harris prayed in his church every morning from six-thirty until seven o'clock. Having dealt with the spiritual he then attended to the physical and ran a circuit of roughly three miles round the parish. Turning in at the Rectory door, he jogged straight up to the bathroom and took a shower, singing vigorously whilst he did so. As soon as the singing stopped Caroline began preparing his breakfast: two Weetabix, with full-cream milk and a banana chopped up on the top, followed by a boiled egg with wholemeal toast and plenty of butter and marmalade. Having concluded his daily ritual he then turned his attention to Caroline.

'Come here, my darling girl, and spend some time with me before you disappear into the vampire department.'

'Vampire department? Peter, that is dreadful! Don't let any of your parishioners hear you say that, or they'll get terrible ideas about what I do.'

'Tell me why you didn't let Lady Bissett come to tea on Monday.'

'It's not often I take an instant dislike to people, but I'm afraid Sheila Bissett and I will be clashing swords before long. If she conducted herself as the person she really is I could quite like her, but instead she gives herself such airs. She honestly believes she is the modern equivalent of the squire's wife. I know for a fact she used to work behind the bar in The Case Is Altered in Culworth.'

'Who told you that?'

'Willie Biggs. If you need to know anything about anybody, ask Willie. I've made a point of becoming a friend of his.'

'How have you done that?'

'By diagnosing his ailments for him.'

'Caroline!' Peter tipped her off his knee and pretended to slap her bottom for her. Caroline laughed, kissed him full on the mouth with a lingering relish which reminded Peter how much he loved her, and dashed off to the hospital. Peter cleared the table, washed up and went into his study.

Hearing a noise not unlike the chattering of a brood of nestlings, he glanced out to see what it was, and passing the window was the girl he had noticed in church on Sunday. Her silvery-blonde hair was held back by an Alice band so that her charming rosy-cheeked face could be clearly seen. She had a long, perfectly straight nose, round curving cheeks and brilliant blue eyes. Her colouring was echoed by the three little girls who were walking hand in hand beside her. One was round, one very thin, and one just right. All three had long plaits swinging behind as they hopped and skipped on the pavement. Their mother looked up at the study window and raised her hand in greeting. For some unexplained reason, Peter's heart almost stopped beating. He waved back and then bent his head to open the post. His heart righted itself and he tried hard to concentrate on his work, but couldn't. He was being quite ridiculous. His post that morning was considerable – most of it addressed to the now deceased Revd Arthur Furbank.

The phone rang. 'The Rectory, Peter Harris speaking. How may I help you?'

'It's Michael Palmer here, Headmaster at the village school. Could I possibly come round some time in the next day or so, and have a chat with you? We are a church school so you'll be very much involved.'

'Certainly, I shall be delighted. This is the first time I've been directly concerned with education and I'm looking forward to it. Now, there's no time like the present, is there? I would be free to see you about eleven this morning. How would that suit you?'

'Fine, I'll see you then.'

Peter put down the receiver, leant back in his chair and contemplated the study. Hanging above the fireplace, in which a two-bar electric fire tried defiantly to warm the room, was a crude peasant-like painting of the Virgin Mary. The only thing that was good about it was the face. Who did it remind him of? – Caroline? No, not his darling girl. Then he knew who it was. The over-bright blue eyes and the rounded cheeks reminded him of the girl who'd been in church on Sunday and who had caused his heart to jolt only moments ago. Peter's self-discipline enabled him to push his feelings into the background. He leapt up, took down the painting, and placed it face downwards on top of the filing cabinet. Above the fireplace there was now a light buff-coloured square where the picture had hung. Peter moved another picture from the wall and realised that the wallpaper was very dirty indeed. So were the bookshelves which were waiting for him to unpack the tea chests full of books stacked against the far wall. The carpet was threadbare and dirty, the desk where he worked grimy and slightly sticky to the touch. He should never have agreed to take the Rectory as it stood. He ought to have insisted on furnishing it himself. Caroline had worked wonders with the kitchen; this, being his domain, he would have to work upon by himself.

Within ten minutes of rolling up his sleeves, Peter had removed all the pictures from the walls, and unplugged the ancient electric fire. Once it had cooled down, he put it, flex and all, into the bin. The desk, filing cabinets and the sofa – ancient and falling apart – had all been pulled or pushed into the hall. The easy chairs had been stacked against the hall wall, too, and all that remained was the removal of the carpet. As he began to roll it up, thick dust fell from it and made him cough. He opened the study window and waved his arms about trying to dispel the clouds of dust and found himself once more face to face with Suzy Meadows returning home with Pansy and Rosie. His heart jolted again as he looked into those sweet, Madonna-like features.

'Good morning, Mr Harris. I'm Suzy Meadows, this is Pansy and this is Rosie. Say good morning, you two.' The tiny girls smiled and hid their faces in her skirts.

Peter's voice boomed out onto the pavement. 'Good morning, Mrs Meadows. I'm just—'

'Call me Suzy – everyone else does.'

'Suzy, then. I'm just clearing out the study. Sorry for the dust blowing about.'

'The binmen come on Tuesdays. If you're quick they'll take anything you don't want – and if it's the rector they'll most likely do it for nothing. They'll be along here in about half an hour.'

'Right, thank you. Most of it needs to go.'

'There's a furniture place in Culworth if you're needing some replacements. I bought a lovely pair of hall chairs there for an absolute song. They've always got plenty of easy chairs and things.'

'Thank you for your advice. Hello, Pansy and Rosie. What have you done with your sister?' Neither of the two girls offered a reply so Suzy answered on their behalf.

'Oh, she's gone to play with Hugh Neal in Glebe House. They're both learning the recorder at school and Liz Neal has promised to help Daisy with it. Be seeing you soon, Mr Harris. Bye!'

'Bye.' Peter watched her disappear down the road and recognised his feelings for what they were. Shatteringly, for a man so devoted to his wife and his Church, he felt disastrously attracted by her. Why, he had no idea. It was just one of those things which happened and over which one appeared to have no control. Peter left the clearing of the study and went across to the church. Here, surely, he would find help before it was too late. How could such a thing have happened to him? Every cleric, young in years, had his quota of young women who made sheep's eyes and for a while became devoted to the Church until they realised they were making no progress, but this was it in reverse. He knelt before the altar and prayed. '*Dear God, help me, a miserable sinner . . .*'

Willie Biggs, needing a rest from labouring in the graveyard, crept quietly into the church by a side door and sat munching his morning break in the gloom by one of the pillars. His Mars bar was nearly finished when he spotted the rector, head bent in prayer. Funny that, he thought – only halfway through the morning and needing to recharge his batteries. Already been here for half an hour first thing. The man must be troubled. Willie kept silent and still, hoping Peter wouldn't see him when he went out and Peter didn't, because he went across to the organ and, switching it on, began playing a jaunty hymn tune. Willie, whenever he heard the organ being played, always thanked the good Lord that it no longer required him to work the bellows at the back. Years he'd done that, till some benefactor or other, needing to put in a good word with God before departing this life, had paid for it 'to be electrocuted' as Willie described it. My word, he thought, now that Rector can't half play. Mrs Peel'll have to look to her laurels and no mistake. The music throbbed through the church with a kind of lively triumph which Willie found quite moving. Brass band music was more to his personal taste, but he mightily appreciated the beauty of the rector's playing.

Peter concluded his performance with a flourish, switched off the organ and quietly made his way home. He heated a pot of coffee and carried the tray with two cups on it into the sitting room. As he put down the tray the doorbell rang.

Standing on the step was Michael Palmer, schoolmaster extraordinaire of Turnham Malpas for the last twenty years. What had been meant as a stepping stone had become a millstone, and here he was still teaching a new generation of children, holding onto life by the merest thread. His square, weatherbeaten face topped by thinning hair smiled benignly at Peter, who stood looking down upon him from his great height, Michael reaching only five feet six in his socks. The two men shook hands and Michael winced at the strength of Peter's grip.

'Delighted to meet you, Mr Harris. Or shall I call you Peter?'

'Yes, please. Coffee?'

'Thank you, black, please. It seems odd using your Christian name. We always knew the previous incumbent as Mr Furbank – it would have felt impudent to have called him anything else. It was time we had some new blood; he'd been here far too long. Sorry for being outspoken, but it's the truth. Mr Furbank took a great deal of interest in the children but I'm afraid he didn't have the right touch and I had difficulty preventing the children from giggling at his absent-minded ways. He came into school every Friday morning to take prayers and then gave the children a little talk of some kind. I don't expect you to follow exactly in his footsteps, so I wondered what kind of presence you would like to have?'

Peter took a sip of his coffee whilst deciding how to answer. 'I should very much like to take prayers one morning a week, but how about if it was held in the church?'

'What a good idea.'

'I'm very keen to encourage the children of the village to come into church and centre their lives around activities here. I intend to start Beavers and Brownies as soon as I can find suitable helpers, and also Muriel Hipkin has suggested that a playgroup would be a good idea. She feels that a lot of the children come into school at five not having any real experience of joining in with other children and knowing how to share. How would you feel about that?'

'I should be delighted – it's a perfectly splendid idea! There are quite a few children from the farms hereabouts who come to school quite afraid of what they have to face. A playgroup would be excellent. Where would you hold it?'

'I had thought of the church hall.'

'If we can get permission from the County we could hold it in the school itself. I have a spare classroom and the facilities like toilets and equipment would all be available with very little extra expense. I'll have a word with my assistant – she takes the infants so she would be more involved than me. I'm sure she'll be delighted.'

'Does your wife help in the school?'

For a moment Michael didn't answer. He carefully placed his cup on the little table, took out his handkerchief and dabbed his moustache dry. Peter noticed his hand was shaking as he put the handkerchief away.

'My wife died three years ago.'

'I'm so sorry. Please forgive me, I didn't know. What an intrusion.'

'Not at all – how were you to know? She did teach, but over in Culworth. No, my assistant is Toria Clark, one of the new breed with plenty of energy and fresh ideas. The children love her.'

Peter put down his cup and offered Michael more coffee. The two of them talked for another hour about the village and the possibilities of change. Peter sensed that Michael was a fine schoolmaster, and Michael thought what a blessing it was for Turnham Malpas that Peter had accepted the living.

To keep himself occupied and push his current problem to the back of his mind, Peter had raided Caroline's plentiful supply of paint in the garden shed and, having washed the walls and paintwork, was finishing putting a muted shade of antique gold on the study walls when he remembered he needed to go to the village store to buy meat for the evening meal.

Jimbo Charter-Plackett stood by the door discussing politics with Sir Ronald. Jimbo was wearing his butcher's apron and straw boater, a get-up he'd adopted to give style to his store. He raised his boater as soon as he recognised the Rector.

'Good afternoon, sir, welcome to Turnham Malpas Village Store. It's an honour to serve you. See you later, Ron . . . Sir Ronald.' He waved a dismissal to the self-appointed squire and made room for Peter to enter. 'Perfectly ridiculous man. Now, Rector, what can I get for you?'

'Caroline has asked me to buy lamb chops for dinner tonight.'

'Come this way.' Jimbo led him to the meat department. The Charter-Placketts had bought the next door cottage and by pulling down walls and reorganising the space available, they had made an excellent store out of what had originally been a small village shop in the front room of a large cottage.

'I have never seen such an incredible shop in such a small village before,' Peter exclaimed. 'Is there anything you *don't* sell?'

'Not much. You name it we sell it – and if we don't, we soon will.'

'Forgive me for asking, but how on earth do you make it pay?'

'Well, we don't sit here waiting for people to pass the door. We run a mail-order business selling farm products to the nation, and also have a catering business providing food for weddings and the Hunt Ball. This year, we've won a contract for catering for the VIPs at the Game Fair in the next county. I buy almost all our fresh food from the local area and all our cakes in the freezer and on the counter are made by local farmers' wives, so I provide work for the people hereabouts as well as giving a good service to the local inhabitants. I pride myself that there are not many villages with as good a village store as Turnham Malpas. Now, these four chops are on the house, Rector – a small token of our delight at having youth in the Rectory for a change. We loved the old boy but he should have gone years ago. When it comes to the Harvest Supper, Harriet and I would like to provide all the meats free of charge as our contribution.'

'How extremely kind and generous of you, James.'

'Jimbo, if you please. Here, put this box of sugared almonds under your good lady's pillow with love from Harriet and me.'

'You're more than generous, Jimbo – she'll be delighted. Must press on, got to finish painting my study. Thank you very much indeed.'

The lamb chops, delicately flavoured with rosemary and grilled to a turn by Caroline, were a gastronomic delight.

'These chops are a vast improvement on the ones we used to buy in the supermarket, aren't they, darling?'

Caroline, chasing the last of her mint jelly round her plate, nodded her agreement. 'Everything in that shop is fresh,' she enthused. 'The fruit, the vegetables, the cakes, the meat, the cheeses . . . it's a positive wonderland. They must have to work terribly hard, Peter, to keep it all up to scratch. That Jimbo is a bit of a lad, you know. Willie tells me that they swim "nakkid" every day in their pool at the back.'

'Naked, eh? I bet that set the village tongues gossiping.'

'In fact, one could get quite carried away with Jimbo. Harriet must have her work cut out keeping an eye on him.'

'Caroline, really! Is there any of that cheese left that we had last night?'

The sugared almonds came to light when Caroline searched under her pillow for her nightgown.

'Darling, what a lovely surprise! I do love you for it.'

'Don't thank me, thank Jimbo Charter-Plackett – he gave them to me for you. Said I should put them under your pillow. Maybe it's a secret method of his for getting his evil way with Harriet.'

'Well, you can have your evil way with me right now. Hurry up.' She put the box of almonds on her beside table and lay on top of the bed 'nakkid' with her arms outstretched in welcome.

Peter made love to reassure himself that everything was well between his darling girl and himself, but as he fell asleep the face of Suzy the Madonna floated into his mind. He rubbed his forehead to push her away.

3

The busy life she led keeping her three girls well care for, compensated Suzy for the lack of her husband's companionship. He was the archetypal mad scientist. She knew it when she married him so she'd no right to complain, but at the time it had seemed an endearing quality. Now, with lawns to mow and decorating to be done and the new sitting-room fireplace still laid out in pieces on the floor waiting to be fitted, Suzy was feeling bleak. Daisy, Pansy and Rosie were the delight of her life; without them she would have left Patrick by now. She'd willingly given up her career to have babies and had wallowed in motherhood for five years, but right now there was a powerful feeling that her life lacked purpose. Then she laughed at herself. Considering the mound of ironing waiting to be done she didn't need to be looking for anything else to do. But the window wide open and the girls playing in the garden and the daffodils in the narrow-necked glass vase on the kitchen window didn't provide the deeply satisfying feeling that had always lifted her spirits. Lonely, that's what I am – lonely, she thought. She stood ironing Patrick's shirt and felt that this was the closest she came to him nowadays. He'd provided her with the babies she wanted, and then almost departed this life. Self-absorbed and erratic, he hadn't wanted sex for nearly a year, and she was only thirty-two. Agreed he was forty-five, but the difference in years hadn't seemed to matter to start with, although now it seemed like a yawning void. Maybe all men went off sex when they got to their middle forties – it wasn't really something she could discuss with the mothers from the school. Even the girls all looked like her and not a bit like Patrick. Anyone would think she'd had three virgin births. It seemed as though he'd had nothing to do with them right from the first.

Suzy contemplated how many other wives stood ironing, wondering where their husbands had gone. For all practical purposes they might as well be dead. Perhaps there were thousands of women all over Britain who felt as she did this morning. A new hairstyle, a pretty nightgown, expensive perfume, a special candle-lit dinner when the girls were all in bed . . . she'd tried everything. And it had all been a total waste of time. She held Rosie's tiny socks to her face and enjoyed their warmth and the recalling of Rosie's delightfully happy personality. How she loved them all. For their sakes she had to keep going.

She heard the front door open and then bang shut. Patrick stood in the hall looking shattered. He'd come home to pack a bag en route to America to read a paper at a conference there. The researcher who should have done it had been taken ill and he'd stepped in at the last minute. She made him some sandwiches which he ate while she packed his bag. He was in a tremendous hurry and after he'd left she realised she didn't know which hotel he would be staying at. Still, he would only be gone three or four days at the most; not much could happen during that short period.

The next time she heard someone at the door it was Miss Hipkin. She couldn't expect anything of a world-shattering nature from her.

'Good morning, Miss Hipkin. Do come in.'

'Good morning, Mrs Meadows. Have you a moment to spare?'

'Yes, of course. I'm just going to make a drink for myself and the girls. Would you join us?'

'Oh yes, please. There's nothing I'd like better.'

Muriel stepped eagerly into the hall of Suzy and Patrick's house. Laura Ashley had had a field day here. Muriel loved the delicate grey carpet and the complementary wallpaper. These old houses really were worth the effort of doing them up.

The three little girls stood shyly in the hall watching their visitor. Muriel made a special point of remembering children's names as she felt it was so important to them. Daisy knew her from the infant school music lessons.

'Hello, Daisy and Pansy, and you, little Rosie.'

'Hello, Miss Hipkin. Have you come to see me?' Daisy enquired.

'Well, your mother really, but I'm delighted to see you, Daisy. Are you enjoying the holidays?'

'Want to get back to school, I like that best. After the summer holidays Pansy will be going too.'

'Yes, I know. I saw Mr Palmer putting her name on a list only the other day.'

Suzy brought the girls Ribena and wholesome-looking oatmeal biscuits. Muriel and Suzy had coffee.

'Mrs Meadows . . .'

'Suzy, please.'

'Well, Suzy then, I've come on a little fishing expedition. Peter, you know, Mr Harris, is wanting to start a playgroup for the little ones. They are hoping to have it in the church hall, although that's not definite, but they will be looking for someone to lead the group and for other helpers as well. It occurred to me that you might be interested in running the group. I know you were a teacher before the babies came along and I thought you would be an ideal person. Mr Harris, Peter, you know, doesn't know I've come to see you, so it's all very secret at the moment.'

'You must be the answer to a prayer. I would *love* to do it. What an opportunity! I could bring Rosie with me because she's the right age. Oh, Miss Hipkin, I could kiss you! In fact, I will!'

Suzy stood up, took Muriel by the shoulders and gave her a hearty kiss on each cheek. 'Seeing as we're in the Common Market you can have a continental kiss.'

Muriel hadn't been kissed since she couldn't remember when. Her mother hadn't been one for kissing, and there wasn't anyone else. She blushed bright red.

'It isn't definite yet, because Mr Harris doesn't know I'm here, but if you seriously mean you want to do it then I'll have a word.'

'Oh, I do, I do. It will be such an advantage for the children to have a playgroup. Just think of all the children on the farms and the ones from the Big House. Those poor little mites will be in their seventh heaven.'

'This coffee is lovely, thank you very much for it. I'll go and see the rector now and tell him of our plan. Dr Harris says she thinks it will have to be a mother and toddler group until we get proper permission from the County. We must walk before we run. Bye bye, dear girls.'

'Bye bye, Miss Hipkin,' they said, their mouths full of crumbly biscuit.

'My head's exploding with plans, Miss Hipkin. I shan't be able to sleep tonight for thinking about it.'

'Mr Meadows won't mind, will he? I know some men can be funny about their wives having jobs outside the home.'

'Oh, don't worry about Patrick. He probably won't even notice I'm doing it. Anyway, men don't mind wives having jobs nowadays. Let me know as soon as you can about the playgroup. Liz Neal would probably help as well.'

'Of course, I'd forgotten about her. Bye bye . . . Suzy.'

Muriel stepped along past the infant teacher's cottage to the Rectory and rang the bell.

Peter answered the door wearing his decorating trousers and an old shaggy jumper relegated to the bin by Caroline but rescued just in time.

'Come in, Muriel, you've caught me finishing painting my study. How do you like the colour I've chosen?'

'Lovely, it's really lovely. I'd no idea this room could be so light. What a difference! The white woodwork sets it off so nicely. It takes courage to choose such strong colours. I'm afraid my house is white or magnolia and that's that. I've really come to see you on parish business. You remember we were taking about starting a playgroup? Well, I think – with your approval of course – that I've found the very person to be the leader.'

'That's excellent, Muriel. Who is it?'

'Suzy Meadows. She can take little Rosie with her and when I mentioned it she jumped at the chance.'

Peter turned to look out of the window to hide his consternation. Muriel awaited his grateful thanks.

'She used to be a teacher, you know, before the girls were born and I think she would enjoy getting back into the fray, so to speak.'

'What a good idea, Muriel. I should never have thought of asking her. Are you sure it won't be too much for her with those three girls to look after and her . . . husband?'

'This new generation of women are much more energetic and determined than their mothers used to be. She's very keen.'

'Very well. We'll get the ball rolling. I'll make arrangements to meet her and get down to brass tacks. Thank you for being so inspired, Muriel.'

'Not at all. I'm looking forward to it all starting. Good morning, Rector. I'll see myself out.' And Muriel shut the Rectory door behind her.

Her next stop was the village store, where both Harriet and Jimbo were working. As Muriel entered, Harriet was serving Sharon and Scott from The Royal Oak.

Sharon was choosing her shopping with a disdainful expression on her face. 'You haven't got no convenience foods, have you, like what we sell in Tesco's. Lovely Chicken Kiev and things all ready to pop in the oven, we have there. Scott, put that KitKat down. Mum said you weren't to have no more chocolate today.'

'Shut up you, I'll do as I like.' Scott picked up the KitKat, tore off the wrapper and began eating it.

Jimbo fumed. 'You'll have that to pay for, Sharon.'

'He can pay for it himself, I'm not paying.'

'Can't, our Sharon. Haven't got no money.'

'Wait till I get you home, I'll tell Mum about this.'

'If you do I'll tell her about where you were last night.'

Muriel felt compelled to intervene. 'That's not the way to talk to your sister, Scott. You should pay for it. Come to think of it, you shouldn't have taken the chocolate in the first place if your mother says you shouldn't.'

'Shut up, Miss Prim Hipkin. Miss Neat an' Tidy, Miss Dull an' Boring, mind your own business.'

'Well really.' Muriel blushed bright red. This nasty little boy had spoken out loud something she'd been thinking about herself for quite a while. But it was disconcerting to hear the truth from one so young.

Jimbo marched round from the cheese counter, took hold of Scott by his collar and removed him from the store.

'Out, you, and stay out. You can come back in when you've apologised for your bad behaviour. And if your father wants to know why I've sent you packing, ask him to come round to see me.'

Sharon didn't even have the grace to apologise for her brother. She paid for the goods she'd bought and sauntered out of the shop, putting her tongue out at Muriel as she went.

Harriet sat Muriel down on a chair and gave her a coffee from the machine provided for customers.

'Sit here, Miss Hipkin, and drink this. I'm sorry he was so rude. The parents are to blame, not him – remember that.'

Jimbo was fuming. 'And you remember, Harriet, that Scott McDonald is not allowed in here until he has apologised – and I mean it.'

'Jimbo, The Royal Oak is a very good customer of ours.'

'I know, I know, but I won't have him in. He'll be shoplifting next.'

Muriel found her tongue. 'He's very difficult in school, you know. Mr Palmer has to keep him on a tight rein. He always plays up in music lessons.'

'Doesn't get enough attention at home, I suppose.' Harriet had turned away to press on with collecting ingredients for some cheesecakes she was making for the freezer.

Jimbo went into the meat department to find some trimmings from a hindquarter of beef that he'd just cut into joints for a customer. He presented them to Muriel in a smart dark green plastic bag with 'Turnham Malpas Village Store' printed on it.

'To Pericles from Jimbo with his compliments.'

'How kind you are, Mr Charter-Plackett. Pericles will enjoy himself. You indulge him too much.'

'Not at all, it's my pleasure.'

After Muriel had made her purchases she wandered off home. As she paused to check the road before she crossed, Scott McDonald approached from the green and, ramming something into her shopping bag, ran off laughing. When she looked inside she found his KitKat wrapper. He'd quite spoilt her day. It had begun so well, solving the problem of the playgroup leader and admiring Peter's colour scheme and looking forward to shopping for her little bits and pieces – and now Scott had ruined it all. She couldn't demean herself by speaking to Mr McDonald. She didn't go into The Royal Oak: ladies didn't. She had to hope it would all blow over. However, Pericles enjoyed his fresh meat and eventually her usual cheerfulness reasserted itself.

Muriel's visit had left Suzy Meadows all of a dither.

'Come on, girls, we'll go round to Mrs Neal's and tell her about the playgroup. I know it's not official but I'm bursting to talk to someone about it.'

Rosie shrugged on her anorak and asked her mother what a playgroup was.

'A school for little girls and boys who are not old enough to go to Mr Palmer's school.'

'Where?'

'In the church hall, I expect.'

'Oh.' Rosie popped her thumb in her mouth whilst she sorted out her feelings about it.

Liz was pruning her roses in the front garden. Guy and Hugh were racing madly about on their bikes.

'Liz, I just had to come round. Muriel Hipkin has told me that the rector is thinking of starting a playgroup in the church hall and she is going to suggest me as the leader.'

'I know, I know.'

'How do you know?'

'Peter's been round to see me this morning. It's not going to be in the church hall – well, it might be to start with – but then with any luck it will be moved to that spare room in the Infants.'

'Liz, has he asked you to be leader?'

'Of course not, I'm not a teacher. He just wanted to know if I would be willing to help you, and help form a committee.'

'Would you mind working with me?'

'I'd love to. We both need some kind of outlet and this would be just the thing. Hugh, leave Pansy alone – she doesn't want to ride your bike. Stop it, please. Let's all go inside and get Chinese Checkers out or something. Come on, all of you.'

When Suzy left Liz's house she decided to take the bull by the horns and call on Peter.

He answered the door and invited them all inside.

'I hope you don't mind me coming to call,' Suzy began rather shyly. 'Have I caught you when you're busy on anything? No? Well, Miss Hipkin has been round to ask if I might be interested in starting a playgroup and I've come to say yes, I'd be delighted.'

Peter had lifted Pansy onto his knee and given her his watch to play with. Rosie was trying hard to get it off her.

'Let me see if I can find something for you to play with.' He opened a drawer in his desk and took out paper and a pencil. 'There you are – draw me a picture. I would be delighted, too, if you would do it,' he said, finally meeting Suzy's bright blue eyes. 'We need enthusiasm but we also need expertise, and it will make it much easier for us to get the use of the room in the school if the person in charge is known to be properly qualified for the job. I envisage a really lively playgroup doing a real job, not just keeping the children out of their mothers' way. Would that be how you would feel about it?'

'Yes, of course. It will make Toria Clark's job so much easier if the new intake have had the experience of a good playgroup. Liz Neal is very willing to help. I don't know about charges, though. I'll ask around some of my friends in London and see what they pay.'

'I hadn't thought about charges, but of course there will have to be one. You ask around and I'll draft a letter for the Council and get someone to come down and view our facilities. If we can have it in the school that would be the best. If not, the church hall.'

'I won't keep you any longer, Peter. Come along, girls. Isn't it exciting? I can't wait to get started!'

'My daddy's gone to America this morning.' Pansy looked up at Peter as she told him her news.

'Oh, I see. Will he be away long?'

'No, just three or four days.' Suzy took hold of Rosie and set off for the door.

Peter saw them out and stood watching them walk along the pavement. They lived next door but one. He heartily wished it hadn't been Suzy who was the most suitable candidate for the job.

Two days later Suzy, her head full of lists and jobs to do towards the successful opening of the playgroup, answered a knock at the door. Expecting it to be Muriel with more news about the project, she had a shock when she found a policewoman and what looked like two detectives standing there. The older man showed her his warrant card and then asked if she was Mrs Patrick Meadows.

'Yes, I am.'

'May we come in?'

'Yes.'

They stood looking at one another in a group in the hall.

Finally the policewoman said, 'I'm afraid we have some bad news for you, Mrs Meadows. It's your husband. I'm sorry to say he has died.'

'*Died?* You must be mistaken – he's in America. No, no, you've got it all wrong. It must be another Patrick Meadows. My husband is giving a paper to the Commission. He'll be home tomorrow – won't he?' Her voice trailed off as she recognised the embarrassed sympathy in the faces of the officers.

The policewoman took her into the sitting room and helped her to a chair.

'I'll go and make a cup of tea for you, Mrs Meadows. Where are the children?'

'How do you know I've got children?'

The policewoman pointed to the bottom bookshelf where the children kept their books.

'They're at my mother's for a couple of days. I'll make the tea.' She started to get up out of the chair but the WPC gently pushed her back down again and disappeared into the kitchen. The two detectives stood in front of her. The younger one was looking about the room as though expecting clues to come leaping out of the walls.

Suzy managed to find some words to say. 'How did he . . . how did . . . what happened?'

'He died in his car.'

'You mean he had an accident?'

'Well, no, it appeared to be intentional.'

'Intentional? What do you mean, "intentional"?'

'He used the exhaust pipe and a piece of hose.'

'You mean *suicide*? Patrick wouldn't commit suicide. He's not that kind of person!'

'In view of the top secret job he was doing, Mrs Meadows, could we be allowed to look through his papers and belongings to see if we can find a reason for what has happened? If not today, perhaps another day when you're feeling more able to cope.'

'Where was he when he . . . he . . . did it?'

'He was found this morning at first light. He'd parked his car on the cliffs near Flamborough Head in Yorkshire.'

'Oh well, it definitely isn't Patrick then, because he went to America three days ago. I packed his case for him.'

'He never actually left the country, Mrs Meadows. He had no passport, no currency, no ticket – nothing to indicate that that was what he intended to do.'

'He said he was going. He never told lies – he was scrupulously honest.'

'Had he been behaving oddly recently?'

'He always behaved oddly. Everyone thought he was odd, but it was normal for him. His mind was always preoccupied with his work; he didn't socialise or bother with the children. There was nothing different about him that day he left.'

'We found this letter addressed to you. I'll put it here on the mantelpiece and then you can read it when you feel ready. If there is anything in it that might throw light on his state of mind or why he did it we'd be glad to know.'

'Thank you. That's his desk over there. You can look in it if you wish.'

Suzy laid her head back, unable to grasp what had happened. Her mind was racing over the happenings of the last few weeks before Patrick had left for America. Had there been some clues which she'd failed to recognise? Suddenly she shot bolt upright. 'However am I going to tell the children? Oh dear God, what am I going to do?'

The matter-of-fact voice of the policewoman broke in with a kindly, 'Here's your tea, Mrs Meadows.' She didn't notice that the tea was scalding hot, she was so thirsty. The senior one of the two detectives had begun searching Patrick's desk: methodically, drawer by drawer, file by file, letter by letter. His filofax was in the top drawer. Suzy knew when she saw the detective begin to look through it that Patrick had never intended to go to America. He took the filofax with him whenever he left the house. It was filled with names, addresses and messages, all necessary to his work. So he had acted out of character, even before he'd left for work that last morning.

'He was frightened – that was it. He was frightened that morning when he left,' Suzy told the policewoman in a shaking voice. 'I don't know what he was frightened of, but he was.'

'Did you do much entertaining of people from the office or the laboratories, Mrs Meadows?'

'Well, sometimes we did, but not often. Patrick wasn't a very social being. Occasionally we had people from abroad. They stayed here – they liked the idea of the typical English village.'

'What nationality were they?'

'Middle Eastern sometimes, or European, and once an American.'

'Was everything all right between the two of you? You know, were you close enough for him to confide in you?'

Suzy felt as though she was carved out of wood. There was no part of her of which she was in command. All control had gone. Slowly tears began to trickle down her face. Not huge rolling streams of tears but a steady trickle like drizzling rain. She knew she'd have to get to the lavatory quickly or she was going to wet herself. She found herself in the cloakroom, where she suffered violent diarrhoea. It must have been almost ten minutes before she had sufficient control to leave. The policewoman knocked on the door twice to ask if she was in need of help but Suzy's voice had gone and she couldn't reply. Finally she came out and went back to the sitting room. She sat trembling uncontrollably. The room was so cold.

'We'll leave now, Mrs Meadows. I'm taking this filofax to the station to see if I can find anything that might be of help. I'll give you a receipt for it. Debra will stay with you. If there's anything you think of that might be of help, tell Debra and she'll let us know.' The three of them went into the hall and Suzy could hear them quietly talking. Debra came back in, took off her jacket and sat down in the chair opposite her.

A few minutes after the detectives had gone the door-bell rang. Debra answered it. Whoever was at the door was invited in and stood talking in the hall. The sitting-room door opened and framed in the doorway with his head bent because of his height stood Peter Harris. He was wearing his white marriage cassock. He appeared to Suzy like an angel sent from God to comfort her.

'Mrs Meadows, I saw the police car outside so I came to see if you needed help. The policewoman has told me what's happened. I'm so sorry.'

Peter took her hands in his and automatically rubbed them to bring some warmth to them. She smiled at him. 'Thank you for coming.'

'I'm sorry I'm wearing this cassock, I've been conducting a service. Do we know why it happened?'

Debra explained that they knew no reason for it but that Mr Meadows had left a letter for Mrs Meadows. She seemed glad of an opportunity to mention it as though anxious to know what was in it, but sensitive enough not to suggest opening it.

'Would you like to open it while I'm here, Mrs Meadows?' When Suzy nodded Peter picked up the letter and handed it to her. She gave it back to him and asked him to read it to her.

'I really can't do that, Suzy: Patrick meant it for you. It will be very private. Perhaps we'd better leave it till later when you feel more yourself.' He held her hand and she held his as though by doing so she held onto reality.

'I shan't have a funeral service for him. It would be an absolute mockery if we did. He had no time for the Church. I'll just have him cremated. No hymns, no prayers. There'll be no afterlife for him, Peter. He's finished. Give me the letter.'

'"*Suzy,*"' she read. '"*The research I have been doing for the last three years has proved to be based on a total misconception, a complete falsehood. I am so appalled by my colossal mistake, that I have destroyed all my notes and the paper I was preparing, so no one will find out what a horrifying waste of time these last three years have been. I might as well never have lived at all. I can't face my colleagues, so I am obliterating myself.*"

'Peter, here – you read it.'

He took the letter expecting to read a loving farewell. He'd read suicide notes before, but this was the cruellest. Hot tears began to fall on the hand Suzy held. He looked into her face and saw her Madonna-like features crumpled with grief. He held her close whilst the tears fell. Gradually the tears lessened and Suzy spoke.

'Did you notice, Peter, that there was nothing in the letter about me or the children? Nothing about what will happen to us now, or how we shall live? Nothing about "how much I have loved you or sorry for what has happened"? Losing him is bad enough, but to know he hadn't a thought for us is what really hurts.'

'I think you need someone to be with you. We ought to get your mother to come and bring the girls home.'

'Oh dear Lord, how on earth can I tell them? What words do you use? "Your father's killed himself because he can't live with himself any more? He didn't care a fig for you all"?'

'Perhaps your mother could help you to find the right words. Whatever you say it won't be easy, I'm afraid. We should contact Patrick's parents. I'll tell them for you if you would like me to.'

'His parents both died when he was in his twenties. He has no one, except a distant aunt who never bothers with him. Will you ring my parents and get them to come and bring the girls? The number's here.'

After a pause she said, her voice trembling: 'I'll sit here waiting. I don't know what I'm waiting for, but I am. Patrick will be home soon. He's always early on Thursdays.'

4

First thing next morning, before she left for the hospital, Caroline placed a vase of flowers on Peter's desk with a little note telling him how much she loved him. She looked out of the study window to see what the weather was going to be like. Outside on the pavement were four or five photographers and press reporters, grouped around Suzy's door. Their cars were parked haphazardly on the village green. So the ghouls had arrived. She could just imagine the headlines: '*Nuclear physicist dies. Was it murder?*'

'Peter, come here a minute. Look at this.'

He was horrified. 'This simply won't do. I'm going out to stop it. First I'll ring the police – they ought to be here.'

'I'll ring them. You go out and have a word.'

Peter swept out of the Rectory door and down the pavement, his cassock swishing angrily as he walked.

'I would be most grateful if you would kindly move away from here and leave Mr Meadows' widow and her children in peace.' The reporters clustered around Peter, holding their microphones up ready to catch his words.

'Can you give us some information about Mrs Meadows? How many children has she? Did she realise something was seriously wrong? Will she come out for an interview?'

'Have you not listened to what I said? I asked you to move away from here. Get in your cars and go. Please.'

'Now, sir, you can't expect us to leave a headline story like this, the public have a right to know. A top nuclear physicist is found dead in his car . . . something must be *very* wrong. Could be a breach of national security.'

'Has his wife being playing away?'

'Is it marriage problems? You'll know, sir, being the vicar.'

They all clamoured around him.

'Can you get us an interview?'

Peter towering above them all caught a glimpse of the little girls watching from a downstairs window and the hurt this must be causing them made him angrier still.

'Come into my study and I'll tell you everything I know,' he promised, saying the first thing that came into his head just to get them away.

'Right, sir, you lead the way.'

Having got them away from Suzy's house, Peter then had to think what on earth he would say when they reached his study. At the same time, he remembered why he was wearing his cassock: the children from the school were coming to church for their morning prayers. As he opened the Rectory door to let the reporters in, the police arrived. The local sergeant, beefy and belligerent, made his views known.

'Now then, gentlemen and ladies, we don't want Mrs Meadows troubled by all of you stood about. Have some consideration, if you please. Those cars will have to be moved. It's an offence to park on the green, and I shall put the owners on a charge if the vehicles are not moved immediately. Constable, you can stand on duty outside Mrs Meadows' house. Let's have these cars moved pronto, if you please. The Royal Oak will be open soon so you can go and sit in there for a bit. They've got a car park, too.'

When the group of eager journalists had dispersed, he turned to Peter. 'Thank you, sir, for moving them on. Never thought they'd be on to it as quick as this. Reckon they must be telepathic.'

'Mrs Meadows needs to be protected from these people. She has quite enough to contend with.'

'You're absolutely right, Rector. I'll see to it. Nice to meet you, sir, sorry it's in such difficult circumstances.'

'Thank you. Must be off, got a service to take.'

There must have been almost thirty children gathered in the church for their Friday morning prayers. Muriel Hipkin was seated at the piano playing gentle 'settling down' pieces. She'd often fancied trying out the organ but felt it was beyond her. In any case, Mrs Peel would have had something to say about that; she jealously guarded her position of organist. Michael Palmer stood as Peter entered the church and the children followed suit. Everyone, that is, except Scott McDonald, who was feeling anti-everything that morning. Muriel frowned at him but he stuck out his tongue and ignored her.

Peter, well practised at attracting everyone's attention, had Scott out at the front as his assistant before he knew where he was. He cooperated wonderfully and displayed an intelligence at odds with his usual silly behaviour. However, as he passed the piano on his way back to his seat he made a rude gesture to Muriel. She turned her bright pink face to the music and played the tune for going out. That boy really was obnoxious. She didn't like using that word about a child but it fitted him exactly.

Peter argued with himself as to whether or not he should go in to see Suzy again. Best not, he eventually decided. He might find himself holding her hands in a most un-rector-like manner, and that would never do. As he settled down at his desk to commence his notes for Sunday's sermon he noticed the flowers and the note propped up against the vase.

'*To my dearest Peter, to keep you cheerful till I get back. All my love, Caroline.*'

He leant forward so that he could appreciate the scent of the flowers. It was gestures like this which made Caroline so endearing. The two of them were like one person and he never wanted to spend even a single night away from her. If he lost her through death like Suzy had lost Patrick, his life would be over. A large family would have completed their happiness, but God in His wisdom had seen it differently. Perhaps if Peter had had children he would not have been able to devote his life so entirely to the Church. He'd never replaced the crude painting of the Madonna which he'd taken down that day, but nevertheless the image of her face kept reappearing in his mind. Suzy – a rather ridiculous name, but it suited her. She might move away then he would have a chance to forget her. He recollected her face crumpled in grief. Why on earth hadn't the man said something in his letter about how he felt? Why hadn't he said the kind of things Peter had read in other suicide notes, like: '*You will be well provided for,*' or, '*The insurance policies are in the bottom drawer,*' or '*I love you. Please forgive me.*'? There had been nothing of his relationship with his family at all. Peter pushed to the back of his mind thoughts about Patrick's relationship with Suzy. If he was as icy-cold in his life as he had been in his letter of death, maybe their marriage had not been idyllic.

The phone rang.

'Caroline here. Is everything all right with Suzy? I had to dash, I was running late.'

'Yes. The police have moved the reporters on and there's a constable outside the door. Darling, can I come into Culworth and take you out to lunch?'

'I'd love that – what a nice surprise! See you about twelve-thirty outside Casualty. Bye, darling.'

When he got back from his lunch with Caroline, Suzy's mother called round to say that she and her husband were taking Suzy and the girls to live with them for a few days. They'd be leaving tomorrow. Could Peter call in this afternoon while they took the children out and advise their daughter about Patrick's cremation? Suzy didn't want the girls to overhear, as she had no intention of them going to it . . .

It was about three o'clock when Peter saw the girls set out with Suzy's parents. He waited five minutes and then went round. The constable had gone and the reporters were nowhere to be seen. Suzy answered the door. He'd expected her to be in black but she was wearing a bright pink shirt and white trousers, with her hair tied up in a pink ribbon. Only the dark shadows under her eyes showed her distress. She took his hand and drew him in. They discussed Patrick's cremation. The police had told her that it would be some time before his body would be released: post mortem etc, etc.

'I want no one there. I'll go by myself. I shall put his ashes in the bin. No, no, it's no good protesting, I shall do just that. And I'm staying in this house. The children are upset enough without moving them to a strange place. And, Peter, I don't want you at the cremation. No one – just me. Then I can forget him. Do you know, we had not made love for over a year? Fancy that. I've not told anyone that but you. Don't really know why I'm telling you. Yes, I do. Yes, I do. Please comfort me, please.'

Suzy reached out her hand as she finished speaking and took hold of his arm. Peter lifted her hand and held it to his cheek, then turned it over and kissed the palm.

5

Muriel, taking Pericles for his afternoon walk, had stopped for a rest on the seat under The Royal Oak on the green. She'd seen Peter go into Suzy Meadows' house and had decided to have a word with him when he came out. She needed to know if Suzy wanted help with the children. Muriel quite fancied having the three of them for the afternoon some time. Poor little mites. She hoped they were too young to understand fully what had happened. Little Rosie in particular would never remember her father. He'd always been strange, had Patrick. It really wasn't surprising that he had committed suicide – though with so much to live for at home, how could he leave them all?

The sun had gone in and it had become quite chilly. She decided that she was only making an excuse to have someone to talk to. That was it – she was so lonely she had to make up excuses to talk to people. What must it be like, to be grateful for a moment of peace and quiet? Fancy being so busy, so very busy that being left alone felt like a bonus.

That was it, then. She would march purposefully across the green, down Shepherd's Hill and cross the spare land and walk by Turnham Beck. Pericles liked rooting about on the banks. Do something positive, she had read in a magazine article. Yes, *positive.* Her brown walking shoes made quite a brisk noise as she set off determinedly for the beck.

It must have been over an hour before she came back into Shepherd's Hill and turned up Jacks Lane. As she came out at the top of the lane and crossed to her house she glanced towards the rectory and saw Peter leaving Suzy's house. Poor dear, she must be very distressed. How thoughtful of the rector to spend so much time with her. Muriel waved enthusiastically to him but he didn't see her. It must be very draining, she thought, dealing with people who are bereaved.

*

The following Tuesday was not one of Muriel's better days. She played the piano at the school from 10.30 to 11.30; half an hour for the Infants and then, while they were out at play, half an hour for the Juniors. The first half hour she always enjoyed. Toria Clark was a lovely, lively girl just right for tiny ones, but the Juniors were another story. How Mr Palmer controlled them she didn't know. So calm he was, and yet they did as they were told.

Muriel had very nearly been late for school. She'd begun baking early for a coffee morning, but somehow the cakes had not been ready to come out of the oven and she'd had to wait around. Finally, she'd got to school. She usually put her coat and her keys in the tiny teachers' room, but being late she'd left them on top of the piano. Halfway through the Juniors' lesson, half a dozen infants had come running in, shouting: 'Miss Hipkin! Peri-what's-it is in the playground.' They were closely followed by what appeared to be the entire Infant Department. Miss Clark also came hurrying in, hoping to retrieve the Juniors' singing lesson before it was too late.

Pandemonium reigned. The entire school rushed out to help catch the errant poodle, but by that time, Pericles was over the wall and well on his way down to the beck. With a booming command, Mr Palmer stopped the children from crossing Shepherd's Hill just in time, and ushered them all back into school. Meanwhile, the singing lesson forgotten, Muriel stumbled on the rough ground as she hurried after him. 'Pericles, Pericles!'

She shouted in vain. He scampered on, leaving her well behind. Tears began to run over the edges of her eyes and trickle down her face. She hadn't anyone who cared, apart from Pericles, and even he had decided to desert her. She struggled on, calling his name. Just as she had given up on him and decided to sit down on the grass and wait, Sir Ronald appeared with Pericles tucked under one arm and Lady Bissett's Pomeranian under the other.

'Found him digging a big hole down by that rabbit burrow in the bottom field. 'Fraid he's dirty, Miss Hipkin. Now, now, don't take on so. He's safe and sound.' He handed Pericles to her and she thanked him profusely. Muriel didn't enjoy being under an obligation to such a common man but she had to tolerate it.

'Thank you very much indeed. How he got out of the house I don't know. I do appreciate your kindness, Sir Ronald. Thank you again.'

When she got back to school the caretaker was getting the hall ready for dinners.

'Sorry to trouble you, Mrs Duckett. I left my coat and keys on top of the piano.'

'Here's yer coat but there ain't no keys with it, Miss Hipkin.'

'Oh, there are. I left them there.'

'Only yer coat. There ain't no keys whatsoever.'

Muriel looked under the piano and moved the chairs about in the hope that they had been knocked off in the excitement.

'I've just put all them chairs ready for dinners, do you mind!'

'Sorry, Mrs Duckett. Maybe I never locked the house at all – perhaps that's how Pericles got out. Oh dear, I do hope I haven't been burgled!'

'Don't put that Prickles down in 'ere, this floor's clean.'

'Sorry. I'll be off then.'

She hurried home to find the back door wide open but the front door locked and no sign of her keys. She spent most of the afternoon worrying herself to death. She must pull herself together. Sixty-four didn't mean you were in your dotage. The keys must be at school somewhere. Her spare ones were hidden under a plant pot in the back garden. She'd use those till the others turned up. What a mercy she'd hidden the spare set in case she ever locked herself out.

The next two nights were uncomfortable ones and she didn't sleep at all well. On the Thursday when she went to school to play for movement lessons, Michael Palmer greeted her, jangling her keys in his hand.

'Look what I've just found amongst the music in the piano stool. I was sorting out what we needed for this morning and there they were.'

'Oh, thank you, Mr Palmer. What a relief! How foolish of me.'

The postman rarely called at number 1 Glebe Cottages, but on the mat the next morning was a lovely thick envelope. Inside was a gold-edged invitation card. Harriet and James Charter-Plackett invited Miss Muriel Hipkin to dinner to celebrate James's fortieth birthday. Formal dress. Never, ever, had Muriel attended any event at which the gentlemen wore dinner jackets. The incident of the keys dwindled into insignificance. Two weeks today, no – two weeks and one day. What on earth should she wear? And what should she buy Jimbo for his birthday? Equally important, who else had been honoured with an invitation? Her finances were stretched to the limit just living from day to day; extra expense caused havoc. The only answer would be to dip into her capital. After all, this *was* the highlight of her year. Surely she could afford to live dangerously for a while? A visit to Culworth and the Building Society was a must and while she was there she would look for a suitable present and for a dress.

Wednesday would be the best day to go. Monday didn't seem the right day for shopping in her mind; there was too much washing and ironing to do and tidying of the house after the weekend. Tuesday and Thursday she was needed at the school, and Friday morning she played for the morning prayers in the church, which meant that she would miss the only bus into town. So Wednesday it was.

Tuesday evening there was a knock at the door and on the step stood Caroline Harris.

'Hope I'm not intruding. I felt like a chat – have you the time?'

'Of course! Do come in. Shall we have a cup of tea, or would you like a sherry? I do have a very nice one. It's years old and very good.'

'Sherry would make a delightful change from the gallons of tea I drink at the hospital. I swear if there was a shortage of tea the whole place would grind to a halt. What a lovely house you have, Muriel. That does sound rude but I can't help but comment.'

Muriel disappeared into the sideboard cupboard and re-emerged with a bottle of sherry and two very attractive crystal glasses. A little tray with a neat white cloth on it and a china plate with dry biscuits arranged in a circle completed her hospitality.

'I heard all about Pericles escaping,' Caroline said. 'I'm glad you found him safe and sound.'

'Well, actually, it was Sir Ronald who found him. He'd been digging for rabbits – Pericles, that is, not Sir Ronald.' They both giggled at the prospect of Sir Ronald digging for rabbits.

Caroline took a sip of her sherry and a nibble of her biscuit, dusted the crumbs from her skirt and cleared her throat.

'We've had an invitation from Jimbo and Harriet to Jimbo's fortieth birthday party.'

'So have I – isn't it exciting? I'm going into Culworth tomorrow to buy a present for him, though I haven't any idea what to get.'

'I'll give you a lift if you like. I always leave by eight-thirty – would that be convenient?'

'Oh yes, it would, then I'll come back on the bus.'

'Muriel, I do hope you won't take offence, but have you decided what to wear?'

'That is a problem. I have nothing at all suitable, because I've never been to a smart dinner like this. One can't wear a nice wool dress, one must be a little fancy.'

'Look, I don't see any point in you spending money on a dress you'll not get a lot of wear out of. You and I are about the same height, so how about if I lend you one of mine? If I've given offence I'm sorry. It was just a suggestion.'

'Not at all. Do you really mean that?'

'Of course I do. Because we're new here no one's seen my smart clothes so they will never know. Look, it's dark outside so we wouldn't be noticed – why not sneak across now and have a try on?'

'What a splendid idea. Mr Harris won't mind, will he?'

'Of course not. He'll be glad to be of help.'

It was embarrassing for Muriel to be undressing in Caroline and Peter's bedroom. They'd not got round to decorating it yet, but on the old carpet Caroline had spread a huge off-white rug which felt luxuriously comfortable to Muriel's stockinged feet. On a chair in the window was Peter's running kit, and his trainers lay on the floor beneath. Caroline's nightgown – a peach-coloured silk confection – lay on the bedspread beside Peter's Paisley pyjamas. It felt almost indecent to see their night-clothes in such close proximity, as if she was peeking into their private life. Out of dear Mr Furbank's huge old wardrobe came three delightful evening dresses.

'This black one with the bead decoration on the bodice would look good on you, Muriel, don't you think?'

'It's beautiful. The beadwork is quite splendid but for someone my age, I think the arms would be too bare, don't you?'

'Ah, but you see there is a long-sleeved jacket to wear over the top for dinner. It's in the wardrobe somewhere – ah, here we are. Try it on.'

The beaded dress fitted Muriel exactly. If she'd been to a shop, this would have been the very one she would have bought. When Caroline fastened the tiny georgette bolero over the top she gasped at the change in herself.

'Why, this is wonderful! Do you really mean that I can borrow it? I shall have to do something with my hair.'

'When I've worn it before I've used this hair ornament to hold my hair back. Look, like this.'

The black velvet clasp holding her hair smoothly back from her face suited Muriel beautifully. All she needed was to find those black court shoes she'd had since the sixties.

'I'm going to wear this cream thing, I think. Peter loves me in this.'

Muriel had changed back into her own clothes and stood looking at herself in the long mirror of dear Mr Furbank's wardrobe. Given half a chance and the money, she might have made something of herself, but it was too late now. The two of them wrapped the dress and jacket in a carrier bag and went downstairs. Peter was on the phone. 'Yes, certainly I'll come round. Yes, straight away.' He hung up and turned to Caroline.

'Darling, that was Suzy Meadows. She wants me to go round. She didn't go to her mother's after all. Will you come with me? Sorry, Muriel, good evening. I'm forgetting my manners.'

'I was going to have an early night, Peter.'

'I'll say good night to you both, and thank you, Caroline, for thinking of this. I'll be here not one minute later than eight-thirty tomorrow.' Muriel held the carrier bag up in thanks and swiftly made her way out of the Rectory and home past Willie Biggs' cottage and St Thomas à Becket, and into her own Glebe Cottage. There she stood with her back to the door for a moment holding the bag up out of Pericles' way as he jumped and pranced celebrating her return.

Upstairs she carefully took the dress out of the bag, and laid it on the bed. Her clothes were off in a jiffy and the dress back on again. She tried it first of all without the bolero. There was a small hint of her brassière strap showing white against the black. Dare she wear it without a brassière? Since no one could see her at the moment she tried it without. Her size 34A brassière would not be missed, she thought. Who would know? No one but herself. Dare she? Why not! Lots of girls did nowadays, she'd noticed. The georgette bolero gave the finishing touch. She brushed her hair back and put the black velvet clasp in. She'd buy a little gift for Caroline tomorrow – some of those special Belgian chocolates from that expensive shop in Culworth. She would like that.

What Caroline *didn't* like, was Peter wanting her to go to Suzy's at this time of night.

'You've never asked me to go visiting with you before, darling.'

'We didn't live in a little village like this one before. I want you to be there, in case she needs a sedative or something.'

'It's not ethical for me to be dishing out drugs to other doctors' patients, you know that. Anyway, I'll come.' She reached up and kissed him on his lips, pushing her tongue against his teeth, enticing him to kiss her properly. He put his arms round her and kissed her as though he wouldn't be seeing her for a thousand years. His hands gently massaged her back and then slid down and pressed her body to his so that from toe to head she felt welded to him.

'Never forget that whatever might happen, I love you more than life itself. My love is always there for the asking.'

'Peter, I love you too, from now and for ever. I can't imagine my life without you. Now come on, down to earth if you please.' Laughingly Caroline pulled herself free and said, 'We're only going next door but one. Come on, she'll be wondering where you are. We'll finish this conversation in bed when we get back.'

When Suzy opened her door to them she was hysterical. She flung her arms around Peter, clutching his coat and alternately crying and screaming. Caroline's matter-of-fact voice in the background saying, 'Suzy, let us in or all the neighbours will be round,' brought her head up with a jerk.

She produced a handkerchief from her sleeve, wiped her eyes and drew back.

'I'm so sorry.' This was said more to Caroline than to Peter. 'I know I'm being ridiculous but the press will not leave us alone. They've been pestering my mother, they keep ringing me, they've been to the school where I used to teach, they've even found out where *I* went to school and have been asking friends what I was like at school. Nasty suggestive things like, "Was she very interested in boys? Did she have a lot of boyfriends? Did she take drugs?" They're trying to dig up dirt about me for their articles. I just need someone to consider my feelings. I'm sorry for asking you to come.' She burst into tears again and sat down with her head almost on her knees.

Caroline rooted about in the sideboard and found a bottle of brandy.

'What you need, my girl, is some brandy and a good night's sleep. Here you are – drink it slowly.' Caroline stood over her while Suzy, protesting, drank each and every drop.

'I don't want it.'

'Well, it'll do you good. Now to bed if you please, while you're feeling warm inside. I'm not going to leave you; I'll spend the night on the settee.'

Suzy vehemently shook her head. 'No, no, I can't have you do that for me! Please, I shall be all right.'

Caroline insisted and got her way. She found a pillow and a duvet and arranged them on the settee.

'Be a darling, Peter, and go home and bring me my night things. Or you stay here and I'll go.'

'No, I'll go.'

When he got back Suzy was tucked up in bed and Caroline was reassuring her that she would listen for the children. She peeped into the two bedrooms where the girls slept and wished she had to go the rounds in her own house every night before *she* went to bed . . . Peter came back to the house, gave her what he'd brought, kissed her and quietly left.

When, finally, the body was released for cremation, Suzy was free to put Patrick in the bin as she'd said she would. Caroline tried to persuade her to have the ashes buried at the crematorium, arguing that at the moment she felt that was what she wanted to do, but in later years she might think differently. Suzy disagreed.

The day the urn came home, she waited until it was dark and the children were in bed, then she put the urn in a Sainsbury's plastic bag and marched through the village to the beck. She couldn't quite bring herself to put the ashes in her own bin, so she was going to use the Council bin by the little footbridge. Watching the water flowing by, however, she decided it would be preferable to scatter her husband's last remains over the surface of Turnham Beck and let them rush away, eventually down to the sea perhaps and out into the world.

Suzy turned for home, feeling as though a door had been shut on a part of her life. There was nothing to do now but step forward into the next stage. Patrick's pension would be adequate if she lived carefully, and what with the playgroup and things she would be busy enough. Perhaps one day she might meet someone else whom she could love. But not yet. She needed to live for a while entirely for herself. For a start she'd find someone to babysit for her, perhaps Toria Clark would do it, and she would attend Jimbo's birthday party. Why not? She'd be a person again wholly unto herself, not having to worry about Patrick causing offence with his withdrawn, offhand manner.

6

Muriel had wrapped the pen she'd bought for Jimbo, written the card, washed her hair and manicured her nails, using that little manicure set in the leather case she hadn't bothered with for years. She'd taken a long lingering bath, and Pericles had been turned out in the garden for nearly an hour so he'd be all right till she got back. Her borrowed dress was laid out on the bed, her court shoes were gleaming and now she was putting some perfume on. 'Panache' it was called. Not the most expensive, but delightful just the same. A touch behind her ears, a touch on her wrists – well, perhaps more than a touch – and some at her throat. The clock said six-thirty. Oh dear, an hour before she needed to be there. She was ready much too soon.

Muriel lay on the bed in her underskirt reading this week's book from the mobile library – *A Horseman Riding By*. A most enjoyable story; what a lovely young man he was. When her little china clock said seven o'clock Muriel got up, refreshed herself with more Panache, put on her dress, tied the little bolero beneath her now unrestrained bosom, eased on her court shoes, picked up the evening bag she'd used at the annual Young Conservatives' Dance all those years ago, kissed Pericles on the top of his head and sallied forth to Jimbo's party.

She'd done that unforgivable thing, arrived first and too early. Seven-thirty for eight, the invitation had said, and look what she'd done – arrived at twenty-five past seven.

'Come in, Muriel, come in. Delighted to see you!' Jimbo kissed her warmly on both cheeks. 'You're not a customer tonight, you're a guest so I can call you Muriel and give you a kiss. I must say, you're looking stunning tonight. Where did you pick up that little number?' Muriel blushed. 'You three come here and greet Miss Hipkin.'

Out of the sitting room popped the boys Fergus and Finlay and then little Flick, all dressed in their best. 'Daddy, Daddy, can we give Miss Hipkin her sherry?' Flick asked excitedly.

'Don't worry, Muriel, they're not staying up for the dinner, just long enough to welcome everybody and then off to bed. We like our children to be sociable beings and to know how to behave. Yes, you may, gently now.'

'I'm much too early, I am sorry.'

'Not at all, it's good to see you. Harriet has everything under control. Excuse me while I attend to the wine.'

The children took Muriel into the sitting room. The boys led her to a chair and Flick brought her a sherry.

'How did you know I like sherry?'

'Daddy said you would. The others will want gin and tonics but he says you belong to the old school and you'd want sherry.'

'Oh, I see. Are you enjoying school?'

The boys pulled funny faces but Flick said, 'Oh, yes! Miss Clark is lovely. She's so funny, she's always making us laugh. She's not coming tonight, though. She's sitting in for Mrs Meadows.'

'Is Mrs Meadows coming, then?'

'Oh, yes. Mummy said it would do her good to mix a little.'

'How old are you, Flick?'

'Six, why?'

'You seem to know a lot of what goes on.'

'Mummy and Daddy think we should know. Anyway, I listen when I shouldn't.'

At that moment, Harriet came in with her mother and mother-in-law.

'Muriel – can I introduce my mother-in-law, Katherine, and of course you know my mother Sadie.' She took them to shake hands with Muriel and left them talking.

Katherine settled herself importantly in the chair next to Muriel, leaving Sadie Beauchamp to stand beside her.

'So, Muriel, you're one of the village people, are you?'

'I live in the village, yes.'

'All this seems rather a bore to me. Jimbo should never have organised this party. I've only come because I didn't want to let him down. He had a great career in a merchant bank, you know, doing famously until he got this idea that he would leave the rat race as he called it and come down here to be a grocer.'

Muriel felt bold enough to be controversial. Perhaps the sherry had gone to her head and not to her knees as usual.

'I'd hardly call him a grocer. He and Harriet have a very good business here. They're doing—'

Sadie indignantly interrupted. 'Sometimes, Katherine, you are extremely rude. They are making a great success of this business! I'm here every day, so I should know, and I can also see that Jimbo is in much better health than he was.'

'Allow me to know what is best for my own son.'

Sadie's gin and tonic began trembling in her hand. 'What's more, the whole atmosphere here is much better for the children. There's no more of that keeping up with the Algernons and the Arabellas; it's much better for them at the village school.'

Katherine snorted and turned her attention to making Muriel feel small.

'What have you done with your life – Muriel, is it?'

'I was a secretary to a solicitor until I retired. Now I live in Glebe Cottages.'

'I must say, you know how to dress – rather surprising for a village person. Though I don't suppose you get much chance to wear an ensemble like that. Who is this gorgeously handsome man coming in?'

Sadie smiled and told her he was the rector.

'The *rector*? What a perfect waste of a man. He should be in a city parish heading for a bishopric. His wife looks very stylish. I assume it *is* his wife, and not his mistress. One had to be so broad-minded where the clergy are concerned nowadays.'

Muriel stood up to welcome Caroline and Peter and introduce them to Jimbo's mother. Sadie they already knew from church. Muriel took this opportunity to escape and spend some time with Suzy, who had just arrived with Michael Palmer. Suzy was wearing a bright scarlet skintight dress which revealed more than it concealed. Muriel felt it was hardly suitable for a new widow. Which indeed Suzy knew it wasn't, but she was in a defiant mood. Mustn't cast a cloud over the festivities: Jimbo had a right to enjoy his party.

Harriet gently guided everyone into the dining room, so the children reluctantly went off to bed while the adults settled themselves at the table. How Harriet had ever found the time to lay the table, let alone provide all the wonderful food, Muriel could not understand. The table had been spread with a delicate pink cloth, down the centre of which were small glass candle-holders, each containing a pink candle gently illuminating small pink and white flower arrangements – just the right height not to obscure the face of the person sitting opposite you. There were three crystal wine glasses at each place setting, and a pink linen napkin arranged in the shape of a swan. The hors d'oeuvre were already in place. She knew Sadie came every day to help, but even that couldn't explain how all this food had been cooked to such perfection.

Peter and Caroline were seated opposite Muriel, and on either side of her she had Suzy and Katherine. Next to Caroline was Lady Bissett, with Sir Ronald next to his wife. It seemed an unfortunate choice to have Sheila and Caroline together, but Harriet wasn't to know they didn't get on. Jimbo sat on one end, with Harriet and her mother at the other. In between were Michael Palmer and Liz and Neville Neal; Neville being Jimbo's accountant.

The food was unusual and quite superb, and by the time Muriel had chosen hazelnut meringue for her dessert she'd no idea how she would find room for it. Three different wines at one sitting had made her very talkative and the wine had also loosened the tongue of Lady Bissett.

'We shall be very busy next weekend, shan't we Ron . . . ald?'

'Yes, indeed. We have Neil and Glenys coming for the weekend, you know.'

Caroline stopped eating her zabaglione and, all innocence, asked: 'Neil and Glenys? Should I know them?'

'Of course you know Neil and Glenys Kinnock! He's going to be the main speaker at the Labour Party rally in Culworth. We suggested they stayed with us – typical English country weekend and all that. Give them a chance to relax.' Sir Ronald had answered her in all seriousness, but Lady Bissett guessed Caroline was being provocative.

Peter gave Caroline a nudge but she ignored it, continuing: 'I do hope there won't be an overspill in the village, and that we shan't be inundated with banners and marchers. I understand that the rally is quite crucial as far as the Party is concerned.'

'No one will even know they're here – it's being kept secret. Well, the police know, of course. Thanks to his position in the Party they have to check out where Neil is.'

'I see.' Caroline put down her spoon and leaned over towards Lady Bissett, enquiring confidentially: 'Do they have any particular quirks which Central Office have had to tell you about?'

'Quirks? Certainly not. They're very nice people.' Lady Bissett turned to Peter. 'We do hope that now you're settled in here we shall soon be hearing the patter of tiny feet at the Rectory, Peter.'

After a short pause Caroline answered on his behalf. 'That you will not be hearing . . . Sheila.'

'Oh, you're one of these modern women who doesn't believe in having children, is that it? You're a career woman then?'

'It is a matter entirely between my husband and myself, and no concern of yours. I think you are being offensive.'

Peter interrupted with a kindly, 'To our great regret we are unable to have children, Lady Bissett.'

'It will soon be the Village Flower Show, Lady Bissett. What do you have in mind for it this year?' Muriel strove to change the conversation, but Sheila Bissett would have none of it.

'Being a doctor I would have thought you would have known what to do about it. There's all kinds of ways nowadays, you know. I don't know where I'd be without my Bianca and Brendan.'

'I have no need to resort to having children in order to justify my existence.'

Caroline was dangerously near to tears and Jimbo, receiving distress signals right down at his end of the table, sprang to his feet and offered Sheila Bissett more wine, thus diverting her from Caroline. Katherine Charter-Plackett intercepted a glance between Suzy and Peter. She leant towards Muriel and whispered in a loud voice: 'What's between the gorgeous Rector and that red siren? There's something going on.'

Muriel was horrified. Fortunately Caroline was occupied getting her feelings under control and missed Katherine's comment, but Peter didn't. He looked very distressed.

Neville sat back, well satisfied with his meal. 'Harriet, that was wonderful! You ought to open a restaurant, you know. You've got the talent and the experience.'

Harriet playfully put her hand over his mouth, as she spotted a sparkle come into Jimbo's eyes when he overheard the remark.

'Be quiet, Neville. Don't put any more ideas into his head, there's enough there already. No, Jimbo, down, boy, down. I'm not falling for that one.'

Neville continued making his point. 'There's that cottage next to Sadie's house going for a song, *and* it's got spare land at the side for a car park. Sadie would be very handy for keeping an eye on it, wouldn't you, Sadie? It would make an excellent restaurant, right opposite the village green and all.' They all burst out laughing but Jimbo didn't laugh; he made a note of it in the filing cabinet he called his mind.

After coffee and liqueurs they retired to the sitting room, where Jimbo had two bottles of champagne on ice. They all sang Happy Birthday to him whilst he opened the bottles.

'Your very good health, Jimbo. Here's to your fiftieth!' Peter said and they all applauded. After that they danced, played games and had a thoroughly riotous time. At midnight Peter said he really must go as he had early service tomorrow, and he and Caroline offered to escort Muriel home. Jimbo went with them to the door. He took Muriel by the shoulders and gave her a huge kiss.

'Thank you so much for my splendid pen. I shall treasure it as a gift from a lovely lady who did herself proud tonight.' Muriel felt bold enough to kiss him back.

Jimbo then kissed Caroline and whispered in her ear. 'Take no notice of my old hag of a mother. I don't. She isn't worth the candle – OK?'

She smiled, took Peter's hand and they went off into the night. The moon shone and the sky was full of stars bright and clear, a perfect ending to a lovely evening.

'Good night, good night and thank you for seeing me home.'

'Good night, Muriel, see you tomorrow.' Both Caroline and Peter waved to her as they turned down Church Lane towards the Rectory. Peter was gripping Caroline's hand tightly. Caroline remained silent. She knew how Peter longed for children and she longed for them, for his sake. The hurt engendered by Sheila Bissett was beyond endurance.

When they were safely tucked up in bed Caroline in a small tight voice offered Peter a divorce.

He sat up, shattered by what she had said. 'A *divorce*! Why?'

'Because you want children and I can't give them to you, that's why. Then you could marry someone who is able to give you children. How I would live without you I don't know, but for your sake I would have a jolly good try.'

There was a moment's silence before Peter answered.

'Caroline, I'm not worthy of you. I married you because you are the light of my life, not for the sole purpose of procreation. You make me feel very small. Don't ever dare suggest such a thing again. That is, unless you yourself truly want a divorce, though heaven help me if you did. Who'd want me anyway? There's only a saint like you could put up with me.'

'That's not true, you're very eligible. In fact, you're really rather superb. I saw Katherine Charter-Plackett looking you over!'

'Her tongue's too sharp. It's time she engaged her brain before she speaks. I'm giving you a good night kiss and then I'm going down to my study to have a word with the Lord.'

'You can have a word with Him here, if you wish.'

'No, you'll distract me. I need to think. Good night, my love.'

Peter went down to his study and wept.

Muriel, having waved them goodbye, unlocked her door and found Pericles looking worried. She hurriedly popped him into the back garden and left him there while she made herself a cup of Ovaltine to help her sleep. What a wonderful evening she had had. The food, the company, the wine, the kindness, everything. She'd never forget it. She opened the drawer to get a teaspoon out and found the cutlery in disarray. The knives were where the forks usually were, and the spoons where the knives ought to be, and the forks where she kept the spoons. How ridiculous! She must have been so excited about the party that she'd mixed them all up. It left an odd feeling in a corner of her mind.

7

Mrs Duckett the school caretaker was the first one in the village to voice an opinion about the change in Muriel.

'Failing, that's what she is. Never seen such a change in a person. One minute as fit as a lop, bit too prim and proper, mind, but still fit as a lop – and now what is she like? I reckon she's got that disease Asmizler yer read about in the papers. This Tuesday she couldn't play a right note to save her life. Mr Palmer looked real fed up.'

Her neighbour Vera Wright nodded in agreement. 'She was in the store the other day and couldn't remember what she'd come in for – and I'll tell you another thing. I think she's neglecting herself.'

'Neglecting herself? What do you mean?'

Their heads drew closer over the fence. 'Haven't yer noticed she's losing weight?'

'No I hadn't, but come to mention it you could be right.'

'She's never been the same since that Jimbo's party you and I didn't get invited to. Good customers we are as well.'

'That dog of hers needs putting down. He's getting old and smelly. Mucky things, dogs. Perhaps she's got a disease off 'im. No self-respecting dog would want to be called Prickles or whatever his name is. Going round The Royal Oak tonight?'

'Might. See how the money stretches when I've done me shopping. Our Rhett's eating me out of house and home. Must be 'aving a growing spell. Yer bring yer own up and then get landed with bringing yer grandchildren up as well. It's not right. Our Brenda was sex-mad and look what that got her – our Rhett.'

Mrs Duckett locked her back door and went off to put the hall to rights for school dinners.

Muriel was just finishing putting the music away.

'Got yer keys have you, Miss Hipkin?'

'Oh yes, thank you, Mrs Duckett. I'm much more careful than I was. Now, where's my cardigan? Oh, here it is.'

'Tell yer what, Miss Hipkin, I don't think you're looking too good. Aren't you well?'

'Oh yes, I'm quite well, thank you. Yes, quite well.'

But she wasn't and Muriel knew it. And she knew why. It was the worry that her memory was going. It had started with little things, but they were a matter for concern. First there was the cutlery. Then another time she'd put a cake out to cool on the rack and when she came back home it had gone. She blamed poor Pericles but she knew he couldn't have reached it. Then she always made her bed when she went upstairs to clean her teeth after breakfast. One morning she came back from school and the sheets and blankets were all pulled back as if she'd just got out of it. Another time she came home and her ornaments had been changed round. Mother's delicate china figures were all back to front and her own little cottages, lovingly collected these last three years, had been arranged along the edge of the hearth instead of being on the shelves she'd bought specially for them.

True, these were only minor incidents but she had come to the conclusion that her brain was softening, as her mother used to say. Before she knew it she would be in a home and her lovely life which seemed to be perking up at long last would be finished.

Muriel went to church and prayed about it. Peter had been playing the organ when she got in there, so she'd let his lovely sad music carry her along. Eventually, he switched it off and came to sit beside her. He took her hand and said, 'God bless you, Muriel. Are you happy to be by yourself or would you like some company?'

'I'd like you to stay and talk if you would.'

'I have the feeling that things are not right at the moment. I was so glad when you agreed to give Mrs Meadows—'

'We all call her Suzy.'

'—Suzy, help with the playgroup. It doesn't do not to be busy, you know.'

'I know that, Peter, and I am busy with one thing and another, but just lately things haven't been right for me.'

'Can you tell me about it?'

'It's all silly, just women's talk. I'll be off now.'

She picked up her bag and fled from the church. Willie Biggs, cutting the grass in the churchyard, watched her escape. Something funny there, he thought, something funny. Peter emerged from the church and made his way down the path to the Rectory.

'Rector, I got some nice geraniums. What do you say I make a flowerbed hereabouts and put 'em in? They're all pink-coloured. Can't abide them bright red things – go against nature, they do.'

'Sounds wonderful, Willie. How's the back?'

'Fine, sir, thank you. Fine. That stuff Dr Harris recommended is grand. Will you thank her for it? I'm not troubled at all now – which is more than I can say for that Muriel Hipkin. What's up with her, do you reckon?'

'Don't know, Willie, and she won't tell me.'

'We went to school together, yer know. We were in the Infants. Her father was head gardener at the Big House. Married above himself, and Muriel was the result. Used to play with Sir Tristan's boys when she were young. Pretty little thing she was. Now she's all spinsterish and that. Pity, really. So, geraniums it is, sir, then?'

'Yes, please. Could I buy some from you for the Rectory garden as well? My wife thinks it's time I made inroads into the weeds.'

'If you're in need of help there, Rector, we might be able to come to some arrangement the two of us?'

'I'd be very glad if you could spare the time, Willie. I'm getting much too involved with the parish to find time to do it. Some amicable agreement could be reached, I'm sure. By the way, that shed in the graveyard needs clearing out. Could you put it on your list?'

'Anything for you, sir. Top of the list it will be. Morning to you.'

'Good morning, Willie.'

Come Saturday afternoon, Willie began clearing out the shed. It was surprising what had collected there. Gardening tools that would have done well on the 'Antiques Roadshow'. Old buckets, old vases, string, old wrapping paper from flowers and – surprise surprise – a plastic container from supermarket sandwiches. Who in their right mind would want to have a picnic in this old shed? There were also two Coke tins and two empty crisp packets. 'Well I never, what next?' muttered Willie. By the time he'd finished there were two full bags of rubbish for the bin men. He stood them out on the path, straightened his back and then noticed Mr Palmer from the school filling his vase at the tap.

'Afternoon, Mr Palmer. Don't usually see you here on a Saturday.'

The headmaster looked up, startled. 'No, you're right, Willie. I thought I'd come earlier this week.'

'Sunday as regular as clockwork you are, sir. Wish some others would care for the graves like you do. It's a pleasure to look at your wife's. Three years it is now, Mr Palmer. She'd have wanted you to find someone else, you know.'

'That's as maybe. Good afternoon, Willie.'

After he'd gone Willie perched himself on the edge of a tombstone and lit his pipe. He rested his elbows on his knees like he did when he was going to have a good think. Three years. He remembered the fuss there'd been. It was the Saturday of the Village Show. Boiling hot day it'd been. Sun beating down, one of the best attended for years. The flowers in the marquee had been wilting with the heat. Lady Bissett had upset all the flower arrangers by taking it upon herself to spray their arrangements with a secret concoction of her own to freshen them up. There'd been some very unpleasant things said that afternoon. Tempers got even more frayed when the ice cream ran out and the little steam train they'd hired had blown up – something to do with the pressure gauge. And it wasn't only the pressure gauge on the train that had got steamed up. Revd Furbank had had the money from the coconut shy stolen from under his very nose. Nice gentle old chap, but he didn't know what made the world tick nowadays. Can't leave a thing about, not even in old Turnham Malpas. Willie blamed the boys from the Big House. A leopard won't ever change its spots.

The late Mrs Palmer had been in charge of the maypole dancing. She'd brought a group over from her school in Culworth, as the village school couldn't muster enough children. Muriel Hipkin had seated herself at the piano which the men had dragged out of the school and into the field, right job that was. She was warming up with a few of her jolliest tunes, the maypole was in place, the children were all ready in their costumes, and the crowds awaited the start. Muriel played a few more tunes, and still Mrs Palmer hadn't appeared to set the ball rolling. The children were getting restless. All apologetic, Mr Palmer went home to see if he could find his wife – and he'd found her, all right. Hanging from the big beam in the school hall. If Stella Palmer had set out to cause a sensation she couldn't have chosen a better moment. And nobody ever found out why. He was a decent enough chap, Michael Palmer. Mightn't set the world on fire, but you can't have everything. He was kind. Maybe that was it – he was *too* kind.

Willie saw Muriel come out into her garden. He went and leaned over the church wall.

'Them daffodils is finished now, Muriel. They wants tying up.'

'Thank you, Willie, that's my next job.'

'You'll never guess who I met in Culworth the other day.'

'Oh?'

'You know where the Market Square just bends a bit and there's that dentist's surgery right on the corner? Well, I'd been 'aving another fitting for me new teeth and who should I bump into on me way out, but Sir Ralph Templeton.'

Muriel perked up a little at this. 'Really? How on earth did you recognise him?'

'He recognised me. Said I 'adn't changed a bit, but since it must be more than forty years since he last saw me I must be wearing well. He's still got all that thick bushy hair 'cept it's snow-white now. Tanned he is, been out in the Far East for years and now he's retired and come back to live in England. In all those years he's never married. Remember that time he put a jumping cracker inside Miss's boots when she'd put 'em by the stove to dry out? He were a lad, he was. Didn't we laugh!'

'What was he doing in Culworth?'

'Visiting some friends, he said. Wanted me to go for a drink but I knew I'd miss me bus if I did. I've been clearing out the shed – amazing what yer find in there. Rector wanted it doing. He's a grand chap, he is. Yer know where yer are with 'im. Mr Furbank couldn't talk to yer, somehow – he never had that touch. Rector's worried about you, Muriel. He reckons yer not yerself at all these days.'

Willie left a pause but got no reply.

'I'll get on then if yer not talking.'

He turned his back on Muriel and heaved the bin bags off to his dustbin corner.

Muriel sat on her little seat by her rose arch, tickled Pericles behind his ears as he settled down beside her and pondered on her predicament. If she told someone, they would have her certified. If she didn't tell someone, she would go mad. Maybe she was already mad and didn't know it. Perhaps one would be the last to realise. If she did one more stupid thing she would give up playing for the school. Last week she had made an idiot of herself with constant wrong notes, wrong timing – and even the wrong tune, once. She couldn't expect Mr Palmer to put up with it much longer. She didn't profess to be a pianist as such but she could play some lively tunes for her age. That was it – her age! She was trying to be twenty-four when she was sixty-four. One glimpse of her reflection in a shop window and she despised herself. She was nothing but a faded elderly spinster, dragging out her life because she was too much of a coward to commit suicide. Death would bring its own reward. Paradise. What greater prize could one have than entering paradise? What an incentive, Thy face to see. Surely the good Lord would let her in? She'd been well-behaved all her life. For this to happen just as she was feeling needed and beginning to enjoy her life . . . One can't even gas oneself nowadays. That would have been a gentle way to go. Drowning? Jumping off the church tower? But she got vertigo simply going up to take the bell-ringers their cocoa on New Year's Eve. She'd never reach the top. In any case, Peter would be so upset . . .

This last incident was ridiculous, but she'd done it. How could anyone leave the oven on at full blast with the door open and all the rings on as well? To say nothing of the gas bill. The house was positively steaming when she got back. She'd had to open all the windows and the doors to cool it down. She hadn't even intended to cook a Sunday dinner seeing as it was 82 degrees. Tomorrow when she went to church she would take particular notice of what she was doing and check everything before she left. That way she'd know when she got back that she hadn't done it. Maybe she had a ghost. Maybe someone from years past resented the cottages being built on church land. There'd been plenty of opposition when they were built – from the living, never mind the dead. If that was it, Peter would have to exorcise it.

Sunday morning came. The sun shone brilliantly as it had done for two months now. Before it got too hot, Muriel watered her most precious plants with water from the butt. She enjoyed turning the little tap on and watching the water come running out. When she'd finished she lifted the lid to check how much water was still left: floating in the top was a drowned cat. A drowned ginger cat. A fully grown, drowned ginger cat. A beautifully fully grown drowned ginger cat! Someone's pet, someone's beloved pet in her water butt. The horror of its drowning whilst she'd been going about her affairs ignorant of its agony, was more than she could tolerate.

She fled out into Church Lane, past the church gate and on to Willie's front door. She banged and banged but he wouldn't answer. Of course – he'd be in the church opening up. She turned round and headed for the church door, hastening up the path, shouting: 'Willie Biggs! Willie Biggs!'

He emerged, wearing his cassock. 'What's the matter, Muriel? What's up?'

She grabbed his arm and began to gabble, trying to tell him about the cat. 'Come on! You've got to come. Please help me, please.' When she showed him the cat she was shuddering with the horror of it.

'Now sit down,' he told her kindly, alarmed at her reaction. 'It's only someone's old cat got in here by mistake. Wasn't your fault.'

'The lid is always on tightly in case children get in the garden. Someone's put it in there, I know it. It's a nasty trick, a vile evil trick.' She began sobbing.

'I'll find a plastic bag to put it in. 'Spect there's one in your kitchen somewhere.'

She watched Willie invade the seclusion of her neat pristine kitchen with his big heavy shoes on, tramping on the small white tiles, defacing them with footprints, the footprints turned here and there whilst their owner found the place where a score of plastic carrier bags were stored, all neatly folded inside a Tesco's bag.

'I'll put it in here and get rid of it in the church bin.'

'It's got a collar on,' Muriel shrieked as he lifted it out.

'So it has. I'll take it off and we'll see whose cat it is. Why, it's Mr Charter-Plackett's cat!'

'Oh no, I can't tell him, I can't tell him. You tell him, Willie, you tell him.' Her voice was frantic.

'I'll have to tell him after church then, 'cos I'm running late. Won't do for the service to be late. You make yourself a cup of tea and then come to the service. Don't sit here by yourself thinking about it. Do as I say, now.'

'Yes, yes I will.'

She didn't hear a word of the service. Her mortal remains sat in the pew but the real Muriel was in the rafters avoiding looking at Jimbo and Harriet and the children. Oh, the children would be so upset about their pet. Such dear children they were, never a mite of trouble in school. There was Caroline sitting in the Rectory pew, wearing a lovely lemon-yellow dress with big splashes of apricot and soft brown on it. What a dreadful thing that Katherine Charter-Plackett had said. 'Red siren' indeed. As if Peter would get involved with someone else when he had Caroline. The scent of the flowers was delicious up here in the rafters. It was like being in some heavenly garden. No weeds here. No need to water the plants. No discovering dead . . . no, she wouldn't think about that. Mrs Peel is excelling herself today. Was it the 'Trumpet Voluntary' she was playing? Heavenly music for a heavenly day. The cherubs, decorating the arches in the roof, had joined her and went swirling about in a kind of celestial maypole dance. She'd loved maypole dancing as a child. The patterns you made with the ribbons so intricate and then you danced again and unravelled them. All her ribbons had got tangled and they wouldn't come straight.

The church was emptying. The chosen of the Lord had walked firmly down the aisle, accompanied by His servants singing a hymn of praise. The sun shining through the ancient coloured glass of the windows had cast strange streaks of reds and purples on their white gowns. They were like Technicolor angels. She must have done it, she must have done it and here she was about to see the face of her beloved Lord.

Caroline took immediate action.

'Peter, we must take her to Casualty. There's something seriously wrong here. She doesn't even know I'm speaking to her. What can have happened?'

'I can tell you that, Dr Harris.' And Willie related the story of the cat.

'Whatever's been worrying her these last few weeks, the cat has been the final straw. Whoever would do such a thing to poor Muriel – or the cat, come to that? She wouldn't hurt a flea.'

'Someone's got it in for her, that's for sure.' Peter tried to rouse Muriel but she sat as though carved from stone.

He and Caroline drove Muriel to the hospital while Willie went across to the Charter-Placketts' to break the news.

'Orlando? How could that have happened?'

'I don't know, Mr Charter-Plackett, but I've got him in the churchyard shed. Here's his collar, sir.'

Jimbo went white when he saw poor Orlando's bright red collar. 'Hardly dare tell the children, but I must. We'll have to have a funeral service and bury him in the garden. I'm surprised at Miss Hipkin, having a water butt without a lid.'

'She did have a lid and she kept it on all the time – tight-fitting it was, too. She only found him 'cos she was wondering how much water she had left in it.'

'It was deliberate, then. How could anyone do such a thing? I'll go in and break the news to the children and Harriet, and then come across and pick up poor Orlando. We left London to avoid dreadful things like this.'

8

On the Monday morning, Jimbo was busy freshening up the displays for the coming week. He hummed to himself while he planned the menu for a dinner party he'd been asked to do for a customer in Culworth. They weren't his kind of people but you can't pick and choose your customers in this business. Harriet sped through the shop on her way to pick up the fresh vegetables they prided themselves on supplying. As she opened the outside door she was brushed aside by the angry figure of Betty McDonald from The Royal Oak.

In her hand was a letter. Her face, normally red, was even more so; now in fact, it was almost puce.

Harriet gathered herself and said, 'Good morning, Betty. Is that your order?'

'Order? *Order?* You'll be lucky if I set foot in here ever again. Where is that two-timing blackguard? You come from London with your fancy ways and your new ideas and before we know where we are you're cutting our throats.'

'Cutting your throats? What do you mean?'

'Where is he?'

'Is someone wanting me?' Jimbo emerged from amongst the bananas hanging along the rail above the vegetables. His face was devoid of expression. Harriet with a sinking feeling began to suspect he'd been up to something she knew nothing about.

'Wanting you? I'll swing for you before long. How dare you do it!'

'Do what?'

'You know full well what I mean. This – this is what you've done!' She smashed her hand onto the letter she was holding and it nearly tore in half. 'This letter is informing me that you have applied for planning permission for a restaurant in old Phyllis Henderson's house, and a car park right on the corner. I'll fight you every step of the way, every single step. If you open up I might as well say goodbye to my morning coffees and my ploughman's lunches and my farmhouse soup. The damage to my business will be devastating.'

Harriet held out her hand. 'Let me see this letter, please.' As she read it her face grew stormy. 'How dare you do this without consulting me? How dare you? Jimbo, I shall never forgive you for this. Have you bought it already?'

'Now hold on a minute, Harriet. I've made an offer subject to planning permission. A chap's got to make progress, he can't just stand still.'

'Stand still? A chap's got to make progress? I'll give you progress, Jimbo. Not one foot will I put inside that restaurant if this goes through. Not one foot. So think on that.' She flung out of the door and the little bell, the delight of Jimbo's heart, rattled till it nearly fell off the door. Then the Charter-Placketts' Range Rover crashed into life and roared off down Stocks Row as if it was the M4.

Betty was triumphant. 'See, even your wife is against the idea!'

'Leave Harriet to me, she'll come round. If it all comes off I shan't be doing ploughman's or farmhouse soup so you've no need to worry about that. I'll be catering for a different part of the market.'

'Don't try to sweet-talk me. It can only do harm. I know – I've been in the licensed trade too long not to know serious competition when I see it. I shall get a petition up and ask everyone to sign it. You won't win this one.' And Betty McDonald marched out of the shop, whereupon the poor bell had another fit as she smashed the door shut.

Jimbo chuckled to himself. He'd have that restaurant before he was much older, and it would turn out to be a right money spinner. It was definitely a box of sugared almonds under Harriet's pillow night tonight. He'd soon have her eating out of his hand: it always worked. He smiled to himself as he served his first customers. The Charter-Plackett charm was up to full strength as usual.

As soon as Jimbo saw Harriet pull up outside he poured out two coffees from the pot brewed for the customers, put them on the counter with a couple of special chocolate biscuits and confidently awaited her entrance. But she didn't come in. He played the waiting game while he served two more customers and then, to his amazement, saw Harriet dressed to kill driving past in the Volvo.

'Sadie, Sadie!' Jimbo shouted into the back where his mother-in-law was doing the mail order parcels. 'Where's Harriet going?'

'Jimbo, I have no idea. She flew past me saying "I'll kill him, so help me, I'll kill him." To whom she referred I have no idea. I assume she's driven off to commit a murder. We'll have to hope it's no one we know.'

'It could be me.'

'You? Why, what have you done?'

'Put in a bid for old Phyllis Henderson's cottage and asked for planning permission for a restaurant. I thought it would be a lovely surprise for Harriet and yet she's absolutely flown off the handle.'

Sadie finished addressing a parcel of Harriet's Country Cousin Lemon Cheese – farmhouse-made with free-range eggs – took off her glasses and said, 'Now look here, Jimbo. As mothers-in-law go I think I give you an easy ride but this time I have to speak my mind. I don't want to interfere but I must. Do you realise that Harriet has far too much to do?'

'I work hard, too.'

'Indeed you do, but you don't also prepare meals and look after the children and cook for dinner parties and receptions and meals at Game Fairs and the like. My daughter never has a minute to herself and it's got to stop. Employ more help. Ease the burden. She only objects to the restaurant because she physically can't do any more than she is already doing.' Sadie's index finger poked Jimbo rather sharply on his lapel and she turned on her heel and left him to think.

The day wore on and still Harriet had not returned. The boys and Flick arrived home from school, accustomed to their mother greeting them with food and sympathy, to find their grandma there instead.

'Where's Mummy? I wish my Mummy was here.' Flick did not take kindly to her routine being upset.

Sadie told the children that their mother had gone out for a change, and that she'd soon be back. Jimbo was feeling exactly like Flick but he didn't voice his feelings. By eight o'clock, anxiety took the place of wishing. He sat at his office desk trying to do the VAT return, but too worried to have much success. About eleven the back door opened and in she came.

Jimbo leapt up to greet her. 'Darling, where have you been! We have missed you.'

'Crawled out from under your stone, have you?'

'Now, Harriet, that's a bit unfair. You know I've always wanted a restaurant. If you say no then no it shall be. I leave it entirely to you.'

'That's emotional blackmail.'

'No it's not, I'm simply being thoughtful.'

'Don't, it's too painful. Goodnight, Jimbo. Good luck with the VAT return.'

'Aren't you going to help me?'

'No.'

When he'd finished he went upstairs, only to find that Harriet was not in their bed. He crept round the bedrooms and discovered her fast asleep on the put-u-up in Flick's bedroom. This was the first time they had slept apart since they were married. Jimbo knew he had gambled once too often. Serious amends would have to be made.

Next morning Harriet saw the children off to school while Jimbo started work in the shop. His first job was to write out an advertisement for the local newspaper.

'*Smart young people needed, full and part-time, to help entrepreneur with busy catering business. Excellent remuneration for hardworking lively applicants. Apply Turnham Malpas (0909) 334455.*'

He telephoned the advert to the newspaper and served some customers, all of whom were eager to know about the restaurant. Most of them were thrilled at the idea, but over in The Royal Oak, some, but not all of the regulars, had signed Betty's petition.

'I've said it once and I'll say it again.' Vera Wright was laying down the law. 'Before we know it, this village will be as busy as the M4. Car doors slamming late at night, headlights on full blast. It won't be the same any more.'

'It will mean more jobs, Vera.'

'Oh yes, more jobs for chefs and the like. How many chefs do you know in Turnham Malpas?'

'Well, none actually.'

'Exactly, Willie – *none.* All it'll do is bring people in from outside. Village folk will get the rubbish jobs like cleaning and doing the vegetables. Aren't I right, Pat?'

'Well, yes, I suppose you are, Vera. Who do we know who'd want to work restaurant hours? Not me for a start, though I could manage evenings, I suppose, and fit it in with the school.'

Jimmy Glover, a regular at The Royal Oak, placed his pint carefully on a beer mat, wiped the froth from his mouth and said, 'What about all these tourists coming to see the murals in the church and the stocks and the like – where can they go for a nice meal? Not here for a start. One look at Betty McDonald's face and it's a wonder they don't all run a mile – to say nothing of the rotten food here. I hope he does get permission.'

'You would, Jimmy. That's you all over. No thought for the village green getting churned up 'cos they can't be bothered to park in the proper places. Oh no. It's time that Jimbo was taken down a peg or two anyway. Too clever by half, he is.'

'Vera, that's not fair. He does a lot for the village.'

'Oh yes? Like what – jumping naked in that pool of his? I seed 'im one morning when I was off to work extra early. By gum, Pat,' she nudged her friend and nearly made her spill her lager, 'he's got nothing missing.' They both laughed raucously.

Harriet didn't begin to come round to Jimbo's way of thinking until she answered the phone to find herself talking to an eager job applicant. After a moment or two of confusion it dawned on her what he'd done. She took the young woman's name and telephone number, and promised that Jimbo would ring her back.

She put the piece of paper down in front of him as he ate a lonely pork pie behind the bread counter. Linda, who ran the post office and the stationery section, was nearly dying of laughter at the sight of Jimbo in the dog-house.

'There's someone who thinks we need extra help on the catering side,' Harriet announced. 'I can't think why they've rung us, can you? That's their number if you think they're needed.'

Jimbo kissed her hand as she turned to go. She hesitated for a moment but then went on her way. She's softening, she's giving in, thought Jimbo elatedly.

As she had threatened, Betty McDonald started a petition, wrote letters, campaigned and spread malicious rumours in an effort to stop Jimbo opening the restaurant, but it was not to be. Plenty of the inhabitants of Turnham Malpas signed her petition, but the majority liked Jimbo and didn't like Betty McDonald. The planning committee met only a month after Jimbo's application had gone in. They could see no reason for withholding their permission and in fact quite welcomed the idea of an up-to-date restaurant, to supply a service to the tourists who visited the village.

Jimbo was beside himself with delight. The three new part-time girls he had employed eased Harriet's burden, while he flung himself into organising the complete refurbishing of his latest project. The whole building required attention: rewiring, replastering, mains water and electricity, decoration, and of course brand-new kitchens. Jimbo whirled around phoning and writing, cajoling and compelling until within four weeks he had completely changed the cottage both outside and in.

A few people had hazarded guesses as to what it would be called, but he had remained mum on that issue. Harriet knew but she refused to tell. The sign was being put up as Pat Duckett wended her way to open up the school. The transformation from tumbledown house to smart village restaurant in such a short space of time had amazed her.

'It's these Londoners, you know. They don't let grass grow under their feet. Their motto is "Time is money". Get taking money in as fast as you can.' Michael Palmer only half-listened to her. He'd had years of Pat Duckett and he knew she'd waste hours talking, so he never encouraged her.

'He's calling it Henderson's, would you believe! Old Phyllis would be tickled pink having it named after her. Fancy Henderson's. What do you think, Mr Palmer?'

'Sounds good enough to me. I shan't be eating there.'

'Time you got out and about a bit, Mr Palmer. Man your age should be enjoying himself, not be shut up with his books every night. You enjoyed Mr Charter-Plackett's party, didn't you?'

'I did indeed. The children will be here shortly, Mrs Duckett. Could we get on, please?'

'Has it gone through yet about Mrs Meadows and that playgroup thing?'

'The committee meet this week. There shouldn't be any problem. It seemed to meet with a favourable response.'

'I'm not looking forward to all that mess. All them wellington boots from them farm kids. Stands to reason the toilets will be a mess, with them all being so young. They make all these arrangements but they never think about the school caretaker.'

'Well, I am right now, Mrs Duckett – and she isn't getting organised.'

'Sorry, I must say. Only passing all the news on, like,' Pat Duckett said offendedly.

'Thank you.'

Michael stood watching the children arriving in the playground. They really were a good bunch – clean, healthy and eager, except for the ones who came from the Big House. The cards life had dealt them were rotten indeed. He doubted if they would ever get their lives straightened out. Come to think of it, he hadn't managed it yet and he was forty-five. If Stella had lived, his life would have been hell. People thought they should feel sorry for him when she died, but in truth the opposite was true. He wasn't any happier since she'd died, but he would have been a sight worse by now if she hadn't. How he could have married her and not known, he had never fathomed. There was something to be said for living together before marriage. Morally he couldn't condone it, but in their case it would have saved a lot of heartache.

Now he had this problem of Sharon McDonald. She'd struck him as a sly child when she was in the Infants, and he'd been right. He opened the window and called out, 'Close the gate after you, please. We don't want the little ones out in the road, thank you.' Experience taught you which children were truthful and which didn't know the truth if it jumped up and hit them, but Sharon had been unfathomable. Now she'd grown up she was still sly. Fancy her seeing Stella in Culworth and following her. She'd harboured the secret all this time. That demonstrated just how sly she was. How to tackle the problem, though? Say 'Tell all and be damned'? There'd be no end to it if he began paying her. Or should he give in his notice and disappear? Or have a word with her parents? Then the cat would truly be out of the bag. Betty McDonald would still be spreading gossip from her grave – he might as well put an advert in the paper.

Just then, Toria Clark rang the school bell and his favourite people began pouring into school, laughing and chattering all ready for another day. Thank heavens he'd chosen teaching; he couldn't think of a more rewarding job.

9

Caroline went into the village store to buy a card and present for Muriel's birthday.

Jimbo asked her how Muriel was.

'It's her birthday tomorrow so I'm getting her a card and taking a present in for her. They've put her in a psychiatric ward. I can hardly bear going in to see her. She sits entirely still and speechless. Whoever did what they did to her needs serious psychiatric help themselves. We know about your dear cat, but we think other things happened before that, and Orlando's death was what finally broke her. What can I buy to take for her, Jimbo?'

'My present will be one of my special birthday cakes. We have them already made – they do for birthdays, weddings or whatever. I'll get Sadie to put "Muriel" on one while you wait. Look round while I organise it.'

Caroline chose a card and a box of chocolates. Muriel had lost so much weight perhaps the chocolates would entice her to eat. Jimbo emerged from the back of the shop carrying a smart cardboard box. He showed Caroline the cake before closing down the lid.

'Why, that's beautiful, Jimbo. What a lovely idea! She'll enjoy giving everyone a slice.'

'Will she be back with us soon, do you think?'

'Not for a while yet, I'm afraid. She won't tell anyone what the matter is, you see. She needs to get it all out of her system before she can get better. Thank you for the cake. I'll remember you when it's Peter's birthday. His is in November. Your restaurant will be open by then – we'll have a meal in it to celebrate.'

'If you see Harriet, don't mention it. It's a sore subject at the moment.'

Caroline laughed. 'See you, bye!'

*

'Good morning, Dr Harris. You're on the ball this morning.'

Caroline put the carrier bag down on her desk and slid out the box containing Muriel's birthday cake.

'I am – I've a lot to do. Don't make it sound as if it's unusual for me to be here in good time, Anne, I always am.' She grinned at her secretary.

'Well, I meant you were bouncing in more energetically than normal. Sorry.'

'I'll see to my post and then I'm going down to the psychiatric ward. It's someone's birthday and this is a cake for them.'

'Oh, can I look?'

'Yes.' Caroline opened the box and they both admired Jimbo's cake. 'It's from our village store. Albeit a very superior village store.'

'It looks gorgeous. Your friend no better?'

'Unfortunately, no.'

'We're short-handed today. Two of the technicians have got this 'flu thing that's going round, and it's ante-natal clinic day as well, so we shall need to get our skates on.'

'Right, here goes then.' Caroline rolled up her sleeves and began opening her post. Samples, drugs, letters, reports . . . endless paperwork. She loved her work as a doctor. The only event which could stop her doing medicine would be the arrival of a baby. For that she would give up everything. Although Peter reassured her often enough that he wasn't the slightest bit bothered about not having children she knew it would absolutely crown their lives together. She'd just finished her medical training when they met. Full of determination and dedication, having arrived at last at the goal she had pursued for more than ten years, nothing was further from her mind than marriage. On her first day as a GP, taking surgery entirely on her own, he had been one of the patients. The moment they looked at one another she knew he was going to be special. Within three months they were engaged and then married three months later. If he had had a call to go as a missionary to some far-flung primitive corner of the world, she would have followed without a backward glance. When she saw him again at the end of a long day her spirits soared as though she were a lovesick girl instead of a professional woman of thirty-two.

Having sorted through the post and allocated it to different trays she gave Anne her work for the morning and then set off down to the psychiatric ward with Muriel's cake and present.

The ward had been made more 'user friendly' in recent years. The high windows, such a favourite with Victorian architects, had been draped with soft net curtains, each bed had pretty curtains around it, the furniture was modern and one end of the ward had been turned into a sitting area where the patients who felt well enough could sit and talk in comfortable armchairs or watch television.

Muriel sat in one of these chairs surrounded by cards and presents given to her by the staff. She'd lost more weight and her hair hung in lifeless strands down each side of her vacant face. She sat motionless, ignoring the other patients, wrapped in her own world like a very old person who is sitting out the years waiting for death.

'Muriel – hello. Happy birthday!' Caroline put the cake on the table beside Muriel's chair. 'Jimbo has sent you a cake. Would you like to have a look at it?'

Her head nodded assent. When the lid was off she peered into the box. Tears began pouring down her thin cheeks. Silent rivers of release. She made no attempt to wipe her tears away but let them flood down. It was painful to watch her.

Caroline didn't try to stop her; she simply held her hand, feeling that the tears were significant and healing.

The ward sister came by and behind Muriel's back gave the thumbs-up sign. 'That's encouraging,' she mouthed.

When the tears had ceased, Caroline wiped Muriel's face and combed her hair for her. It was like attending to a very young child. For the first time in days Muriel spoke.

'It's got my name on it. It's meant for me, just me. It's really meant *just for me.* How kind of Jimbo, such a thoughtful man. I haven't ever had a birthday cake. Mother thought they were a self-congratulatory luxury. She didn't know how much it pained me not to have one. I'll have a slice right now. Will you have one too?'

Caroline organised tea for the patients sitting round the table and they all had a slice of cake. It was delicious and Muriel enjoyed it more than any food she had been persuaded to eat in all the time she'd been in the hospital.

Muriel leant over to Caroline and asked her if she would get Peter to come in to see her. 'I've got things to tell him I can't tell anyone else. He hasn't been, has he?'

'Yes, he has, several times, but you weren't well enough to talk to him.'

'Oh, I don't remember that.' The shutters came down and Muriel returned to wherever she had been before Caroline came in.

'Dr Harris, have you a moment?'

Sister Bonaventure discussed some blood tests she felt one of the patients needed, and then Caroline wended her way back to the pathology lab, calling in at the ante-natal clinic en route to collect any blood samples they might have.

The clinic was busy. Expectant mothers lined the walls, some with little ones in tow, others alone and staring ahead, bored by the waiting. Some of them were exchanging pregnancy experiences, while others read magazines. Caroline stood looking out of the Sister's office window at the full waiting room wondering whether she might like to change to obstetrics. It would certainly be more lively than pathology. It was then she noticed Suzy Meadows, with Rosie on her knee. Suzy must have sensed someone was looking at her because she glanced up before Caroline could avert her eyes. They looked directly at one another. Caroline raised her hand in greeting and then turned away.

She longed to go and have a word with her but as a doctor, professional etiquette dictated she should remain silent. This was one of the problems of being a doctor in a busy county hospital. One met neighbours and friends but had to keep a discreet silence to preserve their confidentiality. Poor Suzy, with another child to bring up and no husband for support. Still, this one might be a boy and that would be a great comfort. Suzy was a born mother. How sad that Patrick had not lived to see his new baby . . .

When Caroline got home she told Peter about Muriel wanting to see him and nearly mentioned Suzy's presence in the ante-natal clinic, but decided against it. Everyone would know soon enough. It wasn't exactly something which could be kept a secret for long.

Peter went with her to the hospital the next day and called into Muriel's ward. She was sitting as before, wrapped in thought.

'Hello, Muriel. It's Peter come to see you. God bless you.' He shook her hand and then held on to it. 'I see you've had plenty of cards for your birthday.'

She turned to look at him and slowly recognition came. 'Would you like a piece of Jimbo's cake? He sent it for me; it's the first birthday cake I have ever had. You will have a piece, won't you?'

'I can't wait. If it's the same standard as that birthday meal of his, then I'm in for a treat.'

'Oh, it's every bit as good.' She waited until he had tasted it and then asked how he liked it.

'It is excellent, absolutely delicious. Happy birthday to you. Thank you very much.'

'I can't go back to my house. Not ever again. Not after the cat . . . and the other things.' There was a long pause while Muriel found her handkerchief. 'I'm not fit to live by myself, you know. I'm doing such silly things. I know it must have been Pericles who ate the cake but I did – Oh, Pericles – where is he? I haven't thought about him once while I've been in here. Has he been shut in the house all this time? Oh dear, how could I have forgotten him? You see, it is my mind that's going, it is, it is.' The tears began again.

Peter leant towards her and said clearly: 'Your Pericles is having the time of his life. Sir Ronald has taken charge of him and he takes him and Lady Bissett's Pomeranian for long walks every day. The two dogs are the greatest of friends so you've no need to worry on *that* score. And Pericles hasn't eaten the cake because it's here.'

'I don't mean this cake, I mean the one I baked at home. I put it out to cool and when I came back it had disappeared. Then I didn't make the bed and I knew I had. Then the ornaments were all turned round and put in the wrong places. It was one thing after another – such silly things I was doing. It all started the day Pericles ran away because I'd left the back door open. I lost my keys and since then I've been soft in the head. Yes, soft in the head. Mother went like that – didn't know what she was doing. But she still kept her sharp tongue. To be truthful, she didn't really want me. Having me spoiled her figure and she never forgave me. She was mean, so mean. Sitting here I can remember things she did.'

Muriel put up the shutters and Peter, after praying aloud that God would make His face to shine upon her and give her peace, left puzzled but at the same time relieved that at last Muriel had spoken – even if he couldn't understand her.

That evening when Caroline came home they exchanged information about their respective days. Peter told her about Muriel.

'She seems to have been doing such foolish things. Yet it all must have happened very quickly because the night of Jimbo's party she was perfectly all right, in fact on top of the world. She natters on about cakes being eaten and ornaments being moved. I can't understand her.'

'Look, I've got her keys. I'm going to have a look in her house when we've eaten. What shall it be – Spanish omelette or fish with chips, or shall we be completely disgusting and have Chicken Kiev out of the freezer?'

'Nothing you could do would be completely disgusting, so we'll have Chicken Kiev. I wonder if they do eat it in Kiev? Bet they've never even heard of it.' Peter laughed and Caroline, catching his mood, flung her arms round him and kissed him. She chattered on about her day while she cooked and Peter sat on a kitchen chair enjoying her gaiety. They'd promised right from the start that they would be completely truthful with each other, but it wasn't always the best thing to be completely truthful to one's beloved. Sometimes one needed to be deceitful in order to save them pain, and that left one bearing the pain alone. Peter didn't like himself.

After they'd washed up, Caroline went over to Glebe Cottages. As she turned the key in the front door of number 1, she thought she heard a noise inside the house. She stood listening in the little sitting room. There was only silence, that kind of hollow silence peculiar to an unoccupied house. She went straight to the back door and opened it. As she looked into the garden she thought she caught a glimpse of something moving swiftly over the wall into the churchyard. Caroline hurried to the wall and looked over, but there was no one in sight. She waited for a moment and then shook her head and went back into the house.

One of the cupboards in the kitchen was open, and as she went to shut it she noticed that there was hardly anything on the shelves. She opened the door wider and saw that it was the cupboard where Muriel obviously had kept her tinned food. Sitting alone was a tin of grapefruit, one of the tiny ones people on their own buy, and a small, partly-used jar of mint sauce. Surely Muriel wasn't so short of money that that was all she had in store? Something told Caroline to search further. The pedal-bin had empty tins in it and an empty biscuit packet. Caroline went into the sitting room and opened the cupboard where Muriel kept her sherry. There was only a drop left in the bottom, yet Caroline knew that when they'd had a drink together the night she'd lent Muriel a dress for Jimbo's party, the bottle had been nearly full. This all seemed very odd. Back in the kitchen she found two cups standing in the sink; she smelt the remains of their contents and recognised the smell of sherry.

Caroline locked the house and sped home to Peter. She told him all her findings.

'Someone must have access to her house. Perhaps they've had access for quite a while and have intended frightening her with these mysterious tricks.'

'She did say this morning she'd lost her keys.'

'That's it, then! She's lost her keys and someone has found them, said nothing and has been going in and out when they've known she wouldn't be there.'

'Caroline, the only way to put a stop to this is to have new locks put on her doors, then the keys will be useless.'

'Absolutely, but we also need to find out who is so malicious as to want to frighten her – and don't forget, they also have a vendetta with Jimbo Charter-Plackett because they deliberately drowned his cat.'

'You make it sound as if we have a pathological killer in our midst.'

'This kind of thing is only the beginning. We very well could have.'

Peter made a decision. 'First thing in the morning I shall get the sergeant to go with me to the house. Give me the keys and I'll put them on the hallstand ready for tomorrow.'

The sergeant had no answers for Peter but he agreed that it was obvious someone was getting in, and there were no signs of a forced entry. He suggested speaking to Muriel about changing the locks, but Peter said he would go and see her about it. A police sergeant arriving could well do more harm than good.

It was two days before Peter had time to call at the hospital. He took the keys with him.

'God bless you, Muriel, I'm here again.'

'Who are you? I don't know you.' Muriel turned herself so she couldn't see Peter's face.

'Yes you do, Muriel. It's Peter from St Thomas à Becket at home in Turnham Malpas.'

She refused to answer.

'I have something to show you. Will you turn round and have a look?'

Curiosity got the better of her and she half turned to look.

'In my hand I have the keys to your house. Look.' He opened his hand and let her look.

'I'm not going home.'

'No, I know you're not. When you lost your keys, how did you get into your house again?'

'I used the spare keys I hid in the garden, till the others turned up again.'

'Oh, so they turned up again then? Where did you find them?'

'Mr Palmer found them in the piano stool.'

'So where are your spare keys now?'

She looked furtively round the ward and then whispered, 'Under the pot with the hydrangea in it in the back garden.'

'Does anyone else know they're there?'

'Only you.'

'I see. If I changed the locks on your house, that would mean that no one could get in, wouldn't it?'

'What would I do with all those keys? I wouldn't know which ones to use.'

'We would throw away these keys and you could use the new ones.'

'It wouldn't stop me doing silly things.'

Muriel switched off and Peter could do no more. He debated about changing the locks and decided to go ahead.

*

A few days later he was sitting in his study reading a book entitled *Why Follow Christ?* when Willie Biggs knocked urgently on his door. He always knew when it was Willie knocking because he didn't give two or three knocks like everyone else. It was always nine or ten, as if his message couldn't wait to be delivered.

'Mr Harris, sir, I've come to report that there's someone living in the churchyard shed.'

'Living in the churchyard shed? Whatever for?'

' 'Cos they've got no 'ome, I 'spect.'

'Who is it?'

'If I knew that I'd 'ave chased 'em off, sir. Can't catch 'em, yer see. I keep finding crisp bags, tins, a tin opener, a plate and a cup, biscuit packets . . . one thing after another, but I can't catch 'em. When I do I'll beat the living daylights out of 'em.'

'I don't think that would look very good in the headlines, Willie. "*Verger beats hell out of homeless boy.*" Of course, it might be a girl, which would look even worse.'

'I'll keep watch. If I sat on that seat in Miss Hipkin's garden by her rose arch, lovely roses they are, yellow with a fleck of pink, I could keep an eye from there right grand and they wouldn't see me. What do yer think, Rector?'

'I think it's a brilliant idea, but you could be there for ages.'

'I don't care and it won't be upsetting Miss Hipkin, her not knowing, like.'

'On one condition, Willie, that you bring to me unharmed whoever it is you catch. Unharmed, mind you.'

'Very well, sir.' Willie tapped the side of his prominent bony nose. 'And mum's the word, sir. It's between you and me. Bet Mrs Rector likes the garden a bit better now. I haven't let on it's me who's been doing it, yer know.'

'No – and neither have I. That's another secret we have, Willie.'

'I'll be off then. Wonder who I'll catch?'

10

Willie had a shock when he recognised the person wandering casually up to the shed. Sitting under Muriel's rose arch he'd contemplated who it might be. The children from the Big House were well known for bringing their town ways to the village. Smoking in the bushes down by the beck and shoplifting if Mr Charter-Plackett didn't keep a sharp eye out . . . more than likely it would be one of them, he thought. Several times he'd caught them wandering round the church, but the rector – old Mr Furbank, that is – insisted that the church must be open for private prayer, and also for tourists to visit and admire the ancient murals and the Templeton family tombs. Willie had kept everything locked that he possibly could. No sense in inviting trouble, he'd thought. This new rector, Mr Harris, wanted the church to be freely available too. Sometimes, the verger of St Thomas à Becket wondered which century these men lived in. What had done before didn't do for now. From the corner of his eye he watched Scott McDonald walking quietly between the tombstones – an unlikely occupation for such a one as he. Willie kept entirely still and waited. Scott approached the shed, went past it and climbed the wall into Muriel's garden. Willie, hidden by the lush growth of the climbing rose, bided his time.

From his pocket Scott took some keys and went to Muriel's back door. He put one key in the lock with confidence, then found it wouldn't open the door. He tried the other key, rattled the door knob and stood puzzled as to why he couldn't get in. Willie crept up behind him.

'Got you, my lad!'

Despite his years Willie was very nimble and with the shock of his discovery and the idle life Scott made sure he lived, Willie had him by the collar before he could make an escape.

'We're going straight round to see the rector. One word from you and I'll cuff you one.'

'Willie Biggs, what do you think you're doing? Leave me alone. Wait till my dad hears about this.'

'Yes, just you wait. If he doesn't give you a hiding, I shall. Upsetting old ladies – whatever next.' Willie marched him to the Rectory and rattled on the door.

'Here we are, sir. I've found him trying to get into Miss Hipkin's house with his own key.'

'You'd better come inside, young man, and sit down in my study.' Peter led the way. Scott by now was beginning to feel uncomfortable. Visiting the rector's study was not something he did from choice. He was completely out of his element.

'I didn't do nothing, Mr Harris,' he whined. 'It's the first time I've—'

'First time, my foot,' Willie shouted. 'I could see you knew exactly what you were doing. You've been in there before.'

'Just a moment, Willie. We'll let Scott speak first.'

Scott looked at Peter and kept his mouth closed. Peter continued waiting for him to speak. The silence lasted and lasted, Peter patiently leaving the silence for Scott to fill. Eventually he did speak, worn down by Peter's searching look.

'It was our Sharon. I found the keys that day old Muriel—'

'Miss Hipkin to you, Scott,' Peter interrupted.

'Well, Miss Hipkin then, that day the dog got out and she raced out of school to catch him. Took 'em home I did, and told our Sharon. She took them into Culworth and got new keys cut. Cost her a packet it did, but she said it was worth it to see the old bat's face when she realised someone was getting into her house. What I did served her right. Told me off she did more than once, the daft old faggot. Why won't the key fit? Always did before.'

'Because I've had the locks changed. Do you know that Miss Hipkin is a friend of mine just as she is to lots of people in the village? We all like her very much.'

'Like her? She's an old bat, a miserable old bat, and it serves her right.'

'What have you done in Miss Hipkin's house?'

'Only daft little things to frighten her. Pinched a cake, moved the cutlery about in the drawer, drank the sherry, switched her ornaments around, things like that.'

'What about the cat?'

'What cat?'

'The cat she found drowned in her water butt?'

'Well, Mr Harris, I don't know nothing about a cat. That's not me. I like cats.' His face suddenly changed as if something had dawned on him which he wouldn't be prepared to talk about. Peter realised Scott had made a guess as to who was responsible.

'Well, Scott, Willie and you and I are going to go to your house to see your parents.'

Scott sprang to his feet. 'Let's keep this to ourselves, Mr Harris. I won't go there no more, I promise. I give you my solemn promise, cross my heart and hope to die. I'll swear on your Bible. Honest to God I will. I won't go there any more if you promise not to tell my mum.'

'It's too late for making bargains, Scott. The tricks you've played on Miss Hipkin have made her very ill. She could prefer charges, you know. Stealing, trespassing – you name it. Your mum and dad are going to have to be told. You've done it not once but several times and we must get the matter straightened out. Come along.'

Peter stood up, took hold of Scott's hand, led him from the Rectory and marched him to The Royal Oak, with Willie following eagerly in his wake. The public house stood prominently on the corner of Stocks Row and Royal Oak Road. Scott resigned himself to the inevitable. There was nothing he could do; Peter was too strong and too big for him to wrestle with.

The bar was open and crowded; his mother was busy serving.

'Two ploughman's name of Coster, here we are then, plenty of pickle like you – And what do you want with our Scott, Rector? Put him down, if you please.'

She and not Mac was the licensee for some reason unknown to the villagers, though frequently hinted at. She stood nearly six feet high and was built on Amazonian proportions. Her jet black hair was piled high on top of her head in a beehive design. Mac had once ventured to say he liked it that way and that way it had stayed. The heat of the bar on this humid afternoon had heightened the usual flush on her face. Her low-cut Lurex blouse exposed rather more of her figure than one wished to see. Her dark eyes glared furiously at Peter.

'Let him go then, Rector. There's no call to hold him like that.'

'Good afternoon, Mrs McDonald.'

'Everyone calls me Betty.'

'Good afternoon, Betty. I wonder if we could go somewhere quiet. We need to discuss Scott's behaviour.'

'Been messing about in your church, 'as he?' She brought her arm back and smacked Scott hard on his face. He ricocheted against Peter's legs.

'Well, no, not in the church.'

'Well then, you've no call to be holding him like that. Let him go.'

Peter held firmly to Scott. 'Betty, I really feel you would prefer to hear this in private.'

'I haven't the time, can't you see we're busy. Out with it.'

'Very well. We have been concerned for some time because someone has been using the churchyard shed. Willie here went to keep watch to see who it was and caught Scott attempting to enter Muriel Hipkin's cottage with a key. He has told us that he'd had the key cut and had been using it for some time.'

Apart from Peter speaking, the whole bar had frozen in anticipation of Peter's news. It was as if someone had pressed 'Pause' on a video machine.

Betty McDonald was totally nonplussed. She glared first at Peter, then at Willie, then at Scott. Before she could say a word, however, the whole bar erupted.

'It's you then that's frightened her.'

'Been stealing, have yer?'

'Might have known it 'ud be him.'

'What about Jimbo's cat, how about that then?'

'He needs horse-whipping.'

'Time you got him under control, Betty.'

Their advice incensed Betty. She rose to her full height, brought her arm back and hit Willie a savage punch right on the nose.

'That 'ull serve you right, sneaking about spying on people. A harmless little boy and two grown men frightening him to death.'

Poor Willie sat down in a chair someone put behind him as his knees buckled. Blood streamed down his face. Someone got him a brandy, someone else found some tissues and tried to catch the blood.

Mac came out from the other bar. 'Betty, that's enough! You lay one hand on the rector and you'll be done for. Mind what I say. Man of God and all that.'

Scott crept quietly upstairs out of the way. He'd seen his mother like this before.

'Man of God? I'll give him man of God, picking on a poor innocent little boy!'

' "Poor innocent little boy"? Come off it, Betty,' someone in the bar shouted.

Peter stood quietly watching the scene, hoping she wouldn't hit him because there was no way he could defend himself against a woman of her size, not when he was wearing his dog collar.

'Mrs McDonald, Scott has caused Muriel Hipkin a great deal of pain. In fact, he is the reason why she is in the psychiatric ward in hospital! You had no cause to hit Willie in that manner. He was only doing his duty by trying to protect church property. It was incidental that he found Scott trying to enter Miss Hipkin's house.'

'If he couldn't get in then he can't have had the right keys, so it can't have been him.'

'He couldn't get in today because I've had the locks changed on Muriel's behalf. Scott has admitted to entering and stealing from Muriel . . .'

'More fool him. He should have kept his mouth shut.'

'That is not the advice a responsible parent should be giving.'

'Are you telling me I'm not a responsible parent?'

'No, I was just saying—'

'Betty! In the back, if you please.' Mac finally made his voice heard.

Betty turned to look at him, and he jerked his head in the direction of the back room. She flounced behind the bar counter and left the field. Willie's nose had almost stopped bleeding. The crowd round him congratulated him on his success as a sleuth.

'Well done, Willie.'

'Serves him right, the little sneak.'

'Muriel will be glad.'

'Drinks on the house!' Mac shouted above the noise. 'What will yours be, Rector?'

'A whisky please, Mac, and the same for Willie. He really deserves it.'

When the hubbub had quietened, Peter asked Mac for a word.

'Here I am, Rector, fire away.'

'Sharon helped Scott, you know. He didn't do it entirely on his own. She went to the key-cutters in Culworth with Muriel's keys and got copies made. I think only Scott went into the house but she definitely aided and abetted him.'

'I am extremely sorry about all this, Rector. The trouble is we're so busy with the bar that the children are left to their own devices too much. We'll have to make a better effort. You know what it's like with teenagers nowadays, they're that headstrong. Our Sharon's like a grown woman and has been for years. You can't say no nowadays.'

'Do your best, Mac. Muriel has the right to press charges, you know, and I wouldn't blame her if she did. I shall have to tell the police, because they came to have a look round the house when we realised someone was getting in. So they might call in here to speak to you even if Muriel doesn't go ahead with a prosecution.'

'I really must apologise for our Betty's behaviour. Sharon takes after her mother – acts first, thinks afterwards.'

*

It took all of two weeks before Muriel felt able to come home. Caroline took her to the hairdresser's in Culworth and made her feel a million dollars by encouraging her to have a perm at Caroline's expense. Peter presented her with her new keys, which gave her the confidence to go home. Someone suggested a party to welcome her back but then they all agreed she'd feel better just quietly sliding back into her own routine.

Jimbo had restocked her kitchen cupboards for her, popping specialities of the house into her fridge as well. Sir Ronald had taken Pericles for a shampoo and a hairdo at the dog parlour and bought him a new lead and collar, bright red and glossy. Lady Bissett had arranged a bouquet of flowers for the middle of Muriel's little dining table and the mantelpiece was filled with 'Welcome Home' cards. Willie had been keeping her garden watered and the grass cut so that when she went home her world was gloriously restored.

Her confidence, however, was only partly restored but she felt that time would heal that. A few days after getting home Peter called with Scott in tow.

'Good afternoon, Miss Hipkin. God bless you. I've brought Scott to see you. He has something to say, haven't you, Scott?'

Muriel began trembling. Seeing Scott brought back all her anxieties.

Scott wriggled free of Peter's restraining hand.

'He says I've to apologise. And I will, but I didn't do the cat, Miss Hipkin – that wasn't me. I like cats. But I did the other things, and I'm sorry I made you poorly.'

'Well, thank you, Scott.' Muriel held back the tears and turned away, hoping Peter would take him away.

'Good afternoon then, Miss Hipkin. Say good afternoon, Scott, please.'

'Good afternoon, Miss Hipkin.' They both went out and Peter closed the door quietly behind them.

A day or two later there was another knock at the door.

'Why, come in, Mr Charter-Plackett! I intended coming into the shop to thank you for your kindness in filling my kitchen with food. I can never thank you enough, and also thank you for my birthday cake. Do you know, it was the first birthday cake I'd ever had?'

'Only too glad to see you back home again. We've all missed you very much. Can I sit down for a moment?'

'Of course, how remiss of me. Here, sit in this chair, it's the most comfortable.'

'I've come because I'm in a bit of a dilemma.'

'Oh dear, how can I help?'

'Well, I don't know if you've noticed but I've got the restaurant opened now. We've called it Henderson's.'

'After Phyllis? What a lovely idea!'

'That's right, yes. Well, it's kind of two restaurants in one. There's Harriet's Tearoom which sells light snacks and coffees and teas and the like, which opens at ten o'clock and closes at five o'clock, and we also have what Flick calls the "posh bit" – which is a proper restaurant for dinners, open in the evening from seven until eleven. I've got waiters and waitresses and chefs, et cetera, but what I *haven't* got for the tearoom is someone whom I can rely on to take the money every day. No matter how careful we are with our accountancy, there's always a way of stealing money if one's employees try hard enough. I've found someone I can trust for four days a week, but I need someone for the other two days. It would be Wednesday and Friday. What I wondered was, well, would you like the idea? If I've given offence, please forgive me. It's a very genteel tearoom, not all taped music and the like – a kind of thirties-style tearoom, you know.'

'Why is it called Harriet's Tearoom?'

'Because I had hoped to get her interested in it, but she refuses. I went about it in completely the wrong way and she's taken her bat home and refuses to have anything to do with it.'

'Oh dear. I thought you were cleverer than that.'

'So did I.'

'I don't know if I feel confident enough yet to help out. It would mean being sure about how much change I was handing out, wouldn't it? I'll give it serious thought and let you know tomorrow.'

Jimbo went off home, well satisfied with his morning's work. Out and about she needed to be, and this ruse might do the trick. Besides which, he really did need someone. Harriet could be extremely difficult sometimes. Even the sugared almonds hadn't worked their usual miracle this time. She needed a holiday. That was it – a holiday. He'd get Sadie to organise something. He amazed himself sometimes with his fertile mind . . .

Jimbo had left Muriel all in a dither. Three years at home without much challenge and no need to keep to someone else's timetable, had lessened her capacity to cope. But she could see herself sitting at the seat of custom like Matthew in the Bible, except she wouldn't be collecting taxes. It would be fun, though, because everyone in there would have gone to enjoy themselves. Maybe she'd have one of those tills which went Ping! when she opened the drawer. On the other hand, knowing Jimbo, he'd have one of those electric things with lots of buttons to push and flashing lights. Even so, the money she would earn would be very useful. She could always come home in the lunch-hour to take Pericles out, and not starting till ten o'clock would mean she could do her little jobs about the house and take him out before she went. Yes, why not? Was it a comedown for a solicitor's secretary? – a bit beneath her? No. If Jimbo could serve in a shop when he'd had a good post in the City in a merchant bank, why should she quibble about serving behind the till? 'Two toasted teacakes and a pot of tea.' 'Scrambled egg, pot of tea and a cream cake.' Oh yes, she could manage that, and there'd be plenty of people to talk to.

Next day, Muriel hastened into the shop on her way out with Pericles. Harriet greeted her like a long-lost friend.

'How lovely to see you, Muriel. I'm so glad you're home, we have missed you. You are looking well. I love your hair, it does suit you.' And then she kissed her on both cheeks.

'Thank you, Harriet, and thank you also for all the food in my kitchen. Your kindness will not go unnoticed in the Book of Good Deeds. Jimbo called to see me yesterday and I promised him I would give him an answer today.'

'An answer? To what?'

'Well, something he asked me to do. Is he about?'

'Can you tell me and I'll pass on the message?'

Muriel shuffled about a bit, checked on Pericles tied up outside and then said, 'Well, the answer is yes.'

'Yes to what? What's all the mystery about?'

'Isn't he in?'

'No, he's out on business.'

'Don't be annoyed with me will you, Harriet? I couldn't bear that.'

'Of course I shan't be annoyed, but if you don't explain soon I shall be thinking you and Jimbo are having clandestine meetings.'

Muriel blushed. 'Oh, Harriet, it's nothing like that! You're teasing me, aren't you?'

'Yes.'

'Well, he's asked me to take the money in the tearoom he named after you, two days a week. You're not angry, are you?'

Harriet burst out laughing. 'Of course not. He urgently needs someone. I don't mind at all.'

'You know, Harriet, you should support him. Husbands need support. He's very upset.'

'Muriel, leave Jimbo to me, I know what I'm doing. I won't have him riding roughshod over me and that's what he did with this tearoom business. He thought he'd bring me round by naming it after me, but I know his little game. I'll come round in my own good time, never fear.'

Pericles yapped out his boredom at the long delay.

'I must be off. I'll call in later when Jimbo gets back,' Muriel said hastily.

She began work the following Wednesday. Once she'd mastered the till and how to check the little bills, Muriel found herself enjoying her new role. Handing out menus and showing people to suitable tables and passing the time of day with them, she was in her element. Jimbo paid her £25 a day – riches indeed. One day's pay went into the savings bank and the other for living expenses. If she was careful she might manage a holiday next year. The continent, maybe?

11

The following Saturday morning Muriel was taking her turn cleaning the brasses in the church, listening while she worked to Peter playing the organ. Sometimes when she heard him she wished he was the organist instead of Mrs Peel. Mrs Peel played competently but Peter played competently *and* with his heart and soul, which made such a difference to the beauty of it. He finished playing, switched off the organ, went to the altar rail and said a few words of prayer and then came across to speak to Muriel.

'God bless you, Muriel. What the Church would do without its women I do not know.'

'Good morning, Peter. In that case, why can't we be ordained priests? I'm not clever enough to be one, but there are plenty of women who would be and could do good service to the Church.'

'I didn't know you were a militant parishioner.'

'I'm not, but I do get annoyed about the whole subject sometimes. I expect we'll win in the end, women usually do. Have you got out Mr Furbank's costume for Stocks Day? I'll give it a good clean and a mend for you if you like.'

'Stocks Day – what's that?'

'Surely Mr Furbank must have left notes about it? We've been celebrating Stocks Day for centuries. The whole village joins in a procession and we all wear costumes and someone dresses as the Grim Reaper and someone else as an angel. After dark the night before, the verger has to dress the stocks with dead or dying flowers. Then the next afternoon, always the last Saturday in June, we all walk twice round the green. The first time we carry sticks and we all beat the stocks when we pass them and knock off the old flowers, and the second time round we carry white flowers and lay them all on the stocks and cover it completely if we can. Mr Palmer knows someone who plays the flute and they come and lead the procession, like as if it was medieval times. Then, weather permitting, we all sit down to a big tea on the green. Some say we've been doing it since 1066, some say since before history began – but I think that's a bit fanciful – and some say since the plague. According to the church records, Turnham Malpas was badly hit by the plague in 1349 so I think that's more likely, don't you?'

'What part do I play in this?'

'Oh, you're the Devil.'

She turned away to collect her cleaning cloths and move on to the altar vases. Peter stood appalled. '*The Devil?*' He followed her to the altar.

'Yes, you wear your marriage cassock underneath your costume and when you reach the stocks for the second time you take off your Devil's costume and then you bless the stocks. You're all in white like the flowers, you see. Purity or cleansing or something, I think. The whole village loves the celebration. They used to hold games and competitions on the green after the tea, but since about 1895 there's been a fair on the spare land behind the Methodist Chapel. So, when the tea is finished, the tables are all cleared away and everyone goes to the fair for the evening. It's a wonderful day.'

Muriel didn't notice the effect on Peter of what she had said. She busily rubbed away at the twiddly bits on the altar vases, remembering processions from her childhood and how much she had enjoyed seeing the transformation of the Rector from a nasty horned Devil to a charming harmless figure dressed all in white.

'The Press always come and take photographs and there's always a piece in the paper about it and lots of people come to watch – to see the villagers playing at being quaint, I suppose. There's an old painting of it on the wall in the corner behind that tomb that Willie Biggs says is haunted – you know, the one with the knight resting his ankles on his little dog. I don't know which rector it is but he's there for all to see.'

Peter beat a retreat to the rear of the church and stood gazing at the painting. The gold frame was old and in need of a good clean and so was the painting, but it was possible to discern a rector of indeterminate century dropping his Devil's mask and costume onto the grass and standing there holding up his hand in blessing. Close by him were an angel and a figure he assumed was someone's idea of the Grim Reaper. Pagan. Definitely pagan. Nothing to do with Christianity at all.

Peter called to Muriel: 'Surely we usually dress a well, not the stocks.'

Muriel came up the church to speak to him.

'Well yes, most villages do, but the only well still in existence is that one in Jimmy Glover's garden and that is foul. Over the years he's been throwing all his rubbish down it. It certainly wouldn't be any good blessing that. Besides, which, he wouldn't let you. Something of a recluse is Jimmy and a smelly one at that. Oh, and there's another one in Thelma and Valda Senior's garden too. I'd forgotten that one.'

'I have grave doubts as to whether I can perform this blessing.'

'Oh dear. Mr Furbank never gave it a thought – he loved getting dressed up. We had the procession right through the war. Whatever's going on in the world, the ceremony always takes place.'

Neither of them realised that they were being overheard. The news about Peter's misgivings was all round the village and the outlying farms before he had finished his soup that evening.

As Peter entered the church the next morning he noticed an increase, in fact a substantial increase, in the size of the congregation. For a split second he wondered if he had forgotten it was some kind of special day but knew he hadn't. The difference he did notice was that only the choir was singing. The congregation stood mute to a man. When he announced the first hymn, scarcely a hymnbook rustled. Mrs Peel played the first two lines and everyone stood. From his position on the altar steps Peter could see that Caroline, Muriel and Jimbo and Harriet had got their hymnbooks out, but none of the real villagers had done so.

He conducted the entire service in his normal joyous uplifting manner but by the end the strain was beginning to tell. When Peter stood at the church door to wish the congregation 'Good morning' he found that apart from those same four people, no one appeared to shake his hand. They had all gone out through the vestry door.

Willie Biggs supplied the answer.

'They've all taken their bats home, sir. Heard you were none too pleased about playing the Devil in the procession on Stocks Day and they is very upset. They've sent you to Coventry till you change your mind.'

'Does it mean so much to them, then? Why can't someone else play the part? Jimbo would do a good job, wouldn't you, Jimbo?'

'No, Peter, indeed I wouldn't. If they gave me the same cold shoulder they've given you this morning, I'd be bankrupt in a week and with a wife and three children to support, I simply can't afford it. It's you they want, Peter. I'd be no substitute, believe me.'

'But it's a pagan ritual.'

Caroline took his arm. 'Let's go home and have a think, darling.'

'Can't you persuade him to do it, Caroline?' Harriet asked as they made their way down the church path.

'I never try to influence Peter where his conscience is concerned. He is the rector, not me. Sorry, Harriet.'

Caroline went straight to the kitchen and began making sandwiches for their lunch, leaving Peter to wrestle with his own conscience. She knew he'd have to fall in with it in the end, but he needed to come to that conclusion himself. This Stocks Day was evidently part of the fabric of village life and sometimes modern theological thinking had to give way when such stout opposition was voiced. She'd been mortified during the whole of the service and had felt desperately sorry for Peter. At one stage she had nearly stood up and told them what she thought about them all, and then she remembered that he was the rector, not she, and that this was a battle he must fight.

During the afternoon she began altering a dress she'd worn in a play at the hospital. It was drab and loose and torn, but just right for a medieval peasant woman taking part in a village ritual.

'Surely to goodness that isn't a dress you intend wearing, is it? It's not your colour at all,' Peter protested as he brought in an afternoon cup of tea as a means of regaining Caroline's favour.

'Yes it is. I'm playing the part of a medieval peasant woman fearful of the plague and trying hard to forget that I've lost my mother, my father, two sisters and three of my children with the dreaded pestilence.'

'Caroline, is this some kind of joke?'

'No, thanks for the tea, no, that's what it's for.'

'Are you joining in the procession, then?'

'Yes.'

'Even though I don't approve?'

'I am not trying to persuade you to change your mind, so you mustn't try to change mine. We agreed on that before we married.'

'But this is something where I need your support.'

'I can't support you when these good people have so vehemently shown you their disapproval. They must feel very deeply about the issue or they wouldn't have been as unkind and rude as they were this morning. It's not in their nature.'

'But this has nothing to do with Christianity. It's a relic of some pagan ceremony, I'm sure it is. The Devil, indeed! There's no such thing, only the evil within ourselves.'

'Who are you trying to persuade now? Yourself or me?' She slipped off her dress and tried on the costume. 'All I need now is to make my hair all drab and disgusting and I shall look a treat. I've got that old pair of Jesus sandals you don't like – they'll come in handy. It's ages since I had my tea on a village green. You'll have to get your own tea that day. I'll leave something in the fridge for you.'

Caroline went into the hall and stood looking at herself in the long mirror. Peter came up behind her and put his arms round her.

'What if I asked you not to join in?'

'It wouldn't work, Peter. I'm part of the village and I must join in. They know it has to be done or things won't be right for them. I look like a too-well-fed peasant, don't I? I'll have to put some shadow on my cheeks and make them seem hollow.'

Peter had a bitter week following his declaration about Stocks Day. Those who did speak to him looked sorrowfully at him; even Muriel was icily polite when he dropped into Harriet's Tearoom for a coffee.

'Good morning, Mr Harris. Would you like a table outside in the garden or do you prefer inside?'

'Inside, Muriel, then we can talk.'

The YTS girl brought his coffee and Muriel sat at the till trying to look busy with her bookwork. Her natural politeness prevented her from being rude but secretly she was very distressed by Peter's attitude.

He chattered on about the playgroup starting and one thing and another of parish interest, and then eventually she could stand it no longer.

'It's no good, Mr Harris. You've got to face up to it, you know.'

'Face up to what?'

'Stocks Day. I knew the village would be upset but I'd no idea feeling would run so high. The ceremony has a great deal of significance for them, you know. It's right there in their bones and they won't feel right if they don't have the rector doing what he should. They'll all be quite convinced that terrible things will happen to the village if they don't keep faith with the past.'

'I've heard what you say, Muriel, but what about my conscience?'

'Pshaw! What's your conscience worth if you lose everyone's trust?'

'It's worth a lot to me.'

'Yes, I know it is, and we wouldn't want it any other way, but please try to see their point of view.'

Other customers came in and she had to break off her conversation with him.

He went across to the school in the hope that he might find some kindred spirit there in Michael Palmer.

The children were all having their dinners when he arrived. The hall was full of laughing chattering children, a sheer delight which lifted his spirits. As soon as they noticed him, however, they fell silent and Peter knew it wasn't out of respect.

'Good day to you, children. God bless you all.'

Micheal Palmer looked sternly at the children and told them to answer. Peter got some shamefaced muttered responses and then the children ignored him.

'Mr Palmer, could I speak to you for a moment?' They went into Michael's tiny office, where Michael offered him the only chair whilst he perched on the edge of the desk.

'You've done it now, Peter. The children can talk of nothing else.'

'I don't know how everyone found out I disapproved.'

'You can't catch cold in this village without they know before the first sneeze. It's no good trying to keep anything quiet. Historically, Blessing the Stocks is part of them, you see.'

'Historically yes, but from the Church's point of view it's a no-go area.'

'You do know the origins, don't you?'

'Well, they're pagan, aren't they?'

'Not really. A Victorian cleric with more time to spare than you have nowadays, investigated old village customs and found that the Stocks Day procession in Turnham Malpas originated because of the plague. A vagrant had come to the village and had been stealing food and clothes from the villagers. They caught him at it and the local Lord of the Manor, namely one of the Templetons, had him put in the stocks. Unfortunately, while he was fastened in there they realised he had begun showing the early symptoms of the plague. They released him but he died the next day. In consequence of this, many of the villagers died. The part of the ceremony in which villagers beat the stocks with sticks to get rid of the dead flowers is their way of getting rid of the vagrant who brought death with him. That's why there is someone to represent the Grim Reaper – though where the angel comes in I'm not sure. Then the white flowers represent a new beginning after the plague had passed, and the rector dressed in white blessing the stocks makes everything right for another year. When you do that, the whole village will feel safe from the outside world. So really it's an historical drama commemorating the past.'

'I see. I suppose that casts a different light on it. But they shouldn't need something like this to make them feel safe.'

'I know, I know, but they do. Presumably they felt the Devil had sent the vagrant in the first place, and they get rid of him by turning him into the rector.'

'Thank you, Michael, for taking time to explain. You'll need to get back to the children now. How's the playgroup working out?'

'Extremely well. Suzy Meadows is excellent and we are all dovetailing in very nicely indeed. She was an inspired choice. While Muriel has been ill,

Suzy's been playing the piano for us. It's early days yet, but I know the children will benefit.'

'Good, I'm glad. Thank you for your help this afternoon.'

Peter made his way out across the playground, smiling at the children and throwing a ball back to someone, but the children would have none of his overtures. He went into church to meditate for a while.

As he stood before the altar wrestling with his conscience he heard firm footsteps approaching and turned to see who had come in. It was Betty McDonald.

'Thought I might find you here, Rector. Seeing as you've been communicating with His Nibs, perhaps you've decided to change your mind about Stocks Day?'

'No, indeed I haven't. I still feel it's wrong.'

'Well, you'd better think again. Who the hell do you think you are? Have you any idea how much money we shall lose in the bar if you don't do it? Stocks Day is one of our busiest in the whole year. We can't afford to lose money. You're all right, it won't affect your pocket but it will affect mine and Mac's.'

'Whilst I would not wish any harm to come to your business, I'm afraid that your public house is not my responsibility.'

'I dare say, but I'm damned if I'm going to let the village suffer just because of your conscience.' She advanced another step and prodded Peter in the middle of his chest.

'You come here with your posh ways and more money than you know what to do with, and think you can dictate what we do. We may not have been to Oxford but we do know what's right and it's time you did too. Take my advice, play the Devil in the procession, and do it with your fingers crossed behind your back then it won't matter, just like we did when we were telling lies when we were kids. Do it you will, or else I shall want to know the reason why.'

She stormed from the church like a ship in full sail. Peter groaned and said, 'Now, Lord, what do I do?' He went out of the church, crossed the green and stood in front of the stocks. Ancient though they were, they were complete. He'd often seen them in other villages and only the bottom half remained, but Turnham Malpas stocks stood as they had done for hundreds of years. He tried lifting the top half and found it was possible to move it sufficiently to put his own legs and hands through and he decided to sit in the stocks for a moment. The strangest feeling came over him as he sat there. He didn't feel like himself at all; he almost became someone else. He looked round the village and observed that the houses facing the green were just as they had been for centuries. That vagrant must have looked out through the pain of his plague symptoms and seen the village more or less as it stood today.

Here and there a new sign could be seen. The tasteful Turnham Malpas Stores of Jimbo's, and the new sign above his restaurant and tearoom were perhaps the only changes. Peter only intended sitting there for a moment but he became wrapped in his thoughts and drifted away in time. He could see that woman Caroline had pretended to be who'd lost her parents, two sisters and three of her children in the plague. She would have joined the procession in a desperate effort to ward off its return, in case any more of her family died from it. The rector himself must have prayed for it never to return because of the burden he would have had to carry comforting the bereaved and burying the dead. History stretched out before him and behind him, and Peter saw himself as part of a pattern in which he felt compelled to participate. He decided to agree to do the Blessing; it was only right.

Peter extricated himself from the stocks and went off home satisfied he was doing the right thing. 'I must not let Betty McDonald think she's persuaded me – that would be the end!'

Peter sitting in the stocks had not gone unnoticed. Pat Duckett had seen him on her way to close up the school, Muriel had seen him from the window of Harriet's Tearoom, and so had Suzy Meadows as she set off to collect Pansy and Daisy from afternoon school. Her heart missed a beat as she saw him, for she still found him tremendously attractive. It wouldn't be long now before he knew. She couldn't disguise her situation many more weeks; she'd never been as big as she was this time. Maybe he already knew, perhaps Caroline had told him about seeing her in the clinic, but she felt he didn't know. He wouldn't have been able to stop himself from speaking to her about it. God knew she didn't want this baby. She'd offer it for adoption. Surely people who adopt a child would cherish it. She quite simply didn't want it. No way. No way.

12

Muriel pressed her costume with loving care. She'd worn the same one for four years now. It was made from an old brown coat of her mother's. Every time Mrs Hipkin had worn it she'd said, 'This coat will see me out.' It didn't. She'd bought another one, but refused the throw the old one away. 'It'll come in for something one day,' she'd maintained. Stocks Day was only two days away and Muriel couldn't wait. The fair had already arrived, Willie Biggs had cleaned all the trestle tables and had them stacked in the church hall awaiting the big day. Tradition had it that everyone brought their own food for the tea so there was no catering to do, which made the event a pleasure for everyone.

Thank goodness Peter had decided to do the Blessing. Muriel wasn't superstitious, but she had a sneaking feeling that if he hadn't, all kinds of dreadful things would have happened in the village. Death and destruction, that's what. The costume, hanging up on its hanger from the door frame, blew gently in the breeze from the garden. The hot weather still persisted. Because her plants were so dear to her she'd managed to get over her fear of the water butt, but she shuddered each time she used it. Those weeks in the hospital had gone by in a blur but they still struck terror in her heart. She'd only to see Scott in school and the horror came flooding back – but she mustn't dwell on it. There were so many exciting things happening to her these days. The part of the week she liked best was Wednesdays and Fridays, when she went to the tearoom. She hadn't realised what a gregarious person she was. All these years she'd taken a back seat and she shouldn't have done.

Peter's costume was hanging from the door frame as well. The mask and horns had had to be seriously renovated but she'd taken great joy in the task. How sensible he was to accept what had to be. He and Caroline were the best thing that had happened to the village for years. They'd brought such light and joy to everyone, and in such a practical way, too. If only they'd had a family. Peter's children would have been beautiful indeed, and Caroline would have made such a lovely mother.

She went out into the front garden to water the roses. Glancing up, she saw Betty McDonald going past.

'Good afternoon, Mrs McDonald.'

'Why do you always insist on calling me Mrs McDonald? Everyone but you calls me Betty. Go on, say it – Betty.'

'Well, Betty then.'

'That's better. It was me made the rector change his mind, yer know.'

'I should think that Pe— the rector made up his own mind.'

'Oh no, he didn't. I went to see him in church. Praying, he was. Said he didn't agree with it, but I told him. "Cross yer fingers" I said, "and pretend you're liking it." It did the trick – I knew it would. Just needed someone to tell him what was what.'

'I don't expect he took any notice of what you said.' Muriel said this politely but firmly.

'See 'ere, I'm telling you it was me what made him change his mind. I told him good and proper. "Mac and me 'ull lose money if the Blessing doesn't go ahead," I said. I told him he'd have me to answer to if he didn't. Next day he's doing it.'

'I see.'

'Time you unbent a bit, yer too stiff and starchy. Come in the bar tonight and I'll treat you to a drink. Mind what I say, I shall expect you.'

Muriel had never been in a public house unescorted in all her life. She dismissed the idea and carried on watering her plants. Pericles dug about in the borders and got under her feet in that annoying way he had when he was wanting to go for a walk. Finally she gave in and got his lead. They wandered down to the beck and met Lady Bissett out with her Pomeranian. The two dogs greeted each other like long-lost comrades so Muriel and Lady Bissett joined forces and chattered about this and that as they walked by the beck.

'I'm to be the angel this year you know, Muriel.'

'I didn't know that. We usually have a – well, a younger person to be the angel.'

'Yes, I know, but the committee said they would choose me on account of all the work I've done in the past for the Village Flower Show and things. It is an honour. I've hired an angel costume from the costumiers in Culworth. Ron . . . ald has gone to collect it this afternoon.'

'Do you think that's wise? After all, it's only a simple village affair.'

'I know, but you must raise standards, don't you think? And what with the Press being there as well, you have to keep up your position. Ronald is delighted. He's the Grim Reaper this year, you know. In fact, if Peter had not changed his mind he was going to volunteer to be the Devil.'

'The verger is the Grim Reaper, by tradition.'

'Well yes, but he has no style, has he? Willie Biggs isn't really suitable for such a part.'

'The verger is always the Grim Reaper – it doesn't matter whether he is suitable or not.'

'Yes, it does. Things must be done correctly. I did consider paying for Peter to have a new costume. It's still not too late. Ron . . . ald could go back tomorrow and get him a real smart outfit.'

'I've renovated Peter's costume. It's the one that has been worn by the rector for something like seventy years.'

'That's what I'm saying – he needs a new one.'

'Well, I disagree. We've all to be thankful he's decided to do it; let's leave it at that.'

'It was me who persuaded him to change his mind, you know. I told him that these small-minded village people have to be humoured. They haven't much in this life and if Blessing the Stocks makes them feel better, then who are we to argue?'

'I think you're being very patronising, Lady Bissett. Just because they live in a village, it does not mean to say they are idiots.'

'Don't take on so. I'll go and see Peter this afternoon and tell him I'm hiring, at my own expense of course, a brand-new Devil's costume for him.'

'You can't. He's away at a Diocesan Retreat all day.'

'I'll ring the company this afternoon and reserve one just in case then, and ask him in the morning first thing and Ron . . . ald can go in again tomorrow morning to pick it up.'

Muriel grew flustered and actually stamped her foot. 'You'll do no such thing! You are an interfering old busybody.'

'How dare you call me that? I'm giving the whole proceedings a bit of style, that's all.'

'A bit of style? If we listen to you we shall all be hiring costumes and that's not what it's about. Some of the costumes are dozens of years old and have been passed down from generations back.'

Muriel snatched Pericles up into her arms as he dashed by, turned on her heel and fled the scene of battle.

Hired costumes, indeed! Whatever next?

Peter declined Lady Bissett's offer. He felt things were in such a delicate state that he daren't trespass so far from tradition. Besides, he didn't want to hurt Muriel's feelings. She'd worked so hard on his costume.

On the day he put it on over his marriage cassock and stood admiring himself in the hall mirror. Caroline joined him and they both burst out laughing.

Wiping the tears from her eyes, she turned to him and said, 'When I promised to marry you I thought we would be at a university church or a big city church and be all posh and dignified. Now look at the two of us!'

'So did I, but this is much more real and much more fun. I'm going to take you on the dodgems tonight – it's years since I went to a fair. I must say, Dr Harris, you look very authentic. What have you used for the shadows on your delightful cheeks?'

'Just a very little soot from the stove in the sitting room, mixed with some wrinkle cream. I've been quite artistic, haven't I?'

'Indeed you have. Now, where are the words I have to say? Oh, here they are in my cassock pocket. Having given in about this thing I must do it right. I wish Arthur Furbank had been a bit taller. My cassock's barely covered by this costume.'

'Never mind, you look very impressive. Come on, it's time we were off.'

They made their way to the starting point where already three-quarters of the village were waiting and the Press had their cameras at the ready. The down-at-heel local reporter stood wearily watching the proceedings for the umpteenth time. He'd been well primed by Lady Bissett with two double whiskies in her drawing room and in return he had persuaded the photographer to take pictures of her standing by the door of her house, but the feather wings she was wearing caught on the thatched roof where it curved round the porch and she had had to be extricated by Sir Ronald. The reporter forbore to take notes on the language she used as her husband rescued her.

It must have been one of the most successful Stocks Days the village had ever had. Because of Peter's initial decision not to take part, a lot of outside interest had been aroused and the crowds watching the procession were bigger than ever. Betty and Mac had a sensational day in the bar, and the fair took more money that evening than on any Saturday night for years. The brilliant weather, of course, had encouraged the crowds. About half-past nine, Pat Duckett decided that it was time she went home, as the children had already spent most of her money. Dean was clutching a huge turquoise teddy bear he'd won on the little shooting range and Michelle was munching her way through yet another toffee apple.

'There's no more money left now so we'd better go home.'

'Aw, Mum, we want to stay for Mr Charter-Plackett's firework display.'

'I didn't know he was having fireworks.'

'Well, he is. It's a secret but we all know at school because Flick told us. She couldn't keep a secret, not if you paid her.'

Michelle took time off from her toffee apple to say, 'It's at ten o'clock, she says. Please can we stay?'

'Well, all right then, but after that we must go. We shan't be able to eat all week if I spend much more. Where's the display?'

'On the green. He started getting it ready as soon as Mr Biggs had cleared the trestle tables away.'

'Righto then. We'll walk round a bit longer then we'll go and stand near the school and get a good view.'

It was almost dark when the three of them went to take their places. A small crowd in the know was already in position.

As the first fireworks went up, the crowds in the fairground came running to watch the fun. Oooh! Aaaah! they went as the huge rockets soared into the sky. Pat Duckett watching Jimbo igniting the fireworks thought how lovely it would be to have the kind of money that could afford a display of such magnitude. To have money to spend just for fun. She turned her head to watch a rocket as it flared into dozens of stars above the school. Right mess I shall have clearing the playground before school on Monday, she thought. As she glanced at the school, she noticed that a light had been left on.

'That's funny – there's a light on in the school. You two stay here and don't move. I'll just go and see everything's all right. Do as I say, now.'

Pat dug around in her bag for the school keys. There they were right at the bottom with her fags. 'Have to clean this bag out some time,' she muttered. She put the huge key in the lock of the main door and to her surprise found it was already undone. The rows of pegs in the narrow corridor leading to the main hall were free of the children's coats and they looked quite forlorn. She pushed open the door into the hall. Only the lights at the far end were on. She walked forward to the bank of light switches and kicked against something on the floor.

She looked down to see what she had kicked. She was so distraught she didn't know she was screaming at the top of her voice. Her hand clamped to her mouth, she ran from the hall and out into the playground. The fireworks were still exploding with massive bangs and no one could hear her screaming above the explosions. She ran to the edge of the crowd and found Willie Biggs.

For once in her life she couldn't speak. She grasped his arm and, still screaming, pulled him towards the school.

' 'Ere, Pat, what's up? Now then, now then, go steady.'

Pat Duckett pushed him through the main door of the school and then stood outside sobbing and gasping for breath. She couldn't bear going inside again.

Willie pushed open the door into the hall and saw what had frightened Pat Duckett. Lying on the floor at his feet was Toria Clark, so badly beaten about the head that she must have died instantly. She still wore the bright red shirt and the close-fitting black trousers she'd put on for going to the fair. Her dark hair was blood-soaked and her face almost unrecognisable from the beating she had taken. By her hand lay the keys which Willie recognised as belonging to the school. He ran outside, turned Pat Duckett's key in the lock, thrust it into her hand for safe keeping and set off for help.

He knew the police sergeant was on fairground duty and he ran as fast as his legs would carry him. He found him at the entrance talking to some boys from the next village.

'Sergeant, you'll have to come to the school. There's been a . . . well, a tragedy. Come quick!'

It was the same sergeant who had come when Suzy Meadows' Patrick had been found dead. The news of Toria Clark's death flashed round the crowd in a moment. The babble of sympathy and curiosity grew in volume as the sergeant arrived. A crowd had gravitated from the finale of the fireworks to watching the activity around the school.

Pat Duckett was being revived with a timely nip from Sir Ronald's hip-flask.

'Terrible sight it is. I shall have to have another nip, my nerves is all shot to pieces. She's laid there dead as a doornail. Can't believe it, always such a nice person she was, nothing too much trouble. There's all that blood. Oh dear, I'm going to faint.'

She slid sideways off the school wall where Sir Ronald had sat her down and fell with a resounding thud onto the pavement.

The sergeant hastened up to the front of the crowd. 'Evening, Rector. Sounds nasty. Thank you for keeping the school locked, Mr Biggs. Can't have everyone tramping on the evidence. You have the keys, sir? Thank you. Stand aside, please.'

Caroline arrived on the scene. 'Sergeant, it's Dr Harris here. Can I help?'

'Would you come in with me, Doctor, please? By the sound of it we're much too late but I should be glad of your opinion.'

'Of course.'

They entered together. Caroline left Toria Clark lying just as she was. She felt for a pulse and listened for any signs of breathing but there were none.

'She's definitely dead, Sergeant. I don't think anyone could survive such a savage beating. I should like to cover her up but we'd better wait for your forensic people, I suppose. Don't want to confuse the evidence.'

'Certainly not, Doctor. Come here and have a look at this.'

The sergeant was standing in the light at the far end of the hall. Laid out on a table was a huge poster made up of two sheets of the paper Michael Palmer used for artwork. They had been joined together by Sellotape with a partly finished message in large letters scrawled on, saying: *Ask Mr P. he knows she was a Lesbian, that's why she died.*

'Very embarrassing this, Dr Harris. Not quite the kind of thing a village like Turnham Malpas is used to. In your opinion, do you think she was – well, you know – what the poster says?'

'We've only been here a few months, as you know, Sergeant, but I've seen Miss Clark on several occasions and she's been to the Rectory for coffee a couple of times and I have never, not for one moment, thought on those lines. Not even for one moment. Whoever wrote this is quite mistaken. But why did she have to die? I can't understand that.'

'Whoever attacked her certainly didn't intend her to live.'

'What did they kill her with, Sergeant? It must have been something fairly thick and heavy like a rounders bat or a cricket bat.'

They were interrupted by a hammering on the outside door.

'That'll be the inspector now, Dr Harris. Would you stay and have a quick word with him, please?'

'Yes of course, though I can't contribute much.'

After Caroline had said what she had found, the inspector asked her to find Mr Palmer and tell him to come into the school and look for anything missing which might have been used as the murder weapon. She found the headmaster patiently waiting in the playground. Caroline explained why the police needed to see him immediately.

'Murder weapon? She really is dead, then?'

'Oh yes, there's no doubt about that. Who on earth would want to murder Toria? She was such a lovely person and so well liked. Whoever did it is accusing her of being a lesbian. They've written a big poster saying that's why she died.'

'Lesbian? Toria Clark? She most certainly wasn't.'

'Exactly my sentiments, Michael. You'd better go in, the police are waiting for you.'

Pat Duckett had been revived and was sitting surrounded by eager busybodies wanting to hear again her vivid description of the body.

'Now, Mrs Duckett, is there anything I could do for you?'

'Oh, thanks, Dr Harris, but I'm feeling much better now. It was a terrible sight, wasn't it? Oh dearie me. I shall never forget it, never. Where's them kids o' mine? Back on the fairground, I expect.'

'Well no, the fairground has been closed by the police. Here they are, look.' Dean and Michelle appeared, surrounded by children from the school all wishing to bathe in their reflected glory. 'I think it would be a good idea if you had a word with the police, told them what happened and then took these two children home.'

'Shall I have to be questioned, then?'

'Well, it was you who found her, wasn't it? You were the first on the scene after all.'

The sergeant came out at this moment and asked to speak to Mrs Duckett. 'Here I am, Sergeant.'

Much to the disappointment of the crowd he took her inside.

Michael Palmer was questioned for much longer than Pat Duckett. He answered every question with genuine truthfulness and was unable to throw any light on the murder at all. He denied all suspicion of his colleague being a lesbian and could furnish no reason why anyone should want to kill her, nor indeed why his name should be mentioned on the poster. They asked if he and Toria had had a relationship.

'Only that of a headmaster and an assistant teacher and no more. We were simply teaching colleagues, that was all. Ask anyone in the village. Her social life and mine were something quite separate.'

Every person in the village was interrogated by the police. Toria's house was thoroughly searched from top to bottom in an effort to uncover some clues as to her death. The television news crews came and went, the newspaper people came too, but the police were no nearer finding a solution to her death nor even a motive than they had been the day it happened. They'd endeavoured to trace everyone who had been at the fair that night and question them all, with no success. The file was kept open but despite all their efforts her murder remained unsolved.

The speculation in the bar at The Royal Oak kept the regulars fully occupied. Pat Duckett's story was repeated time and again.

'I'm 'aving nightmares about it, Vera. Every time I go into that dratted hall I can see her lying there. It's all right them carting off the body, but who is it who's left with the memories? Me. I 'ave the floor to clean and when I see them dear children sitting there calm as you please eating their dinners or doing that dancing they do with Miss Hipkin playing away on that piano all I can think about is Miss Clark and all that blood. I think there was something in it, what was said on that poster. Otherwise why would anyone want to murder 'er? They say there's a lot of it about.'

'A lot of what about.'

'You know, that funny stuff with women.'

'She wasn't a lesbian, Pat. I seed her out with a chap only a few weeks before she died. Nice young man he was.'

'Did you tell the police that when they questioned you?'

'Yes I did, and they found him and questioned him but he'd been away on business when it happened so that ruled him out.'

'I think it's disgusting, people like that teaching our children.'

'I don't think you should talk like that,' Vera bridled. 'She was nice was Miss Clark and you hadn't a word to say against her before she was murdered, Pat, so don't start now. She was lovely when our Rhett couldn't settle down at school and kept running home every playtime. Lovely, she was. She soon got him sorted.'

'It's funny there should be two deaths in that school hall. First Mrs Palmer and then Miss Clark. Course, I know the circumstances were different but we never got to the bottom of Mrs Palmer killing herself, did we, Vera? And what's more, each time it comes back to Mr Palmer, don't it? "Mr P." it said on that poster.'

Jimmy joined in. 'I can think of lots of people called Mr P. What about old Mr Pratt at Bolton's Farm or Mr Planchard what has that cobbler's shop in Culworth?'

'It's hardly likely to be one of them. Can't see Mr Pratt at his age having anything to do with someone as young as Miss Clark!'

Jimmy wiped the beer froth from his mouth before adding his bit to the conversation. 'You never know; he was seventy-one when his Gerald was born, remember. Married a girl of thirty when he was seventy, and Bob's yer uncle – next news they had a baby.'

'So they say, but was it his?' Vera queried sagely.

'Anyways, I reckons Mr Palmer knows more than he's admitting to.'

'That's enough of that, that's not nice, Pat. That's casting a slur. He could have you for libel and then where would you be?'

'There is one thing, the murder certainly put Stocks Day in Turnham Malpas on the map. Nobody will forget us in a hurry.'

But a couple of weeks after Stocks Day, the village had something else entirely to gossip about.

13

Several people had had their suspicions but it was Muriel who first voiced hers in public. 'Harriet,' she said one day when she was the only customer in the shop. 'You know much more about these things than I do, but have you thought that Suzy Meadows, the poor dear, might be expecting another baby?'

'It's funny you should have said that, Muriel. I was thinking on those lines myself, but I hoped I was wrong.'

'Poor dear girl if she is. A posthumous baby – how very sad for her.'

'Well, I'm fairly sure we're right. She's not simply putting on weight. He died at the end of March so the very latest the baby could be born would be the end of December. But judging by the looks of her it will be earlier than that.'

'Let's hope it's a boy. It would be a comfort to her, having lost Patrick.'

'I suppose it would, but a new baby costs money. I don't see how she could afford it.'

'The Lord will provide, I'm sure.'

Peter, busy about his parish duties, having initiated more schemes than he had time to comfortably oversee, was one of the last to hear the news about Suzy. Also, Caroline had given him food for thought with her decision to resign from her pathology post.

'But why, Caroline? You've always loved working at the hospital!'

'I know, but I feel you need me at home more. Just lately you've looked very much like a little boy lost and have been giving me some searching looks as if you don't know who I am any more. So I've decided to have some time to ourselves. I can always go back to hospital work if I get bored with housekeeping. I've worked all the time we've been married and it's time for a while anyway that I spent more time looking after your needs. The money's not important, with your private income as well as your stipend. So I shall be the dutiful wife sitting at your feet admiring your efforts. I might even manage to finish decorating this place, you never know.'

'My darling, I don't deserve your sacrifice.'

'It isn't a sacrifice, Peter, it's a joy and a pleasure. I'd do anything for you if it made you happy, you know that.'

'What I've just said is true, I don't deserve your love. It's absolutely true. One has to earn love like yours, and I haven't earned it. I've tried to throw it away.'

Peter stood up at this point, turned abruptly away and strode off into his study, leaving Caroline puzzled by his reaction. She'd known for some time that Peter was deeply troubled but she couldn't discover what it was. There was definitely something he was keeping from her. She hoped it wasn't that he was going through that period most clergymen had to confront at some time or another – that deeply disturbing time when they questioned whether their faith was real or imaginary, and doubted if they should have taken up the Church. Whatever it was, whatever his decision, she would stand by him. Nothing and nobody would separate her from him. That was, if he still wanted her. The alternative didn't bear thinking about.

Michael Palmer asked Peter if he could have a private word after morning service the following Sunday.

As soon as he had closed the vestry door, Michael dropped his bombshell.

'Suzy Meadows has told me this week that she won't be able to continue with the playgroup for much longer.'

'Why ever not? She's doing such a good job.'

'For the very good reason that she is expecting a baby. In fact not just one, but two.'

'Two! Oh, good Lord!' Peter turned away and looked out of the window.

Michael, full of his news and plans for coping with the emergency, didn't notice the effect his words had had. Peter stood looking out onto the churchyard but seeing absolutely nothing. What he had most dreaded had come about. Dear God, not one but two. He was blinded mentally and physically. He heard Michael saying, 'What do you think, Peter?' and hadn't the faintest idea what he had said. Still apparently studying the churchyard Peter said, 'I'm sorry, Michael, I didn't catch what you said.'

'I said that the education committee had decided to confirm the appointment of the temporary teacher they sent to replace Miss Clark, and that Liz Neal has said she would like to take charge of the playgroup while Suzy has the twins. Do you think that will be satisfactory? I told Liz I would have to consult you first before I could confirm it, but I was sure you would agree.'

'Yes, of course I agree. You decide what is best. We're lucky to have people who can step in.'

'The other thing is that I am thinking of giving in my notice. Toria Clark dying like she did has set a lot of rumours going and I feel it's time I should move on. I always intended to move after a few years but somehow Turnham Malpas has the effect of getting you in its clutches and you can't get away. However, I've decided that now is the time. I'll go at the end of the school year in July. Mind you, I've said this several times before and then changed my mind.'

Peter turned to look at him. 'I shall be sorry to see you go but we all have to move on some time. In fact, I shall be *very* sorry to see you go. Thank you for coming to tell me.'

Michael left, puzzled by the rector's awkwardness. Peter went back into the church and knelt in torment in the seat Caroline always occupied. He found her prayer book, opened it and read on the flyleaf the words '*To my dearest Caroline on our wedding day. Together from this day unto eternity. Peter.*'

Caroline had his dinner ready and when he didn't come she eventually set off to find him. And there he was, knelt in prayer where she usually sat. He had her own prayerbook in his hand. She sat beside him and took his hand in silence, not wishing to interrupt. He gripped her hand until it hurt. When she tried to release his grip he turned towards her, laid his head on her knee, put his arms around her and wept.

'My dear, dear Peter, what on earth is the matter? My darling, for heaven's sake tell me.' She stroked his hair as she would have stroked the hair of a child of hers. 'Whatever is the matter? There isn't anything that you can't tell me, you know.'

Caroline waited patiently for Peter to speak. His voice came out jerkily.

'Suzy Meadows is having a baby.'

'I know.'

There was a long pause before Peter spoke. 'How long have you known? Did she tell you?'

'No. I saw her at the ante-natal clinic several weeks ago.'

'So you don't know anything really?'

'I would have thought that giving birth to a baby after your husband has died was sufficient to be going on with. What else is there to know?'

'Caroline, you remember you said the other day that you thought I seemed strange and needed looking after? I don't need looking after, I need hanging.'

'Hanging? Oh God, Peter, whatever have you done to deserve that? Surely you're not our phantom killer?'

'In my judgement it's worse than that. I have been totally disloyal and unfaithful to you and I think, in fact I know, the result is what I've just told you. Which you already knew – except you didn't know the whole truth.'

'What are we talking about, Peter? Toria's murder or Suzy's baby?'

'Suzy's babies. She's having twins.'

'Twins? Oh good heavens, the poor girl. Now that really is a problem. I shall have to go round to see her. However is she going to manage? Why has that upset you so much?'

'You still haven't understood. The twins are mine.'

The only sound in the church was the steady drip drip of the tap in the choir vestry. The flowers on the altar looked just the same as they had done two moments ago, the great brass cross still hung gleaming above the altar. The old, old wood of the pulpit and the choir-stalls still glowed softly in the summer sun filtering through the stained-glass windows. Caroline still sat cradling Peter's head on her knee, the clock kept ticking, Caroline's heart kept beating. Inside herself she had died. Finally Peter spoke.

'It only happened once, a few days after Patrick died. She needed comforting and she begged me, begged me to comfort her and it went on from there. That isn't any excuse, nor a reason. I could still have gone away, but the first time I saw her I was attracted to her. Not loved her but lusted for her, I suppose. After that one time I kept right away I was so ashamed of what had happened. I thought if I carried the burden of what I'd done all by myself I could atone for the sin of it. I didn't want to hurt you, you see. Didn't want to cause you pain. Even though we had promised each other always to be truthful about our feelings. Now of course the greatest harm has been done. I have given someone other than my beloved, a child.'

Willie Biggs coughed loudly as he came in to switch off the lights. Peter stood up and tried to appear normal.

'Sorry to interrupt, sir. I forgot to switch off the electrics. Just started me pudding when I remembered.'

'That's all right, Willie. Thank you for remembering. Must save on the electricity bill.'

'Exactly what I thought, sir. See you about six, Mr Harris.'

'Yes, of course, Willie.'

Caroline stood up after Willie had gone. She turned to Peter and said in a small defeated voice: 'Why should these babies be yours? Why aren't they Patrick's?'

'She told me they hadn't . . . well . . . they hadn't had relations for nearly a year.'

'I see. It's no good pretending that I'm not hurt because I am. I'm going back to the Rectory now. I need to find out where I stand.'

The following morning Caroline told Peter she was going to take a few days' leave and go up to her family home in Northumberland to give herself time to think. She rang the hospital, made arrangements for her work to be covered and then packed a case and left.

From her bedroom window Suzy Meadows watched her go. Caroline's white strained face told Suzy what she needed to know. After the last of the playgroup children had gone home, Suzy took Rosie by the hand and marched off with the firm intention of calling in at the Rectory on her way home to lunch. 'Grasp the nettle,' her mother always said, and this was some nettle.

Suzy could see through the Rectory window that Peter was sitting at his desk. She knocked loudly on the door.

She looked closely at his face when he opened the door and was shocked to see that he appeared to have aged ten years at least. His normally fresh complexion had turned to a strange shade of grey and his eyes had lost all their fire.

'I need to talk to my parish priest.'

'Please come in.' Before, the sound of his voice would have set her heart zinging but no longer. She had lived an age since anything had had the ability to do that.

Peter stood back and made room for her to enter. 'Come in the study.'

'I need to talk.' Suzy patted Rosie's head. 'Can we occupy her somewhere else?' Peter stood nonplussed for a moment and then suggested to Rosie that she went in the kitchen and played with Mrs Harris' cats. 'Do you like cats, Rosie?'

'Yes I do, Mr Harris,' Rosie beamed at him, and confidently put her hand in his and allowed him to show her where to find the cats. When he returned to the study Suzy was sitting on a chair waiting to speak.

Suzy cleared her throat. 'I realised this morning when I saw Caroline leaving and looking so upset that she knows what has happened.'

'I honestly didn't . . .' Suzy held up her hand to stop him speaking.

'There's no need to say anything at all, just let me speak. I have no intention of anyone knowing that these twins I'm carrying are anyone else's but Patrick's. That's what everyone will think and that's what I shall allow them to think. There is no way that I would ruin your life nor Caroline's by telling the truth. To be brutally frank, Peter, I don't want these babies at all and I shall offer them for adoption. In fact, I've already had a word with the adoption people about that. I have it all arranged. As soon as the babies are born they will be handed to the new parents. Then the adoption will go through when they are about a year old. I've picked out who their parents shall be.'

'You have?'

'Yes. It's quite simply sound common sense. I can't possibly feed and clothe five children. I need to get back to work as soon as I can and with Rosie nearly ready for school that becomes feasible. If I keep the twins it would be impossible. In any case, I can't find any more love in my heart at the moment. There is none to spare for two more babies, be they boys or girls.'

'I can never forgive myself for what happened.'

'Why should you feel guilty? I needed you and you, for the moment, needed me. But Caroline is your life's partner, not me. I wouldn't do at all. I know I sound absolutely hard as nails but at the moment that's the only way I know how to cope. The twins are due in December around Christmas-time, but I expect they'll have to be induced so that fits in very nicely with Patrick's death.'

'Thank you for being so totally considerate towards Caroline and me. I don't deserve it.'

'Not another word shall I say to you or anyone else from now on. What I have said I have said, and that's it. Caroline hasn't left for good, has she?'

A flash of pain crossed Peter's face. 'I don't think so. She's gone home to Northumberland to sort her feelings out. Walking along the coast there has always done her good. If she doesn't come back I shall be finished. I can't go on if I haven't got Caroline.'

Suzy stood up as Rosie came back into the study. 'Some good must come from this, and it will. Two children will have been given life – and what better father could they have than you?'

14

Four days after Caroline had gone to Northumberland Peter had to go to an inter-Church meeting in Culworth. He knew he would be away all day so he fed Caroline's cats, made sure the cat flap was unlocked, patted their heads as being the nearest he could get to kissing his darling girl and left with a heavy heart. Inter-Church services were not foremost in his mind. He'd tried ringing Caroline, though if she'd answered he wouldn't have known what to say. There'd been no reply. He hadn't realised that he no longer functioned as a single person. If he didn't hear from her soon he would go straight up to Northumberland and hang the parish.

He drove back to the Rectory and arrived home about six. There was no letter on the mat as he had hoped. The cats rushed to greet him.

'Cupboard love, that's what it is – pure cupboard love.'

As he hung up his jacket he smelt that special lingering perfume of Caroline's on her coat hanging beside his own. The cats cried for attention and he went to the kitchen to get their food. The table was laid for two. He could smell a casserole cooking.

The cats pestered, so hardly daring to believe that Caroline was back he fed the ravenous beasts while he decided what to do. When he'd put down their dishes he stood listening for a moment and then climbed the stairs. Their bedroom door was open and he could see Caroline unpacking her case. Her back was turned to him and he realised she hadn't heard him come in.

'Caroline.'

'Peter.'

'You're back.'

'I am.'

Caroline turned to face him. 'Mother sends her love. I've put a casserole in the oven. It'll be ready in about twenty minutes.'

'I smelt it when I came in. I've fed the cats.'

'So have I. The greedy things.'

'Shall I get a bottle of wine opened?'

'That would be nice. I'll be down in a moment.'

'I didn't see your car.'

'No, I've had to leave it in Culworth for repair. There's something wrong with the electrics.'

'I was in Culworth. I could have picked you up if I'd known.'

'I caught the bus.'

'I see.'

On a weekday evening they usually made a bottle of wine last two meals but tonight they finished the whole bottle. They exchanged news about the parish, about the weather, about Northumberland, carefully avoiding the major difficulty which consumed their minds. Caroline broached the subject first.

'Peter, I had to get away to get the right perspective on things. Something about not being able to see the wood for the trees, you know. It took me until yesterday to understand how I felt. I stood high up on the cliffs watching the sea coming pounding in onto the rocks, and I thought about the permanency of the sea and that it goes on relentlessly no matter what trivial pursuits Man manages to occupy himself with. I sat thinking about you, thinking about how you are the permanency in my life. I tried to imagine what my life would be like if I turned my back on you now. Sitting there I said goodbye to the Rectory, to the village, to Muriel and Jimbo and Harriet and Willie and all the others. I set myself up in a little flat and got a job in a hospital. I saw myself coming home at night to an empty flat, trying to make new friends, going to evening classes. It didn't work. I thought about you coming home to an empty house. No one to talk your problems over with, no one to love you and make sure you were fed properly, no one actually to care whether you lived or died. And I could see no point in both of us being on our own.'

Peter smiled. 'Are you saying then that the sole reason for you coming back is to make sure the village doesn't sit sniffing the air during the sermon because the rector hasn't washed his socks?'

'Yes, you could say that.' Caroline looked up at him and grinned. 'That's if you want me.'

'A lifetime of washing my own socks couldn't make up for what I've done to you. You make me feel very humble. Could you possibly sit on my knee?'

'Yes.'

They talked well into the night. The cats gave up hoping for their nightly walk around the garden with Caroline and went to bed in a huff. The Aga in need of its usual stoking up went unattended, the Rectory door remained unlocked and the bedroom light stayed on all night.

15

The following Sunday, Peter's sermon dealt with forgiveness. Muriel listened with deep interest. That was exactly what she should be doing to Scott McDonald – forgiving him, even though he had caused her so much pain. She looked round the church to see if there was anyone else who should be listening with particular interest to Peter's powerful, heartfelt words. Well, old Jimmy Glover had put in one of his rare appearances, and he certainly needed to ask forgiveness for the bad language he used when the children threw sticks into his tree to get the conkers to fall. And Vera, who lived next door to Pat Duckett – now *she* needed to ask forgiveness for her disgraceful behaviour outside The Royal Oak on Friday night, when she had had too much to drink. Betty McDonald had had to throw her out – really throw her out, not just ask her to leave. Come to think of it, Muriel supposed everybody had something they needed to ask forgiveness for . . .

After the service, she stood talking to Lady Bissett whose head was full of arrangements for next month's Village Flower and Vegetable Show.

'Well, Muriel, if you go on winning like you do we shall have to ban you to give someone else a chance.'

'I'm not competing this year.'

'Not at all?'

'No. I haven't the time to devote to my garden like I used to. I'm so busy, you see.'

'Of course – I'd forgotten you'd got a job. I've decided to organise more classes for the flower-arranging this year and some more for the children. If they enter things they're bound to bring their parents. Do you think Jimbo might provide the refreshments?'

'He's already promised Peter to provide the meat for the Harvest Supper. We can't go on asking and asking.'

'Oh, come off it, Muriel! He's making a packet out of this village, what with the store and the tearoom and restaurant. He can well afford it.'

'Can well afford what?'

Lady Bissett hadn't realised that Harriet was standing right behind her.

'Ah, Harriet. I was just saying to Muriel here that you and Jimbo might be so kind as to provide something towards the refreshments for the Village Show.'

'It sounded to me as if you were saying we could well afford to provide the lot. It's not Charity Hall, you know. We do actually run a business.'

'Oh, I didn't mean it like that.'

'How did you mean it, then?' Harriet retorted. Muriel felt very uncomfortable. She hated rows and this one looked as if it was going to be a big one. But Lady Bissett was saved from answering Harriet's belligerent question by a loud joyous shout.

'Moo? It is – it's really Moo! What in heaven's name are *you* doing here?'

Muriel turned round to see who had used a name she hadn't been called since she was a girl. The owner of the cultured voice stood about five feet six in his socks. He had thick snow-white hair, big bushy eyebrows, a very tanned complexion, a haughty nose and big laughing bright brown eyes. She blushed bright red as she realised who he was.

'Why it's . . . it's . . . Ralphie! I don't believe it.' Before she could say any more he had clasped her in his arms and given her a hearty kiss on both cheeks.

'What are you doing here, Moo? You left the village years ago.'

Muriel tried to restore her equilibrium but didn't succeed; she was quite breathless. Swallowing hard she replied, 'I did, but when I retired I came back here and bought a little house. What are you doing here?'

'Come to see the old place to find somewhere to live. I've retired, you see – fancied coming back to the old roots. Well, would you believe it! You haven't changed a bit. This is wonderful! Won't you introduce me to your friends?'

In a state of total confusion and almost unable to differentiate between everyone because of a sudden mist which had come down over her eyes, Muriel introduced him.

'This is Sir Ralph Templeton. Ralphie, this is Harriet Charter-Plackett who owns the village store with her husband James who's over there talking to the rector. This is Liz and Neville Neal from Glebe House. This is Lady Bissett, who's husband Sir Ronald you might know, with him being a trades union leader. He's been on TV a lot . . .'

'Living abroad, I haven't had that pleasure.' He shook hands with them all. 'Delighted to meet you, how do you do. What a pleasure to meet Moo's friends! There must be a lot of newcomers to the village, I imagine, and very few of the old families left.'

Muriel found her voice again. 'Well, Jimmy Glover's still here, and Valda and Thelma Senior, the twins. You remember them, don't you?'

'Not the twins!'

'I can't think of anyone else at the moment.'

'Come on, Moo, I'll take you out to lunch. We've lots to talk about – more than forty years to catch up on. You will excuse us, won't you?' he said to those around him. 'I'm sure we'll see each other again before long.'

'I don't think so,' Muriel panicked. 'No, I really can't.'

'Have you other plans?'

'No. Well, yes . . . I have. I like to garden on Sunday afternoons in the summer and—'

Ralphie interrupted, 'The gardening can wait, can't it, surely?'

'Well, I suppose it can, but no, I can't come with you for lunch. It wouldn't do.'

'Wouldn't do? I'm not abducting you, Muriel, simply asking you out for a meal. I'll bring you straight back if you like.'

Harriet gave her a nudge. 'Go on, Muriel. You can't say no, you've so much to talk about.'

'Well, perhaps I might then.'

Before she knew it Muriel was whisked off towards Sir Ralph's Mercedes which he'd parked in Church Road.

'Moo, I'm so sorry – I didn't stop to think. Have you a husband we ought to be taking with us?'

Muriel, who was already blushing at the prospect of the entire village seeing her being carried off by this dynamic personage, went even redder.

'No, but I do have a dog and I can't go anywhere until he's been for a little walk.'

'Where do you live?'

'Here by the church in Glebe Cottages.'

'Go and get him, then. I've got a cover I can put on the back seat and we'll take him out for a run. I know a nice place in Culworth where we could have lunch afterwards.'

The congregation mysteriously found reasons for lingering around the lych gate. They weren't going to miss the chance of watching Muriel Hipkin being driven off in such style. Pericles climbed into the car as though he'd been going for rides in a Mercedes all his life, and when Muriel waved goodbye to the crowd at the gate, she felt quite royal.

Lady Bissett was taken aback by the sudden change in Muriel's social status.

'Who the dickens is Ralphie?' she said too loudly, forgetting she was titled.

Harriet laughed. 'I really don't know, but it doesn't matter.'

Caroline supplied the answer. 'He's just introduced himself to Peter. He's one of the Templetons who used to own the Big House. Apparently, Sir Ralph has retired from the Diplomatic Service and is coming back to live in the village as soon as he can find a house he likes. He's rather nice, isn't he?'

Harriet agreed. 'Nice? He's gorgeous. I would never have dreamt of calling her Moo.' Lady Bissett wasn't sure she approved of someone she looked down on suddenly having such aristocratic connections. It rather put Ron's life peerage in the shade.

The news about the return of Ralph Templeton spread through the area in a flash, and there was much speculation about the difference it might make, having a Lord of the Manor in the village again. Would he buy back the Big House? And wouldn't it be a bit of a comedown, living in an ordinary house after having been abroad, and after growing up on a country estate?

Tucked up safely in bed that night, Muriel gave herself time to think about Ralph Tristan Bernard Templeton. Ralphie was the only one who called her Moo. Her mother used to get furious when he called her that. 'Your name's Muriel and a very pretty name it is, too. Tell him, go on – you tell him not to call you Moo!' she used to nag. But Muriel never did. It was their own special link. They did have something between them, even though they were only children. They were just in their teens when his mother sold up and he went away for ever. She remembered how they'd held hands, on the last bonfire night that there'd been at the Big House. With his father gone, Ralphie had had to light the bonfire himself; the older people, Muriel recalled, had had difficulty in not shedding a tear when they thought about his father, dead in some Burmese jungle and his body not brought home for burial with his ancestors. The two of them had kissed when he left – just a little youthful peck on the lips, but she had carried the memory of it for years. She had been leaving, too, at the time and in the turmoil it had never occurred to her to ask for his address. It all seemed so final, that moving away from their roots. Fancy – she hadn't thought about him for years – and then out of the blue he turns up!

They'd had a lovely lunch, in that posh restaurant overlooking the Cul.

He asked the restaurant manager for some bread and they'd gone out to feed the swans when they'd finished their meal, just like they used to when they were children, feeding the swans on the lake at the Big House with bread Ralphie had pinched out of the kitchen.

She wondered if the colleagues who'd seen him as a pillar of the Foreign Office all these years knew what a naughty boy he'd been when she knew him. There was that time when he started the farm tractor and drove right up to the front door of the House, with her stood up on it clinging to his shoulders. Or that time in the war when he switched on all the lights and opened all the blackout curtains as a gesture of defiance to Hitler. The butler had been furious. Until he was eight, Ralphie had gone to the village school. She remembered he'd been very quick to learn but such a trial to poor Miss Evans. He was far too inventive and all the children had followed his lead.

'I shall have to get up and have another cup of Ovaltine,' Muriel murmured. 'I'm not going to get to sleep, I'm in a whirl.'

As she got warm in bed again and began relaxing, Muriel thought about the thick scratchy tweed jacket he wore and how it had rubbed on her arms when he'd kissed her as he left. There was that slight perfumed smell about him, as if he kept himself particularly clean, and she liked that in a man. Scrupulous attention to cleanliness was a commendable trait.

Next morning, she popped into the store. It was her cousin's birthday and she needed a card.

Jimbo was serving. He raised his straw boater to her and said, 'Ah, good morning . . . er . . . Moo. You've got back home, then?'

'Good morning, Jimbo, of course I have.'

'What a send-off! I don't think there could have been many more people to witness your departure. Did you have a good time?'

'I did, thank you.'

'Shall we be seeing more of him?'

'He's looking for a house to buy, but of course there aren't any in the village at the moment so I don't know what he's going to do.'

Harriet came in. 'Hello . . . Moo. What a sensation! The whole village is agog to hear how you got on.'

'We had a lovely lunch at the George in Culworth and then we drove around a bit for Ralphie to see how things have changed – or not, as the case may be. Then we had afternoon tea at that new café by Havers Lake and then he brought me home.'

'I'm so glad you had a good time. He seems very nice.'

'He is, just like he was as a boy except he's calmed down a lot.'

Jimbo, stacking shelves from the top of a stepladder, called down, 'He could always rent until a house comes up for sale. Those people from London who have the cottage behind the pub are off to South Africa for six months soon. They might be willing to rent to such a nice tenant.'

'That would be a good idea, Muriel, wouldn't it? Which one is it, Jimbo?'

'Number three.'

Harriet suggested ringing up Ralph to tell him about the cottage.

'I mustn't presume to ring him up,' Muriel demurred. 'I don't really know him very well. No, I won't ring.'

'Well, if you do decide to ring, come here and use our phone. Don't use the public one – it's always so smelly.'

'I'll put some money by the phone if I do use it.' Muriel left in haste to avoid being persuaded.

'Now who's playing at Charity Hall?' Jimbo said from the ladder.

'This is a good cause. In fact, a very good cause. I've half a mind to have another dinner party. What excuse could I think up?'

'Too late, Caroline's already arranging one. She has the date to fix, that's all. She's planning the menu with me 'cos she's no time to cook herself at the moment.'

'Who's she inviting?'

'Yours truly, "Moo" and "Ralphie", Liz and Neville, and you if you behave yourself.'

'What does that mean exactly?'

'Come here and I'll show you.'

He leant down from the ladder, clutched hold of Harriet's hair, turned her face up towards his and began a lingering kiss which would have lasted much longer if Muriel hadn't come in and interrupted.

'Oh, I beg your pardon, I'm so sorry. I left the card on the counter. I'll be off now.' She hastened out covered in embarrassment.

'Tell you what, a good kiss like that is just what Muriel needs. It wouldn't half widen her horizons.'

'Jimbo, not everyone is sex-mad like you.'

'*N . o . o . o . o . o . ?*'

'Wouldn't it be fun if the two of them got married?'

'Getting like a typical villager you are, a finger in every pie.'

'I shall pull the stepladder away in a minute.'

'Don't you dare! How is the menu for that Twenty-first coming along?'

'Not too good. The mother likes everything I've listed but the son wants something less traditional. I'm waiting to see who wins. There's another two weeks yet.'

The door burst open and in dashed Linda. 'Sorry I'm a bit late, roadworks for miles. Have you been busy?'

'No. The birthday-card order came in first thing and there's a big envelope of instructions from the post office. It could take all morning, working out what they mean. Something about changes in procedure to make things simpler but it looks a lot more complicated to me.'

'Thank you, Jimbo. Just what I need on a Monday morning.'

Linda's first customer was Sharon McDonald.

'Ten first-class stamps, please, and be quick. I'm in a hurry.'

'Have you got the right money? I haven't unlocked the till yet.'

'No. That's all I've got.' She handed Linda a five-pound note.

'Rightio then, half a mo.' Linda got the keys from Jimbo's pocket, unlocked the till and tore off the stamps.

'There yer go, Sharon. Ten first-class stamps and two pounds sixty change.'

'And then some.'

'I don't understand. You gave me a five-pound note, the stamps cost two pounds forty, and I've given you two pounds sixty change.'

'I gave you a ten-pound note – you know I did. Come on, Linda, pocketing the takings, are you? Nice little earner if it comes off. Jimbo, this Linda of yours is lining her pockets.'

Jimbo strode across the store, his moustache positively bristling. 'That's not a very nice accusation, Sharon. In any case I know exactly how much we leave in the till ready for the day so I can count the notes and tell you what you gave.'

Linda tried to signal a message to Jimbo which, in his annoyance, he failed to interpret.

He sprang open the till and realised that it had not been cleared on the Saturday night, so he couldn't prove anything. He made a pretence of counting up and said, 'Well, by the looks of it the customer's always right. Here you are Sharon, another five pounds.'

'You've been caught with your fingers in the till, haven't you, Linda?'

'It was a genuine mistake. I'm very sorry.'

'So you should be. Don't try it on with me again. It might work with the old bats collecting their pensions, but it won't wash with me.' Sharon bounced out of the shop, her high heels click-clacking on the red tiles.

Linda was very upset.

'Mr Charter-Plackett, I know, I positively *know* she gave me a five-pound note.'

'Don't worry, Linda. I know she did, too, but I couldn't prove it. It was my fault – I forgot to clear the till on Saturday when you were away. It won't happen again, I can assure you. Don't let her upset you, she isn't worth it.'

'She's so rude. One day she'll get her comeuppance.'

16

The police sergeant had never really given up on the murder of Toria Clark. As he said to his wife, his gut reaction was that it was someone local, so he wasn't surprised when he saw what Jimmy Glover brought into the station one day. The sergeant had been watching the news on the television and, through the open door, been keeping half an eye open on the station desk. That was one of the advantages of having the police station and his own home all in the same building.

'Now then, Jimmy, what's this?'

'A rounders bat, Sergeant. Found it hid behind the Methodist Chapel in that long grass that never gets cut. I've handled it careful, like, on account of there being blood on it, like they does on the telly.'

'And what were you doing messing about behind the chapel? Not you been stealing the Scout money, is it?'

'I don't steal from the church. That's lower than low, that is. I was wandering along enjoying the sunshine and decided to sit down on that low wall that's all that's left of the old boiler-house. There it was, tucked down in the corner. Thought your men had searched every inch?'

'We did. I'll enter this incident in my book and pass it on to forensic. Thank you for being so alert and spotting it, Jimmy.'

'I liked that Toria Clark. She allus had a kind word for me, which is more than some people I could mention. If this is what killed her, perhaps it'll help you find who did it.'

'What's that hidden in your coat, Jimmy?'

'Never you mind. I'm off.'

'Hope you haven't been poaching, old son?'

'I have not.' Jimmy was indignant but could not meet his eye. The sergeant laughed. He hadn't been the village bobby for twenty years without knowing about Jimmy Glover's nocturnal activities.

The rounders bat proved to be the murder weapon all right, but there were no fingerprints on it. Mr Palmer had checked the rounders bats on the night of the murder but had forgotten that Toria had brought her own to school until the office had supplied a spare. That had meant there were two in the stock book but three on the premises.

This find supplied the regulars of The Royal Oak with further fuel for their small talk.

'Here, Betty, you heard Jimmy's found the murder weapon?'

'Yes I have, Willie. Just wish them lazy beggars 'ud find the murderer. We pays their wages, it's time they got off their backsides and earned 'em instead of catching me for speeding last week.'

'Now, Betty, they 'as tried, can't say they haven't. They questioned every living person for miles around. It was made more difficult with it being Stocks Day – there was that many strangers hereabouts. If it'd been an ordinary day, there would have been only a tenth that number about. Seems funny to me that whoever it was knew where to find the rounders bat. Makes me think it's someone local.'

'Local? For heaven's sake, Willie, don't put the wind up us all.'

'Stands to reason. If you never went to the village school, how would you know where to lay your hands on a rounders bat? Especially if you were worked up.'

'Just think, there's someone here in this village who might be coming into this bar night after night and they've got that on their conscience. They might strike again.'

'Well, Betty, you'd better not make too many enemies. Yer never know, it might be you next.'

Jimmy Glover laughed at the prospect. 'Fat chance they'd have of killing Betty. It'd take more than a rounders bat to see her off.'

'Here you, Jimmy, just mind yer manners or I'll turf you out.'

The bar burst into corporate laughter. 'Watch out, Jimmy. She'll be clasping you to her bosom next and out you'll go.'

'Cor, it'd be worth it, though, eh?' someone well out of Betty's reach shouted.

The door opened and everyone's attention was taken by the man who entered.

Jimmy shouted, 'Well, if it isn't Ralphie! I'd heard you were about. How do you do, Ralphie, remember me?'

Ralph held out his hand in greeting. 'Why, it's Jimmy Glover! How are you, Jimmy? I'd know you anywhere.'

'I'm find, how are you?'

'In the pink. What are you drinking?'

'Best bitter. Thank you.'

'Best bitter and a double whisky, please, landlord.'

Mac attended to his order and welcomed Ralph to the bar. 'I hear you're thinking of coming to live in the village, sir?'

'I am indeed. I'm hoping Jimmy here will be able to put me up for a while.'

Jimmy's head jerked up. 'Eh, what was that?'

'Only joking, Jimmy. Come and sit over here and we'll talk about old times.' They sat at the corner table Ralph had chosen and enjoyed an hour's chat. The rest of the bar marvelled at the sight of smelly Jimmy being made a fuss of by such a personage as the son of a past Lord of the Manor.

Finally, Ralph rose to go. 'I'm off to see if Muriel will come in for a drink, Jimmy. I'd ask you to join us if you were a bit, shall we say – tidier? I'll be back shortly.'

Muriel answered the knock at the door wearing an old jumper and skirt she'd put on to do her gardening earlier in the day.

'Oh dear, I wasn't expecting visitors.'

'I've come to ask you to join me in a drink at The Royal Oak. How about it, Moo?'

'I've never been in the bar before. I don't really think I could, anyway I'm not dressed properly. I've got my old gardening skirt on.'

'Well, pop upstairs and get changed. I'll wait here.'

'Shall I? Perhaps another night.'

'Don't turn down the chance of an hour on the tiles. Please come.'

'Very well then. I'll be as quick as I can.'

Ralph waited, sitting in the most comfortable armchair in the room, while Muriel dithered about upstairs deciding what to wear. Should she put a touch of that lipstick on that Caroline gave her for Jimbo's dinner party, or would Ralph prefer her without? Which shoes should she wear – her 1960s court shoes or her Clark's walking shoes? Oh dear, oh dear. All these decisions when what she had originally planned was to simply collapse in front of the television and watch that nice play.

Ralph stood as she came down the little spiral staircase.

'Come along then, we'll give the bar a big surprise.'

He chatted to her as they strolled through the village, knowing full well she was feeling apprehensive. Sure enough, the company fell silent as they walked in through the door. Miss Hipkin in the pub, whatever next? Jimmy had disappeared.

Muriel allowed Ralph to choose where to sit, and what she should drink.

''Evening, Muriel.' ''Evening, Miss Hipkin.' She nodded to them all, hoping she wasn't as red in the face as she felt. Why did she never have the courage to face new situations?

Ralph put her Snowball down on the little mat and sat beside her. 'You have nothing to fear, you know. You're with me and I have been in bars all over the world so I know what's what.'

'Have you really been all over the world, Ralphie?'

'Not far off. You get sent to all the worst places when you first start in the Foreign Office and then once you've proved yourself and you have a few strokes of luck, like being in the right place at the right time, you find yourself in the better places. Rome was my favourite, I think.'

'Have you been to Rome? Oh, I would love to go there! I always feel it's larger than life.'

'That's a good way of describing it. "Larger than life" – yes, I like that.'

Sharon came into the bar, having been press-ganged by her mother into clearing the tables. She went round languidly picking up empty glasses and limply wiping up any spills.

'Our Sharon, look lively! I need those glasses pronto.'

She squeezed between the tables and stopped by theirs. 'Finished, 'ave yer?'

Ralph looked up at her. 'Neither Miss Hipkin nor I have finished, as you can well see.'

'All right, all right, keep your shirt on, only trying to help. Surprise seeing you in the bar, Muriel. First time in yer life, I reckon.'

Ralph showed his anger by snapping, 'Miss Hipkin to you, if you don't mind, young lady.'

'Miss Hipkin then, *Sir* Ralph. She'll need more than a Snowball to get her going, yer know. A stiff whisky would do better.'

'That's quite enough of that.' Ralph stood up to assert his authority. 'Kindly leave us alone.'

'OK, OK. Just giving you some advice, Ralphie.' She turned away with a flick of her pert bottom.

Muriel wished the floor would open up and swallow her.

Ralph ordered, 'Drink up, we're leaving.'

He took her arm and as they reached the door he turned to Mac who was behind the bar and said, loudly enough for everyone to hear: 'Landlord, that girl who collects the glasses needs her manners attending to. See to it or I shall not patronise your bar again. Good night to you.'

'Ralphie, I don't know how you dared to speak like that!'

'She was extremely rude.'

'She's their daughter.'

'I don't care whose daughter she is, Moo, she was rude to you and to me. It simply won't do, I'm not accustomed to it. I'll see you to your cottage and then I'll be on my way.'

When they reached her door Muriel daringly suggested he came in for a coffee before he went. She would quite have preferred him to say no but he said yes so she'd no alternative but to open the door and invite him in.

Pericles growled and barked but Ralph patted him and made a fuss and Pericles allowed him in. He wasn't used to male company and felt Muriel needed defending.

They sat drinking coffee and talking until nearly midnight. Ralph had such an easy way with him, and to her surprise Muriel found herself to be quite an interesting person.

As he left Ralph said, 'I'm renting Derek and Bunny's cottage for six months, possibly a year, while they're in South Africa. They leave on Tuesday and I'm moving in on Thursday. Perhaps you would be so kind as to have a meal with me one evening when I get settled?'

'I should like that, thank you.'

'Good. Moo, be very careful of that girl Sharon. There's something not quite right about her.'

'Sharon McDonald? She's very rude and outspoken, but she's all right really.'

'You're too kind. Just mark my words.' Ralph took both her hands and very tentatively kissed her on the lips.

'Good night, my dear. You are one of the few real ladies left in this world, do you know that?'

Muriel closed the door and stood with her back leaning on it. She felt the same thrill that a girl in her teens would have felt at her first kiss. She'd been kissed in Postman's Knock at Sunday School parties in her early teens but never by a grown man. Now she felt she knew something at least of what that kiss she'd witnessed between Harriet and Jimbo must have felt like. Well, just a little maybe, because Ralph's hadn't lasted very long.

She put an extra dash of oil in before she stepped into her bath – frankincense she chose, to help her sleep. The light from the night sky lit the bathroom and she imagined what it would be like visiting Rome with Ralph. Katharine Hepburn had had that fabulous holiday in – Venice, was it? – when she met that two-timing Italian in that film, *Summer Madness.* Katharine Hepburn had had a wonderful awakening. Muriel could see herself standing by the Trevi Fountain with a chiffon scarf around her throat, the ends blowing about in the summer breeze, and Ralph handing her coins to throw in and her wishing, like you should, that this moment would never end . . . but end it would, and they'd have to go back to the hotel. Abruptly Muriel sat up and began vigorously scrubbing herself with the loofah. Got to get to bed, work to do tomorrow.

On the Wednesday before the Thursday that Ralph moved into number three, Muriel was sitting at her 'seat of custom' as she jokingly called it in her mind. She'd not been very busy but then it was market day in Culworth. She was contemplating asking Jimbo to run off a few new menus, as some of the ones in use at the moment were beginning to look tatty and she did like to have nice clean menus for everybody, when the door opened and in walked Sharon. Did she never work? Muriel thought to herself.

The girl was wearing her usual high heels and skin-tight short skirt. She trotted over to a table. Her peroxided hair had taken on an orange tinge and she wore lipstick and blusher to match. Her Walkman was plugged into her ears.

'Hello, *Miss Hipkin.* A coffee and a slice of chocolate gâteau if you please.'

Muriel did hope Sharon wouldn't be rude while she was in the tearoom; if she was, she'd send the YTS girl for Jimbo. But Sharon sat quietly, reading her magazine and listening to her music. Muriel busied herself checking her bills and sorting out which menus she would throw away. She contemplated going to find Jimbo to get him to do them, but decided she wouldn't leave Sharon on her own – for you never knew. There was a lovely smell of burning wood in the air, she noticed.

Muriel had just shown three customers to a table and settled them with a menu when Sharon shouted: 'Oh, look, Miss Hipkin! There's smoke.'

Muriel looked out of the window cautiously; she anticipated that Sharon was playing a joke on her. But sure enough there was smoke billowing into the sky. They must be having a bonfire, though it seemed the wrong time of year.

Sharon leapt to her feet. 'I'm off to see where it is. Get ready to phone the fire brigade.'

She dropped her Walkman on the table and rushed out towards The Royal Oak. Muriel could see her standing in Stocks Row looking up behind the pub.

She came racing back. 'Ring the fire brigade! It's one of the cottages belonging to them London people. It's got a right hold. Hurry up!'

'Oh dear, what do I say?' Muriel dropped the phone in her agitation.

'Here, give it to me.' Sharon dialled 999 and asked for Fire. She gave the address and explained what had happened. 'Cool and calm in a crisis' were the words which sprang to Muriel's mind. How glad she was, that

Sharon had been there. She would have been incoherent if she'd had to phone.

Sharon rushed out again and went round warning everyone. It seemed an age until the fire brigade actually arrived. Someone had rigged a hose up and was trying to wet the thatch to stop the roof burning. Mac and Betty came out to help, as the cottage was very close to the back of the pub and they didn't want their thatch on fire as well. Jimbo hastened across to give a hand. Muriel stayed in charge in the tearoom, thankful for an excuse to keep out of the way. The water from the fire-brigade hydrant soon put the fire out. It was only then that Muriel realised it was the cottage Ralphie had hoped to move into the next day. Then the police came to investigate and the tearoom was kept busy with teas and toasted teacakes and soup for the Press, the firemen and the police. All on the house, of course, for in his inimitable way, Jimbo knew free publicity when he saw it.

Sharon, of course, was the heroine of the hour. Muriel spoke highly of her, saying how calm and level-headed she had been and how well she had explained to the fire brigade about the location of the cottage.

The fire meant that for a while Ralph had nowhere to stay. Caroline suggested that he didn't go back to the hotel but stayed with her until the cottage was sorted out. He jumped at the chance.

'How very kind of you to invite me. I shall be delighted. I'll try to be a model guest, and keep well out of your way.'

'We shall enjoy your company, won't we, Peter?'

'We shall indeed. Bring your things round tomorrow morning as you've planned, but move in here instead of the cottage. We've plenty of room if you need to store anything, haven't we, Caroline?'

'Acres. Anyway, I intended inviting you to dinner on Saturday night, as we're having a few friends in, so you'll be on the spot so to speak.'

'It's extremely kind of you. I do appreciate it.'

'I hope you like cats, because I've got three Siamese.'

'That's fine, I like animals. Never had a chance to have any of my own with moving around such a lot, but when I get settled I shall have at least three cats and a dog.'

'A poodle perhaps?' Caroline's smile was wicked and Ralph had to acknowledge it.

'You never know.' He smiled gently, turned on his heel and thereby terminated the conversation.

Peter was outraged. 'Caroline, you take the biscuit for absolute cheek!'

'It was only a bit of fun. I've decided I'm inviting Suzy to our dinner party.'

'Suzy?' There was a pause.

'I know you might find it difficult but it won't be half as difficult as I shall find it. If I leave her out, tongues might wag. If I invite her I shall have a devil of an evening, but I can't do otherwise. I'll invite Michael Palmer as well, then she'll have a man to partner her. You don't think they might . . .'

'Caroline, between you, you and Harriet Charter-Plackett ought to be running a marriage bureau.'

'It's only kindly interest. Do the police know how the fire started?'

'They assume it was faulty wiring but they haven't had time to be sure. I expect these old houses have had bits of wiring done here and there over the years and most of them could do with a complete fresh start.'

It wasn't until she was in bed that night that Muriel remembered Sharon hadn't paid for her coffee and chocolate gâteau. Well, in the circumstances, Muriel couldn't really remind her about it. She'd have to put it down to experience.

17

'Good evening, Michael. Come in, please. Have you met Sir Ralph Templeton?' Peter was greeting his guests whilst Caroline was performing miracles in the kitchen with the food Jimbo had organised for her.

'I haven't had the pleasure. Good evening.'

Michael Palmer shook hands with Ralph, then followed the two men into the sitting room. Jimbo and Harriet were already there with drinks in their hands. 'Hello, Michael. How are you? Glad the school holidays have started?'

'Not really, Jimbo, no. I love school. There isn't another job in all the world I would rather do. I know people think that being a schoolmaster is some sort of soft option and a skive, but it is the most interesting and rewarding work anyone could hope to do.'

'I don't know how you cope with our little lot.'

'Your little lot as you call them are very very bright, well behaved and a great challenge. They keep me on my toes.'

'That's nice to know.' Jimbo turned and laughed at Harriet who raised her glass to Michael and dropped him a mock curtsy. 'Harriet will live on that recommendation for about a fortnight.'

'Jimbo, that will do.'

Caroline appeared, trying not to look too flustered. She loved dinner parties but worried herself to death about how they were going to work out.

The doorbell went and Caroline answered it. On the doorstep stood Suzy. She was wearing a pale lavender dress with a scarf of a deeper shade draped across her shoulders. Her long blonde hair was brushed back and held up in a comb on the top of her head.

She smiled nervously at Caroline. 'Thank you for asking me.' Suzy spoke in a soft voice so no one else would hear.

'Thank you for coming, you look lovely.'

Caroline slipped her arm through Suzy's and drew her into the sitting room. 'Here we are, everybody, Suzy's arrived. You know everyone, of course, except Sir Ralph. Ralph, this is Suzy Meadows our next-door-but-one neighbour.'

'How do you do.'

Peter stepped forward and asked as naturally as he could what she would like to drink.

'Orange juice, thank you. No alcohol.'

As he handed the glass to her he caught her eye and smiled cautiously. Suzy looked up at him and gave that Madonna smile which had so captivated him. 'Thank you, Peter.'

In order to make conversation with someone he had never met before, Ralph innocently asked whether her husband would be coming along later, or was he abroad or something?

There was a brief silence and then Suzy answered steadily: 'No, my husband has died. To add to my troubles he left me expecting this baby – or should I say babies.'

'I'm so sorry. I had no idea.'

'Please don't be upset – I'm not. He's dead and gone and I've the future to think about. He wouldn't have wanted anyone to feel sorry he'd died, would he, Peter?'

'I didn't know him, Suzy.'

'No, of course not. He never took part in village life. The only good he did with his life was to give me thr – *five* children. Being a nuclear scientist isn't exactly commendable, is it? I understand you're wanting to settle in the village, Sir Ralph?'

'Yes. I'm staying with Caroline and Peter at the moment because I was to have moved into number three behind the pub, but it caught fire, as you know.'

'Oh yes, of course. It doesn't look too serious.'

'No, fortunately it isn't. Sharon McDonald spotted it before it got too much of a hold.'

At that moment Muriel arrived. She was late, breathless, and very tense. She was wearing a slim-fitting black dress, long-sleeved with pearls filling in the neckline.

'Why, good evening, Muriel. How absolutely charming you look!' Peter drew her into the circle and offered her a drink.

'A sherry, please. Sweet, if I may.'

Ralph took it across to her. As he put the glass into her hand he smiled and said, 'You look lovely.'

Harriet and Caroline winked at each other.

When they sat down for their meal Caroline put Michael between herself and Suzy. Though she was feeling desperate about Suzy, she made the greatest possible effort to be a hospitable hostess.

Jimbo came up with an idea for Ralph's consideration.

'I've just had a thought. Toria Clark's house must be coming up for sale soon, Ralph. It would be a good buy if you like it.'

'Where is that?'

'Next door to here.'

'Why ever didn't we think of that? Of course – what a good idea!' Caroline exclaimed.

'Where is Toria Clark going to live?'

Jimbo cleared his throat. 'She isn't. She was found dead a few weeks ago, the night of Stocks Day to be exact. Her house must be going to be sold, I would have thought.'

Harriet, finishing the last of her soup, put down her spoon and gave Ralph a résumé of the accommodation.

'It sounds ideal,' he responded. 'A little on the large side, but then I don't like poky little rooms. Would I be able to have an open fire?'

'Well, Toria had a wood-burning stove so I suppose yes, you could have an open fire. Have you ever been inside it, Muriel?'

'No, never.'

'It's very nice.'

'Stop playing estate agent, Harriet, and let Ralph make up his own mind.'

'Jimbo, you're bossing me again.'

Jimbo apologised and they all laughed.

Muriel was having the greatest difficulty in enjoying herself. Being actually partnered with Ralph made her very self-conscious. This dress she'd bought was so slim-fitting that in fact it was almost tight, and it showed every inch of her figure. She hardly dare bend over to eat because she felt sure the dress would drop forward and reveal her cleavage. She caught Ralph smiling at her and she went bright red. To cover her embarrassment she took a deep drink of her wine and within a few minutes was feeling quite light-headed. Ralph asked her a question and her words slurred as she answered.

She was one of the first to leave, excusing herself on the grounds that Pericles would be needing to go out. Ralph offered to escort her to her door.

'Oh no, thank you, don't come out. I can manage quite well. Please, no thank you.'

'Of course I shall. It's very dark with there being no street lighting. I couldn't possibly let you go by yourself at this time of night.'

He stood up and, taking her elbow, guided her towards Caroline. Muriel kissed her hostess and thanked her confusedly for a lovely evening.

'Not at all, Muriel. I'm glad you could come. See you in a minute, Ralph.'

After the pair had gone, the rest all looked at one another and speculated about them.

Ralph held tightly to Muriel's arm as they picked their way along the path.

'Moo, you've got some very nice friends.'

'They are, aren't they, Ralph? I'm very lucky.'

'Have you thought that they are lucky, too, having you as a friend?'

'They give me far more than I give them.' She put her key in the door, and out of politeness offered Ralph a drink before he went back. The lateness of the hour had persuaded her he would refuse but he accepted. He followed her into the kitchen and helped her fill the kettle and get out the cups. Muriel felt invaded. Her very own space was being taken over. She'd created a safe world, a place for everything and everything in its place, and now here was this masculine person touching her very own belongings. It was an effrontery. Her natural graciousness held her back from being rude and asking him to go, but it was all very disturbing. She'd have to wash all the kitchen things tomorrow, to make them all hers again.

'Moo, sit here. Here's your cup.' They chatted for a while about Toria's house and whether Ralph would like it or not and then out of the blue he asked her a question.

'Have you enjoyed yourself tonight?'

'Yes, thank you.'

'I thought you seemed ill at ease.'

'No, I wasn't.'

'Is it me? Am I crowding you too much?'

'No, it's not that at all.'

'What is it then?'

'I haven't had a real friend since I was a girl. I've known people well but not had friends, and there is a difference, isn't there? Mother never encouraged me to make friends, always afraid they would take me off somewhere and I wouldn't be there to look after her, I suppose. Your coming back has mixed me up.'

'I hope it's a nice mix-up? I know at our age we can't expect to have rich passionate relationships like one does when young, but there's no reason why one can't be happy together, is there?'

'No, I enjoy your company.'

'Good, because you won't get rid of me easily.'

Ralph stood up and pulled Muriel to her feet. 'I'll say good night now and leave you to go to bed. You must be tired. I have to say that you were the smartest lady there tonight. Good night, Moo.' Ralph put his hands on her shoulders and very gently kissed her lips. She stood, arms by her sides, not responding.

'Moo, don't keep people away, let them draw near.'

He left, giving Pericles a pat as he went.

Muriel sat down when he left and cried.

Caroline was crying, too. Peter held her in his arms trying to soothe her distress away.

'My dearest girl, it all went absolutely smoothly. I was so proud of you. The table was lovely, the food was great, they all enjoyed themselves and you carried it all off so well.'

Caroline dried her eyes and tried to gain control of her voice. 'It's not that. Oh, Peter, I *do* wish I could have a baby. Why does someone have the chance to have five and I can't have any? I am so envious of Suzy. It's not fair. Not fair.'

'If it's any consolation to you I love you more than ever and I wish I could take away the pain, but I can't.' She burst into a fresh flood of tears.

'Caroline, Caroline, please, darling, try to stop. How about we try to adopt? That would be a solution, wouldn't it? We're still not too old and we couldn't have better credentials, could we? Now you're leaving work it is a possibility.'

Caroline dried her eyes, laid her head on Peter's shoulder and contemplated a wholly new idea which Peter's suggestion had triggered in her mind.

'What a brilliant idea. What a *very* brilliant idea. I'll think about it.' She turned her face to Peter, looked him straight in the eyes and asked: 'Do you not love her just a very tiny little bit because she is carrying your children?'

'Despicable though it is, no I don't. You're the one for me. Never forget that.'

'Thank you. Ralph's taking a long time to come back.'

'Stop matchmaking and go to sleep. Feeling better now?'

'Yes, thanks.'

'Good night, my love.'

'Good night, Peter. Sometimes you do hit upon some very good ideas.'

Peter slid his arm around her waist and hugged her. 'I am some use then, sometimes. What's the good idea I've come up with?'

'Never you mind. I'll tell you when I'm good and ready.'

18

Never one to let the grass grow under her feet, Caroline asked Suzy the next time she saw her if she could come round to her house for a chat when the children were in bed.

'You want to see me?'

'Yes, if that's possible.'

'Yes, it's possible but why?'

'Well, I can't speak about it now, it's just something I need to discuss with you.'

'About Peter?'

'In a kind of a way.'

'They're usually all in bed by eight at the latest so come round any time after then.'

'I'll come tonight if I may.'

'Very well.'

Caroline knocked on the door by two minutes past eight. Suzy gave her a glass of wine and they both sat in front of the fire. Suzy waited to hear what Caroline had to say.

'I was extremely upset when I found out about . . . about your pregnancy. When I saw you in the clinic quite naturally I assumed it was Patrick's baby. Peter didn't know about you being there because of course I don't discuss patients at home – not by name, anyway. He only found out when Michael told him you wouldn't be able to keep on with the playgroup. That was the day before I went up home to Northumberland.'

'I saw you leaving. I knew from your face you'd heard. It was only the once, and entirely my fault. I was so shatteringly lonely that day. I needed comforting and before we knew where . . . well, anyway, you know what I mean.'

Caroline took another drink of her wine and tried hard not to mind about what Suzy had left unsaid. She had more important things on her mind.

'I've given in my notice at the hospital.'

'Oh, I didn't know that. Whatever for? I thought you enjoyed it.'

'I do – or rather I did. I gave my notice in because Peter and I have never had much time together. I've always worked long hours, ever since we were married, so I decided that I would spend some time at home and then perhaps go back to hospital work when I got fed up with keeping house.'

'I see. Is that what you wanted to discuss with me?'

'No – well, kind of. How are you going to manage with the twins?'

'Do you mean financially?'

'Well, yes – and also, how will you look after them? I mean, two babies and three little girls is an awful lot for one person.'

'Are you fancying being mother's help, Caroline?' Suzy smiled when she spoke.

'No, I'm not. Look – I find it hard to know how to say this.'

'Well, say it and then I'll tell you if you've done it well.'

'Peter knows nothing of what I am about to propose – it's all my idea.'

'Right.'

'I wanted to say: if at any time you found you couldn't face coping with the twins, I would be more than willing to . . . well, I would be more than willing to have them.' Caroline gulped nervously.

'Have them for the afternoon, you mean?'

'No, I didn't mean for the afternoon. I meant for – for always. To keep. That is, if you could part with them, if that was possible at all.' Her voice trembled.

'Caroline, has Peter not told you what I said to him?'

'No. I didn't know you'd spoken to him about them.'

'The day you left, I told Peter that no one – and I mean *no one* – would ever know that these twins were not Patrick's. I told him that I intended to have them both adopted, and that I had already chosen the parents.'

'Oh, I see. Then there's no more to be said. I'm sorry if I've caused you pain. I'll be going.' Caroline rose blindly.

Suzy took hold of Caroline's hand and told her to sit down again.

'I know I sounded as if I was being very difficult, but I wanted to hear it from you, absolutely and completely from you without any help at all, that you, Caroline Harris, wanted to have Peter's children. I had to be sure, you see.'

'But it's no good! You've just said so. Oh please, let me go.' The pain and disappointment were tearing her apart.

'It is, that's the point,' Suzy insisted. 'You've told me, with no help from Peter and no prompting from me, that you want to adopt them. That was what I wanted to hear! You and Peter are the parents I've chosen. I told him so in a roundabout way, but he was so upset about you leaving that he didn't understand what I was saying.'

Caroline sat down again slowly, unable to take in what Suzy had just said. 'You mean you want Peter and me to have them? Is that what you really want? Truly want?'

'Yes. I've no love to spare for anyone at the moment, least of all for two new babies who'll need loving attention for years. I've got to get back to work, Caroline. With three children to feed and clothe, the money Patrick left is rapidly disappearing. I've gone quite dead inside. I don't want to know about obligations to anyone else at all. I just want to get on with working and looking after my three girls. As soon as the twins are born I'm leaving here, so there won't be any worry about me billing and cooing over the pram. They'll be yours completely.'

'As long as I live I shall be entirely in your debt.'

'I won't tell you where I'm going. I shan't want photographs – nothing at all, and I mean that.'

'Suzy, how are you going to tell the girls?'

'Daisy and Pansy can't help but notice things aren't quite what they were. I've explained to them that though I'm expecting two babies, we are not going to keep them because I have no money to feed and clothe them. So what better way is there but for us to give them to someone who has no babies at all? They've both cried about it and said could we keep one and let the lady with no babies have the other one, but I've said you can't separate twins as that would be cruel. Bless their dear hearts, they do appear to understand. Rosie doesn't even seem to have noticed that she can't sit on my knee easily any more, so I'm leaving that till she says something. They won't forget, but at least it will stop hurting after a while.'

Caroline stood up, put her arms round Suzy and kissed her.' Thank you, thank you so much, so very much.'

'When the twins are due I shall want you there. Right there helping.'

'There aren't any words to tell you how grateful I am.'

'What about Peter?'

'I'll tell him in my own good time.'

'We won't let anyone else know what we've planned, Caroline. They gossip so much in this village that all kinds of stories will do the rounds.'

'No, that's right, we'll keep it our secret. Good night. You may say you have no love left for anyone, but I think you must have.' She closed the door and tried hard to walk normally into the Rectory, but it was so difficult, so very difficult. She wanted to skip.

Peter was in his study with a couple who were asking to be married in the church. She took coffee into them, then went off to have a bath. She lay there planning which room she would choose for the nursery and how she would need to buy a twin pram, as well as nappies and cots and . . . then a cold drip from the tap fell on her toe and seemed to chill her through and through. What if the twins were premature and didn't survive? What if Suzy decided to keep them both? What if Peter didn't want them?'

She heard him coming up the stairs. He came into the bathroom and sat on the edge of the bath.

'Someone else taking the plunge. They seem as if they'll be very happy. Sometimes couples come and you want to say to them, "Look, it won't work," but it's very difficult when they're convinced they're doing the right thing. Where have you been?'

'Talking to Suzy.'

'What about?'

'About you not understanding what she was trying to tell you.'

'I don't know what you mean.'

Caroline sat up and began rubbing soap onto her face flannel. She didn't answer immediately. She held up a leg and soaped it right from her toes to the top of her thigh and did the same with the other one. Then she looked up at him and said: 'You know, the twins. Well, she doesn't want them.'

'I know – she told me.'

'She's going to have them adopted and she . . . I asked her if I could have them and she said that was what she had been waiting to hear, and that yes, I can – *we* can. Now I'm frightened they'll die or something, or she'll see them and change her mind. And I'm frightened in case you don't want them.'

'I don't.'

Caroline sat up, startled at the vehemence of Peter's reply. 'You don't? You can't mean that!'

'I do. I most definitely do.'

'Peter, it's what I most want in the world. Please don't do this to me. *Please.* I have never pleaded with you in all the time I've known you, but I'm pleading now.'

'I can't face day in day out the evidence of my unfaithfulness. Do you hear me? I can't do that! It would destroy me to watch you loving and caring for my children, ones that were mine and not your very own. I couldn't bear it.'

Caroline stood up quickly, making the water surge over the edge of the bath onto Peter's feet. She took the towel she'd propped on the edge of the washbasin and wrapped herself in it. When she'd climbed out she stood facing him and looked up at his face. He was in the deepest depth of despair.

'Caroline, you don't realise what you're asking of yourself.'

'So I can care for children who are not mine and not yours – strangers' children – but I'm not allowed to care for yours. Have you no idea how bad I feel about not being able to have your children? Have you any idea what being barren means? What if things were reversed and it was you who couldn't have children? Would you feel a complete person? Because I certainly don't! Suzy *wants* us to have them. She sees it as a very right thing to do. She's told the adoption people all about us and we are the parents she has chosen. Don't break her heart by making her have to give them to people she doesn't know.'

'Caroline, please don't bring Suzy into it. This is for you and me to decide. We have to get things straight between us. Get dried and we'll talk later when we've both calmed down.'

Peter turned and left the bathroom. He went down to his study and sat at his desk with his head in his hands. He'd suffered so much since that day with Suzy that he didn't think God could ask any more of him. To have them here in this house and watch Caroline loving them was too much. No matter how he longed for children of his own, he mustn't agree to adopt them just because of that need. He could only agree if he felt Caroline truly forgave him for his infidelity. If he knew that, then he could accept adopting them. But he'd no right to ask forgiveness of that magnitude from her.

She was in the kitchen making coffee for the two of them when he sought her out.

'I'm deeply sorry for shouting like I did just now. It was unforgivable.'

'I can understand, I was too precipitate. It must have been a quite dreadfully unexpected announcement.'

'I could adopt the children if I knew with my head and my heart that you have forgiven me my infidelity. That's the only way, but I haven't the right to ask such a thing. So that's the end of it.'

'If I tell you that I had forgiven you when I came back home from Northumberland, would you believe me – *really* believe me? You see, I wouldn't have come back if I hadn't forgiven you.'

'Caroline, I don't deserve you.'

'We must wipe the slate clean, Peter. You can't spend the rest of our life together being grateful to me – it would turn me into the most insufferable person. Please don't do it to me.'

'Very well. It would make things very right, wouldn't it, in all sorts of ways if we took the children?'

'Yes, of course it would – and thank you.'

'No, I need to thank you for the immense generosity of your spirit.'

19

Muriel stood stark naked in front of her bedroom mirror looking critically at herself. Her skin appeared to be too big for her: there was a sagging around her bottom, definite sagging down the back of her arms at the top, and her breasts, always small, appeared smaller than ever. How could she possibly imagine for one moment that Ralph, sophisticated, well-travelled Ralph, could have the slightest interest in her? She was sixty-four, heaven help us. Sixty-four! Was it too late for happiness? Ralph had really hit home when he'd told her to let people draw near. That, of course, was half her problem, fending people off all the time. He'd wanted to draw near and she didn't know how to let him. She promised herself that if he kissed her again, she would do as they did on the television – put her arms round him and hold on. She'd watched Jimbo kiss Harriet and Peter kiss Caroline and noticed they fitted each other like a glove; all she'd done was stand completely still. Dare she invite him to dinner, then perhaps he might kiss her again and she could try harder. She'd been to number three after he moved in, but those friends of his from Culworth were there as well so there'd been no opportunity.

She called round with a little note and popped it through the letter box of number three. '*Dear Ralphie,*' she had written. '*Would you care to come for a meal Thursday of next week? Perhaps seven for seven-thirty? Yours sincerely, Moo.*' It was brief because there wasn't anything else to say.

She got a note back accepting. '*Dear Moo, I shall be delighted to come for a meal. See you just after seven o'clock on Thursday. Many thanks, Ralph.*'

It was no good attempting to cook something she wasn't familiar with. She laboured over the menu, trying to plan something which wouldn't keep her tied to the kitchen and yet would be tasty – after all, he was accustomed to eating exotic meals all over the world. The menu she finally settled on was Baxter's Tomato and Orange soup, followed by chicken and broccoli in white wine sauce, with new potatoes, baby carrots from the freezer and peas, followed by her own speciality – home-made chocolate mousse. She debated about the mousse; maybe a lemony dessert would be better for the palate. Yes – lemon passion, that's what she'd make.

Muriel asked Jimbo about which wine to choose.

It cost her £4, but would be well worth the money, he told her. She bought most of the ingredients for the meal from Jimbo and he had the greatest difficulty in not enquiring whom she was entertaining. When she got into bed Harriet complained, 'Why ever didn't you ask her?'

'Because she was in a dither and she has a perfect right to invite whomsoever she pleases. It's nothing to do with us, we just sell her the goods.'

'I bet it's Ralph, I bet it is.'

'It very probably is, but don't say a word. For people their age, romance is a very delicate thing. People our age take it for granted.'

'I wonder if he's kissed her yet?'

'Harriet, you are the limit. Turn over and let me show you a bit of romance of your own.'

'Certainly not! I'm an old married woman and I've decided to live a celibate life in future. It's the modern thing to do, you know. Leaves time for one to contemplate the world and its meaning, instead of clogging up one's thinking processes with all that emotional see-sawing.'

'That's what you call it, is it, emotional see-sawing?'

'Jimbo, stop it, please. Oh, that's nice. *Mmmmmmm.* I do love you.'

'I am forgiven then about the restaurant?'

'You know you are and have been for some time, but don't pull a trick like that again. I might not be so forgiving next time. I wonder how Muriel's feeling tonight? It's a big step for her, to invite someone into her home, did you realise that?'

'Harriet, concentrate on me for a while, will you, please?'

Muriel lay awake unable to sleep. She too was contemplating the dinner. The time-table for the preparation of the food was pinned on her little noticeboard and she was planning what they could talk about afterwards. She should never have asked him. Why *had* she asked him? Yes, why indeed? Did she actually want to get involved with him? What did 'involved' mean? On those Australian soaps, they call it 'being an item'. Did being an item mean you were going to get married?

Muriel hastily hid her head under the bedclothes as though by doing so she could hide from the consequences of the question she had posed herself, but it was no good evading the subject. If Ralph Tristan Bernard

Templeton asked her to marry him, would she? Give up her solitude, her privacy – her own personal space? And in return for what? Companionship, more money, a better life-style? And dare she say it, SEX? Did one have sex at her age? Ralphie seemed to be a very virile kind of person, but maybe they could marry for companionship – yes, that would be it – companionship. He could take her abroad and drive her about in that beautiful Mercedes and she would have a wedding ring on her finger and that would be that. Better without SEX. If he asked her, that is what she would say: no SEX. Bit late to start with that now.

The only problem with that decision was that by the time they had finished their meal and Muriel had cleared away, leaving only Ralph's brandy and the coffee on the little table, she was actually wishing he would kiss her. She put it down to the wine.

'Moo, shall I light the fire for you? I think you look cold.'

'If you like, yes. Now the evenings are drawing in, a fire is welcome. It's all laid – we only have to find the matches.'

Ralph pulled the sofa round closer to the fire when he'd got it going and the two of them sat on it watching the flames flicking up the chimney.

'I missed an open fire when I was abroad. If I get Toria Clark's house I shall keep her wood-burning stove. They warm the whole house and there's a lovely crackling sound and a nice woody smell.'

'You're looking forward to your own home, aren't you, Ralphie?'

'Yes. It will be the first real home I've ever had.'

'That will be nice for you. Would you like some more coffee?'

'Yes, please.'

They sat in silence watching the fire. Ralph put down his cup, swirled the last drops of his brandy round the sherry glass, which was all Muriel could find to put it in, and then took hold of her hand.

'I should very much like to kiss you, Moo.'

'Oh, I see.'

He put his arms around her shoulders and drew her closer. She shut her eyes and waited. Ralph burst out laughing. Muriel's eyes sprang open. 'Moo, you're not in a torture chamber! Kissing is supposed to be fun.'

'Fun?'

'Yes, fun. Come here.'

Muriel did most of her deep thinking in bed. Reflecting on the evening's events, she arrived at the conclusion that yes, Ralphie was right – it *was* fun. They'd progressed from little pecks to touching each other's tongues as they kissed. She recollected the stirrings of feelings she hadn't known existed, feelings which went all over her body and were quite incomprehensible. Ralphie certainly seemed to know what he was doing. But what had given her the most food for thought was his suggestion that they went to Rome together.

'I want to say this right now before we go any further, Moo. It will be all above board. Separate rooms, no obligations of any kind. We shall go as two friends each in need of companionship.'

'Oh yes, that's right, I understand. Companionship. That's how I would want it.'

'I don't wish to give offence but I have plenty of money. What with my bachelor existence and my family money, I've managed to save all my life and I know that things might be difficult for you, so if I may I should like to pay for the flights and the hotel myself. Absolutely no strings attached. There's no pleasure in travelling alone and having no one to share, and it would give me great delight to show you Rome.'

'I'll think over what you suggested and let you know tomorrow.'

As he left, Ralph kissed her hand and said, 'Don't be afraid of what life offers you, Moo. It's too short for letting chances pass you by. Do say you'll come.'

She'd have to ask Jimbo for time off and tell Mr Palmer she couldn't play the piano for him that week. Oh dear, and what about Pericles? He'd have to go into kennels, that's what. Second fiddle he'd have to play for a week. She'd give him his favourite chicken meal when she got him back. No, she'd better not go, it wasn't fair to Pericles. He'd never been in kennels before. She'd tell Ralphie. It wouldn't do at all, going to Rome with a man. It simply wasn't done. But she would have loved to see the Coliseum, and the Trevi Fountain and the Sistine Chapel, and to have walked in St Peter's Square. Well, it wasn't to be. Pericles was her staunch friend and she couldn't desert him.

Ralph was very disappointed. 'I don't wish to be intrusive, Moo, but are you saying no because of me?'

'Oh, not at all. You said as two friends and for companionship and that's how I would want it. But it's Pericles, you see. He's never been in kennels before and he's too old to start now. It would be cruel. I'm so sorry, I would have loved to have gone. I've got to go. It's time I was at the tearoom. Thank you for asking me, though.' She trailed off towards Harriet's Tearoom with a heavy heart. It was no good, you couldn't cast off old friends just because you'd found new ones. One must be loyal.

Jimbo came bustling in about eleven. 'Come to hearten the troops. How's things this morning, Muriel?'

'Very good, thank you, we're having a very busy day.'

'You sound as if you don't enjoy us having a busy day.'

'Oh, I do, I do.'

'Well then, what's the matter?'

'If I told you something in absolute confidence could I rely on you not to tell a soul?'

'Of course. Cross my heart and hope to die.'

'Ralphie – you know, Sir Ralph – has asked me to go with him to Rome. We'd be going as friends and for company, you understand, and I've said no and I wish I didn't have to say no.'

'Well, why do you have to say no?'

'It's Pericles. I'd have to put him in kennels, and that would be cruel.'

'Ah, right. Now, if I could solve that for you, would you go then?'

Muriel stopped to think for a moment. 'I don't know if I should.'

'Why not? Why not have some fun! He's a lovely chap.'

'Yes, then I would.'

'Right.' He dashed out of the shop and left her on tenterhooks wondering what he was going to do. Jimbo couldn't have Pericles because the children had got two new kittens to replace the one drowned in her water butt. There – she'd said it without flinching. She must be improving.

Jimbo returned after half an hour. 'Right, that's settled. I've told Sir Ronald that you've got the chance to go abroad and would it be possible for him to have Pericles like he did when you were in hospital and he jumped at the chance. Says Lady Bissett's Pom loved the company. So that's sorted. I'll look after the till while you go and make your arrangements.'

Ralph and Muriel spent five days in Rome. In her whole life she had never had a holiday like it. Never even been abroad. Mother always wanted to go to Eastbourne or Torquay, when Muriel in her soul had longed to visit far-distant lands. Ralph treated her like a queen, and to his sophistication she brought genuine childlike delight to everything they saw. They dined in pavement cafés, followed in the footsteps of the Christian martyrs, nearly had her bag stolen by children at the Trevi Fountain, stood in St Peter's Square and saw the Pope appear at the window, and held hands as they wandered through the Basilica. He bought her anything she took a fancy to. She felt like a child being indulged in some kind of fairyland. On the last night they had dinner in a smart restaurant and then went walking by the Tiber.

'This is a far cry from Turnham Beck, Ralphie.'

'It is indeed. One day we'll go to India and see the Ganges. That really *is* a sight.'

'I don't know if I could bear to see the poverty in India. That would upset me dreadfully. All those children with flies crawling on their faces.'

'You would have made a lovely mother, Moo, if you'd had the chance.'

'It's too late to be crying for the moon.'

'Too late for children, but you could still have happiness and friendship.'

'You've given me that and spoiled me quite dreadfully. I shall never forget this holiday, not if I live to be a hundred.'

'There could be more like this – Paris, Venice, New York, Hong Kong . . .'

'Oh, don't, Ralphie, I couldn't possibly go to all those places. I'm quite satisfied to have come here. Thank you, thank you, thank you.'

Muriel leant towards Ralph and placed her lips on his. It was the first time she had chosen to make contact with him and she felt she might develop quite an appetite for it.

20

The bar of The Royal Oak hummed with the news of Muriel's return from Rome.

'Have you seen 'er, Betty?' Jimmy Glover enquired.

'Not likely to, after what he said about our Sharon last time he was in here. Flipping cheek.'

'Could be a good customer of yours if she apologised.'

'That's as may be.'

'Well, your Sharon is rude. And them clothes she wears leaves a lot to be desired.'

'Listen who's talking.'

'I'll have you know I've turned over a new leaf, haven't you noticed?'

Willie, seated at a table close to the bar shouted, 'Well yes, I've noticed. I've stopped wearing a peg on me nose when I come in 'ere.'

Jimmy went over to sit with Willie. He took a draught of his best bitter and leaned confidentially towards him. 'Reckon he'll make an honest woman of her then, now they're back?'

'I'll let you know if they put up the banns.'

'By gum, I bet Muriel's had a surprise. Spinster good and proper all these years, and then this. She must be sixty-three or four, I reckon.'

'Must be – on the other hand, it could be purely platonic. "Just good friends" like all them film stars say.'

'That's likely, I don't think. Our Ralph looks to me like a man who would enjoy a bit of that there 'ere.'

'And what do you know about it in your vast experience?'

'Well, Willie, I have been married, which is more than can be said of you.'

'True, true, but even so I might have had more experience than you have. They say there's some married men who never find out what it's like. Their wives put their foot down on the honeymoon and *finito* – they never even get started. D'yer remember old Fred Armitage? He once told me his wife had ne—'

Their confidential exchange was curtailed by the sound of Betty shouting in the back.

'You're *not* going to an acid-house party! I don't care where it is, you're *not going*! For a start I need you in the bar tonight, we're short-handed, and for another you're not staying out all night.'

'Bit rich, you starting to take notice of me after all these years. Since when have you ever bothered about me and Scott? It's been "the bar, the bar" all my life. I'm off and that's that.'

'You're not. I shall tell your dad.'

'Some good that'll do. He's been under your thumb for years. He's forgotten he's got a mind of his own.'

'That's enough, our Sharon. Do as I say.'

'Who the hell do you think you are, telling me what to do? I'm nineteen and can do as I like.'

'Not under my roof you can't.'

'Under your roof, is it? Well, in that case I'll find somewhere else to live.'

'Right, you do that – and good riddance to yer!'

'And good riddance to you too.' The sound of furniture falling and the distant noise of flesh on flesh resounded through the bar.

'Mac, hadn't you better go and see what's happening?' one of the women shouted.

But Mac carried on stolidly washing up glasses. 'They'll sort it out without me,' he grunted.

Obvious sounds of a fight were now filtering through.

'Mac, get round there and do something!'

The door from the house into the bar burst open and Sharon and Betty appeared, wrestling with each other. Glasses and bottles on the bar and shelves behind began cascading onto the floor. Willie and Jimmy leapt up and went to help Mac separate them. Eventually mother and daughter were forced apart. Betty was breathing heavily, her carefully structured hair awry and her gold chains in complete disarray around her throat. Sharon was laughing.

'What a sight you look – mutton dressed as lamb. You won't get away with this. I'll have my own back, just you wait and see. You're welcome to 'er, Dad.'

Sharon trotted back into the house, leaving the inmates of the bar scandalised. The hubbub continued for some time. Betty went to reconstruct her hair and Mac cleared up the mess. He was philosophical. 'They've had rows like this before. It'll all blow over.'

Michael Palmer, absorbed in listening to *Aida* on a new CD he'd bought at the weekend, jumped when he heard the hammering on his front door.

'Drat it, I wonder who that is at this time of night.'

His heart sank when he saw Sharon McDonald standing at the door with her case. A large bruise was making itself noticeable all down one side of her face, and there were tears brimming in her eyes.

'Oh, Mr Palmer, please can you help me? I've nowhere to go and Mum's turned me out. Please help me.' Tears began to fall and she sniffed helplessly.

'Whatever are you doing with a bruise like that on your face?'

'Mum did it and I'm too frightened to go back home. I've packed my case and climbed out of the window. I've always tried to do what she wanted but I can't please her. Could I stay the night while I decide what to do? Please let me in. She'll never think to look for me here.' The tears trickled down her bruised cheek and she fumbled unsuccessfully in her pocket for a handkerchief.

'Here, come in. I'll find you a tissue.' Michael's immediate reaction, that he mustn't have anything to do with this girl, was overridden by his schoolmasterly instincts to care and protect children in distress. 'We'll have a cup of tea and talk things over. Perhaps if I come back home with you we could sort it out with your mum and dad. It's not right for you to have nowhere to go.'

He found a box of tissues and went in the kitchen to put the kettle on. Sharon followed him in. 'I'm scared to be on my own. Can I sit in here while you make the tea? Oh, Mr Palmer, all my life my mum's been hitting me. Now I'm old enough to leave but that means our Scott will be left on his own. She's terrible to live with, you know. I have thought about going to the Social about 'er but who'd believe me?'

'Well, of course they would, Sharon. You've got the evidence now.'

'Yes, that's right I have, and they couldn't make me go back 'cos I'm nineteen. But who'd protect Scott then? He's the one I worry about.'

'That's very commendable. Let's go and sit down by the fire and see what we can sort out.'

'You are kind to me, Mr Palmer. I always liked you when I was in school. I know I gave you a lot of trouble but with all the rows at home it was hard to behave right.' The tears began falling again.

'Now, now, Sharon. Drink your tea up and you'll feel better. I've only got digestive biscuits, will they do?'

'I love digestive biscuits, Mr Palmer. They're so homely and that's something I've never had, a real home.'

Michael pondered the predicament in which he found himself. He'd no idea that the girl had experienced such a difficult childhood. She'd kept it to herself all these years. No wonder she'd been such a trial! He had really misjudged her . . . Sharon adopted a brave smile. She touched the bruise on her face and grimaced.

'I'll get some ice for that, Sharon. At least we might keep the swelling down.' They sat chatting for a while and as it grew later and later, Michael realised he had no alternative but to put her up for the night. He didn't fancy tackling Betty McDonald until the clear light of morning. No one would know, anyway.

'See here, Sharon, just for tonight you can sleep in the spare bedroom. It's downstairs next to the bathroom. So you go and use the bathroom and I'll put clean sheets on the bed. There are fresh towels in the airing cupboard in the bathroom.'

He kept well out of the way while she got ready for bed; he didn't want her to think he had any designs on her – which he hadn't, heaven forbid. He called, 'Good night, Sharon,' through her closed door as he went up to his bedroom. He'd never got rid of the double bed he and Stella had used, and as he got into it he suddenly felt quite lonely. Being a widower had its compensations, but sometimes it would be nice to have someone sharing the bed, even if it was only for keeping warm and conversation. Despite the events of the evening he fell asleep almost directly, firmly convinced that in the morning he would go across to the McDonalds' with Sharon and lay down the law.

During the night, he turned over and woke with a start. Close beside him was a female form. Convinced he was dreaming, he put out a hand to assure himself he was alone, but it came it contact with another hand which guided his to a warm ample breast. He leapt out of bed. There was a soft chuckle and Sharon's voice.

'Oh, come on, Michael, I'm used to this kind of thing. A handsome widower like yourself must be in need of some hanky panky. Come on, get back in. I'll give you a good time. Don't be shy.'

'Sharon, get out immediately – this minute! Go downstairs to your own bed.'

'It's cold and lonely down there, and I need someone to hold my hand. Come on, no one will know. It'll be our secret. I bet I can teach you things you've never even dreamt about. Let's face it, that Stella of yours wouldn't have given you much joy, so take your chance now while you can.'

'Do as I say. Get out of my bed this instant!'

'Don't waste your breath coming the schoolmaster with me. You want me, so for once in your life let go and enjoy yourself. I don't kiss and tell and I'm panting for you. Come on.'

'Absolutely not. Get out.'

'Well, in that case you can be cold all night because I've got cosy. Good night. If you feel in need of a cuddle, climb in any time.'

Defeated and unable to get her out without dragging her out – which would give her the chance she wanted – Michael went downstairs. He found an eiderdown and wrapped himself up on the sofa. What a blithering idiot he'd been. He should never have let her in in the first place. She'd totally deceived him. Her acting abilities merited an audition with the RSC. He woke a couple of hours later needing to go to the bathroom, and saw that the spare bedroom door was open and Sharon's case had gone. Oh God, had she moved into his bedroom – surely not? But she hadn't, she'd disappeared. Thank heavens for that. At least no one would know what a fool he'd been. And he had been right all along – she *was* sly.

All that boasting about knowing about sex, a girl her age! On the other hand, she'd been in Culworth very late at night and seen Stella there; she'd already threatened him with that. From the back of his mind pieces of a puzzle began coming together. Pieces were missing and he could be wrong, yes of course he *must* be wrong, unless it was that Toria Clark had found someone writing the pos . . . That was it! Sharon had been writing the poster to leave in the school, and had been interrupted by Toria Clark. But Sharon wouldn't kill someone, would she? How could she? She was a village girl who'd gone to school there, grown up there . . . No. No. No! But it fitted. Sharon was the only one who knew about Stella being lesbian. It was Sharon who'd driven Stella to suicide with her threats of exposure. The poster referred to Stella, not to Toria Clark. That was the mistake they'd all made. They'd all thought the poster meant Toria. He'd have to tell the police what he thought, and a right fool they'd all take him for. He wouldn't be able to hold his head up any more; he'd have to resign. Would he need to tell the police that Sharon had stayed there all night? He could say he'd been thinking things over and had decided to tell them what he knew.

Betty and Mac went to the police the following day.

'Our Sharon's missing.'

'How old is she now, Betty?'

'Nineteen.'

'Well, she can do as she likes, you know. It's no crime at nineteen not to come home one night.'

'Look, Sergeant, me and our Sharon have had our differences but she'd no money with her when she went – we've found her purse in her bedroom. She was only doing it to frighten me. She didn't intend going any distance at all. You've got to do something for us, Sergeant, no messing.'

'I'll make some enquiries in the village and see what I come up with. But if she's decided to leave I can't bring her back.'

'She's always led such a sheltered life. I won't let her go to these all-night parties or anything like that. We've always been so careful with her, haven't we, Mac?'

'Yes. Well, fairly careful.'

The sergeant questioned everyone in the village. The row in the bar came to light and also another factor which caused the sergeant's pen to hesitate for a moment as he took notes.

'You saw her going inside?'

'Oh yes, Sergeant. He opened the door and he closed it behind her. I saw him with my own eyes.'

'This is very serious, you know. Mr Palmer is a well-respected gentleman in this village, so you'll have to be very careful about this. Are you absolutely certain it was Sharon McDonald?'

Pat Duckett nodded her head in agreement. 'Who could miss that cheeky backside and those sticking-out boobs of hers? And I couldn't be mistaken about the house, could I? It's the only one in the school playground. It was only because I was going out for a drink and knew I'd left my purse in the school kitchen that I happened to be there. I thought, "the dirty old man," so I did.'

'That's enough, Pat. Nothing's been proved about anything. Keep mum about this; you might be needed to give evidence and if I hear you've been spreading this story around I might remember about that shoplifting your Dean's been getting up to in Culworth. Remember that.'

Muriel went into school the following day at her usual time. The atmosphere was tense. Suzy came out of the playgroup room and told her that Mr Palmer was helping police with their enquiries so Mrs Hardaker the new teacher would be taking the children for singing and she and Liz Neal were going to keep an eye on the children in the playground for her.

'Helping the police with their enquiries? Whatever do you mean?'

'I'm not quite sure, but the poor man has not been himself for a day or two and now he's at the police station in Culworth. Also, Sharon McDonald's gone missing.'

'Oh dear, whatever next is going to happen in this village? When I was a girl nothing happened, apart from Jimmy Glover's father being caught poaching and someone once setting fire to a farmer's hayrick when they were up to naughty things with a girl. Well, I never.'

She told Ralph about what had happened when he collected her to go into Culworth for some shopping for his house, and asked him what he thought.

'I never cease to be amazed at what goes on in this village now. Do you suppose it all happened before and we were too young to hear about it?'

'I don't know, but I can only think it's all connected with his wife's death, and Toria Clark's murder and Sharon's disappearance. Where shall we go for lunch?'

'I do believe you're beginning to enjoy all this tripping about we do.'

'I am. It's opened up a whole new side of my nature.'

'I haven't decided yet. Where do you fancy?'

'I don't mind. Somewhere quiet where we won't meet anyone and we can talk.'

'So be it.'

Ralph chose the restaurant by the River Cul where they'd first had lunch together. They'd reached the coffee and liqueur stage when Ralph cleared his throat and began to speak. Muriel, enjoying her After Eight mint – she never could resist them – brought her head up with a jerk when she realised what Ralph was saying.

'I know we can't expect to have a mad passionate affair, but why should the two of us live, one in one house and one in another, when we could share so much?'

'Why can't we have a mad passionate affair?'

'Moo, my dear!'

'Why should we miss out on it because we're older? We'd appreciate it a lot more than when we were younger, wouldn't we? We'd be so grateful to have the opportunity. In fact, you can kiss me now in front of everybody.'

'It hardly seems the place to be kissing.'

'I'm feeling daring. All my life I've held back, been too quiet, not said what I felt, let everyone else have all the fun and it's time I came out of my shell. It's like you said, I've been fending people off and not letting them get near. All these old fuddy duddies will be jealous of me. You're such a handsome man, Ralph. I'd be proud for you to kiss me.'

They neither of them noticed the scandalised looks they got from the other diners. Ralph's hands were trembling as he signed the credit card voucher and Muriel, hiding in the Ladies from this new person she had become, could hardly control her hand long enough to renew her lipstick. Ralph took her to a department store and insisted on buying her some new perfume. She dillied and dallied choosing first one and then another till she couldn't distinguish which perfume she liked the best. Finally Ralph chose on her behalf – Obsession, the largest bottle he could find. He then marched her purposefully towards a jeweller's.

'I'm buying you a necklace. Don't argue, I am.'

They emerged after an hour with Muriel carrying a box in which was laid a beautiful pendant of garnets and seed pearls on a long gold chain. They went back to Turnham Malpas without the furniture they had gone for.

Ralph made afternoon tea for them both, and they sat together on his sofa holding hands. 'Put your necklace on, Moo.'

'It's much too good for everyday.'

'No, wear it now – I want to see it on.'

He helped her with the clasp and kissed her throat before leaning back to see the effect. 'Excellent! It looks lovely.'

'My only regret is that I am not young and beautiful, Ralphie. I never have been, come to think of it. I've always been Plain Jane all my life, even as a young woman.'

'I'm not exactly an Adonis, am I? You wouldn't give me a second look if you were as young and beautiful as you would like to be. Oh, I'm so sorry, that didn't come out very well. I do beg your pardon.' They both laughed and Muriel caught hold of his hands and held them to her chest.

'That's what's nice about us. We can laugh, can't we?'

'Oh, my dear.' Ralph took her in his arms and they kissed as they had never kissed before. They fitted like a glove. Ralph's fingers traced the line of her collar bone and then the line of her jaw and he kissed her ear and then her forehead and then her mouth again. He began to undo the buttons of her blouse. She very nearly protested but didn't. Modesty had got her nowhere in the past and it seemed right for Ralph to do as he did.

He suddenly said, 'We must stop.' He rebuttoned her blouse and stood up. 'I must be absolutely truthful with you, Moo. It pains me to say it, but I do not come to this relationship as pure as you do.'

'I thought not.'

'I felt you should know. I've got to be quite open about it to you. I don't mean I had frequent casual one-night stands, but there have been others. Not that I am asking for a serious relationship with you.'

Her eyes began filling up with tears. 'I can't understand what you mean, Ralphie.'

'I mean, I'm not going to expect a sexual relationship with you, Moo. I want something better than that.'

'Oh. I thought you meant you didn't – you wouldn't be seeing me . . .'

'When the time is right I shall ask you to marry me.'

'Oh, I see.'

'I'll see you to your door.'

'No, don't do that. The village is gossiping quite enough about us as it is and it's not dark yet. Pericles will be needing a walk.'

Marriage. Heavens above. And she wouldn't be plain Mrs Templeton, she'd be Lady Templeton. She couldn't marry him – could she? Whoever heard of a solicitor's secretary becoming a titled person? It was perfectly ridiculous. It wasn't five minutes since she'd been promising herself no SEX and yet today she'd been saying, 'Why can't we have a mad passionate affair?' What had come over her?

Ralph was so generous, beyond anything she had imagined. Maybe that was part of the attraction – maybe she wanted financial security. That was it, she liked him because he could provide her with the things she had never had. She wouldn't accept anything more from him and next time they went out it would be her treat. No more kissing and holding hands and gifts, strictly platonic till she'd had time to sort her feelings out. Play it cool, as the Americans would say.

21

Michael Palmer was allowed home by the police. He asked for leave of absence from school and the Office agreed that it would be for the best. He'd explained all he could when he was questioned; what hurt most was having to let Stella down by telling them about her secret life. He told them about the threats which Sharon had made and how she had duped him by pretending her mother had treated her so badly. He felt as if his whole life had been laid bare to satisfy his interviewers' insatiable appetite. Finally they could hold him no longer, but he knew they would be keeping a close eye on his movements. The police also had another problem in Turnham Malpas. From being a sleepy, well-regulated village carrying on its life as it had done for centuries, it had become a thorn in their flesh. Peter had discovered that some items of the church silver plate had been stolen. It happened the night Sharon went missing.

Willie, ever mindful of the need for security, always locked the Communion paraphernalia away immediately after use. They didn't have a safe as such but he had a very strong cupboard bolted to the wall with thick doors and a stout lock. In the past that had been all that was needed. Peter had spoken of buying a safe for the valuables but had decided the expenditure was not possible. The village sergeant sighed at the prospect of yet another problem on his patch. The beautiful eighteenth-century chalices had been given by the Lord of the Manor at the time, a Sir Tristan Templeton, in memory of his wife and daughters who had drowned on board a ship which had gone down in the Channel in a violent storm. The vessels had been in constant use for two hundred years.

'Whoever took them, Sergeant, cannot have realised that if they tried to sell them they would be instantly recognised. It was an amateur for certain.'

'Not necessarily, sir. Organised crime can find outlets abroad for items like Eucharist chalices. You know the story – "Church short of funds must sell to survive" kind of thing and they were beautiful. Some families have been taking Communion from those chalices for generations. The whole village is very upset.'

The habitués in The Royal Oak concluded that no good would come of it.

'Stealing from the church, how could anybody do it? Talk about the wrath of God, it's a wonder they weren't struck dead as they forced the cupboard open.'

'Believe you me, Willie, whoever's took 'em will come to no good. Their lives'll be blighted. Might not happen this week or this year, but as sure as I sit 'ere they'll have a bad end.'

Jimmy leant closer towards Pat and Willie, checked Betty wasn't within earshot and whispered, 'I reckon it's that Sharon, night she disappeared.'

Pat agreed. 'Bad lot, she is. I haven't told a living soul but if you promise me not to breathe a word I'll tell you what I saw the night 'er and Betty 'ad that row in here.'

'Go on, then. We won't split, will we, Jimmy?'

'Definitely not.'

Pat took a long drink of her lager, settled her bottom more securely on her stool and told them what she'd said to the police.

Willie shook his head. 'I don't believe it, Pat. Mr Palmer's a gentleman. He wouldn't have that Sharon calling at his house like that. He's not that kind.'

'You calling me a liar?'

'No, I'm just saying you're mistaken.'

'I'm not. Is there anyone else roundabouts who looks like Sharon? How many houses is there in the schoolyard? One – and that's Mr Palmer's.'

'Let's face it, he must have been the last to see her, that's why the police have been questioning him.'

'Exactly, Jimmy. Exactly.'

Betty strode across. 'Finished with your glasses, 'ave yer, and yer tittle tattle? Pity you 'aven't got something else to talk about. I can see the glances yer keep giving me, making sure I can't hear yer. Yer ought to be feeling sorry for Mac and me with all the worry we have with our Sharon missing, not gossiping about us.'

Willie stood up. 'Right, that's it. I'm coming in here no more. If I can't talk about what I like when I'm having a quiet pint with me friends then I'm off. You're an interfering old buzzard you are, Betty. I've drunk in this pub for forty years and more but I've reached the end of me tether. Good night, Pat. Good night, Jimmy.'

Betty was incensed. 'That's right, cut yer nose off to spite yer face. Now where will you go?'

'I shall cycle down to Penny Fawcett and drink in The Jug and Bottle. Landlady's a sight more welcoming there than you are, or so I'm told.'

'If yer 'ad a tandem I'd come with yer, Willie.'

'Well, I haven't, Jimmy, so yer can't.

Peter was very distressed by the theft of the chalices.

'If only I'd bought the safe!'

'Well, you didn't because the finance wasn't there so you can hardly be blamed.'

'I shall buy a safe myself, Caroline, and the Church can pay me back when they can manage it. These treasures are priceless in the life of a small parish like this one. They belong not only to the Church but the parishoners as well, simply because their families have used them for so long. Think how you must feel if you can take Communion knowing that your grandfather, your great-grandfather and your great-great-grandfather and further back than that in some cases, have all drunk from the same chalice. I can never forgive myself.'

'Maybe a dealer will be offered them and he'll contact the police.'

'Let's hope so. I must get on, there's a thousand and one things to be done this week.'

'Is there anything I can help you with, now I'm not working?'

'Are you enjoying your freedom?'

'Yes. My mind is obsessed with the twins. I can't think about anything else. If it's two boys, what about Thomas and Joshua? If it's two girls, what about Elizabeth and Sarah? If it's one of each what about Thomas Joshua and Elizabeth Sarah?'

'Don't build up your hopes too much, Caroline. I can hardly dare to think about it. I expect all prospective parents get the shivers sometimes worrying about whether the baby will be all right, and that's the phase I'm going through at the moment.'

'Peter, you mustn't. I know in my heart of hearts that this will all come right.' There was a loud knocking on the door. 'I'll answer it, it sounds like Willie knocking. Hello, Willie, the rector's in his study. Come on in.'

'Mrs Harris, the police is here. They've found the chalices. Can the rector come, please?'

'Thought it was a bomb, sir, they did – as if they'd plant a bomb on Culworth Station. Got the bomb squad in and found it was our chalices. You've to formally identify 'em, they say.'

'I would think you'd be better at that than me, Willie. You've been familiar with them a lot longer than I have.'

'Never mind that, sir. You're the official person as yer might say.'

Inspector Proctor from Culworth was waiting for them in the vestry.

'Good morning, Rector. The cups have been tested for fingerprints, sir, so it's all right to handle them. They are yours, are they, sir?'

'Yes, indeed they are, Inspector. Thank goodness we've got them back – undamaged, too. Where did you find them?'

'In a case on Culworth Station. Left there by the thief. Might I suggest, sir, that when you're allowed to have them back they are kept either in a bank vault, or that you provide better security for them than a stout cupboard?'

'Certainly, Inspector. I shall deal with it as soon as you leave. Thank you very much indeed for all your efforts. No news of Sharon McDonald, I take it?'

'None at all, sir. I wish there was, for there's a few loose ends that she could tie up for us if we could find her. No need to say this, sir, but if you should hear anything of her wherebouts, you will let us know?'

'Of course, Inspector. We are most indebted to you, thank you again.'

The inspector went round to The Royal Oak after leaving the church. He was carrying a small case. He hammered on the door. A voice called through, 'We're not open yet.'

'Police here, can we come in, please?'

The bolts shot back and the door was opened by Mac. 'Have you found our Sharon?'

'No, I'm sorry to say we haven't, but we wonder if you recognise this case?'

'I'll fetch Betty. She'll know better than me.'

Betty came through from the other bar still wearing her dressing gown.

'Mrs McDonald, do you recognise this case?'

'Oh, have yer found her?' She clutched the bar counter for support.

'No, we haven't, but we've found this case and we wonder if it's hers?'

'Well yes, it certainly looks like one I bought a few years back. I'll go and check.' She nodded to the inspector when she returned. 'That's right, mine isn't there, so I expect our Sharon borrowed it to put her stuff in. Have you no clues where she went, Inspector?'

'We know she went to Culworth Station in the early hours of the day she disappeared and left this case under a seat in the Ladies, and we expect she caught the first London train but we can't trace her after that.'

'London? She doesn't know anybody there.'

'Lots of young people go to London. Think they won't get found, with it being so big.'

'Anyway, Inspector, I've a bar to run so you'll have to excuse me.'

Mac asked the inspector if the case was empty when they found it.

'No, Mr McDonald. Inside were the two chalices stolen from St Thomas à Becket.'

Mac sat down heavily on the nearest stool. 'Is there no end to it? What will that girl do next! I'm right sorry Mr Palmer's been involved. It wouldn't be him, you know. It'd be our Sharon – man-mad she's been for years. I daren't think what she used to get up to in Culworth.'

'Well, we've a pretty good idea. But don't trouble yourself with that at the moment, Mr McDonald. If you hear or see anything, let us know straight away, won't you?'

'Of course.'

Jimbo was surprised to find that Muriel had not turned up for work. She had never been absent before, except when she had gone to Rome. Harriet promised to go round to make sure she was all right.

'Maybe she's forgotten it's Wednesday. I've got one or two things to do and then I'll pop across. Have you seen my action list anywhere? I always put it here by the order book and I can't find it. Dammit, I'll have to start remembering all over again. I'll go and see Muriel first and then make a new list when I get back.'

Harriet knocked on the door and stood admiring Muriel's winter pansies. However did she find the time to keep her garden so lovely! Every flower was meticulously manicured and all the flowerbeds were so neat and tidy, not a single weed. When Muriel didn't answer the door she decided to go round the back and knock on the kitchen door. There was still no answer, though somehow she felt sure there was someone about. Round at the front door again she knocked once more. The door opened a little and there stood Muriel in her dressing gown.

'Yes? Oh, good morning, Harriet.'

'It's only me, come to ask if you're all right. It's Wednesday, you see, and you haven't come to the tearoom.'

'I've got a tummy upset and I'm afraid I can't leave the house.'

'I'm so sorry. Look, is there anything I can get you?'

'No thank you, I've got everything I need.'

'I'll call again tomorrow and see how you are. Are you sure you don't need a doctor?'

'Oh no, thank you, not a doctor.'

'Hope you'll soon feel better. See you tomorrow.'

Muriel closed the door and stood with her back to it. The knife Sharon was holding was only a foot away from Muriel's chest.

'Well done, Moo. We'll make an actress of you yet.'

'I'm going to get dressed now.'

'Oh no, you're not. You stay like that. Make me some breakfast now.'

There was absolutely no alternative, Sharon had the upper hand. Neither of them had slept all night and Muriel genuinely felt ill. Her mind struggled round and round her problem. She'd called Pericles in from the garden last night and left the door open for him to come in. She's turned from making her Ovaltine to find Sharon – dishevelled, grimy, without make-up and desperately cold, standing in her kitchen. To think the girl had been hiding in the shed in the churchyard all day, waiting for the village to go quiet before coming to the door. Sharon had taken one of Muriel's Sabatier knives they'd given her at the office when she left, so there was no alternative but to do as she said and hope. During the night Sharon had told her the whole story. It was the hot chocolate and the piece of ginger cake which had weakened Sharon's armour. Muriel made it about two o'clock, more for something to do than any real need.

'This is nice, Moo. Real homely. That's what you like, isn't it, things comfortable and homely, not too challenging? Me, I like change and excitement. Poke the fire a bit, it's getting cold. Put some more coal on. Neat and tidy, smart and clean, that's you all over. Mind – there's a bit of coal-dust on the rug. Whoops, that won't do, will it? It was a good fire I made at number three, wasn't it? Nice mess that created. Your Ralphie shouldn't have told me off that night in the bar. That Ralphie of yours, has he been to bed with you? Don't be embarrassed, Moo, it's what makes the world go round. Men – that's all they want, yer know. King Street in Culworth, you should see the kerb-crawlers there. Nice market town, real piece of Olde England but they're all at it. I should know. I've earned more money there in one night than in a whole week at Tesco's.'

'Sharon, I don't believe you.'

'No, well, you believe the best in everybody. You won't find any best in me. I'm rotten through and through.'

'No one is as bad as that.'

'Oh yes, I am. You won't believe the things I've done. Climbed into Michael Palmer's bed night before last, really fancied him but he jumped out like a frightened rabbit. Cor, you should have seen him. Remember his wife Stella? Lesbian, yer know she was. Followed her one night in Culworth, saw her go into a pub there what specialises in people like her. I told her I'd tell good and proper about her goings-on. She gave me money to shut me up. Then she hanged herself. Good riddance to her, who wants rubbish people like that.' She moved the knife into the other hand and pointed it at Muriel.

'No one ever found out it was me who'd threatened her, police running round like chickens with their heads cut off.' She flicked the knife sharply as though decapitating one. 'But I kept mum. Who'd think a girl of sixteen could bring off a coup like that, eh? They ran round like two chickens with their heads cut off when they found Toria Clark. She was a bloody idiot, challenging me and trying to stop me writing that poster. She didn't know what power I had. That night I was so full of power nothing and nobody could stop me.'

'Sharon, are you making all this up?'

'You stupid old cow, don't you believe me? Someone's got to believe me. You've got to take notice of what I say, or you'll be like all the others. My mum never listens to what I say. My dad never listens and our Scott's not even worth bothering about, the little toad. All my life I've heard other children at school saying "This weekend, mum and dad are taking us to Weston for the day and my dad's promised to take me out in a boat" or they were going to the zoo or up to London. What was Sharon doing? Sitting upstairs with some chocolate watching telly and looking after our Scott. Weekend after weekend. So when I got older I found my own entertainment. I made that Jimbo sit up though when I drowned his cat. He treated me like dirt in his shop, so I paid him back. All the money in the world he has, and thinks he's so superior.'

'He works very hard all day and every day. He earns every penny he gets.'

'More fool him. I like easy money. Have you got any money?'

'Only a few pounds. I don't keep money in the house.'

'When I go I'll take that.'

'Where are you going?'

'I don't know but it'll have to be a long way away because they'll be after me.' Sharon's eyes became crafty. She looked about the room. 'Where's Pericles?'

'In his basket asleep.'

'Fond of him, are you?'

'Of course.'

Sharon's mind darted from one thing to another. 'If you steal from the church, will something evil happen to you?'

'Was it you who stole the chalices?'

'What if it was?'

'Where are they now?'

'Under a seat in the Ladies in Culworth Station. Got worried, yer see, stealing from the church, so I thought if I left them there the police would think I'd gone to London, put them off the scent like they do in detective stories.'

Sharon stood up and taking the knife with her, went into the kitchen pushing Muriel in front of her.

Pericles was asleep in his basket. 'See him? One peep out of you and I shall stick this right through him, right the way through and you'll be able to hear him screaming.' She put the point of the knife close to his ribs and prodded him with it. Pericles jumped up and snapped at her.

'See – even the dog don't like me. Come back here for a pat, you nasty little thing. *Come here!*'

'He won't come if you shout, he's not used to it.'

The girl changed her tone to a wheedle: 'Come on, then, little Pericles. Come to Sharon, there's a good boy, there's a good boy.' She grabbed his scruff and pointed the knife close to his eyes. 'Remember, remember, you little sod.' When she released him Pericles scrabbled along the floor towards Muriel. She bent down to pick him up, but Sharon grabbed at her arm. 'Oh no, Moo, he doesn't deserve a cuddle. He tried to bite poor Sharon, he did.'

Muriel ignored her and scooped him up. The knife quickly arrived at her throat.

'Put him down, Moo. Do as I say – now! That's better. I've murdered once and I can do it again. The second time is easier, they say.'

She motioned to Muriel to return to the sitting room. They both sat down and remained in silence. If I can keep awake, thought Muriel, she might drop asleep and I can creep out. Oh dear God, if she kills Pericles whatever shall I do? Ralphie, why aren't you here? This would never have happened if you had been here. Please, Ralphie, come and find me. You'd know something was wrong. If he comes to the door how can I let him know, without Sharon understanding, that something is wrong? Shall I blink my eyes? Talk rubbish? My word, her eyes are beginning to close. I'll count to one thousand before I get up. It's three o'clock. No one will be about. The phone box, that's it – the phone box and 999. *One hundred and four. One hundred and five. One hundred and six.* She didn't actually murder Stella Palmer, *one hundred and fifty*. Killing with a rounders bat, that was vicious. How dreadful. The clock ticked, *two hundred and two*, the fire crackled and Sharon still sat with her eyes closed.

The counting in Muriel's head went on and on. *Two hundred and forty, two hundred and forty-one.* I shan't wait to one thousand, I'll have a try at five hundred. *Three hundred and seven.* It's so hard to keep awake. *Four hundred and fifty-nine.* She still hasn't opened her eyes, but is she asleep or playing with me like a cat with a mouse? *Four hundred and seventy-six. Four hundred and seventy-seven.* A coal in the fire dropped suddenly and sparks flew up. *Four hundred and seventy-nine.* She didn't move; she didn't hear it. *Five hundred.* Muriel placed her feet slightly apart on the carpet, checked where the rug was so as not to trip over it and slowly, slowly stood up. A knee cracked as it straightened. No movement. No movement. Inch by inch she walked forward. Please God, don't let Pericles decide to get up and come in. Inch by inch. Don't breathe, don't breathe. Two more feet and she'd be at the door. When the door opens run like the wind. Slippers won't make a sound. One more step. She turned to check that Sharon was still asleep and bumped into her, nose to nose. Muriel screamed.

'Thought you'd escape, did yer, Moo?' Sharon had Muriel's hair in a tight cruel grip. She'd spent the rest of the night tied tightly by her dressing-gown cord to Sharon's wrist. 'One move and I shall know. Just one itsy bitsy move and Pericles will be a goner.'

'You'll have to come to the bathroom with me. I want to have a bath. I haven't washed for two days.'

'Very well. There's plenty of hot water. I'll sit outside the door.'

'You won't, you'll be in there with me.'

'But you'll be having a bath.'

'So? Never seen a woman in her birthday suit before? Something new every day when you're with me.'

She made Muriel run the bath for her.

'No bubbles? I like bubbles.'

'No bubbles, only oil.'

Sharon dropped her clothes on the floor and stood in front of the mirror.

'Cor, I do need a bath. Got yer eyes shut, have yer? You daft old cow. Moo, that's the right name for you. Moooo. *Mooooo.*'

Muriel did open her eyes and wished her body looked like Sharon's. It was a pity Sharon had abused it so.

When the bathing was over Muriel was forced into the bedroom and made to get out fresh underwear and a skirt and blouse and a cardigan. When Sharon had the outfit on she stood in front of Muriel's mirror and laughed.

'Oh God, what a sight. It looks awful on you, but on me it's a disaster area. Time that Ralphie bought you some clothes with a bit of style. That's what you lack – style. We'll go downstairs now and you can make me something else to eat.'

They were halfway down the spiral stairs when a knock came at the door.

The knife-point pricked Muriel's back very slightly.

'They might go away. Keep still.'

'I'll have to answer. It's probably the postman with a parcel. I am expecting one.'

Sharon whispered, 'Answer it then, but I'm right behind you. Where's Pericles?'

'Shut in the kitchen.'

They walked like two halves of a pantomime horse towards the front door.

Sharon hid behind the door and Muriel opened it slightly. Thank God it was Ralph.

'Good morning, Moo. I've just been in the tearoom to see you and have a coffee but Jimbo says you're ill this morning. Is there anything I could get for you?'

'No, nothing . . . thank you.'

'Would you like me to come in and make you some camomile tea or something?'

'No, thank you. I shall be all right. Ralphie, you know you asked me about going to the theatre tomorrow night to see *The Waiting Game*? Well, yes, I'd like to go. It's a thriller, isn't it?' She managed to wink.

Ralph looked puzzled, hesitated and then said, 'Right, I'll try to get the tickets. I'll let you know tomorrow. Hope you'll soon be better.' He looked her full in the face, waved and went down the path.

The knife-point prodded Muriel somewhere around her kidneys. 'What you playing at?'

'I had to tell him. He asked me to let him know and we don't want him back again asking if I've decided to go, do we?'

'No.'

Ralph backed off, puzzled by Muriel's suggestion. He'd never asked her to go to the theatre. What on earth was she talking about?

He went round to see Jimbo again and told him what Muriel had said.

They checked the paper and could find no mention of the play being performed locally.

'She winked, you see. She didn't really mean it.'

'Muriel was ill a few months ago. I do hope it's not starting all over again.'

'She wasn't dressed, which isn't like Muriel, is it? – even if she's not well. I know this sounds mad but I had the feeling that Muriel was being overheard.'

The problem unsolved, Ralph went off to find Peter. He'd decided to agree to becoming a church warden. Time he got involved. He wandered up the church path hoping the rector would be about, and when he couldn't find him, he had a walk around looking at the gravestones. He was trying to decipher a very ancient one near the churchyard wall when he saw how conveniently the wall was situated for seeing into Muriel's house. Looking around to make sure he wasn't being watched, he walked along the side of the wall to find the best spot for seeing easily into the back windows of her house. He propped himself on an old headstone and sat with his head barely visible above the wall.

He'd only been there a few minutes when he spotted Muriel, still in her dressing gown, obviously beginning to prepare food. Then he saw what he had suspected: someone else was in the kitchen, and that someone was wearing Muriel's clothes. Someone as fastidious as she, did not lend their clothes willingly. For a moment only, the other person came close to the back window. Peroxided hair . . . where had he seen that before? Who on earth was it? It was that daughter from The Royal Oak, Sharon what's-her-name. Suddenly, Muriel's odd behaviour became absolutely clear to Ralph. Sharon was hiding in her house and Muriel was very frightened. Ralph felt terribly cold and very afraid. *The Waiting Game.* Of course, that was what Muriel was having to play! 'The Waiting Game'.

When the sergeant heard Ralph's story his insides did a somersault. He'd have to appear calm, but this really was above and beyond the duties expected of a village policeman. Metropolitan police, yes, but not the Turnham Malpas village bobby.

'I shall need to get on to my inspector, Sir Ralph. Would you take a seat for the moment while I contact him.'

'Whatever you do, you mustn't have them barging up there with their big boots on. That girl is dangerous. I've warned Muriel about her before.'

Sharon sat in front of the fire eating her lunch of scrambled egg on toast with two rashers of bacon and baked beans, and tea and a piece of gingerbread for afters.

'This suits me down to the ground, Moo. Once it gets dark I'm going. Waiting here is getting me nowhere. I've got to get away. Pity you don't drive, then you could take me in the car in the dark and drive me away. When I tell you to, you must fetch me all the money you've got.'

Muriel tried to eat her lunch but it would keep sticking in her throat. If only it would get dark right now, but there were another three hours before sunset. Could she keep her nerve until then? Oh, Ralph, please understand what I was telling you, please. *Please.*

'I'll wear a coat of yours and a scarf and get myself to Culworth on the tea-time bus. There's never no one on it going to Culworth.'

'I shall have to let Pericles out or he'll be wetting the floor.'

'I'll come with you when you open the door. I don't want you running out.'

She picked up the knife, took hold of the back of Muriel's dressing gown and marched her to the kitchen. Pericles dashed out of the door. They both stood, Muriel in front and Sharon holding the knife to her ribs, watching the dog in the garden. For one brief moment Muriel thought she saw a head move behind the wall. She glanced at Sharon but she was standing a bit behind and didn't get quite the same view as Muriel did.

A small flame of hope flared in Muriel's heart. Pericles came back in.

'Well now, Sharon, shall we wash up?'

'You can, I'll watch.'

Talk to your captors, make a relationship with them. Be friendly, be sympathetic. Where had she read that?

'I'm sorry I haven't got much money in the house, my dear, but there'll be enough for the bus and something to eat. Would you like me to make a picnic for you to take with you?'

'What's this – trying to win me round? You won't get me to give myself up, you know. Couldn't bear being locked up. Got a thing about it, you see. I've got to have freedom, that's me. Yes, you can make me a picnic. Put some of that gingerbread in and a nice jam sandwich.'

Sharon sat on a stool watching Muriel wash up. The small kitchen made her proximity hard to tolerate. Muriel didn't like people in her house at the best of times but this was suffocating. They watched television during the afternoon and then had another cup of tea. Before it grew dark Muriel made the picnic, found Sharon a coat and a big scarf for her hair.

'You'll miss the tea-time bus, Sharon, if you don't hurry.'

'Right. I'll go over the wall and round the back of the church through the graveyard and wait for the bus behind the wall, then no one will see me.' Sharon put the knife in the plastic bag holding her picnic.

'Sharon, don't take the knife. You don't need it.'

'Oh yes I do. It's a big bad world out there.'

Muriel opened the back door and said, 'Good luck, Sharon.' The girl tossed her peroxided head and without another word ran into the garden and headed for the wall.

The terrifying scream which tore across the night sky as Sharon disappeared over the wall shattered Muriel's self-control. She collapsed unconscious.

22

Ralph thought his heart would burst with fear. Surely, surely, she wasn't dead? Not when they were about to find happiness together after all these years.

He gently rolled her over, fearing the worst. She was ghastly white and scarcely breathing, but not apparently hurt in any way. He needed a phone. 'I shall put a phone in for you, Muriel, immediately,' he whispered.

A constable followed him in. 'Is she all right?' Ralph demanded.

'I think so, sir – just fainted with shock. But she'll need to be checked over all the same. I'll call for another ambulance.' While the constable did this on his radio, Ralph covered Muriel with his coat, gently rubbed her hands between his warm ones, and spoke her name, desperate for her to come back to life.

'How's Sharon?'

'Dead, sir, I'm afraid. The knife went straight through her as she fell, and the blood just pumped out. She was dead in a moment. There was nothing we could do to save her.'

'Poor girl, what an end. Have her parents been told?'

'Someone's gone to tell them now.'

When Muriel came round she was neatly tucked up in bed with Ralph sitting beside her holding her hand. Caroline was there too and they both sighed with relief when she spoke.

'Sharon – I heard her scream. Is she all right? That poor girl.'

'Don't you worry about her, Muriel. Let's be thankful you're OK.'

'She died, didn't she? *Didn't she?*'

'Yes, I'm afraid she did. She saw the police waiting for her and she was so startled she slipped and fell on a knife she was carrying. She died almost instantly.'

'Can I have a drink of water, please, Ralph? I'm so terribly thirsty.'

Caroline supported her head while Ralph held the glass for her. She took a few sips and then lay down again.

'You understood then what I meant about *The Waiting Game.*'

'It took me a while but in the end I did. You've been very brave, Muriel . . .'

'You've called me Muriel. You must be growing up.' She smiled.

'And you've called me Ralph.'

'So I have.'

'The police will need to see you when you feel better.'

'Sharon made Mrs Palmer kill herself and then she killed Toria Clark. And it was Sharon who set fire to number three. It's perhaps as well she's died, she couldn't face being locked up. She was only a little girl really, you know. She needed an awful lot of love and she felt she never got it from anyone. I felt quite sorry for her when she left.'

Caroline said gently, 'That's because you have a very kind heart, isn't it, Ralph? Harriet is devastated that she didn't cotton on.'

'She couldn't help it. Sharon said I was a good actress. It wasn't Harriet's fault.'

A nurse came bustling in. 'Message for Dr Harris. Ah, there you are. You're needed in Maternity as soon as you can make it, Doctor.'

'Oh, am I? Right, well, I'll come then. Bye bye, Muriel. I'll leave Ralph to take care of you. Perhaps I could pop in to see you tomorrow if you're still here?'

'Of course, Caroline. Thank you for coming.'

Caroline arrived in Maternity, puzzled about why she should be required.

'Good evening, Sister. You've sent for me?'

'Yes. Mrs Suzy Meadows from Turnham Malpas has insisted we inform you she's been brought in. She says you're a friend.'

'That's right, I am. Ah, the twins are on their way then? Will it be in order for me to be here? Her husband has died and she did say would I be here to support her, purely as a friend.'

'Of course, as a friend. I appreciate you asking my permission.'

Suzy lay in bed pale and anxious.

'Oh, Caroline, you've come – I'm so glad. What's all this about Muriel and Sharon McDonald? I saw the police about during the afternoon but I wasn't feeling up to going out to find out why and then Mother arrived and I came straight in.'

'At the moment it's nothing for you to worry about, but Muriel is quite safe and they're taking care of Sharon. This is earlier than expected, isn't it?'

'Yes, but I'm glad, I couldn't have coped much longer. I do not want to see the babies at all. I shall have my eyes closed and don't let them give them to me, please. You take them. Promise me, will you promise me?'

'Suzy, I shall quite understand if, when it comes to it, you want to keep them.'

'I don't. Oh, please, you mustn't let me weaken. I mustn't weaken. I don't want them, but I'm not strong enough to see them and hold them and then not want them. Tell the Sister, please. Tell her that you're looking after them, not me.'

Suzy closed her eyes and began breathing steadily. She drew a self-imposed wall around herself and concentrated on giving birth and getting it over with. Caroline felt excluded. She went in search of Sister.

'It's all most irregular,' the woman frowned, 'but of course there is no law which says a mother has to love and want her babies. If she is getting them adopted then I can quite understand her not wanting to see them: she's too vulnerable at the moment to be emotionally strong. But it's preferable for the babies to relate to someone immediately. That's how I like to work. It's not only the mothers who have rights, you know. Babies are not parcels.'

'Well, that person is me. She wants my husband and me to adopt the twins and has been making arrangements with that in mind.'

'I see, you and the rector. Well, highly suitable parents I must say. What does your husband think about this?'

'He is delighted. We can't have children of our own, you see.'

'Proper arrangements must be made before the babies are allowed out of the hospital. I can't let them go off willy-nilly with anyone.'

'Of course not.'

Peter sounded anxious when he answered the phone. 'My darling girl, where are you?'

'Sorry, Peter, I learnt about Muriel and Sharon before I left so I've been to reassure myself Muriel's OK, so if anyone asks you can tell them she's conscious and quite unharmed apart from shock. But Suzy has been brought in in labour so she wants me to stay here till the twins are born. Darling, I'm terrified.'

'Oh God, this is it then. Shall I come to the hospital?'

There was a pause and then Caroline said, 'I don't think so, do you? It wouldn't look right somehow. Look, I'll ring as soon as there's any news. Do you love me?'

'You know I do. Take the greatest care, my darling, and keep a rein on yourself. There's always a risk, you know. I don't want you to be heartbroken.'

'I know, I know. I am trying hard to be sensible. I won't leave the hospital without ringing you so take the phone to bed, won't you?'

Peter went into the church. It was about eight o'clock. He stood in the darkness before the altar. His tall figure, topped by his thick, bright-bronze hair, was quite motionless. In the darkness his black cassock made him almost disappear as though only his head was present. Inside he was in turmoil. This day perhaps or at least within a few hours his children, please God, would be born safe and well. He daren't let Caroline know what it meant to him. All these weeks he had been trying to play the role of bystander, the cautionary man, the detached onlooker, when all the time these new powerful emotions were coursing through him. His gut reaction, his primitive instincts were that of pride that he had reproduced, that his bloodline would continue. He knew now what was meant by the words 'my own flesh and blood'. To hold in one's arms the product of oneself must be an unbelievable experience and one for which he was not altogether sure he was equipped.

He knelt before God and prayed, for forgiveness for his sin, for the life of his children, and for the life of their mother. He prayed for his darling Caroline and the wonderful way in which she had decided to take his children into her care. Then he rose from his knees, bowed his head and went across to the organ, where he began playing a sad piece by some obscure seventeenth-century composer that exactly fitted his mood. The music poured from his soul and he concluded with a triumphant Bach Fugue.

As the last note finished he heard someone clapping.

'Wonderful, wonderful. You should have been a musician, not a clergyman. You played from the heart, Peter.'

Ralph stepped forward into the light.

Peter, in a strange mood and not welcoming company, switched off the organ, swung his legs over the organ seat and went towards Ralph.

'I didn't realise I had an audience,' he said quietly. 'How is Muriel?'

'Very well, all things considered. She's had a dreadful time. I'm sorry Sharon has died, but there couldn't have been anything other than a bad end for the girl. Have you seen her parents?'

'Yes. I spent half an hour with them. Betty is distraught but Mac is fairly calm. What a terrible thing for a parent to have to face.'

'Well, that's something we aren't likely to know anything about – not me, certainly. Bit late now.'

'That's right. What's the time?'

'Half-past nine.'

'I'd better get back to the Rectory. I'm expecting a call.'

'Good night, Peter. What an eventful life I've led since I came back here. I thought it would be peaceful in Turnham Malpas. Some chance of that.'

'Too true. Good night then, Ralph. You know you and Muriel could be very happy together.'

'Perhaps. We'll see, we'll see.'

The phone went at 1 a.m.

'Hello, Peter. You're a daddy. Peter, are you there?'

'Yes, I am.'

'They're both fine, a bit small but both fine.'

'I see. I see.'

'Peter, you sound funny.'

'No, I'm not. What are they?'

'A perfect family – a boy and a girl.'

'That's wonderful. Are you all right?'

'I'm in seventh heaven.'

'Is . . . is Suzy . . . ?'

'Yes, she's fine. She's very upset but still determined that she doesn't want the babies.'

'I see. That's good, isn't it? Are you coming home now?'

'In about an hour, when the babies have been weighed and washed and everything. I held them as soon as they were born. They are beautiful, just beautiful. Wait till you see them. You could come tomorrow, couldn't you?'

'I can't wait.'

When he held Alexander and Elizabeth in his arms, Peter had tears in his eyes. His own two, very own two children. He'd thought that joy like this would never be his and yet here he was. Caroline stood looking down at him. He glanced up at her and smiled.

'Aren't they beautiful, my darling?'

'Absolutely. We are blessed.'

'We are indeed. God be praised. Caroline, my darling girl, thank you from the bottom of my heart.'

'You've got two darling girls now. Muriel's coming down to see them before she goes home. I couldn't wait to tell someone that they are going to be ours.'

'They seem very tiny.'

'Well, they only weigh just over four pounds each so they won't be coming out until they get a bit bigger.'

The midwife had given Alexander to Caroline as soon as she'd cut the cord. The tiny tiny being lay bawling and squawking in her arms, his weeny arms waving in indignation at the disturbance his birth had caused him. She'd pulled aside the sheet Alexander was wrapped in and examined his ten little toes, touched his minute fingers, admired his fingernails, stroked his wet, blood-streaked hair which looked as though it would be the same colour as Peter's, and noticed how very long he appeared to be, with what seemed like two quite large feet fidgeting away as he cried. She'd smiled to herself. What else could she expect from a baby of Peter's, but long legs and big feet and bright, almost strawberry-blond hair? There was no mistaking whom Alexander belonged to. She laid him in a cot, carefully placing him on his side, and covered him over. When the midwife handed the second baby to her, Caroline found herself holding a neatly made, composed little girl. She'd lain in Caroline's arms stretching and occasionally opening her eyes but mostly preoccupied with sucking her thumb. She had perfect little feet. Elizabeth – that's it. Elizabeth, she'd decided.

Sister interrupted her reverie. 'What a wonderful job you've done, Suzy. Absolutely brilliant. No complications like we'd anticipated, you've been a model patient.'

'I'd like to have the babies taken out, please. Now.'

'Of course. Nurse, jump to it, if you please. Dr Harris? You too – out you go, please.'

Caroline went across to Suzy, bent over her and kissed her and said: 'Thank you from the bottom of my heart. God bless you.'

Suzy nodded as silent tears began trickling down her cheeks. She made agonising choking sounds as she endeavoured to control the pain rising in her chest. All she could think was 'I mustn't weaken, I mustn't weaken.' Surely when she was so positive that she didn't want these children, surely the pain wouldn't last? She mustn't ask what they were. Mustn't ask who they looked like. Treat it like a miscarriage, a late miscarriage – that was it. That was how she'd solve it. She'd go straight to her mother's from the hospital and then there'd be no chance she might see or hear the babies. Twenty-four hours, that was all she'd stay in this place. Mother would see about moving their belongings and selling the house. Then she'd make a new beginning away from memories of Patrick and Peter. A completely new life. Oh God, please take away the pain.

When Muriel came down to the ward to see Alexander and Elizabeth her feelings were confused. Delight for Caroline and Peter. Distress for Suzy. Anticipation at seeing the two tiny babies, and fear of returning to her own home with all the memories of the last forty-eight hours so fresh in her mind.

Peter and Caroline were both there when she walked in. They greeted her and then she walked over to the cots. The shock she received as she leant over Alexander's obliterated her own anxieties, for there, nestled in a hospital shawl, lay an exact replica of Peter. Fond parents go on about how like their father or their mother a baby is, yet no one else can detect much likeness at all. But there was no doubt here. She stood touching his tiny clenched fist and stroking his bright hair whilst she composed herself.

'Why, he's beautiful! So perfect.'

'And this is Elizabeth.'

Muriel bent over the second cot and saw a tiny, perfectly angelic-looking baby sucking her thumb. Her mass of blonde hair and her fair peaches and cream complexion made a beautiful picture and Muriel loved her from that moment. Had Caroline realised how like Peter Alexander was? Muriel raised her eyes from the two cots and looked straight at Caroline. Their eyes met and without speaking Muriel knew she was right. Caroline dropped her gaze to the cots and said, 'Aren't we lucky, Muriel, to have been given these two babies? A family all at one go.'

'Indeed you are. Congratulations.' Muriel kissed Caroline and then turned to Peter.

'Congratulations, Peter. These two children couldn't have hoped for better parents.' She reached up and kissed him. 'If you don't mind, I should like to get home now. Any time you need a babysitter, just ask me. I shall be delighted. I don't feel up to seeing Suzy yet, but she does need support so you won't forget her, will you?'

'No, of course not. Thank you.' Caroline patted her arm and saw her out of the nursery.

When she'd gone Peter and Caroline stood holding hands looking down at their children.

'Mr Harris, I think that Suzy's parish priest should go to see her. It's only right.'

Peter took his hand from Caroline's and said, 'Yes, of course. Are you coming with me?'

'No.'

Peter knocked on the door of Suzy's private room. She'd been put in there in preference to the general ward. Sister had insisted on that in the circumstances.

'Come in.'

He felt as if his entrails were being burned before his very eyes; he deserved it too.

'Good morning, Suzy. May I come in for a minute?'

'Of course, Peter, find yourself a chair. If you've come to tell me how grateful you are, and what a heel you feel, and is this really what I want, because you would quite understand and so would Caroline if I changed my mind, don't bother.'

'I won't, then.'

'Good. What I don't need is sympathy. I intended being out of here tonight but I've got a slight infection and Sister refuses to let me go home. Well, I'm not going home, I'm going to Mother's – and I never want to hear the words Turnham Malpas ever again. It has been a disaster for me from the word go. Is Muriel all right?'

'Yes. She's just been to see— She left hospital this morning.'

'Poor Muriel. I would love to know whether or not she marries Ralph, but that's something I shall have to speculate on because I never want to hear another thing about the village.'

'I can understand you wanting to sever your ties. How are you of yourself?'

'Better than can be expected, in the circumstances. Take hold of my hand. Don't worry, I'm not going to go all sugary and weepy. Peter, I won't be putting Patrick's name on the birth certificate – that wouldn't be right. I'm putting yours on, you are their father after all. When they are old enough you will be truthful to them, won't you? Don't deceive them. Children can't cope with parents who lie, they see it as a betrayal. Will you give me your blessing and then go?'

'Of course.' Peter stood with his head bowed for a moment. 'Dear Father God, bless this precious child of Yours, standing at the crossroads of her life. Take her into Your loving care and watch over her in the task she has set herself. Bless her little girls, Daisy, Pansy and Rosie, ensure that they will be a joy to her throughout their lives. Bless her for her generosity of spirit, her courage, and her moral strength. Make Your face to shine upon her and give her Your peace. Amen. May God bless you, Suzy.'

'Take care of them for me, won't you? Go now while my eyes are shut.'

'Thank you, Suzy, for your blessed gift.'

Peter bent over, kissed Suzy's forehead and left.

23

The village bubbled with the news of Suzy's twins going to the Rectory.

Pat Duckett treated Michael Palmer to one of her monologues the first morning he was back at school.

'The rector and the doctor will be delighted. Only right, too. How could Suzy Meadows feed and clothe all them children? Very sensible. Funny her not coming back to empty her house, though. Still, what with Mr Meadows committing suicide and then the twins being born, 'spect you can understand. The twins might be home by Christmas, so I hear. Mighty busy Christmas Rector'll have. Busiest he's had for some time, I reckon. Dr Harris should know how to manage, I daresay. Plenty of offers for babysitting they'll be having, mind. Alexander Peter and Elizabeth Caroline – nice names they are. Going to call 'em Alex and Beth, apparently. Old-fashioned, but nice. You glad to be back, Mr Palmer?'

'I am indeed, Mrs Duckett. The school seems to have managed very nicely without me, though.'

'Don't you believe it. Oh, nothing's gone wrong, it's just that something was missing and it was you. That Mrs Hardaker, hard by name and hard by nature she is. Told me off good and proper about the boys' lavatories. I said, if you can kill that smell then you go right ahead and do it. I does my best, Mr Palmer, but that smell won't go. I reckon the drains isn't right. Shall we report it to the Office?'

'I'll check them out myself and see what I think. Isn't it a lovely morning, Mrs Duckett? Nearly Christmas but quite mild still.'

'Muriel Hipkin's gone back to her house, yer know. Never thought she would. Thought she'd be living it up at Sir Ralph's. He asked her but she put her foot down and said it wouldn't be right. I ask yer, at their age. Makes yer laugh. They're not likely to get up to anything, are they?'

'I wouldn't know, Mrs Duckett. I'll go and tackle the boys' lavatories, while you get done in here. The children, the best people of all, will be in soon.'

'Don't know about best people of all, they makes a lot of work.'

'Children are the whole reason for the school's existence. Remember that.'

He went off whistling to his appointed task. Life felt a great deal better than it had done for years. A whole load had lifted off his shoulders. Sad that it had taken Sharon's death to do it, but there you were.

When he went to his house at lunch-time there was a letter on the mat. He didn't recognise the handwriting, so when he slit it open he looked first at the signature. Marjorie Vickerman. Who on earth was she? He went back to the beginning of the letter and read,

> 'Dear Mr Palmer, I know you will wonder who this is writing to you, but I am Suzy Meadows' mother. I feel very upset that Suzy wishes to cut all ties with the village. People have been extremely kind and helpful to her and you especially. She loved being with you in the school because, as I am sure you realised, she is a born teacher. She is at home with me now and will be for some time. She is going to apply for teaching jobs shortly. Her address certainly for the next year will be 24, Little Orchards Lane, Beckhampton, Nr Gloucester, GL14 9PJ.
>
> 'I can't help but feel very sad that I shall never know what happens to her and Patrick's twins and I would be so grateful if from time to time you could let me know. I am a loving grandmother, you see. DON'T write to Suzy, write to me at the address above. Many thanks for your kindness to her. Yours sincerely.'

His heart skipped and danced. He was glad he'd not lost contact with her. She must be heartbroken, giving her babies away like that. Poor girl. He could see in his mind's eye her charming round face and her long silvery-blonde hair. She was small in stature but big in personality and in heart. They'd had some good talks when she'd been leading the playgroup. Real communications, not simply talk.

After lunch he was launching himself into football practice when he saw Betty McDonald coming through the school gate. Oh no, not just now, Betty.

'Good afternoon, Mrs McDonald. Keep going, boys, I'll be back. Come into my office, won't you?'

He propped himself on the edge of the desk and waited for Betty to speak.

'I've come to tell you our Scott will be leaving school soon. We're moving. It won't be for a month or two but move we must. Our Scott and Mac can't stand it here any more so we're off to make a fresh start. Thought I'd better let you know. Sorry you've had all this trouble. She was a bad girl, was our Sharon, and we didn't help. But there we are, it's too late now. Thank you, Mr Palmer, for all you've done.'

'Mrs McDonald, I've only done what a good schoolmaster should have done. Your Scott is a very clever boy, you know, if he'd only let himself do some work. He is actually university material – I don't know if you realised that? With encouragement from you, he'll make it, believe me. Thank you for coming to tell me.'

Betty stood up. Michael opened the office door for her and she went out. He watched her walk across the playground between the footballers, looking like someone who, as his mother would have said, had had the stuffing knocked out of her. The edifice she called hair was not so high, her shoulders were slumped and she'd definitely lost weight.

'Right, where's that goalie? Watch out then, here I come down the right wing. And here we go – and it's a goal!'

'Cor, Mr Palmer, that was a good 'un!'

Muriel stood leaning on the school wall watching the boys. She applauded Michael's goal and then carried on behind the chapel towards Turnham Beck.

Pericles scampered about as though he'd never been there before. He was ten now and still full of life. What a dear little friend he was. She must keep an eye on the time, Ralph was coming for her to go Christmas shopping in Culworth. Not that either he or she had much to shop for. She'd buy something for Suzy's twins. Oh dear, she must stop thinking that. *Caroline's* twins, and a nice gift for Peter and Caroline. How on earth had that strange situation come about? Suzy and Peter, and there stood Caroline knowing all about it. Muriel knew she knew, even though Caroline had said nothing. 'If I know,' Muriel mused, 'how about everyone else? Surely they'll notice?' They were beautiful babies though, and Caroline had got her heart's desire. So had Peter, come to that.

Pericles needed a new basket. What on earth could she buy for Ralph? He had enough money to buy anything he wanted. 'Only one hour to go and he'll be here,' she hummed to herself. 'I can't wait. He's so lovely. Such good fun and so charming and well-mannered. I can hide behind his *savoir faire* wherever we go. He knows exactly what to do. I do wish I had better clothes, though. It isn't that I don't know what is good taste, it's that I can't afford it.' She turned for home.

'Come, Pericles. This way.' Out of the bushes ran Lady Bissett's

Pomeranian. 'Oh, hello, PomPom, where's you master? That will do, Pericles, don't be so silly. Calm down now, you're upsetting PomPom. Oh, hello, Sir Ronald, lovely day, isn't it?'

'It is indeed. Not going away again, are you, Muriel?'

'No, why?'

'Well, your Pericles and our PomPom get on like a house on fire. When Pericles isn't there, we've all on to get PomPom out of his basket, but when they're together they race about all day long.'

'Well, not for a while that I know of. I did appreciate you having Pericles for me when I went to Rome; it was a relief to know he didn't have to go into kennels. Any time you and Lady Bissett want to go away I would gladly have PomPom for you.'

'Thank you very much. I keep hoping you might be going away on a honeymoon.'

Muriel blushed. 'I really don't think so. We're quite simply old friends from the past – there's nothing like that in it.'

'If he asks you, you accept. What's the point of not taking hold of life and getting on with it? You can be too retiring and then spend your last years regretting it. Don't let opportunities pass you by, remember that.'

He raised his tweed hat to her as they parted. How dare that man advise her what to do!

Ralph arrived on the dot, eager to be off. Muriel put on her new winter coat, well, it was three years old but it was her newest. The Mercedes had been polished to within an inch of its life and Ralph looked particularly sparkling. They drove to Culworth and started their shopping by having an early lunch.

Ralph had kissed her in the car before they set off. He kissed her when they parked in the multi-storey car park and held her arm tightly as they crossed the road. Muriel's heart began doing head-over-heels. She felt most odd.

He'd emptied the last drops from their bottle of wine when he said: 'Muriel, I have something special I want to say. You don't have to answer me now if you don't want to, but please give it your utmost consideration.'

She mopped her mouth with her napkin and paid attention.

'I want to know if you would like to visit Australia with me.'

'Australia?'

'Yes, but not as my companion, like when we went to Rome. As my wife.'

Muriel clasped her hands together on her lap to stop them shaking. 'I . . .'

'Don't answer yet, think about it. I have various friends in Australia and they have suggested I go out there in the spring and visit them and I thought it would be nice, well absolutely perfect, if I could tell them that my wife would be coming, too. I don't want to rush you. I want you to give it your utmost consideration.'

'I see.'

'Muriel, I hope I haven't rushed my fences.'

'No you haven't, and I am very honoured that you should want to marry me. It's just that . . .'

'What?'

'When I retired I made up my mind that I was quite satisfied with living on my own. I had had years of caring for Mother and being at her beck and call night and day. When I got my own house it meant I could do exactly what I liked when I liked and furnish my home as I wanted it, not as someone else had chosen. I don't know if I can give up that freedom. I've got my life nicely sorted out and I don't think I want to change it. Don't think I haven't thought about what it would be like being married to you, because I have.'

'I see.' Ralph took a long sip of his wine and sat staring into his glass.

'I enjoy your company so much. I can't imagine what it would be like not to see you and go out with you, but that's as far as I want it to go. I'm very sorry. It's not you, it's the whole idea.'

'You mean the whole idea of being truly married?'

'Yes, I think so. Oh dear, I'm not doing very well here, am I? I'm so sorry.' Muriel got out her handkerchief and dabbed at her eyes.

Ralph still sat staring at his wine. He looked up from his glass.

'I thought, you see, we would be able to make a go of it. Marriage for companionship's sake isn't actually marriage at all, you know. It's simply a piece of paper. That's not for me, Muriel – it's all or nothing. I'm sorry I have embarrassed you by jumping the gun. Shall we go?'

They sat in silence all the way back to Turnham Malpas, Muriel staring fixedly out of the window, wishing she could bring herself to say yes. But there was no two ways about it: she couldn't bring herself to think about being in bed with him. Going out and enjoying a little kiss now and again, or going on holiday as companions was fine but that final commitment . . . No. No. No! That was the truth of it – it wasn't because she preferred to live on her own, she didn't, not any more. She couldn't face up to being 'married'. If she made a list when she got home of the pros and cons of marriage she wondered how many points there would be on each side. Muriel glanced at Ralph's profile as he drove. It was a handsome one, but there was no way she could wake up each morning to find that profile laid at the side of her. Imagine actually getting into the same bed! She preferred her neat white single bed in her neat and tidy room in her neat and tidy cottage. No, she'd done the right thing. It was only fair to be truthful and refuse straight away.

Ralph parked the Mercedes outside Glebe Cottages. He got out and went round to open Muriel's door. She stepped out of the car and led the way to her front door expecting that Ralph was following as usual. But he wasn't.

'Aren't you coming in, Ralph?'

He was standing halfway between the car and the front door. She went back down the path and stood beside him.

'God, what a mess, Muriel. I won't come in, thank you. I'll be in touch.' He spun on his heel and went straight back to the car. She stood watching him drive away, expecting he would turn round and head for his own house down Church Lane, but he didn't. He drove off in the direction of Penny Fawcett. What was he doing? Didn't he know where he lived? She worried about him all evening and wished she'd had more sense and insisted that he came in. When she took Pericles for his evening walk she deliberately went past Ralph's house. There were no lights on so he must have either gone to bed early or not yet got home.

The following morning she found a note from Ralph in her letterbox.

> 'Dear Muriel, After your refusal yesterday I have decided we both need time to ourselves, so I am going abroad for a while – at least for a month. After that my plans are vague. I may go to Australia during the summer as I have lots of friends there whom I would like to visit, as I told you. Take care. Ralph.'

She burst into tears. Hot scalding tears ran down her cheeks and fell into her lap. She hadn't cried with such abandon since her childhood. Like Ralph had said, what a mess. What a stupid, blindingly disastrous mess. She rushed up her little spiral staircase and into the bathroom, turned on the cold tap and splashed her face time and again with the torrents of cold water till her hands and face were numb. Then she dried her face and the edges of her hair where the water had caught it. She combed it vigorously with no attention to style, ran downstairs, pushed Pericles out of the way and fled down Church Lane to Ralph's house. It was all locked up. She was already too late. He'd gone. She couldn't even wish him a good holiday or offer to water his plants or anything. He wouldn't be home for Christmas and that nice little surprise she'd had of inviting him for Christmas dinner wouldn't materialise.

24

A few days later, Caroline called in at St Thomas à Becket.

'Willie, are you there?'

'Yes, Dr Harris, I am.'

'Ah, Willie, have you found my gloves yet?'

'Picked them up this morning. You'd left them in the vestry when you were waiting for the rector to finish. I'll get them for you.' Willie's cassock beat a rhythmic tattoo as he strode briskly down the aisle into the vestry.

'Here we are, Doctor. Safe and sound.'

'Thank you, they are my favourite pair.'

'Will you be having the twins home for Christmas, do you think?'

'Well, I think it's going to be after Christmas now. They've been slow at putting weight on and the hospital want to be sure they're thriving before I get them home. Inexperienced as I am, I'm quite glad in a way, though the rector would have loved to have them home for Christmas, whatever weight they were.'

'Never mind, you have the rest of their lives to enjoy them. By this time next year they'll be running around and wearing you out!'

'Heavens, Willie, of course you're quite right, they will be!'

As Caroline headed for the door she saw Muriel polishing the brasses.

'Hello, Muriel. Soon be Christmas. Have you got your Christmas shopping done?'

'Yes.'

'I'm off to the hospital this afternoon to sit with the twins and give them their feed. I'm getting quite nervous about looking after them all by myself. Still, I can't wait to get them home.'

Muriel sat back on her heels and looked up at Caroline. 'You've taken hold of life and got on with it, haven't you?'

'What do you mean?'

'You knew those babies were Peter's, didn't you, and yet you decided to take them into your home for his sake.'

Caroline sat down with a thump on the pew nearest to Muriel.

'I realised you'd guessed when you saw them in the hospital. I love Peter more than life itself. It took a great deal of agonising on my part before I could cope with what had happened, and then when I got the idea of adopting the twins it seemed to put everything right.'

'That takes courage and that's what I haven't got.'

'What do you mean? Is there something the matter?'

Muriel put down her dusters and sat on the pew next to Caroline. 'Have you noticed that Ralph isn't home at the moment?'

'No, I hadn't. Where's he gone?'

'I don't know.' Muriel got out her handkerchief, blew her nose and took a deep breath. 'You see, he asked me to marry him and I said no. I didn't even say I would think about it. I said no. Unequivocally, no.'

'Ah, and now you wish you'd said yes?'

'No, well, I don't know! He's gone away and won't be back until after Christmas. He put a note through my door. I ran round to his house but he'd already gone, so I couldn't even say goodbye or anything.'

'Oh, Muriel, he must have been very upset.'

'He was. You see, I made the excuse that I'm perfectly satisfied with my life as it is. Now he's gone I'm not so sure.'

'It's being actually married that's your problem, isn't it?'

'To be honest, yes. I've been a spinster for sixty-four years. It's such an invasion of one's privacy sharing a house and a . . . a bed.'

'I'm sure that such a well-travelled man has had plenty of experience. I'm absolutely certain that Ralph would be the most wonderfully considerate lover.'

'Lover? Oh dear. Oh dear.' Muriel got out her handkerchief and blew her nose again to cover her confusion.

'Isn't that what you mean?'

'Yes, I suppose so. It's a big step, isn't it, at my age? He has had experience – he's told me that.'

'Well, there you are, then – and being married to him would make your life so exciting. All that foreign travel and that nice house he's bought and all his money. You would have a wonderful life, so rich and full. Think hard about your decision, Muriel. Life can be very lonely in old age.'

'It's lonely now with him away. He may never ask me again.'

'Perhaps you'll have to orchestrate that yourself.' Caroline stood up, patted Muriel's hand and bent over and kissed her. 'Come for dinner on

Christmas Day. It may be my last dignified Christmas dinner for years – thank goodness!'

When Caroline got back to the Rectory she found Peter checking his action list for the midnight service.

'Peter, I feel as if I have lived a thousand years since last Christmas.'

'We have come a long way since then. Are you happy, my darling girl?'

'I am indeed. I thought I would miss being a doctor but I don't. I simply can't wait for the twins to come home.'

Peter reached his hand out towards her and pulled her on to his knee. 'This Christmas Service is going to be the best they've ever had. Ralph has bought all the boys new surplices and Sheila Bissett has massive plans for decorating the church and Mrs Peel is practising like mad for the big day. Things have improved, haven't they?'

'They have and all thanks to you. I've invited Muriel for dinner on Christmas Day. Ralph has gone off into the wild blue yonder and won't be back until after Christmas and Muriel's upset because she's to blame.'

'Why, what's Muriel done?'

'Refused to marry him.'

'Oh dear, what a lot she's missing.'

'That's what I told her.'

Muriel was getting ready for the Christmas Eve service in the church. There'd been rather a lot of secret meetings and enigmatic smiles from people about this service but she'd been so obsessed by the dilemma of Ralph and his disappearance that she'd been too self-absorbed to take much notice. She did know that Peter had completely transformed the whole concept of the midnight service and she was looking forward to it. Last Christmas Eve she'd been getting ready to listen to one of Mr Furbank's lacklustre sermons. Well, she didn't think they were at the time but when she looked back she had to admit that was exactly what they were. Heavens above, if she'd married Mr Furbank, oh dear, oh dear, what a tepid life she would have lived!

She got out her new coat: a warm wine red, with a thick black fur collar and a matching black fur hat. Not real fur, of course, she wouldn't have liked that. Her new black court shoes pinched a little but they would soon get better when she'd worn them a few times. Her pride was the beautiful black leather handbag Ralph had brought her back from London. It had clasps and pockets and zips all over the place and in it she put a clean handkerchief and her purse. She drew on her new black leather gloves.

When she looked at herself in the mirror she wished Ralph had been coming to collect her and they could have walked to the church together and sat side by side and had Christmas dinner to look forward to. She'd had long days and nights to think about her decision. She was much nearer saying yes than she had been when he'd first proposed, but now of course she had missed her chance. Sometimes she had to admit she stood back from life far too much and she ought to grasp chances with both hands. Maybe that dreadful Ronald Bissett was right. She realised she was ready about half an hour too soon. Would she never learn! She sat down to read the paper for a while.

She glanced at the clock. Mother's clock. Whatever would she have said if she'd been here? She'd have said, '*No!* At your age, you stupid girl? And what about me? How would *I* manage?'

That could have been one very good reason for saying yes.

The phone interrupted her thoughts. Oh no, she'd never get used to answering the phone. Ralph had insisted she had one, bu she knew hardly anyone who would ring her anyway. Who on earth could it be at this time of night?

'Hello, it's Turnham Malpas 23235 here.'

'Muriel? It's Ralph.'

'Ralph? Oh, Ralph, you've just caught me. I'm getting ready to leave for the midnight service. Where are you?'

'In Singapore.'

'Singapore, oh my word. How are you?'

'Not nearly as well as I should like. How are you, my dear?'

'Not nearly as well as I should like.'

'I see. What are you doing tomorrow?'

'I'm having dinner at Caroline and Peter's. What will you be doing?'

'I'm about to have my Christmas morning breakfast. I've been awake a long time in the night thinking about the village and what you'd all be doing. I should never have gone away so abruptly.'

'I've bought you a little present for when you get back.'

'Thank you, Muriel. I might decide to go home earlier than I planned.'

'That would be nice, Ralph.'

'Would it?'

'Yes, it would. I should enjoy seeing you back again.'

'Good, so be it. Happy Christmas, my dear.'

'And to you, Ralph. Bye bye.'

'I won't say goodbye. I'll say, see you soon. Sleep well, my dear, and give everyone Christmas greetings from me.'

The phone went dead. Muriel snatched up her bag and gloves, patted

Pericles on his head, slammed the front door shut and raced with a glad heart to the church.

She stood in the doorway full of surprised delight. St Thomas à Becket had been transformed. In every window were huge, bright-red candles burning; at the foot of each candle were circular arrangements of holly and fir cones. Each of the stone columns supporting the roof had a necklace of ivy and artificial poinsettias around the top, and trailing downwards were long strands of ivy interspersed with shiny red curls of holly-red ribbon. The altar was ablaze with red candles and at the front stood two beautiful flower displays made up with the blooms Willie had got from the hothouses at the Big House. At the foot of the lectern a marvellous artificial display of poinsettias and Christmas roses and holly had been placed, with red ribbons looping their way to the floor from the top of it. Standing to one side was a beautiful Nativity scene – not one of those tinsely things one saw in shop windows, but splendid carved creatures and lovely painted figures of Mary and Joseph. Even the font had not been forgotten: it had pure white ribbons and small white chrysanthemums in a kind of crown around the top, with a large fat white candle in the centre illuminating the display. Over all was the faint smell of frankincense. All the lights had been turned out so that the church was lit only by the candlelight. Mrs Peel was playing completely new pieces and putting her heart and soul into it, quite different from her normal mechanical playing.

Harriet and Jimbo were there with the three children, and Sir Ronald and Lady Bissett, she dressed in her rather alarming leopardskin coat, he in his usual tweeds. Even Jimmy Glover had come and he was wearing a new suit. What had come over everyone? How lovely the church was and full to overflowing, too. Willie had to bring some extra chairs in from the Sunday School. When was the last time we had to do that? Muriel thought.

The organ rose to a crescendo. The choir processed down the aisle looking extremely pleased with themselves, for they were wearing their brand-new bright-red cassocks and new surplices with stiff white ruffs around their necks, which transformed a raggle taggle group into angels. Peter was smiling triumphantly at his flock. They all sang the first carol: 'All my heart this night rejoices'.

She caught Caroline's eye and they both smiled.

Talk of the Village

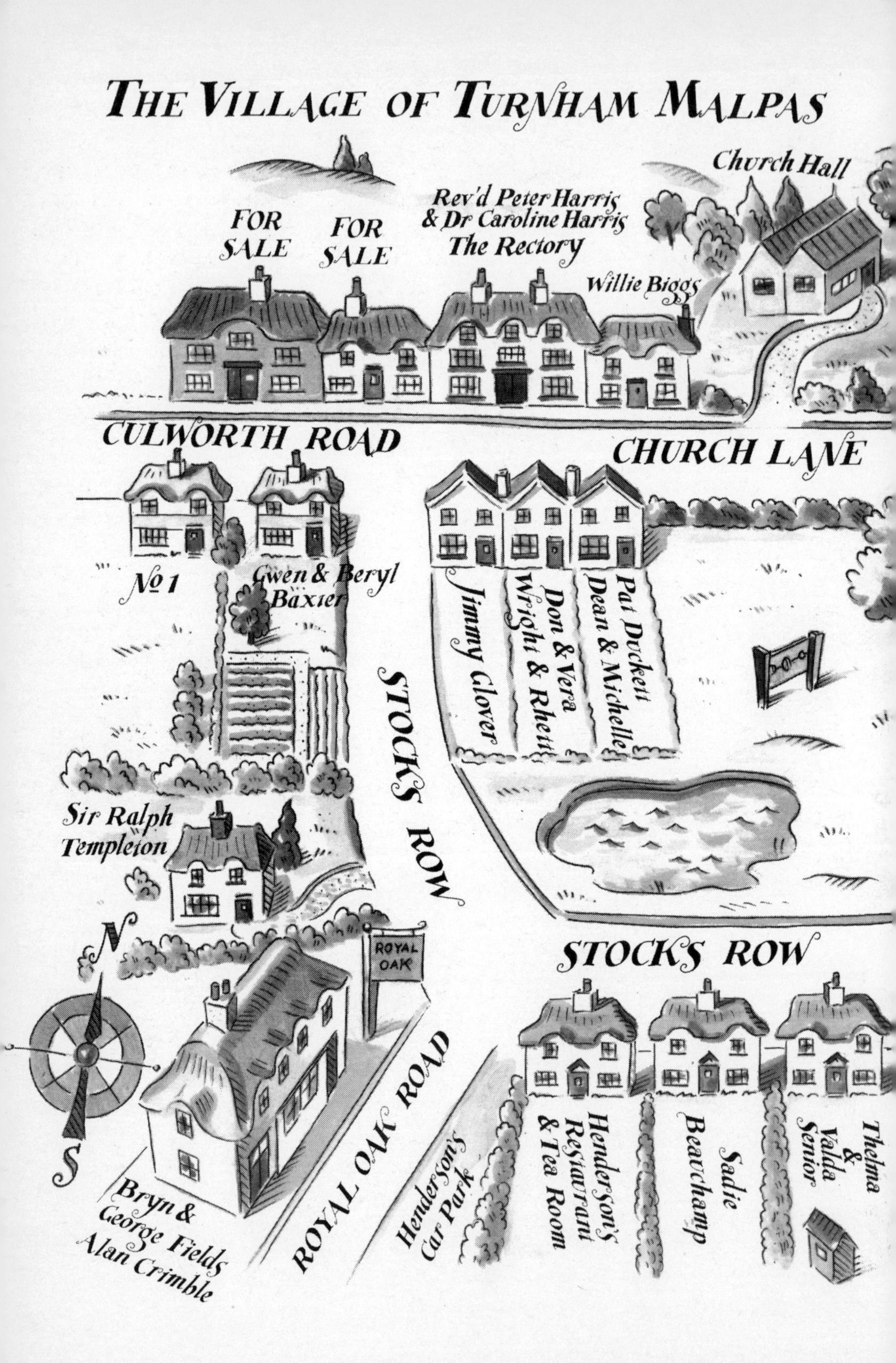
THE VILLAGE OF TURNHAM MALPAS
FOR SALE
FOR SALE
Rev'd Peter Harris & Dr Caroline Harris The Rectory
Church Hall
Willie Biggs
CULWORTH ROAD
CHURCH LANE
No 1
Gwen & Beryl Baxter
Jimmy Glover
Don & Vera Wright & Rhett
Pat Duckett Dean & Michelle
STOCKS ROW
Sir Ralph Templeton
N
S
ROYAL OAK
STOCKS ROW
ROYAL OAK ROAD
Bryn & George Fields Alan Crimble
Henderson's Car Park
Henderson's Restaurant & Tea Room
Sadie Beauchamp
Thelma & Valda Senior

St Thomas à Becket
Muriel Hipkin
Anne Parkin
Liz & Neville Neal
Guy & Hugh
GLEBE COTTAGES
GLEBE HOUSE
CHURCH LANE
Village Store
Jimbo & Harriet Charter-Plackett
Fergus, Finlay & Flick
JACKS LANE
School House
Michael Palmer
STOCKS ROW
Swimming Pool
Turnham Malpas School
SHEPHERDS HILL
Methodist Chapel
FD'01
Sir Ronald & Lady Bissett
pond
SPARE LAND
BECK
TURNHAM
footbridge

Inhabitants of Turnham Malpas

Gwen Baxter	A spinster of the parish.
Beryl Baxter	Her twin sister.
Sadie Beauchamp	Retired widow and mother of Harriet Charter-Plackett.
Sylvia Bennett	A villager from Penny Fawcett.
Willie Biggs	Verger at St Thomas à Becket.
Sir Ronald Bissett	Retired trades union leader.
Lady Sheila Bissett	His wife.
James Charter-Plackett	Owner of the village store.
Harriet Charter-Plackett	His wife.
Fergus, Finlay and Flick	Their children.
Alan Crimble	Barman at The Royal Oak.
Pat Duckett	Village school caretaker.
Dean and Michelle	Her children.
Bryn Fields	New licensee at The Royal Oak.
Georgie Fields	His wife.
Jimmy Glover	Poacher and ne'er-do-well.
Revd Peter Harris MA (Oxon)	Rector of the parish.
Dr Caroline Harris	His wife.
Muriel Hipkin	Retired solicitor's secretary. Spinster of the parish.
Jeremy Mayer	Owner of Turnham House Health Club.
Venetia Mayer	Co-owner of the Health Club.
Michael Palmer	Village school headmaster.
Sir Ralph Templeton	Retired from the Diplomatic Service.
Vera Wright	Cleaner at the nursing home in Penny Fawcett.
Don Wright	Her husband.

1

Praise be! Ralph had come home at last. Muriel stood gazing up at his bedroom window, Pericles beside her on his lead impatiently awaiting his morning run. The bedroom curtains were closed, so he was still in bed. She'd checked his house every morning for the last five days and now her vigil had been rewarded. Muriel glanced at her watch, a quarter to nine. She'd take Pericles for his usual walk and then when she'd dried his feet and shut him in the house, a visit to the Store would be next on her agenda. A nice home-made cheese cake, some fresh rolls, with some of Jimbo's special oak smoked ham on the bone would make a nice lunch for her and Ralph.

As Muriel gazed up at Ralph's bedroom window she felt an unexpected surge of excitement. It filled her heart and spread all over her. Suddenly she wanted Ralph's arms around her and thought it would be the best thing that had ever happened. So reassuring, so comforting, so right, yes, that was it, so right for her and for him too, she hoped. Muriel tried to imagine what Ralph's face looked like, but the image of it had almost disappeared from her memory. Surely that couldn't happen in one month. Then the clean sharp smell of his after shave seemed to envelope her and with it his face and the whole feel of him came back to her. He was the first man, no, the first person she had wanted to be close to in all her life. How could she have said no so emphatically. This business of not knowing her own mind would have to stop. Sometimes she really was a fool.

Pericles, bored with waiting, lay down on the pavement. Muriel felt the pull of the lead and looked down at him. 'Ralph's back Perry, isn't that lovely? Come along let's be off. Quickly now, no time for lying down.' Pericles stood up and shook himself, but the red wool coat he wore stopped it from being the refreshing activity he had hoped for. He trotted after Muriel pleased that her dilly-dallying was over.

As they walked past the Store, Jimbo came out to inspect his window display.

He raised his straw boater. 'Good morning Muriel. How's things?'

'Very well thank you, Jimbo. Isn't it a lovely day?'

'It is indeed. You seem very chipper this morning, looking forward to the New Year Party?'

'New Year . . . oh yes, that's right, I am. I'll be in later.' She left Jimbo still assessing his new display. Harriet came out to join him.

Harriet tucked her arm in his. 'Darling, I really think you've done the best display ever. I like the way you've tilted that basket with the dried flowers, and the way you've stacked the cheeses, kind of haphazard but planned if you get my meaning. Very effective.' She peered closely at the flower arrangement. 'I seem to recognise those dried poppy seed heads. Jimbo! They're from my display on the landing, it will be ruined now. Really. The corn dollies are a nice touch, bit out of season but appropriate.'

'Considering I was in a merchant bank a little more than three years ago plaiting nothing but paper, I've got quite good at this window lark haven't I?'

'Well, if this doesn't sell off the Christmas cheeses I don't know what will. We'll do a tasting shall we?'

'Why not? Organise it if you please.'

'Certainly sir. Oh there's Linda. 'Morning Linda.'

Linda waved to the two of them. Jimbo with his striped apron, his white shirt and the bow tie matching the ribbon on his straw boater, bowed to her, Harriet in her 'taking out the Range Rover to pick up the fresh supplies from the farms outfit', curtsied and the three of them laughed.

Harriet said, 'They're queueing for their pensions already Linda.'

'Sorry I'm late.' Linda rushed in to begin the business of the day. Harriet went to start up the Range Rover and Jimbo went inside, well satisfied with having stayed up until twelve the night before to finish the window.

An hour later the door bell jangled and Jimbo looked up from serving a customer to find Ralph had entered the Store. Ralph was thinner, much thinner but tanned, his white hair even whiter if that was possible. But he was looking as aristocratic as ever. His holiday, or whatever it was that had made him disappear so surprisingly, had obviously done him good.

Jimbo went to shake hands with him.

'Delighted to have you back Ralph, we've missed you, specially over Christmas. How are you?'

'Very well, thank you Jimbo. You appear to be in tip top condition. Nothing seems to have changed in my absence.'

Jimbo clapped his hand to his forehead in mock despair. 'I slaved until midnight last night doing that window display and you say nothing has changed!'

'Blame it on jet lag, I've not come round yet.'

'Been somewhere exciting?'

'Visiting friends. I need to shop for my breakfast, Jimbo, I've nothing fresh in at all.'

'Oh, I see . . . didn't Muriel get you anything in?'

'No, she doesn't know I'm back.' Ralph took a basket and began collecting what he needed from the shelves. Jimbo went to serve another customer.

When Ralph went to the cash till to pay for his breakfast Jimbo wished to ask why he had gone off so suddenly, but a tactful phrase simply wouldn't come to mind, so he had to reluctantly open the door for him and wish him good morning. In the hurly-burly of a busy pre-New Year shopping spree, Jimbo scarcely noticed that Muriel had been in to buy lunch. Working without Harriet, combined with having given his part-time girl an extra day off for working so hard before Christmas, he battled on by himself with little time for conversation. Muriel on her part was glad to escape without having to give an explanation of why she was buying two slices of cheese cake instead of her usual single slice.

When she got home she put the ham in the fridge and the cheese cake out on the worktop to defrost and then having been in the bathroom to titivate herself and spray on some of the perfume Caroline, dear Caroline, had given her on Christmas Day she sauntered as casually as she could down to Ralph's house. She wore her new, well, newest coat, wine red with a black fur collar and carried the black leather bag Ralph had brought her back from London. Muriel's fair hair, well, nearly white hair, peeped out from under her fake fur hat. She hoped her dark red lipstick didn't exaggerate her pale skin. One day I shall try some blusher she thought, but right now she was blushing without any artificial aid and trembling inside too. Oh good, he was up. The knock on Ralph's door had not been loud enough. She tried again. Oh dear, that was enough to wake the dead. The door was opened abruptly and there he stood, smiling tentatively down at her, his lovely fine-boned hands held out in greeting.

'Muriel my dear, come in.' As he took her hand Muriel burst into tears. She hadn't expected to, so she'd no handkerchief available. Ralph gave her his own and his thoughtfulness made her cry even more.

'Oh, Ralph, I have been a fool. Such a fool.'

'Never, Muriel, never a fool my dear.'

'Yes, yes. A complete fool.' She wiped her eyes dry and smiled shakily at him. 'Could you possibly come for lunch?'

'I've just finished breakfast, but for you I'll eat lunch too.'

'Oh not yet, I meant later about one o'clock.'

'I'll bring some wine shall I?'

Muriel was scandalised. 'In the middle of the day?'

'You drank it in the middle of the day when we were in Rome.'

'Of course I did. Yes then, bring some wine.'

'So be it.'

Muriel studied his face. She reached out to touch his arm. 'Ralph you've lost weight, have you been ill?'

'In my heart.'

'Your heart? Have you got heart trouble?'

'Don't you remember almost the last word you said to me?'

Filled with sadness she answered, 'I said, "No". Forgive me for causing you so much pain. I did say I'd been a complete fool. I'm sorry I was so dreadfully unkind.' Muriel reached up, pecked his cheek and said, 'See you shortly.' She spun round and went out before she could reveal any more of how she felt. As she hurried along Church Lane past the Rectory Caroline came out and almost collided with her.

Caroline clutched hold of her. 'Steady Muriel.' They both laughed at each other. 'Where are you going in such a hurry?'

'Oh Caroline, I'm going to take your advice.'

'My advice? What about?'

'Ralph's home and I'm going to do what you said and orchestrate a proposal!'

'About time too. Peter will be delighted. He hasn't had many weddings to conduct lately, he was saying the other day he'd be losing his touch.'

'Oh dear, yes of course. Oh dear. I must be off I've got lunch to get ready. Oh dear. Oh my goodness.'

'Muriel, do try to be happy, it's the first day of the rest of your life.'

'Of course, yes . . . what a lovely idea. Yes, of course it is. Bye bye.'

Caroline watched her dash off down Church Lane. Today was the first day of the rest of Caroline's life too, but she hadn't wanted to take away from Muriel's happiness by telling her. Today she, Caroline Harris would become a mother. A real honest to goodness mother of two. She and Peter were going at two o'clock to collect the twins from the hospital. Never again would she have to worry about Peter not having the children he wanted, because now he had his very own two children. Alexander and

Elizabeth. Alex and Beth. Beth and Alex. Caroline stood watching Jimmy's geese as they grazed on the village green. In her mind's eye she could see the twins snuggled in their cots in the hospital, their tiny hands clenched tight, their eyelids fluttering a little as they slept. Thank God they'd decided to put weight on instead of losing it. Maybe they'd not fed eagerly because they were grieving for their mother. No that couldn't be it, could it? Still, they'd finally decided to feed well and gain weight so she needn't worry about them now. Just to get them home. Home! That sounded wonderful. She decided she was going to make a really successful job of bringing up the twins. Try to make them each feel they were the only one that counted. Full of anticipation she pushed open the door of the Store, in her pocket the list she'd made of the food she needed to fill the freezer before she became too busy to shop.

As Caroline dumped yet another basket of food by the till Jimbo asked, 'My word Caroline, I know Peter's a huge chap and has a big appetite but this is ridiculous. Do you know something I don't know? Is there going to be a siege or something?'

'Can you keep a secret?'

'Cross my heart and hope to die,' said Jimbo suiting the action to the words.

'I'm stocking the freezer because . . . well, we hardly dare believe it but the twins are well enough to come home, and we're collecting them this afternoon. I'm sure they'll be OK but you never know with them being so tiny, do you?'

'Caroline, I'm delighted for you.' He came round from behind the counter and hugged her.

Harriet coming out from the storeroom grinned. 'That's enough Jimbo please, hugging the customers. Whatever next? Is this a new sales gimmick? As the rector's wife, you ought to know better than to encourage him Caroline!'

Jimbo whispered, 'Hush Harriet, Caroline is collecting the twins this afternoon.'

'Oh how wonderful. I won't tell a soul or you'll be overwhelmed with visitors. Everyone is so excited and I'm so jealous of you having new babies in the house. I feel quite broody. We've made sure we've plenty of "new baby" cards in stock haven't we Jimbo?'

Caroline pulled their legs about their sharp eye for business. Having paid for the food she realised she should have brought her car round. 'I don't know what I'm doing this morning, I'm a complete idiot and so is Peter. He tried to start his car without the keys in this morning and wondered why it wasn't moving. Then he realised he'd left the Communion wine behind and had to come back for it. If we're like this before the twins come home, what will we be like afterwards?'

Harriet assured her that things would all work out, and suggested she should bring everything across to the Rectory in the Range Rover which was still outside.

'Thanks very much. I appreciate that. Bye Jimbo.'

Mother's clock was striking a quarter to one when Muriel heard Ralph at the door. She checked her hair and face in the little mirror she kept for the purpose in her tiny kitchen and hastened across the living room to open the door. The small dining table in the window was already laid, all she needed to do was put the food on it.

Momentarily the two of them were silent as they looked at each other across the threshold.

'Shall I come in?'

'Oh yes, I'm so sorry, please, yes, please come in.'

'I'm early, I know, but I couldn't wait to come.'

'It doesn't matter, everything's ready. I shall never learn to be late. Sit down Ralph and I'll put the things on the table. Oh you've brought the wine.'

'Yes, I've had it in the fridge since you called, it should be just right.' Their hands touched as she took the bottle and Muriel felt as though she'd had an electric shock.

'Oh Ralph.' She stood on tip toe and pressed her lips to his. When she stepped back her face was flushed and she apologised. 'I'm so sorry, I beg your pardon. You sit down, I'll get on and make the coffee.' A wisp of hair came down across her forehead. Flustered and embarrassed she reached up to push it away only to find Ralph taking hold of her hand and putting it to his lips to kiss.

'It tastes of ham, smoked ham. Let me see, yes, that's right, vintage Jimbo Charter-Plackett.'

Muriel laughed. 'That's right.' She scurried away into the kitchen hoping for a moment's respite but Ralph followed her in. Being such a small kitchen Muriel felt smothered by his presence there. She was acutely aware of him and couldn't avoid savouring the smell of his after shave or was it cologne or . . . She turned to pick up the coffee pot and bumped into him. In a moment his arms were round her and they were kissing as if their lives depended on it.

'Muriel, Muriel, I have missed you.' Ralph buried his face in her neck and she reached up to stroke his head.

'I've missed you too Ralph. If you still feel the same I desperately want to change that "No" to a "Yes".'

Ralph drew back and looked closely at her. He cupped his hands around her cheeks and said, 'Muriel Hipkin are you proposing to me?'

'Well, yes, I think I must be.'

'Hallelujah. What a day. Let's open the wine and drink a toast.'

He expertly removed the cork, poured them each a glass and raised his in a toast to her.

'To Muriel, my best beloved.'

'To Ralph, *my* best beloved.' Muriel sipped her wine and then said hesitantly, 'You haven't answered me yet.'

'The answer, my dear, is yes. I shan't let you forget you proposed though. Who would have imagined the day would come when you did that?'

'If my mother knew what I'd done she be ashamed of me.'

'Mothers don't always know best. To save you any further shame I'll ask you. Muriel Hipkin will you marry me immediately?'

'Yes. A thousand times yes.'

After lunch, during which they'd interrupted almost every mouthful to say something meaningful to each other, Ralph with a twinkle in his eye said, 'Do you remember when we were children I used to tease you about that initial "E" in your name and you would never tell me what it stood for. I used to try to guess, Ethel, Eloise, Edna, Enid, Elise, Evadne, Elsie . . . but you never told me. Seeing as I am shortly, very shortly, to become your husband will you tell me now?'

'Husband, oh my word. Oh dear, I shall be Lady Templeton. Oh, Ralph, what have I done?'

'Nothing yet, but you still haven't told me what the "E" stands for.'

'I have to have something of mystery about me, anyway it's so excruciating I can hardly bear to think about you knowing.'

'More wine my dear?' As he leant across to fill her glass he said, 'Still, I shall know on our wedding day because Peter will have to use your full name. I can wait.'

'Will he really? Oh dear, the whole village will know then.'

'Don't worry it will only be a nine days wonder.'

'Ralph!'

'By the way Muriel, in my male arrogance I assumed that when I proposed you would say yes . . .' Muriel reached across the table and stroked his hand. 'I am sorry about that, but you wouldn't have wanted me to say yes before I was sure would you?'

'No, my dear I wouldn't, so I made arrangements to buy Suzy Meadows' house as a surprise . . .'

'Oh Ralph, really? I thought you were going to buy Toria Clark's cottage.'

'So I was, but I decided it wouldn't be big enough for a married man. It's all signed, sealed and delivered now, or it will be by the end of next week, so I intend moving shortly. Do you think you could live in Suzy's old house or would you prefer somewhere else?'

'Oh no, I've always liked her house.'

'We could always redecorate if you wish.'

'No, certainly not, I like it as it is. I shall really enjoy working in her garden.' Muriel couldn't help feeling sad at the prospect of leaving her beloved cottage. 'I shall miss my view of the churchyard. When I sell this house I hope the person who buys it loves it like I do.'

'We could live here if you want,' said Ralph.

'Certainly not, it wouldn't be suitable. And there isn't room for all your things and mine.'

'Well, I have got boxes and boxes in store which I have never looked at since I came home to England.'

'Well, there you are then, we need Suzy's house.'

After lunch Muriel cleared away. Ralph helped and they washed the dishes together talking about where he had been, and trying to decide where to go for their honeymoon.

'That does seem a foolish word to use, Ralph, for people as old as we are.'

'I'm hoping that even though we are older we shall still have a wonderful time together. It's the first time for both of us Muriel, so it can be as exciting or as dull as we choose to make it.'

Muriel was worrying and didn't know how to phrase the next thing she wanted to say. To give herself time she tested the little plant she kept on her window sill to see if it needed more water. She felt Ralph's hand on her arm. He turned her round and held her close and then stood away from her and smiled. 'You're very quiet, is there something you want to say?'

'Not just now . . .'

'Have you got some doubts?'

'Oh, no. No. It's not that.' Muriel rinsed the tea pot out again and dried it till it gleamed. It had been mother's favourite pot. She could almost see her mother's face reflected in the shining brown roundness of the pot. Her mother had never discussed anything to do with being a woman, not in all her life. Muriel realised she was as ill prepared for marriage at sixty-four as she had been at sixteen.

'I'm still here.' Ralph was leaning against the washer, arms folded, patiently studying her face.

'Ralph, you'll have to help me. I shall need help, you see, to get it right. I don't understand how to feel inside myself, because I've never had those kind of feelings. I don't know how it feels to want a m . . . I think passion is the word I mean. It's an old fashioned word but that's what I mean. I know you want us to be truly married, and so do I but . . .' Muriel blushed bright red and turned away from him to look out of the window. Her winter garden was just beginning to get a little colour, she could see the snowdrops peeping green through the soil. But soon she'd be leaving it for a whole new life and it would be someone else's winter garden. The enormity of what she'd done struck her and she felt intensely shy of the future. Why had she used the word passion? Now she'd have to face up to something she had avoided thinking about all her life.

'Muriel,' Ralph said gently, reminding himself as he spoke of the gentle delicacy of Muriel's nature and not wishing to trample all over it with some kind of hearty ho! ho! "it'll be all right on the night" kind of speech. 'I love you and you love me and because of that we'll make our married life absolutely lovely and satisfying in every way. We shan't rush things, we'll go steadily because that way we shall both reap rich rewards. I'll help you to feel passion, my dear, and I do love you all the more for your reticence. You can have confidence in me.'

'I can, can't I? You'll look after me, won't you Ralph?'

'Of course.'

'Please Ralph, let's go and see Peter about getting married. Can we get a special licence or something? If we wait a long time I shall get doubts and want to change my mind.'

'Very well, we'll go and tell Peter you can't wait to get married and which is his first free Saturday.'

'Ralph! You mustn't say I can't wait.'

'Well, I certainly can't.'

'Neither can I! I'll get my coat.'

They arrived at the Rectory door still laughing.

It seemed a while before Peter answered their knock. 'Why, Ralph, hello. Caroline said you were back.' He shook Ralph's hand. 'Lovely to see you, you're looking well. Have you had a good trip? We missed you over Christmas. Come in both of you. Hello Muriel, God bless you.'

'Hello Peter. Ralph has something to say.'

'Can we talk privately?'

'Certainly, come into my study. I'd offer you tea but Caroline's busy at the moment. Have you come to tell me something exciting? You both look very pleased with yourselves.'

Peter led the way into his study, and sat his two visitors in the easy chairs and then himself in his chair by the desk. Ralph cleared his throat, took Muriel's hand in his and asked Peter if he could fit in a wedding ceremony during the next few weeks.

'What? Oh I am delighted, absolutely delighted, I couldn't be more pleased. That's really great. Wonderful.' He stood up to shake Ralph's hand and then kissed Muriel on both cheeks. 'Just what we've all been waiting for. Is it a secret or can I tell Caroline?' Muriel nodded.

He opened the study door and shouted, 'Caroline, can you spare a minute?'

The moment Caroline saw the two of them in the study she knew they had come to arrange their marriage.

'Don't tell me, let me guess. You're getting married. I'm so pleased for you both, so very pleased. Peter, this calls for champagne.'

'Well, we have that bottle ready in the fridge for tonight. We don't *have* to wait till then do we?'

'In fact it might be best to have it now while all's quiet.'

Muriel looked curiously at the two of them. 'All's quiet? What's going to happen tonight?'

Caroline and Peter grinned at each other. 'You've only just caught us in, we've been to the hospital this afternoon . . .'

Muriel stood up quickly full of joy. 'You've been for the twins!'

'Yes.' Caroline hugged Muriel and she in turn hugged Caroline and then Peter.

'Oh where are they? Please let me see them.'

'Come on then, you too Ralph.' The four of them went upstairs into the nursery to gaze with love and admiration on Alex and Beth, each firmly tucked up in matching swinging cribs. Alex lay quietly sleeping, wisps of his bright blond hair just showing above the blanket, his tiny fists held close to his face. Muriel gently drew the blanket back and saw he still strongly resembled Peter, and felt uncomfortable at the thought of what the villagers would make of that. She rather hoped no one would notice. Loud sucking noises were coming from Beth's crib, and when Muriel peeped in she saw that little Beth had her thumb in her mouth.

Muriel clapped her hands with glee. 'Aren't they lovely Ralph? Just perfectly lovely. You must both feel so happy to have them safely home.'

'We are, but I'm terribly nervous. They'll be waking up any minute now for a feed and I shan't know where to begin, but we'll learn, we'll have to.' Caroline tucked the blanket a little more firmly around Alex and smoothed her hand around the top of Beth's head.

'How much do they weigh now, Caroline?'

'Alex is five pounds two ounces and Beth only just five pounds. But they are gaining a little every day now, thank the Lord. We'll go get that champagne before they wake up.'

They touched glasses and Peter said, 'May God bless all four of us on this very special day in our lives. Ralph echoed his thoughts with 'God bless us all and give us all great happiness in the future.' Muriel clinked her glass with Caroline's and said 'Amen to that.'

2

Jimbo, balancing on the top step of his ladder, was attempting to fasten a banner above the sign on his new restaurant. When he'd finally secured it, he leant back as far as he dare to read the words. 'CONGRATULATIONS ON YOUR WEDDING DAY.' That would give Muriel and Ralph a lovely surprise when they opened their respective bedroom curtains this morning. He climbed down from the top of his ladder and stood back to admire his endeavours. Turquoise and silver hydrogen-filled balloons, three at each end of the banner, were blowing briskly in the early morning breeze. A work of art Jimbo admitted to himself. In such good taste too. Oh well, lots to do, must get on. There was the cake to finish, and the bride to give away, to say nothing of the food to prepare for the village reception that evening. He folded up his ladder and turned to go inside, pausing for a moment's peace at the beginning of his hectic day, to look at the sleeping village.

Best day's work he'd ever done moving to Turnham Malpas. He'd been on a treadmill at that damned merchant bank. Living on his nerves and for what? A smart house, smart friends, smart garden, smart clothes? Trading it all in for a country store had seemed exceedingly rash at the time but what a superb business he, well Harriet and he, were making out of it. And the children were growing up in peace and quiet, that was the bonus. The sun was now well over the tops of the Clintock Hills; it shone on the Church of St Thomas à Becket and the old white-walled houses, making the village look at its best. This was a great day for them all. True, Sir Ralph wasn't Lord of the Manor any more, but he still carried that aristocratic air and all the old villagers acknowledged him as such, even after nearly fifty years without the Big House at the hub of their lives. As for Muriel, what a very exciting day it would be for her. Jimbo bustled inside. Lots to do, lots to do.

By five minutes to twelve the church was filled to overflowing, for the guests invited to the wedding and the breakfast afterwards had been joined by dozens of villagers. All eagerly awaited the bride's arrival. The choir was in place and the rector, Peter Harris, stood on the altar steps dressed in his white marriage cassock and his best surplice. The entire congregation was hushed in anticipation.

At a signal from the verger, Mrs Peel the organist burst into Mendelssohn's *Wedding March*. Sir Ralph rose and stood next to his best man, an old university friend whom no one knew, as Muriel Hipkin entered the church on Jimbo Charter-Plackett's arm. She wore a pale turquoise suit, matching shoes, and a tiny stylish turquoise hat with a fine veil softening its outline and covering her hair and forehead. In her trembling fingers was a small bouquet of white flowers. Muriel was nervous but triumphant. She'd been awake since first light, thinking about giving the whole of her future happiness into the hands of this man, Ralph. The momentous decision to marry Ralph, once she had made it, was so absolutely right.

As Muriel approached the altar steps she saw that Ralph had turned to greet her, his strong features softened by love and by the sheer delight he felt at her arrival and at her charming appearance. He reached forward to take her hand and Muriel gave it to him without any reservations. Ralph leaned towards her and whispered, 'You look beautiful, my dear.'

When it came to the time for making their vows they turned to face each other and spoke steadily in firm, confident voices. The choirboys, dressed in their best ceremonial cassocks and ruffles, had to stifle giggles when they heard Peter say '. . . *this woman Muriel Euphemia Hipkin* . . .' Peter's address during the service brought some members of the congregation close to tears.

'I shall first read St Paul's thoughts on love, from Corinthians Book One, Chapter Thirteen.

' "Love is patient and kind; it is not jealous, nor conceited, nor proud; love is not ill-mannered nor selfish nor irritable; love does not keep a record of wrongs; love is not happy with evil, but is happy with the truth. Love never gives up; and its faith, hope and patience never fail. Love is eternal."

'It is only a short time ago that we welcomed Ralph on his return to the village after a long absence. His work in the Diplomatic Service has taken him worldwide, but the ties he had with the place in which he was born brought him winging his way back here when that work was done. He didn't know when he made the decision to return that Muriel, a childhood friend, had already come back. Some of you will recall that the bride and groom played together as children and that where Ralphie went, Moo was sure to follow. Recently we have watched them revive those early years. We all kept hoping that they would finally make it to the altar. There were some ups and downs, and at one stage it seemed we had all hoped in vain, but at last they have stood before God and declared their love. Muriel and Ralph, you have made your vows, secure in the knowledge that between you there is love which knows no bounds, love which *is* eternal. May God bless you both as you begin your married life together.'

When the wedding service was concluded the guests and villagers went out into the spring sunshine to watch the photographs being taken. They clutched their unopened boxes of confetti, mindful of Willie Biggs' ire should they sprinkle it around within the church precincts. The children from the village school formed a guard of honour down each side of the path. Dressed in their best and firmly instructed by their parents in the behaviour expected of them, they waved their Union Jacks and smiled until their faces ached. The bells of St Thomas à Becket rang out across the village filling the air with exultant sound. Everyone wanted to shake hands with the bride and groom and wish them the very best.

'Congratulations.'

'All the very best.'

'You look lovely Miss Hipkin . . . oooops Lady Templeton, beg yer pardon.'

'Lovely service.'

'Could 'ear every word you said, Muriel, and we all thought you'd be too shy.'

'Good luck to you both.'

'Get in the photo, Rector. At the back please, seeing as you're so tall, sir.'

'Them choir boys need keeping in check. Giggling all the time. Still 'er name was funny. Euphoria was it?'

'Wonder if they'll 'ave separate bedrooms, all them Dukes and Duchesses 'ave their own rooms.'

'Shut up, Pat. Now's not the time for that.'

Cameras of all shapes and vintage clicked and clicked again.

Once Ralph and Muriel were safely through the lych gate there was a concerted rush to shower them with confetti. Finally they were free to leave for their reception. Waiting in Church Lane was a beautiful open carriage and pair. The horses had their tails and manes plaited with turquoise and white ribbons and the driver wore a black coachman's coat and top hat. Ralph handed Muriel into the carriage with a flourish and seated himself beside her. Top hat in hand he acknowledged the cheers and good wishes with a wave as the carriage pulled away.

Harriet turned to Caroline and said, 'Don't they look splendid? What a send off.'

'They do. And they look so very happy.'

'I thought Peter's address struck just the right note.'

'He really laboured over it, it's so easy to wax dreadfully coy with a marriage service and he knew Ralph wouldn't like that at all. I'm just going to check that my parents are coping with the twins, so we'll see you at The George, Harriet.'

'Right. I'll find Jimbo and we'll be off too. He's in his element today. See you there.'

After the bridal party and guests had departed for the wedding breakfast at The George in Culworth, the rest of the villagers went home with the evening reception to look forward to. Lady Sheila Bissett longed to get home to kick off her shoes, she should never have bought them half a size too small just because they didn't have her size in stock. She'd be glad to get home anyway, because Ron was pestering her about her leopard skin coat. He'd never liked it but she did and that was what counted. Anyway, it was winter even if it was a wedding. And just wait till he saw her tonight, she'd show them all how to dress.

They'd had lunch and were fast asleep in front of the TV when Lady Bissett was awakened by frenzied barking. Oh no, not Flick Charter-Plackett's cats again. Pom and Pericles were behaving like crazed animals. Why Ron had promised to have Pericles while Muriel went on her honeymoon she never would know. They each encouraged the other where the cats were concerned. One whiff of a cat and they both went berserk. Sheila was sure that Chivers and Hartley came into their garden just for the fun of it. She looked out of the window. The two cats had just decided where they preferred to relieve themselves when Pom and Pericles pounced. Caught in mid stream as it were, the cats were at a disadvantage but fought their attackers with spirit. The spitting and snarling, the barking and growling could not be ignored.

Sir Ronald came out with Sheila hard on his heels. She was raucous in her annoyance.

'Ron. Ron. Get them both. Those bloody cats will tear their eyes out. Oh, Pom, come here darling.'

The protagonists ignored her cries. Pom and Pericles raced down the garden in hot pursuit, the cats spitting and clawing as they went. Sheila, abandoning any pretence of gentility, was shrieking at the top of her voice.

Sir Ronald charged down the garden carrying a large spade, looking as though he intended to flatten any cat within reach. By now Pericles had really caught the spirit of the exercise and was doing his best to murder

Chivers. Confused by all the barking and still only half awake, Sir Ronald launched himself at Hartley, missed his footing and plummeted headlong into his ten-by-eight premoulded glassfibre pond with two shelves at differing depths for water plants, where his Harris tweed suit, purchased to make him look like a countryman, rapidly absorbed a good deal of water. Forgetting the dogs Sheila went to his rescue. As she gave him a hand to climb out the cats left the scene of battle and hurried out of the garden. Pom and Pericles, well satisfied with the mayhem they had caused, returned to the house, drank deeply from their water bowls and then lay down, each in his own bed, to contemplate their part in the chase. What Ron and Sheila had not realised was that Flick had been watching the whole proceedings from the side gate, her screams of protest unheard in the general mêlée.

Sir Ronald stood in the back porch removing his clothes while Sheila went inside for a large bath towel. The damage done to the garden and the pond by the skirmish was more than she could bear. The fish would sulk for at least a fortnight and the herbaceous border, just when the plants were beginning to grow again, would most likely take all summer to recover. By the time she returned with the bath towel Sir Ronald had undressed down to his underpants. An angry voice boomed over the gate.

'Sir Ronald, a word if you please.' Jimbo CharterPlackett, still wearing his morning coat, was striding into the garden. 'Got back early from the reception to find Flick running down Stocks Row in floods of tears saying you've tried to kill her cats with a spade.'

Unhinged by the ridiculous position he was in Sir Ronald stormed out of the porch and confronted Jimbo, his dignity considerably dented by the wet underpants clinging to his thick, overweight body and the pondweed coating his head and face.

His wife rushed after him with the towel but he waved her angrily aside.

'I'm sick of your bloody cats. They wander about all over the place. We're not the only ones who complain. Ruin my garden they do, they use it as a damned public convenience.'

Sheila tried desperately to rescue what little was left of Ron's dignity, 'Ron, Ron, please put this towel round you.'

'Shut up Sheila. Do you hear me Jimbo? It's open war from now on. I shall use cat powder and any other device I can think of to defend my garden.'

'Come, come now *Sir Ronald*, they're only young cats and it's caused Flick a great deal of distress. It's not fair to threaten them with a spade. What have you been doing to yourself, by the way? You look perfectly ridiculous in those drawers, man. Get yourself covered up.'

'Covered up? It's your cats I shall be covering up, dead and buried they'll be if I have my way.'

Jimbo stepped forward and prodded his finger sharply on Ron's fat wet chest. 'Lay one finger on those cats and I shall have you prosecuted and I mean that. Flick's already had one cat drowned as you know, she can't cope with any more tragedies. Now go inside and get yourself attended to before you make any more of a spectacle of yourself.' Jimbo in a blazing temper turned on his heel and marched forcefully out of the gate, banging it shut and nearly breaking the catch. Sir Ronald took the towel, wrapped it round himself and strode, with what little dignity he had left, into his house.

Sheila knew when to keep quiet and now was the time. Normally she ruled the roost in the Bissett household, but there were days when even Sheila knew that silence was golden. She could hear Ron stamping about in the bathroom. He was so careless of all her frills and flounces: heaven alone knew what the lavender carpet and bath mat would look like when he'd finished. She'd chosen them so carefully to tone with the navy fitments. The cover on the toilet lid was lavender as well. She'd bought them all in Marks & Spencer and knew the moment she saw them that they would give the right effect. But it was the white basketwork shelving holding the glass jars of guest soaps and bath pearls and the lace tissue-holder which were the delight of her life. And the nets at the bathroom window, frilled all round the edges and draped tastefully over the frosted glass, were white as well with little sprays of flock flowers. The bathroom was one of her triumphs. Since she'd married Ron life had not had many delights for her financially, but these last few years, with his broadcasting fees and all the trips abroad he'd had with the Union and the expense account, things had improved considerably.

Sitting at her bow-fronted dressing table, Sheila heard the bathroom door slam shut. Ron came in stark naked.

'I've told you before, Ron, not to walk about like that.'

'Who's to see me?'

'Well me for instance, and it's not nice.'

'I'm not concerned whether it's nice or not I'm too occupied thinking about how to stop those damned cats from ruining our garden.'

'I thought Jimbo had rather a lot too much to say. Such a temper he has . . .'

'Barbed wire that's the answer. Cat powder only puts them off when they've got in, I've got to stop them getting in at all.'

'Barbed wire? We'll look like Colditz.'

'I don't care. Barbed wire it is. Or else we'll get a bigger dog who'll kill the blasted beggars.'

'Ron, you know I don't like language like that.'

'There isn't a word in the English language that fits those blasted cats.'

'In any case Pom wouldn't like another dog here. It would upset him dreadfully.'

'Might do him good, brighten his ideas up a bit. You make him too mamby pamby Sheila, I've told you about it before. He only comes alive when Perry comes to stay.'

'So you say. I think he's all right on his own. You should never have volunteered to have Perry. Three months' honeymoon in Australia, I ask you. That Muriel Hipkin's never been further than Bournemouth I should think, not till Sir Ralph came back. First Rome and now Australia . . . she's played her cards right, and no mistake. Managed to land him at last. What on earth he sees in her I shall never know. Ron, do you think they'll . . . you know . . . ?'

'Eh? Oh that, I haven't any idea about that. I might as well put on the clothes I'm wearing tonight at the reception. Wish it could be my tweed suit. Bloody cats.'

'It wouldn't have been suitable anyway. People like us have to show the villagers the right way. You need your funeral suit love. With that nice spotted tie Bianca bought you for Christmas.'

'I'll look like a dog's dinner. You know I don't like that suit. I should never have let you persuade me to buy it.'

'Men in your position need to look smart. Whatever would they think if you went on telly with a ginger tweed suit on? Right country bumpkin that would make you look.'

'When I ordered that tweed outfit you said it would make me look like a country squire.'

'Well it does, but the telly people wouldn't see it like that would they?' Sheila concentrated on her nail varnish. One stroke down the middle of the nail and then one each side. This pale apricot would look splendid with her new dress. She couldn't wait to put it on. She'd never bought anything in Thoms & Curtis before, but one did have to set standards in the village. So easy to let things slide. The clothes that Caroline Harris wore, considering she was only a rector's wife, were unbelievably beautiful. Still, she had been a doctor all those years so she must have earned a lot of money in the past. And she did have style. Those twins, though, they must be hard work. Hardly any sleep at all some nights. They were lovely babies. Amazing how like Peter the little boy was. They say that about adopted children, how they start to resemble their new parents as they get older. But they must only be about eight weeks old at the most. Wonder what Harriet Charter-Plackett will wear tonight. Another of her Sloane Street creations no doubt. Still, wait till they see me in my outfit.

Sheila got up from the dressing table now her nails were dry and took the dress out of the wardrobe. She had little pot pourri bags hanging from each coat hanger to keep her clothes fresh. She bought them from a local girl who made anything and everything, edged with lace. Sheila was always popping in for something. One of her best customers she was. The dress was made of lime-green flowered brocade with a pleated peplum around the back which went flat as it came over the hips and across her stomach. It had a stand-up collar with large revers which crossed over just below where her cleavage began. Either side of the collar below her collar bones was a neat design of pearls sewn around the shape of one of the brocade flowers. She'd seen Ron look askance when she'd tried it on in the shop. She knew he didn't like her to display herself, but the dress was so right she couldn't resist.

She laid it on the quilted white satin bedspread and slipped off her négligé revealing a dumpy figure clothed in a Marks & Spencer slightly-too-tight underslip. When the dress was on, she turned this way and that inspecting herself in the mirrors on her wall-to-wall wardrobes. Yes, it was just right for the occasion, and just right for church in the summer, too. She'd make their heads turn. They were all beginning to accept that she was the lady of the village now. Her flower arranging and her organisation of the Village Flower Show had given her a real solid position in village life. They couldn't manage without her in Turnham Malpas now, no siree. Her black strappy high heels were uncomfortable but they'd soon wear in.

'You're ready too soon Sheila.' Ron yawned.

'I know. I thought I'd go and sit downstairs and give my shoes a chance to wear in a bit. There's a nice programme on the telly I can watch.'

'I wanted to see the sport.'

'Well, you watch it up here and I'll go downstairs. I'll spoil my dress if I lie on the bed.'

Sheila let the dogs into the garden seeing as she and Ron would be out for a long time at the reception. That Pericles was a right card. Seemed to really enjoy being able to race about instead of being all stiff and starchy with that prim Miss Hipkin. She made their dinners for them and then installed herself in the sitting room. All the cushions on the beige Dralon three-piece had shiny curly fringes and huge embossed flowers in the centre. The arms were thick and solid and never failed to give Sheila a thrill when she looked at them. Perhaps they were a bit on the big side for an old cottage, but even so they added a real touch of class.

On the mantelpiece above the inglenook fireplace stood the wedding invitation card. *'Sir Ronald and Lady Bissett'* it read. Sheila ran her fingers along the embossed lettering and smiled with pride. They'd come a long way she and Ron. She switched on the telly and got out a box of Newberry fruits. She didn't rest her head against the cushion in case she ruffled her strawberry-blonde hair. She'd had the roots done only a week ago so it was looking its best. Hope this reception was worth all the trouble, she thought as her eyes began closing.

3

By six o'clock that evening there was a steady stream of people heading for Henderson's Tearoom and Restaurant. Many of the guests lived so close they were able to walk to the reception. Most joined up with others and chatted and laughed their way through the village. Two of the guests walked alone. In the dark they were barely discernible and in their black coats and hats they appeared to the fanciful eye to be ghostly wraiths wending their way to some macabre feast. In fact they were Gwen and Beryl Baxter who'd lived in the village at number two all their lives. As children in the village school they'd always been considered odd, but in later years their oddities had become more pronounced. They rarely spoke to anyone and certainly no one could remember ever having been inside their house. If their windows were anything to go by, the habitués of The Royal Oak opposite guessed the house must be filthy. They were right. It was. Only Gwen went out and that was to the Store for food. Tonight the two of them were making one of their rare sorties out into the world.

They bumped into Peter and Caroline as they pushed their way through the restaurant door.

'Good evening to you both. How nice to see you.' Peter's hand, extended to shake theirs, was ignored.

'Isn't it lovely having a village party for Ralph and Muriel?' Caroline tried. There was no reply.

'You go in first, ladies,' Peter suggested. He and Caroline followed them in.

Caroline looked up at him. 'Will Mother be able to cope do you think? I'm so worried about Alex's runny nose.'

'My darling girl, your mother has had four children and she *is* a doctor and so is your father. Just be thankful they were free to come to stay, otherwise we wouldn't be here at all. Anyway, they've only got two minutes' walk to find us, haven't they?'

'Yes, you're right. I must make myself enjoy this evening. What I'd really like to do is go home and sleep all night without a break. That's the best present anyone could give me at the moment.'

'Evening Rector. Evening Dr Harris.'

'Left them two babies, Dr Harris? Hope they're in good 'ands!'

Peter and Caroline acknowledged the greetings. It was obvious the villagers were hell bent on enjoying themselves. Peter took his wife's arm and gently guided her through the crowd into the bright lights of the restaurant. Jimbo and Harriet had decorated the two rooms with pale turquoise and white flowers, and streamers complemented by silver garlands and bells. The food was already laid out on the tables, and an enormous three-tier wedding cake stood on a table by itself surrounded by a circlet of delicate white blooms.

Ralph and Muriel stood in the entrance greeting their guests. Muriel reached up to kiss Peter. 'Thank you, Peter, for conducting such a lovely service this morning. Ralph and I did enjoy it. You said all the right things.'

'I was only too delighted to take the service for you. My best wishes to you both. I know you'll be very happy.'

Caroline kissed Ralph and then Muriel. 'I do hope you will, no, I'm sure you will, both be as happy as Peter and I. I couldn't wish anyone anything better than that.'

'Thank you Caroline, I'm so glad you were able to leave your two little ones and join us all.' Ralph leant forward and kissed Caroline on both cheeks.

'Give my love to Australia won't you Ralph? I was there for three months one summer when I was at university. I grew quite fond of the place.'

'Caroline, we shall be delighted to do just that. Come now, help yourselves to a Buck's Fizz and go and join in the fun.'

'Peter, don't they both look happy?'

'They certainly do. Now my girl, drink that Buck's Fizz and then another one and you'll be in just the right mood for a party.'

The party was in full swing, the band playing, the people dancing, the food rapidly disappearing when the door opened and in came Sir Ronald and Lady Bissett at full tilt and exceedingly flustered. Full of apologies they searched for Ralph and Muriel.

'We're so sorry we're late. We didn't realise how the time was going. Congratulations to you both. So nice for you at your time of life to have such a lovely sending off. Ron . . . ald could you pass me a drink please?'

Sheila and Ronald circulated, Sheila feeling she must make everyone feel at home. It was difficult for village people to know how to mix and make small talk. One had to do one's bit to make things go with a swing. She waved delightedly at Caroline, deep down experiencing that dreadful inadequate feeling when she saw Caroline's beautiful midnight blue floating creation. She might have known her dress would have been superb.

It was their misfortune to come face to face with Jimbo and Harriet, and Ron's drink spilled a little as he swerved to miss bumping into them. Harriet jumped back to avoid getting splashed.

Jimbo couldn't resist a jibe. 'Must say you're looking better than when I saw you last. Dressed in water and pondweed he was, Harriet. To the point of indecency.'

Sir Ronald spluttered his annoyance.

'It was your Flick's damned cats as you well know. Sick of 'em I am. Don't blame me if they don't get back home one day.'

'I've warned you about threats like that. Two cats in a garden the size of yours? What's the worry? Good for the soil I'd say.' Harriet, sensing Jimbo was brewing up for one of his big "put down" speeches, hastened to smooth ruffled feathers.

'Isn't everyone enjoying themselves tonight? I thought Muriel looked lovely at the wedding, like a ship in full sail coming into harbour.'

Sheila looked non-plussed by this flowery description of Muriel, 'Yes, I suppose so. Come Ron . . . ald I need another drink.' Sheila shepherded him, protestingly, on his way. Ron took a drink from a tray on the side and rapidly drank it down. Sheila recognised the signs.

'Don't you dare show me up by getting drunk. This is *the* social event of the year. I've spent a lot of money on this dress and I'm blessed if I'm going to have to go home before the party is well and truly over. We've missed quite a bit of it already with falling asleep.'

'It was you fell asleep, not me.'

'You could have woken me up, you knew the time all right.'

'I didn't, I was enjoying the football.'

'Just you remember we have a position to keep up. You're a national figure and they expect you to know what's what. Go and talk to Peter Harris or someone and keep well away from those two. And behave like a gentleman if you know how.' She said all this between clenched teeth and all the while smiling at anyone who came near. She'd kill him if he made a fool of himself. Kill him she would. If only Bianca and Brendan had been here. They would have kept their father in check. He was so proud of them both. Bianca in that new job at the bank helping small businesses start up, she'd done well for herself, and Brendan with his computer business. His degree from East Anglia had been a real stepping stone for him. Admittedly it was only a third but he could still put B.A. after his name. First one either side of the family who could do that.

'Hello Lady Bissett. How are you? What would you like to drink?'

Sheila turned to find Sadie Beauchamp, Harriet Charter-Plackett's mother, offering her a tray of drinks. If there was anyone in the room who could make her feel small it was Sadie Beauchamp.

'Thank you, I'll have a Buck's Fizz. It is a lovely party isn't it? I understand the children are to have an entertainer when they've finished eating.'

'That's right, Punch and Judy and then a magic show. Ralph and Muriel are so thoughtful. I love your dress, where did you get it? It's rare to come across something so unusual.'

'It's from Thoms & Curtis in Culworth. I saw it on display in the window and couldn't resist it.'

'I must remember that. I didn't know they sold such . . . interesting clothes.' Sadie made her way through the guests. Sheila watched her go. The slimfitting understated floor-length black dress Sadie wore proclaimed money and taste and Sheila felt sick.

Harriet came to join Peter and Caroline.

'Good evening Caroline.' Caroline turned to answer her.

'Hello Harriet. Isn't this a lovely party? I like this idea of having an evening "do" for everybody in the village. Especially for Ralph with his past history of being Lord of the Manor so to speak.'

'Definitely Lord of the Manor no more.'

'What do you mean?'

'Didn't you realise? They've already started work on turning the Big House into a health club. The lorries have been going in and out of the gates for weeks.'

'A health club? I don't believe it!'

'True. True. Some people called Venetia and Jeremy Mayer have bought it and are spending thousands on it. And I mean thousands. Entirely new decor, swimming pool, jacuzzi, running track, gymnasium, aerobics classes.'

Peter asked Harriet how anyone could get permission to make such radical changes to such an old house.

'By dishing out backhanders to the Council, or so Neville Neal says and he should know shouldn't he? Considering the strings he pulled to get Glebe House built. Oh, of course that was before your time. Anyway now's your chance to get fit.'

Caroline groaned. 'Fit? I haven't time for anything but keeping my head above water at the moment. I don't know how two such small human beings can cause so much work, to say nothing of the lack of sleep. Every three hours they need feeding. There's no time for anything. Does Ralph know about the health club?'

'I don't know.'

When everyone had circulated and eaten and examined the wedding presents which were on display in a small side room, it was announced that the happy couple would shortly be cutting the cake. As many as could gathered round, and cameras clicked and photographers jostled as Ralph and Muriel stood holding the silver knife and smiled first this way and then that. When they'd done the cutting Ralph took hold of Muriel and kissed her for rather longer than necessary. The guests clapped heartily and Muriel blushed, which made them all clap and laugh even more. Ralph took her hand and kissed it with all the aplomb of an eighteenth-century suitor.

'Ladies and gentlemen, thank you very much indeed for accepting our invitation to join us on this very special day. My wife and I . . .' cheers resounded through the room and Ralph laughed while Muriel blushed again, 'would like especially to thank Jimbo and Harriet. Jimbo for giving Muriel away and both of them for providing such a splendid reception for us and decorating the room in what can only be described as a tasteful and exuberant manner. And thank you one and all for the lovely presents you have given us. We have been quite overwhelmed by your good wishes. We both look forward to coming home again to you and enjoying many more years sharing in the life of the village. The children's show has finished, so would you all care to come outside and watch the firework display? Thank you.'

The guests just about allowed Ralph and Muriel to get outside first before they all stampeded onto the green. Jimbo's firework displays were renowned and they didn't want to miss one moment. Gwen and Beryl delayed leaving with the crowd, as they had designs on the food remaining on the table. The two of them wrapped sausage rolls and vol-au-vents, cakes and quiche in paper napkins and stuffed them into their handbags and pockets. Between them they had enough food for two or three days. Well satisfied with their haul they sauntered outside to see the last of the fireworks. There being no street lamps the fireworks showed up brilliantly from the first moment they escaped their containers. The children ooh'd and aah'd and the adults joined in. The grand finale consisted of a tableau made of Catherine wheels in the shape of the bridal couple's initials. They all clapped Jimbo's genius. Soon afterwards someone brought Ralph's Mercedes up close to the crowd. It was decorated all over with balloons and “Just Married” signs. Muriel was handed courteously into the front passenger seat by Ralph, who then got into the driving seat and the Mercedes slid quietly away down Church Lane with the guests waving and cheering their goodbyes.

Sheila had managed to prevent Ron from getting drunk and apart from her twinges of envy about Sadie Beauchamp had thoroughly enjoyed herself. She wouldn't half be glad to get these blasted sandals off though, they were cutting into her toes. She kicked them off as soon as she got in. Ron got the dogs' leads and set off for a sharp walk to exercise Pom and Pericles before he went to bed. He'd been lumbered with walking the dogs because Sheila always considered it a man's job to take the dogs out late at night. Come to think of it she thought it a man's job first thing in the morning and during the day. Ah well, it was a small price to pay for peace.

As he passed The Royal Oak, Ron heard the sounds of loud laughter through the open door. Well why not? He tied Pom and Pericles to an ancient hitching post outside the saloon bar door and pushed his way into the crowd. As he neared the bar Ron remembered that the new landlord had taken over only this week. It seemed odd after all these years not having big Betty McDonald behind the bar pulling pints.

‘A double whisky please, landlord,’ he shouted. The landlord's round shining face was dominated by a huge ‘Flying Officer Kite’ moustache which more than made up for the lack of hair on his head. For such a youngish man he was certainly very bald. In the shiny smiling face was a pair of twinkling grey eyes. By any standards he was a big man. ‘Good evening sir, and welcome to The Royal Oak. I'm Bryn Fields and this is my wife Georgie. Come here Georgie and introduce yourself.’

His wife was a petite and pretty blonde with a warm laugh. She reached over the bar to shake Ron's hand.

‘Good evening, very pleased to meet you. And you are?’

‘Sir Ronald Bissett.’

‘Welcome to The Royal Oak. You know your first drink is on Sir Ralph with it being his wedding day?’

‘Yes, I did know. Thank you very much. I hope this week is the start of a long and happy time for you here in Turnham Malpas. I see you've got a new barman too.’

Bryn called out, ‘Come here, Alan, and meet another customer. This is Alan Crimble, Sir Ronald, he's been with us for what is it . . . fifteen years now. We couldn't manage without him.’

Alan nodded a greeting to Ronald, who wasn't much impressed by Alan's weedy figure and ingratiating smile. ‘Best cellarman in Britain is Alan.’ Bryn clapped Alan on the back as he returned to serving drinks.

'Here you are then Sir Ronald, here's your whisky. Good health and a long life to Sir Ralph and his bride.'

'Here's to that.'

Ron downed his whisky and immediately asked for another. After all he had been nearly drowned today, he could be catching a severe chill. Pom and Pericles waited and waited. They were unaccustomed to being tied up for long and when boredom set in they began playfully snapping at each other. This rapidly became more than a game and before they knew it they were having a real fight. Neither could escape as both were firmly tied up. A passer-by unfastened their leads intending to pull them apart and then find their owner, but they took their chance and escaped. Their first thought was to continue the fight but having been released they changed their minds and raced for home. Pericles went to Muriel's house out of habit and Pom to Ron and Sheila's, where he sat yapping outside the front door.

Sheila, already in bed, woke up with a start when she heard him. She popped on her négligé and went to the window overlooking the front door. When she saw Pom sitting there with no sign of either Ron or Pericles she feared the worst. She went to bring in Pom, expecting that Pericles would be out there with him somewhere. He wasn't. She hung about nervously in the hall for a few minutes hoping Ron would return with Pericles. When he didn't Sheila went upstairs and got dressed with the intention of going over to Muriel's to see if Pericles had gone to his home by mistake. Sure enough she found Pericles shivering and crying outside Muriel's front door. As she wearily put the key in her own door on her return, she heard a burst of laughter from The Royal Oak.

'That'll be it,' she said out loud. 'He'll be in there drinking himself silly. Well, if he thinks I'm going to make a fool of myself dragging him out he's got another think coming.'

Sheila had been asleep about half an hour when she was woken by a loud thumping at the door. She snuggled down under her goose down duvet and deliberately ignored him for a while. Eventually she relented and went down to let Ron in.

Ron was standing unsteadily on the door step. 'Couldn't find the key, Tsheila. Tsorry.' He came over the threshold clinging to the door frame for support. He patted her arm, almost pulling her négligé from her shoulders as he slipped on the polished floor. 'You're a wonderful wife Tsheila. Best day's work I ever did marrying you. No one anywhere has a better wife than you. Blow Tsadie Beauchamp and that lot, I like something cuddly to get hold of. Give me a woman with curves I tsay. Come 'ere and give us a kissh.'

'Certainly not. What would the union people think of you now Ron?'

'They'd tsay good luck to yer Ron.'

He went into the downstairs loo, pale green fitments with pale yellow accessories and a spray of artificial flowers tastefully arranged in a vase the shape of a penguin. She could hear him vigorously splashing himself with water. Ron came out rubbing his head and face with the pale yellow towel. More dirty washing.

'You're a big disappointment to me Ron. I try hard to turn you into a gentleman and you ruin it by coming home drunk as a lord.'

'I am a lord or very nearly. But you've tsome room to talk. That blasted fur coat, I told you not to wear it. I hate the blessed thing.'

'I don't know what it is that makes you think you know all there is to know about women's clothes.'

'I have got eyesh Tsheila, I can see what Tsadie Beauchamp wearsh, what Dr Harrish wears and it's not like what you choose.'

'Well, thanks very much. Been out having a good time without me and then come home criticising me and my clothes. Thanks very much Ron Bissett. I'm off to bed and think yourself lucky if I ever speak to you again.' Sheila stormed off to bed hurt almost beyond endurance by his cruel words, made worse by the fact that underneath all her bluster she knew he was right.

4

The Monday morning after the wedding Peter followed his usual habit of praying from six thirty until seven and then going for his half hour run. He'd been awake since five helping Caroline to feed the twins so it already felt like the middle of the morning to him. He went down Jacks Lane, crossed Shepherd's Hill and then onto the spare land behind the Methodist Chapel and set off along Turnham Beck. He had the steady economical action of the experienced runner and having followed this route for nearly a year now, he didn't need to take particular notice of his direction. Just past the footbridge he became aware of someone coming at speed towards him. Lifting his head he saw what appeared to be a large oriental butterfly winging it's way down the path. It began running on the spot. Peter stopped to speak. 'Good morning.' The gaudy creature was dressed in an electric pink plush tracksuit with a matching sweatband holding back jet-black hair, which seemed to spring in a dense mass out of her scalp. Round her ankles were purple slouch socks and on her feet a pair of expensive snow-white running shoes. Her wrists and fingers were covered in bright jewellery, the kind Caroline would never dream of wearing.

'Hi! I'm Venetia Mayer from the new health club.'

'Oh right, I'm Peter Harris. Great day for a run isn't it?'

'It certainly is. Be seeing you. Bye.' She carried on her way, leaving Peter shaking his head in amazement. He did a lot of thinking on his runs and this morning he was contemplating how he could best sort out Caroline's problems. Very soon she was going to be ill. The children being so small needed feeding frequently and were taking so much of her time both night and day that she was close to collapse. Much as he would have loved to stay in to help her he had his own commitments which she knew could not be ignored. What she really needed was another pair of hands all day long.

He stopped to rest for a moment, leaning on the gate into Sykes Wood. That was it, another pair of hands. But whose hands? There was no one in the village who sprang immediately to mind. No doubt the answer would come to him. Today, Lord, for preference, he prayed.

Mondays he tried to spend in Penny Fawcett, the first village travelling west from Turnham Malpas and one belonging to his parish. Its own church was long gone and the churchgoers from Penny Fawcett came to St Thomas' for their services. They still had their own village centre and there was always a mini market there on Mondays, so he knew he'd meet plenty of his parishioners. Peter parked his car and was about to go into the centre when a voice hailed him from across the road.

'Mr Harris, isn't it? Good morning. You won't remember me but I met you at the Hospital Garden Party last summer. My name's Sylvia Bennett.' She held out her hand to shake his. Peter racked his brain trying hard to recollect her, then, as he walked across the road he remembered.

'Oh. I know, you're a supervisor there. Yes, that's right, Caroline introduced us. How are you?'

'This is my cottage, come in and have a coffee before you go in the mini market. My coffee's a lot better than that stuff out of the paper cups they serve in there, their rubbish could rot your insides. I'll be glad for some company.'

They took their coffee from her bright shining kitchen out on to a little bench by the back door and sat catching the best of the winter sun while they talked. Peter warmed to her lovely kindly face and her big candid grey eyes, which never seemed to stop twinkling.

'Having a day off are you Mrs Bennett?'

'Well, yes, except it's a long day off I'm afraid. Been made redundant after fifteen years.'

'But you were a supervisor.'

'Makes no difference sir, nowadays. Re-organisation and out went Sylvia and got replaced by a young manager barely out of nappies who couldn't supervise a chimpanzees' tea party let alone a work force of twenty cleaners. Added to which I'm soon to lose my cottage. Landlord's coming back from abroad and has nowhere else to live, so out goes me. In fact it's not like me but I do feel a bit low today.'

Sylvia paused to put her cup down beside her on the path and then asked, 'How's Dr Harris? She was well liked at the hospital; we did miss her when she left. No edge you know sir, you'd as likely find her in the broom cupboard joking with the cleaners as find her perched on a desk in a consultant's office, explaining to him that he really shouldn't keep sick people waiting for hours while he played God with his private patients.

Many's the one who's been hauled over the coals for it by Dr Harris. And what's more they did as they were told. And her so young compared to them.'

'At the moment she feels very far from young. You know, I expect, that she isn't able to have children, well, we've been very privileged to be able to adopt twins . . .'

'I had heard. I bet she's thrilled, she'll make a lovely mother.'

'Yes, she does, but she's exhausted. Living in the Rectory the phone is going continuously and she's trying so hard to do well by the twins, but they are tiny and they are much harder work than she'd anticipated. Well, no not that, we just didn't know what hard work such tiny babies are. There's lots of parish things she's involved with and she is a perfectionist as you know.'

Sylvia asked him if he'd like more coffee.

'No thanks, must be off. Lovely talking to you Sylvia, I'll tell Caroline I've met you. Thanks for the coffee. See you again sometime.' How could he introduce the idea of Sylvia helping out without giving Caroline the feeling that she wasn't coping. Lack of faith in her at the moment could cause serious damage to her already shaky confidence.

'Guess who I met today in Penny Fawcett?'

'Can't. I just want to get my dinner down before those two horrors of ours wake up. I'm sorry it's one of Jimbo's frozen dinners . . .'

'I don't think he'd appreciate the apologetic tone in your voice. He considers his frozen dinners are of gourmet standard.'

'Well, they are, but you know what I mean. Who did you meet?'

'Sylvia Bennett.'

'Oh, from the hospital. How is she?'

'Redundant.' Peter chose another roll and energetically buttered it while Caroline digested his news.

'Redundant? Has she got another job?'

'No, and another few weeks and the landlord wants her cottage back.'

'I see. I always liked Sylvia. We got on very well.'

'She likes you, she gave my darling girl very good references.'

'Did she? Jimbo's right, these dinners are good. Though I could eat a horse tonight. I got no time for lunch at all. Sylvia's a good cook you know.'

'Is she?' Peter continued enjoying his dinner, leaving a silence for Caroline to fill with her own thoughts.

'She doesn't know much about babies.'

'Doesn't she?'

As she finished the last morsel of her dinner Caroline said, 'She would be good for everything else though, wouldn't she?'

'Are you thinking what I'm thinking?'

'What's that?'

'She might be able to help us a bit here, just occasionally, you know from time to time.'

'Peter, you must be telepathic. Except I'd go one further than that.'

'You mean have her here every day?'

'Well, there are four big bedrooms here and . . .'

'So long as we always have one spare for visitors or the odd tramp in need of accommodation she could . . .'

Caroline triumphantly finished his sentence for him. 'Live in. Brilliant. We can afford it for a while, and she would save my life you know. She's very discreet, she wouldn't be a pest. Just till she found somewhere of her own you understand.'

'Of course.' Peter silently thanked the Lord for his intervention.

He came out of the church the following morning to find Jimbo limbering up outside as though he was about to take part in an Olympic marathon. He was wearing a pair of old rugger shorts from his university days and a sweat shirt with *Support the Whales* emblazoned across it.

'Good morning Jimbo.'

'Morning Peter. I'm taking up the challenge.'

'What challenge is that?'

'My beloved and valuable mother-in-law has said she will give me £10 each time I go for a run with you. She says I shan't manage it but I'm determined I shall. She ought to be called sadistic Sadie. She says I'm fat,' Jimbo patted his bulging midriff as evidence, 'so I'm definitely going to get fit.'

'Right, well, I shall be glad of your company. Here we go. I usually do a circular tour round Sykes Wood and back. Is that all right?' Jimbo quaked at the prospect but put on a brave face. He couldn't afford to allow his mother-in-law a laugh at his expense.

'Of course, nothing to it.' Peter set off at his regular brisk pace and almost immediately Jimbo realised he wouldn't make the grade. Just before he had begun showing serious signs of stress Venetia Mayer came into view wearing her pink track suit. She waved enthusiastically.

'Hi there.' She continued running on the spot while chatting, without any sign of shortness of breath.

'Good morning Venetia, have you met Jimbo from the village store?'

'Hi Jimbo. How perfectly delightful meeting two such fine specimens of manhood at this time in the morning. It seems to me that you are both prime candidates for membership of the health club when we open at the end of next month. Peter, I must say your physique is superb. Are you a sports fanatic?'

'Not really Venetia, simply a man who wants to keep fit.'

'Well, come to see me at Turnham House. I'll see you keep fit all right. We shall be holding "Executive Trim" classes, which I think will be ideal for you. What about you Jimbo? You need my services more than Peter. You don't strip quite as well as he does. Looks to be lots of flab to be attacked with our special exercises. How about if I offer the pair of you an introductory course at half price. How's that for a bargain?'

Peter and Jimbo agreed it might be a good idea.

'Two Tarzans you would be before a month was out. Then all the women in the village would be after you both in a trice.' She laid a hand on Peter's arm, tweaked his muscles and winked at him. 'A few hours on a sun bed and you would look superb. There's nothing like a tan to increase a man's sex appeal!'

'Well, we must be on our way Venetia, thanks for the offer, we might take you up on it.' Jimbo hastened off, followed by Peter who couldn't stop laughing.

'I don't think she realises who I am, do you?'

'No, Peter, I don't. The woman really is the limit. Has she gone yet?' Jimbo turned round to check. 'Yes she has. It's no good I shall have to turn back. Do you think I can claim I've been for a run?'

'In all conscience, no, you can't.'

'You're right, I can't. You carry on Peter, and exercise your jungle man body. I can't keep it up.' Peter waved and carried on with his run. Jimbo turned back and slowly jogged his way home.

Sadie, having listened to their encounter with Venetia, was highly amused.

'How far did you run then Jimbo?'

'Not far enough. But I'm working on it.'

'So my ten pounds is safe then?'

'For the moment. I might take her up on the offer of membership. Keep the old flab at bay. Would you like to join, Harriet?'

'Yes, I would. Time I paid more attention to my body. In any case I can't let you and Peter loose up there with no one to keep an eye on you. If you're going in the jacuzzi, you'll go in it with me not Venetia. What's Jeremy like? Have you seen him?'

'No, and if he's as sexy as her we'll both have some fun.'

Sadie took hold of a fistful of Jimbo's sweat shirt. 'No straying James.

You're married to my daughter and don't you forget it. I'm very handy with the garden shears.'

'Ouch! That's positively mediaeval. You wouldn't be so cruel would you darling?' He placed an arm round Harriet's shoulders and hugged her.

'Just try me.'

'Remember the garden shears James, that's all I ask.' Sadie laughed as she headed for the office to catch up on her mail orders.

Harriet's curiosity about Jeremy was satisfied later that morning when he came into the Store to enquire about the possibility of ordering food for the health club.

'I'm looking for quality food, fresh, well-presented and appetising. Ideally I need someone willing to provide all the food at competitive prices. There's no way we shall have time for shopping here and there and everywhere once we open. I must admit I cut prices to the bone, there's no fooling me when it comes to overheads. And I shan't hesitate to change my supplier at a moment's notice if I feel I'm being taken advantage of.'

'We are not in the business of cheating anyone. Fair prices and consistent good quality is what we guarantee. In return we expect our bills to be paid on time. There's absolutely no credit.'

'Well, at least we understand each other.'

'Coffee?' Harriet stood with her hand poised on the lever of the customer's coffee machine.

'Yes, please.' She had to admit that Jeremy was a disappointment. Having heard about his wife Harriet had anticipated an Adonis. Instead he was thick set, if not downright chubby with a large bald patch in the middle of his grey hair. His heavy glasses enhanced him not one jot. She couldn't see him doing an early morning run with his wife. More than likely he was tucking into bacon and eggs sunny side up while she was out jogging.

'How long have you been in the health club business, Jeremy?'

'New venture, actually. Venetia has the beauty and the experience and I have the brains and the money. This coffee's good.'

'Jimbo is out on business at the moment. If you could give me some idea of the kind of food you would be wanting and how you would like deliveries made and how often et cetera, when he gets back we could have a discussion about it.'

'Certainly. I've written down my thoughts on the subject so I'll leave them with you to browse over. Could I have another cup of coffee, please?'

'Of course. I've been wondering where you're going to get people from to fill up your health club. There's not many people around here who could afford to be members let alone stay there.'

'I have lots of business contacts and we intend promoting it as a place to send executives for a social as well as a physical weekend. Build company loyalty and morale and all that jazz. All paid for by the employers, of course.'

'I see. Well, here's hoping you have lots of success. I'm sure you will. As you say, with Venetia's beauty and your brains you're bound to be onto a winner.'

'Exactly. Must be off. There's our card. Give me a ring and we'll arrange a meeting. Remember though I'm in business. It's not a charity, so no fancy prices. Good day to you.' He left the store in a hurry, climbing into his BMW with more haste than grace.

'And so much for you Jeremy Mayer. No fancy prices indeed! If we didn't need the business I'd tell him what to do with his orders,' Harriet muttered to herself.

'Who's that just disappeared in a cloud of dust?' Caroline asked as she manoeuvred her pram in through the door.

'Good morning Caroline. That is the famous or is it *in*famous Jeremy Mayer from the health club. He's not anything like I'd expected.'

'I wonder if he knows his wife's been making passes at the rector? I shall be having a thing or two to say to her if she doesn't stop.'

'Don't take it too seriously Caroline, Peter's not so foolish as to be taken in by her. Can I lift Beth out?'

'Yes of course. I can't find my list, yet I know I put it out to bring with me.' Caroline tried all the pockets of her jacket and eventually found it tucked down the side of the pram mattress. 'I really think I've lost my marbles since I got these two. I don't know what I'm doing most of the time.'

'Would you be without them, that's the question.'

'Certainly not. But it does take some adjusting to when one's led an adult, shackle free existence for so long and then suddenly your life is not your own any more.'

'That will pass. Now, little lady, I'm going to put you back in your pram and pick up your brother for a cuddle. Mustn't show favouritism must we?'

Harriet picked up Alex and kissed the top of his head. 'What darlings you are.' Harriet cuddled Alex against her face. 'Mmmm little babies are lovely. I'm very jealous of you do you know that?' Harriet put Alex back in the pram and said, 'I'm thinking of joining the health club. Jimbo fancies it and I'm going to keep an eye on him. What do you think?'

'No time really Harriet. Peter might join but I won't. I'm not into exercise and all that right now.'

Whilst Harriet was putting Caroline's shopping together for her, Venetia dashed in. She'd changed her pink track suit for a pale green one, all colour co-ordinated with her headband and slouch socks. Emblazoned across her back were the words *Turnham House Health Club.*

'Harriet, hi! I met your husband this morning. I'm trying to persuade him to join our health club. Do you think he will? Would you like to join as well? We're expecting a rush for membership so you'd better make your mind up quickly. He was out with this gorgeous man called Peter this morning. Now, he really is a superb physical specimen. Just the kind I like. Tall, well made, fair haired, with surprising muscles. I told him a few hours on a sunbed would just set the seal on him. My dear, he's devastatingly attractive. I could really make music with him. Can't think what he's doing living out here in the sticks. Do you know him at all? Of course you must, if he was out running with your Jimbo.'

Harriet tried to hush her up but it was no good. Caroline grew steadily more and more angry as Venetia blithely enthused over Peter's physique.

'Are you aware that you are speaking about my husband?' she asked finally. Venetia turned to study Caroline. 'You should be delighted to hear his praises sung so enthusiastically.'

'I'm not delighted, I'm very angry.'

At this Venetia only laughed and said, 'All's fair in love and war.'

Caroline left the Store without her shopping. She strode home in a furious temper and then burst into tears as soon as she got inside the Rectory door. Alex and Beth, sensing her distress, also began crying. When Peter got home a few minutes later he found the house in uproar.

'Darling, whatever is the matter? Come here to me.' Peter took hold of Beth and put his other arm round Caroline as she sat herself on his knee holding Alex. She wept.

'I've been such a fool. I've made a complete idiot of myself. That dreadful Venetia Mayer came into the store and what had been a nice conversation with Harriet turned into a steaming row with Venetia.'

'What about?'

'You.'

'Me?'

'Yes, you. She thinks you are absolutely superb and wants to make music with you. Sunbed and all.'

'Did she not realise who I am?'

'No, not till I spoke up. I should just have laughed and made light of it, instead I got furiously angry.' Caroline began laughing through her tears.

'I really was a fool. I expect it's because I'm so tired, I take umbrage at almost anything. I shall have to apologise to her.'

'Don't do that, I'll go and see her, do the apologising and warn her off.'

'You'll do no such thing. *I'll* do the apologising. It was me who blew my top. She doesn't know you're the rector and I didn't enlighten her. I couldn't hide behind that as a reason for her to hold off.'

'I do love your sound commonsense Caroline. You do know I haven't encouraged her don't you?'

'Yes, I do. Absolutely. She's the threat, not you. I shall apologise the very next time I see her.'

5

Caroline met Venetia a few days later when she was in Harriet's tearoom having morning coffee. She'd left the twins with Sylvia who'd promised to keep an eye on them while she did the ironing. Caroline was glad to escape for a little while and become a person again in her own right. Life was beginning to get a certain balance to it since Sylvia had come to live in. Her parochial duties having taken second place since the twins had arrived she was becoming aware of her neglect of Peter's flock. So this morning she would rectify the matter. And where better to meet people than in the tearoom?

It was half full when she went in. There was the usual sprinkling of tourists come to view the ancient tombs, the church murals and the stocks on the green and, dotted amongst them, were villagers out to meet anyone and everyone who might have some news to impart. She greeted the parishioners, smiled at a few of the strangers then took a seat at a table near the back. She ordered her filter coffee and a slice of Harriet's famous carrot cake and sat back to enjoy a grown-up interlude.

Venetia entered carrying a large poster. Her voice carried right to the back of the tearoom.

'I'm Venetia Mayer from Turnham House Health Club.' She spun herself round so the cashier could see the words printed on the back of her track suit. 'I'd like you to display this poster in one of your windows. I'm going round to the store to ask Jimbo if I can put one on his Village Message Board but I thought one in here might be a good idea.'

The cashier looked warily at her. Caroline sensed a feeling of resentment in the look.

'Leave it here behind the counter and I'll ask Mr Charter-Plackett if I can put it up.'

'Oh, but I want to put it up now. You might forget.'

'I'm sorry, Mr Charter-Plackett employs me and I have to ask his permission before I put up notices. We can't have every Tom, Dick and Harry littering the place with posters. He's very particular, is Mr Charter-Plackett. Doesn't want to spoil the ambonce he says.'

'Oh very well, but you won't forget, will you? I'll have an orange juice please.'

'The girl will come to your table and take your order. I deal with the money.'

'It's a wonder to me you get any customers in here at all with an attitude like yours. I wouldn't want to employ you at the health club.'

'No cause to worry yourself about that, I wouldn't want a job there anyways.'

'Well really! How rude. I shall have words about this with Jimbo. Such rudeness to a customer. Oh hello there, you're Peter's wife, aren't you?' She trotted down between the tables.

'That's right.' Caroline pulled out a chair. 'Come and sit with me.'

'These people are extremely rude. Are they always like this?'

'No, they're not. But I was very rude to you last time I saw you. I owe you an apology. It was entirely due to lack of sleep, I suppose. I'd been up with the twins a lot during the night and couldn't see straight at all. But that's no excuse. I'm so sorry.'

'That's fine. I didn't take any notice of you anyway. But you have to admit he is gorgeous. You are very lucky. I unashamedly admit I married money. Lots of it.'

The girl brought her orange juice and banged it down with little grace.

'See what I mean? They are thoroughly unpleasant people.'

Venetia sipped her orange juice and commented on its quality. 'We're buying all the food for Turnham House from Jimbo and Harriet. I imagine they provide some good stuff.'

'Oh yes, they are excellent. They've only been here for about three years, I understand. Jimbo used to work in the city but decided he hated it and it wasn't a good life for his children, so he and Harriet resurrected the village shop and they've made a great success of it.'

As Caroline finished singing the praises of the Turnham Malpas Store, Mrs Peel the organist left her table and came across with an envelope.

'Could you give this to the Rector for me, Dr Harris? Save me knocking on your door. He asked for a list of music I fancied buying for the Services. Said he'd pop into Culworth and order it.'

'Certainly Mrs Peel. I loved the pieces you played on Sunday. I thought that Scarlatti delightful.'

'Thank you, Dr Harris, I don't often get compliments, except from your husband, of course. Since he came I've felt that at last here's someone who could appreciate and inspire an organist.'

'I'm glad about that. The music is so important.'

'Old Mr Furbank never cared that much for the music. I could have played nursery rhymes and he wouldn't have been any the wiser. Good morning to you Dr Harris.' She gave a curt nod to Venetia and went out.

'Caroline! I had no idea that your Peter is the rector. What a laugh. Oh, well, maybe I brightened his day. What on earth is such a super man doing being a rector? Oh my word.'

'Because he is a committed Christian, that's why.'

'Well, I may as well be honest. He won't be seeing me in church, I've no time for it. Hope to be too busy on Sunday mornings to go, even if I wanted to. See what I mean about the villagers though? She virtually ignored me. They don't want to know. Well, they'll have to put up with me because I intend staying and making a success of this place. Cheery bye. I'm off.'

Venetia waved a carefree hand and set off towards the door deliberately smiling and nodding at everyone as she went. The village people did not respond.

The regulars in The Royal Oak had plenty to say about the health club. Willie Biggs, the verger, confided to his drinking partner, Jimmy Glover, that it was an excuse for a sexual orgy like them Romans used to have.

'Wouldn't go as far as that Willie, but by Jove that woman in the tracksuit has plenty going for her. Nice bit of crackling and not half.'

'She ain't a woman, she's a walking sexpot skellington. See her eyes when she spots the rector. He's 'ad to change his route for his morning run to avoid her. They say she made eyes at him not knowing who he was. Dr Harris had a row with her in the Store because of it, and she's made sheep's eyes at Jimbo before now. Huzzy she is, Jimmy, a huzzy.'

'What I don't like is them making the Big House into a circus. Jaccersys and them naked Swedish steam things. Goes against nature. All them beautiful walls and them lovely paintings. I remember as a boy when we all went up from school to sing carols and then had mince pies and orange squash in the music room. Miss Evans getting bright red doing the conducting and then fidgeting with 'er 'ands and staring at her shoes when Sir Tristan made his thank you speech. Remember that, Willie?'

'I do. I looked forward to that from one Christmas to another. And then Bonfire Night. Remember the cook used to do dozens of baked potatoes and yer ate 'em with yer gloves on 'cos they were that hot. Them bonfires were grand. That high they used to be, yer don't get bonfires like that nowadays. I could just fancy going this November to one o' them fires. Remember Sir Tristan used to come out and give each one of us a toffee apple to take home? Say what you like they were special people up at the Big House.'

'And where is it all now? Madame Butterfly won't be dishing out toffee apples, more likely condoms.'

'Shut up, Jimmy, what are yer thinking of?' Willie glanced round to make sure Jimmy hadn't been overheard.

'Well, I'm right. Everybody thinks the same; the good old days are dead and gone.'

''Ave you got that Sykes in 'ere? Yer know Bryn doesn't like dogs in.'

'Doesn't matter. I don't care. He never makes a sound, nobody knows 'e's 'ere.'

'I do 'cos I can smell him.'

'That's only 'cos he's drying out, he's been out in this old rain and he got soaking. In any case 'e's partial to a drop of Guinness as you well know, so we share a glass.'

'All right, all right. You're soft in the head where that dog's concerned.' Willie put down his pint of Tetley's and waved to Pat Duckett, beckoning her across to join them. 'Sit 'ere Pat and tell us the latest from the school. Still wearing you out, is it?'

Pat carefully placed her plump behind on the settle and launched into the story of Venetia's visit to Mr Palmer.

'Headmaster, I ask yer and there she is prancing about in the playground demonstrating some exercises he could do to correct his stoop. "Come up and see me sometime," she says, sounded like Greta Garbo in that film. Or was it Marlene Dietrich? Anyways them children were all gathered round with their mouths open listening to all this. I had the kitchen window open on account as I was washing up in there and it was steamy. I could hear every word what she was saying. I heard Mr Palmer say, "I'm afraid the subscription would be beyond my teacher's salary, Mrs Mayer." "Oh," says she, "call me Venetia do." Waggles her bum and dances off.'

'Been making eyes at the rector an' all,' said Jimmy determined to inflame Pat's wrath.

'Never. That's it then, she is a tart. Whatever would Mrs Rector think if she knew?'

'She does.'

'Never. The poor dear. She might be a Doctor and well brought up but she is pleasant to everybody. No hoity toity with her. Tell you what, I wish

Sir Ralph was up at the Big House and it was like my mum remembered it before the war. The Village Flower Show in the grounds, all them side shows and the flags flying . . . that's how it ought to be, not all tarted up like she's making it. Our Dean went up there on his bike the other day, says it's like a building site. That Jerry Mayer bossing 'em all and diggers and machines all about. It'll never be the same again. Never.'

'It's what's called progress,' Willie moaned. 'But it will mean jobs. They've been advertising.'

Pat banged her lager down. 'If she offered me a king's ransom I wouldn't work up there. All them bare folk plunging about, it's not decent. My Duggie would turn in his grave if I worked up there, God rest his soul.' She raised her eyes piously to heaven and sketched a cross with the hand that wasn't holding her glass.

'Your Doug didn't have much time for God when he was down here Pat. Reckon he went up there do yer?'

'That's enough from you Jimmy Glover. Yer'll be civil when yer talk about my Doug. He was always kind to me.'

'I could tell that by the black eyes he kept giving yer.'

'That's as maybe, but he didn't mean it.'

They were sitting right by the door so they had a full view of the stranger when she walked in. She had a kindly fresh country face, with twinkling eyes. Well, they had the potential to be twinkling, but she was nervous just now. She wore a royal blue coat and smart high heeled court shoes which helped to increase her height. She went to the bar and asked for a white wine.

'Who's that?' Jimmy asked.

Pat nudged him and said, 'Isn't it Sylvia Crossman that was? Worked over at Culworth Hospital for years as a cleaning supervisor. Wonder what she's doing here?'

Sylvia looked around the bar for a table but they were all occupied. Pat caught her eye and, hitching further along the settle, invited the newcomer to sit down.

'You're Sylvia Crossman that was, aren't you?'

'Yes, I'm Sylvia Bennett now.'

Jimmy introduced the three of them to her and then followed it up by saying they hadn't seen her in the bar before.

'No, well, I only moved into the Rectory this week. Dr Harris needs help, what with that big house to run, and the twins, and helping the rector and answering the phone all day long. I rented a little cottage over at Penny Fawcett for years but the landlord wants it for himself now and I couldn't afford a bigger rent, everywhere I looked the rents were far too high, so Dr Harris suggested I lived at the Rectory for a while till I find something. I've got a lovely room and I have my own bathroom too. They're both so pleasant to work for. Do you know them very well?'

Willie didn't answer so Jimmy answered for him, 'Willie 'ere, who seems to have been struck dumb, is the verger at the church.'

'Oh well then, you won't need me to tell you how nice they are. Those babies are a delight. I love looking after them. Dr Harris feeds one and I feed the other and we sit chatting, or watching the TV. It makes a real change from supervising at the hospital, I can tell you. I've never been in here before.'

'We all know one another and we get on fine. Some of the newcomers are a bit pushy . . .'

'Who had you in mind Pat?' Jimmy asked, knowing full well to whom she would be referring.

'Well, that Sir Ronald and Lady Bissett. Ron and Sheila really, but they stand on ceremony a bit. Think they're somebody special 'cos he's on telly now and again. Most folks is all right. Funniest folks is Gwen and Beryl Baxter. They've lived here all their lives, if yer can call it living.'

Pat, sensing a chance to pass on some local gossip, hitched herself closer and began regaling Sylvia Bennett with the story of Gwen and Beryl. Willie hadn't spoken because he couldn't. He felt as though he'd been poleaxed. He stole glances at Sylvia when she wasn't looking, and found himself more delighted with her than he could possibly have imagined. Every move she made fascinated him. He'd been around a bit, but it was the first time he'd ever met a woman who had affected him in this way. One glance from her lovely grey eyes and his insides melted. He felt ridiculous. His heart was racing, his blood pressure seemed to have gone clean through the roof and he was sweating as though it was high summer and he was hay making. At his age . . . fifty eight and his heart beating twenty to the dozen. It must be this new beer the landlord was selling. That was it, it was the drink. He stood up, pushed back his chair and, cutting across Pat's monologue, said abruptly, 'I'm off home. Goodnight.'

'What's up with Willie?' Jimmy inquired as Willie pushed his way past a crowd coming in. 'He's in a hurry.'

Willie went home to his little cottage between the church and the Rectory, bewildered by his reaction to Sylvia Bennett. He took one look around his sitting room and his heart sank to his boots. He saw everything with new eyes as if he'd never been in his own cottage before. He'd never noticed how awful it was. Something would have to be done. If ever he plucked up courage to invite Sylvia in he'd be mortified. In fact he couldn't invite her in. It was all too dreadful. He'd do what he'd been promising himself for years, dip into his savings and get it done up. He needed a new bathroom for a start. Couldn't ask Sylvia Bennett to go up the garden to that old privy when she got caught short.

6

The news about Willie's improvements not only to his cottage but to his general appearance too, caused a great deal of interest in Turnham Malpas. The first meeting of the newly inaugurated Flower Festival Committee provided a good moment for an exchange of views, as Willie, co-opted onto the committee to advise on the feasibility of their plans, was unable to attend due to a severe cold. Peter had arranged the chairs in a circle to give the impression that no one person was in charge though nominally it was himself. Harriet Charter-Plackett, Mrs Peel the organist, Lady Bissett and Sylvia Bennett with Peter and Willie constituted the committee. Their speculation as to the cause of Willie's sudden burst of activity drawing no conclusions, they had to reluctantly begin the business of the meeting.

Lady Bissett removed her imitation Burberry and got down to brass tacks immediately. 'I'm full of ideas for this Flower Festival. We did one in Culworth Church, and it was compliments all round. Good organisation is the key.' Sheila Bissett had a vision of all white arrangements punctuated here and there by soft green foliage.

'Why all white, Sheila?' Harriet asked.

'Because it is restrained and tasteful.'

'Downright boring if you ask me,' Harriet retorted. 'There's no variety in that. I'm not much of a flower arranger but even I know there's not much to catch the eye if every arrangement is white.'

'Believe me I do know,' Sheila bridled. 'I've been a member of the Culworth Flower Arranging Society for the last five years. They did a very effective one in the Cathedral only two years ago. The variety comes in all the differing shapes of the petals and the foliage.'

Harriet pressed her point, 'The Cathedral is very light though, full of huge windows, while our church is small, dark and mediaeval. We have those beautiful murals and the painted tombs. Surely it would be better to echo the colours in those?'

'I agree,' Sylvia said. 'I think the colours of the murals and the tombs would look good. Rich reds and purples and pinks and blues. Quite excellent.'

'Who's the one with the experience here? Me. I'm the only one who is even a member of a society. Please allow me to know what is best.' They could see Sheila was beginning to lose her temper.

Adept at stepping in when storms were brewing, Peter cleared his throat and said, 'Were we celebrating Easter, marriage, baptism or confirmation then I'm quite sure Lady Bissett, that your idea of an all white display would be highly appropriate and very effective, but we are celebrating summer and the beauty of our church. Mrs Peel and I have been planning some very buoyant and cheerful music for our recital and I think that coloured arrangements would be more suitable at this time. We'll let the committee vote, shall we? Those in favour of coloured arrangements please signify.'

Every hand bar Lady Bissett's went up.

'That settles it then: arrangements reflecting the colours of the church. Now Lady Bissett, do you think that your society would do us the privilege of arranging the flowers? We would foot the bill for the flowers of course. Their expertise and your flair would I am sure provide a wonderful display. The money we raise will go towards urgent church repairs. I wish we were well enough off to give it for charity, but I'm afraid that's not possible. I think cups . . .'

'Just a moment Mr Chairman, I haven't said yes.'

'I'm so sorry, I thought you'd accepted the decision of the committee.'

'I have not. The way I feel at the moment I could very well say that I won't have anything to do with the Festival at all.'

'Come now Sheila, you can't have everything all your own way,' Mrs Peel objected.

'If it's about flowers I can. I've worked my fingers to the bone over the church flowers and now when it comes to the best bit, my wishes are completely disregarded. It's not fair. I think all white arrangements would set off the colours in the church beautifully.'

Peter, trying to be as diplomatic as possible, argued that the committee had voted and they had to take the decision of the majority.

Sheila drew herself up and said with tight lips, 'I know why they voted like they did. It's not because they didn't want white flowers, it's because they don't want me.'

'That's hardly fair, Sheila. We all know we couldn't manage without you,' Harriet protested.

'Well Rector, the decision is yours. Either we have all white flowers and I do it or you have coloured ones and someone else does it. I would have thought that you of all people would have backed me up.'

'We are doing this to help the church, not to satisfy our own egos, and I feel that . . .'

'Are you saying I'm wanting my own way for the glory of it?'

'No, not that at all. It's just that . . .'

'Oh yes, you are. Well, that's that then. I shall have nothing to do with your festival at all. You can organise it all by yourselves and then we'll see what a mess you make of it. You'll soon be crawling to me to do it for you, but I shan't. I wash my hands of it completely.' Sheila stood up, pulled on her raincoat and stormed out of the vestry.

'Sheila won't you recon . . .' But Peter's words went unnoticed.

The remainder of the committee sat silently for a moment gathering their thoughts.

'We've done it now, Peter,' Harriet murmured.

'It looks very much like it. But it's no good, I don't honestly think all white would be a good idea.'

'Neither do I. I have a friend,' Sylvia said quietly, 'who is a member of a flower arrangement society and I'm sure she would be delighted at the opportunity to organise a festival in such a lovely church as we have here. She would accept it as a real challenge and she's very talented. Would you like me to put it to her?'

'That sounds a very good idea, don't you think so Mrs Peel?' Harriet said, seeking support.

'Indeed I do. We've all had enough of being bossed about by Sheila Bissett.'

'I don't think we should be too critical. She has put in a lot of work while I've been here.' Peter shuffled his papers together and suggested that Sylvia should contact her friend and perhaps could let him know the outcome as soon as possible. With that the meeting closed.

Sheila spent the next morning in readiness for Peter coming to apologise and agree to her suggestions. She'd plumped the cushions, vacuumed the carpet, re-arranged the flowers, and given her houseplants a spray of leaf shine. She'd dusted the coffee table, left a few of her flower magazines on it and put some new drops of essence in the pot pourri on the bar. Should she offer him a drink or would it be better just to offer coffee? Coffee would be best. Sheila got her best coffee set out in readiness.

When it got to one o'clock and he still hadn't come she knew she'd lost. 'Ron, who else could they get to do it? They'll be cancelling the whole thing next, just you wait and see.' But in the church newsletter the following Sunday the date and details of the festival were announced. Sheila seethed with annoyance. 'I shan't be going to church any more. That's the thanks you get for being a stalwart. Christian indeed! Some Christian that Peter Harris is. That's definitely settled it. I'll get my own back and I know how.'

She didn't tell anyone how she intended doing this, but the very next morning she was in Harriet's tearoom nice and early. She settled herself at the table in the window, waiting for a suitable listener.

She didn't wait long. Before the morning was out a considerable number of the villagers were convinced that Peter was the father of the twins whom he and Caroline were adopting. Sheila had started it off by questioning the babies' parentage. 'Isn't it odd how much like the rector little Alexander is? It's a funny coincidence isn't it, seeing as how Suzy's husband had dark hair? Before it had been passed on more than a few times it had become a fact.

Harriet overheard two of her customers talking about it in the Post Office queue.

'And Lady Bissett says that she knows for a fact that the twins are the rector's own.'

'No! Well, I don't believe that. Surely to goodness, it can't be true.'

'Well, she says it is. Says how little Alex is so like the rector they can't deny it. And he is yer know.'

'Well, he is the same colouring I expect. Well I never, whatever next.'

'Rector having a bit on the side, takes some swallowing that does.'

'It's Dr Harris I feel sorry for. If it's true I think she's been very brave taking them on.'

'So do I.'

'Question is, who do we really want, a lovely young rector who's strayed a bit or that Lady Bissett as she likes to be called. I know who I prefer.'

'Well yer right there, that Lady Bissett isn't half a pain in the arse. He's lovely and he's worked so 'ard since he came, what with the Cubs and the Brownies and the Women's Meeting and the pensioners' Luncheon Club. I don't know how we managed with that old faggot Mr Furbank. It was time the good Lord gathered 'im to His bosom and no mistake. My turn is it Linda? Two second class stamps. Thanks.'

Harriet at her first opportunity went in search of Jimbo. He was sitting worrying over his accounts.

'It's no good you know. The restaurant is not pulling its weight. I shall have to think seriously about . . . Why whatever's the matter?'

'Jimbo, I don't know what to do. Two of the customers have been saying that Sheila Bissett has said that Alex and Beth are Peter's.'

'We know they're Peter's; they're adopting them.'

'No, they mean actually *Peter's.* You know, that he's the real father and that's why they've adopted them.'

'You mean Suzy Meadows and Peter . . . No, no, no. I don't believe it. That can't be right. Peter would never let Caroline down like that. I mean God, he's the rector. No, of course he wouldn't. Absolutely not. I'll have a word with Peter, man to man when we go for our run in the morning. Devil of a job bringing up the subject though. But this gossip will have to be stopped. I can't believe it's true. Spreading lies like that. The woman's malicious.'

'I know why she's done it, it's because we wouldn't do as she said about the Flower Festival. She expected Peter would go running round next morning and apologise and beg her to run it, but he didn't because Sylvia Bennett asked a friend of hers to do it and she's jumped at the chance.'

'I feel desperately sorry for Caroline. Do you suppose it really is true and she doesn't know it?'

'I haven't the faintest idea. We are good friends, but she wouldn't tell me something like that would she? It's much too private.'

When Jimbo met Peter the next morning he wasn't quite sure how to broach the subject. Then Peter himself mentioned Sheila Bissett, saying she'd resigned and how difficult it made things.

Almost as an aside Jimbo asked, 'Have you heard the rumour she's spreading as her revenge?'

'No. What is she saying?'

Jimbo stopped by a farm gate and leant on it. 'Let's have a rest before we turn back.'

Peter wiped the sweat off his face with the sleeve of his running shirt and said, 'Well?'

Jimbo, breathing heavily as much from the quandary in which he found himself as from the running he'd done, looked Peter straight in the face and came out with Sheila's malicious gossip.

'No good beating about the bush. I feel very awkward telling you this, but you've got to know. Sheila Bissett is spreading the story that your Beth and Alex are really yours and Suzy's . . . you know . . . that you well, you are their real father. That's why you're adopting them. There, that's it in a nutshell.'

Peter went pale, turned his head away from Jimbo's direct glance and said quietly, 'What's that old saying? "Be sure your sins will find you out." ' He leant on the gate looking across the fields towards Sykes Wood. 'We didn't have an affair. It happened the week Patrick died. She was desperate for comfort and I have to admit I was stunned by her, quite stunned. Then I found out she was expecting twins and I thought it was the end of everything, my marriage, my vocation everything. Caroline was magnificent, said it wasn't to be allowed to make any difference to us. We were partners for life and she wouldn't permit something like that to separate us. What Suzy longed for and planned for, was that Caroline would want to adopt the twins, and that's exactly what she did want.'

Jimbo silently absorbed what Peter had said. God! What a situation. What was there to say? He waited a while for Peter to compose himself and then said in a matter of fact tone, 'Then you've nothing to fear: the two of you can stand together on this. I know in my heart that the whole village will be behind you. They don't like Sheila Bissett, but they do love you and Caroline.'

'I promised Suzy faithfully that we would never disclose the truth, just as she promised us that she would never tell, either. How has the woman found out?'

'She's put two and two together and made five. That's what.'

'I must get straight home.' Peter turned away from the gate and set off at such a cracking pace that Jimbo couldn't keep up. When he got back to the Rectory, Peter went straight up to the bathroom for his shower. He arrived in the kitchen for his breakfast already dressed in his cassock for the regular Friday morning school assembly in the church.

'Sylvia, do you think you could leave Dr Harris and me for a moment, I need to speak to her about something.'

'Of course Mr Harris, I'll just get on making the beds. Your eggs are ready.'

'Thank you.'

Caroline, who was loading the washing machine, reminded him to ask Michael Palmer about the children doing some singing in the church on the day of the festival.

'Caroline come here.'

'I really am busy, Peter. I shall have to start bathing the twins soon and I've the drier to empty and a thousand other things to do. Can't it wait?'

'No, it can't. Please come here and sit down.'

'Be quick then.' She sat on the edge of the chair ready for immediate flight.

'My darling girl, the one thing I don't want to do is to hurt you any more than I have done already. God knows I've done enough damage one way and another, but there's something I must tell you. You know we promised that we would never explain about the twins? Suzy promised and we did for everybody's sake. Well, I'm afraid that someone has put two and two together and arrived at the conclusion that they are mine.'

'Oh please God, no. Oh no.' Tears began brimming in Caroline's eyes and she got out her handkerchief to wipe them away. 'Are you sure?'

'We should have known we couldn't get away with it. We should have been honest from the start.'

'C . . . c . . . c . . . could we deny it?'

'That wouldn't be right would it, not in the long run?'

'No, it wouldn't. Oh, just when everything was going so well. Just when I was beginning to feel like a normal woman instead of a peculiarity.'

'Was that how you felt?'

'Yes.' Caroline wiped away the new tears beginning to run down her cheeks. 'The barren woman syndrome, you know. I was beginning to forget. What the hell are we going to do?'

'I've not had time to think. Jimbo's just told me.'

'How does Jimbo know?'

Peter finished buttering his toast before he told her, 'Because Harriet overheard someone talking in the Store.'

'Then they all know.'

'Yes, I'm afraid so.'

'Who started it?'

'Sheila Bissett.'

'I might have known. I've never liked that woman, always pretending to be something she isn't. Now she's really done for us. What are we going to do?'

'Go and have it out with her.'

At that moment the door bell rang and Caroline composed herself and went to answer it. Jimmy Glover was standing on the step holding a plastic carrier bag.

'Morning, Dr Harris. Thought you might like a couple of rabbits for the pot. Fresh this morning they are and I've dressed 'em all ready like. There's nothing to do 'cept rinse 'em and pop 'em in the pot. Rector'll like a bit of rabbit I expect.'

'That's very kind of you, Jimmy. Can I give you something for them?'

'Not at all, Dr Harris, they're a gift from me as a thank you for all you and the rector do for the village. We all appreciate you both and them babies. Good morning.' Jimmy raised his foul old cap and stepped briskly off across the road back to his cottage.

She closed the door and tears came into her eyes again. He hadn't said anything specific, but she knew what he meant.

'Peter that was Jimmy Glover with two rabbits for us. He knows and he's trying to tell us he doesn't mind. Isn't he lovely?'

'Yes, he is. I wouldn't have thought it of old Jimmy. Rascal that he is. That will test the cook tonight. I bet you've never cooked rabbit before have you?'

'No, but I'll get Sylvia to give me some ideas. It doesn't help what's happened though does it? What shall we do? I'm so upset.'

'I'm going to see Sheila Bissett straight after I've taken the school assembly. I've got to face her with it and get the matter cleared up. We can't have it festering away for ever.'

'You've got more courage than I have.'

'Well, in my book it has to be done.' Peter drained his cup and then said, 'Must be off. Don't worry about it too much my darling, I'll get it sorted out. We'll have a difficult few days but there'll soon be something else for people to talk about.'

When the school assembly was finished Peter lingered in the church for a while. The prospect of facing Sheila Bissett was causing him anguish. One of the reservations he had had about taking on the twins had been this very thing. Maybe in the long run being completely truthful, after Suzy had left, would have been the better course of action. He'd dreaded the hurt Caroline was now feeling, to say nothing of how he felt. One mistake, just one fall from Grace and he was still paying for it. Rightly so, but Caroline shouldn't have to pay too. The children were flesh of his flesh and he was bound by ties he never knew existed before they were born. He'd even found that he would kill for them rather than have them hurt in any way. For a man who claimed to be a pacifist that was a strange thing to discover about oneself. Waiting for the adoption papers to be processed was torment. Caroline felt so certain that it would all go through without a hitch, but he lived in dread until it had all been signed and sealed. For Caroline's sake he had to find the right words. He knocked on Sheila's door and waited for a reply. Sheila opened it and looked defiantly at him.

'Good morning, Rector. You've managed to call then at last.'

Peter looked down at her and gave her a tentative smile. 'Good morning. May I come in for a moment Lady Bissett?'

'You may.'

He followed her into the sitting room. She indicated the sofa with a nod of her head. Peter clasped his hands and took a deep breath.

'It has come to my notice, Lady Bissett, that a rumour is going round the village to the effect that Alexander and Elizabeth are my children by Suzy Meadows.'

'Is there?' Momentarily, Sheila looked uncomfortable and then defiant.

'I can't deny it, because it is the truth. I won't go into the circumstances which brought it about, but I will say this; my wife, the one person in the world who should have felt entitled to take her revenge on me, in fact did not do anything of the kind. When she found out that Suzy couldn't keep her twins, Caroline asked to adopt them, as much for my sake as for her own. As you know she can't ever be a mother herself, but out of some great store of compassion, she decided that adopting the twins would make everything right for everyone. Suzy wanted that too. If Caroline can find such love and understanding when she has the most right to feel deeply hurt, is it not possible that you could find it also?'

Sheila didn't answer.

'I have no right to ask for sympathy for myself, but perhaps I have a right to ask for it for Caroline.'

Still Sheila didn't answer. With her hands resting on her lap she sat staring at Peter, waiting for him to continue.

'There really isn't anything else to say. I hope that you can find it in your heart to show some of the compassion which Caroline has shown me, and that you will endeavour for her sake not to make life more difficult for her than it is. Please don't encourage the gossip, that wouldn't be right, but put the situation in the best light that you can?'

'I like your wife, and in the circumstances I wouldn't want to make matters worse for her. But it's only for her sake not yours. You can't be forgiven for what you have done, not a man in your position. Just as you can't be forgiven for letting me resign.'

'With regard to your resignation, we ran the Flower Festival through the committee and the others didn't want all white displays. We did decide democratically, Lady Bissett. I'm only sorry that we have not the opportunity to benefit from your flair and expertise. I have been giving the matter some thought and I wondered if you might like to put some all white displays in the church hall? Everyone will be going in there for refreshments and will have plenty of opportunity for seeing the displays. The hall is rather bare as it is now isn't it?'

'Would I have a free hand?'

'Absolutely.'

'Then I shall be in charge of the church hall flowers on the day.'

Peter stood, and so did Sheila. He took her hand and, looking straight into her eyes, thanked her for her understanding and told her that there were few people in this world who could have overlooked the committee's decision with such generosity of spirit. Sheila found herself blushing with delight. She squeezed his hand and assured him of her intention to make a real success of her task. 'You won't regret asking me, Peter. And I'll remember about Caroline.'

'Thank you, Sheila. Thank you.'

Caroline, knowing she must be brave and go out to meet people, set off for a walk with the twins on the pretext that they wouldn't settle so she thought perhaps an outing in the pram might get them both to sleep. Pat Duckett was leaving her cottage on her way to get ready for school dinners. She called across to Caroline, 'Morning Dr Harris. Isn't it lovely? Just right for getting the twins a breath of air. Aren't they coming on?' She poked her head in the hood and tickled Beth and then Alex under their chins. 'You two be good for your mum. My they are looking great. You must be so proud of 'em.'

'Yes, I am, Pat.'

'Bye then, I must be off. I tell you what, I wish you'd bring them in for the children to see. I'll ask Mr Palmer if it's all right shall I?'

'I don't think he'd want me coming into school.'

'He would if I asked him. Walk round with me and I'll ask him now. Come on. No time like the present.'

The children were delighted. They asked her questions about how the babies could be twins when they were a boy and a girl. Caroline explained as best she could. They all wanted to cuddle them, and eventually when the twins started getting fractious, Caroline said she must be going. Michael Palmer came to the gate with her.

'You and Peter have their loyalty, you know. Never doubt that.'

'Thank you, Michael, very much.' She smiled at him, trying hard not to let him see how much she was affected by their kindness.

When she called in the Store to do a bit of shopping she found Harriet deep in conversation with Venetia.

'Why, hello, Caroline,' Venetia enthused. 'How lovely to see you. When we have our opening night will you and Peter be able to attend? I wondered if he would take the first swim in the pool that night as a way of celebrating our little enterprise? He's such a good advertisement for a healthy body.'

'Oh come on, Venetia, let it rest. There's plenty of other men who could do that for you with a lot more verve and sex appeal than Peter.'

'I tell you what, after the rumours I've heard this morning, I realise now why you're so touchy about him. I think it's very courageous of you to take on those twins. Not many women would do it.'

'I'd better leave, Harriet, before I say something I shall regret. I'll come back later when you have more time.' And Caroline opened the door wide and pushed the pram out, blinded by tears she was determined not to let Venetia see.

Harriet exploded. 'How dare you make a remark like that? How dare you?'

'I was complimenting her on her courage.'

'Complimenting her? Oh, so that's what you call it. We are all very upset about this nasty gossip that Sheila Bissett has been spreading and we're standing behind them both on this. There was no need for you to say what you did. I'm so mad I think we'd better postpone our discussion to another day. If indeed I ever feel like discussing it with you ever again.'

'You're letting sentiment get in the way of business Harriet. Jimbo wouldn't let that happen. Have it your own way. Perhaps Jimbo has more of a business brain than you. I ought to have known.'

She tripped out of the Store leaving Harriet fuming at the woman's lack of sensitivity. She went through to the back office in search of someone to whom she could let off steam.

'Jimbo, where are you? Isn't he back yet Mother?'

Sadie looked around and said, 'No, he isn't. She's right you know. You did let your feelings get the better of you. No one can afford to turn business away nowadays.'

'You agree with what she said then?'

'No, but it is a free country.'

'Not in our Store it isn't.'

Peter found Caroline in the kitchen with Alex and Beth fast asleep in their pram.

'Sorry it's taken me so long to get back I . . .'

'Shush . . . keep your voice down. I've just got them to sleep. What did she say?'

'Sylvia in?'

'No, she's having some time off. How did you get on?'

'Reading between the lines, Sheila had been expecting me to go round the morning after the Flower Festival to apologise and agree to her all white job. When I didn't go, she decided to get her own back. I have unashamedly used every trick in the book to persuade her of the error of her ways. I told her she was quite right, that Alex and Beth are mine, but that we had decided to say nothing both for the children's sake, for Suzy's and for yours. It seemed the best of all the options. So we've come to a compromise. She's apologised to you through me, I've apologised for the

Flower Festival Committee being a bit high-handed and disregarding her wishes, and in return she's doing flower displays in the church hall where we shall be serving refreshments all day. I've no doubt they will be so magnificent we shall be able to charge for visiting the hall as well. So honour is satisfied all round.'

'Thank God for that. I feel shattered about it all. You were quite right, we couldn't really expect to keep it a secret. Let's hope it's a nine days wonder. I've received nothing but kindness from everyone, except from Venetia Mayer. The woman is totally lacking in tact. She could cause a lot of trouble for you, Peter. Apparently she wants you to be the first to dive into the pool at the Health Club on opening night. Something about you being an "excellent advertisement for a healthy body".'

'Oh help, what will the woman think of next? I'm glad Jimbo's running with me at the moment. At least there's safety in numbers!'

'I think maybe we shall weather the storm. Do you?'

'Yes, I do. You don't regret adopting Alex and Beth, do you Caroline?'

'Never for one moment. Except sometimes in the night when I've had hardly any sleep then I *do* wonder if I'm right in the head. But not seriously.'

'I love you, my darling.'

'And I love you too.'

7

When Peter heard the heavy hammering on the Rectory door he knew it was Willie. Willie always knocked as though there was a major emergency on hand. He opened the door to find his verger standing on the step holding a large box full of plants.

'You're looking very smart today Willie. I hardly recognised you.'

'Thank you sir. Thought I'd spend a bit of money and get done up.'

'You've certainly got done up and no mistake. If I didn't know better I'd think you were courting. I assume those plants are for me. Are you staying to put them in?'

'Well I could, sir, if you like. I'm not dressed for it, but I don't mind.'

'I'm going to get Sylvia to make me a coffee. My wife's taken the twins for their injections this morning so Sylvia's in charge. Come into the kitchen and we'll get her to make one for you as well.'

'Right, thank you Rector, I will.'

The two of them went into the kitchen to find Sylvia almost hidden behind a pile of ironing.

'You know Willie our verger, don't you Sylvia?'

'Yes I do, Mr Harris. How are you, Willie?'

'Fine thanks Mrs Bennett.'

'Sylvia's the name.'

'Right well, Sylvia then.'

Peter offered to make coffee. But Sylvia declined his offer.

'I shall be glad of a break thank you. I'll do it.'

They all three sat down in front of the Aga with their coffee. Peter asked Willie how his house alterations were going on.

'Very well indeed Rector thank you. Nearly completed they are.' The telephone rang and Peter went to answer it.

Willie cleared his throat and asked Sylvia how the Flower Festival was going on.

'Very well indeed. You know Lady Bissett is doing the flowers in the church hall, do you? She tried to take over the whole thing but we wouldn't let her.'

'Sounds just like her. I was in Culworth yesterday. I see they've got a nice musical on, done by the Operatic Society, *The Mikado* it's called. Have you seen it?'

'No, I never have.'

'I just wondered. I fancied going.'

'Oh, I see.'

Willie drank some more of his coffee trying to think how to phrase the big question without risking a rebuff.

'Do you get plenty of time off while you're here?' he began casually.

'Usually every evening. And most weekends, unless there's something special on.'

'I see. So if you wanted to go out you could.'

'Yes, I can and I do.'

'So if I came up with two tickets for it you'd be free to go?'

'Oh yes.'

'Shall I do that then?'

'Willie Biggs, are you asking me out?'

Willie pondered the implications of this question and then decided that in for a penny in for a pound.

'Well, yes I am.'

Peter came back in. 'Old Mrs Woods in the almshouses in Penny Fawcett is dying and she's asking for me. I've got to go out there straight away. Tell Caroline I shan't be back for a while, will you Sylvia?'

'Certainly Rector.'

'I'll settle up with you for the plants when I get back, Willie. Next time I see you we'll have a word about clearing out the boiler house store room.'

Bracing himself for Sylvia's answer, Willie looked up vaguely at Peter and said, 'Right sir.' Peter smiled to himself and hastened off to old Mrs Woods.

'Very well, Willie, if that's an invitation I'm accepting.'

'Accepting? Oh right then. I'll see about the tickets and let you know.'

He banged down his cup by the sink said, 'Thanks for the coffee' and hurried out without a backward glance. Sylvia, washing up the cups, was bent over the sink laughing. He didn't expect a yes I bet. Well, why not? What have I got to lose? Nothing at all. And he's nice enough. Thinks I haven't noticed he's smartened himself up. Usually means a woman in tow when a bachelor smartens up. Done his house up too. Must be serious.

*

After Willie had put the plants in the Rectory garden he went home to admire his cottage. He'd given it a good clean and tidy up after the building work and he was almighty satisfied with it. Having done all the work he'd have to pluck up courage to ask her back after *The Mikado* and no mistake. Since he'd had the bathroom made and the kitchen fitted out with those units from MFI that were going for a song, he'd realised how much the new things showed up the rest of the cottage. As a result he'd acquired a new carpet, new curtains and new chairs for his little sitting room. He'd also bought some house plants and special pots to put them in. Altogether home was beginning to look like one of those places he'd seen in the magazines at the dentist's when he'd been forced to go with that raging toothache; cosy but a bit special. The old stuff had gone on a bonfire in the churchyard along with a lot of other rubbish he'd kept ever since his mother had died. Sylvia wouldn't be going in the bedroom, so if he kept the door closed while she was there he could set about clearing that out in his own good time. She didn't know it, but he'd bought the tickets on the off chance when he was in Culworth yesterday. He'd call round tomorrow and tell her he'd got them. He just hoped he hadn't shown how agitated he was, he'd only to come near her and he felt like a boy of sixteen with his first love. Well, she was his first love and . . . The door bell rang. Willie went to answer it, hoping it wouldn't be Sylvia saying she'd changed her mind.

It wasn't. It was Gwen Baxter.

'Hello Gwen, what can I do for you? First time since I can't remember when that you've knocked on my door.'

Gwen always spoke as though she was on the bridge of a ship during a violent storm. Willie stepped back to avoid not only the smell emanting from her but to lessen the impact of her gruff voice. 'Wouldn't be knocking now if I wasn't needing help. There's something wrong with the tank on the roof and we need help. Beryl's standing watching the bucket. It's filling up with water nearly as fast as she can empty it.'

'What do you want me to do?'

'Attend to it of course.'

'I'm not a plumber, Gwen.'

'I know that. But you could look at it for us.'

'Well, I'll look, but I'm not promising anything.'

She marched across to her cottage with her long strides, Willie dashing along in her wake. The stench which greeted him as he walked through the back door made him feel sick. She took him into the little hallway. The shoulder-high piles of newspapers baffled him. They'd go up like tinder if ever there was a fire. He squeezed between the towering columns and followed Gwen upstairs. Every step had things stacked at each side till it was only possible to put one foot at a time on the step. Basking in the righteousness of his own recent clear out and the improvement it had made, he suggested to Gwen that she had a bonfire too.

'A bonfire? Whatever for? We need all these things.'

Beryl appeared at the head of the stairs carrying a heavy bucket. She waited till they got to the top and then raced downstairs as fast as she could to empty it.

'I shall have to get in the loft, you know,' Willie told Gwen.

'There's a trap door in the ceiling in our bedroom.' She opened the door to their room.

'Have you got a ladder?'

'Yes. Wait there I'll get it.'

Willie looked round. It was not the kind of bedroom he would have liked to sleep in. His own was a prince in comparison. Every item in here needed either throwing away or a thoroughly good wash. Preferably throwing away. He began to itch, first on his ankles and then further up his legs. Oh Lord, surely they hadn't got fleas? The sooner he was out of here the better. He saw Beryl galloping up the stairs with an empty bucket. Gwen appeared with the ladder and he managed to push open the trapdoor and heave himself up into the loft. It was a burst pipe. A major joint, botched by some amateur plumber in years gone by, had opened up and water was pouring from the slit through the floor onto the landing below. He shouted down.

'It's no good Gwen, there's a big slit in the pipe up here. I'll have to turn off the water and you'll need to get a proper plumber.'

'Can't you do it?'

'No I can't, I haven't got the right equipment.'

Willie dropped down onto the ladder and pulled the trap door shut.

'Where's the stop tap?'

'Under the sink.'

He pushed his way between the newspapers and went into the kitchen. Willie bent down and after a great deal of effort turned the tap completely off. 'It'll be a while before the water stops running. You really will have to get a plumber to come, Gwen. Use the phone in the Store.'

'So far you've told me to have a bonfire, get rid of our belongings and now phone the plumber. Anything else you'd like to instruct me about?'

'No. I'm only offering advice.' Beryl rushed through with another bucket and emptied it with more vigour than sense into the sink. Willie stepped out of the way just in time.

'Well, don't offer any more and what's more don't go out and tell people about our house. What we do under our own roof is our affair. I don't want you tittle tattling about us in The Royal Oak. I've seen you going in there.'

'No harm in that.'

'Drink is the devil's work and I ought to know.'

'You mean yer father.'

Gwen swung round and glared into his eyes from only a few inches away. He had all to do not to get his handkerchief out to hold over his nose.

'What do you mean by that?'

'Well, we all know what he was like, Gwen. Went home rolling drunk six nights out of seven didn't he? Be honest.'

'What he did six nights out of seven was his affair.'

'How your mother put up with it I don't know. She was such a clean woman, always washing and scrubbing you all.'

'You find something odd do you in her being so clean?'

'Now, don't take on so.'

Beryl dashed past again with another bucket.

'Well, do you?'

'No, I don't, it just seemed such a pity that she tried so hard and he undid it all. It must have been a relief when he died. Pity she went first. Anyway I must be off.'

'Off to see your lady friend are you?'

'Lady friend?'

'Yes, Sylvia Bennett. Going out for a bit of that there 'ere. Disgusting it is. Disgusting.'

'Later today the rector has a funeral to conduct and I am going to make sure the church is looking its best and to contact the funeral director in the absence of the rector to make sure everything is in order. And I'll thank you not to make nasty remarks about my private affairs.'

'Affair is it now. That's why you've had your house done up. Making it nice for taking her back there. I've been watching you. I know what your evil designs are.'

'Next time you want any help don't send for me.'

Willie went out through the narrow opening of the back door, enraged at Gwen's dirty mind. He had a good wash in his new bathroom and as he changed his clothes discovered bites all the way up his legs. All during the funeral he had to exercise the utmost control to stop himself from scratching. He explained to Peter when the funeral party had gone.

'Sorry, sir, if I've been behaving a bit odd during the service, but I'm afraid I must have got fleas.'

'Fleas? Where from Willie?'

'Gwen and Beryl Baxter's. They've got a leak and I went in to investigate it. They need a plumber but I bet they won't bother with one.'

'Have you had to turn off the water?'

'Had to else that house of theirs would be flooded. Mind you, not a bad thing. It's foul, like their minds, begging your pardon Rector.'

'I'd better go across and see if I can help. They can't manage without running water.'

'I wouldn't if I were you. They'll only be abusive, sir. Not fit for your ears.'

'Willie, I have not lived in an ivory tower all my life, I have been around a bit.'

'Very well sir, as you please.'

Peter tried knocking on the front door and, getting no reply, went round to the back. He knocked loudly and then did as he did at most of the village houses, he opened the door and said, 'It's Peter here from the Rectory, can I come in?'

He pushed open the door as far as it would go and stepped in.

'Hello, Miss Baxter, are you there?' He stepped further into the kitchen. 'Hello?'

There was a sudden rush of feet and Beryl entered the kitchen with a carving knife held threateningly in her hand.

'It's only me, Miss Baxter – Peter from the Rectory. It's all right.'

'Yes?'

'I've come to see if I can help about the leak you have. Have you rung the plumber?'

'That's for Gwen to decide.'

'Is she here?'

'Yes.'

He heard more footsteps and then Gwen burst in through the kitchen door.

'What do you think you are doing entering our house without asking?'

'I'm sorry but I usually knock and then walk in when I go visiting. In future I'll knock and wait for you to answer. I've come about you having to get Willie to turn the water off.'

'Well, he's done it.'

'How are you going to manage without running water?'

'Quite well thank you.'

'We could let you have some water from the Rectory if that would help until the plumber gets here.'

'We don't want any favours.'

'If you like I'll phone the plumber on your behalf and in the meantime Willie and I will bring you some water across.'

'We do not require help from someone who professes to be a goody goody and then fornicates with his neighbour. I don't think Jesus had that in mind when he said love thy neighbour.'

Peter had no answer to that.

'Don't think that because we don't socialise we don't know what goes on. We have a complete view of the comings and goings of this place from our windows. Nothing goes on that we don't know about. I saw you go round to see that slut and saw how long it took you to leave. Then when we saw her getting bigger, we knew. Oh, yes we knew. Then your wife tries to cover your tracks by wanting to adopt them. What a joke. Standing by her man. Ha. No man living deserves loyalty like that. Not one of you. You're all scum. Scum, do you hear?'

'I think it would be better if I take my leave. No person is totally perfect and I above all am aware of the fragility of both man and woman, but we can ask for forgiveness. Perhaps you need forgiveness for thinking the way you do. May God bless you both.' Peter forced open the door and left.

'Get out, get out and don't ever come back. Fornicator.'

When he got home he went straight upstairs, undressed, showered, put fresh clothes on and went into his study and got out what Caroline called the 'parish whisky'. He poured some into a glass and sat at his desk trying to erase from his mind the evil he had just encountered. Caroline came in carrying Beth who was in her permanently happy mood. Nothing ruffled her calm.

'They actually live in this village day in day out and their lives are so foul, Caroline, I can't believe it. How on earth can it have happened, that they turn out like that?'

'Here, nurse your daughter for a while, she'll restore your faith in human nature. I would have thought that by now you could no longer be surprised by the infinite variety of the human condition.' Peter took Beth in his arms, propped her carefully against his shoulder and rubbed his cheek on hers to remind himself that there was still something beautiful left in the world.

'This is something much, much worse. You can feel the evil in the air. To say nothing of the smell. Don't ever call on them Caroline please. Nor let the children near them either. There's something very wrong there, believe me. Beryl came into the kitchen brandishing a carving knife.'

'You mean holding a carving knife?'

'No *brandishing* it. They must be unhinged. Completely unhinged.

Apparently they watch all the comings and goings from their window and claim nothing goes on that they don't know about.'

'Heavens above, I shall hardly dare go out.'

'Exactly.'

Had Peter been able to see them at that moment he would have seen them struggling to get the top off their old well. Running water had been put in when their parents bought the house on their marriage, and the old well had been covered up. More than sixty years of rain and earth and neglect had wedged the lid tight. Beryl found a spade and dug away some of the earth and grass. Gwen got a steel rod from the shed and used that to prise it loose. Eventually they got the lid off and both peered in. Beryl picked up a stone and threw it down. They listened for the sound of it hitting the water.

'I didn't hear it, did you?'

'No. Throw another one in.'

She did and they both heard it hit the water. In the shed they found a long piece of rope. Beryl emptied the metal rubbish bucket from under the sink and they tied the rope to the handle and dangled it down the well.

After several attempts it came up filled with water.

Gwen grimaced.

'I knew we didn't need a plumber. Interfering sods those men are. Go fill the kitchen sink with it and we'll let it down again.'

Beryl put the plug in the sink and emptied the water from the bucket into it. Things were swimming around. Funny little things with lots of legs and some that wiggled along with no legs at all. And it was green.

'Gwen, I don't think it's fit to drink.'

'We'll boil it.'

'There's funny things in it swimming about.'

'We'll sieve it first.'

'What if it makes us ill?'

'We'll get used to it. Take this bucketful. That'll do us for today, better than tap water with all the chemicals they put in it nowadays.'

'Well we shan't need the plumber shall we?'

'No. We don't use much water anyway.'

8

No one realised that Gwen and Beryl had been taken ill through drinking the well water. The first day they drank it without concern, but then after that they developed serious intestinal infections which laid them low.

It was only when Willie noticed their curtains had not been drawn back for two days that anyone decided to do something about it. Willie, Jimmy and Pat went across together. They tried the front door but couldn't get in so they went through the side gate and pushed open the back door as far as they could. Pat got her handkerchief out and covered her mouth and nose. Even Jimmy, used to a very haphazard regime in his own home, was appalled at what he saw. They called out downstairs and looked in the sitting room but there was no sign of the two sisters. Willie suggested they made their way upstairs together. They tried to push open the main bedroom door and found it almost impossible because of the newspapers piled up from floor to ceiling. They tried the next bedroom and found the two of them prostrate in bed. They had used various containers to be sick in as well as having been sick in the bed, and they lay there, two gaunt, exhausted and unconscious women in dire need of help.

'Right Jimmy, out to the Store, dial 999 and get an ambulance. Tell them what you like but they've got to get here quick.'

'What about asking Dr Harris to come while we wait? Maybe she could give 'em something to 'elp,' Pat suggested.

'Certainly not, we can't ask her to come into this mess. It's enough to make me ill just looking at it. In any case she might get something and give it to them babies. No, that won't do. Have you gone yet Jimmy?'

'I'm just off.'

Pat reached out and tentatively shook Gwen's hand as it lay over the edge of the bed.

'Is this Gwen, Willie, I can't tell the difference? Gwen are you all right? Gwen? Gwen?'

'She's breathing I can see. Go round the other side and try the other one.'

Pat did. She could see that Beryl or Gwen, whichever one it was, was breathing, but she got no response.

'I reckon we've caught 'em only just in time Willie.'

'So do I.'

It must have been all of twenty minutes after Jimmy got back before the ambulance came. Even they, who must have seen some dreadful sights in the past, were appalled at what they saw. They wrapped the sisters up, put them on stretchers and with Willie and Jimmy's help manouevred them down the narrow staircase.

When they'd gone Willie locked up and went to tell Peter what had happened.

'I reckon they're touch and go, sir. Don't know what's caused it, but by Jove they aren't half poorly.'

'I'll ring the hospital and then go in to see them tomorrow. Though if my last encouter is anything to go by it will be far from pleasant.'

'They's too ill to be nasty sir, far too ill.'

'Right Willie. My word, they are two very peculiar women, aren't they?'

'Peculiar is putting it mildly. They weren't that bad as kids. They've gone funnier and funnier since they got into women. You should see the house.' Sylvia came down the stairs and Willie smiled and nodded to her.

'Hello, Sylvia.'

'Hello, Willie.'

Peter tactfully retired to his study.

'There's a good film on in Culworth this week. Funny title, *Fried Green Tomatoes in a Whistle Stop Cafe*, or something. I'm told it's good. Wondered if you'd like to go see it.'

'I would indeed. And when we've been perhaps you'd like to come back here for a coffee.'

'Right you're on. I'll look up the times.'

'I'm buying myself a little car, if it's arrived by then, we could go in that.'

'Didn't know you could drive.'

'Well, I had a car for years for getting into work and then it packed up. But I've decided to get another one. Only an old banger mind.'

'Never mind so long as it goes. I'll be in touch.'

Peter couldn't get to the hospital for two days but he reassured himself by phone that they were recovering. When he did manage to visit them they were unrecognisable, not only because they had lost weight but because they were so scrupulously clean.

'Sister Murphy, how are you?'

'Why, hello, Mr Harris, long time no see. These two parishioners of yours are going to be all right, though heaven knows why. They were in a terrible state when they came in. Dreadfully dehydrated, absolutely filthy and in need of a lot of loving care. Could you come into the office and give me a few details.'

Peter told all he knew and then went to speak to them. He hardly knew which was which.

'Hello, Gwen? Is it Gwen? It's Peter here from the Rectory. How are you today?'

Her eyes opened slowly and focused on his face.

'Go away.'

'I've come to see you because you've been very ill.'

'I don't need you.'

'Very well, my dear. You're in good hands. All you have to do is get yourself better, then you can go home.'

He went to the next bed, took hold of Beryl's hand and spoke her name.

'Beryl, are you awake?' She opened her eyes, looked him full in the face and whispered, 'I told her we shouldn't drink it. I told her.'

'What did you drink Beryl?'

'It was the well.'

He could learn no more from her. She'd fallen asleep again.

The sisters were due home at the end of the next week. Apart from Peter no one had visited them. He organised a plumber to attend to the burst pipe but other than that he did nothing to the house, outfaced by the enormity of the task and afraid of intruding.

The social services were there when he called at the hospital a couple of days before they were to go home.

'We really cannot understand how two people have been allowed to live like they do. Does no one in your village have a conscience about them at all?'

'I know things look very bad and that the house is in a terrible state, but these two women will allow no one in. They shun all friendship, all overtures and totally refuse to accept that they need help. The reason why they drank the water from the well was because they didn't wish to have a plumber in their house. You tell me how to help them in those circumstances?'

'It is difficult I know. But you must persist. In the 1990s it's wicked for old women to be living like they do. The whole village should take responsibility for them. No wonder we find old people have been lying dead in their houses for days before anyone realises. Someone should check them regularly.'

'Well, how about if you talk to them. You've seen the house, you know how unhygienic it is, in fact downright filthy. You offer them help to clean up and decorate or whatever it is you have the ability to instigate and see what kind of a response you get. You can't force people to have help if they don't want it. And they don't. As far as they are concerned their home is all right. It's just how they want it.'

'I'll have a word, I'll persuade them to let us help.'

'I've paid for a plumber myself and he's been in and mended the leak so the water is turned on again and they won't need to use the well. So at least they won't be back in here.'

'Well, that's something. I have a fund which I can use to help them, so I'll see about it straight away.'

Peter nearly said, 'And the best of luck' but didn't, being mindful that he might need their help at some future date for other parishioners.

Despite Gwen and Beryl stoutly refusing all offers of help the social services came to the village, borrowed the key from Peter and cleaned the twin's bedroom and the downstairs rooms and took away all the out of date packets and tins which had accumulated over the years. So when the twins went home from the hospital at least the worst of what had taken place while they were ill had been cleared up.

Gwen and Beryl were horrified when they found out and sent the social worker away with stern reminders that she was not to call to see them under any circumstances and that now they were well again she could cross them off her list.

The day before they were due home Sheila couldn't resist going round and taking a peep through their windows. A golden opportunity she called it. Ron, unwilling to allow her to go alone, found himself sneaking through the side gate. They had a peep through the windows.

'Ron, just look at this kitchen. It's absolutely antiquated. They haven't even a washing machine. No wonder they always look dirty.' Sheila reached up on tip toe and by holding on to the rotting window sill could see into the pantry.

'There's scarcely any food in the pantry, but the shelves have all been wiped. How can they live in there? Someone should do something about it.'

'You offer to go round and clean then.'

'Who'd want to clean up in there I ask you?' She turned round to hear his answer but he'd gone.

'Where are you Ron?'

'I'm down the garden looking at this well.'

Sheila struggled through the undergrowth. She knew she shouldn't have put her high heeled sandals on, but she pressed on. Ron was on his knees throwing stones into the well.

'It's mighty deep is this well. Fancy drinking water straight from this.'

Sheila peered down and sniffed the damp mossy odour. 'It's like those caves we went to see, near Bath was it? Why do they have their house like it is? Anyway no one can help them. The social services have helped a bit but they've not done enough. What do we pay all these taxes for?'

'Let's be off.'

'Shouldn't we put the lid on the well, Ron?'

'Yes, OK.' He pushed the heavy rotting old lid over the top as best he could. 'Surprises me they could move it in the first place. They must be stronger than they look, those two.' He stood up, dusted the earth from his trouser knees, and they walked towards the side gate. As they approached, Gwen and Beryl appeared from the front path.

Gwen became immediately enraged. 'How dare you, what do you think you're doing? Thought we weren't home until tomorrow did you? Well, we discharged ourselves early. Couldn't cope with their interfering ways. What do you think you're doing creeping about our garden like this? Get out, go on get out.' Gwen was angry, but Beryl was frightened. 'Go away, please go away,' she called.

Ron tried some of the assertiveness training he'd learnt on a course for union leaders. Assuming his most authoritative voice he marched towards them saying, 'Now Miss Baxter we've been in to make sure the lid was on the well securely. Couldn't take the risk of one of you falling down it could we? All's well, now I've attended to it, you've no need to fear. Glad you're well enough to come home. Take care of . . .'

Ron got no further. Gwen picked up an almost bristleless broom and raised it above her head, obviously intent on hitting him with it. The head of the broom caught Ron on the side of his head with an enormous thwack. The words he'd just used about her being stronger than he'd thought came back to him as she struck him again and again. Sheila intervened in an attempt to help Ron, but Beryl came behind her and gripped her arms. Suddenly Gwen stopped. She went quite pale and very short of breath.

Beryl let go of Sheila and went to Gwen's aid. The two of them unlocked the back door and Gwen and then Beryl squeezed inside and shut the door.

'Ron, Ron, let's get home before anyone finds out.'

'Quick, through the gate. I feel such a fool.'

Inside their own home, Ron turned on Sheila.

'Can you tell me why I listen to you? It's you who got me into this predicament. I've that interview to do tomorrow for the ITV programme. All kinds of a fool I'm going to look with a bruise and a swelling the size of an egg on the side of my head.' He tenderly examined his head with the tips of his thick fingers. 'You're nothing but a confounded nuisance Sheila and after all these years it's time I stopped listening to you. In future *I* say what we do.'

'Well really, when I think of how I wait on you hand and foot, you don't do a hand's turn in the house and now you say I'm a confounded nuisance.'

'Well, you are. Don't ever suggest that we have anything to do with those two damned women ever again.' He stamped off upstairs to Sheila's navy and lavender bathroom, angry about the impression he would give on the TV programme. Maybe if he sat on the left hand side of the discussion group the lump would not be too obvious to the audience. The media certainly made one conscious of one's image. Talking of images, he wished Sheila looked more like Harriet Charter-Plackett or Caroline Harris. No not them, more like Sadie Beauchamp. Now she always looked stylish. Sheila never quite got her clothes right. And that dyed hair, he'd have to have a word about that.

His afternoon tea was ready when he got downstairs. Neat little brown bread sandwiches and a plate of scones with jam. No cream because of his cholesterol. The china teapot, the tea strainer and a neat little pink serviette for his knee. He'd much rather have had a big cup of strong tea, at the table in the kitchen and some well fried bacon between two slices of fresh white bread.

'There's a possibility I might get a chance to sit on the Question Time panel Sheila.'

'Honestly? Why didn't you tell me straight away? Oh Ron that really is something. Question Time, well I never. Could I sit in the audience?'

'It's not quite the thing to do that. In any case I wouldn't want you there.'

'Would I make you nervous?'

'No, embarrassed.'

'Embarrassed? That's nice.'

'I mean it. You spend ridiculous money on clothes and somehow you never quite make it. That leopard skin coat will have to go for a start.'

'My leopard skin?'

'Don't keep repeating what I say.'

'I don't keep repeating what you say.'

'You do, you've just done it again. Anyway, that coat'll have to go. And when you go into Culworth to the hairdresser's you can get your hair made back to what it ought to be.'

'It cost a lot to get it like this.'

'It's not worth it, believe me. If I'm going to move in Question Time circles you've got to move with me. Hair done like when you were serving in The Case is Altered is not right now. We've moved up from then.'

'I do try.'

'No, you don't, you've stayed stuck like a gramophone needle. I bet Sadie Beauchamp spends no more money on clothes and hair than you do but she looks like a lady.'

'If I don't look like her and she looks like a lady, what do I look like then?'

'What you always looked like, a barmaid.'

'A barmaid?' Sheila's feelings were hurt in a way she couldn't remember ever before. This then was the thanks she got for trying. She stood up, scattering her sandwiches over the coffee table, 'This will cost you and not half Ron, not half. You wait and see.'

'Yes I will. You're Lady Bissett now, not Sheila with her brassy hair, twinkling away to get the punters to buy more drink. When I get back tomorrow night from Birmingham we'll lay some plans.'

9

As Harriet dashed across to the church to help water the arrangements the flower society had worked on the day before, she noticed Ralph's Mercedes parked in front of his and Muriel's house. Oh good they're back. And in time for the Festival too. How nice to see them again.

She got there and found Sylvia had arrived first.

'Good morning, Sylvia. You're early.'

'Well, I decided to get absolutely in front of myself this morning, because Dr Harris and the rector and I want to spend time here today and of course the rector is giving the recital too, so we're sharing the work load so that we can all enjoy the Festival in turns.'

'It's a lovely day. Let's hope it brings the crowds and we make lots of money.'

'Let's hope so.' They went from arrangement to arrangement feeling the oasis and deciding how much water, if any, the holders needed. The church looked quite the best it had ever done. Willie Biggs had worked marvels with spotlights and floodlights emphasising the flowers in all the right places.

'There's more to Willie than meets the eye isn't there Sylvia? Who'd have thought he would have had the sensitivity to know how to show the flowers and the murals and tombs to such good effect?'

'Yes, there is more to him than one thinks. He certainly has an ear for music.'

'Oh how's that?'

'Well, to tell the truth we went to see *The Mikado* together in Culworth last week and he can sing some of the songs really well. If he wasn't the verger, he should be in the choir.'

'I didn't know you and he were . . .'

'Well, we are just good friends that's all.'

'Just like they used to say in the papers! Have you any water left in that jug? This arrangement under the pulpit needs a drop more.'

'Yes, here you are. I don't need to ask you not to say anything do I?'

'I shall be as silent as the grave, Sylvia.'

'Thank you, Mrs Charter-Plackett. He'd be so embarrassed if he thought everyone knew.'

'You won't keep it a secret for long as he well knows. Nothing can go on in this village without everyone knowing. Although come to think of it there have been a few well kept secrets in the past.'

Sheila chose the morning of the Flower Festival to launch her new image. Ron had been with her to Culworth to help choose her outfit. After a lot of wrangling on Sheila's part, he had persuaded her to buy a very expensive suit which he declared would come in useful for all sorts of occasions. It was a soft olive green and Ron had chosen a delicate cream blouse to wear with it. The collar of the blouse flowed over the neck of the collarless jacket. The most astounding difference was her hair. It had been made a soft mousey colour with slight blonde highlights and cut quite short but flatteringly around her face. Instead of her usual strappy stilettos she had chosen a pair of medium heeled dark chestnut shoes with a small matching handbag. Ron had surreptiously been making mental notes of the way Sadie Beauchamp made up her face and had supervised Sheila's make up, having slyly hidden her rouge and the bright blue eye shadow she normally affected.

She purposely arrived in the church hall a little late pretending to be checking whether or not her flower arrangements needed more water. Several early visitors to the Festival didn't recognise her. 'Why Lady Bissett, we didn't see you there.' They would have bitten their tongues out before they could be friendly. They hadn't quite forgiven her yet for pointing out that young Alexander was so like the Rector. After all some things were best left unsaid. Out of the corner of her eye Sheila saw Sadie Beauchamp arrive for her morning coffee. This she knew was the great test. Sheila went to buy her third coffee that morning quite coincidentally at the same time as Sadie.

'Why hello, it's Sheila. I hope you don't mind me making a comment but, I must say, you look absolutely charming. And your hair too!'

'Thank you.'

'Where did you buy your suit?'

'Fisk's.'

'They have some lovely things in there. You've made a good choice.'

Ron watched the exchange from across the hall and felt well satisfied with his campaign.

The church hall had a continuous queue of customers for refreshments. Harriet had to go back to the Store three times for more milk and bread and cakes, and also for another ham to carve for the rolls and sandwiches. The flowers in the church hall were not all white as Sheila had insisted upon. They were mainly white but here and there she had placed pale yellow flowers to give warmth and they were pronounced a great success. To her delight several customers said they'd put an extra fifty pence in the cash box as a fee for viewing her flowers.

There was such a steady stream of visitors to see the flowers in the church that Willie was in attendance all day keeping a watchful eye on anyone who might be a threat to the arrangements. Sylvia's friend, who'd been in charge of the church arrangements, blushed with delight when Peter complimented her on the effective way her society had picked up the colours of the stained glass windows and the murals.

'Wonderful, truly wonderful and we do appreciate you standing in at such short notice,' Peter said, whereupon Sylvia's friend blushed again to the roots of her hair and had to retire to the church hall for a cup of tea while she recovered. The organ recital, given by Mrs Peel and Peter, filled the church and most satisfactory of all, it was full again when the school choir did their performance prior to the church closing at seven.

Ralph and Muriel, having travelled through the night from the airport, didn't put in an appearance until the school choir was performing. Willie Biggs, adjusting some lights so they shone on the children while they sang, was the first to notice their arrival.

He whispered, 'Welcome home Sir Ralph, Lady Templeton.'

Muriel whispered back that he had no need to stand on ceremony, they were still Ralph and Muriel as before.

Harriet, standing at the back, gazing full of love and motherly pride on Fergus, Finlay and Flick singing on the front row of the choir, felt a slight nudge at her elbow. When she saw Muriel she broke into a delighted smile and whispered, 'See you afterwards.'

When the church was finally closed for the night Harriet suggested that Ralph and Muriel, Peter and Caroline should come over to her house about eight thirty when she'd had a chance to get the children to bed and they could all catch up on Ralph and Muriel's news.

Caroline arranged with Sylvia to babysit for a while. 'I shall be glad to, my feet are nearly killing me. Would it be all right if I asked Willie in for a bite to eat? It'll be his first chance of a meal all day. I thought afterwards we'd watch TV.'

'Of course, that will be fine. I've got the twins to sleep so they shouldn't be any trouble. Go and ask him to come in. Peter and I are nearly ready to go. Don't forget to switch the baby alarm on in case the twins cry, will you?'

'I'll do that. I won't be a moment asking him.'

Caroline grinned at Peter. 'As fast as we get one romance sorted out there's another one to be tactful about.'

'I don't think anything will come of it, do you really?'

'Come here, your shirt is out at the back. Why not? One should grab happiness while one can. There's too little of it in this world.' Peter turned round and linked his hands around Caroline's waist.

'Except here in this house. I thought I was completely happy before, but I had no idea what happiness was till now.'

'Thank you for saying that. I know I gave you a hard time when I found out about Suzy; I honestly believed the end of my world had come. That was until I recognised how much I needed you.'

'I love you my darling. Give me a kiss.'

'Peter, we mustn't start kissing. Sylvia will be back with Willie, and we've got to go.'

'Have we? Well, yes, I expect we have. Just one then. Did you notice Sheila Bissett today? I hardly recognised her.'

'Bought her outfit in Fisk's in Culworth.'

'How do you know?'

'I asked her when I complimented her on how charming she looked. Ron grew about two feet taller.'

'Shall I check Beth and Alex?'

'Yes please. You played beautifully today, Peter.'

'Thank you, my darling girl.'

Willie was installed in the kitchen with Sylvia cooking an omelette on the Aga when they got downstairs.

'We shall only be about an hour, Sylvia.'

'Be as long as you like Dr Harris. Willie and I are going to watch TV so we shan't notice the time. We'll listen for Beth and Alex.'

'Good night Willie.'

'Good night sir.'

Sadie was already there when they arrived at Harriet and Jimbo's.

'Good evening you two, escaped for a while from your family cares?'

'Good evening Sadie. No, we've escaped from playing gooseberry.'

'Playing gooseberry?'

Caroline winked at Sadie and put her finger to her lips.

'Not able to disclose.'

'Oh I see. It's Sylvia is it?'

Harriet pushed a drink into her mother's hand. 'Hush, mother, you're getting into a real village gossip. Don't pry.'

'My dear Harriet, what else is there to talk about but the goings on in the village? I swear I could write a column every week for the local rag on the comings and goings in this village. "Village Voice", I'd call it and I wouldn't be short of items for it either. A couple of evenings in The Royal Oak and I'd have enough material for three columns in no . . .'

'You never go in The Royal Oak.'

'I could always start. Do you suppose the Culworth Gazette would pay me for it?'

'Don't say you need the money,' Harriet retorted.

Peter laughed. 'Compose your first column Sadie, right here and now.'

'OK here we go. Item one. Venetia and Jeremy Mayer are opening their new health club in two weeks' time. The local rector is performing the opening ceremony by being the first to dive in the pool. He has been chosen because of his superb athletic figure, Venetia Mayer told your reporter. Local people are expected to gather in their hundreds to witness their trendy rector performing this duty.'

'Oh no he's not,' Peter declared amidst a lot of laughter.

'Item Two. What is this we hear? Villagers are no longer friendly caring people as in the past. Two local residents lay ill for three days before anyone realised. Their lives were saved by the prompt action of the verger. Village life is not what it was in days of yore.

'Item Three. What has prompted the said verger to spruce up his house, put a bathroom in and a new kitchen and buy new clothes? Is there romance in the air we ask?

'Item Four. A local aristocrat has abandoned her unbelievably tasteless clothes and become quite civilised. The hairdresser in Culworth has thrown away her last bottles of peroxide. Her best customer has gone mousey.'

'Mother, that is cruel.'

Caroline agreed. 'Very cruel Sadie. She has made a real effort.'

'Yes, you're right, it was cruel. She is trying, I have to admit.'

Peter suggested that Sheila was quite nice once she'd dropped her pretence of being landed gentry.

The door bell rang and Jimbo went to answer it, to find Muriel and Ralph at the door bearing gifts.

'Come in, delighted to see you both. Have you had a good trip?'

'Absolutely wonderful Jimbo. But we're so glad to be back. We couldn't wait another night. Ralph drove us straight here from the airport.'

'Hello, everyone.'

Muriel stood in the doorway looking tanned and radiant. Sadie went towards them crying, 'Why, Muriel you look ten years younger, what have you been doing?'

Harriet blushed, 'Mother really, what a thing to say to someone just back from their honeymoon.' Muriel took the innuendo in her stride. Her arms were full of presents.

'We've brought presents for everyone. This boomerang is for Fergus, this is a fearsome Aborigine carving for Finlay, and these carved wooden beads are for Flick. Harriet this is for you. It's a wrap for you to put on when you come out of your pool. Jimbo, we've bought you a beach shirt from Bondi Beach. Here are some toys for the twins, Caroline. I nearly got them some clothes but I wasn't sure of the size, babies grow so quickly. The huge parcel Ralph is carrying is a sheepskin rug for you Peter and for you Caroline. I do hope you like it. Sadie this is a silk scarf for you. I hope I've made a good choice, you're always so clever with your clothes. I do hope you all like them.'

'Muriel spent most of the honeymoon choosing those presents. To say nothing of all the things she's bought for the house and for me.'

'Ralph, I did no such thing.' They all smiled at Muriel's indignation.

'Let's all have drinks while we open our parcels.'

When they'd opened their presents and caught up with some of the news from Australia and Turnham Malpas, Harriet suggested they went into the kitchen and collected whatever they liked from the leftovers of the Flower Festival catering. And if Jimbo opened some wine they could sit down and talk some more.

Caroline, about to put a roll filled with ham and cream cheese into her mouth said, 'This ham looks delicious Jimbo. In fact everything you sell is delicious. You don't sell rabbit do you? We had some a while back. It was gorgeous. We used a recipe of Sylvia's grandmother's, all herbs and spices and things. Why don't you sell them in the Store, Jimbo? I'm sure Jimmy Glover could keep you well supplied and it would be a nice little addition to his income for him.'

Jimbo glanced questioningly at her and said, 'Jimmy gave you them did he?'

'Yes, that's right.' She unconcernedly continued eating until Jimbo said, 'I'm surprised at you Caroline.'

'Surprised at me, what have I done?' Harriet tapped his knee and shook her head but he ignored her. 'I wouldn't have thought you would have condoned eating an animal that had been trapped and no doubt been in excruciating pain most of the night.'

Caroline put down her fork and looked at Jimbo in surprise. 'What do you mean? He *shoots* the rabbits . . . doesn't he?'

'No, he traps them.'

'You're wrong, Jimbo. I've seen him with a gun.'

'That's as maybe, but he traps his rabbits. Ask any of the villagers, they all know he does it.'

'He wouldn't give me rabbits he'd *trapped* now would he? You're quite wrong Jimbo, isn't he Peter?'

Ralph answered her question. 'He does trap rabbits, Caroline, and has done all his life and his father and his grandfather and no doubt his great-grandfather before him.'

'I don't believe you. Traps them? I thought that all stopped years ago.'

Ralph shook his head. 'It may have declined but Jimmy still does it. Prides himself on using the same type of snare his father used. I'm sorry Caroline.'

'Not as sorry as I am. It's barbaric, absolutely barbaric. And I ate them. I feel terrible.'

Peter stood up and went across to her, taking her plate to prevent the contents sliding onto the floor. 'Darling, please don't upset yourself. You didn't cook them knowing how they'd . . . died, did you?'

'That's the kind of remark people make about torture and mass executions. What could we do about it they say, we didn't know and they think it makes it all right. They think that takes away the guilt. It doesn't. He has to be stopped. Peter, I very nearly gave the twins a taste, but decided the gravy was too rich. I can't bear to think of how I would feel if I had done that. Oh God.' Caroline shuddered.

'There you are then, at least they haven't eaten them.'

'But they could have done. What time is it, I'm going round to see Jimmy right now.'

Jimbo, who'd spent the last couple of minutes feeling decidedly uncomfortable and trying to avoid Harriet's angry looks, decided he must pour oil on the trouble he had stirred up.

'No good going tonight Caroline, I expect he'll be in The Royal Oak by now. Sleep on it, you'll feel better in the morning.'

'Sleep on it? Ignore it, it'll go away. The rabbits won't feel the hurt so much if Caroline sleeps on it, is that it? I've eaten one of those rabbits. Actually eaten one and it makes me feel sick. The children have rabbits on their eiderdowns and they look so sweet, they're doing head over heels all round the edges, and I do love them.' She looked up at Peter, her eyes filling with tears.

Peter started to feel real concern about Caroline, he couldn't remember when he'd seen her so distressed, apart from . . .

'I think we'd better be getting home, we've left Sylvia quite long enough and it is her day off really.'

Caroline jumped to her feet. 'I know, you go home and I'll go into the pub and look for Jimmy.'

Muriel, wishing the floor would open up and swallow her, murmured quietly, 'Don't you think The Royal Oak is a bit public for a discussion of this nature?'

'Muriel! I thought you of all people would be on my side.'

'Oh I am, I am, but I think you need to sleep on it first. Don't be too hasty.'

'Ralph what do you think? And you, Harriet, where do you stand?'

Harriet answered first. 'Frankly, I'm on your side but I'd want to act quietly rather than making a big public fuss.'

'And you Ralph?'

'Well Caroline, I suppose you could say I am at heart a country man having spent my childhood here and I have to admit to going poaching with Jimmy's father when I was a boy. When I think of the sum total of all the agony in the world, a few rabbits in Sykes Wood are a very minor incident aren't they?'

'I'm afraid I can't agree with your argument.' As Sadie had contributed nothing to the discussion Caroline asked her how she felt.

'Frankly one more or less concerns me not at all, there are far more pressing problems in this world than the demise of a few rabbits,' Sadie yawned. 'In any case I'm off home now.'

Caroline pulled a disapproving face and said, 'Right, Peter, we'd better go, as you say. Thank you for the supper Harriet, I do hope I haven't upset things too much but . . . Anyway I must go.' Caroline marched for the door leaving Peter to follow. He thanked Jimbo and Harriet for their hospitality, wished Ralph and Muriel a goodnight and went out after his darling girl.

As they passed the church she said, 'It's no good, Peter. I'm going to see if he's in the pub. You go on home.'

'Please Caroline, please don't.'

'When we married we both agreed that there would be no trespassing on each other's moral ground. You are always free to behave according to your dictates and now I'm behaving according to mine.'

'Please darling, I think you're rather overwrought, you've had a long day and . . .'

Caroline turned to face him. 'I sincerely hope you are not humouring the little woman, Peter.'

'Oh no, of course not, no, no, but I do think . . .'

'See you later.'

Caroline pushed open the door of the saloon. Being Saturday the bar was full. From every corner there were great gales of laughter and smiling faces. Such a contrast to the desolation she was feeling. It seemed as though three-quarters of Turnham Malpas were here tonight. And why not? It was a lovely summer's evening and they were all out to enjoy themselves. The glass doors into the little courtyard at the back were open and she could see people sitting out at the tables Bryn and Georgie had put there. In the far corner near the other entrance to the bar, ensconced on the settle, were Pat Duckett and Vera Wright. Jimmy sat opposite with a pint in his hand. Alan asked Caroline what she wanted to drink, but she refused. He shrugged his shoulders and stood watching her threading her way between the tables. Nice bit of stuff that rector's wife he thought. Well off too, by the looks of it. He'd remember that.

Pat moved up to make more space. 'Good evening Dr Harris. Would you like a drink? You'll have to be quick, it's nearly closing time.'

'No thanks.'

'Getting away from them twins for a bit are yer? How are they getting on?'

'Very well thank you. I've come to see Jimmy actually.'

'What can I do for yer Dr Harris? How did them two rabbits turn out I gave yer?'

'That's what I want to talk to you about, Jimmy. It has been suggested to me tonight that you snared the rabbits you gave me. Is that correct?'

'It is.'

'Has it ever occurred to you that it is a very cruel way of catching an animal?'

'No more cruel than most kinds of deaths.'

'But they'd've been there all night probably, terrified out of their minds struggling to escape.'

'Well, they is only rabbits yer know, not people.'

'They are still God's creatures aren't they? I'm very upset by it. I can't bear to think that I ate animals killed in that way. What's worse, I did contemplate giving the twins some of the gravy but decided it was too rich for them. If I had done, I can't imagine how I would be feeling right now.'

'But that's what life's like in the country. It's a townie way of looking at things to think the country is all little lambs frolicking about and fluffy Easter chickens. It isn't. The country's tooth and claw, really yer know, and I'm part of it.'

'If I asked you to stop would you do that for me?'

Pat weighed in on Caroline's side. 'Jimmy I've told you before about them rabbits, you know I've stopped 'aving 'em from yer. Our Dean's dead against 'em since he saw yer coming 'ome that morning with that one with its leg dangling.'

Vera, incensed by what she saw as disloyalty to one's own, snapped, 'You've been glad enough in the past to 'ave Jimmy's rabbits. Saving money was 'ow you saw it, but now suddenly you've got principles.'

Caroline intervened, 'Well, Pat, I admire you for changing your mind and sticking to it, now all we've got to do is to get Jimmy to stop.' Something brushed against Caroline's leg and she jumped. 'What's that?' She looked under the table and saw Sykes, Jimmy's dog, under there. Beside him was an empty tankard.

'It's only Sykes, mi dog. I gave you those rabbits because I'm glad you're both 'ere, and I'm glad you've got them twins, and because I was mad that time when Sheila Bissett was spreading them rumours, which most of us knew already but weren't telling. This is the thanks I get.'

Alan called out, 'Time gentlemen please. Come along now.'

Caroline silently absorbed what he'd said. 'I appreciate your kindness Jimmy, nobody appreciates it more than me, but will you stop Jimmy?'

'No, Dr Harris, I won't. I've been catching rabbits all mi life and I'm not going to stop now. I 'ear what you say and I'll think about it. Can't be fairer than that.'

'I really wanted a promise to stop altogether.'

'That you won't get.'

Vera chipped in with, 'Quite right Jimmy, it's a free country.'

'Not for them rabbits it isn't if Jimmy goes on snaring 'em.' By now Pat was getting very indignant. She liked Caroline and had no intention of her coming off the worst in the argument.

Vera chipped in, 'It is a free country Pat. There's few enough things we can do nowadays like what we want so what the heck, you keep right on going Jimmy.'

'Don't come looking to me when you want to borrow a couple of pounds for the insurance man, Vera Wright. You've had the last borrow of my money believe me.'

'Righteo then, at least we know where we stand.'

'Yes, we do. And what's more Jimmy, you can give some thought to what Dr Harris has said. Just think of them poor babies eating that gravy. It makes me want to chuck up.'

Jimmy drank the last of his pint, wiped his moustache dry with the back of his forefinger, stood up and said loudly, 'I shall continue to catch rabbits in whatever way I think fit.'

Caroline pleaded, 'I wouldn't mind if you shot them Jimmy, at least they wouldn't suffer would they?'

'They might if I didn't kill 'em straight off. Then they'd go away and hide and still die in agony.'

'Well, why kill them at all?'

'It's my right. Good night. Sykes.' Sykes crept out alongside Jimmy, as though he knew full well dogs were not allowed in the bar.

Alan watched, and smiled to himself. He wasn't prepared for the uproar which erupted once Jimmy had left.

'Quite right Dr Harris, quite right.'

'It should be stopped, it's wicked.'

'He gets the social, why does he need to torture poor rabbits, he always catches more than he can eat.'

'He has got rights yer know.'

'What rights?'

'Something to do with the rights of villagers on common land, I think, from way back.'

'Sykes Wood belongs to Home Farm. He's trespassing.'

'Still, he isn't stealing is he? Tain't as if Home Farm know how many rabbits they've got.'

'If you decide to get a petition up I'll sign it Dr Harris.'

'Oh well I hadn't thought about doing that.'

'Well, it does need stopping.'

Finally Alan had to become quite stroppy with his customers. 'I need to lock up ladies and gentlemen. Please. I don't want the Sergeant coming round or Bryn will kill me, to say nothing of what Georgie will do.'

Caroline went out, wished everyone goodnight and headed for home.

Peter was feeding Beth and Alex was crying.

'Where's Sylvia? Why isn't she helping?'

'She and Willie have gone for a walk. It *is* her day off you know. Alex's bottle is ready, just check it first.'

When Caroline had got Alex settled with his bottle, Peter asked her if she'd found Jimmy.

'Yes, I did. He won't stop and said as much to everyone in the bar. We've had a big argument and he's defiant. They've all had a row. Pat and Vera are on opposite sides, and I'm exhausted and angry.'

'You sound to have caused a real furore. Enjoy feeding Alex and we'll get them both to bed and get off ourselves.'

'Apparently most of the villagers had guessed already about these two babies of ours, but were keeping mum.'

'Oh, my word. Had they?'

10

When Ralph woke during the night after only a few hours' sleep he knew he would be awake until breakfast time. Jet lag seemed to affect him more as he got older. He turned over in bed hoping he wouldn't disturb Muriel.

'Ralph,' Muriel whispered. 'Are you awake?'

'I'm so sorry my dear, did I wake you?'

'No, you didn't. I've been awake for ages. I didn't realise that flying could upset one's personal clock so much. I didn't notice it when we went out to Australia. I suppose that was because I was so excited. How long will it be before I'm back to normal?'

'A few days that's all.'

'Ralph isn't it lovely to be back home again?'

'Yes my dear, it is.'

'You don't sound as enthusiastic as I am.'

'Oh I am, I'm all mixed up I suppose. You see, it's coming home for you, but I haven't quite found my feet yet.'

'It feels as if you've always lived here.'

'Does it?'

'Yes.' Muriel turned over, snuggled up to Ralph and put her arm around him. 'Doing this, putting my arm around you, feels the most wonderful thing in the world. You see I've always had a bed of my own, a room of my own, and now sharing it with someone I love is so comforting. No matter how afraid or upset I am now, I've always got someone who will listen. It's surprising, isn't it, what one can tell someone in the dead of night when the curtains are closed and the whole world is asleep.'

'And what kind of things would you like to say to me at this moment? Have you some dark secret you have refrained from disclosing, Lady Templeton?'

'Doesn't that sound grand? Definitely not. I am very worried about Caroline.'

Ralph released himself from Muriel's grasp and got out of bed.

'Would you enjoy a cup of tea and a slice of toast?'

'Yes Ralph, but I'll get it.'

'No, no, I will. You rest there and allow your beloved husband to wait upon you.' He searched under the bed for his slippers, put on his dressing gown and went downstairs. Muriel lay back in bed admiring the pretty wallpaper and matching curtains. She was pleased she had resisted Ralph's insistence on redecorating. She loved the Laura Ashley papers and in any case the house had seen enough sorrow; it needed leaving alone for a while. Poor Suzy giving up her babies like that. Still it was the best decision in the end. They had two wonderful parents now.

After a while Ralph returned to the bedroom. He'd found the best tray, Muriel's favourite tray cloth and the morning tea set her cousin had bought them for a wedding present. The toast was keeping warm under a silver cover with the family crest on, from Ralph's old home. Muriel couldn't help but reflect on how affronted an earlier generation might have been to find their son and heir tucked up in bed with their head gardener's daughter. Things had changed.

Ralph poured the tea and presented Muriel with her toast and a paper napkin. 'My mother would have fainted at the prospect of paper napkins. White starched linen was *de rigueur*, so starched it nearly cut one's mouth if one was so foolish as to use one. What a ridiculous set of standards they had.'

Muriel popped the last piece of her toast in her mouth, and drank the remains of her tea. Ralph got up. 'Here let me take your things.' He put their cups and plates on the tray and got out of bed to place it outside the bedroom door.

He took off his dressing gown, climbed back into bed and took hold of her hand. She squeezed his hand with both of hers and smiled.

'What do you think about Jimmy and the rabbits, Ralph?'

'Frankly, I think Caroline is making much too much fuss. If we went into it I'm sure we'd be horrified at the way chickens are killed, and the way cows and pigs and sheep are killed. A few rabbits hardly matter in the scheme of things do they?'

'That's not quite the point though, is it Ralph? Just because others are suffering it doesn't mean to say it's all right for those rabbits does it? It's like people say, "Oh, well, everyone else is taking pens and paper and equipment home from the office so it's all right if I do it." It's still stealing isn't it?'

'Yes, you have a point. But I'm not going to join her in her "Freedom for Rabbits" campaign. I'm too much of a countryman at heart.'

'Well, I'm afraid I'm on her side. It has to stop.'

'Muriel, please, you will not get embroiled.'

'Why not?'

'Because I don't want you to.'

While Muriel mulled over a side of Ralph's character she hadn't met before, he turned towards her and began caressing her neck in the way he knew she enjoyed. He tried to turn her to face him but she resisted.

'Ralph, it's the middle of the night.'

'Not to me it isn't, but in any case is the time relevant in some way?'

'No, but we haven't sorted out about the rabbits. I hate being at cross purposes with you, Ralph.'

'I didn't know we were.'

'*You* said you didn't want me to get embroiled, I didn't say I wouldn't.'

'Well, leave it for now and we'll sort it out in the morning.'

Ralph was still caressing her neck and Muriel could feel her bones beginning to melt; a sensation she had grown to appreciate these last few months. 'Very well dear. Ralph I do love you. Listen! What's that noise? It's Perry drinking the tea out of the bottom of our cups! He is a naughty dog, but it's so nice to have him back. I have missed him.'

'There's a little girl in you who has never quite grown up and every now and again she emerges. It's that youthful quality of yours which I love.'

'Is that all I am, just a little girl?'

'Come here and prove otherwise.'

The two of them were very late waking the following morning and to Muriel's chagrin they missed morning service. 'Oh Ralph, I did want to hear how much they'd got with the Festival yesterday. Peter will think us very neglectful not getting to church.'

Ralph picked up the clock and saw it was already eleven. 'When I see him I'll tell him why you slept in.'

'Ralph!'

'Stay another half an hour, and then we'll have brunch and this afternoon we'll take Pericles for a long walk, have an early tea and go to evening service.'

'What a good idea. It's so nice to have someone to make up my mind for me. Put your arm round me and we'll have a little doze.'

She changed her mind about going for a walk, deciding she needed to answer some letters which were awaiting urgent attention. Ralph had only been gone a few minutes when Muriel heard an urgent knocking at the door. She opened it to find Jimbo there.

'Muriel, please, have you seen Flick?'

'Flick? No, why?'

'We can't find her. She was with the Brownies this morning in church and we went home with the boys, thinking she would follow in a little while when Brown Owl had dismissed them. She hasn't though. We've looked everywhere. I've even been up to the Health Club and Venetia and I have searched up there, but there's no sign of her. I've left Jeremy looking round the grounds and the people from Home Farm are searching their barns. We're absolutely at our wits' end. Harriet's being so sensible but underneath she's terrified.'

'Oh Jimbo, I'm so sorry. I'll get my cardigan and keys and I'll come to help you look.'

'Is Ralph in?'

'No, he's gone out for a couple of hours. I'll set off and walk with Pericles along the beck. She might have gone wandering off with her cats.'

'Thank you. We're getting really desperate now. It's been an hour and a half you see.' Having tried each house in the immediate vicinity of the green Jimbo went home to Harriet.

'Harriet, I've had no luck. Have you heard . . . no obviously you haven't.'

'Jimbo, it's time to ring the police.'

'I know, I know. Look phone round some more of her schoolfriends will you. She might have gone off with one of the Brownies, fancying having lunch with them or something. You know what children are like. "Oh I've asked Mummy and she says it's all right." Go on, darling, ring. Ah, Sadie, you're back.'

'She's not at my house hiding or anything. Have you been angry with her about something Jimbo?'

'Not at all. As far as I know she is perfectly happy. God I'm going mad. Harriet's ringing up some more of her friends. If she has no luck then I shall contact the police. It's no good relying on the local Sergeant, we need more brains than his.'

Harriet came back into the room. 'Mother, what's the name of that girl whose mother held the barbecue and nearly set the father alight?'

'Now she tells me. What kind of friends do we have?' Jimbo grunted. 'Idiots?'

'She's called Jenny something,' Sadie remembered, 'I know, Jenny Barlow.'

'That's it.' But Harriet returned, having drawn a blank. She said she couldn't think of anyone else to ring. 'I know, I'll ring Brown Owl and see if she noticed where Flick went. I should have done that in the first place.' And she went off to the telephone once more.

'Jimbo, I didn't like to ask this in front of Harriet, but did you try at the Baxters' house?'

'Yes, Sadie, but there was no reply.'

'Well, I think we should try again.'

'So do I, but they're not going to let me in, are they? And if I ask, they'll say no they haven't seen her, even if they have. That's why I want the police. They can insist on looking, whereas I can't.'

Fergus and Finlay were standing listening.

'I know I've asked you two this before, but do you have any clue at all about where Flick might be?'

'None at all Daddy. We finished before the Brownies did, 'cos they'd got a lot of notices. She didn't say anything to us.'

'Have you been needling her?'

'No, we've been very good today. Aren't we going to find her Daddy?'

'Yes, of course we are. Don't be silly. We will, won't we Grandma?' Jimbo appealed to Sadie as much for reassurance for himself as for the boys.

'Yes, we will. Let Grandma make you a nice drink. I think I might be able to find a KitKat for each of you, if I have two sensible boys.'

'We'll save one for Flick for when she gets back.'

'Of course.'

As far as Jimbo was concerned, that last remark of the boys made up his mind for him.

'Right Harriet, no news from Brown Owl?'

'No. Jimbo what are we going to do? I can't think straight.'

'Neither can I. It's the police next, there's no doubt in my mind.'

The Sergeant, roused from his afternoon sleep brought on by a surfeit of Mrs Sergeant's jam roly poly pudding, knew that this meant the end of his Sunday and possibly his Monday as well. They'd gone for years in this village without so much as the theft of a bicycle bell and now this. Murder, suicide, sudden death. It was all happening in Turnham Malpas. Now worst of all, a missing child.

'I have to tell you this Sergeant, the only house where I have had no response is the Misses Baxter's. All the other people have answered their doors, looked in their sheds and gardens, and done their best to help. Three quarters of the village is out looking for her, but there's no news yet. I don't know what to think any more. I do know that something serious needs doing though.'

'Right Mr Charter-Plackett. It seems to me that we can't dismiss this on the basis that she will turn up shortly. It's been two hours now, you say, and all she had to do was walk from the church to your house. That would take one minute at the outside. I want you to go find Willie Biggs and get him to search the churchyard with you and the church and the church hall as well. I'll get onto the station in Culworth. Keep looking in all the most unlikely places. She may have got locked in somewhere.'

'That's it! She could be locked in the vestry or something, couldn't she? I'll see Willie straight away.'

The two of them searched the church, unlocking the vestries and the boilerhouse, looking behind the old tombs and in every nook and cranny. They then began methodically combing the churchyard. Willie kept the grass between the graves absolutely immaculate so the chances of her being found there were nil, but they still persisted. Jimbo wished the churchyard was overgrown and that he would find her hidden in the long grass with a broken ankle or something. Anything but this total blank.

When he got back to the house, the police from Culworth had arrived. Harriet was showing them a photograph of Flick. The Sergeant took the Detective Inspector on one side and after a short consultation the Inspector went off with his Detective Constable to the Baxters' cottage. Meanwhile the village Sergeant accompanied Jimbo to the school to knock on Michael Palmer's door and ask to search the premises.

Detective Inspector Proctor had no preconceived ideas about the Misses Baxter. So far as he was concerned this was just another house in a dead alive hole which he wouldn't live in if his salary was doubled. DC Cooper knocked loudly on the front door and they both waited. The Inspector thought he saw the curtain move slightly but couldn't be sure. He always said it was his wife who was intuitive but today he acknowledged his own instincts were sending signals that all was not as it should be in this house. 'Knock again Cooper,' he growled impatiently. 'I haven't all day. God what a dump.'

There was still no reply. 'Right. Down the back and see what you can find. I'll have a dekko through the window, that's if I can make anything out through the filth.'

The Constable went off round to the side gate while Inspector Proctor shaded his eyes with his hand and peered through the dirty glass. He recoiled, startled to find himself staring straight into a pair of brown venemous eyeballs as close to the glass as his own. He jumped back and then knocked on the window and pointed to the front door shouting, 'Open up please!'

He waited for the sound of footsteps coming to the door but there were none. Cooper came round the corner and said, 'No reply, guv. Not a sausage. We could find all sorts 'ere. The garden's like a jungle; wouldn't surprise me if Tarzan didn't come swinging through it shortly.'

'Good, we might be needing him. They are in, I've just seen one of 'em looking at me through the window. Not a pretty sight. They're a queer lot. We're definitely not going without seeing them. Go round the back again and make a pretence of searching the garden. That might flush 'em out.'

'Right guv.'

'Cooper we're not filming *The Bill*; drop the guv bit. It's either sir, or Inspector.'

Cooper thrashed about with the broom that Gwen had used on Sir Ronald. He waved it this way and that, pushing the grass aside as he went. He glanced once or twice at the kitchen window to see if they were watching him, but he didn't catch them looking. Inspector Proctor came through the side gate. He banged on the back door and shouted, 'It's the police. Open the door or I shall have to break it down. Come along now, please, we only want to ask you some questions.' A small crowd of villagers had gathered by the front garden of the house. Amongst the crowd was Sheila Bissett.

'They are mad you know. I bet it's them have got her. You wait and see. I just hope she's still all right.'

'Come on, Lady Bissett. What harm could they have done her? We know they's crackers but they won't murder no one would they?'

'Wouldn't they? Don't you be too sure.' The crowd watched the police officers standing outside the back door. The Detective Constable and the Inspector had a whispered conversation and then they said, 'One, two, three!' and barged at the door with their shoulders. Their combined weight and force broke the latch and the door burst open. Inspector Proctor was unmoved by the condition of the kitchen. There wasn't much that could surprise him about people.

'Hello there, it's the police. Can we have a word?'

Gwen appeared. 'Just you keep well away from me. We don't want you here.'

'Believe me madam, we wouldn't be here at all if it wasn't for the fact that we have a little girl missing. Yours is the only house we haven't been able to check, and check it we must.'

'Where is your warrant?'

'We haven't time to waste getting a warrant. Everyone else has co-operated willingly. We need to make sure she hasn't been shut in somewhere by mistake.'

'What are you accusing us of?'

'Nothing, madam. It is simply a case of looking to make sure she hasn't been taken ill somewhere and can't get help or has locked herself in an outhouse and can't make herself heard.'

'You can search the shed if you want. You'll find nothing in there. It's always locked.'

'Give me the key and my Constable will look.'

Gwen put her hand in the pocket of her apron and handed him the key. While Cooper searched the shed, the Inspector questioned Gwen. 'Did you go to church this morning?'

'Certainly not.'

'Where's your sister?'

'Having a nap.'

'Could you get her to come down to see me?'

'No. She's not at all well.'

'Then in that case I shall go upstairs to see her if you will accompany me.'

'You won't.'

'If you won't go with me then I shall have to go alone.' He made to brush past her into the hall. Gwen stood aside, then changed her mind and went up the stairs in front of him.

Beryl lay huddled in the big double bed they shared, apparently asleep.

'Wake your sister for me.'

Beryl stirred at the sound of his voice.

'Good afternoon Miss Baxter. I'm making inquiries about a little girl who's gone missing. Felicity Charter-Plackett. I understand she's always called Flick. Have you seen her today?'

Beryl's eyes slid from his face to Gwen's and then back again. 'No.'

'Would you recognise her if you did?'

'Yes.'

'Have you been out today?'

'No.'

'Has your sister been out today?'

'No.'

He looked at Gwen and said, 'There's a Sunday newspaper in the kitchen. Mr Charter-Plackett doesn't deliver newspapers, so how have you got it into the house?'

'Well, that's all I've done. I didn't think you meant popping out for two minutes for a paper.'

'What else do you think I hadn't meant?' He heard Cooper return to the house. Cooper shouted up the stairs. 'It's full of old clothes, guv . . . sir. I haven't moved everything, we'd have to clear the whole shed out to do that.'

'Do it, Cooper.'

'Yes, guv.'

Gwen glared at him. 'You'll have it all to put back again.'

'We will.'

The Inspector went back downstairs again but not before he'd opened the big bedroom door and looked in. He estimated that the piles of newspapers hadn't been disturbed, though he could be wrong. He opened the sitting room door next, looked in and then returned to the kitchen. Moving a pile of papers from a kitchen chair he sat down to wait for Cooper to empty the shed. He looked round the kitchen hoping to unnerve Gwen and make her say something. She stood watching him. He picked up the Sunday newspaper and began reading.

'Nothing better to do with your time than sit there? What about repairing that door?'

'We'll send someone round.'

Jimbo came to the back door to report that they had had no success in the school.

'We're being invaded. Get out, go on, get out.'

Cooper came back from the shed sweating and dirty. 'Nothing in there guv.'

'Thanks, Cooper. Put it all back.'

'Back?'

'Yes, back.'

Jimbo, by now almost incoherent with anxiety, asked Gwen if she knew where Flick was.

'Please Miss Baxter we need to know.'

'I don't know.'

'Are you absolutely sure you haven't seen her going past the house? I know you like to watch people going by. Perhaps you happened to see her after church. Or you saw someone stop to speak to her. Think Miss Baxter, think.'

'No, I didn't.'

'We'll search the garden now, Miss Baxter.' The Inspector stood and turned to go out. Jimbo followed him and they went to the far end of the garden and began looking section by section. They unearthed an ancient mangle, a roll of rotting carpet, and various old boxes and an old mower, but of Flick they found nothing. It was Jimbo who came upon the lid of the disused well.

'Oh my God. I didn't know they had a well. Inspector, come here.'

'That's recently been disturbed.' Jimbo went deathly white. The Inspector looked at him. 'Go and find the village Sergeant for me, will you, Mr Charter-Plackett, and ask him for his torch. He'll have one with a powerful beam.' Jimbo hurried off, glad to be of use.

'Now we've got him out of the way, we can get the lid off and look down.'

Between them they managed to lift it off. The Inspector threw a stone down. 'It's very deep. Go and get the torch from the car, Cooper.'

Willie arrived to offer his help. 'You don't think she's down there do you, Inspector?'

'We have to look at every possibility. My instincts tell me there's something odd here. I can feel it in my bones as they say. Good lad, Cooper.'

He shone the torch down the well. The surface of the water gleamed greenly back at him. He moved the beam of light slowly up and down the walls of the well. There were no signs of anything having rubbed against the brickwork as it was pushed down. He decided to have another go inside the house. They heaved the lid back on again.

Jimbo arrived with the Sergeant's torch.

'Oh thanks, sir, my Constable remembered we had one in the car. I'm glad to say there's no sign of your little girl down there.'

Gwen and Beryl were both in the kitchen when he returned to it.

'You're feeling better are you Miss Baxter?'

'Yes.'

'Right, Cooper. Upstairs. And search properly, every drawer, every cupboard, don't miss a thing. Both bedrooms.'

This upset Gwen and Beryl. They both rushed to block the door.

'You've already searched. You can't search again. We won't let you.'

'I'm afraid I can. Move to one side please.' He noticed Beryl's eyes stray momentarily towards a chest of drawers, which was standing in front of what was obviously the understairs cupboard. When he looked at the floor he saw marks which showed that the chest had been dragged across to its present position. How had he missed that?

'Cooper, move this chest.'

Cooper pushed and strained but couldn't budge it, so Willie went to give him a hand. At this the two women became more and more agitated. Suddenly Gwen snapped. She went straight for Cooper and lunged at him and beat him with her fists.

'This is our house. Stop it, stop it! You've no right!'

Inspector Proctor took hold of her and forcibly restrained her from attacking his Constable. She kicked and struggled to get free, shouting at Willie and Cooper to stop. The two men pulled open the door of the cupboard and Cooper shone the torch inside.

'Here we are sir. She's here.'

He knelt down, reached inside and came out backwards on his knees, holding Flick in his arms. She had been bound and gagged and lay limply. Constable Cooper bent his head and listened for her breathing.

'She's OK. She's breathing.' He laid her down on the kitchen floor. Jimbo undid the gag, unbound her arms and ankles and then held her to him and forced back the sobs which, despite his strenuous efforts to retain self control, would keep coming into his throat.

'I'll go tell her mother, Mr Charter-Plackett,' offered Willie and he ran from the house shouting. 'She's all right, we've found her.'

The crowd outside cheered. They caught snatches of Inspector Proctor saying, 'I arrest you both . . . and anything you might say . . . I must ask you to accompany me to the station.'

The procession to the police car was followed by dozens of pairs of eyes. Pat Duckett shouted, 'Yer nasty pair of old baggages. Yer deserve all yer get. What did yer want to harm a poor little girl for?'

The Sergeant, who had arrived too late to help, importantly cleared the way. 'Move along please, move along.'

'Harriet are you awake?'

'Yes, I've not been to sleep yet.'

'Neither have I, and what's more I don't think I shall. God what a day. Never again.'

'I'm going to check if she's all right.' Harriet went across the landing to Flick's bedroom and stood looking down at her. Flick was curled on her side, her hand tucked under the pillow in its usual position. Harriet gently stroked the hair from her cheeks and pulled the duvet a little closer around her shoulders. She went back to bed and lay staring at the ceiling.

'She's fine, sleeping like a baby. Never *ever* do I want to go through a day like today again.'

Jimbo lay on his back staring at the ceiling. 'I've been thinking: it's my fault this happened.'

'Your fault? How could that be?'

'I've put everything into making a success of this business . . . mostly for my own satisfaction but also as one in the eye of those City people who said I'd be back there inside six months. It's made me ignore my own children.'

'You haven't.'

'Yes I have. I don't mean I ever stopped caring about them. How could I? They're our own flesh and blood, for God's sake. But today, when I thought we'd lost Flick I realised that under pressure from me we've let that bond between ourselves and the children grow weak. That's why she feels free to just wander off as she likes. Because we don't put restraints on her. We're always busy and, to be honest, we've been quite glad if she's not bothering us.'

'But we take such care of them. The boys don't go off and they're older.'

'They don't seem to feel the need. You see, there's two of them so they always have someone to share games with. It makes Flick quite an outsider, you know.'

'So what's the remedy?'

'From now on, I don't care what it costs, but whenever Flick and the boys aren't at school I want you home there for them. I know it means employing people in the shop and the kitchens when you're not there. But no matter what it costs, that's what we're doing. We came within a hair's breadth of her being dead. I can't imagine what hell that must be but I know it would be double hell if we had ourselves to blame. I just can't take a chance of that happening.'

'But I enjoy working in the shop.'

'I didn't say you would do nothing, Harriet, I said you weren't going to be involved whenever the children are at home. And that's final. I'll work twice as hard to make it possible. You are their mother and I want you to be there.'

'Jimbo, since when have you told me what to do?'

'As of now, but then I've never been so frightened as I was this afternoon. You know, waiting to see if a big deal had come off when I was at the bank, the old adrenalin would be riding high, my palms would be sweating, my nerves at top pitch, and that awful patch of fear at the pit of my stomach would be there gnawing away. But it was nothing compared to today. I am not going through that again.'

'She ought to be able to go about alone in a place like this.'

'She ought, but obviously she can't.'

'You're quite right of course, and I shall do as you say. And tomorrow when the police come to question her, make certain they don't frighten her, won't you? We don't want to make matters worse than they already are.' They were quiet for a while, then Harriet said, 'All that trouble with Caroline and the rabbits last night doesn't seem very important today does it?'

'But, Inspector, I didn't go in. I saw Chivers running down Church Lane when Brown Owl dismissed us. He's always wandering off, and I'm frightened he'll get lost, he's only small, he's not even had a birthday yet. I ran after him and he went to Misses Baxter's side gate and climbed over. I went to the gate and called "Chivers, Chivers".'

'Did you open the gate Flick?'

'No..o..o.o. I stood looking over, calling. Daddy said I mustn't go in people's gardens after my cats. So I didn't. But then she came out.'

'Who came out?'

'Gwen.'

'What did she say?'

'Nothing.'

'I can't understand why she was so very very cross with you if you didn't go in.'

Flick looked uncomfortable and glanced anxiously at her mother. Harriet patted her arm and said, 'Just tell the Inspector the truth, Flick.'

Flick swallowed hard and whispered, 'Daddy's told me not to go in people's gardens after my cats, but I did twice. They like Miss Baxters' garden because it's all messy and piled with rubbish and they like to play in there, it's such an *interesting* garden for cats you see. So they've told me twice not to go in there and shouted at me and she said, that is Gwen said, she would punish me if she caught me again. This time I didn't go in but she just opened the gate and before I could run away, she grabbed me and dragged me inside. I told her Mummy would be cross. But she wouldn't listen. She used some naughty words I've heard the boys use, and Daddy once when he dropped a box of baked beans on his foot. She held me tight and Beryl said, "Let her go. You must let her go." But Gwen didn't listen.'

'Where did she hold you? Pretend you're Gwen and get hold of me like she got hold of you.'

Flick grabbed Inspector Proctor's neck and his arm. 'Like that but really tight. I couldn't get away.'

'What happened next?'

'She told Beryl to get some old cloths and then she tied me up and stuffed me in the cupboard. It was so hot and I couldn't breathe and then Daddy was holding me. I don't know how long I was in the cupboard.'

'Did Beryl help to tie you up?'

'No. She was crying and saying "No, no, no." She said she was so upset she'd have to go to bed.'

'So Beryl didn't do much then?'

'No. Beryl must be nicer than Gwen, mustn't she?'

'Well, I'm not too sure about that, she didn't stop Gwen or go to get help did she?'

'No, she didn't. Can I go and play now?'

'Is there anything else you need to tell me. Your Mummy is here and we don't have secrets from Mummy do we? So tell her and me right now if you can remember things I've forgotten to ask.'

'I've told you everything. I'd like to go now please.'

'Are you quite certain you've told us everything that happened? Did they take you anywhere else besides the kitchen?'

'No, nowhere else. Nothing else happened at all. Will they go to prison for being nasty to me?'

'We'll wait and see.'

'May I go now, please?'

'Yes, but before you go I want to say something. Your cats know you love them Flick, because you look after them so well. They're not daft, they know when they have a good home. So don't, whatever you do, go looking for them again. It might be a while before they get back home, but they will. Thank you for answering all those questions. You've been a great help. Off you go.'

Flick got down off the chair and went to find the boys. She thought she'd go back to school tomorrow, they'd all want to know what had happened, and she'd be able to tell them about the doll Venetia had sent her that morning. It was absolutely gorgeous and had the most wonderful lace dress on and beautiful long blonde hair. She didn't know which was lovelier, the doll or the box it had come in. She'd call it Venetia, that was a perfectly splendid name for a perfectly splendid doll.

When she left, the Inspector stood up to take his leave. 'Thank you, Mrs Charter-Plackett. There's bound to be some after effects, like bad nerves and nightmares. Your daughter will need lots of love and reassurance. We shan't be able to keep those women locked up for ever, much as we might like to, so take care. If Felicity lets slip any more information, no matter how slight, will you phone me at this number? If I'm not there leave a message to ring you. I'll be in touch.' The Inspector shook hands with Harriet and went out to his car.

11

Despite Caroline's anxiety about Flick she still felt as strongly about Jimmy and the rabbits and was determined to swing public opinion onto her side. She made a point of mentioning the subject to everyone she met. Some villagers met her idea with downright hostility. But aided and abetted by Pat, who made it her business to introduce the subject to as many of the school parents as she was able, many of the villagers came round to her way of thinking. Michael Palmer, having listened several times to the story of what had happened in The Royal Oak on the Saturday night, agreed with Caroline.

'Knew yer'd see it her way, Mr Palmer,' Pat commented gleefully as she tidied the hall after school dinners. 'She's a lovely lady is Dr Harris, she's really cut up about them rabbits, feels right bad about 'em. I don't understand how some people don't see her point of view. I tell yer who would be on her side . . . Mrs Meadows. Now she was always very keen on kindness to animals. She had that campaign d'yer remember? Not long after she got 'ere, about stopping foxhunting. Yer remember she got the Council to stop the hunt going across the Big House land. 'Spect that Health Club lot won't care two hoots about poor foxes. Do you ever 'ear from Mrs Meadows, Mr Palmer? I always thought you two got on really well.'

Michael Palmer hesitated for a moment and then gave an emphatic 'No'. Pat smiled to herself. She hadn't lived thirty-nine years without learning something about human nature. She guessed from his answer that it wasn't strictly the truth.

In his pocket Michael had the latest letter from Suzy's mother, this time at the bottom was a short note from Suzy herself sending him her good wishes. It was the first time she'd written anything at all and the first time he realised that she knew he'd been writing in response to her mother's request. In future he'd have to be careful what he said about the twins. It was one thing divulging news to a devoted grandmother, quite another telling a mother news of the babies she'd given away. He fingered the envelope, carefully tucked away in the pocket of his tweed jacket. One day perhaps she'd write a real letter to him. In his mind's eye he could see her long fair hair, her lovely rounded cheeks and the sweet, so sweet smile which lit up her face. He imagined his hands cupping her cheeks and himself placing a kiss on her dear mouth . . .

'Shall you be having football this afternoon, Mr Palmer, with it being wet? 'Cos if you are I'll put newspapers down in the cloakroom, that floor's murder to keep clean.'

'Shall I be having what?'

'Football, yer know with the boys.'

'Oh right, yes, I shall.'

'I hope you'll bring it into your nature and science lessons about cruelty to rabbits and explain to them children about using snares . . . Our Michelle can speak up about it, our Dean's explained it all to her.'

'We'll see, we'll see.' Michael gazed out of the window and saw Caroline coming across the playground. Oh no, not more rabbits he thought.

'Good afternoon Dr Harris, what can I do for you?'

'Hello Michael. I want to know if I can persuade you to talk to the children about cruelty to animals. Especially in connection with the way in which we kill them, in particular the killing of rabbits. If you don't feel able to, will you let me have a word?'

'Mrs Duckett has already informed me several times as to my duty to the children concerning this matter. If you would like me to do it then I shall. I feel quite as strongly as you do.'

'Oh thank you Michael, I do appreciate that. I've been so upset about it all. If we can teach the *children* that it's wrong then that's the most important thing, even if we can't convert diehards like Sir Ralph.'

'Country people do see things differently Dr Harris.'

'I know, I know.' One of the children came to Michael with a problem about his football kit. 'I won't keep you. Thanks anyway. Bye.'

'Good afternoon.'

Caroline, on her way back to the Rectory, met Muriel out with Pericles for his afternoon walk. 'Hello Muriel. Isn't it a lovely day?'

'It certainly is. Now, are you feeling any better? I thought you were quite drained on Saturday night, and greatly in need of a rest.'

'Muriel! Is that how you saw my protest? As some kind of hysterical outburst?'

'Oh no, I didn't mean it like that. I think you're quite right about Jimmy, but I did think at the same time you were needing a change.'

'Well, perhaps I am, and perhaps not. But I'm still angry about Jimmy, it doesn't alter that does it?'

'No, it doesn't. I'm afraid Ralph and I are on opposite sides. It's a bit uncomfortable.'

'Oh Muriel, don't let it upset things for you, that's the last thing I want.'

'I can't do as Ralph says *all* the time can I?'

'No, that's right you can't, but don't let it come between you. I can fight my own battles, you know, when it comes to it.'

'I know that Caroline, but you must be careful. These last few days there's been an awful lot of upsets over this rabbit question. I understand there was a row in the Store in the pension queue on Monday. Jimbo had to step in and sort it out. He refuses to be drawn on the matter, of course, because he has customers on both sides, though we both know how he feels. Linda slapped the change down for some person who'd declared themselves on Jimmy's side and they complained to Jimbo and he had to tick her off in front of everyone and she had yesterday off, said she was sick, but Jimbo's not too sure about that. First day's sickness she's taken in two and a half years. Lady Bissett's given someone a real telling off at the flower arrangement class because they criticised you. One of the members confided in me that she'd used language more suited to a saloon bar than the church hall. Some of the ladies quite ruined their arrangements they were so upset.'

'Oh, Muriel, I'd no idea things were so serious. It won't affect Jimmy will it though? It won't make him change his mind?'

'I doubt it, he's very thick skinned. Must go, Pericles is getting impatient.'

Peter stormed into the Rectory half an hour after Caroline got home. She was unprepared for the onslaught she got from him.

'Cup of tea Peter?' she called from the kitchen. 'You've timed it nicely, darling.'

He came into the kitchen and sat down at the table. 'Thank you.'

'Biscuit?' She turned round to hand him the tin and saw how angry he was. His eyes were almost black with temper and his jaws were clamped so tight his cheeks were white.

'Peter, what's happened?'

'What's happened? I'll tell you what's happened. I've spent, what is it, eighteen months? carefully nurturing this village back to life. Back to being a caring community, back to church, back to having some social life together. I've started Brownies and Cubs, a women's group, a luncheon club for the elderly, I've revitalised the choir and the music, I've improved the finances and heaven knows what else. And now *you* are destroying all my work. I can't believe it of you, Caroline, I really can't.'

'What have I done?'

'You know full well what you've done. It's these damned rabbits.'

'Peter!'

He dragged the lid off the biscuit tin, chose a biscuit and banged the lid back on again. But he was so enraged he had to put it down uneaten, his hand shaking with anger as he laid the biscuit on the table. 'I've said nothing these last three days, but I can keep my own counsel no longer.' He began ticking off facts on his fingers. 'One, Bagheera and Brown Owl aren't speaking, so the Jumble Sale they are supposed to be holding jointly a week on Saturday to raise money to help parents who can't afford uniforms is in jeopardy. Two, two of my senior choirmen have resigned because the choir master has instructed the boys about the cruelty of snaring rabbits and they think it is none of his business to indoctrinate them, which it isn't. Three, Mrs Peel has had a row with Willie and he refuses to unlock the church early and to make sure the electric is switched on so she can practise first thing on Wednesday and Saturday mornings. And four, old Mrs Woods' son and daughter, who were coming to see me about their choice of some elaborate kind of headstone for her grave, have argued so fiercely about the rights and wrongs of killing rabbits, the daughter has declared she is about to become vegetarian, and neither of them can keep the appointment about the headstone because, though they live in the same house, they are no longer speaking. You knew my calling from the first day we met in your surgery. I cannot lay that calling aside as you well know. As my wife, Caroline, you should behave more circumspectly. Your actions are causing serious damage to the parish, and I must ask you to reconsider before it all becomes irretrievable and, for me, unforgivable.'

Caroline was defiant. 'Because I am the wife of a priest I am not permitted to have opinions then? I must allow things I disapprove of to happen and stay silent? None of this is my fault anyway.'

'Whose fault is it then? I've just met Pat Duckett and she was praising you to the skies for having got Michael Palmer to instruct the children in the school on the rights and wrongs of the situation. Is there no end to your activity on behalf of these rabbits?'

'The fault is Jimmy's not mine.'

'Jimmy has been killing rabbits in this way for years. Until you decided to begin this crusade nobody minded.'

'Then it was time their consciences were woken up.'

'Woken up? They've certainly been that. Caroline, I don't know when I have been so angry. The repercussions have been far beyond anything I expected. Far beyond. Irreparable damage is being done.'

'Go and see Jimmy then and persuade him to stop. I can't.'

'Oh no, you go and see Jimmy. This hornet's nest is all your doing.' Peter stood up, and taking his cup of tea with him stormed off to his study. Sylvia put her head around the kitchen door and asked if there was any tea going or should she beat a hasty retreat?

'Come in Sylvia, the storm clouds have departed. Are the children OK?'

'Yes, they're asleep in the garden in their pram and yes the cat net is on.'

After a moment Caroline said, 'Peter has never spoken to me like that in all the time I've known him. I have never seen him in such a temper. It's very . . .' Caroline got out her handkerchief and blew her nose.

Sylvia poured herself a cup of tea. 'Well, to be honest, Dr Harris, it has caused a lot of trouble believe me.'

'It would all blow over if I could just get him to stop it.'

'You won't, only an instruction from the Almighty could stop Jimmy. I'm sorry, Dr Harris, but you're going to have to let it go.'

'My conscience won't let me.'

'Willie says Jimmy is such a law unto himself anyway, that all this trouble will bother him not one jot. Seeing that the rector is so upset, maybe you'd better just let matters rest.'

'But that's it, that way nothing gets done, no reforms are made, no bills through parliament, no injustices righted. When I think of eating those rabbits I feel so sickened.'

Sylvia took a deep breath and spoke her mind. 'If it had been Beth missing on Sunday instead of Flick, believe me, Dr Harris, you wouldn't be worrying your head about rabbits this week.'

Caroline looked at her in horror. As she leapt to her feet, her chair crashed over onto the floor, but she ignored it and rushed out into the garden. Sylvia stood the chair up and went to the window. She saw Caroline lift Beth from the pram and hold her tightly to her chest. Sylvia watched as she began to sob, deep, searing sobs which tore at Sylvia's heart. She tapped on the study door. 'Excuse me, Rector, but I think Dr Harris needs a hand.'

Peter looked up from his desk. 'Needs a hand?'

'Yes, she's in the garden crying, sir.'

Peter strode out and gathered Caroline and Beth into his arms. He stood stroking her hair and kissing her, hushing her as though she was a little girl.

'My darling, my darling, I'm so sorry for what I said. Please forgive me, please. I can't bear you being so upset. Please, please stop. I should never have spoken to you like that. I know how devastated you felt about the rabbits and I'm deeply sorry for the way I spoke. If you want to crusade for the rabbits you can, I shan't mind.'

Caroline raised her head from his chest and looked up at him. 'Oh Peter, what if it had been Beth missing on Sunday?' Peter felt as though he'd been kicked in the solar plexus: the breath went from his body. He forced air back into his lungs with a great heave of his chest. He couldn't trust himself to speak, so he took out his handkerchief and wiped her face dry with his trembling hand. When he'd composed himself he said, 'Caroline, I'm sorry it was Flick, and, I sound selfish, but I thank God it wasn't Beth. She's here safe and sound with us, loved and cherished, fast asleep in her mother's arms. What more could a baby ask?'

He bent down to kiss his little Beth, who was blissfully asleep and unaware of the crisis unfolding around her. Peter stood holding the two of them closely in his arms comforting Caroline, hugging her and telling her she was safe with him. When he felt her relax and no longer shaking with sobs, he stood back from her and said, 'There we are, now let's put her back in the pram with Alex, and we'll leave them to sleep the afternoon away.'

They walked back together into the kitchen. Sylvia had gone.

'Come and sit on my knee, and we'll finish that cup of tea you were having.' He refilled her cup and the two of them took turns drinking from it. The hot tea gave Caroline back her voice. 'I'm so tired Peter, so tired.'

'I've been thinking about that. Can I be in charge for a while and make some positive suggestions?'

'Anything you like.'

'I'm going to do some ringing up and some organising and hopefully you're going up to your mother's for a few days.'

'Oh, I couldn't manage driving all that way with the children. I couldn't face it.'

'I know that. You're going on the train by yourself, and Sylvia and I will look after the children between us, and if we get desperate Willie can come in as support troops. Or Harriet or someone. We shan't be short of volunteers believe me. Three or four days walking along your beloved cliffs, with the wind blowing your cobwebs away, will do you all the good in the world.'

'It sounds wonderful. But I've been such a failure. How can an intelligent woman, with a loving husband, with all the help I have available and the babies I desperately longed for, be so hopeless?'

'My darling girl, you're not hopeless, you're a brilliant mother, and that's the problem. You're suffering from exhaustion, brought on by hard work and lack of sleep, that's what.'

'I would be so grateful for a respite. Mother will be pleased. Please forgive me for this rabbit business, I shouldn't have been so persistent. Never having lived in a village before I didn't realise that everyone would be taking sides. I still mean it about the rabbits though, it must be stopped.'

'Of course.' He held her close, then said, 'I don't know how I shall manage without you.'

'Don't worry, you'll be so busy I shall be back before you know it! Thanks for being so wonderfully understanding. Give me a kiss, a real proper humdinger of a kiss.' When he released her she said, 'M..m..m..m.m. Let' s have another.'

12

Pat Duckett sat waiting on her favourite settle right by the door where she could see people coming in. Her port and lemon stood on a little brewery mat in front of her. If she sipped it slowly it might last half the evening and then Jimmy or Willie might buy her another one. No good hoping Vera might, for Vera was as strapped for cash as herself. She was tired, she'd had a hard day. It had been raining and the school floors had got muddy footprints all over. It had taken her ages to get them cleaned up. Sometimes she wished she could give the job up, but what would she do for money then? Bringing up two children on your own wasn't much fun and the bigger they got the more they ate and the more it cost for their bally clothes. The door opened and in came Vera and Jimmy.

'Hello, get yourselves a drink and come and sit down.'

'Hello Pat.'

'Evening Pat.'

When Jimmy and Vera had settled down with their drinks Pat said, 'Have you heard that Dr Harris has gone up 'ome for a few days?'

Vera looked surprised. 'No, I hadn't. Has she taken the twins with her?'

'No, the rector's looking after 'em with Sylvia.'

'Sounds as if he's put his foot down then about her rabbit crusade.'

'Well, it did cause a lot of bother and, come to think of it, I don't know why I'm drinking with you, Jimmy. Anyways, I understand they had a blazing row, and then she cried and next day she's off to Northumberland.'

'Last time she went there was when . . .'

'That's right, when she found out about . . .' Pat glanced round to make sure she wasn't being overheard, 'about Suzy Meadows and them twins. Heaven's above you don't think it's happened again?'

Jimmy scoffed at their speculation. 'For crying out loud you two, I'm not that keen on Dr Harris at the moment as you well know, but he can't be straying again. Surely to goodness 'e's learned 'is lesson.'

'You have to admit Jimmy, he's very handsome. There's many a one would fancy 'im and no mistake.'

Jimmy laughed. 'You're wrong. She's gone away for a rest, believe me.'

'Who says?'

'Willie, 'cos he and Sylvia are giving a hand at sitting in when the rector has to go out.'

'I wouldn't be sur . . .'

The door burst open and in came Vera's Don. 'Guess what?' he panted. 'Them two's released pending trial.'

'What two?'

'Gwen and Beryl.'

'Released? Never.'

The news flashed round the bar in a trice.

'Disgusting.'

'Whatever next?'

'Them courts have a lot to answer for.'

'We shan't be safe in our beds.'

'We don't want 'em 'ere.'

'Definitely not.'

'They should be locked up forever.'

'That's right, locked up till they're dead and gone.'

'The nasty wicked beggars that they are.'

'Have you ever been in their house? Willie says it's disgusting.'

'I bet it is.'

'We don't want them in Turnham Malpas with their dirty ways.'

'We should get rid of 'em.'

'That's right we should.'

And their voices rose to a crescendo, filling the bar with clamour.

Bryn and Georgie tried to lighten the atmosphere but the customers wouldn't listen.

'Now ladies and gentlemen let's take this calmly please. We'll all have a drink on the house and settle down. The two of them do belong here and they haven't been proved guilty yet.'

'Not been proved guilty? It doesn't need a trial, we were all there when they brought little Flick out. Double whisky for me.'

Bryn and Georgie regretted offering drinks all round. The whole bar was inflamed at the news, and the extra alcohol only made matters worse.

The more hotheaded among the regulars came to the conclusion that the police wouldn't do a thing to make sure Gwen and Beryl didn't do worse than hiding Flick in the cupboard. 'Murder it'll be next,' they said. 'Let's clear 'em out ourselves,' they said. 'Right come on then! We'll soon see off two old bats like them. Let's be rid of them. We want our village to be safe.'

There was a concerted dash for the door and the bar emptied. Bryn and Georgie decided to ring the Sergeant. The crowd surged down Stocks Row and into Culworth Road. They stood outside Gwen and Beryl's cottage chanting, 'Out out out. Out Out Out. OUT OUT OUT.' Someone found a stone on the road and threw it at the house. By chance it hit a downstairs window and broke it. Someone else found a bigger stone and aimed it deliberately at another window which shattered with a resounding crack. Incensed by the injustice of Gwen and Beryl's release and inflamed by the sound of the breaking glass the crowd began throwing stones in earnest. Being so close to the road the windows were an easy target. The chanting began again, 'Child molesters. Filthy women you are. Get out get out get out.' The sound of their chanting rose to a crescendo.

The Sergeant, summoned by Bryn's phone call, pushed his way to the front of the crowd, but they shouted to him to get out of the way.

'Your lot have let 'em out. It's no use you coming, you're on their side, go on shove off before you get hit. Out out out.'

The Sergeant shouted above their noise, 'I shall charge you all with a breach of the peace! Now please go away to your homes before you do something you regret. Move along there please. Come along now, go to your homes. Justice will be done but leave it to the law.'

'We've done that and look what's happened. Move away Sergeant. Out out out.'

Peter came across from the Rectory and pushed his way through. Standing in front of the cottage door he faced the angry crowd. 'Please, please, everyone, have you forgotten who you are? This *must* stop. You must *not* take the law into your own hands. Tomorrow morning, in the clear light of day, you will be ashamed of what you are doing tonight. What will your children think of you when they hear what you have done? Shame, that's what they will feel. Absolute shame. And I am ashamed, that you are part of my flock and you behave in this way. In the name of God go home, before something more terrible befalls this village.'

The steady quietness of Peter's voice and the strength of his argument cooled their tempers, and after some muttering and resistance the demonstrators gradually began to thin out and make their way home.

The Sergeant was shaken but relieved that the trouble had been resolved and he thanked Peter for his help.

'Let's go inside and see how they are,' Peter suggested.

The two of them went round to the back of the house. Peter knocked on the door and tried to push it open but it was bolted and he couldn't move it.

He shouted through a broken front window, 'This is Peter from the Rectory. Are you all right in there?'

Gwen came to the window. 'Yes.'

'Can I help in any way at all?'

'No, we shall manage.'

'Very well, but if you need help you know where I am don't you?'

'Yes.'

Gwen turned away from the window and the Sergeant asked Peter what on earth he could do with people like them who wouldn't allow themselves to be helped.

'I honestly don't know. But I'll tell you one thing Sergeant, you must see to it that they are not attacked in this way again. Law and order is your responsibility, and the safety of these two women is essential if justice is to have any credence at all. If I think for one minute that you have neglected your duties to these two people, I shall not hesitate to make it known. They deserve your protection, and turning a blind eye will not do.'

'No sir. I'll see to it.'

'Indeed you will.'

The next morning the village woke to the sound of hammering. Gwen was boarding up the windows. Only the window at which Gwen used to sit watching the comings and goings of the village was left intact. The Sergeant went round later in the morning to check they were all right, but Gwen came to the one remaining intact window and signalled to him to go away.

Later that morning she went as usual to the village store to buy her newspaper and get the groceries.

Jimbo and Harriet had already talked about what they should do.

'If they can't get their food here, Jimbo, they will starve to death.'

'Peter would certainly give me a hard time if I refused to serve them. On the other hand, it isn't his child they nearly suffocated.'

'In all conscience we can't refuse to serve them.'

'I can't serve her.'

'No, and neither can I.'

They consulted Linda and she said she would come out from behind the Post Office counter and take Gwen's money if they wished.

Jimbo thanked her. 'I feel very un-Christian behaving like this, but they threatened Flick's life.'

Gwen's arrival was greeted with silence. There were only two other customers in and they were from Penny Fawcett so they weren't aware of any problem. When she had collected her shopping Linda came to the cash desk and took her money. Gwen never spoke, and neither did Jimbo or Harriet.

Peter came in later that morning. 'I'm truly sorry about all this trouble with Gwen and Beryl, Jimbo. It must be very distressing for you, I'm sure.'

'It is, Peter. If we don't allow them to shop here they will starve, but it's very hard to be Christian about it in the circumstances.'

'I'm quite certain it is. If it was a child of mine who'd been threatened I don't know how I would react. But the fact remains we cannot take the law into our own hands. The two of them came within an ace of being lynched last night. I was appalled by the hatred everyone felt. It was mob rule and no mistake. I feel this morning as if I am a complete beginner as a judge of character. The behaviour last night was positively mediaeval. I couldn't believe it. It's a wonder they didn't put them in the stocks and stone them to death.'

'It's hard for us, Peter, to condemn them. They were doing it in outrage at what happened to Flick.'

'I know, but you wouldn't want anything but justice for them would you?'

'No, we wouldn't.'

Peter's sermon the following Sunday had as its text 'Let he who is without sin amongst you cast the first stone.' There was coffee for everyone in the church hall afterwards and Peter set about rebuilding the bridges he had so painstakingly constructed during the last year.

13

The morning following Peter's sermon was the first day of Ron and Sheila's membership of the Turnham House Health Club. In preparation for this day Sheila had bought a plush tracksuit, not the same pink as Venetia's but very similar. She'd toned down her choice of colours since her conversion to more refined dressing, brought about so insistently by Ron. Joining the Health Club was a move in the right direction she was sure. One had to move in the right circles and have the opportunity to meet the right people. You never knew where it might lead. When Sheila counted up how long it was since she'd worn a bathing costume, no, she musn't say that, a swimsuit, she discovered it was thirty years. The one she'd bought was in pink to match her tracksuit. Ron had made sure she bought the correct size. She knew he was right, she always bought her clothes too small. She didn't like to admit she needed a sixteen whereas before she'd worn size twelve.

It was a fine, warm morning so Sheila wondered whether they should run up to the Health Club or take the car. Ron shook his head.

'I think we should go in the car. No sense in arriving dead beat. Better wait till we get fit, and then run up there.'

The reception hall was cool and elegant. The girl at the desk checked their membership cards, handed them fresh, pale pink towels with Turnham House Health Club emblazoned on them and was directing them to the pool when Venetia came across the hall to greet them.

'Hi there, come for your first dip have you? Glad to welcome you to the Club. I'm sure you'll get great benefit from coming here.'

'I'm sure we shall.'

'Give me a knock on that door over there when you're ready to try the gym. I like to plan your personal exercise routine myself. I make sure you take things easy to start with and gradually build up to maximum. Have a nice day.'

Ron and Sheila met at the poolside. There were huge, plastic palm trees arranged in gargantuan pots along the perimeter of the pool, interspersed with white plastic chairs and loungers for relaxing in. The enormous glass windows were closed but could be opened wide on really hot days. There was a terrace outside with another batch of white plastic chairs for people to sun themselves.

Sheila lowered herself into the jacuzzi. The warm pulsating rhythm of the water throbbed around her bottom and she suddenly understood why they came so highly recommended. Oh my word, she thought, there's more to this than meets the eye.

Ron was swimming backwards and forwards slowly and somewhat painfully. She had to admit that no one seeing him stripped off in public could describe him as athletic. Lumbering might be a more appropriate description. She hoped that Venetia wouldn't get designs on him. She was getting too old to fight off opposition. But someone like Venetia wouldn't be interested in an overweight man of mature years would she? Though come to think of it, that was exactly what Jeremy was. Overweight and lacking sex appeal. Like Ron.

Ron suggested they had a sandwich lunch from the pool bar. They'd just settled themselves nicely in two of the plastic loungers by the pool when Venetia appeared, wearing quite the smallest bikini it was possible to imagine. It was a sharp, bold purple colour which gave Sheila spots before the eyes. She watched Venetia poised on the edge of the pool, giving them the maximum opportunity to admire her slim, taut body and then she dived sleekly into the azure water. Sheila turned to make a sneering remark to Ron about exhibitionism, but she looked at his face and bit back the words. Ron was avidly watching the bronzed and purple blur which was Venetia racing back and forth down the pool. Sheila tapped him on his thigh and said, 'Ron? Ron?' but he ignored her. Venetia finished her swim and came over to them, tossing her thick dark hair from her face and shaking her limbs to rid them of water. Her well-toned flesh trembled as she did so. She reminded Sheila of a cat which had got wet in the rain. Feline. That was it.

'When I've got dry would you like to come to the gym, Ron, and we'll plan your schedule?'

Sheila answered on his behalf, 'When we're ready we'll come and give you a knock.'

She watched Ron's face as Venetia jogged off to the changing rooms. He was positively relishing the sight of that woman's behind.

Ron was about to knock on the door marked 'Private' to ask Venetia to come to the gym, when Sheila stopped him. The door was partly open and they could hear voices inside.

'Look here, Sid, you said you'd got it in the bag.'

'I know I did. They promised twenty staff for each of six weekends starting this coming weekend. They wrote and promised it, there's the letter. Now this has come saying that due to the recession they're having to lay people off and make economies wherever they can. One of their economies is cutting out these special weekend incentives.'

'But that means we've no one here for the next six weekends now.'

'Don't state the obvious, Marge. It doesn't take much of a brain to come to that conclusion.'

'Don't call me Marge here. You might do it in front of the clients.'

'What clients?'

'What the hell are we going to do? You'll have to get out on the road and look up some of your old contacts. Offer them weekends at special introductory rates or something. You know, to give them a taste of the fabulous opportunities for body health or whatever.'

'Hell, what a mess.'

There was a pause and Ron took this opportunity to knock on the door. Venetia came out and headed with enthusiasm to the gym.

She got Ron and Sheila onto the exercise bikes. It seemed to require a lot of stroking of Ron's legs and extra special placing of hands on his thighs as he made the pedals go round. She didn't help Sheila at all. Sheila was told she was performing excellently and she must have been on an exercise bike before. She protested she hadn't, but noticed that Ron needed an awful lot of attention considering all he had to do was make his feet go round. The worst of it was, he was lapping up the attention with a silly grin on his face.

Later that day, Sheila went to the Store to get something special for their evening meal. Jimbo was in there entertaining his customers with his usual gusto.

'Hello there, Sheila, you're looking sprightly today. Been up to the Health Club, have you?'

'Yes, for the very first time. It's very nice up there. Have you been yet?'

'Harriet and I go quite regularly. We've both taken out membership. I like the gym and the running track, but I'm not too keen on the pool. It's not very big, is it?'

'No, it isn't, but then you don't need it with having a pool of your own. I tried the jacuzzi and found it most enjoyable. We had lunch there as well which was very pleasant.'

'All supplied by Turnham Malpas Store, you know, so it should be.' Jimbo raised his boater and took a bow.

'There was only us there this morning. I expect it will be busier in the evenings.'

'Let's hope so for their sakes. They've got groups coming for the next six weekends so that will help. We've just been planning the menus for them.'

'Oh . . . I don't know if I should tell you this, but by mistake we overheard Venetia and Jeremy talking, and they've had a cancellation and those people aren't coming. We heard them say that they had no one now for the next six weekends.'

'They haven't told us.'

'Well, that's what they were saying. I think they only heard this morning.'

'I'll give them a ring and ask a few questions about the food and see if they tell me anything. Thanks for letting me know, Sheila.'

'There's something else as well. Her name's not Venetia.'

'What is it then?'

'It's Marge.'

Sheila and Jimbo burst into hysterical laughter. Sadie came through, asking what the joke was. When they told her she had to lean on the counter for support. She got her handkerchief out and wiped her eyes.

'Never. I don't believe it. Oh my word what a laugh.'

Sheila, enjoying centre stage said, 'That's not all. You'll never guess what Jeremy's real name is.'

Jimbo hazarded a few guesses but in the end Sheila had to tell him, 'Its Sid.'

Sadie laughed till she had a pain in her side. 'Marge and Sid. Sid and Marge. Oh help, wait till Harriet hears this.' And she went off in search of her daughter.

After Jimbo had calmed down he asked Sheila what she wanted and when she pointed to some fresh salmon, he cut her two generous steaks and gave them to her as a gift.

'You and I haven't always seen eye to eye Sheila, but I'm very grateful for your warning. Accept these as a peace offering.'

'That's extremely kind of you, Jimbo, Ronald loves fresh salmon. So much nicer than those nasty tins.' She chose vegetables and a homemade blackcurrant cheesecake from the freezer and went home.

Jimbo rang the Health Club number with his list in his hand of the meals he'd planned. Jeremy answered the phone. 'Turnham House Health Club, how may I help you?'

'Good afternoon . . . Jeremy. It's Jimbo here from the Village Store. Got some menus worked out. Could I run a few ideas past you? I'd fax them but the dratted thing has gone on the blink and I can't make it transmit.' He crossed his fingers because of the whopping lie he'd just told.

'Ah, right. I'm listening.'

'I know it's only Monday but I'll need to get the food ordered you see and I don't want to find I've asked for things which aren't suitable. Can't afford waste in these hard times, as you well know.'

'Indeed, indeed. Fire away.'

Jimbo read out his list, trying to decipher from Jeremy's response whether or not the man was bluffing or whether Sheila Bissett had got it wrong.

Jeremy's voice came back down the line confidently agreeing to Jimbo's menus, 'Excellent, Jimbo, excellent. Just what we want.'

'In that case then we'll go ahead and order?'

'Yes, do that please.'

'I'll deliver very first thing Friday morning. Give your cook time to sort himself out.'

'Of course. We're lucky to have such excellent service so close at hand.'

'Payment on delivery as agreed?'

'Of course, of course.'

Jimbo put down the phone, took off his boater and stood looking out over the green. Either the man was a very convincing liar or Sheila had made a mistake. Only time would tell. All the salad stuff would be a pain, he'd have most of that to throw away. And he'd never sell the ten litres of carrot juice. Such waste. He couldn't bear it. However, when the Friday came he delivered the food, received his payment, and came to the conclusion that Sheila Bissett had misunderstood what she had overheard.

Harriet planned to go up on the Saturday with the children and see for herself what was happening. Jimbo was still sticking to his decision about her being with the children whenever they weren't at school, and she'd found herself enjoying their company more than she had expected. Sometimes when she saw Caroline's pram she almost fancied having another baby herself.

At the Health Club the receptionist checked their membership card, gave them the appropriate number of pink towels and they finally got to the pool. The children all swam like fishes so Harriet gave herself the luxury of lounging in the jacuzzi while they swam and played with the floating toys provided by the management.

She was soon joined by two couples. They began chatting to each other and Harriet lay listening with her eyes closed, enjoying the warm water and the feeling of relaxation it engendered. They chattered on about how much they were enjoying the club and one of the women said, 'Nigel, how come we got invited for free? Do you know this Jeremy chap well?'

'Not that well. Met him a couple of times in our local hostelry and he gave me the chance to come for nothing so I suggested I brought friends as well, and he was well chuffed. In fact, everyone here this weekend is here for free. Shan't be taking out membership though, too far away from my usual haunts. No doubt the sales pressure will be administered before we're much older.'

That was Jimbo's answer then. The guests were all there on a freebie.

She told her news on her return and Jimbo's mouth went down at the corners. 'They won't last long at that rate then. Better watch our backs where they're concerned. Blast it! I was hoping the income from the Health Club would balance the lack of earnings from the restaurant. Something will have to go. We can't keep Henderson's open when it's such a drain on our resources. I can't tolerate failure. Damn and blast it.'

Ron and Sheila went four times that week to the Health Club. Sheila was not nearly as keen as she had been but couldn't permit Ron to go up there on his own. Heaven alone knew what might take place in the sauna. Ron had taken a great liking to them.

'Help me to lose weight you know Sheila, which is just what we want isn't it?'

'Yes it is.' Privately she wondered if she would be better off keeping Ron overweight.

The crunch came when Sheila lost Ron one afternoon. They'd both been for a swim and done their scheduled exercise plan which was taking longer now they were getting better at it. Then Sheila had got changed and they'd arranged to meet in the pool bar for a drink before they went home.

Sheila ordered her gin and orange and sat perched on one of the high stools watching some children swimming and waiting for Ron. She assumed he'd be along soon. After twenty minutes she went in search of him. She tried to appear casual, not wanting to have to admit to losing him. She opened the door of the men's changing room and called in a loud stage whisper, 'Ron, Ron are you there?' There was no reply. She wandered around for a little longer, looking here and looking there until besides the treatment rooms, there was only the gym left to check. Sheila looked through the glass panel in the door. Ron was laid on his back working hard on a weights machine, pushing up and down, up and down under the close supervision of Venetia. She was alternately holding his hands and helping him push and then holding his legs to stop him lifting his knees. Ron was working away as though he was a young man of twenty not an old man of sixty-six. The stupidist grin imaginable was creasing his face. She marched in and stood beside them. They were so preoccupied that at first they didn't notice her.

'What are you trying to do to him? Kill him?'

Ron let go of the handles and sat up abruptly. Venetia stood up and said, 'You've got a much better movement now Sir Ronald. You just needed a little help.'

'Let's get home. I've been waiting twenty minutes for you Ron.'

By the time Sheila had made their bedtime cup of tea, Ron wished he hadn't been born. It was all so innocent he kept telling Sheila, but she wouldn't listen.

'It was an excuse for getting her to paw you all over. And what's more you were enjoying it. I wasn't born yesterday Ron. She's a nympho . . . whatever it is. Look how she pursued the rector. Disgusting that was. She's man mad and anyone will do.'

'That's not very flattering to me.'

'One more word out of you and I shall tell the world and then where will your political career be? Down the pan that's what. And what's more I don't care. And another thing, first thing tomorrow I'm getting my leopard skin coat out of store and wearing it as soon as it's cold enough, so you can put that in your pipe and smoke it.'

'No, Sheila don't do that.'

'You're in no position to tell me what to do Ron Bissett. I listened to you about going up in the world and dressing like Sadie Beauchamp. Well I'm not listening any more. In fact I think I shall ring the *Sun* tomorrow and let them know, anonymously of course, what really goes on up there.'

'If you did that, membership would rocket. It would really take off.'

'You're right it would.' Sheila caught Ron's eye and they both started laughing. 'Honestly Ron, what were you thinking of?'

'Just an old man flattered by her attentions. At bottom I knew it was all a sham. I couldn't have done anything about it if I'd wanted to, could I?'

'I doubt it, though if you got fitter you might.' Sheila sat up and looked down at him. 'That's it Ron, get fitter and perhaps we could resume diplomatic relations.'

'Right then old girl.'

'Not too much of the old girl Ron, I'm not drawing my old age pension yet. Shall we keep going and both of us get fit? You hear about these pensioners who have an exciting sex life. Let's have a try shall we Ron? There's not much else on the horizon is there? You get fit and me as well and I won't get my leopard skin out of storage and then we'll go for a second honeymoon. We'll have to hope you don't have a heart attack that's all. And remember no getting Venetia to pay you undue attention, 'cos you'll have me to answer to if you do. I'll maim her for life . . . right where it hurts.'

14

Sylvia broke the news to Caroline on her return from her holiday with Willie.

'Have you a moment Dr Harris?'

'Of course Sylvia, if you don't mind me burping Alex while we talk.'

'No that's all right. I've managed to find somewhere else to live.'

'Oh Sylvia, you don't mean you're leaving me?'

'Oh no, well, that is if you still want me to work here.'

'Well, of course I do. We get on so well together. Peter and I really appreciate your help, you know that. Where will you be living? Is it in the village?'

'Well, yes, it is.'

'Oh where? I didn't know there were any cottages empty.'

'There aren't. I don't know how to say this, but I'm going to live next door, with Willie.'

To give herself time to think, Caroline carefully wiped Alex's mouth where some food had spilled out when he burped. Sylvia, stacking the dishwasher, cast sidelong glances at her while she worked.

'It's no one's business is it, but mine and Willie's?'

'No, that's quite right. Have you thought this out properl . . . Sorry. Sorry, Sylvia, of course you have, you're not a child, you've a perfect right to do as you wish.'

'I can't contemplate marriage yet, you see.'

'Why not?'

'Because I got such a rotten deal the first time round. My first husband was a womaniser. The pain I suffered was intolerable. I put up with his unfaithfulness for fifteen years and when he got killed, I had all on not to cheer. No woman should be asked to put up with what I did. They wouldn't nowadays, you know, Dr Harris. They'd divorce them straight off. I wish I'd divorced him years back. But marriage is marriage and I stuck to what I'd promised.'

'I'm sorry you had such a hard time of it.'

'That's why I can't marry Willie, not yet anyway. When I said those marriage vows before, I meant it and I stuck to 'em. I daren't make them again until I'm really sure.'

'Willie's not like that though Sylvia.'

'No, but I've yet to be convinced. Trouble is, he daren't tell the rector.'

'He's no need to, I shall. Your private lives are your own. We can't avoid him knowing but I don't know what he'll feel about it. He's old fashioned where things like that are concerned. Church's teaching and all that.'

'He might not want me to work for you then?'

'He will, because I can't manage without you. Leave it to me.'

Caroline suggested Sylvia went out for the evening. She wanted her out of the way while she tackled Peter.

He loved treacle pudding and she'd made an especially good one for him. He sat back after his second helping and complimented her on the sheer perfection of it.

'That was splendid Caroline. How you manage such delights with so much to do I don't know.'

'I wouldn't if I didn't have Sylvia to help me. You'd be making your own treacle pudding if I didn't have her.'

'If she looks like leaving give her a rise. We can't afford to lose her.'

'I know. Do you want to finish the wine?'

'I'll have another drop, do you want some more?'

'No thanks. You finish it. Have you seen Willie today?'

'Yes, of course. Why?'

'I just wondered. Was he all right?'

'Bit quiet, but he seemed OK. Why are you so concerned about Willie?'

'I'm not. You couldn't manage without him could you, just like I can't manage without Sylvia.'

'Caroline, is this leading up to something?'

'Well, I have to be truthful. Yes it is.'

'He isn't leaving is he?'

'No, he's taking in a lodger.'

'A lodger. In that little cottage? Who is it?'

'Sylvia.'

Peter put down his wine glass, stood up and went to look out of the dining room window.

'Can you tell me why? Are they getting married?'

She explained what Sylvia had told her.

'I see. Well, they sound like good reasons.'

'They are.'

'But I can't be seen to condone it. It's quite against my principles.'

'I promised myself some time ago that I would never use what I am going to say next in any discussion we had. I made that a sacred vow to myself. But on behalf of your reputation in this village I have to remind you that where marriage vows are concerned the rector must be seen to tread extremely warily. After firing that particular salvo I shall retire to stack the dishwasher and empty the drier.'

Caroline had set the dishwasher going and was folding nappies onto the top of the tumble drier when Peter finally came to find her.

'I can't accept that what they are doing is right, because it isn't. Willie is the verger here and as such should be showing some example to the parish. However, as you so rightly and tenderly reminded me I am in no position to comment. Forgive me Caroline.' Peter stood waiting for her reply. She finished folding the nappies, held the last one to her cheek, relishing the soft warmth of it and then turned to him.

'My darling, you know I forgave you months ago. I may not forget, I have two constant reminders day and night and I can't avoid the memories, but I have forgiven you. Lock stock and barrel forgiven you.'

Peter held out his arms and drew her to him.

When Willie met Peter in the churchyard a few days later, he knew he had to say something about Sylvia. They'd both kept silent about it and Willie didn't enjoy being estranged from the rector. It made life very difficult; the air needed clearing.

He leaned against the side of the shed, took out his pipe and when he'd got it going to his satisfaction he looked at Peter and began his apology. 'I know, sir, that as rector you won't agree with what Sylvia and I have arranged.'

'That's right Willie.'

'I also know that as the verger I ought to set an example, but it's like this. When I was a boy I fancied girls like all boys do, but the years went by and I never met one I wanted to share the rest of my life with. A quick roll in the hay, begging yer pardon sir, and goodbye was my philosophy. Then I clapped eyes on Sylvia and wished both she and I were thirty years younger. But we're not. We haven't got a right lot of time left, well not enough anyways. She's the first one I've met I'd really want to share my life with, not temporary but permanent like. She's told me all about 'er first, and I can understand why she can't make 'er mind up. She's got to be sure and she isn't yet. So I've had to compromise, as you might say. I can't face spending the rest of my life without her, so at the moment it's second best as far as I'm concerned. As soon as she's sure we shall be up that aisle.'

'I'm glad to hear it, Willie. Let me know when she decides and we'll regularise things. Meanwhile, we won't discuss it any more. You're both grown people and know full well what you're doing. I do know this, she's a tremendous help to my wife and lovely to have around. You've got good taste.'

'There'll be a lot of gossip in the village and I shan't like it but I expect it'll be a nine days' wonder and then they'll get something else to talk about. I'd be glad if you didn't say anything about me hoping to get married. It might make Sylvia feel obliged when she isn't.'

'I shan't say a word Willie. And if, when the time comes, you want to keep the wedding a secret, then so be it.'

'I'll be round tomorrow to dig that border for yer sir. Yer know your good lady guessed all along it had been me and not you doing your garden, but she never said a word did she?'

'No, she didn't, not to me anyhow.'

'She's a lovely lady sir. You're well blessed and so am I with my Sylvia.'

'Indeed we are both well blessed. By the way Willie I've asked several times about you giving me a lift down with that tin trunk in the boiler house store room, but we haven't got round to it yet. How about it?'

'Can't find the key sir.'

'Well, then we shall have to saw through the padlock.'

'I'll be round like I said to do the plants.' Willie spun on his heel and disappeared into the shed.

Two days after Sylvia had moved into Willie's cottage, she went shopping for the Rectory and bumped into Gwen collecting her groceries. Gwen's coat button caught on her basket. As she tried to disentangle them she said, 'I'm sorry Miss Baxter.'

'Not sorry enough, you slut.'

'I beg your pardon?'

Gwen raised her voice. 'Slut, I said.'

'What do you mean?'

'You know very well. Listened to Willie's sweet talk have you? Let yourself get persuaded eh? Not even his ring on your finger.'

'I think you need to mind your own business.'

'We've got eyes. We see what you're up to. Tainted, that's what you are, TAINTED. A scarlet woman.'

Gwen's voice grew louder and brought Jimbo out from behind the meat counter.

'Miss Baxter would you please pay for your groceries and leave.'

'Leave? Oh yes, I'll leave. I wouldn't want to be consorting with women like her. Harlots and sluts. Toys for men's pleasure, that's what you all are, toys. You'll all end in hell.' She glared around at the customers who were all staring at her, wagged her finger at them and then went to pay Linda who stood waiting by the till to take her money. Sylvia blushed bright red, put down her wire basket and fled from the Store to the safety of the rectory.

By the time Gwen had left, those who hadn't known about Willie and Sylvia now certainly did. The hubbub in the Store was raised several decibels.

'Wonder where that Gwen thinks she'll end up, considering what she's done?'

'Lucifer 'ull have it nice and hot for her I bet.'

'Nasty old besom she is. Open that door, Mr Charter-Plackett, and let some fresh air in. After what she's done I don't know how you can let 'er in 'ere to shop. If it was me I'd refuse.'

'Can't do that, they'd both starve.'

'Serve 'em right for what they did to your Flick. Mind you she was right about them two.' The speaker nodded her head in the direction of Willie's cottage. 'And 'im the verger too.'

'Like rector like verger,' someone at the back said and laughed rather too loudly.

Pat Duckett waiting in the Post Office queue interrupted. 'No cause for you to say that Bet, he's lovely is our rector and 'is wife is too.'

'Oh yes he certainly is, too lovely if you ask me,' Bet said, nudging the woman next to her and winking.

'Nobody asked you, it's no business of yours, seeing as you come from Penny Fawcett.'

'He's our rector as well yer know.'

'Not like 'e is ours.'

'No, but I can offer an opinion.'

'Oh no you can't, you old cow.' Pat left her place in the queue, marched to the back and swung her handbag resoundingly round the head of the woman from Penny Fawcett.

Before Jimbo knew where he was he had a fight on his hands.

'Ladies, ladies, if you please.' He waded into the mêlée intending to extricate Pat, but his boater was knocked off and he came close to getting a black eye. Peace eventually restored, he retired to the mail order office and sat, considerably shaken, on Sadie's stool.

'There are times when I wonder if it's all worthwhile trying to make a living. Those women were at it tooth and claw. That Gwen has a lot to answer for.'

'I heard the skirmish and saw you disappear into the fray. Masterly it was, Jimbo.'

'All right Sadie, enough of your sarcasm. The sooner those two women are in prison the better.'

'I think they'll get off due to their age or something.'

'Surely not?'

'Wouldn't surprise me. The law is such an ass nowadays. I'd get prison for a motoring offence, but I bet they don't for kidnapping Flick.'

'Heaven alone knows what will happen if they do get off.'

15

That week Harriet and Jimbo got notification of the date for the court case. What they had dreaded confronting was about to become reality. They decided not to tell Flick until nearer the time. There seemed no point in her worrying for days before there was any need. The letter revived all their hatred of Gwen and Beryl.

The following day Harriet noticed that Gwen seemed very confused when she came in for her regular shop. Harriet got Gwen's newspaper out for her and put it ready on the counter. She watched Gwen move vaguely along the shelves and pick up a loaf of brown bread and two Chelsea buns. Then she went to the greengrocery and chose some parsnips. All the time Harriet had been in the Store she'd never seen Gwen buy parsnips. Carrots and swede yes, but not parsnips. Then Gwen went to the meat counter and selected a small pack of braising steak and a piece of pork fillet. She went back to the greengrocery and took a long time choosing two apples and two pears. Then she went to collect their two pensions. Linda came out from behind the Post Office counter and took her money and she wandered distractedly out of the store.

Harriet was very busy that day and dismissed the incident from her mind. The next day Jimbo was serving when Gwen slid into the shop and wandered around. She made completely different purchases from those she'd made the previous day. When Jimbo offered her her newspaper she shook her head. She paid for a portion of cheesecake, a tin of corned beef and a packet of tea and went out.

On the Monday Flick was in there after school sorting out the birthday cards. Jimbo paid her one pound a week for keeping the card display tidy. She loved doing it. The boys plagued her about the extra pound but she knew they only did so because they were jealous.

Her job that Monday was to put out loads of new cards with ages on them. They'd got really low. As she bent down to slot in the 50, 60, 70, and

80 birthday cards she smelt that peculiar smell which surrounded Gwen and Beryl. To Flick it smelt like a mixture of the boys' old football socks when they'd forgotten to ask Mummy to wash them, that awful French cheese Daddy said was like nectar and of unwashed clothes. Plus for Beryl the smell of garlic. Flick crouched down by the card displays and stayed as still as a mouse. Her breathing became rapid and that same terrible fear she had experienced in their cupboard came back and washed all over her and nearly made her wet herself. She couldn't get out without being seen so she stayed curled up, hiding her face, praying for her to go.

After she'd paid and left the shop Harriet spoke to Jimbo, 'Do you know Jimbo, Gwen is going peculiar.'

'Going peculiar? Don't you mean even more peculiar?'

'Well, yes. She has always bought exactly the same things each day of the week. But she hasn't had a tin of that dreadful Spam we keep in for her for nearly a week. Two days last week she never came in at all and now when she does she buys unusual things. I think she's finally lost her marbles.' Harriet felt Flick clutch hold of her skirt. 'Flick, you're pulling my skirt off! Oh, darling, I'm so sorry. I didn't think. Here, hold my hand tightly and we'll get out of here and go rustle up some food for the ravening hordes we call our menfolk.'

Harriet settled Flick on a kitchen stool and gave her the job of cutting up the cherries for a pudding she was making.

'Feeling better now, darling? I'm sorry I didn't realise you were there. You must have felt dreadful.'

'That wasn't Gwen.'

'When we go out on Satur . . . What do you mean that wasn't Gwen? They're twins, you can't tell the difference.'

'It wasn't, it was Beryl.'

'Beryl never shops.'

'She does now, that was Beryl.'

'How do you know?'

'She smells different from Gwen.'

'That's not very polite, Flick.'

'No, but she does.'

'Is that how you tell the difference?'

'Yes. Gwen is old football socks and Daddy's French cheese with unwashed clothes and Beryl is the same but with garlic as well.'

'Well, of all things! What an awful way to tell which is which.'

'I thought everybody knew them by their smell.'

'We all know they smell but no one has said anything about the smells being different. Are you absolutely sure it was Beryl?'

'Oh yes. Is that enough cherries?'

'Yes, that's plenty. In fact you can eat a few if you like.'

'I'm going to watch children's telly now.'

The following day when Beryl, or was it Gwen? went to the till to pay for her purchases, Harriet deliberately didn't ask Linda to come to take her money. Harriet asked innocently, 'Is your sister keeping well?'

Beryl looked at her, nodded and began to back out of the Store.

Harriet was determined to find out what was going on. 'And how are you today Miss Baxter. Keeping well?'

The dark brown eyes stared nervously at her.

'Yes.'

'It will be winter before we know where we are, won't it?'

'Yes.'

Harriet watched her hesitate and almost begin to say something but she changed her mind and fled from the shop leaving half her purchases on the counter.

'This is my moment Jimbo, I'm going after her with these things.'

'You're doing no such thing. If she wants them she can jolly well come back for them.'

'Someone's got to find out what's going on. Gwen could be lying seriously ill in there and Beryl too frightened to do anything about it. You and I pick up the phone as easy as we comb our hair, but to Beryl it's a major undertaking.'

'Have you heard what I've said Harriet? You are not going to their house!'

'You are getting far too dictatorial James Charter-Plackett, do you know that? Do this, Harriet, don't do that, Harriet, I shan't allow et cetera, et cetera. Well it won't do. I'm going.'

'Then I shall come with you. Linda can you manage for five minutes while I escort my bossy wife across the green?'

'Yes, of course I can. If you're not back in ten minutes I shall send for Inspector Proctor.'

'You do just that. Come on, Harriet, put it in one of our carriers and we'll be off, though what you expect to find I don't know.'

They set off at Jimbo's usual brisk pace. He dreaded going to their cottage, but wouldn't admit it for the world. His memories of that awful day when Flick was missing rose in his throat as they neared the house, and almost choked him. He found he could hardly breathe.

As they passed the front of the cottage they saw Gwen sitting bolt upright on a chair by the one window which hadn't had to be boarded up, her head resting against the high back of her chair. They waved and signalled to her to come to the door but she ignored them.

They knocked and knocked but got no reply.

'We'll put the carrier by the back door and then go,' Jimbo decided.

They went back to the Store and faced the morning rush, but at the back of Harriet's mind she kept seeing Gwen sitting so still by the window. It was all very odd.

'Half a pound of braising steak and two pork chops? Right you are Mrs Goddard. How's life in Little Derehams nowadays? Still as lively as ever?'

'We leave all the lively happenings to you in Turnham Malpas, Mr Charter-Plackett. That's why we all shop here, so we can learn the latest gossip. Apart from the fact your food's the nicest of any hereabouts, of course!'

'Thank you for that kind compliment.' Jimbo raised his boater in acknowledgement.

Mrs Goddard went out of the shop and returned immediately. 'Quick! Ring for the fire brigade, there's a cottage on fire. Look! Over there! The other side of the green!'

'It's the Baxters' cottage. Oh Look! Clouds of smoke there is.'

The customers rushed outside to see. Smoke was curling steadily up from the thatched roof and beginning to collect in a huge pall above the thatch. Harriet dashed inside to the phone and Jimbo rushed out across the green. Ron and Sheila were coming out of their house as he passed. Jimbo banged on the door of the sisters' cottage. Surely to God that wasn't Gwen still sitting in her chair? He peered in through the one remaining window. Oh God she was. Then he realised with horror that Gwen looked as if she might be dead. There was no smoke in that room yet, so she must have been dead before the fire. Where the hell was Beryl? Willie, Jimmy, and Peter along with Bryn from The Royal Oak had all arrived.

'We'll have to break in round the back and get them out,' Peter said urgently.

'It's too late for Gwen. She's already dead. Look.'

'Oh dear Lord, whatever next.' Peter took charge. 'Willie, go and get my hose pipe from the Rectory and get Caroline to fasten it to our kitchen tap. Bryn, see if Sir Ralph is in and get him to fix his up too. We'll have to move quickly, at best the fire brigade won't be here for twenty minutes.' In no time at all they had two hoses struggling to keep the fire under control. 'Play it on the thatch there Bryn. That's right. Jimbo and I will go in round the back. Willie and Jimmy you come with us. That's right Ralph, pour it in through the windows. Plenty of water onto those flames.'

They pushed open the back gate and threw their combined weight into opening the door. It burst open and clouds of smoke billowed out.

'You're not going in there sir,' Willie shouted. 'The smoke'll get you before you've gone two strides. Don't let him Jimbo.'

'Do as we say Peter, you don't go in there.'

'We must save them.'

'Gwen's already dead . . .'

'Already dead?' Willie couldn't believe what he'd heard.

'We'll pull down the boarding from one of the front windows and get in that way,' Peter shouted. They rushed round to the front of the house, getting drenched by the water from the hoses. By now a crowd had gathered and Bryn had organised a chain of buckets which they were filling from Jimmy and Vera's kitchen taps.

'She's sat in the window, get her out. Overcome by smoke that's what.'

'It's Beryl we're looking for. Has anyone seen her today?' They all began shouting 'Beryl. Beryl.'

Peter pulled a piece of boarding from the window. As it came away the outside air rushing in caused flames to belch out. Gwen could no longer be seen from the window.

'I'm going in.'

Willie grabbed Peter. 'Oh no, you're not, sir. Here stop him somebody.' Jimbo held Peter's other arm and refused to let go.

'You're not going in there Peter. Thank God here's the fire brigade. They'll go in with breathing apparatus.'

The firemen sized up the situation and began releasing the hoses and getting out their breathing apparatus.

'How many are we looking for?'

'Well, one sister is already dead sitting in a chair in the front room here and there should be one other sister.' Peter wiped the sweat from his forehead and took over the hose pipe from Ralph.

Two firemen named Barry and Mike were soon kitted out. They entered the blazing cottage. Those onlookers not fully occupied with the chain of buckets waited with bated breath to see who they brought out. Within moments Barry emerged carrying the body of Gwen. He laid her on the green. Peter took off his cassock and covered her with it. 'We can't find anyone else in there, are you sure they were both in?'

'Well, they hardly ever go out.'

'There's mountains of paper smouldering in there. It makes searching very difficult. One more try Mike, eh?'

'Right.' Barry and Mike disappeared again. The other firemen were playing their hoses into the upper windows, from which they had dragged Gwen's boards.

'There's only the old lady we've already brought out,' Mike announced when he emerged through the smoke.

The Sergeant arrived on his bike, having been contacted on his radio at a farm he was visiting.

'This is a right do this is,' he grunted. 'Have you got both of 'em out?'

'We can only find one old lady and she's dead.'

'Which one is it?'

'She's under the rector's cassock on the grass there.'

The flames had died down now but the piles of newspapers were still smouldering and clouds of smoke were pushing up into the sky. The entire village was out on the green watching. It must surely have been the most interesting day they'd had for years.

'I shall have to send for the Inspector. Can I borrow your phone, Rector?'

'Certainly.' The Sergeant bustled off across the road.

Georgie came across from The Royal Oak carrying a tray filled with mugs of tea. Behind her trotted Muriel, also holding a tray filled with mugs.

'You firemen get first call on the tea, and then the bucket brigade, and after that anyone else who helped,' Georgie shouted.

'Peter?'

'Caroline! What are you doing?'

'Helping. She's been dead for a few days, I'd say.'

'I suspected as much. Beryl's left her sitting in the chair. Why on earth didn't she get help.'

'Too frightened, I expect. I'm glad Jimbo stopped any heroics on your part.'

'You heard.'

'I did. The smoke would have killed you.'

'Wish we could find the other one.'

'She's not inside, by all accounts. Do the fire brigade know how it started?'

'Not yet.'

Caroline stayed till the ambulance came to take Gwen away. They all assumed it was Gwen because it was always she who watched the comings and goings of the village from the windows. Caroline spared a thought for how Beryl must be feeling. It all looked decidedly disturbing.

*

The fire brigade stayed for nearly four hours before they were satisfied there was no chance of the fire restarting. But there was still no sign of Beryl. Muriel, mindful of her obligations to Pericles, had abandoned her ministrations behind The Royal Oak teapot and gone home to take him out.

They went on his favourite walk, down Jacks Lane, across Shepherds Hill and onto the spare land behind the chapel and then down by Turnham Beck. The rabbiting opportunities were legion around here. He raced from one hole to another his tail wagging furiously whenever he got the drift of rabbit. Then he began yelping in earnest. Muriel smiled. 'One day you'll catch one Pericles and then you won't know what to do with it.'

As Muriel stood watching Pericles searching for more rabbits, she felt a tug at her sleeve. She jumped with the surprise of it, unaware thanks to the hullabaloo Pericles was making, that someone else was down by the beck.

Standing behind her, bowed and distraught, was Beryl. Never looking particularly clean, Beryl looked even worse than usual. She had been crying and there were streaks of dirt and tears all down her face. Her hands were dirty as though she had been digging in the earth with them.

'Why Beryl, we've all been so worried about you,' Muriel said kindly. 'Where have you been my dear?'

Beryl rolled her eyes and then hid her face in her hands and stood trembling and mute. Then she pulled her oversized cardigan over her head as though she thought, childlike, that if she couldn't see the world the world couldn't see her.

'Beryl can you tell me what happened at the cottage? Were you there when the fire started?'

At this Beryl sat down and tried to hide the whole of her body inside her cardigan. Her desperate writhings put Muriel in mind of a sick animal burrowing to find a place to die.

'My dear, let's go and find Peter from the Rectory. You know Peter don't you, he's tried to help you before. Get up and we'll go there together. He'll be sure to help us. Come along.'

It was all so beautiful there in the field, with the sound of the beck trickling its way along as it had done for centuries. The willows were bending their graceful twigs down to the water's edge, the grass almost emerald green with all the rain they'd had and the sun getting low in the sky. The contrast of that peaceful scene with Beryl's agony was almost more than Muriel could bear.

'Please, Beryl, get up. Let's go and find Peter. He's so kind, you can tell him everything that's happened. We'll ask Caroline to make us a cup of tea and we'll get warm by her stove. It's so comfortable in the Rectory kitchen.' Muriel called Pericles and clipped on his lead.

She bent over, put her hand under Beryl's elbow and heaved her up. The two of them began a slow walk towards the Rectory. Beryl's head stayed hidden in her cardigan. Muriel didn't even know if Peter was in but Caroline seemed the best person to find. Harriet and Jimbo could hardly be asked to help. No, Caroline was best with her being a doctor. Yes, that was it. Caroline and Peter.

'We'll have a nice hot cup of tea and then we'll talk,' Muriel promised. 'Come along, keep going.'

More police had arrived at the scene of the fire and were in deep consultation with several of the firemen. They all looked at Muriel as she guided Beryl across to the Rectory. Muriel signalled to them to leave Beryl alone, and pointed to the Rectory saying, 'We'll see you in there.'

Inspector Proctor and Sergeant Cooper followed them across the green. Cooper knocked at the Rectory door, while Muriel tied Pericles to the old boot-scraper still standing sentry duty on the Rectory step. Caroline answered the door, holding little Alex in her arms.

'Ah, hello,' she said, surprised to find this curious collection of people on her doorstep.

Inspector Proctor was the first to speak. 'Can we bring Miss Baxter in Dr Harris? As you can see she's very distressed and we can't take her to her own home.'

Muriel said, 'I've told her Peter will listen and understand.'

'Of course, of course. I think we'd better go into the kitchen. There's too many of us for Peter's little study. I'll put the kettle on and we'll all have a cup of tea.' Caroline led the way and settled Alex on Sergeant Cooper's knee, while she put the kettle on and went to find Peter.

Muriel sat Beryl down in Caroline's rocking chair by the stove. Beryl was still holding her cardigan over her head.

Inspector Proctor asked Muriel where she'd found Miss Baxter.

'Down by the beck, Inspector. She won't speak. She's like an animal who has lost all reason.'

'I'm afraid we've made a rather unpleasant discovery at their cottage.' Peter came in and the Inspector stood. 'Ah good afternoon sir, sorry for intruding, but we didn't seem to have anywhere we could take Miss Baxter.'

'That's quite all right, Inspector. Where else but the Rectory for such a problem as this?'

Peter went to Beryl and rested his hand on her head and patted it.

'God bless you Beryl, you're quite safe here, my dear. My wife Caroline is making a cup of tea for you. I'm sure you must be ready for it. It's been a very tiring day for you, hasn't it?'

Peter pulled up a chair, Caroline gave him a mug of tea for Beryl and he handed it to her under the canopy of her cardigan.

'Do you take sugar?'

From inside her cardigan she whispered, 'Gwen says no.'

'Well, she isn't here at the moment so we'll put some in. It will do you good. I like to have a biscuit with my tea, do you?'

'Can't.'

'Why not?'

'They make you fat, Gwen says.'

'I'm sure she won't mind you having one out of my special tin just this once. Here you are, it's got chocolate on one side.' Beryl grabbed the biscuit and hurriedly crammed it into her mouth. Then she took a second one and ate that more slowly. The Inspector began to fidget. He looked at his watch and coughed pointedly.

Without taking his attention from Beryl Peter said, 'I can't hurry this, at least she's started talking. There we are Beryl, I'm sure that feels better.' He took the empty mug from her hand and then held her dirty hands in his and asked, 'Now what were we saying, oh yes, I know, about when you started the fire.'

'I didn't.'

'I know you didn't do it on purpose.'

'Wanted candles for Gwen. Couldn't put her in church. He'd never done us a good turn in all our lives, so why should we bother with Him she said. She didn't believe.'

'I know she didn't.'

'I wanted to light candles for her . . . hands shaking, she shouldn't have gone. She should have waited for me. Where is she? Dropped the candles you see and the rug caught fire and then the newspapers. She would keep the newspapers.'

'Why did she keep the newspapers?'

'To hide it. Make a wall.'

'Ah I see, she stacked the newspapers up to hide it.'

'Don't tell that bobby. Don't want him to know.'

'I realise that Beryl. But I need to know don't I?'

Caroline quietly took the sleeping Alex from Sergeant Cooper and left the kitchen. Muriel and the Inspector sat completely still, their minds racing to guess what Beryl was trying to tell them.

Beryl was shuffling and twisting about under her cardigan and then the rush of words began to come, stumbling over each other in Beryl's urgent need to tell.

'Gwen smothered it you know. It was her. When it came I wanted to keep it but Gwen said no. The shame she kept saying, the shame. It won't take a minute to smother, not a minute. I cried. I cried, but she wouldn't listen. It's a bastard twice over she kept saying, twice over. Its an abomination, that's what it is. An abomination. But it wasn't, it was lovely and I wanted to keep it.' Under her cardigan Beryl shaped her arms as though cradling a baby. 'She said, this way it will never grow up, it will never need to leave this house. So that was when she did it. Then she put . . . it . . . it . . . in the tin trunk and we hid it with the newspapers.'

Muriel wished she was anywhere but here. All these terrible happenings and no one knew. What a frightful secret. When Caroline came back Peter asked her to get a brandy for Beryl.

'No one found out though did they Beryl?'

'No. We were clever. I never left the house once I got fat. She made me stay upstairs. Gone to a sanatorium for TB she told the people at the factory where we worked. But that wasn't it really. She called me a slut and a harlot. But he'd done the same to her, hadn't he?'

'Oh. I didn't realise that.' Peter gave her a glass of brandy. 'Drink this Beryl, I think you need it. It's not easy telling me all this is it?'

Muriel was beginning to feel very faint but held on for everyone's sake. This story had to come out now or it might never be told. Her collapsing would break Beryl's thread. The Inspector, keeping well back, was taking notes as Beryl spoke. Caroline sat perched on the edge of the table, both absorbed and horrified by what she was hearing.

Still under her cardigan Beryl blurted out, 'I haven't told a soul. She said I mustn't. All those years it went on. That was why Mother was always scrubbing and cleaning and washing our clothes. She thought she'd wash away the sin, but you can't do it as easily as that. She could have helped us. As soon as Mother died in nineteen forty-seven Gwen decided it would be Father next. She said he deserved to die slowly, but in the end we smothered him the next time he came to our room. "This'll be the last time," she said. "The very last time. You'll do it no more to us." And we both pressed hard on the pillow and he struggled for a while but we won in the end. Then we carried him back to his own bed and covered him up and told the doctor next day that we'd found him dead. We got away with it because he'd been ill on and off for a while, and they thought he'd died in his sleep.'

Muriel was feeling distinctly ill, and wished Ralph would come to rescue her. Beryl had come out from under her cardigan and was staring Peter full in the face.

'We couldn't help it, you see. Father started coming in our bedroom when we were in our early teens. We tried to stop him but we couldn't. I knew Mother knew because she wouldn't look at us the next day. That was why Gwen said the baby was an abomination, because it was his. So I've had nothing and no one to love all these years. We couldn't let anyone in the house in case they found . . . you know . . . that . . . thing in the trunk. Then when we got the letter about the court case Gwen took ill and I found her dead in the chair. I didn't know what to do.'

Peter looked in on the twins before he went to bed. He touched their smooth cheeks and smelt their lovely sweet cleanliness. How true what someone said about the sweet innocence of a child's sleep. They neither of them knew anything about what had happened, nothing of the pain and horror in that cottage over the way. Please God they would never need to know of such things in all their lives. No, that was unrealistic, please God they would have the strength to cope with such evil, and come through it.

He lay in bed unable to sleep. It had taken all his skills to get Beryl to go quietly to the hospital. Caroline had volunteered her help and Muriel, feeling that moral support would be needed, had gone with them. The Inspector had wanted her to go directly to the police station and give a formal statement, but eventually even he realised that he was never going to get that from Beryl. A permanent bed in a secure mental hospital was the likely option. It was when Beryl had decided she would be safe with Peter that his worst fears were realised. Hell, what a situation to be in. As a Christian he ought to have said, 'Yes, of course.' But how the hell could one invite a known murderer to share one's home when it contained two precious children besides his darling girl? She would more than likely have become obsessed with the twins and none of them would ever have known a moment's peace. No, it had to be somewhere secure where she could get help. At least she would be kept clean and well fed which was more than had been the case for a very long time.

He heard Caroline at the door.

He ran down the stairs and she almost fell into his arms.

'Peter, I am so tired I can hardly stand up.'

'My darling, it's so late. Whatever happened?'

'I'll tell you everything when I'm in bed.'

'I'll help you.'

Once he had got her settled in bed and his arms were round her she said, 'She'll never be free again, you know. They've put her in the psychiatric ward but she'll have to be moved somewhere more permanent. She has absolutely cracked now. When we got her out of the ambulance she was so meek and mild, but as soon as we stepped into the hospital she ran amok trying to escape. Fortunately Terry was on duty, he's the nurse I told you about who's built like an ox and is very fleet of foot. They always call him when there's trouble. Anyway he managed to catch her and restrain her. Muriel was terribly upset and I didn't know which one of them to comfort first. However, we calmed her down and I had the inspiration to give her a bag of dolly mixtures I had in my bag. She's like a child; it took her interest and she sat calmly munching them, while I filled the registrar in on what had happened. Then when Muriel and I tried to leave she decided she was coming with us. So we had another set to. She clung to Muriel and they had to pull her off. There's no Gwen, you see, to tell her what to do. What an awful mess. How did we not realise what was going on?'

'We knew things weren't right, but how could we possibly have guessed how terribly wrong they really were? This has taught me a profound lesson, I shall not give up so easily next time I sense something is not as it should be. Thank you for all your help, darling. What did it feel like being back at the hospital?'

'It's nice being able to pull strings because of who you are, but I'll tell you something and then I'm going to sleep. I much prefer my life as it is now, thank you very much, and you were wonderful today.'

Peter kissed her and gave her a hug then found she was already fast asleep.

16

Peter laid his morning post on his desk without even a glance. Dressed in his oldest clothes he had plans for clearing out the old trunk in the boiler house store room, the one which Willie had so adamantly refused to attend to. Today was Willie's day off and Peter was taking his chance whilst he could.

'You never know, Caroline, I might find documents in there which are of no use to the church but could be sold and the money used towards the new heating system.'

'Well, you're certainly dressed for it. I threw out that pullover about six months ago. How come you're wearing it?'

'I found it in the bin and rescued it. Sylvia washed it for me and now it's being put to some use.'

'Sometimes you do cling to your old things. Is it your security blanket?'

Peter kissed her and declared she was his security blanket thank you very much. He played for a few minutes with the twins who were rolling about on a rug on the kitchen floor. 'Before we know where we are these two will be walking . . .'

'And then your troubles will begin.'

Peter laughed. 'Right, I'm away. I'll open the post when I get back.'

The trunk was far heavier than he had expected and it took all his strength to lift it down from the shelf. Thick, grimy dust lay all over it. Peter rooted about in the cupboard where Willie kept his cleaning materials and found a brush and a cloth which he used to clean the outside. The padlock on it was stoutly made and as he had no key available, Peter had to saw through it to get it off. He had difficulty in forcing up the lid, and it creaked stiffly as he pushed it fully open. Inside were dozens of papers and files filling the trunk right to the top. Some of the papers were minutes of parish meetings from years long gone. Some were old letters belonging to Victorian rectors, even one from a bishop telling the Reverend Samuel Witherspoon that he would be visiting the parish on the 15th May 1867 at precisely two thirty. All very commendable but scarcely of much use as saleable objects. At the very bottom of the box was a thick, leather-bound book. In copper plate handwriting on the inside page were the words Turnham Malpas Parish Charity Fund. The first entry was dated December 1st 1761. After the date it was recorded that James Paradise had received the sum of ten shillings for food for his family.

Each subsequent December the names of villagers who had received money from the Fund were recorded. Names of families Peter recognised as still living in and around Turnham Malpas. The last recorded distribution was 1st December 1916. The sum of £1 had been given to each of four Glover brothers; Cecil, Arnold, Herbert and Sidney. Since then there had been no further distributions. Why had the distributions stopped and why had the book been so carefully hidden beneath all the other much older papers?

Peter put all the papers back in the trunk. He brushed the dust and dirt from his trousers and sweater, rubbed as much as he could from his hands, took the Charity Fund book with him and placed it on his study desk.

Caroline took his coffee into him and he drank it while he opened his post. There were several letters, three items of junk mail, his credit card statement and a letter from the County and Provincial Bank. Puzzled as to why he should be receiving a letter from a bank he didn't use Peter opened it first. Inside was a statement saying that the Turnham Malpas Parish Charity Fund had twenty-three thousand four hundred and thirty-three pounds thirty-four pence to its credit. The bank manager had enclosed a letter suggesting Peter visit the bank to discuss more advantageous investment of the money.

Peter opened the study door and called out, 'Caroline, come here a minute.' She came into the study with a baby wriggling under each arm.

'Yes?'

'I've opened this letter and it says we have all this money in the bank, in a Charity Fund. Curiously enough I've found an old book in that trunk, here look, with the words Turnham Malpas Parish Charity Fund on it. Distributions went on right up until December 1916 but there's no further record in it after that. Isn't it odd that we've never heard of this fund before and yet on the same day the book turns up and the bank make contact? And why has there been no further money given out? I can't believe there has been no one in need of help for the last eighty years, can you?'

'How very odd. Look, I'm putting these two to bed for a sleep before lunch. I'll be back in a while and have a proper look. Twenty-three thousand pounds! Just think what the church could do with that!'

'Exactly. This could be the answer to a prayer.'

The bank manager gave Peter an appointment for that afternoon and he set off straight after lunch. Caroline used to comment derisively on the speed he drove at, but since becoming a father he'd reduced it by at least fifteen miles an hour and drove far more cautiously. He was familiar with the little cross roads three miles from the village, heaven knows he'd crossed it often enough, though there was always that bend in the road which blocked a driver's vision. It did make one hesitate and check carefully before driving on. Suddenly, out of nowhere, a tractor crossed in front of him. He braked, and swerved viciously to the right to avoid an impact. The car lurched and juddered as it shot across the road, straight towards the ditch. Peter braked even harder but couldn't prevent the car from going down into it where it lay tipped at a crazy angle, front end right down in the nettles, the back wheels spinning in the air. The tractor driver, apparently oblivious to other road users, appeared to melt into thin air. Peter waited a moment to collect his thoughts before attempting to climb out. His knees had come sharply into contact with the edge of the dashboard and both felt amazingly painful. He managed to force open his door and climb out onto the road.

The first Caroline knew about it was Peter arriving home in a breakdown truck.

'What's happened? Are you all right? Where's the car?'

'Thanks for the lift Brian, I'll ring you tomorrow about the car.'

'That's fine, sir, we'll do our best.'

Peter came limping into the Rectory. 'Don't panic, I'm only bruised.'

'Show me, show me.'

'The car went into a ditch, I managed to struggle out, hailed a passing lorry and got a lift into Culworth.'

'You didn't go straight to the bank?'

'Yes.'

'You should have gone to casualty.'

'I thought perhaps I'd come home instead.'

Peter undid his trousers and pulled them down so Caroline could examine his knees. 'Not much problem there I think. I guess you'll have massive bruises by tomorrow. They are already swelling. I'll make you a cup of tea with plenty of sugar in it. Explain how it all happened.' Peter dressed himself and told her the story of the phantom tractor.

'That tractor driver is an absolute pig for not stopping.'

'Well, never mind, I'm not badly hurt.'

'And the car?'

'Well, that's another story. The front end is badly damaged, headlights gone, radiator stoved in, bumper badly damaged, bonnet buckled and that's what you can see before it's been examined inside. I think I'll get it repaired and then sell it. Cars never feel right once they've been involved in an accident.'

'What did the bank have to say?'

Peter sipped his tea. 'That tastes good. They are as surprised as I am about the bank account. They've got a new manager and in the way of new managers he's something of a new broom. They're having a massive face lift and really bringing the bank into the twentieth century, so every nook and cranny is being cleared out. He found a file pushed down the back of a cupboard which hadn't been moved since the year dot. In it were details of the Charity Fund. None of the money was on their computerised system and no one can understand why not. They've done all the necessary with calculating the interest over the years, which must have been very complicated, and that's what it amounts to. He recommends that I write to the Charity Commissioners and get things sorted out.'

'It's all very odd. How could a bank have money hidden like that and no current record of it?'

'He doesn't know either. What amazes him is the fact that we both unearthed evidence of its existence in the same week. It's all very strange.'

When Willie realised that the rector had got the trunk down and broken in to it, he was very upset and indignant.

'I did say, sir, I'd look for the key.'

'Yes, Willie, I know you did, but you didn't actually bother did you?'

'No, sir. But there was no call to go investigating it though. That trunk's been on that shelf for years, there's nothing in it of any use. It was best left where it was, untouched. You 'aven't taken anything out of it 'ave you, Rector?'

'Yes, I have as a matter of fact. A book with entries in it to do with a Parish Charity Fund.' Peter could have sworn that Willie blanched, but he dismissed the idea as ridiculous.

'Right, well, I'll be off.'

'Don't you want to hear the rest of the story, Willie?'

'No.' He walked off without so much as a good morning, leaving Peter feeling affronted by his attitude. It was so unlike Willie to be bad mannered.

In The Royal Oak that night Willie was very quiet.

Jimmy asked him if he wasn't well.

'I'm OK, but the rector soon won't be.'

'Clairvoyant are yer then? Or 'ave yer been poisoning 'is soup?'

'No. 'Nother drink Sylvia?'

'Yes, please love.' While Willie waited at the bar for the drinks Sylvia told Jimmy she was quite worried. 'He keeps going on about a trunk the rector's opened up, says he's no business bringing up the Charity Fund again. Says no good will come of it.'

Jimmy looked pensive and then offered his opinion. 'Ah, well, he could be right at that. How's the rector going on about 'is car?'

'They've lent him one from the garage while his gets repaired. Though I don't know if he'll be well enough to drive. He's looking real poorly tonight. Dr Harris is quite worried about him. She's sent him to bed. Flushed and coughing a lot he is. When I told Willie he said, "and no wonder" whatever that might mean.'

Willie came back with the drinks and they began talking about other matters, in particular what Jimmy would do when he got this massive win he expected from the pools.

'You've been filling in the pools for twenty years that I know of. Whatever you get you'll deserve it, you've spent a fortune on them pools.' Willie laughed and Jimmy snorted his annoyance. 'You wait and see.'

'I will.'

Peter was diagnosed as having a virus. For a week he lay in bed with a high temperature unable to eat and scarcely able to get to the bathroom unaided. He lost a great deal of weight and caused Caroline and their GP serious anxiety. Then he developed a secondary bacterial infection and a patch of fluid on his lung. The curate from Culworth came to conduct his services and he prayed with the congregation for Peter's recovery. There was a continuous stream of parishioners at the Rectory door, some inquiring after the latest news, others bringing gifts for the invalid. Calves foot jelly and beef tea had to go down the waste disposal. Caroline said to the jelly and the tea, 'Sorry about doing this to you. I know you have the best of intentions, but he can't eat you.'

She was having the most harrowing time of her life. She rather wished she wasn't a doctor as ignorance of the true state of affairs would have been bliss. The specialist who had come to the house felt that Peter would be better left at home, especially after Peter became very distressed when he realised there was a possibility of going to hospital. And Caroline was, after all, medically qualified. One evening, when it had taken Peter three hours to decide he couldn't eat a small piece of grilled trout, Caroline asked Sylvia to keep an eye on the twins and Peter for a while, took Peter's keys and let herself into the church to pray. She turned on the small lights by the altar and went to kneel in the Rectory pew. Gazing up at the beams of light illuminating the brass candlesticks and ornaments and the huge, ancient cross hanging above the altar, so beloved by Muriel, Caroline prayed for Peter's safe deliverance, reminding God that she didn't often ask for things, but that this time she really meant what she asked.

She recollected sitting in this very pew with Peter when he told her about the twins. The desolation she felt then was as overwhelming as what she was feeling now. If I lose him whatever shall I do? Keep going for the sake of his children, that's what I would have to do. She thought of them being fatherless and she a widow and then shook herself. This morbid dwelling on death would have to stop. She allowed her common sense to get the uppermost of her thoughts and finished her prayers with the words, 'Your will be done.'

In The Royal Oak, Jimmy told Bryn that nothing, not even prayers, would cure the rector. Bryn, recognising the curious village persona which existed and to which he wouldn't belong even if he lived there fifty years, asked him, 'Now, why Jimmy, I mean why? People come in here, ask how he is and then wisely nod their heads and say, "Well, there's no wonder he's so ill, is there?" What has the rector done to deserve whatever it is?'

'Interfered where 'e shouldn't that's what. Interfered 'e 'as. Like Dr Harris did over me and my snares. Stuck 'er nose in where she shouldn't, and so's he. 'Cept this time it's more serious.'

'Interfered with what? He seems a charming, enthusiastic and very genuine chap to me. Just what the village needs in the church.'

'He is, but this time he's over stepped the mark.' Jimmy tapped the side of his nose with his forefinger and took his drink to his seat opposite the settle to await Pat and Vera and perhaps even Don; a bit of male company would be nice seeing as Willie appeared to have gone into a decline, and was refusing to socialise nowadays.

It was three weeks before Peter was well enough to venture outside. Ralph suggested he came to have coffee with him and Muriel for his first outing.

'Sit down here Peter in this big chair. It's more suited to your frame. I must say though, you've lost a lot of weight.'

'A stone and a half actually Ralph. Caroline is busy feeding me with suet puddings and meat pies trying to build me up, but I've very little appetite for them I'm afraid. I have never been so ill in my life. Never. I've walked from the Rectory to here and feel exhausted.'

Muriel came in with the tray of coffee. 'Here we are Peter, and I've brought some shortbread too, do you think you can manage a piece of it?'

'I think so.' Muriel handed him his coffee. 'Thank you, you're very kind.' He sipped his coffee and said, 'This is lovely Muriel.'

'How are your legs after the accident?'

'Fine thank you. I've been so ill, a couple of very bruised knees paled into insignificance!'

When he'd drunk his coffee and finished the shortbread, Peter asked Ralph if he knew anything about the Charity Fund.

'I'd heard that was what you'd been meddling with.'

'Meddling with?'

'Yes, meddling with. Best leave well alone, Peter.'

'How can I leave twenty-three thousand pounds alone? Just think what we could do with that money. The new heating system, the pointing which needs doing, the organ serviced. It would help us out of a big hole wouldn't it? And Neville Neal would be smiling for once.'

'Even Neville as Treasurer wouldn't want you to use it.'

'So he knows why, half the village knows why, you know why, but I don't.'

'No, Neville doesn't know why. But I've told him he mustn't use it even if he gets permission from the Charity Commissioners, because the village will come out in open revolt. Your accident and illness have only served to confirm their fears. If you used it for repairs they would expect the church to fall down on their heads, literally. Make no mistake about that.'

'Will you tell me what it's all about?'

Ralph hesitated and then said, 'No. Partly because I don't know the full story and partly because I can remember my father saying, "The village won't stand for it, so it's best to leave well alone." '

'Is there anyone who *will* tell me?'

'Go see Grandma Gotobed in Little Derehams. She's well into her nineties, but don't imagine for one minute that means she's soft in the head. She rules her two unmarried daughters with a rod of iron and won't even allow them to bake the bread, because she reckons they're too young to get it right. And believe me neither of them will see seventy again!'

Muriel laughed and then said, 'Oh Ralph, how can she know about the Charity Fund? The Gotobeds lived in Little Derehams when we were children.'

'If Peter looks in the old records he'll see that the Gotobeds were originally a Turnham Malpas family. They only moved to Little Derehams towards the end of the First World War.'

Peter asked Muriel if she knew anything about the Fund.

'Nothing at all. My parents protected me from anything and everything, and the nuns told me nothing. I didn't even know how babies came till I was sixteen, and even then it wasn't my parents but a girl in my class at the secretarial college who told me.'

'Quite right too. Children know far too much, far too soon nowadays,' Ralph retorted. Muriel reached across and kissed Ralph's cheek. 'You're behind the times, dear, I'm afraid.'

Peter stood up to go. 'My new car is being delivered this week, so as soon as I'm feeling up to it I'll drive out to Grandma Gotobed's and see what she has to say. Thanks for the coffee, hopefully I shall be back to work next week.'

17

That same week Sheila called in at the Store to speak to Jimbo.

'Is he in, Linda?'

'Oh yes, I'll give him a call.' Linda left the post office counter and called through into the store room, 'Mr Charter-Plackett, Lady Bissett would like a word.'

Jimbo came bustling through into the Store, raised his boater to Sheila and asked her if she liked the new, scarlet ribbon Harriet had put round it.

'Very smart I must say, Jimbo. You always keep things so stylish here. I like that new display area for the meat. Very "olde world" isn't it?'

'Strikes you like that does it?'

'Mmm, very tempting. You're a good salesman. I've come with another snippet of news for you about the health club.'

'Thought you weren't going there any more?'

'Who told you that?'

'You know how news gets around.'

'Were you told why?'

'No,' Jimbo declared innocently.

'That Venetia was trying it on with Ron in the gym. I soon gave her short shrift.'

Jimbo drew closer, looked around the Store to ascertain whether he was being overheard and repeated, 'Trying it on? What was she doing then?'

'Making ten times too much fuss helping him with the weights machine, holding his hands and pressing his legs down. Making him work like a maniac at his age, too. I was really angry about it. Anyway, what I came in to say was that this weekend, all the people there were having it free again.'

'Venetia's very liberal with her favours isn't she?' Jimbo laughed.

Sheila giggled, 'Really! You know full well what I mean, Jimbo. I meant they were *staying* there for free.'

'This can't go on, can it? I'll go up there myself tonight and nosy around a bit.'

True to his word Jimbo went to Turnham House with Harriet. Besides them there were only three other clients. The two of them plunged into the pool and swam vigorously back and forth and then went into the jacuzzi. Venetia appeared wearing another of her miniature bikinis. 'I shall be joining you soon. I'll have a swim first.'

She poised on the edge of the pool and then dived in, scarcely rippling the water.

'Give her her due she can dive.'

'Jimbo, shall I go for a sauna and leave you to her mercies?'

'What a good idea.'

'Find out all you can, won't you?'

'And some.'

'Remember Mother's garden shears though won't you, darling?'

'Ouch, don't remind me.'

Harriet climbed out of the jacuzzi and made her way to the sauna, while Jimbo lazed with his eyes shut waiting for Venetia to strike. When she slid into the water and sat opposite him with her feet touching his, he pretended to be surprised.

'Why Venetia, hello. Harriet was just saying how beautifully you dive. Quite spectacular.'

'Thank you Jimbo.' Venetia smiled at his compliment. 'I thought with having a pool of your own you wouldn't be interested in swimming here. The gymnasium would be really useful to you though. Have you got an exercise programme?'

'No, I haven't. Are you the one to give it to me?'

'Yes, I will. We do have a gymnast but it's his night off tonight. When you're ready, we'll go in to the gym and I'll take your pulse and things and show you how to pace yourself.'

'In that case I'll get my gear on right now. Harriet's in the sauna so she'll be a while.'

'Let's stay here a little longer Jimbo.' Venetia slid along the seat and sat very near to him. Jimbo nestled close.

Jimbo took his chance. 'How's business then? Looks as if things are going well. I wish I could say the same of Henderson's.'

'Isn't it going well?'

'Comme ci, comme ça. Not bad, but not good enough unfortunately. You're a businesswoman, Venetia, have you any advice?' Jimbo's leg came in for some sympathetic patting from Venetia who then said, 'I'd no idea things weren't too good. Jeremy could advise you I'm sure.'

'What I need is some sensational happening to create a lot of interest. A customer of mine, who's a member of a health club up in town, was telling me that membership was none too buoyant, until one of the girls in the gym began giving "extra mural" tuition to the men in the sauna, then membership soared. News like that travels fast. The owners were feeling well chuffed and rubbing their hands with glee, till they got a visit from the police and the girl had to be sacked. They came close to being accused of running a brothel.'

'That's something one has to be very careful of in this business. It's so easy for clients to get the wrong impression.'

'What is really happening here? Membership wise I mean?'

'It's building up and will soon be a roaring success. Jeremy is very confident, and so am I. These things take time, that's all.'

'That's OK so long as the money doesn't run out.'

'It won't run out believe me. Anyway, you get paid on delivery for what you supply, so you should worry.'

'Cheques are fine so long as there's something in the bank to back them up. I might need to ask for cash soon if I get edgy.'

'You must do that if you wish. Here's Harriet. Bye, I've got things to do.'

Harriet joined Jimbo as Venetia left.

'She is a liar I'm afraid. They are in grave difficulties.'

'That's not what she said.'

'No, I know it isn't, but I haven't worked in the City for years without getting a sixth sense about money. They are mortgaged up to the hilt I bet. No more food Harriet, unless they pay cash. Remember.'

After she'd dried and changed Venetia went to the private office to find Jeremy. He was seated at a desk covered with well-fingered files, his latest cheap bodice ripper novel spreadeagled on top, ash trays stacked with cigar stubs and a pile of Snickers, Jeremy's latest craze. He unwrapped his third since tea and sat gloomily reading a letter he'd already looked at innumerable times that day.

'It's no good reading the same thing time after time, Jeremy, action is what's needed.'

'I can't believe that things have gone so badly wrong. I mean, old Arnie having to call in the receivers. He and I have known each other for years. If anybody was to go down I wouldn't have thought it would be him. I can remember watching him getting a huge roll of banknotes out of his back pocket and peeling off a few to give his son to go to the cinema with. Generous to a fault, he was. Now look what's happened.'

'Well, he won't be peeling any banknotes off for us will he? He was our last hope.'

'You know, Venetia, we have got to stop these free weekends, all this entertaining trying to persuade the punters to part with their money. There quite simply isn't the cash for it any more.'

'What the hell are we going to do? We've got so much on HP and a bloody gigantic overdraft. I feel sick, absolutely sick.'

Jeremy buried his head in his hands and groaned. 'When I think how much time and money I spent greasing the palms of pathetic councillors to get planning permission for this place, God I could weep. They're all sitting pretty, safe as houses grinning all over their faces while we're in queer street and no mistake. All the time it took convincing people to lend us the money too. They'll be after me like rockets once I stop paying the interest. There must be a way out.'

'And there was me going round telling everyone you were rich.'

'You shouldn't have done that. Most of it was borrowed. Added to which the alterations all cost far more than we thought they would.'

'I only did it to give everyone confidence you know. Well, you're supposed to be the business brain, get thinking.'

'My brains have dried up completely. All I can see is us being saddled with a massive debt for the rest of our lives.'

'You'll be saddled with it, Jeremy. Not me. It was your idea.'

'We went into it together.'

'I know we did. But you borrowed the money, I didn't.'

'I did it for you.'

'Yes, but none of it is in my name is it? Remember? It had to be all Jeremy. The big I am. "Look what I can do for the little woman." I can walk out of here tomorrow and no one can touch me.'

'Look, Venetia . . .'

'Don't you Venetia me. You signed all the papers, you talked to the bank. Second class citizen that was me. It's all yours lock stock and barrel.'

Jeremy leant forward and lowering his voice said one word.

'Fire.'

'Fire?'

'Shush, don't talk so loud.'

'What do you mean?'

Jeremy beckoned her closer. 'I mean, we'll start a fire. Burn the place down and then collect on the insurance.'

'Jeremy you wouldn't.' Venetia peered closely into his face. 'You would,

I can see it in your eyes. You can't do that to this lovely place it would be sacrilege. To say nothing of the risk you'd be taking.'

'*We'd* be taking. We'd have to be very clever. Being a listed building there'd be an awful lot of investigation. Look at the chap who came a couple of weeks ago. Went through the place with a fine tooth comb to ensure we were attending to the upkeep as we should. He spent ages poking about at that west corner. His report should be here soon, let's hope he found nothing too serious. It's not a question of setting fire to this place and doing a runner, then they'd know it was on purpose. We've got to be around and need to be rescued or even to ring the fire brigade when it's all too late. No staff here, us out for the evening, back about two in the morning to find the place in flames.'

'Surely it won't come to that?'

'We'll keep it in mind anyway.'

'How do you start a fire?'

'They're so clever nowadays, a pile of rags near the curtains and petrol poured on won't do at all. They'd soon tipple to that little scheme. We've got to be more subtle. Much more.'

'Let's hope it won't come to that. Surely the recession won't last much longer.'

'It will. Our game is a luxury not a necessity and businesses like ours go under first.'

'Oh God! Whatever are we going to do?'

'Like I said, put a match to it. Well, not literally but almost.'

'If we get found out you'll go to prison.'

'Oh, will I? And what about you?'

'They wouldn't send someone like me to prison, now would they?'

'Yes.'

'Would they?'

'Of course. Why not? This whole thing was your ridiculous idea in the first place. I should never have listened to you. You aren't in the right class for this kind of enterprise. Turnham House is a far cry from 'Let Pam Pamper You' unisex salon in Soho. If the police had had anything about them it would have been closed down.'

'They couldn't very well, half the clientele were senior police officers. That was the reason we didn't get shut down.'

'I'll do some thinking and see what I come up with.'

Jeremy and Venetia's regular food order at the Store for the following weekend had to be cancelled now that freebies were out. Jimbo had to come to some decisions of his own.

'Harriet. Council of War, my darling, if you please.'

'When the children are in bed, Jimbo. We don't want them worrying their heads about money, that's our problem.'

'Fine. Eight thirty sharp then, in Sadie's office, then we'll be well out of hearing.'

A little before time he carried a tray in. There on it were Harriet's usual gin and tonic and a whisky and water for himself. He began his drink while he waited for Harriet to come in. He'd done his figures and he knew what he was suggesting was the only valid solution.

'There's no other way Harriet. Last month we lost nearly a thousand pounds in Henderson's, and now the health club is apparently on its way out. Jeremy says it's only a blip and things will come right but you and I know different, so we've lost that income which did help a bit to offset the losses. The areas where we are actually making money are with the mail order, with the catering side and to a lesser extent with the Store. Rather than bleed those areas to death supporting a restaurant which is failing, I propose we close it. Much as I hate admitting defeat it will sink us if we don't. What do you think?'

'As a director of Charter-Plackett Enterprises I agree. But what the blazes do we do with the building?'

'I very much doubt we could sell it as a going concern. I propose we sell the kitchen equipment and the tables and chairs and, hold your breath here, re-vamp it into a house again and move in. That would give us more living space there and more room for the catering side and the mail order business here. You would be the first to admit we are very cramped in here anyway, we've always said that.'

'You mean use the whole of this building for the business and live separately over in Henderson's?'

'Yes, what do you think?'

'I think that's brilliant. In fact it fits in very nicely with some news I have for you.'

'News for me? What news?'

'I feel like one of those blushingly coy wives in a Victorian melodrama. We shall need that larger house fairly soon.'

'Blushingly coy? What do you mean?'

'I don't mean I'm really blushing, I thought it might do your ego good in these difficult times to know you are good at something. I think I must be expecting again.'

'Harriet!'

'Well, I'm a week late so it's early days, but I'm sure I'm right.'

Jimbo leapt out of his chair. 'Darling I'm so thrilled. That's wonderful. Are you sure it's all right with you?'

'Absolutely. I'm completely delighted, you've no idea how thrilled I am. It will be such fun, we had the other three so close together there was hardly time to enjoy them being babies. With this one we shall all be able to enjoy it. Having a house completely for our own will be marvellous.'

'Does your mother know?'

'No, she doesn't and I'm not telling anyone till we're sure and it's been confirmed. It can be our secret.'

'Come and sit on my knee. I don't mind nearly so much about the restaurant now. We'll expand on the catering side, which I'm sure I can do when I haven't the worry of Henderson's and we shall do fine. Well I never, I can't believe it. It's all come right hasn't it?'

'Yes, Jimbo, I knew you'd be pleased.'

'I couldn't be more pleased. I found out what the children meant to me when we thought we'd lost Flick. Another one is wonderful.'

'Early days Jimbo, we'll keep our fingers crossed.'

'It'll be all right you'll see, it was meant to be. There's life in the old dog yet. I feel positively frisky.'

In the middle of the night Jimbo, planning where he could sell the kitchen equipment, had the inspiration that Bryn and Georgie Fields might like some of the stuff in The Royal Oak. This could be their chance to open up their food side. With this in mind he drifted over there the following day and when there was a quiet moment he broached the idea to Bryn.

'Settled in now are you Bryn?'

'Yes, thank you, we could do to be making more money but I expect that will come slowly as we get known. I don't think the previous licencee encouraged new customers. Trade was very low when we took over.'

'Well, they did have problems you know. They made a lot of enemies and then their daughter was killed and it about finished them. You've improved the bar no end. It's much brighter and more inviting now. What's the food side like?'

'I get too much competition from a certain person sitting not too far from me. But it's picking up.'

'What if the certain person told you he was giving up with the restaurant and tea room? What would you say?'

Bryn stroked his moustache into order while he thought of the implications of Jimbo's question. 'Do you mean that? Really?'

'Yes, I do.'

'Well, of course that would make a tremendous difference to us. All the tourists and the locals would have to come here wouldn't they?'

'You know the barn down the side at the back? Wouldn't that make a good food area if you knocked through into it from that wall at the end of the bar?'

'We thought about that but with you open it wouldn't have been worthwhile. Now it would be. Georgie, have you a minute? Come and listen to this.' Georgie listened and her eyes lit up at the prospect.

'Wonderful, that's good news Jimbo. Well, sorry, not for you, but it is for us! It would be a big investment though, they're such sticklers for everything being absolutely hygienic nowadays with all these new regulations.'

'Not many miles from where you are now, is someone with nearly new equipment for sale.'

'Of course,' Georgie grinned. 'That's the answer. We could go in for meals in a big way then couldn't we? Would the chairs and tables be for sale too, Jimbo?'

'They wouldn't come cheap, but, yes, I'm sure we could come to some arrangement beneficial to both sides.'

'We'll keep quiet about our plans till we've reached a proper financial agreement, then the sky's the limit. Thank you Jimbo for letting us know.'

'OK then, I'll be in touch when I've worked something out.' Alan Crimble, under the pretence of needing more clean glasses, had been listening to their conversation. He grinned at Jimbo and tapped the side of his nose knowingly. Jimbo didn't acknowledge the gesture, thinking it was none of a barman's business listening in on his employer's private conversations, but Bryn and Georgie didn't seem to mind.

Harriet had misgivings about Jimbo's arrangement.

'If we can't make a go of it why should they? I'd feel awfully guilty if they failed.'

'The business decision to start proper meals is theirs Harriet, not ours. They have been wanting to do meals but realised our enterprise prevented them. I simply suggested they purchased our equipment, they didn't have to go for it. Anyway they'll do much better. They won't be making it into a top class restaurant as I tried to do. It'll have wider appeal.'

'We'll close this Saturday shall we?'

'Yes, I've written the notice out for the doors and we'll put a message on the answer machine in the restaurant for when clients ring up to book. Good riddance is all I can say.'

18

The villagers saw the notices and many of them made a point of needing to buy something in the Store in order to find out more.

'Sorry you're having to close the tea room and the restaurant Mrs Charter-Plackett, too much for yer was it?'

'Not making money Vera, that's the top and bottom of it. Glad to be rid of it.'

'I see, well it was a bit ambitious wasn't it? Don't know where they'll all go for their cups of tea and that when they've looked round the church and had their photo taken in the stocks. Do you?'

'No, I don't. Is there anything else?'

'No thanks, that's all for now.'

Vera complained in The Royal Oak that night.

'She told me nothing, shut up like a clam she did. 'Ave you heard anything Jimmy?'

'Can't say as I have. Been out all day with Sykes. Walked to Penny Fawcett and then over by Turnham Rocks and then home. Best part o' fifteen miles I reckon.'

'Have you got that smelly dog in here with yer?'

'Keep yer voice down. He's under the table. Bryn'll turn him out if he knows.'

'Well, take 'im home then, you haven't far to go.'

'I will in a minute. He's me friend yer know Vera, I don't like to leave him on his own too much.'

'Been setting yer snares then?'

'Not yet, thought I'd have a drink first and then pop into Sykes Wood before I go to bed. What's it to you?'

'Nothing, I don't mind, but plenty do.'

'Well, that's up to them. I mind mi own business and they should mind theirs.' Jimmy took a long drink of his beer, and then glancing round to make sure he wasn't being watched he placed the glass under the table. Sharp ears could have heard Sykes quietly lapping the remains of the drink.

Vera launched into a story about a woman from Penny Fawcett who'd been seen with a man other than her husband in the cinema in Culworth. 'Back row in them double seats they were, he was nearly eating 'er. Her cousin Lily told his Aunt Polly and there's been a right row. Are you listening?'

'No. I'm off now. Set mi snares before it gets dark. If I get one do you want it or have *you* gone all soft as well as everyone else?'

'Yes, I'll 'ave one thanks.'

'I'll skin it for yer.'

'Right, thanks.'

Sykes, having business of his own in Little Derehams with a Westie bitch on heat, left Jimmy to set the snares. When Jimmy was ready to leave, no amount of calling brought Sykes to heel, so he reluctantly set off for home. He made himself a cocoa, took the last of the 'Mr Kipling' almond slices out of his cake tin, switched on his ancient black and white TV and watched till nearly midnight. Before he went to bed he opened the back door and called again but his little white and black shadow, the best friend he had in the world, wasn't home yet. 'Damn 'im for being so randy, it'll be that Westie bitch again. I don't know where 'e gets it from, the little beggar. If all 'is wives meet up one day there'll be a right show down. Well, 'e might as well enjoy 'imself, life's short enough.'

Early the following morning Jimmy rolled out of bed, dressed, drank a pint pot of extremely strong tea and went off to inspect his snares. He missed Sykes running along in front of him. If he didn't come home by lunchtime he'd walk along to Little Derehams and see if he could find him. There were times when he wished he'd had him 'done' but his scruples wouldn't allow it, after all he couldn't ask Sykes' permission could he?

As Jimmy climbed the stile in the fence which divided the field in front of the Big House from Sykes Wood, he thought he could hear crying. His astute countryman's ears picked up that it was the crying of a dog or a fox in pain. His heart, with a tremendous lurch, somehow found its way into his throat. He began running. There was nothing in the first snare and it wasn't until he reached the third one that his worst fears were realised. Sykes was caught round the neck in the wire. He tried to greet Jimmy and his little white tail wagged faintly but then he began yelping again. Very gently, trying not to hurt him more than necessary, Jimmy slowly loosened the wire, and slipped Sykes head out of the noose. The dog slid slowly to the ground and lay panting with relief. He tried to lick Jimmy's hand as though thanking him for his rescue. All round his neck, where the wire had been pulling tighter, as he struggled to free himself, the flesh was gouged open and hung around his throat almost like a necklace. There was plenty of congealed blood around the wound but releasing the wire had caused more bleeding and it was dripping onto the grass. For one dreadful moment Jimmy thought he could see his neck bones.

Off came Jimmy's old poaching jacket. He laid it on the ground and, picking up Sykes as gently as he could, he laid him on it. Sykes appeared to have fainted, if dogs did such a thing. The journey home almost broke Jimmy's heart, Sykes lay so still. How he could get into Culworth to that vet he'd used once, he didn't know.

When they got home Jimmy warmed some water in the kettle, poured it into a saucer and added some honey and a teaspoon of brandy. Sykes obliged by trying to drink but he was too weak to make the effort. Jimmy sat down trying to think of a plan of campaign. Ralph, that was it, Ralph. He'd ask him to drive him in. He'd do it. He understood about country ways.

But Ralph wasn't in. 'I'm sorry, Jimmy,' Muriel said, 'Ralph's gone to London on business. He left about half past six to miss the worst of the traffic. Why not ask Peter, he'll just be finishing prayers, it's almost seven.'

'No, no I can't ask him.'

'Yes you can, if I was dressed I'd ask him myself. He's always willing to help anyone in trouble. I'm so sorry about Sykes, he's such a nice little dog.'

'I'll go ask then. There's no one else up and I can't delay he's that poorly.' Jimmy left Muriel and went up the church path. As luck would have it Peter was just locking the church door.

'Why, good morning Jimmy, you're up and about early.'

Jimmy took off his old cap and stood twisting it in his hands. Being of an independent mind, asking favours didn't come easily. 'Rector, I know you and I are not best friends at the moment . . .'

'Don't say that Jimmy, please. We are always friends.'

'Well, we've 'ad our differences, but it's Sykes, he's injured and he needs the vet real urgent like. It's all the way to Culworth sir, I don't really like to ask. Ralph's already gone to London or I'd 'ave asked 'im, so Muriel said why not ask you, sir.'

'I'll get the car out straight away. Let's ring the vet first and let him know we're coming in.'

'Will you do that sir? I 'aven't a phone.'

'Of course, come in the Rectory.'

'No, I'll get back to Sykes. The one I went to years ago was Forsythe and Blair, the one at the bottom of Abbots Row.'

'See you in a couple of minutes then.' Peter returned to the Rectory to find Caroline just going into the kitchen to start the breakfast.

'Jimmy's Sykes has been involved in an accident and he needs to get to the vet's so I'm going to take him.'

'Oh poor thing, what's he done?'

'I don't know, but Jimmy's very upset. It sounds serious. I'll ring the vet and go straight away. Don't know how long I'll be.'

Around lunchtime Caroline heard knocking at the door. Peter had returned from Culworth hours ago, leaving Jimmy to return on the lunchtime bus. It was he standing on the doorstep. His normally ruddy brown complexion was pale with anxiety, his thin cheeks were more hollow, and his stoop more pronounced; all told he was a sorry figure. They hadn't spoken since the night of the rabbit incident, but when she saw how strained his face was, she could feel nothing but compassion.

'Oh, sorry. Thought it would be the rector. It's 'im I need to speak to.'

'The rector isn't in Jimmy, he's sick visiting today. But tell me how Sykes is. Look, please come in.' She opened the door wider and waited for him to enter.

'No, no, it wouldn't be right.'

'Yes it would, come in and tell me all about it.'

Jimmy stood on the doormat, cap in hand. 'I don't know how to tell yer. It's the judgement of the Almighty, that's what it is. The Almighty, yes, that's right.'

'What is?'

'Well yer see Dr Harris, I'm afraid . . .'

'He hasn't died has he?'

'No, but it wasn't an accident, well, it was I suppose, but it was my fault. All my fault, 'e got caught round 'is neck in one of mi own snares. 'E ran off last night yer see when we went to set the snares, 'e right fancies a b . . . a lady dog down Little Derehams way and I expect he came back to find me after I'd gone and that was when he got caught.'

Caroline put her hand on his arm. 'Oh Jimmy! I'm so sorry, so very sorry. Look, the twins are having a nap, I'm about to have lunch, come in the kitchen and at least have a drink of tea or something.'

He followed her in and sat in her rocking chair by the Aga. She busied herself boiling the kettle and making sandwiches, leaving Jimmy to pull himself together.

'Yer see Dr Harris, it's a punishment isn't it? You wanted me to stop, I didn't stop and now look what's happened.'

'Vets can perform miracles nowadays, you know, with all these new drugs they have. He'll probably be up and about in no time, you'll see. Peter said you went to the Abbots Row Clinic. I use them for the cats, they're very good.'

'Septicaemia is the worry. The wire wasn't clean yer see.'

'Ah right. Yes, I see. Here's a sandwich and your tea, it's turned out rather strong. Is that all right?'

He left after lunch with Caroline's words of reassurance ringing in his ears. 'While there's life there's hope.'

But by the weekend the vet held out little hope. Jimmy had had Sykes eleven years and he was already fully grown when he got him, so his age was against recovery. Septicaemia set in and by Saturday evening Jimmy was begging a lift from Peter to get to the surgery before Sykes died.

Jimmy stood stroking Sykes as his life slowly ebbed away. All Jimmy could do was wait for the end and comfort him as he lay motionless on his sheepskin bed. Suddenly Sykes shuddered and let out a long sigh. ''As he gone, vetnary?'

Mr Forsythe listened with his stethoscope and gently nodded his agreement. Jimmy bent down to place a kiss on Sykes' head and then turned away to look out of the window. He surreptitiously took out his handkerchief and wiped his eyes. In a moment he said in a curiously thickened voice, 'Do yer reckon dogs go to 'eaven?' Mr Forsythe said he was sure there was a heaven for dogs where the sun always shines and the rabbits all run slowly.

Jimmy turned from the window and gave a slight smile. 'That's a grand idea, what a grand idea, that's very comforting. Well 'e was always randy, lets 'ope there's plenty of bitches there too, then 'e'll be well content.' Jimmy nodded his head, 'Yes, well content.' No one saw Jimmy for a few days, then he came out of his cottage door, with a huge bunch of flowers he'd picked from his garden, and was seen walking across to the Rectory. Caroline answered his knock.

'Morning Dr Harris.'

'Good morning, Jimmy, do come in.' Jimmy stepped inside and said, 'You'll know, of course, about poor Sykes. I've come with these flowers to thank you for being so kind to me, you and the rector, when you'd every right to be annoyed and say "Serves you right." '

'I wouldn't ever say that, Jimmy, of course not.'

'Well, thank you for everything, and these are for you and I'd like yer to know I shan't be setting mi snares again. Ever. I've given it up. When I saw 'ow frightened my Sykes was, and 'ow much pain 'e suffered it made me think. I've bundled 'em all up and buried 'em in the wood near where I used to set 'em, deep down where they'll never be found.'

'Well, I'm sorry it took Sykes dying to make you stop, but I'm glad you're not going to kill rabbits in that way anymore.'

'Aye well, that's that then. Good afternoon, Dr Harris.' Caroline stood at the door watching Jimmy walk back to his cottage. He looked so woebegone. Her victory, won at such a price, seemed very hollow.

19

Muriel, despite being Lady Templeton, still cleaned the church brass once a fortnight. This time it was three weeks since she'd done the polishing because she and Ralph had been to the south of France for a week. She'd loved Cannes and Monte Carlo and Monaco and had come back with renewed zest to her quiet, country life. She was standing on a chair cleaning the big brass cross above the altar when she saw the sun had come out from behind a cloud and it was shining through the stained glass window covering her with curiously shaped streaks of colour. Her delight in the rich colours made her rub even harder and the old cross gleamed. No one knew how long the cross had hung there but Muriel liked to think it had been there since the Middle Ages and had seen the village through wars and calamities, joys and celebrations, for hundreds of years.

Only the noise of her cloth, rub rub rubbing on the cross disturbed the silence. Satisfied there was no more room for improvement she held onto the altar and stepped down. The chair, given by an ancestor of Ralph's in memory of a young and much loved husband who had died in a hunting accident, belonged at the side of the altar for Peter to use when the choir sang an anthem or a visiting preacher or a parishioner was reading the lesson. She gave it a pat as she replaced it. There was such comfort to be had from familiar things. Muriel collected her cloths and the tin of polish and went to clean the brass work on the lectern. It was then she heard the sound of weeping. Seated in the pew in front of the tomb Willie always insisted was haunted, was Venetia Mayer, her head bent, her shoulders shaking with sobs.

For a few more minutes Muriel continued to clean the lectern. Venetia Mayer was not her kind of person and she'd hardly spoken to her in all the time she'd been in the village. What really stuck in Muriel's throat was the damage done by the modernisation of the Big House. She couldn't quite forgive her for that. Eventually her soft heart could ignore the crying no longer. Muriel went to sit beside her. To Muriel's conservative outlook Venetia's apparel seemed hardly appropriate for church. She wore her brightest pink, plush velvet tracksuit with a purple headband and purple slouch socks. Because she was bent over as she cried, Muriel could see the words 'Turnham House Health Club' emblazoned across the back and they caused Muriel pain; it was such an insult to that lovely gracious old house.

Holding Venetia's hand Muriel said, 'Now, my dear, is there any way in which I could help?'

Muriel's sympathetic voice made Venetia sob even louder, so Muriel put her arm around her and rocked her gently saying, 'Hush, hush, nothing can be so bad that it can't be solved. Come, come, my dear.'

The crying lessened and Venetia lifted her head and looked at Muriel. The false eyelashes on her right eye were coming unstuck, her thick black mascara was running down her face in tiny black rivulets. Where the tears had run down her cheeks there were light coloured trickles amongst her tan makeup. Where had the super confident Venetia gone?

'Whatever is the matter? You can tell me, or if not, I'm sure the rector would be only too pleased to help.'

'Oh no, not him, not Peter, that wouldn't do. No, I don't want him to know.'

Muriel took Venetia's handkerchief from her and tried to wipe her face dry for her, but the streaks became even more pronounced, 'Here, my dear, I have these two clean tissues in my bag, use them.'

Venetia wiped her face as clean as she could without the aid of a mirror, and said, 'Lady Templeton isn't it?' Muriel nodded, 'I'm sorry for making such a fool of myself, but we're in such trouble, you've no idea.' Venetia sniffed into the tissues.

'I am sorry about that.'

'We can't pretend any longer.'

'Can't pretend what?'

'That everything's all right.'

'All right?'

'With the Health Club I mean. We've been pretending for weeks that the clientele was slowly building up, but sod it, it isn't. We're going to have to close. We were so full of excitement, this was really going to be the big deal, the big opportunity and this bloody recession has killed it.' Muriel's embarrassment at her swearing in church showed in her face and Venetia apologised, 'Sorry, sorry for that.'

'I see, so it isn't Mr Mayer that's the problem then?'

'Well, it is, and it isn't. I tell people I married him for his money, well now he hasn't *got* any money, well not much. He borrowed it all and . . . and . . . and . . .' Venetia broke down again. Muriel hugged her again, puzzled as to what the problem really was. 'Now, now dear, pull yourself together. It's something else besides the business isn't it? You can tell me. A problem shared is a problem halved.'

Between her sobs Venetia said, 'I don't know what I'm doing sitting in a church. I've done something terrible and you'll think it's terrible too and that I don't belong here at all.'

'That's not so. Don't let Peter hear you say that. He would say no one is outside God's love.'

'Well, when I tell you what I've done you might think I am.' She hesitated for a moment and then said, 'I've just had an . . . well, I've just had an affair you see.'

Muriel sat speechless while she absorbed what she'd just heard then she said, 'Oh dear, oh dear, no wonder you're upset.'

'I've been the biggest fool, you've no idea.'

'No, I haven't.'

'He came to the Health Club and I fell for his charm, hook, line and sinker. He was so good looking and I did need cheering up. He gave me a wonderful time, treated me like a queen and then dropped me like a red hot brick. Men can be cruel. Now Jeremy's found out and well, we've had a terrible row.'

'I'm not surprised.'

'Anyway it's over with and I've said I'm sorry, but Jeremy's really cut up about it. I do like excitement in my life you see and with everything going wrong at the Club and Jeremy being so worried I got carried away. I've been such an idiot.' The tears began falling again and Muriel searched in her bag for another tissue. 'Here you are Venetia, another clean tissue. Wipe your eyes, my dear, and cheer up. Hopefully Jeremy will come round.'

'Oh he will, he's such a kind man really. I could kill that man for egging me on like he did. He's a slimeball.'

Muriel flinched at the word. Taking a deep breath she said, 'We all make mistakes at some time or another, so you must learn from your experience and resolve not to make the same mistake again.'

'Yes, you're right, but he was so lovely and so well off. I shall miss him.'

Muriel smiled wistfully at her. 'Time is a great healer you know.'

Venetia sniffed loudly. 'Still let's face it, he wouldn't really have wanted to take someone like me seriously would he? On top of all that upset and the Health Club failing I don't know what to do anymore. We don't know which way to turn.'

'Mr Mayer must be very upset too, with this . . . well with your problem and then the business failing. Oh dear, I am sorry, so sorry.'

It was Venetia's turn to comfort Muriel. 'Please don't upset yourself, I'm fairly tough you know, I'll get over it I expect. If I could just come up with a solution, you know, find a buyer or something. But what hope is there of that in these times? No one has money, no one at all.' Inspiration came to her and her eyes lit up. 'I don't suppose Sir Ralph would . . .'

'No, definitely not, he hasn't that kind of money.'

'Oh I see, just a thought.'

'Come with me to the house and we'll have a coffee and a good think.'

Venetia shook her head. 'I shouldn't really you know. Anyway, I look such a mess.'

'You can have a wash and brush up while I put the kettle on.'

'Righteo then.'

Ralph, who'd been in the bedroom changing into some old clothes in readiness for cleaning his car, emerged to find Venetia coming out of the bathroom. He couldn't hide the shock he felt. To find her in his house at all came as a surprise, more so as it was hard to recognise this drained looking version of the colourful Venetia.

'Oh, beg pardon Sir Ralph, I'm sure.'

'That's quite all right . . . Venetia isn't it?'

'Yes, Lady Templeton asked me in. We're just having a coffee. Are you going to join us?' She flicked her hand up to her hair and rearranged her head band. Something of the old Venetia was coming through despite her problems.

Ralph hastily declined. 'Thank you, no, I won't. I'm going to clean the car, so I'll leave you ladies to enjoy a good chat on your own.'

Muriel made three cups of coffee and took one out to Ralph as he hosed down the car.

He thanked her and then in a stage whisper said, 'Muriel, what the blazes have you asked that dreadful woman in for? You know I don't like her. She looks terrible this morning. What a sight to find on one's landing!'

'Yes, she does look terrible, but it's because she has a lot of problems and needs help.'

'Whatever you do, *don't offer money*!'

'Of course not. I'll explain later. When she's ready to go would you drive her back to the Big House?'

Reluctantly Ralph agreed, 'Very well, but you're far too soft hearted Muriel.'

When he returned from taking Venetia home Ralph asked Muriel for an explanation.

'So you see Ralph I couldn't leave her there could I?' Muriel concluded.

'No, in all honesty you couldn't, but there is no way that you and I could buy it back. It makes me very sad to see my old home receiving such cavalier treatment. I expect really it's ruined forever. Wars have repercussions one doesn't always bargain for don't they? If my father hadn't been killed in Malaya the Big House would have been as it always was. Ah well, much as I should like to live there it is quite impossible, my dear. Still, thank you for being kind to her. I don't like the woman but she obviously needed your help. Now, afternoon tea in Culworth I think. I have a mind to buy my wife, my one and only wife something special to celebrate her kind heart.'

'Ralph, you indulge me far too much.'

'Why not? I love you. It was the best day's work I ever did coming back here to live and finding you.'

'Thank you, dear. I think you can buy me that suit I saw in Fisk's. It's terribly expensive but I do love it and it's my size. Let's go now Ralph, buy the suit and then have lunch at the George. I have a feeling it might be sold if I don't hurry.'

Venetia had waved an exaggerated farewell to Ralph as he swung the Mercedes round and headed back to the village. Now *he* really was something despite his years, and so charming. She found Jeremy seated at his desk, head resting on his arms fast asleep. He'd obviously been working at some figures as his calculator was still switched on, his glasses carelessly flung aside and a pen lay between his fingers. His pudgy fingers, his thick wrists, his balding head, his fat ears, his solid shoulders, his suit with flakes of dandruff scattered on the collar, revolted her; whatever had made her fancy him in the first place? Was there any point in staying with him? The debts were all his, her name was on nothing at all. He'd lost all his capital. All he had was the home he'd used as collateral for some of the borrowings. Even that was rented out so they couldn't live in it. Get a job in a beauty salon, or a leisure centre? Only trouble with getting a job was it wouldn't keep her in the manner to which she had become accustomed since she'd teamed up with Jeremy. It would have to be the fire idea after all. But how dangerous. Found out, and she'd be in prison. In any case you couldn't do that to such a lovely old house.

He stirred, opened his eyes and stared vaguely round. He patted amongst the clutter on the desk, found his glasses and put them on. 'Oh, Venetia, you're still here. I dreamt you'd left me. It was a terrible shock. I wept, in my dream, I really wept. You wouldn't leave me would you? I love you, ducky. I know I don't show it, but I do.'

'I know you do.'

'Feeling better now old girl?'

'Better?' Venetia looked up questioningly. 'Oh, yes.'

'You don't look it, in fact, you look quite odd.'

'Thanks. I've been having coffee with Lady Temple . . .'

'Lady Templeton! She didn't offer . . .'

'No. Neither did he.'

'Oh well.' Jeremy hesitated and then said, 'I've let you down badly.'

Venetia looked shamefaced for a moment and then patted his hand. 'I've let you down badly too, and I'm sorry. I shall go see Jimbo. Maybe he might have some bright ideas, he's the only business man hereabouts.'

'It's my place to go.'

'No, I'll go. Jimbo is very susceptible to feminine charm.'

'So am I.'

'Yes, but you haven't the money, have you Jeremy dear?'

20

Peter drove to Little Derehams not expecting to hear a very accurate recollection of the story behind the Charity Fund. One couldn't expect an old lady in her nineties to be able to recall all the details. Nevertheless he'd no alternative. He wasn't sure where she lived as the Gotobeds didn't come to church and he'd never had the opportunity to meet them before. Along the Turnham Road he saw a girl playing with some children in the garden of a neglected cottage. He realised he knew her. Peter got out of his car and went to speak to her.

'Good morning Mrs Paradise, how are you?'

Simone stopped pushing the home made swing and lifted the baby from the seat.

'Don't be polite Peter, get round it by calling me Simone.'

'Right, Simone then. Young Valentine is looking better than when I saw him last.' Simone pushed back her long brown hair from her eyes and agreed. 'Valentine's coming on fine now, Peter, thanks. The operation's been a complete success. Say "Hello" to the rector, Valentine.' Simone held his plump brown arm and waved it up and down, then grinned engagingly at Peter. 'How are your two coming along?'

'They're both doing fine, thank you.'

'Good. Mrs Gotobed lives at Weavers Cottage, last one on the right before the T-junction.'

'How did you know that was what I was going to ask?'

'I'm a mind reader didn't you know?'

Simone laughed and popped Valentine back on the swing. Peter said goodbye and returned to his car. He shook his head in disbelief, one really couldn't catch a cold in this parish but they all knew before you did.

The door knocker at Weavers Cottage was a bright brass Cockington elf rubbed almost smooth with years of polishing. A sprightly woman in her seventies opened the door. She was like an elf herself, so tiny was she, with bright, shining brown eyes and a mass of snow white hair.

'Oh good afternoon, Rector, how nice to see you, do come in.'

Peter shook hands, 'Good afternoon to you Miss Gotobed.'

'I'm Primrose and this is my sister Lavender just coming from the kitchen.'

Though older by some years, Miss Lavender Gotobed was very like her sister, a round chubby woman with round chubby cheeks, sparkling brown eyes and a mass of curly, undisciplined, snow white hair.

'Mother's having a cup of tea, she will be pleased to see you. Would you like a cup too?'

'Yes, please, I would. I'm sorry for calling unexpectedly.'

'That's quite all right, we're always ready for visitors.'

The tiny cottage sitting room was furnished as it must have been some eighty years ago. Clean to within an inch of its life the room was welcoming with, despite the warmth of the day, a fire blazing in the hearth.

Mrs Gotobed, with her apple cheeked face, looked the epitome of a lovely ancient country woman. Her fine white hair now grew so sparsely her pink scalp could be seen through the well washed strands. She struggled to rise from her chair to greet him.

'Please, please, stay where you are Mrs Gotobed. Don't get up on my account.'

She ignored him and stood to shake hands. 'In my day the rector was given great respect in this parish and you still are as far as I'm concerned, sir. I don't hold with all this Christian name business for the rector, it's not right. Now sit down. I hear you haven't been well.'

'I have had a bad dose of something or another, but I'm much better now thank you.'

'Lavender, where's the rector's cup?' Mrs Gotobed's thin piping voice penetrated every corner of the tiny sitting room. 'That girl is just as slow as she's always been. I don't suppose I can expect any improvement now, it's much too late. Now, sir, have you a special reason for coming to see me.'

He knew by the intonation of her voice that she was aware of his mission. He explained the curious coincidence of both the book and the bank statement turning up on the same day and how Sir Ralph had suggested she would be able to tell him the whole story. Mrs Gotobed interrupted him, 'And as soon as you found them you had your accident and then you've been very poorly. No wonder they're all getting in such a state.'

'Can you explain what it's all about?'

'Well, I will, because I'm old and if I popped my clogs tomorrow it would be a blessing for all concerned. So I'm not afraid you see. Now drink that tea and have a piece of Primrose's parkin, it's about the only decent thing she bakes, while I tell you what happened.'

'It all started with those Glover boys. They didn't want to know about hard work. A bit of labouring here and there, poaching, helping put up the roundabouts when the fair came, helping at harvest time, working in Culworth at Christmas, anything and everything so long as it wasn't sensible work needing application six days a week. Well, of course, the war was on, that's the first one you know, and not one of 'em was in the army. Caused a lot of ill feeling that did, but they didn't care. Somehow they'd managed to avoid it even though they were all fit as lops.

'They were that handsome, those boys. I quite fancied Cecil myself except Jonathan Gotobed had decided I was marrying him. Sixteen, that's all I was, but he was determined. I used to laugh, I was much too young to be settling down and those Glover boys did have a lot of dash especially Cecil.'

She paused for a moment and smiled secretly to herself. Then recollecting her story she went on, 'Then late in 1916 they got their call up papers. They were always short of money and when the time came for parishioners to apply to the rector for some help for Christmas from the fund, they applied. Said they needed it to set themselves up with stuff for when they went off to war. Well, of course, it wasn't for young men who could fend for themselves and the rector told them so. But one night after they'd been in The Royal Oak and drunk far more than was good for them, they called at the Rectory, all four of them, and threatened the rector and made him give them the money. The verger was there too. Now what it was the Glover boys knew I can only guess at, like all the rest of the village did. But they must have had some sort of hold over the two of them, because they didn't harm the rector nor the verger, but before you could say knife the four of them emerged from the rectory each with a pound in their hand.

'It might seem a small thing in itself, but it was as though the results of their badness were never ending, like the ripples on a pond when you throw a stone in.

'The verger was a widower and his only child died of diphtheria on Christmas Day that year. He saw her buried decent and then gassed himself in his kitchen, where Willie Biggs lives now. Then, would you believe it, on New Year's Eve the rector, what was his name? my memory isn't what it was, was coming home from Penny Fawcett. In those days of course he rode in a carriage, little it was, just big enough for a lone bachelor. Just by Havers Lake Woods his horse took fright at some gun shots and it bolted. He was thrown out and killed. No one put two and two together then, it all just seemed like dreadful coincidences and after all we had so much else to worry about, what with the war and the food shortages and young men dying right left and centre. There seemed no end to the horror.' Mrs Gotobed stopped for a moment lost in thought.

Peter sat patiently waiting, wondering if she'd fallen asleep.

'Where was I, oh yes, so the worst was yet to come. All four of the Glover boys were at the front by the following summer. Within the space of three weeks their parents received telegrams, one by one, informing them that they had all been killed. Went down like ninepins they did. Terrible. Terrible. Turnham Malpas almost died too. It was a dreadful blow. None of us could hardly lift our heads to the light of day for months. Then as people talked about it, all the tragedies seemed to come together and everyone became convinced that the deaths were caused by the Glover boys getting money from the rector by force. Since that Christmas of 1916 not a single person hereabouts has dared to ask for a penny from the Fund, for fear of what might happen. Blighted it is, blighted. Christmas 1917 the new rector tried to distribute some money but no one applied and it's been like that ever since.'

'If all the Glover boys died who was Jimmy Glover's father?'

'Ah well, there were the four boys who died, they were the eldest, and then came three girls and then Jimmy's dad. He was only eight when it all happened. How they all squeezed into that little cottage of Jimmy's I'll never know.'

'Thank you for telling me all that. I don't know how you remembered so clearly. I won't stay any longer, I don't want to tire you.'

'You won't try to use the money for the church will you? The village won't tolerate it, you know. Heaven alone knows what might happen if you do. You're a grand young man with a lot of good work still to do, and we don't want anything to happen to you. It nearly did you know, you've come very close to it killing you.'

Somewhat shaken by Mrs Gotobed's warning Peter laid his hand on her head and gave her his blessing. As he finished making the sign of the cross on her forehead, she smiled up at him and took hold of his hand. 'And when my time comes, you make sure my funeral service is a happy one, don't want everyone sat there looking glum, they've to sing Hallelujah! After all, I've gone to my reward.'

'I'll remember, I promise.' Peter turned at the door and said, 'So why did the Gotobeds come to live in Little Derehams?'

'Because my Jonathan was too frightened to live in Turnham Malpas any more, so we moved here when we married, and I've never been in Turnham Malpas since that day. What's more I shan't, so you'll have to hold my service in Culworth, and I want you to do the service, not that young whippersnapper of a curate they've got there now, all microphones and guitars. And I'm to be buried there too, alongside my Jonathan. Right!'

'Right!'

When Peter got home for lunch he told Caroline the full story.

'In that case then Peter, leave well alone.'

'You're as bad as Mrs Gotobed, threatening dire consequences if I so much as mention the Fund.'

'Have you seen the local paper today?'

'No, I haven't had the time.'

Caroline put the Culworth Gazette on the kitchen table. She pointed out a news item with the headline '*LOCAL BANK MANAGER DIES*'. Peter went very quiet. '*The new manager of the Culworth Branch of the County and Provincial Bank collapsed and died of a heart attack in his office, early yesterday . . .*' he read.

'The poor chap, such a nice man too. This is pure coincidence though and you know it. It's quite preposterous to imagine there is any connection. How you, level headed and thoroughly sensible, can imagine that there is anything . . .'

'Peter! Take note. Please take note. I *know* it's silly but . . . well, anyway, I don't often insist about matters which are rightly your own concern, but just this once do as I say, please, and be thankful you've been spared. I know I am.' She reached across the table to kiss him.

21

Muriel was still worrying about Venetia. Ralph felt that hers and Jeremy's affairs were quite outside their concern.

'I fail to see why you should worry about her.'

'I know Ralph, but I can't help feeling that beneath all that dazzle she is sad and it hurts me that she has no one to sympathise with her.'

'She's got Jeremy.'

'In the circumstances he won't feel like comforting her will he? Should I tell Peter? Oh no, I can't because she doesn't want him to know. So you see, she has some scruples.'

'Not enough by the sound of it!'

'Ralph!' Muriel picked up her purse and a Liberty shopping bag Ralph had bought her when he last went to London. 'I'm going to the Store, is there anything you want?'

'Order me some cigars will you, my dear? Jimbo knows the kind I smoke.'

'Very well. I shan't be long. Are you going into Culworth today as you said?'

'Yes, come with me Muriel, I hate going alone.'

'Very well, on the understanding that we have lunch at the George to celebrate.'

'Celebrate?'

'Yes, this week it's one whole year since you came back to Turnham Malpas.'

'A year? It doesn't feel like that it feels more like tw . . .'

'Twenty. I know. I know. You're a tease Ralph Templeton.'

Muriel laughed as she escaped Ralph's embrace and headed for the Store. Only one whole year yet her life had been transformed. She couldn't believe that there was a time when she didn't know how to love. Her heart leapt with joy as she heard the birds singing, and saw the flowers blowing in the breeze, and to cap it all, she was going out to lunch with her best beloved.

Jimbo's adored brass bell jingled fussily as she entered the Store. Unusually at that time in the morning Muriel found the Store quite empty. Linda always had her coffee break about now. Fifteen minutes and no matter how busy it was, she always, much to Jimbo's annoyance, took her full time. Muriel collected a basket and began to consult her list. She decided that if they were going into Culworth she wouldn't have much time for cooking so she went to the freezer and chose gourmet fish pie and two of Harriet's delicious individual sherry trifles. When she'd collected milk and bread too she went to stand by the till. She waited a few moments and when no one came to take her money, went into the back to find Jimbo or Harriet or even Linda, if she could be prised away from her coffee break.

Muriel went hot all over with embarrassment when she looked in the storeroom. Standing close, very close together were Jimbo and Venetia. His boater abandoned on a nearby shelf, he was holding her tightly and hugging her, and she was hugging him, her arms around his neck, her cheek laid against his. Neither of them noticed her horror-struck presence. She hurriedly retreated back to the Store. Confused and upset, Muriel left her wire basket near the till and fled for the security of Ralph, bumping into Bet from Penny Fawcett in the doorway of the Store who was just coming in. 'Oh oh-h-h-h,' Muriel said unable to find anything else to say. 'Good morning Lady Temple . . .' Muriel didn't hear the rest, she was rushing on flying feet for home. Her own door was open to catch the sun and she burst into the hall shouting, 'Ralph, Ralph, where are you?'

'In the study, my dear,' Ralph called out. She stood just inside the door of his study and began weeping. Ralph rose to his feet. 'Why, whatever's the matter?'

'Oh Ralph, I don't know what to do.' She got out her handkerchief and wept into that.

'Muriel, my dear, have you been attacked or something? What's happened, please tell me?'

'It's Jimbo . . . and . . . and Venetia.'

'Yes?'

'They're embracing in the storeroom.'

'Embracing? You must be mistaken.'

'No, I'm not Ralph, I know what embracing is.'

'Of course you do, my dear, I'm not doubting your word. I'm just amazed. There must be some very good reason for it, though one doesn't spring to mind very easily.'

'I couldn't pay for my shopping, so it's still there on the counter. I can't go back it's so embarrassing.'

'I'll go. Make yourself a cup of tea while I see what's happening.'

'You don't normally go shopping Ralph, I always go.'

'Well, we'll break with tradition shall we? Shan't be long.'

'No, I'll come too.'

When Ralph and Muriel entered the Store, Jimbo was standing by the till, puzzling over Muriel's abandoned basket. He raised his boater in greeting.

'Good morning Muriel, good morning Ralph. What can I do for you this fine day?'

'This is Muriel's basket she left it because there was no one here to take her money, so I've come back with her in case there was anything wrong.'

'Wrong? No, just busy in the back, and Linda's got half a day for a rather nasty dental appointment. Sorry about that Muriel, I'll check your shopping for you then.'

As he was putting Muriel's things into one of his smart green carrier bags the bell jangled madly and in stormed Harriet.

'Back from the antenatal clinic and feeling on top of the world and who's just stopped to speak as I got out of the car? Bet Whatsername from Penny Fawcett.' Harriet imitated Bet's high pitched voice. ' "Oh," she says with a malicious glint in her eye, "I think you ought to know, Mrs Charter-Plackett, I've been to have a word with your husband about the bread rolls for the Village Centre Fair, and found him and that floosie from the Health Club hugging and kissing in the back. So embarrassing it was, really." I was so astounded by this juicy piece of information I actually thanked her for it, though I can't think why. Well, what the hell's going on?' She glared furiously at Jimbo who looked flustered but innocent.

'Now look Harriet, she's completely exaggerating the situation. Venetia was very upset and I took her in the back to give her a chance to calm down. You know perfectly well I wouldn't dream of hugging and kissing her.'

'Do I? You're a sight too friendly with some of our women customers Jimbo, I've spoken to you about it before.'

'My dear Harriet, it's all good for trade. You're well aware that's why I do it; a smile here, a chuckle there, here a nudge, there a wink. Muriel knows I wouldn't put myself in a compromising situation, don't you Muriel?'

There had been many times in her life when Muriel had wished the ground would open up and swallow her and never more so than now. 'Well, it's like this you see I . . .'

Jimbo jumped in with the assumption that Muriel was about to agree with him. 'There you are, Harriet, I couldn't have a better testimonial than one from Lady Templeton could I?'

Muriel held onto Ralph's arm as she replied, 'I didn't say what you think I said.'

'What did you say?' said Harriet hopping with temper, and clutching at any straw that might justify her suspicions.

Ralph spoke on Muriel's behalf. 'This is all very difficult but the truth of the matter is . . .'

The door opened and in came Jeremy. 'Good afternoon all.' He looked round the assembled company and nodded to them in turn. They all stood in stunned silence. 'I've come to see you Jimbo. Venetia's just found me in the pub and told me all about it, so I've come straight round.'

Muriel went deathly white and grabbed Ralph's arm. 'I'll take Muriel outside for some air, she's feeling faint,' he decided.

The two of them went to sit on the bench thoughtfully provided by Jimbo.

'Whatever am I going to do?'

'Nothing, my dear, nothing at all. Leave them to sort it out. Jimbo's quite capable of taking care of himself.'

'Oh Ralph, I forgot to order your cigars, and I still haven't got my shopping.'

'Never mind. We'll get it all in Culworth. We're best out of the Store for a while.'

'I would hate anything to go wrong between Jimbo and Harriet, especially now when she's expecting their baby. Oh dear, life is so complicated sometimes isn't it?'

'None of this is your fault is it, so don't fret about it.'

'You see, Peter and Caroline have a much stronger marriage than Jimbo. They could withstand, and have withstood, serious trouble and still come through, but I'm not as sure about these two. I do hope Harriet doesn't get too upset.'

'Don't worry. They'll sort it out.' Ralph patted her hand and then said, 'You look a better colour now, so do you feel able to walk gently home?'

'Oh yes, I shall be glad to get out of Turnham Malpas today. I'll take Pericles . . .'

'No, I'll take him for a walk. When I get back with him we'll set off. Put your new suit on Muriel. I like you in that.'

'But we're only going out to lunch.'

'Yes, but we're celebrating aren't we? Had you forgotten?'

Harriet lay in bed that night with tears rolling down her face. Jimbo was sitting beside her drinking a medicinal whisky. 'It's all right you laughing now Harriet, at the time you were livid.'

'Livid? I could have throttled you. I don't know when I've been more angry. It'll be all over the village and then some. You'll never live it down.'

'Poor Ralph, he just didn't know how to cope.' Jimbo held his side to alleviate the pain he had there with laughing so much.

'I really thought Muriel was going to faint. She went deathly white when Jeremy walked in. You do realise that Muriel had seen you, don't you?'

'Oh God, no. Really? Are you sure?'

'Pretty sure.'

'So that was why she abandoned her shopping, of course.' Jimbo began laughing again. 'And then when he said, "Told me all about it and I've come straight round." Oh God, I thought she'll be killing me with one of my butcher's knives.'

'Or he would. I certainly nearly *did*.' Harriet started laughing again. 'Tomorrow I shall go round to see Muriel and apologise. I wonder what they had for dinner tonight? It certainly wasn't individual sherry trifle preceded by gourmet fish pie!' They looked at each other and Jimbo laughed uproariously.

'Harriet, darling, I do love you.' He bent over and gave her a kiss.

'Good, because you came very close to the garden shears this morning Jimbo. I won't tolerate unfaithfulness you know. That's one of the rules I live by and one of the rules we agreed upon when we married. I know lots of our friends in Wimbledon thought nothing of spreading it around but that isn't for you and me.'

'I know that. I enjoy women's company, Harriet, I can't deny that, but it is only harmless flirting and absolutely nothing more. I can swear that on the Bible, please believe me.'

'Well, I've calmed down now, and of course I do know that darling.' Harriet began to giggle. 'Venetia must have thought it was her birthday!'

'She was *so* grateful! She clung on really hard. She's done that once too often though, if what she told me is true.'

Harriet sat up. 'What did she tell you?'

'She told me in confidence, and I can't reveal a confidence can I?' Harriet began tickling him. 'Tell me, tell me.'

'Stop it Harriet I can't bear it, stop it and then I'll tell you. I don't suppose she'll mind me telling you. She told me,' Jimbo glanced round the bedroom as though making sure no one was listening, 'she told me she'd had a tempestuous affair with a chap called Nigel who came to the health club on a freebie. He's an acquaintance of Jeremy's.'

'No o o o o. I met him one Saturday when I went up there with the children.'

'Added to which . . .'

'Go on then.'

'She isn't married to Jeremy at all. He picked her up in some kind of massage parlour in Soho. He's borrowed thousands, she's not sure how much. In addition they have a sleeping partner and so he's going down with them too.'

'A massage parlour? Whatever next! Hell, what a mess. So why was she weeping in *your* arms?'

'She came to me for advice seeing, as she said, I was the only one around with a business head on my shoulders.'

'Was it your head she was interested in?' At this Harriet started laughing again, till Jimbo said, 'You must calm down Harriet, just remember you're pregnant, you've had enough excitement for one day. You're not as young as you were and we don't want anything going wrong because you've got overwrought.'

Harriet picked up a paperback from her bedside table and beat Jimbo over the head with it. 'And how old does that make you then?'

After he and Harriet had settled down with their arms around each other, they talked about Jimbo's plans for the Big House. 'This business of a staff training house somewhere away from the bustle of the City is quite the thing with lots of the big companies now. The Big House has the extra filip of having the sports and leisure facilities already there. I could try Drew Turnbull, he's chief on the personnel side at my old firm, he might be able to put me in touch with someone, or, I know! There's always Declan O'Rourke, property manager of Reilly, Buckton and Shears. Now he might be a very good lead. He's a terrible gossip and knows everyone and everything. I'll try him first.'

'When you think about it, establishments for staff training purposes won't need a full catering staff all year long will they? Times like August and Christmas and weekends there won't be any staff there to train, so the domestic people will be twiddling their thumbs. Being on the spot so to speak you could put staff in as and when.'

'Of course, of course. Having put A in contact with B and got a sale I shall then be able to tender from a strong position. At least they will know that with my City background they're not dealing with a complete country bumpkin.'

'I always knew I'd married a brilliant brain.'

'Thank you and good night.'

'I wonder if they could find a job for Venetia?'

'Now that really is magnanimous of you.'

22

Sylvia was taking advantage of the twins having gone visiting with their mother, and the rector being out at a meeting in Culworth, to get some housework done without interruptions. She began by cleaning the bathroom Peter and Caroline used. She'd tidied up Caroline's bottles and jars, changed the towels for fresh pale green ones and given the taps an extra polish. Standing back to admire the sparkling bathroom Sylvia noticed the curtains needed a wash, so she took them down and opened a window to let in some air. It was late September but still quite mild. The Rectory garden, since Willie had worked on it, was looking splendid. Beyond it she saw a car wandering down Pipe and Nook Lane, and watched it till it disappeared behind Sir Ralph's hedge. Her little car was still going strong. Pity Willie had never learned to drive. She really preferred to see the man driving the car. That was just what Willie was. A MAN. A tender loving man. That fool she'd married in the first flush of her youth hadn't as much tenderness in the whole of him as Willie had in his little finger.

She picked up the used towels and put them in the linen basket on the landing. It seemed an age since breakfast so she went downstairs for a drink. The kitchen felt warm and welcoming and when she'd made a coffee she decided to sit down and read the newspaper. With her elbows resting on the table she sipped from her mug. It had some unknown tropical flower decorating it and Sylvia smoothed her fingers over the pinkness of the petals and thought about Willie and his garden. There couldn't be much wrong with a man who had green fingers. Sylvia added up Willie's qualities. Since she'd gone to live with him she'd found he was kind, considerate, tender, sensitive, thoughtful, a good laugh, and, surprisingly, she'd found him passionate. He did have a sense of humour, you needed that in a relationship. A loud hammering at the door made her jump and she spilled her coffee. That'll be Willie.

She heard his footsteps coming down the hall and him shouting, 'It's me, Sylvia, where are you?'

'In the kitchen wiping coffee off my blouse.'

'What made you spill your coffee?'

'You, banging on the door like that. Is there a fire?'

'Fire? No.'

'You should really have waited for me to answer the door you know.'

'Well, I knew they were both out, so I thought I'd come and cadge a coffee with my Sylvia.'

'Nevertheless, I work here, Willie, it's not my house, and you should wait. It's only right.'

'Give us a kiss and then I'll remember next time.' He grabbed her round the waist and pulled her to him. 'By Jove, Sylvia, but you're grand. You always taste so sweet.'

'Willie.' Sylvia struggled to get free. 'At your time of life! Kissing in the middle of the morning. Really. Anyone would think you were in your teens.'

'I am. Where's that drink, I'm a working man and I need it.'

Willie sat at the other side of the table from Sylvia, stirring his coffee. He glanced at her from under his eyebrows and relished what he saw. Sylvia became conscious of his penetrating eyes and looked up. For a moment, with not a word said, they spoke directly to each other from their souls. Time stayed its hand. Then Sylvia heard the kitchen clock begin ticking again and her heart righted itself. Willie's spoon rattled against the side of the mug because the hand that held it was trembling.

Their silence was broken by the sound of Caroline's voice. 'Sylvia! Can you take Alex for me please?' Sylvia jumped up guiltily. 'Willie, you shouldn't be here.' Caroline was holding Alex and keeping the front door open with her foot to stop the wind banging it shut on her. 'You take him and I'll get Beth. Thanks.'

Sylvia propped open the door with the wedge and stood watching Caroline getting Beth out of her car seat. She'd have to apologise. She felt her face. It was still hot from the aftermath of that stare of Willie's.

'I hope you don't mind Dr Harris but Willie came in for a coffee. We thought you wouldn't be back just yet.'

Caroline looked at Sylvia's flushed face, with a twinkle in her eye she said, 'I hope I haven't interrupted something?'

'Oh no, no, not at all.' They took the twins into the kitchen. Willie stood as she entered. 'Good morning Dr Harris.'

'Good morning Willie. My friend had left a note pinned to the door.

"Sorry gone to casualty, Piers has fallen and I think he's broken his arm." So I've come straight back home. I think these two could manage a drink, Sylvia, please and I'd like the coffee I missed. No, no, Willie, you stay and finish yours.'

Willie sat down again embarrassed by the tumultuous feelings he'd experienced when he'd looked into Sylvia's eyes and by the fact he'd been caught out doing his courting in the Rectory kitchen.

With Alex and Beth seated in their high chairs each with their feeding beakers and a biscuit, Caroline took time to speak to Willie. But he hadn't much to say and as quickly as he could he finished his drink and left.

Caroline, bending down to the floor to pick up Alex's biscuit which he'd knocked off the tray said, 'You know, Sylvia, your face was the colour of a beetroot when I came in and the atmosphere in here was electric. You're going to have to capitulate and marry that man.'

'I can't make up my mind.'

'It seems to me the chemistry is right, oh so right. What's holding you back?'

'I don't know.'

'Neither do I. Don't break his heart, Sylvia. He's a good, kind man and he feels it quite badly you not being properly married, you know. Sometimes I see him look at you very wistfully. He doesn't just want his socks washing with no commitment on his part. Have courage.'

'I know. I can't believe he's fallen in love like a young man would do. I'm so afraid he'll wake up one day and find he's been fooling himself.'

'Have *you* fallen in love? That's the other half of the equation you know. Only time will tell. Now I must press on.' But the door bell rang and it was Muriel on the step.

'Good morning Caroline, I've come about the fund raising for the refurbishing of the small hall.'

'Come right in Muriel. Isn't it a lovely day?'

'It certainly is.'

Caroline showed Muriel to a chair in the sitting room and settled herself in another close by. 'I've been meaning to tell you Muriel, I've been to visit Beryl Baxter.'

'No! You make me feel very guilty. I never gave her another thought. How is she and where is she?'

'She's in a secure mental hospital in Brackley. Rather a grim place but they've done their best to make it bright and homely. At first apparently, Beryl simply sat motionless and they had to do everything for her. Feed her, wash her, dress her, put her to bed. Then one day she disappeared from the ward and they couldn't find her. She'd wandered into the occupational therapy area and joined a class of people learning to paint watercolours. They gave her a brush but she sat staring at the paper and didn't paint. This went on for days, going in there, holding the brush staring at the paper. Sometimes she sat there for two hours without moving and then wandered off back to her bed again.'

'Oh the poor thing.'

'Then miracle of miracles one day she dipped the brush in some paint and painted like a small child would, just hectic brush strokes all over the paper. But the significant thing was that she smiled at it. It was the first emotion she'd shown.'

'How wonderful.'

'Now she goes in there every day and paints. There's no therapy at the weekends but it's doing her so much good and as it's the only way she can express herself, they allow her to sit in there unsupervised at the weekends. Gradually her painting is improving and one can see what she's trying to paint now, and they have great hopes that she is going to cure herself through it. Normally she doesn't speak to anyone at all, but when she paints she talks to herself, so there is a ray of hope there. Isn't that wonderful?'

'Oh, it is Caroline. I don't think I'd be brave enough to go see her myself but, when you go again, would you let me know and I'll send her a present.'

'Of course. I won't be going till next month but I'll let you know when I am.'

'Harriet came round to see me you know.' Caroline looked questioningly at Muriel because the tone of her voice seemed strange. 'Yes, she came to apologise. It was all a misunderstanding.'

'Was it?' Caroline was nonplussed.

'Oh, don't you know? I thought you would have heard. Yes, you see Venetia was very upset because the Health Club has failed and Jimbo was comforting her.'

'Oh I see. How do you know all this?'

'Because I found them in the storeroom. I was so embarrassed I left my shopping and fled home to Ralph.'

'Oh, Muriel.' Caroline collapsed with laughter. 'What a fix to be in! What's happening about the Health Club?'

'I don't know. Jimbo's trying to rescue it but I don't know how. Venetia's not too bad when you get to know her. In fact I have developed quite a soft spot for her. She confided in me one day you see.'

'You have been a busy person Muriel.'

'I have, very busy in fact. You'll never guess what I've done this morning.'

'No, tell me.'

'Well, I met Michael Palmer in the Store and he asked me if I would play the piano for him at the school for a while as I used to do before I married. Doesn't that sound wonderful? "Before I married." I am glad I did what you said. Where was I? Oh yes. So we got talking, he's such a lovely man and so alone. However, I asked him if he ever heard from Suzy Meadows.' The moment the name was out of her mouth Muriel regretted it. 'Oh Caroline, I'm so sorry, I'd completely forgotten, how thoughtless of me. I'll leave and come back another time. I'm so sorry.'

Caroline, knowing Muriel could never be guilty of duplicity, nor intentionally take any action which would cause distress, smiled painfully. She and Peter had an unspoken rule about not mentioning Suzy's name. To hear her name spoken in her own sitting room was shocking to her and Caroline had to struggle to keep control of her feelings. She covered the stress by taking time to remove an imaginary piece of thread from the hem of her skirt. Having done that she looked up and said, 'That's all right, Muriel. I can talk about her and wish her well. After all, in one sense I owe her so much. But I never mention her name in front of the children, it's ridiculous but it feels almost indecent. I know when they are older we shall have to speak the truth, because Peter has promised he will, but for now her name is never mentioned in front of them.'

'I see, well, I must apologise for causing you such distress. I just didn't think. I won't say any more.'

'Please do. They're with Sylvia and not within earshot. I don't wish her harm you know, I do want her to be happy.'

Her lovely piece of news had been spoiled for her but Muriel decided she would look silly if she didn't carry on telling it. 'Well, apparently he is in touch with her mother, you know the twins' grandmother, all because her mother wrote to him wanting to have news of her twins, because after all they are her grandchildren aren't they? So she would wouldn't she?'

'Yes, she would.'

Muriel cleared her throat. This was so difficult, why ever had she launched herself on this story. 'So I told Michael Palmer that they'd always got on well and that if he liked the idea why didn't he go ahead and begin courting her. He went red and said she had started writing to him occasionally, you know, putting little messages on the bottom of her mother's letters, so I said, take life by the scruff, Michael. We only have one life to lead why not plunge in and grasp the nettle. Oh dear, I seem to have got things mixed up but you know what I mean?'

'Yes, I do and thank you for telling me. What did he say?'

'Well, he said that was just what he was going to do and winked. So, yes, I am going to play the piano for him until he gets a new permanent teacher who can play, which will be straight after Christmas, and it does look as if he is going to do something positive about . . . Suzy. Which will be lovely won't it?'

'Yes, it will.'

'Only what I've told you is in complete confidence, except of course you wouldn't want to talk to anyone about Suzy would you seeing how things are? Oh dear, I am sorry, that came out all wrong too. I'm so confused.'

'No, I won't divulge it to a soul. Thank you for telling me. Now about the fund raising. I have been giving it a lot of thought and I wondered what you . . .'

'I really think I'm too exhausted to think about it now, and you're very busy, can I come back another time please?'

'Of course. It truly is all right Muriel, honestly.'

'Yes, well, I still think I will go. Ralph will be wondering where I am. I'll come back another day. Don't worry I'll see myself out.' Muriel let herself out thankful to have escaped. What a stupid silly thing to have done. So thoughtless. She shut the front door, stepped off the stone step into the road and bumped into Sir Ronald and Lady Bissett.

'Oh I'm so sorry, I didn't see you there.'

'Are you all right Lady Templeton?' Sir Ronald took her elbow and steadied her.

'Why, yes, of course. My goodness Sir Ronald you look to me as if you've lost weight.'

Lady Bissett answered on his behalf, 'He has, a whole stone and a quarter *and* our best bit of news is we're off to the States, aren't we Ron . . . ald. We've been married forty years this year so it's a kind of second honeymoon.'

Muriel blushed. 'Oh, how lovely. It certainly suits you being slimmer, Sir Ronald. How long will you be gone?'

'Four weeks, coast to coast we're going.'

'How lovely. I've never been to the United States. Would it be helpful if I have Pom for you?'

Sheila looked grateful. 'Oh it would! I was dreading him going into kennels, he's not used to it you see, and I didn't like to ask.'

'Of course I'll have him. Pericles will be delighted.'

Sheila patted Muriel's arm. 'I've been thinking, how would it be if you called us Ron and Sheila? We're not really titled in the proper sense of the word and it would be much more friendly wouldn't it?'

'Well, yes, it would, in that case you call me Muriel.'

'Very well we will. Bye bye Muriel. Be seeing you.'

'Bye bye Sheila, and bye bye . . . Ron.' At home Muriel sank gratefully into her favourite armchair and consoled herself with a cup of tea and a biscuit. She'd had just about all she could take this morning. There were times when she wished she was a hermit.

23

'Good afternon, Turnham House Health Club. Venetia speaking. How may I help you?' Venetia gripped the receiver between her jaw and her shoulder while she hitched herself onto Jeremy's desk.

'Hi Venetia. Jimbo Charter-Plackett here. How are you this fine bright day?'

'Bloody awful.'

'You don't sound too perky.'

'I'm not and neither is Jeremy. We are completely at the end of our tether.'

'Hold on Venetia, surely things can't be as bad as that?'

'You know full well they are. I wish I was in Timbuktoo, anywhere but here.'

'I jolly well hope you won't be in Timbuktoo on Monday.'

'On Monday? Why?'

'Because I have been incurring a huge phone bill beavering away on your behalf.'

'Yes?'

'A-n-n-d on Monday of this week, at precisely eleven thirty a certain company chairman in the City will be coming to give the Big House the once over.'

'The once over?'

'Venetia, you're not very bright eyed and bushy tailed this morning.'

'Run it past me again and then it might sink in.'

'A person by the name of Craddock Fitch is coming to look over Turnham House with a view to purchasing it for his company. He'll be arriving at eleven thirty on Monday morning.' His announcement was met with total silence. 'Hello. Hello. Venetia, are you there? Hello. Hello.' It sounded as though the receiver had crashed to the floor. After a moment Jimbo could hear a voice quite unlike Venetia's screaming, 'Sid,

Sid.' He heard footsteps and then faintly, 'Sid, get up and come down.' The footsteps returned.

'Are you still there Jimbo? Oh God, I can't believe it. A buyer at last. Thank you, thank you, thank you. I don't know what else to say.'

'Now see here, I only said he was coming to *look*. There are no promises at all. A sale depends on the impression he gets. Can I be brutally frank?'

'Of course.'

'He is a very important person, Venetia, really important. He's coming because he is *seriously* interested. I happened to speak to him on the right day at the right moment, and he happens to be in the area at a weekend house party and is calling on his way back to London. You must, absolutely *must* give a good impression. On no account wear your screamingly dazzling track suit or bikini. Get out your darkest suit, your whitest blouse, tone down the old makeup, hide the gold jewellery in the drawer and wear only one small well chosen piece. In other words behave like a nun. Right? Get Jeremy togged to the nines in a dark suit, white shirt, restrained tie, well polished shoes. Have everywhere totally spick and span. Clear Jeremy's desk and in particular make sure there are no Snickers bars evident. Lots of flowers about, cushions plumped et cetera, create a kind of country house atmosphere. Get the picture?'

'Oh yes, oh yes. I'll start clearing up now. Right away. I can't thank you enough. Jeremy's right beside me and he's dancing up and down.'

Privately, Jimbo thought that wouldn't be a pretty sight. 'Don't build your hopes too high, just play it cool. Most important don't pretend you've someone else interested. He'll see through that immediately. He's not an idiot.'

'Will you be coming up?'

'No, I'm quite certain you can manage the whole thing without me holding your hand. Got the date and time?'

'It's engraved on my heart. Thank you Jimbo.'

'Anytime. The ball's in your court, let's hope you win the match. Bye.'

Jimbo banged down the receiver. 'Well, Harriet, I've done all I can. The rest is up to them.'

Jimbo was having a quick lunch with Sadie in her mail order office on the Monday when the phone rang. Sadie answered it. Jimbo heard her saying, 'I'm sorry I can't tell what you're saying. Yes. Yes. Oh Jimbo. Oh yes, he's here. Hold the line.' Sadie put her hand over the mouth piece and said, 'Some incoherent idiot wants darling, darling, Jimbo.'

'Jimbo is that you?'

'As ever.'

'Jimbo, it's Venetia, he's just gone and he's very, very keen. We did exactly as you said, and he is very enthusiastic. He'll let us know by the end of the week. Jeremy and I can't thank you enough. We're just having a toast to good fortune. We're so thrilled.'

'Hold on a minute, nothing and I mean nothing, as Jeremy well knows, is definite until you've got his signature on a piece of paper. Don't believe your troubles are over until then. Please. Do you understand?'

'Yes, of course, Jimbo, I'm not a fool. Oh, he really was dishy. Have you met him?'

'Only at business receptions, haven't spoken to him much.'

'He's one of those older men who still has that indefinable something. He's so handsome in an aristocratic kind of a way. I quite took to him.' Jimbo groaned. 'I did most of the talking.' Jimbo groaned again. 'Jeremy's so devastated by what's happened he can hardly speak. So I took charge.'

Jimbo interrupted her, 'Put Jeremy on the phone please.' He waited a few minutes while Venetia found him. He heard Jeremy's heavy footfalls nearing the telephone.

'Good morning Jimbo, things do seem to be working out don't they? Just opening the champagne.'

'Look here, I know in this day and age women no longer take a back seat and quite rightly so, but, men like Craddock Fitch still don't subscribe to that view. Please in future *you* must take the lead. You're the business man not Venetia. I know you've had a body blow, but please stand up and be counted. I know these kind of people and I know I'm right.'

'Righteo, yes, righteo. I'll do that. Thanks again.'

'Anyway, glad things are looking more hopeful. Keep me informed. Bye.'

Knowing Peter was out and that Caroline had gone to the dentist's, Willie called at the Rectory. He hammered on the door like he always did but dutifully waited for Sylvia to open it.'

'Come in, I expect you're wanting your coffee?'

'Yes, please.' He followed her into the kitchen. He hadn't been in many kitchens so he hadn't much experience to judge by, but this Rectory kitchen always took his fancy. It glowed with comfort, yes, that was it, glowed. This morning the twins were playing on a big rug spread out on the kitchen floor. Their brightly coloured toys added to the welcoming feel of the kitchen. There were some gold chrysanthemums in a creamy vase on the window sill and the sun, the warm, autumn sun was shining in, casting a lovely colour on his Sylvia as she stood at the table stirring his coffee. Wholesome she was, downright wholesome. He bent down to give

Alex back a ball which had rolled out of his reach. The sun picked up the reddish glints of the baby's hair. It was Peter's smile that he gave Willie when he got the ball. For a moment Willie felt sad that he would never see his own smile on the face of a child. Too late for that, but not too late for joy.

He took his mug from Sylvia and their fingers touched as she relaxed her grip on the handle. There was that thrill again, the sheer physical shock of touching her. They might live together and share the same bed, and you'd think the excitement of her presence would have waned a little by now, but for Willie the vibrance was as rich as ever and he wanted to claim it for his own.

Sylvia cleared her throat. 'I've been thinking Willie, it might be nice to get away for a few days.'

'I've got some holiday due to me, so I suppose we could. Where do you fancy?'

'I've always had a liking for Cornwall. I went there once when I was a little girl. My grandmother took me. Land's End we saw and I really thought it must be.'

'Must be what?'

'Land's End of course.'

'Oh, I see.'

Willie took a sip of his coffee, contemplating Cornwall. They could walk along the cliffs hand in hand, now that would be a romantic place for a proposal. She'd have a scarf on which blew loose in the wind and wrapped around his face, he'd have to tuck it in her coat for her and she'd smile and touch his cheek. He could hear the violins in the background and in his mind's eye he could see him taking her into his arms, the wind blowing wildly and their passion mounting as she . . .

'Willie, did you hear what I said?'

'Pardon? No I didn't.'

'I said a friend of mine went to Cornwall on honeymoon.'

'Nice place for a honeymoon, Cornwall.'

'Yes, it would be.'

Beth began to cry. Alex was dragging her toy from her. Sylvia sorted them out by taking Alex onto her knee.

Smiling, Willie chucked Alex under his chin. 'That's one of my great regrets that is Sylvia, that we can't have children together. I'd have liked a nipper or two.'

'Bit late for that.'

'But of course, I wouldn't have wanted them to be bastards.'

'Willie! What a word to use in front of the children. Dr Harris won't allow them to hear bad language or anything about killing and guns and things. Good job she isn't here.'

'Sorry, but I wouldn't. It would have to be all legal like.'

'That's what pains you isn't it? Us not being married?'

'I'm willing to wait.' His head was bent and he was studying the table top as if he'd never seen one before in his life. Alex reached out to grab Willie's mug and had hold of it before either of them could stop him. The contents streamed across the table and onto Willie's lap. He leapt up. Sylvia put Alex back on the rug and went to get the kitchen roll.

She pulled off a good length and handed it to him to wipe his jumper and trousers with. He made only a half hearted attempt to mop himself so Sylvia took charge and vigorously set about cleaing him up. He took hold of her hand removed the sodden paper from it and put his arms around her waist.

'I hardly dare to ask this, because I don't want to hear you say no. But I'm going to say it. Would *you* like to go to Cornwall on your honeymoon with me?'

She laughed. 'Oh yes, Willie, I would.'

'Sylvia, do you mean that? Are you sure?'

'Oh yes, I am, I am.'

Willie kissed his precious Sylvia, his heart bursting with joy. 'Cornwall it is then. Right? We'll talk about this later, I don't want Dr Harris catching me in here again. I'll do my very best to make you happy Sylvia. We may be getting married late in life but the next thirty years will be the best believe me.'

'I know that, Willie, and I'm sorry I couldn't make up my mind sooner, but I had to be sure this time.' Sylvia kissed his cheek and smiled.

Willie had to get away to give himself time to assimilate what had happened. He almost skipped his way back to the churchyard. As he went through the lychgate he suffered a massive explosion of energy, he leapt up and punched the air with his fist. He'd have the mower out and cut the grass for the last time this year. Next time he got it out he would be a married man. Married to his Sylvia, the light of his life. By Jove, but life was good and not half.

Which was just what Jeremy was thinking when he dialled Jimbo's number the following Friday.

'Hello, Jimbo that you? Jeremy here. Well we've done it. Craddock Fitch has taken the bait, he's buying.'

'Brilliant, brilliant. I'm so glad for you. Price right?'

'Oh yes, I had to bargain a bit with him but yes we are very satisfied. He came himself you know. Been here most of the day which was a bit unexpected. The little woman had to hurry off upstairs to titivate herself and leave the men to conduct the business. But yes, a very satisfactory conclusion I must say.'

'Good, good.' Jimbo's curiosity got the better of him. 'Been able to negotiate terms for staying on to manage?'

'That's in the melting pot, but I'm pretty certain I shall be able to organise that to our mutual satisfaction. Altogether a very successful day's work.'

Jimbo smiled wryly. 'I'm glad. It's certainly saved your bacon hasn't it?'

'Well, I was pretty confident we'd clinch it.'

'Oh yes, that was very obvious.'

'When you've been in business as long as I have it doesn't take long to negotiate a deal does it? If you're holding all the best cards it's a matter of standing your ground. They soon come round when they realise you aren't going to budge.'

'Exactly. Well, busy, busy, got to get moving. Keep in touch Jeremy won't you?'

'Of course.'

Jimbo quietly put down the receiver and said, 'Well, thank you very much Jimbo for all your hard work. We really appreciate what you've done for us. You've pulled us right out of the mire, and we were in it up to our necks. How about a little dinner to celebrate?'

Harriet heard him. 'Talking to yourself are you, darling? It's the first sign you know.'

'Not a single word of thanks, I can't believe it. When he came that day he was on the floor, now he's bounced back up like a rubber ball, riding high and deceiving himself into thinking he's achieved it.'

'Let it go Jimbo, he isn't worth bothering about.'

'Dammit, I need cheering up. Let's ask Ralph and Muriel and Peter and Caroline for a meal tonight. Nothing fancy just something out of the freezer. What do you say?'

'What a good idea. I'll get onto that straight away.'

Harriet was still struggling in the kitchen when the first of the guests arrived. 'Jimbo,' Harriet shouted. 'Answer the door please. Flick don't overfill the jug. They won't be able to pour. Fergus! Don't you dare. You two boys upstairs and watch television for a while. Here's a tray with some goodies on and leave enough for Flick please. In bed eight thirty sharp, but you can read for a bit if you wish. Don't argue Finlay, please, I'm too busy for that. Where's the carving knife. Oh there. Now look, Flick I think you've done all you ca . . .'

Muriel put her head around the kitchen door and said, 'Good evening, sorry we're early.'

'Hello, Muriel. Just about ready. Shoo, shoo children. Off you go. Mind how you carry that tray Finlay, I don't want to have to shampoo the stairs carpet tonight.'

'Hello, children.'

Flick liked Muriel and slipped her hand in hers as she greeted her, 'Hello Miss Hip . . . oh no, hello, Lady Templeton. Mummy's got some lovely food ready for you. We're off upstairs now.'

'Hello Flick dear, I expect you've been a great help to your Mummy, haven't you?'

'Yes. I'm learning to cook like she does and then I'm going to be on TV when I get older, showing people how to cook.'

'And why not? That sounds like an excellent ambition.' Flick let go of Muriel's hand and went off after the boys. 'Harriet, we shouldn't really be allowing you to go to all this trouble when you're expecting a baby.'

'Nonsense, I'm perfectly fit and able. In any case Jimbo needed cheering up.'

'Did he?'

'Yes, it looks as if he's solved Jeremy and Venetia's problems and he's upset because they haven't even thanked him.'

'Oh dear, I expect they're so excited it's slipped their minds. So is it still going to be a health club?'

Harriet put her finger to her lips. 'Can't divulge until it's all signed and sealed. As Jimbo's told them, nothing is definite until the money is in the bank, but they're so relieved to have found a buyer, they're behaving as if it's all gone through. Take these starters in for me will you Muriel?'

'Of course. Peter and Caroline are late.'

'Yes, perhaps got problems with those babies of theirs.'

It was ten minutes past eight when they arrived from the Rectory.

'Sorry we're late,' Peter said as he came up the stairs two at a time into the sitting room. 'Been celebrating.'

'Celebrating?' Muriel asked.

'For once I know something the entire village doesn't know first! Willie and Sylvia have become engaged to be married today.'

Muriel clapped her hands with delight. 'Oh I'm so pleased. I'm sure they'll be very happy.'

'I'm sure they will. We've left the happy couple drinking the remains of the champagne, sitting close together on our settee looking like a couple of teenagers.'

Caroline laughed. 'We'll cough loudly when we get back, so as not to catch them in a compromising position!'

'Caroline! If you please.'

'Oh Peter, don't be stuffy, darling. It's what makes the world go round isn't it Jimbo? And you should know from what I've heard.'

Jimbo groaned, 'Please be kind to me, don't mention that particular incident. Judging by the sly grins and innuendoes I've had to put up with, the story has been spread throughout the entire county. I wish someone would do something really wicked to deflect the flack from me. Here Ralph, your whisky, and for you Caroline?'

'Orange juice same as Harriet, please.'

They talked about plans for Christmas both at the church and for themselves and Ralph asked if anything more had been heard about the Charity Fund. Caroline shuddered when she heard the question. 'Please tell Ralph quickly and then we'll talk about something else.'

Peter gripped her shoulder and gently shook her. 'Don't let yourself get upset darling, I'm here OK?'

'I know, but it always makes me shudder when I think what a close shave you had. Please tell them and then we'll change the subject.'

'Briefly the Charity Commissioners have agreed that the parish can nominate a charity and the money can go to it. I suppose it would have been a good idea to share it out amongst several good causes but to be honest I just want rid of it. My greatest regret is that we can't use it here in Turnham Malpas.'

Ralph shook his head, 'Absolutely not. No.'

'I agree,' Jimbo said as he offered Muriel more sherry. 'This village persona business is so peculiar. You would think that the influence of TV and newspapers and films and videos would have wiped out such strange collective fears, but they do still exist.'

'Well, they haven't and they won't. Look what happened about Peter and Stocks Day. If he hadn't agreed to take part he'd have had no church left at all. Well, except for us here that is.' As she was speaking Harriet became aware of a strange noise out in Stocks Row. 'Someone celebrating!' The noise grew louder and sounded like children blowing on trumpets.

Ralph, being nearest to the window, got up to look. He drew back the curtains and looked out. Standing outside in the road in front of the Store were Jeremy and Venetia. He was dressed in a sweater and jeans so tight Ralph wondered how he managed to walk. On his head he had a huge tricorn shaped paper hat, giving him a musical comedy Napoleonic look, in his mouth a toy trumpet of the kind given to children at birthday parties and he was blowing it for all he was worth. Venetia was dressed in her purple velvet tracksuit, on her head she had a huge shiny pink cardboard hat which sported a large purple feather curving down around her chin. She too was blowing a toy trumpet and was holding what looked like presents in her hands. Both of them carried bottles under their arms.

Venetia looked up as the light from the window caught her attention. She waved enthusiastically and shouted, 'Open the door, we're going to have a party.' By this time they were all crowding to the window to see who was there. Jimbo laughed and went to let them in.

They heard Venetia's light footsteps coming up the stairs and she burst into the sitting room. 'We've come. We've come. Get the champagne glasses out, we're going to have a party all night. So glad you're all here, thought there'd only be Jimbo and Harriet.' Momentarily she remembered her manners. 'I do hope you don't mind us gate crashing, but we had to come to thank our good friends for their wonderful help didn't we Sid?' Jeremy rolled in, obviously already the worse for drink.

'We certainly did, didn't we Marge?' He hugged Venetia and the two of them almost toppled over. 'Ooops sorry old girl. Now Harriet, a formal presentation. I expect you already have a watch but we've bought you an extra special one, as a thank you for all you've done for us.'

'I didn't do anything, Jerem . . . Sid. It was Jimbo.'

'I'm coming to him in a moment.' He lurched unsteadily and grabbed the edge of the table. 'I hereby present you with this gold watch in grateful thanks for saving us from certain ruin.' He held out a jeweller's box. Harriet took it from him, hesitated and then kissed his plump cheek. He flung his arms around her and hugged her, almost crushing her ribs in his enthusiasm. Then he nudged Venetia. 'Your turn now, old girl.'

She gave Jimbo his present and when he opened it he found a beautiful gold pen engraved with his initials, and before he could thank her Venetia placed a big kiss full on his mouth. 'No need for thanks Jimbo, it's worth every penny for what you've done for us.' Jimbo gave her a hug, glancing out of the corner of his eye to check Harriet's mood. But she was laughing as she watched Jeremy going round shaking hands with Ralph and Peter and kissing Caroline and Muriel. Harriet giggled to herself, poor Muriel was looking horrified and dishevelled, Jeremy's hug had pulled up her dress and she was struggling to straighten it and at the same time smooth her hair which had somehow become entangled with the trumpet Jeremy still had in his hand.

When he'd finished kissing and shaking hands Jeremy shouted, 'Out with the glasses Jimbo, I've had the champagne in the fridge at the Club, so it's all ready for drinking.' He gave several blasts on his trumpet as

Venetia opened up a roll of streamers and threw them across the room. The streamers caught Peter and Ralph so that the two of them stood entwined, with the curly coloured strands decorating their heads and shoulders. Muriel relaxed when she saw Ralph was catching the mood of the evening and was looking amused. While Jimbo opened the champagne Harriet thanked Venetia for her watch. Taking it from its box she said, 'This is absolutely lovely, there really was no need to be so generous.'

'Of course there was, you've saved our lives.'

'Look Venetia, why don't you and Jeremy stay for dinner? It's only a scratch one, but there's plenty. Do say you'll stay, we can soon lay two more places.'

Venetia couldn't hide the delight she felt at being invited to stay.

'Oh Harriet we'd love to, really love to, thank you very much. Jeremy will be delighted.'

The sound of the sitting room door opening made Venetia look up. Standing in the doorway were the three children, blinking in the bright light, and looking puzzled by the noise and excitement.

'Drinkies for the children,' she shouted. Venetia asked Harriet for three more glasses and poured a small amount of champagne into each one. 'Here you are children, you can drink a toast as well.' She patted Flick's head and kissed the two boys, whereupon they blushed and vigorously rubbed their cheeks where her lips had touched.

Venetia climbed on a chair and raised her glass.

'Ladies and gentlemen and children drink a toast to the future of Turnham House and to all our very good friends.'

They all clinked their glasses with each other's and then drank.

Jimbo helped Venetia down from the chair and then said, 'May I propose a toast?'

'Everyone shouted, 'Yes!'

'To Venetia and Jeremy! Long may they be with us here in Turnham Malpas.'

'Hear! Hear!'

Village Matters

THE VILLAGE OF TURNHAM MALPAS
Church Hall
Sir Ralph & Lady Templeton
FOR SALE
Rev'd Peter Harris & Dr Caroline Harris The Rectory
Willie Biggs
CULWORTH ROAD
CHURCH LANE
No 1
No 2
Jimmy Glover
Don & Vera Wright & Rhett
Pat Duckett Dean & Michelle
STOCKS ROW
No 3
N
S
ROYAL OAK
STOCKS ROW
ROYAL OAK ROAD
Jimbo & Harriet Charter-Plackett Fergus, Finlay & Flick
Sadie Beauchamp
& Valda Senior
Bryn & George Fields Alan Crimble

St Thomas à Becket
Dicky Tutt
Anne Parkin
Liz & Neville Neal
Guy & Hugh
GLEBE COTTAGES
GLEBE HOUSE
CHURCH LANE
School House
Michael Palmer
Village Store
STOCKS ROW
JACKS LANE
Swimming Pool
Turnham Malpas School
SHEPHERDS HILL
Methodist Chapel
FD'01
Sir Ronald & Lady Bissett
pond
SPARE LAND
BECK
TURNHAM
footbridge

Inhabitants of Turnham Malpas

Barry's mother	A village gossip.
Sadie Beauchamp	Retired widow and mother of Harriet Charter-Plackett.
Sylvia Bennett	Housekeeper at the Rectory.
Willie Biggs	Verger at St Thomas à Becket.
Sir Ronald Bissett	Retired trades union leader.
Lady Sheila Bissett	His wife.
James Charter-Plackett	Owner of the village store.
Harriet Charter-Plackett	His wife.
Fergus, Finlay and Flick	Their children.
Alan Crimble	Barman at The Royal Oak.
Pat Duckett	School caretaker.
Dean and Michelle	Her children.
Bryn Fields	Licensee of The Royal Oak.
Georgie Fields	His wife.
H. Craddock Fitch	New owner of Turnham House.
Jimmy Glover	One time poacher and ne'er do well.
Revd. Peter Harris (MA Oxon)	Rector of the parish.
Dr Caroline Harris	His wife.
Alex and Beth	Their children.
Jeremy Mayer	Manager at Turnham House Training Centre.
Venetia Mayer	His wife.
Michael Palmer	Village school headmaster.
Sir Ralph Templeton	Retired from the Diplomatic Service.
Lady Muriel Templeton	His wife.
Vera Wright	Cleaner at nursing home in Penny Fawcett.
Rhett Wright	Her grandson.

1

Peter shivered in the cold morning air. His prayers finished he got stiffly to his feet, stood back from the little altar in the war memorial chapel and crossed himself. At seven o'clock on a spring morning the church was certainly chilly. The old mediaeval stone walls kept the church cold right through the year, even in the hottest summer.

He went to stand in front of the main altar and looked around his church. Soon he'd have been in Turnham Malpas two whole years. When he'd first come here he hadn't realised how attached to the place he would become. He loved the deep colours of the stained glass windows, the ancient tombs slumbering there through the centuries, the banners, withering away at their posts for almost as many years, and the lovely country graveyard which was as much a part of St Thomas à Becket as the church itself. Still treading the village paths were people whose ancestors had for generations rested so peacefully within the precincts of this consecrated place. There was an ongoing feel about a village church, stretching back through the years and on into the future with an amazing sense of permanence. A city church didn't have quite the same feel about it.

He began to add up all the things he had achieved since his arrival. The Rectory cleaned and decorated and modernised and refurnished, the Scout troup, the Brownies and Girl Guides, the Luncheon Club for the pensioners, the women's meeting, the play group . . . for a moment his face clouded. The play group. That brought Suzy Meadows to mind. She'd still perhaps have been here running it if they . . . But they had and they shouldn't have. He still couldn't avoid the pain somewhere around his diaphragm. It knifed deep into his gut when he thought of her. No, it wasn't the thought of *her* as such, it was the thought of the crushing pain he'd inflicted on his darling Caroline which caused his agony. When she'd begged him to adopt the twins Suzy had given birth to because of him, he had thought he would die of it. But now he'd only to see their beaming smiles, feel their tiny hands grasping his, feel their soft sweet flesh against his own, and he knew Caroline had been right. It was the only course open. They were his, after all.

He glanced at his watch. Time he was off.

Peter's running shoes made no sound as he marched purposefully down the aisle to the main door. He carefully locked it behind him, checked it was secure, and then stripped off his tracksuit and placed it in a plastic carrier bag he kept for the purpose, under the bench in the porch. Underneath he wore his old college running vest and a pair of navy rugger shorts. He hid the huge key beside the grave he and the verger, Willie Biggs, had decided upon, and set off down the path. Jimbo Charter-Plackett was limbering up by the lych gate. Jimbo had been running with him for some time now and the flab he'd been anxious to lose was beginning to go. He was still a less fit looking man than Peter, for Jimbo was older, shorter, rounder and going bald: in contrast Peter was a good six inches taller, with an excellent head of blond hair, and an athlete's physique.

'Morning Peter. Lovely fresh day, isn't it?'

'Morning Jimbo. It surely is.' The two of them did their stretching exercises together and then at a nod from Jimbo they set off down Church Lane, then right into Jacks Lane and onto the spare land. Half way round their three-mile circuit was a five-barred gate where they always stopped for a chat. It led into a huge field and from it they had a view of Sykes Wood. It was a vast ancient wood, once part of a king's hunting forest, but belonging to Turnham House for the last three hundred years and possibly more. To one side where the trees were not quite so tall, the chimneys of the Big House could just be seen. After he'd wiped the sweat from his forehead with the hem of his running vest, Peter nodded towards them.

'Catering contract working out OK then, Jimbo?'

'It is. At least the money's more reliable than it was when it was the Health Club. Fitch plc certainly pays up on the dot, thank goodness.'

'Nice chap, is he?'

'Like all chairmen of big companies he thinks the world revolves round him, and his word is law, but as he knows I was a City man myself I do get a bit of respect for my opinions. They certainly do a good job with their staff training up there. Cracking computer equipment, video, cinema stuff and the rest. Technology gone berserk. That Jeremy Mayer's strutting around throwing his weight about, completely forgetting how grateful he should be that he's managed to sell on to Fitch and still keep a roof over his head.'

'What does Venetia do?'

'Mrs Venetia Mayer organises the leisure time for the staff, and Mrs Venetia Mayer organises diversions in the leisure department for the chairman of the company I think, but don't quote me. I've a soft spot for Venetia despite her permanent come-hither look.'

Peter laughed. 'Come on then, I've got school prayers at nine, must get back.' They turned to go, Peter leading the way.

Jimbo followed on, thinking about his jobs for the day. First, on his way home, he'd stand outside his Store and appraise the window displays. Each window had to be changed alternate weeks. Thinking up new ideas for them was a pain, but it was one of his rules. It had to be done. No fly-blown displays with bleached crepe paper hanging loose for Jimbo. Oh no! That kind of thing belonged to the 1950s, not the 1990s. Just recently with the opening of the training centre at Turnham House there'd been quite a few young trainees in, spending their money, another boost to the profits, and summertime was always good, his sales curve went ever upward with the money spent by the visitors to the church and the old stocks on the green. In fact all told, this year looked good. The mail-order business was booming, due to some clever advertising thought up by Harriet, his outside catering was also booming and the Store itself, the hub of it all, was also doing better than he and Harriet could ever have imagined.

What next could he turn his hand to, to make money? By Jove he was going to need it, with this new baby on the way. He gave a skip and a jump when he thought about the baby. Not bad for a forty-one-year-old chap. Number four. And Harriet so well, and he'd keep her that way. More help. Yes, he'd need more help. Peter turned round to wave and continued on to the Rectory, Jimbo nodded and turned down Stocks Row and round the green to his house. The windows! He'd forgotten the windows. He turned back and went to stand outside his Store. Easter. Easter. Fluffy chicks. Yellow ribbons. Chocolate eggs. A raffle? Huge great egg as the prize. That'd bring 'em in. Just get them in and they'd be buying other things beside the raffle tickets. Twenty-five pence each and five for a pound. Maybe twenty pence each, six for a pound, some of the villagers weren't that well off. He'd work out on his calculator how many he'd have to sell to break even, and then decide. Full of ideas he was this morning. Full of 'em.

'It's only me! Harriet!' The front door slammed shut. He stood, leaning on the hall table trying to get his breath. Sweat was pouring off his face and he wiped it with the sweat bands he wore on his wrists. Flick had bought them for him for Christmas. His dear little Flick. She came dancing down the stairs at that moment.

'Hello, Daddy, I'm not going to kiss you, you're all smelly and disgusting.' She wrinkled her nose and headed for the kitchen. 'Mummy! Daddy's back. You boys hurry up, your porridge is ready.' Flick seated herself at the table and watched her two brothers pretending to box. 'Men do find some funny things to entertain themselves with, don't they, Mummy?'

Harriet laughed. 'They certainly do!' She glanced up and saw Jimbo grinning at her from the doorway. 'Quick Jimbo, get under the shower – I can smell the sweat from here.'

'Thanks a million! A chap's doing his best to keep fit and his womenfolk do nothing but complain.'

'I've been thinking about an Easter raffle.'

'So have I. Great minds!'

'Boys come along now, that's enough. On your chairs. Look, Flick's already seated.'

'Trust her,' Finlay shouted as he dodged another blow from Fergus.

'Miss Goody Two Shoes! Miss Goody Two Shoes!' Fergus danced around the back of Flick's chair tormenting her. Tears began to well in her eyes and Harriet put a stop to the teasing.

She indicated his chair with a sharp finger. 'Enough. Thanks. That's enough! Sit down and eat.'

By the time Jimbo came downstairs the children had disappeared to clean their teeth – or so Harriet hoped – and he sat down to his bowl of muesli, his orange juice and wholemeal toast.

'Coffee or tea this morning?'

'Tea, please. I thought about a huge Easter egg for the first prize.'

'So did I. We get on remarkably well together in business, don't we Jimbo?'

'Yes, we do. And we don't get bored with each other. It would be so easy to be bored to death seeing each other at work *and* at home. Feeling OK?'

'Of course. I've never felt better than this time. Linda has another appointment at the dentist's tomorrow. Will you manage?'

'Yes, I expect so. Hope this is the last one for a while.'

'It is, the poor girl can't help an abscess, can she?'

'No, I suppose not. More tea, darling, please. I'm going up to the Big House this morning, just to keep an eye on things. Will you be around?'

'As ever.'

Jimbo stood up from the table. 'I'm off then. Don't overdo it will you, Harriet? I couldn't bear it if things went wrong.' Harriet stopped clearing the table and took time to look at him intently. 'You're all I've got, you know,' he said.

She reached across to kiss him. 'I know. I know. Believe me I will take care, but I mustn't be mollycoddled. That's not my scene.'

'See you then.' He went to the foot of the stairs and called up. 'Daddy's going now. Bye you lot.'

Flick shouted downstairs, her voice impeded by her toothbrush. 'Bye Daddy, have a nice day.' Jimbo winced at the Americanism. 'Bye now. See you later, Harriet.'

'OK.'

The weather was good for the time of year. Jimmy Glover's geese were out and about as usual. They were grazing close to the edge of the green. He wondered if it was true that they were as good as a dog for protecting their owners. They looked remarkably relaxed this morning. But as he came closer and paused to watch them, the geese began to stretch their necks and honk menacingly. Two of them left the grass and came onto the road, their beaks, on a level with Jimbo's knees, opened threateningly. He shouted and skipped a few steps to avoid them, waving his arms; they lost interest and left him to press on. Blessed geese, if he had his way . . . Then he caught sight of his Store and his heart swelled with pride. He'd turned it round and no mistake. He remembered the depressing aspect of it when he and Harriet had first come to Turnham Malpas to view it. They'd looked at each other and mouthed 'No', but old Mrs Thornton had noticed, and they'd felt obliged to show some interest.

At the time the shop had been Mrs Thornton's front room. The stock was almost non-existent, the trade negligible. But once they'd realised that the cottage next door was for sale too, Harriet had grown enthusiastic. Now look at it. Jimbo took the keys from his pocket and opened up. He picked up the bundle of newspapers from the shop doorway, moved the two advertising boards out onto the tarmac, checked to see that the litter bin by the seat he'd provided wasn't overflowing, noticed the telephone box needed a clear out, and then entered his domain.

Quarter past eight. He was late. It was half an hour before Linda would come to open up the post office section, so after he'd laid the newspapers out on their shelf ready for sale, he decided to begin collecting Easter eggs and all the paraphernalia he needed for dressing the window. Scissors, measuring tape, sellotape, drawing pins, stapler, ribbons, yellow and white crepe paper, silver paper. First, though, he'd dismantle the current display. But his plan was thwarted, his first customer entered. The little brass bell jingled furiously.

'Morning Willie. Come to collect your paper?'

'Yes.' Willie went to help himself. Took it to the till and handed Jimbo the exact money.

'Keep thinking we shall be hearing wedding bells for you, Willie, but you don't seem to have set a date, or have you?'

'Sylvia and I are taking our time about it. We're not in a great bursting hurry like we would be if we were younger.'

'Well, there's one thing being the verger, you won't have any problems making the arrangements. Will Sylvia keep working at the Rectory?'

'Oh yes, she enjoys that job, much better than at the hospital. Mrs Rector couldn't manage without her, not yet. I'll be off, rector's got all sorts of plans for Easter so we're having a conference today.' Willie went briskly out, leaving Jimbo confident that Willie knew exactly when he was getting married but he wasn't saying.

Arranging the windows was very therapeutic for Jimbo and he rapidly became absorbed in his work. The bell jingled again and in came his three children.

'Daddy, it's only us. We've come for something for playtime.' Jimbo reversed out of the window and went to supervise their choices. They were never allowed simply to help themselves, they always had to pay for whatever they chose. His mother-in-law laughed at his insistence on the matter, but he knew he was right. 'That's twenty-three pence for you Fergus, twenty-two for you Flick, and thirty, thirty? for you Finlay. That's a bit excessive isn't it?'

'Well, Daddy, we should really be getting them for free you know, it is our shop.'

'I'm not debating that question this morning Finlay, we've had it all out before. Out! Out!'

As they went out his mother-in-law, Sadie, came in. 'Bye darlings, be good.'

'Bye Grandma!'

'Good morning Jimbo. That word "Grandma" makes me wince, I start fumbling for my pince-nez.'

'You're early.'

'Do I detect a hint of sarcasm there?'

'No, no, not at all, but you are!'

'Well, I've lots to do today. Being in charge of the mail order doesn't give me much time to spare. Did that woman come with the jars of marmalade yesterday? She promised she'd have them made by Thursday last week.'

'Yes, she did.'

'Thank God for that. I hate letting our customers down. I'll have coffee when you're ready.' Jimbo groaned. He'd never get the window started. He began refreshing the coffee machine he kept in constant readiness for his customers. Just as he switched it on the door burst open and in came Pat Duckett from the school. Under her coat she had her school cleaning apron on, and her thick hair was standing on end, almost as though she'd used her head on the school hall floor, instead of her polishing mop. In her hand she clutched the school keys.

Pushing back her hair she whispered, 'Mr Charter-Plackett! Have yer got a minute? I haven't slept a wink all night for worrying. Can we go in the back where we won't be 'eard?'

'Heavens above, Pat, what's the matter?'

'It's that Mr Fitch, yer know, Mr Fitch plc? He's stealing the church silver and I don't know what to do about it.'

2

Jimbo took her into the store room at the back and sat her on his stool. He removed his boater, and laid it on a nearby shelf. Seating himself on an empty mineral-water crate, he said, 'Now what's it all about?'

'Well, yer know I went up to the Big House last night to 'elp out, with that waitress being off with the 'flu? Well, there was a right flap on. 'Ave to admit I made it my business to find out, 'cos I'm a bit of a nosy Parker like you are.' Jimbo began protesting but then admitted to himself he did like to hear all the latest gossip.

'Apparently,' Pat took a deep breath, 'apparently they'd been doing some more alterations. Don't know if you've 'eard but Mr Fitch is 'aving some rooms done up for a private flat for himself, anyway this room he fancied for a sitting room, he calls it 'is drawing room but we all know it's where 'e's going to sit, he starts examining the panelling. Beautiful it is, really old, bit of woodworm here and there and he wanted to get it done. Starts tapping the panelling and finds that one bit sounds 'oller.'

'Oller?'

'Yer know, no wall at the back, empty like. Anyway when 'e stands back to look 'e sees that that piece of panelling is a bit different from the rest, as if it 'ad been put in later. Course, he couldn't bear, 'as to have a look. Well, he gets the carpenter to remove this piece of panelling and lo and behold there's like a small room. An alcove thing. No windows, just a space and there, low and behold in cardboard boxes, stuff wrapped in old newspapers. They drag 'em out and believe it or believe it not it's all old silver things in there.'

'Whose silver things? Sir Ralph's?'

'I'm just coming to that. Apparently he gets unwrapping the newspapers and finds communion cups, two big silver plates, for like propping up on the altar, a pair of beautiful candlesticks, wonderful ones, and one that big, when the pieces are fixed together it stands on the floor. All really old. Well, he looks at the dates on the newspapers and they're dated June 1940!'

'June 1940?'

'June 1940. Yes, but, and 'ere's what's up, he says he's bought the house so they belong to him and he's going to sell them to help with the cost of his alterations!'

Linda came in. 'Hi! Mr Charter-Plackett, just wondered where you were. I'll carry on.'

'Yes, thanks, Linda. Won't be a minute.' Bemused, Jimbo didn't answer Pat for a moment. Had Fitch got a point here? He had bought the house, did everything in it belong to him? But church silver, he could hardly sell it. Could he?

'Look Pat, I've got to get on, there's only Linda and me this morning till Harriet gets here. Keep all this under your hat. Come back at lunchtime after you've finished at the school and we'll have another talk.'

'But it could be urgent. Yer know what a go-getter 'e is, it could all be sold by tonight. Then what would we do? The rector's going to be none too pleased, is he? What I can't understand is why it's there in the first place. Why isn't it in the church?'

'I don't know, Pat.' He stood up to retrieve his boater from the shelf. 'Look, I still think we've got time. I'm due up at the Big House later this morning, I'll have a scout around and see what I come up with. Leave it with me.'

'Will you tell the rector?'

'Or perhaps we should tell Sir Ralph, after all his family still owned it in 1940 didn't they?'

'Did they? Yes, I expect they did. I'll call after I've washed up the dinner things. Right?'

'Right!'

'See yer then. Yer can understand why I'm worried, can't yer? If the village finds out what he's done there'll be hell to play.'

Jimbo placed his boater at a jaunty angle and led the way into the front shop. Linda was trying to serve and deal with the post office too, so for the moment he had to put the whole story to the back of his mind.

Jimbo dropped down to third gear as he went up the long drive to Turnham House. He loved sauntering up the drive, taking in the feel of the place. It mattered not one jot that it had been a children's home then a health club and now a training centre, the old house with its parkland and gardens still had dignity and beauty. Try as they might, the twentieth-century entrepreneurs hadn't spoilt that ambience. One mile long, exactly. He'd measured on his milometer. As he rounded the last curve the lovely old redbrick house came into view. The Big House. Even the village people who hadn't been born when Sir Ralph's mother had to sell because of Ralph's father's death in the War, still looked upon it as the hub of the village. He drew to a halt on the freshly laid gravel at the front of the house and, climbing out, left the car unlocked and went inside. Give him his due, Fitch had retained the lovely entrance hall in its entirety, and had had the sensitivity to place an antique desk for the receptionist to use.

'Mr Charter-Plackett! What a delight! How are you this bright morning?'

'All the better for seeing you, Fenella! What news on the Rialto?'

'You haven't heard then? No, of course not, you weren't up here yesterday.' Fenella's large blue eyes glowed with intrigue. She glanced round the hall, checked no one was within hearing, and leaning across the desk whispered: 'Buried treasure! Well, not buried exactly, but hidden!'

'Fenella, you've been watching too many late-night movies, I've warned you before.'

'Cross my heart and hope to die.' Jimbo took her hand in his. Holding it close to the revers of his Jaeger overcoat he said, 'Tell me more.'

'All the stuff's locked in the safe now. Mr Fitch found it. Thrilled to bits he is. Really thrilled – I've never seen him so excited. He's always so self-controlled.'

'Fitch! Excited? I'd like to have been here to see that.'

'He's gone to Budapest first thing this morning, won't be back in London till Tuesday, so he's locked it up till he's time to deal with it.'

Jimbo's mind raced. 'But you'll need to get in the safe between now and Tuesday, how are you going to manage? I was hoping my cheque would be here. End of month as we all know.'

'Fenella has the key!' She tapped the front of her silk shirt.

'Not down there?' Fenella nodded. 'The sacrifices you career girls make. I am filled with admiration. Have you seen the treasure?'

'I've to guard this key with my life. Mr Fitch has gone all mediaeval since we took this place over, if I lose it I shall be hung drawn and quartered. If you promise me not to tell, I'll open the safe for you, let you see it.'

'You've got to open it to give me my cheque, so . . .' The telephone rang and he waited for her to answer it. When she'd finished speaking she said, 'I'll get one of the girls to take over and we'll go in the office and I'll let you take a peep.'

Fenella had the key on a chain hanging round her lovely slender neck. She bent down in front of the huge safe and, using the key and twiddling the knobs in a combination known only to a chosen few, unlocked it and swung back the door.

Jimbo felt privileged to handle the beautiful things Fenella brought out of the box. They'd all been carefully wrapped in tissue paper and it rustled invitingly as he removed it. But he didn't need enticing, the pieces were breathtakingly beautiful. There was no doubt, the silver belonged to the church. The chalice he was holding in his hand was dated 1655. Around the base were the words 'Thanks be to God'. The matching cup had the same date and the same words engraved. The big silver plates were engraved 'St Thomas à Becket 1739'. Fenella took out one of the candlesticks. It was engraved 'Sir Tristan Templeton 1821–1859'. The other one of the pair said 'Lady Mary Templeton 1824–1859'. His fingers traced the pattern winding round the stem of the candlestick and he noticed there were still traces of wax in the top and a drip of wax down one side. There was one magnificent candlestick which, as Pat had said, was tall enough when the three pieces were fitted together to stand on the floor.

'Why, Fenella, they're wonderful aren't they? Quite wonderful. They belong to the church, don't they?'

'Well, obviously they do.' She began to look upset and started hastily packing them away again in the safe. 'Better lock them up now.'

'Has he told the rector what he's found?' Jimbo said this knowing full well he hadn't.

Fenella locked the safe, replaced the chain round her neck and pushed the key down her shirt front.

'No. More than that I cannot say. Sorry. Going into the kitchens now are we, Mr Charter-Plackett?'

'Now look, I've known you two months now, it's about time you began to call me Jimbo. Please do. All my friends do. And thank you for showing me those things; it was a very precious moment for me. A real privilege.' He waved goodbye and went through the baize door and headed for the kitchens. But his mind wasn't on his work. Damn and blast. He had to act before Tuesday. That fool Fitch would probably send a chap down from a London auction house and the stuff would be spirited away and that would be that. In all conscience he couldn't let it happen. But who should he tell? How had the stuff got there in the first place? And why? Maybe Ralph would know. Yes, of course, Ralph would know. No one could hide those treasures in a house without the inhabitants knowing. All that banging and hammering putting the panelling up. Of course, he'd know all about it.

Jimbo left the Big House around twelve thirty, fully intending to call at the Store to check everything was in order and then go across to Ralph and Muriel's. As he was turning right out of the drive into Church Lane, Peter came past in his car. They both pulled up to hold a conversation through their open windows.

'Good day to you, Peter, had your Easter conference with Willie?'

'Jimbo, is there anything you *don't* know? Yes, I have. Everything OK with you? Good to see Harriet's looking fit and well.'

'Yes, she is, thanks. I say, in your perambulations around the paperwork in the Rectory have you come across any details of gifts of altar silver to the church?'

Peter studied the question for a moment and decided no, he hadn't. 'Why?'

'There's some turned up at the Big House. They found it hidden behind some panelling yesterday. I've chatted up the receptionist and she's let me have a look. It's beautiful. Seventeenth, eighteenth and nineteenth century. Wonderful stuff. Can't stop now. I'll let you know more later today. What time will you be back?'

'Fourish.'

'OK then, see you around.'

He pulled up outside the Store. There was no escape. There was a queue for the post office and one at the till. Pat came in about a quarter to two. She took a chance by jumping the queue to hand him one of his own carrier bags.

'Eh! Pat, can't yer see there's a queue? Gone blind or something?'

'All right, all right, it's just a message.' She turned her back to everyone so they couldn't see the contents of the bag. Lowering her voice she said, 'Sneaked this out of the bin last night. It's some of the newspaper they were wrapped in. OK?'

Jimbo tapped the side of his nose with a forefinger and said, 'Thanks. Mum's the word. See you later when it's quieter.'

'Right.' Pat strolled past the queue, nose in the air, leaving them all wondering what was going on between her and Mr Charter-Plackett. They could wonder. Pat was determined that Mr Fitch plc wasn't getting away with this one. She might not go to church, well, except at Christmas, but there was a limit. You couldn't mess about with church stuff. Look at that time with Sharon MacDonald. Pinched them chalice things and next news she's knifed clean through from front to back. Dead as a dodo. So yours truly had to do something about it, or else. She shivered at the thought and trundled back to her cottage, wishing for the millionth time that she wasn't a widow with two kids to bring up. And what was worse, her Dad perhaps coming to live with her, now it looked as if he was losing his job with the council cuts.

*

Ralph wasn't at home when Jimbo called so he went next door to the Rectory and rang the bell. What a difference Caroline and Peter had made since they came. Old Mr Furbank hadn't bothered at all, dust and cobwebs everywhere.

The door opened. Caroline stood there, a twin on either hand.

'Jimbo! How nice. What a rare treat. Do come in. Say hello, you two.' The two of them hid their faces in her skirt and refused to speak.

'Alex! Beth! say hello to your old Uncle Jimbo. No? Never mind then. Peter in yet?'

'Yes, he's in his study drinking tea, would you like a cup?'

'Yes, please, had no lunch today, been so busy.'

'Go in then, and I'll find a piece of Sylvia's gingerbread for you.'

'Lovely.'

While he drank his tea and ate the gingerbread Jimbo filled Peter in on the story. When he'd finished Peter said, 'Sell it? How could he? It's patently obvious from what you say he can see it belongs to the church.'

'Exactly. If anyone should sell it, it should be the church. I say, wouldn't it help the old finances if we sold it? Just imagine what we could do with the money. This is a piece of the newspaper it was wrapped in.'

Peter took it from him and gently opened it out, smoothing the crumpled paper and laying it on his desk.

'June 1940. 1940. Yes, of course. Do you know what? I think they hid it up there because of the threat of invasion. Dunkirk, the Germans just across the Channel, all that valuable silver, to say nothing of the value to the villagers. Yes, I bet that's what happened. So Ralph's father would know about it, and whoever was rector at the time. And the joiner or the estate worker they used to fix the panelling. Quite a skilful job if it's never been noticed for the last fifty or more years.'

'Thing is, there's no one around now who could possibly remember.'

'Except Ralph. He'd only be a little boy. Let's ask him though.'

'Not at home today. I tried him first. We've got till Tuesday anyway. Till Fitch gets back.'

'You say it's beautiful?'

'Oh yes, in brilliant condition. We've got to get it back to the church, Peter. Even if we decide it's too valuable to have on the premises and decide to sell some of it, at least we could use the money for something specific and say we bought this and this with it. But I would dearly love for us to keep it and bring it out on high days and holy days. That would be bliss. It would have to be secured in some way, otherwise the insurance companies wouldn't touch it with a bargepole. I wouldn't like to be in

Fitch's shoes if he sells it. You know what this village is like. He'd probably find his body cut into little pieces and burnt, and his head stuck on a pole and paraded round the village.' Jimbo shuddered at the thought. 'We'll see Ralph during the weekend, and then I'll ring on Tuesday and ask my tame receptionist when he's coming down again.'

'Should we all go together, do you think?'

'Well, I found out, Ralph used to own the house and his father certainly did when the stuff was hidden there, and you have a very definite vested interest. So, yes, we'll all go.'

Although it wasn't his day for being early Jimbo made sure he was in the Store the following morning to take the opportunity of having a word with Willie about the silver.

He came at his usual time.

'Morning Willie, come to collect your paper?'

'Yes.' Willie went to the shelf where the papers were displayed and selected the one he wanted.

Jimbo said. 'Willie, have you heard any rumours about old silver being found which belongs to the church?'

Willie's head came up from looking at his handful of change. 'Silver? Silver? What silver?'

Jimbo explained quietly, to one side so any customers coming in wouldn't overhear.

'Well, now, June 1940. Let me see.' He scratched his head and looked into the middle distance as he pondered the problem. 'Well, now, in June 1940 my old Dad was the verger. Yes, that's right. My Dad.'

Jimbo looked eagerly at him. 'He isn't still alive, is he?'

'No, no he died in 1943. Pneumonia got 'im when he was forty-four. Would garden in the pouring rain, he would. The rector then would be let me see, Reverend Edgar Levett, that's right, Reverend Edgar Levett. He's dead though. Went to London to 'is sister's funeral and got killed with a flying bomb. Ralph's father's died, of course, in Malaya, so there's no one left. They'd keep it very secret anyway, wouldn't they? Wouldn't be the sort of thing you'd tell in The Royal Oak of a night. Perhaps they were the only three who knew where it was. Silver you say, and you've seen it.'

'That's right. Beautiful stuff, Willie. We can't let the old fox get away with this.'

'Get away with it? It's as plain as the nose on your face, he'd be stealing it. He'd be a thief. That'd look good in the papers. "Company chairman steals parish silver". My paper would be rare and glad to get hold of a tale like that.'

'True. True. Mum's the word, Willie, don't tell a soul. The rector knows, and I know, and now you. Well, Pat does, because she's the one who found out.'

'Pat does? Hell's bells. All t'village'll know by teatime. Well, the rector 'ad better do something about it and quick, or that Craddock Fitch'll need to flee for his life. You'll have a job on keeping it secret if Pat Duckett knows.'

'Willie! She's promised me faithfully she won't breathe a word.'

'Oh yes? I'll be off. I've a grave to dig, and a dozen and one things to attend to before my Sylvia and me get off on our 'olidays.'

Jimbo watched him leave. Everyone dead. What a blow. Still it was more than fifty years ago, it was only to be expected. He amused himself by imagining the newspaper headlines if it got out. Fitch plc would certainly be hopping about. Jimbo grinned. Then he remembered about his catering contract at the Big House and the money it was bringing in each month.

But it was to be more than two weeks before he needed to resolve that dilemma, for Craddock Fitch went from Budapest to Moscow and then on to Helsinki before returning home.

3

Pat Duckett wandered early into The Royal Oak, hoping Willie and Sylvia would be in tonight. They'd be back from their holidays now, full of news. All week it had been quiet with only Jimmy and Vera to talk to. Might be a bit more lively if they came in. She pushed her way through the crowd hoping their favourite table might be free. It was. Pat took her port and lemon over and sat down on the settle. She surveyed the crowd. The bar was really buzzing tonight and not half. There were plenty of the real villagers in, but also a lot who'd come out from Culworth and around to enjoy the country atmosphere and the good beer Bryn stocked now. Not that Pat drank it. Rotten stuff. The downfall of her Duggie and not half.

Pat was determined not to mention about the silver being found up at the Big House. It would try her self-control and no mistake, but with her job with Jimbo at stake if she let on, she'd an awful lot to lose just for the sake of five minutes in the limelight. If she could prove to him she was irreplaceable with this bit of income on the side, ten pound notes in her hand and no questions asked, she might just start to have a bit better life. The kids cost so much to feed and clothe nowadays. And what with Dean doing so well at school he wouldn't want to be leaving at sixteen. Duggie would have been so proud. She watched the door hoping someone she knew would come in. Tonight it didn't matter who it was, she just needed to talk.

The swing doors suddenly burst open. It was Jimmy Glover waving a newspaper in the air.

'I've won! I've come up! After all these years, I've made it. I 'ave. I 'ave yer know, I've made it!' Jimmy shouted at the top of his voice.

Bryn came out from behind the bar. 'Jimmy you never have! You've never won the pools!'

'I 'ave, it's 'ere in black and white. I've just checked mi pools and I'm right, I've won.'

'How much?'

'Don't know. I don't know. But I've won and I'm pretty sure it's a lot of money. Twenty-five years I've been filling in the pools and tonight I've made it. At last! At last!'

Excitedly Pat stood up. She experienced a momentary shaft of jealousy. Why couldn't it be she who'd won? Not much chance of that seeing as she'd never got the hang of filling in pools coupons. She hastened across to congratulate him. 'Wonderful. Wonderful. I'm that pleased for yer, Jimmy, that pleased yer've no idea. What a turn up for the book. How much d'yer think yer've got then?'

'Dunno, but it'll be a lot. What will yer 'ave Pat?'

'Gin and tonic, seeing as you're paying. Aren't you lucky Jimmy? I can't believe it. Brilliant! Absolutely brilliant!'

Bryn shouted for his wife. 'Georgie! come out here, come on, come out here. Alan, get Jimmy a drink on the house in honour of his win. It could be thousands, Jimmy, thousands.'

'It could be a million but it won't, thousands'll do for me. Where's that Willie Biggs? 'As 'e come in yet? He's been telling me all these years I couldn't 'ope to win but I 'ave, I 'ave.'

'He'll be in soon, saw him come back from his holidays a couple of hours ago.' Bryn slapped Jimmy on the back and the customers gathered round to add their congratulations.

'By Jove, Jimmy, yer'll be able to buy a new cap.'

'You'll have plenty of friends now Jimmy, and not half.'

'Congratulations Jimmy.'

'There'll be no speaking to you now, we shall 'ave to touch our forelocks to yer.'

'Some 'ope, I can remember Jimmy with the seat of his trousers 'anging out and Miss Evans lending him a spare pair she kept for when anyone wet 'emselves.'

'Aw shut up.'

Jimmy, quite beside himself with the thrill of his win, told Bryn it was drinks on him for everyone and he'd pay when he got his winnings.

'That new ale for me Alan, and don't be mean with it.'

'Gin and orange here, and a Cinzano and lemonade for my old girl.'

'You've a cheek, I'll give yer "old girl".'

'Ale for me, Alan, and be sharp about it, I've a thirst on me like I don't know what!'

Alan Crimble the barman, with his habitual ingratiating smile on his face, attended to their requests. Georgie, petite and pretty, added her congratulations to Bryn's.

'Wonderful for you Jimmy, I'm really pleased. Take care of it though, however much it is it'll soon disappear. Have you any plans?'

'I've thought about tonight many a time and I decided years ago that when it 'appened I'd set miself up in business.'

The whole bar erupted with laughter. 'You, set yerself up in business! That's a right laugh. What as?'

'A scrap-metal merchant?'

'A rag and bone man?'

'How about a gamekeeper? He'd be good at that. Plenty of experience!'

'No. I bet he's going to be a merchant banker.'

'By gum, the City 'ad better watch out. Jimmy'll 'ave 'em by the scruff inside a week.'

'International banking scandal, that'll be it.'

'No, no, "Unknown pools winner takes City by storm".'

Jimmy began to look hurt, and Georgie took it upon herself to stop the ribbing. 'That'll do. You lot watch out, Jimmy'll be showing you all the way to go home before long, won't you Jimmy?'

Jimmy tapped the side of his nose with his forefinger and grinned at her. 'They can laugh but I'll 'ave the last laugh.' He leant over the bar counter and whispered in Georgie's ear. She listened intently and the customers who'd been pulling his leg strained to hear.

'What a good idea that is.' Georgie winked at him and then said, 'You lot wait and see. You're all in for a surprise. When will you know how much you've won, Jimmy?'

'Monday or Tuesday, but I'll know for definite on Wednesday how much it is, that's when they declare the dividend. Perhaps they'll be arriving in a big Rolls Royce to let me know. I can't wait. Just fancy, the first Glover to be in the money! I shall celebrate by 'aving half a pint of cream delivered with the milk tomorrow, that Malcolm'll 'ave a shock and not half.'

'Might be an idea if yer paid yer bill, he told me last week he'd soon be stopping calling.'

'Don't worry, he'll be paid good and proper when I get mi 'ands on mi money.' Glass in hand, Jimmy went to his favourite spot opposite the settle nearest to the door and sat down with his newspaper to relive his excitement.

The other customers collected their free drinks from the bar and returned to their seats to mull over the unfairness of a ne'er-do-well coming into money when they'd spent all their lives working hard to earn a pittance. But Jimmy Glover didn't care. His day had come. Excitement got the better of him and he called out, 'I'll have a bag o' them salted nuts please, Bryn, if yer don't mind.'

Someone shouted: 'Oh, the last of the big spenders, is Jimmy.'

He remembered a saying of Miss Evans at school, and it was about all he did remember, '*There is a tide in the affairs of men, Which taken at the flood, leads on to fortune*'. He would do just that. He looked impatiently at the door, wanting Willie to come through it so he could tell him of his good fortune.

Jimmy sat relishing his time in the limelight. He'd show 'em. At last a chance to succeed, a chance to pull himself out of the mud and sit out in the sun, where often it seemed as though everyone sat except him. When he'd got organised he'd get another dog. A little Jack Russell like Sykes. Wouldn't call it Sykes though, there'd never be another Sykes. A lump came to his throat when he thought about his old friend. Eleven years of devotion, that dog had given him. Ah well. The emotion of the evening turned into a moroseness he found hard to dispel. As customers left they came across to thank him and congratulate him again, but he couldn't quite raise himself above his melancholy. If only his Mary had lived, he could have made her life so comfortable. All he had left of Mary was a few faded photos and her wedding ring in that carved wooden box of his mother's where he kept a lock of their baby's hair. And who had he to share his money with, now it had come? Nobody.

Pat went back to her favourite settle and sat opposite Jimmy.

'What *are* yer going to do with yer money then, Jimmy?'

'Don't know yet, Pat.'

'First thing yer can do is buy a new cap.'

Jimmy ignored her remark. 'I'll see how much it is first and then decide. I'd like to do mi cottage up. Put a bathroom in and 'ave a new kitchen. Get it painted and that, and then I'll set miself up in business.'

'What kind of business though?'

'Not telling.'

'That's mean. Not telling! What are you qualified to do then?'

'Nothing much. Look out, 'ere's Willie! Over 'ere Willie, a drink for Mr Biggs, Alan, if you please.' Willie bustled across and held out his hand. 'Let me shake hands with you Jimmy, Thelma knocked and she told me yer good news. First chap I've known who's won on the pools, after all I've said too. Congratulations, I'm really pleased and my Sylvia sends her love and says she's thrilled for yer. By Jove, eh Pat, it'll be a pound to speak to him now.'

Jimmy grunted. 'It will not. Like all these big winners say "it won't make any difference to me, I shall turn up for work on Monday as usual".'

'What work?' Pat and Willie began laughing, but stopped when they realised Jimmy was offended.

'You'll be able to go on holiday now, you'll be able to afford one of them glamorous cruises to the Caribbean on the QE2,' Willie said as he nodded his head in acknowledgement of Alan bringing his drink across to the table.

'Never mind about me going on holiday, you've just come back from yours. How was Cornwall?'

'Well, I have to admit my wife and I had a lovely time, the weather was excellent, the sun shone most days and . . .' Pat and Jimmy looked at him as though they were in shock; Jimmy almost choked on his beer and Pat's mouth dropped open. 'We were able to go out every day. It's a lovely place is Cornwall for a honeymoon, have you ever been?' He looked innocently up at them, then took a long draught of his beer whilst he waited for their reactions.

'Willie!' Pat shouted. 'You 'aven't gone and got married without telling anyone, 'ave you?'

Jimmy looked incredulous. 'Married? You never 'ave, Willie, 'ave yer?'

Silence fell in the bar. All eyes were on Willie. He looked down at his drink, his face glowing with pleasure.

'Yes, as a matter of fact we 'ave.'

The other customers gathered round to hear the news.

'Where?'

'Here in the church.'

'Here in the church? Well, I never! When?'

'Day we left.'

Pat protested unbelievingly. 'But you left at half past nine, I saw the taxi come.'

'The rector married us at eight and we left at half past nine.' The customers offered their good wishes to Willie and his bride. 'Thank you very much indeed, I'll tell Sylvia when I get back, she'll be delighted.'

Pat registered her disappointment. 'We never 'eard nothing about banns being read.'

'Special licence.'

'Oh right. Crafty that was, crafty. Well, I'm right surprised at you, Willie. Verger at the church and sneaking in to get married and saying nothing to nobody. We'd have liked to give you a big send-off. I'm really disappointed.'

'Well, that was just it. Sylvia wanted a quiet wedding.'

'It was certainly that and no mistake.'

'Our wedding service was very important to us Pat, and we wanted to be able to concentrate on what we were saying, so that was what we decided to do. Rector and Dr Harris were a bit disappointed, but they agreed with us in the end.'

'Who else was there? 'Cos whoever it was, they've kept mum and no mistake.'

'The rector of course, Dr Harris with the twins, Sir Ralph and Muriel.'

'Oh I see, they could be there but we couldn't who've known you all these years. I'm right offended Willie and no mistake.'

Jimmy grunted, 'A chap 'as a right to get married 'ow he likes. At least he's made an honest woman of 'er.'

Willie objected. 'That's enough, thank you. What's between Sylvia and me is entirely private.'

Pat laughed. 'All right, Willie, keep yer hair on.' She turned to Jimmy and asked, 'Will you be next then, now you've got all this money?'

Jimmy brushed his moustache with the back of his forefinger and smiled wryly. 'Well, I 'ad thought of popping the question to you, but maybe it wouldn't be a good idea.'

Pat was enraged at the thought and told him so in no uncerain terms. 'Married to you? Not Pygmalion likely. I've enough on my plate without adding you and yer smelly clothes and yer ferrets and geese to mi troubles. If I marry it'll be to money.'

'But that's just what he's got, Pat, now. Money.' Willie grinned at her and for a moment she hesitated, and then said, 'He'd have to be a millionaire before I'd marry 'im.'

'Well, he might be, yer never know.'

Jimmy offered his congratulations to Willie and said he was right pleased for him and he hoped they'd be very happy.

The conversation in the bar was rising to a crescendo, the news of Jimmy's win and now Willie's marriage causing consternation. 'We don't get far but we do see life,' they were saying. It was nearly as good as that night when poor Sharon McDonald, God rest her soul, and her mother had that fight here in the bar, or that day when the bar was packed and Betty McDonald thumped Willie on the nose and came close to punching the rector. A few left earlier than they had intended so they could spread the news. Others stayed on in the hope that even more news might be revealed before the evening was over, and better still, more free drink.

Jimmy interrupted a story of Pat's about the school and said, 'I've been thinking that now Bryn's dining room has been open a whole week and they'll have got into the swing of things, would you like to join me for a meal tonight?'

'Well, Jimmy, that would be lovely,' Pat said not admitting that she had already eaten at home, but it had only been beefburgers and chips with ice cream to finish. She couldn't bear the thought of missing a free meal. It was the first time Jimmy had ever offered anything of the kind.

'What about you, Willie, do you fancy going and collecting your Sylvia and joining us? We could 'ave a joint celebration as yer might say. You owe it to us for us 'aving missed yer wedding. I'm paying. Bryn'll see me all right till next week.'

'Well, thank you very much.' Willie stood up. 'I'll go get her right now.'

As he walked home up Stocks Row, Willie added up how many days he'd been married. Nine days, nine whole days. How on earth they'd managed to keep it secret he would never know. He chuckled to himself when he recollected how Mr Harris had leapt about from the organ to the altar steps and back. Good job he could play the organ as well as be rector! Lovely music it was, he couldn't half play. When he saw his Sylvia coming down the aisle he couldn't believe how lovely she'd looked. Dressed in a kind of silvery grey she was, which just matched her lovely big grey eyes. She'd put her hand in his with such love in her eyes he felt very humble. Then of course Sir Ralph couldn't find the ring and searched every pocket till it finally came to light in Muriel's handbag. Her face was scarlet and no mistake. They'd all laughed. That was the best thing about a quiet wedding it was so much more, what was the word, friendly, yes that was it, more personal like. The rector had played some lovely triumphant music when they'd walked down the aisle, stopping as they reached the door so that the village wouldn't hear and wonder what was going on. Then they'd had a lovely champagne breakfast in the Rectory and hey presto, the taxi was there and they were off. Not many men in his position had a baronet as his best man.

They'd posed for photos in the church itself. Dr Harris had taken them, and now they were home and he'd seen them he knew it really had happened.

'Sylvia, where are you love?'

'In here, have you seen Jimmy?' Willie found her in their little kitchen just beginning to make their evening meal.

'Yes, he's thrilled to bits, he wants to know if we'd like to go over there for a meal in Bryn's new dining room to celebrate with him.'

'That would be lovely. Right now? Tonight you mean?'

'Yes. They all know, love, about us.' He stood behind her and linked his hands around her waist.

'How did they find out?'

'I told 'em.' Willie kissed her ear.

'Willie!'

'Why not? I'm that proud of yer. They're all gobsmacked and not half. All the village will know by morning.'

'And why not? Shall I get changed?'

'No, yer lovely as you are. Come on, love, I'm starving. We can take the wedding photos round to Ralph and Muriel on Monday, I'll be too busy tomorrow with it being Sunday. Come on then, put that down. Let's be off.'

4

Sir Ralph was just finishing his breakfast and enjoying the whole experience of being looked after by his adoring wife when they heard the postman at the door. Muriel never could resist seeing what he had brought the moment it came, so she'd left the breakfast table to pick it up from the mat. Pericles, his black nose shining bright against his white coat, yapped as vigorously as his age permitted, and stood on the letters. Muriel pushed him off and as she bent down, there came loud, urgent banging on the front door. It made Muriel jump. She opened the door to find Willie Biggs standing there.

'Oh it's you, Willie, you made me jump. Good morning, how are you?'

'Very well, thank you, and you?'

'Very well, thank you.'

'I know I'm early but I've a lot on this morning with being away. I've brought our wedding photos. Sylvia and I would like you to choose what you want and let me know and then we'll have them done as a gift to you and Ralph.'

'There's no need . . .'

'Absolutely, I insist. It's not every day a man gets married.'

'No, that's right. Well, thank you, thank you very much. I'm really looking forward to seeing them. Goodbye Willie.'

'Good morning.' He stepped briskly away. Muriel returned to the dining room.

'Look, Ralph dear, the wedding photos. I can't wait to look. Let's clear a space, we mustn't get them messy.' Muriel smiled at Ralph and his heart turned over. He never quite got over the delight of being with her again after all their years apart. Coming back to the village and finding her and persuading her to marry him had been the best day's work he'd ever done. He smiled back and then moved his plate to make room. Caroline's photographs had come out excellently and they were delighted with them.

'Oh! Look at this one, Ralph, you do look serious.'

'It's a serious business giving away a bride, and being best man too. This one of you is good, very good indeed. We must have that one. Look at this one, Willie's grinning like a cat that's been at the cream! That one of Sylvia and me is good.'

'Let's have another look later on and decide which we want. We mustn't ask for too many, they're not that well off. You've a lot of post this morning, Ralph. Shall I put it in your study?'

'Yes, please, my dear. I've nearly finished. Is there another slice of toast?'

'Of course, as many as you like.'

Muriel took Ralph's extra slice in to him and as she handed it to him she kissed the top of his head. She stroked his white hair, kissed him again and said, 'Your hair needs cutting.'

'Yes. I know, that's on my agenda for this week. In fact, I think I'll go up to town to get it cut.'

'Up to town? Don't you mean Culworth?'

'No. Town. Come with me and we'll go to the theatre, or the opera if you prefer, and you can do some shopping. I have a few business matters I need to attend to, so you could shop while I . . .'

'Ralph! I'd love that, except I shall go sightseeing instead of shopping. Yes, definitely I'll come. Have you finished, dear?'

'Yes, thank you. That marmalade is excellent, you must compliment Jimbo on it the next time you go in the Store. Tomorrow it is then. Look in *The Times* and choose a couple of theatres and we'll leave tomorrow morning first thing. I'm sure Ron and Sheila will have Pericles for you at short notice. I'll open my post while you do that.'

'I'll clear the table first and tidy the kitchen and then I'll look.' Muriel busied herself clearing away and putting her kitchen to rights. Moving to this bigger house had been a wrench at first but now she wondered how she had ever managed in such a small house as Glebe Cottage. London, how she loved it. They'd been to the South of France and Ralph was planning for them to go to New York later in the year, and she'd seen masses of places in Australia when they'd had their honeymoon there, but London she loved best of all. Her heritage she called it, and Ralph always smiled when she said that.

Muriel was putting the bread knife in the dishwasher and giving her kitchen a final inspection before switching it on, when Ralph shouted: 'MURIEL!!!' She jumped so much she dropped the bread knife and it crashed to the floor. She clutched her heart and said, 'Oh, Ralph, whatever is it?' She rushed into the study expecting to find him taken ill.

Ralph was sitting at his desk holding a letter in his hand, his face, his handsome face, red with excitement. As soon as he caught sight of her he said, 'Had you heard that the Methodist chapel is closing?'

'Closing? No, is it?'

'Well apparently, yes. They are closing this one and building a large extension to their church in Little Derehams. They've always been a funny lot in Little Derehams.'

'Ralph! Really.'

'Well, you know what I mean.'

'Why should the Methodist chapel closing be so important to you? You've never attended there.'

'No, my dear, I haven't. This letter is from the council telling me all about it.'

Muriel sat down on a chair and decided to await Ralph's explanation. He turned over the page and continued reading. Muriel sat admiring him while he did so. In fact she never tired of admiring him, and to think that at one time, to her shame, she didn't fancy the idea of his lovely aristocratic profile being beside her on the pillow each morning. What a foolish, misguided person she'd been. The Methodist chapel closing. Well. It had been there, on the spare land, for something like one hundred and forty years.

Ralph put down the letter and said, 'The spare land, as everyone calls it, belonged to my family. It was my great-great-grandfather who gave permission for the Methodists to build their chapel, on a kind of token rent basis. One florin each New Year's Day, it was. I remember them coming up to the Big House to pay my father for it. I always understood that my mother sold the entire estate to the council after my father was killed, including that piece called the spare land. But they can't find the deeds for it in the archives and have discovered that though the council *assumed* they'd bought the spare land at the time they bought the estate, they now find that the land was never legally transferred to them. So-o-o, I still own all the land surrounding Turnham Beck, would you believe. What I need to do is to find the deeds for it.'

'But what use is it to you, Ralph? It's all rough scrub land. Though the trees are beautiful, I always love the beeches in the spring, their leaves look so fresh and most especially green then, and the willows with their twigs dabbling in the beck, and I do look forward to the ducklings in the spring.'

'Use to me? If it is proved that the council have never in fact owned it and it has been mine all these years without me knowing it, then I shall be able to do what I've always wanted to do and provide houses for village people to rent.'

Muriel jumped up, horrified. 'Houses on it? Oh Ralph, how could you?'

'But don't you want villagers to be able to stay in the village? Young married people can't afford to buy the houses now. If they could rent they would stay, if not the village will die.'

'But the beech trees Ralph, they'll all be chopped down. And the lovely beck! Pericles loves sniffing about down there and paddling in the water. It would be dreadful to destroy it. Quite dreadful.' As though on cue Pericles came trotting in to the study, reminding Muriel it was time for his walk. She bent down to pat him.

'Muriel, my dear, just because I am proposing to build houses it doesn't mean I shall get rid of the beck, where on earth would all the water go if I did? No, it would be incorporated in the design, and you'd still be able to walk Pericles there because it's a public footpath right from ancient times and would have to be preserved.'

'Are you sure?'

'Yes, I am.' Ralph firmly nodded his head and then said, 'Anyway it isn't definite yet. When you come back we'll go in the attic and get down that old trunk from the Big House and go through the papers in there to see if we can find anything to throw light on the matter.' He stood up, took her hand, raised it to his lips and kissed it. 'Don't let yourself become distressed my dear, and don't tell anyone of our conversation this morning. Not a word.' Ralph pressed a finger to her lips and smiled. Muriel smiled faintly at him and then retreated to find her coat and gloves and Pericles' lead.

Apart from their disagreement about Jimmy and him snaring rabbits, Muriel decided this was the biggest conflict they had had to face since they got married. As she unclipped Pericles' lead and watched him scamper off, how did he manage at his age? she paused to enjoy the trees and the sound of the beck running along. Houses here on this lovely piece of land. Even though spring had not yet come, with all the rain they'd had, the grass and the trees were looking quite fresh, and just here and there were the first signs of new life rising in the trees; tiny buds coming on the twigs and the grass looking perkier after the long winter. She stood on the little footbridge which the council had constructed over the beck and leant on the rail to watch the water dashing over the pebbles. Pericles leapt in and paddled under the bridge. She called to him and as he appeared from underneath he looked up and wagged his tail. She tried to imagine houses, houses, houses. Fences and garages, lawns and herbaceous borders, bicycles abandoned on the footpaths, children's slides peering over the tops of the fences . . . Oh no, Ralph, it simply wouldn't do.

When she and Pericles got home Ralph was not downstairs. She called his name but got no response. Then she heard loud thuddings coming from the attic, where she found Ralph already struggling with the trunk.

'You're back, my dear. Shall we get the trunk down the stairs or shall we look at the papers up here?'

'Ralph, I don't want you to build houses on that land.'

He looked at her with surprise. 'Look at it another way, Muriel. Already three of the village cottages are in the hands of weekenders. In addition your cottage is sold to someone who is only here from time to time. Toria Clark's old cottage is going the same way because Dickie and Bel Tutt are never here. Let's suppose some young couple from the village want to live here and bring up their family. Where would they live? Nowhere. And that means that the school numbers will slowly get so small it won't be worth keeping it open. Then there will be an even bigger decline because we shan't be able to attract people to live here if they have a family. They won't want to be busing their little children into Culworth every day, will they? Jimbo's store would suffer, the church would suffer and The Royal Oak would suffer . . .'

Muriel couldn't help smiling. 'That mightn't be a bad thing after Saturday night's rumpus!'

Ralph laughed. They still hadn't got over watching half the village doing a conga round the green after closing time, led by Jimmy who must have had the hangover of all time the following morning. 'Still, he did have something to celebrate, didn't he?'

'Yes, he did. I do see your point, Ralph, about the school. Michael Palmer was talking to me about it only the other day, he said if there were any more cuts in education, closing the school will be one of their next economies. Let's take the trunk downstairs and have a coffee in front of the fire and look through the papers. It could take us all day, but never mind, we've nothing else on our agenda today.'

They had both coffee and lunch sitting by the fire sorting out the trunk. Ralph kept getting waylaid by reading the papers and reminiscing about the old life. He even found some old estate account books in which Muriel's father's name as head gardener appeared. 'Look, Muriel, Henry Hipkin £4. Again here the following week, Henry Hipkin £4. That was before you were born. He was quite well paid for those times, wasn't he? Because he'd have the house and all the fruit and vegetables he could eat. Possibly they'd even provide him with meat when they slaughtered a pig or a sheep.' Muriel despite her reluctance about the whole project became quite excited, and delved into the trunk with delighted cries when she found something of interest. Then, as she went to take their lunch tray into the kitchen, Ralph gave a triumphant shout. 'Here we are, I've found the deeds.' To Muriel it sounded like a death knell.

When they set off the next morning for London Ralph had the deeds in his briefcase, along with the letters which had been exchanged when the estate was sold.

That morning Linda arrived at the Store buzzing with news. Last minute as usual, she was hurriedly unlocking the post office grille and setting herself up for business and at the same time telling Jimbo what her cousin Kev had said.

'So-o-o our Kev knows all about it because he works in the planning department, you see. That'll be one twenty-five, Mrs Goddard. Lovely day isn't it? Thank you. Next! Twenty-five pence first class, right thank you. Where was I? Oh yes, so he says that the spare land where the Methodist chapel is or was as you might say because they're leaving, did you know? Anyway they are, and I shouldn't be telling you this but I can't keep it to myself, he says the spare land all these years has belonged to Sir Ralph and not to the council. And there they've been building the footbridge, putting the wastebins there, cutting the trees down when all the time it wasn't theirs in the first place, and letting it to the fair each Stocks Day and keeping the rent. I bet Sir Ralph could claim all that money back. Nice little packet for him and no mistake, don't you think, Mr Charter-Plackett?'

'I don't think the rent from the fair would amount to enough for Sir Ralph to make a fuss about. Linda, can it keep, if it's top secret this isn't the place to be discussing it, is it?'

'Sorry Mr Charter-Plackett, I'll tell you the rest in my coffee break.'

Jimbo didn't have to wait until Linda's coffee break, because the very next customer who came in launched herself into the latest piece of gossip.

'Have you heard, Mr Charter-Plackett, that the council's building a hundred houses on the spare land when the chapel goes? Doesn't seem right, does it?'

'A hundred houses? They couldn't surely, it isn't big enough.'

'Well, that's what the council's going to do. Scandalous isn't it? Downright scandalous. I bet Sir Ralph won't like that at all. He'll want to keep the village like it's always been. We'll have to get a campaign up. It'll carry some weight though with a titled person leading it.'

'Where did you learn this?'

'From my niece, she works in the council offices doing the tea trolley. She hears everything that goes on there, believe me. And there's certainly plenty going on. The management there 'as wild parties, you'd be surprised at what they get up to. Oh, yes! Disgusting! They do say' – Jimbo's customer leant closer and whispered in his ear – 'they do wife swapping at their parties!'

Jimbo got a piece of paper and a pen from behind the till and said, 'Give me the telephone number and I'll see if Harriet and I can get invited.'

For a moment the customer took him seriously and then realised his eyes were twinkling. 'Oh, Mr Charter-Plackett, you nearly caught me there. Anyway I'll keep you informed.' She winked at him, picked up her groceries and left.

Jimbo contemplated the idea of one hundred houses and what it would do to his turnover. Magnificent. A completely magnificent idea. Still, if the land belonged to Ralph like Linda said it did, there wouldn't be a hope in hell of houses being built on it. Someone had got their wires crossed. Still, a hundred houses. With all those new customers the Store would thrive, with his outsider catering flourishing like it always did, the mail-order business coming along nicely under his mother-in-law's eagle eye and with the contract for the catering at the Big House already in the bag, they'd really be in the money. Jimbo rubbed his hands together at the prospect.

'And why is the proprietor of the Turnham Malpas Village Store rubbing his hands with such glee?'

Jimbo swung round and saw Harriet. 'Darling! Where did you spring from?'

'The mail-order office, Mother needed an extra pair of hands so I've been helping in there.'

'I did say you musn't, not in your condition as they say.'

'I'm as fit as a flea, Jimbo, and with three months to go I've still got some energy to spare.'

'Don't overdo it, darling, please.'

'I won't. So why were you rubbing your hands?'

Jimbo took her arm and led her into the store room. With Harriet seated on his stool, he told her the morning's gossip. 'So we shan't say a word. I don't care who the hell builds the houses, but they will mean a big increase in business for us.'

'It will take years, absolutely years, to get them built. By the time they've had protests and inquiries and things we could be looking at three or four years before anyone even puts a spade in.'

'I rather think they'll need more than a spade to dig the foundations for a hundred houses.'

'We'll see, we'll see. Ralph and Muriel will be opposed so we shall have to tread carefully.'

'Exactly. We shan't come down on either side, we shall remain aloof from the hurly-burly.'

'Some hope, some hope.'

5

The following Saturday night Willie and his Sylvia went by arrangement to have a drink in The Royal Oak with Pat and Jimmy, Pat's neighbour Vera, and Vera's husband Don. They would have infinitely preferred to have stayed at home and watched a video they'd borrowed from Jimbo's newly installed video lending library, but Jimmy had been insistent.

'Vera and Don were away last week at that funeral so they didn't 'ave a chance to have a drink to celebrate you getting wed and me winning the pools. So you'll 'ave to come, yer both getting into right homebirds and it won't do.'

'All right, all right,' Willie reluctantly agreed. 'Seven o'clock sharp then.'

'Well, that's good and dress up a bit and I'll take you for another meal in Bryn's dining room, I'm getting a right liking for it. So don't eat before yer come out.'

Willie passed the message on to his Sylvia and they both made a special effort to look smart. About five minutes to seven they entered the bar. There were scarcely any customers and their host held centre stage. Sylvia gasped when she saw Jimmy standing at the bar. It was his feet she noticed first – instead of his old calf-high, well worn dirty boots, he was wearing brand new black shoes. He stood with one well-shod foot resting on the brass rail below the front of the bar, an elbow propped on the bar counter.

'Why Jimmy, you do look smart. Look at him, just look at him Willie.'

The transformation didn't stop at his feet. Gone was the foul old flat cap, gone the old green jacket and the innumerable jumpers he always wore. They had been replaced by a smart dark grey suit, white shirt and a dazzling tie. He was clean-shaven and his hair well barbered. His moustache, which had been a village institution from time immemorial, had gone too; the newly shaved top lip looked pale in contrast to his narrow well tanned face.

Willie nudged his elbow. 'I can't believe the change, Jimmy, you're almost unrecognisable.'

'Shows what money can do!'

Sylvia felt the quality of the material the suit was made of. 'It certainly does. You look a right catch and not half.'

'Thanks, Sylvia, thanks. I'm glad yer like me like this. Never had money to spare before, yer see.'

'Well, go on,' Willie said. 'Tell us 'ow much yer've got.'

'Seeing as I've known you since we were in nappies, I'll tell yer, but I don't want them busybodies to know.' He nodded his head in the direction of the three other customers. 'Don't want 'em coming begging, yer see.' He mouthed rather than spoke the words. 'Fifty thousand one hundred pounds and seventy-five pence.'

Willie whistled in amazement. 'I don't believe it. I never thought you'd do it, yer know. It's nothing short of a miracle.'

'That's 'ow I see it. A miracle no less.' Sylvia reached up and gave him a kiss. 'I'm really, really glad for you Jimmy. Make the best of it, don't fritter it away.'

Jimmy tapped the side of his long thin nose and said, 'I 'ave mi plans and not 'alf. Wait and see.'

Vera and Don Wright and Pat arrived to join the party. They chose a bigger table than usual and all sat down. Willie made a suggestion. 'Hadn't we better organise a table in the dining room? It might get full with it being Saturday.'

Jimmy assured him that he'd already taken care of that. Vera was pressing him to reveal how much he'd actually won when the door opened and in came the rector. Peter, his head bent because of his height, stood in the entrance looking at the occupants of the bar. He looked anxious and out of breath.

Willie put down his glass, wiped his mouth with the back of his hand and called out, 'Good evening, sir, are you looking for me?'

'Ah, there you are. Good evening everybody. Willie, I'm afraid we have an emergency on our hands. You'll have to come, there's been a break-in at the church hall.'

'Oh no! Have they taken much?'

'Well, I thought you'd know that better than me. Can you come right away? Sorry to break up the party.'

Don said, 'We'll all come, Rector, they might still be in there.'

'Right, thanks, that's a good idea.' The men stood up to go, and Pat and

Vera with them. Willie suggested that the womenfolk shouldn't come, it wasn't safe, but Pat said, 'And miss all the fun? Not likely. Come on, Sylvia, bring yer umbrella, we might need it.'

The six of them hurried down Stocks Row, round into Church Lane, through the big double gates and up the drive to the church hall. It was in darkness. Willie went first and tried the main door. 'It's open!' He felt on the wall for the main switches and flooded the hall with light. It was completely empty.

A lone trumpet burst into 'Here comes the bride' and from nowhere came accompanying voices lustily singing the words. When the song was finished the doors from the kitchen and the small hall opened, and out into the main hall poured almost every friend and neighbour and child Willie knew. Sylvia blushed bright red with sheer delight. They all surged forward to shake their hands and wish them happiness.

'Weren't at the wedding so we had to celebrate somehow!'

'Bet that's surprised you, hasn't it?'

'It was all Dr Harris's idea, wasn't it, Rector?'

Peter laughed and nodded. 'Yes, you're right, it was.'

In the midst of the excitement Willie turned to Peter and said, 'Now, sir, that was a trick you played on us and not half. Hall broken into, what a tale!'

'It was true, it was true. All these people broke in, I had to come and tell you, didn't I?' Peter smiled at him, enjoying the joke.

'Is Dr Harris here?'

'She's at home with the twins, I'm going back shortly and she's going to come over to join you.'

Jimbo Charter-Plackett climbed on a chair. 'Ladies and gentlemen, before we go any further with tonight's proceedings, my daughter Flick has something to say. Come along, Flick, where are you?'

There was a moment's hesitation and then Flick appeared in the kitchen doorway, carrying a huge bouquet. Everyone smiled. They all loved Flick; they loved her happy personality, they loved her smile, they loved to hear her chatter. They awaited her speech.

She curtsied and then said, 'Mr and Mrs Biggs, these flowers are for you from all of us, to say how pleased we are that you have got married, and we all hope you will be very happy.' She whispered confidentially, 'And there's lots of presents in the small hall, you wouldn't believe how many!' She curtsied again and gave Sylvia the flowers. They all laughed and clapped and Sylvia bent down and gave her a hug and a kiss.

Jimbo climbed back up on the chair. 'Right, ladies and gentlemen, quiet please. Quiet please. Now's the time to let the bridal couple lead the way to the buffet. A right royal buffet we've laid on for a right royal pair. Forward march!'

They all held back while the bride and groom reached the front of the crowd and then followed them into the small hall. From end to end of the far wall was a table laden with food and in the centre of the table was a beautiful two-tier wedding cake, with a small silver vase of flowers decorating the top. The flowers were deep pink and around the edges of the cake were icing sugar-flowers in varying shades of pink complementing the real flowers on the top. Swirls of silvery white and pink ribbons decorated the table around the cake. On another table presents were piled high, awaiting presentation. Sylvia burst into tears of joy. Willie lent her his handkerchief, and then put his arm around her shoulders, his face alight with pleasure.

'Speech, speech,' the guests demanded.

'My Sylvia and I would like to thank you for this lovely party, it must be the best kept secret in Turnham Malpas for centuries, we'd absolutely no idea.' Someone at the back shouted. 'We'll go some to keep a secret better than you, Willie Biggs! Marrying without any of us knowing.' Everyone laughed. Willie acknowledged the quip and continued his speech. 'And as for you, Jimmy, you conniving old so-and-so, I'll see you later. Thank you again and again, we shan't forget all your kindness in planning this. We're both very happy, we hope you all will be too. Here's to a wonderful evening!'

After everyone had finished eating, and Willie and his Sylvia had cut the cake, Venetia Mayer, who had disappeared moments before, struggled in through the doorway with a gigantic box, wrapped in wedding gift paper. Everyone crowded round. What on earth could it possibly be? Trust Venetia to come up with something dramatic! Jeremy refused to tell. 'Wait and see,' he said, 'wait and see.'

Sylvia began tearing off the paper. She opened the lid and out floated three huge heart-shaped silver hydrogen-filled balloons. They all craned their necks to see what was written on them. One said 'Congratulations', the second one said 'Willie loves Sylvia' and the third 'Sylvia loves Willie'. Willie tied them by their ribbons to a chair and they all cried 'Give the bride a kiss.' So he did. Then Jimbo put on a tape and they began dancing. Willie and Sylvia started off the first dance all by themselves. Willie wasn't up to dancing, he hadn't done it since he used to go to the Palais in Culworth as a young man, but he made a brave show for his Sylvia's sake.

Caroline let herself into the Rectory at eleven o'clock that night. She called upstairs, 'Peter, I'm making myself a cup of tea, would you like one?'

'Yes, please, darling. Had a good time?'

'Excellent, I'm exhausted! Won't be long. Twins OK?'

'Both fine, not a peep out of them all evening.'

Caroline took the tea upstairs and put it on Peter's side table. She looked in on the twins and tucked the blankets more closely around Beth, who had a habit of kicking off all her bedclothes and waking chilled to the bone in the middle of the night. Alex lay on his back, a hand either side of his head, sleeping deeply, his likeness to Peter increased as the weeks went by. There was no hiding the fact he was his. None at all.

Caroline got ready for bed and climbed in beside Peter, who was sitting up reading. He asked how she'd enjoyed the evening.

'Wonderful. I'm so glad the idea came to me. We couldn't let them get married so secretly and the village not have a chance to celebrate, could we? I have to admit to wondering if they would both cope, but they did. We've had a fantastic night. Jimbo's a brilliant master of ceremonies, he gets everyone going, however resistant they are. We've danced and sung and played games, but I suddenly went dreadfully tired so I've left them all to it. Jimbo has put Scottish dancing tapes on now and Alan Crimble, who says he's part Scottish, is teaching them the dances. They were all laughing so much I don't think they'll learn anything at all. What a night!'

'It was the most superbly kept secret, darling. Here's your tea.'

'Thanks, it was, wasn't it? I don't know how we managed it, knowing the propensity of this village for gossip! Whilst I was at the party I had a talk with Pat Duckett. I'm going to ask Jimbo if he can find some more work for her with his outside catering. She is very strapped for cash, she was telling me at the party how hard things are for her.'

'I thought you went to enjoy yourself, not be a rector's wife.'

'Can't help it, people will confide in me. I must have that kind of face.'

'Well, I love that kind of face. Jimbo, Ralph and I are going up to the Big House on Monday for our appointment with the renowned Craddock Fitch. I feel Jimbo is slightly less enthusiastic than he was, but Ralph is furious about the whole affair.'

'Did he know anything about them hiding the silver?'

'Nothing at all, he was away at prep school when it all happened. In any case they wouldn't tell a little boy, would they? It would have been too much to expect him to keep it secret. He's determined, however, to get it all back where it belongs, even if we decide to sell some of it to help with the repairs to the tower. I can see we could be in for some fireworks. I really don't see how Fitch can possibly lay claim to it at all. He must be off his trolley.'

'Perhaps power has gone to his head. That tea was lovely, I felt so dry.'

'Let me take your cup. Happy?'

'Oh yes, in paradise actually.' Caroline snuggled down under the duvet. Peter lay down beside her. He took hold of her hand and held it to his lips and kissed it.

'I'm glad. So am I. God bless. Goodnight.'

6

Jeremy Mayer greeted them at the door when they arrived.

'Welcome to Turnham House, Rector.' He shook hands with Peter. 'And welcome to you, Sir Ralph, pleasure to see you. Hello, Jimbo, how goes it?' Jimbo observed that Jeremy had put on even more weight since his life had become secure. His podgy hand clasped Jimbo's in a damp grip and Jimbo unobtrusively returned his now clammy hand to his trouser pocket and rubbed his palm on his handkerchief.

'Good morning, Jeremy,' Peter said. 'Long time no see.'

'Been busy, Rector, you know how it is, new project, new fields to conquer, all takes time. Would you like to come this way? Ah! Here's Venetia. Looking delightful as always.'

Venetia, looking very trim, was wearing a white plush tracksuit decorated with a purple yoke and a purple stripe down the legs of the trousers. Her excessively black hair was held away from her face by a white towelling band. Her tan, assisted by heavy makeup, was as deep as it could be. She greeted them as though they'd just returned from a hazardous expedition to some distant shore.

'How wonderful to see you, Peter!' She offered her cheek for a kiss. He bent his head and dutifully complied. Jimbo she greeted by flinging her arms around him and kissing him soundly on both cheeks.'Jimbo! you darling. I must remember to visit the Store more often, I'd forgotten what a lovely man you are.' She turned to Ralph and coyly offered him her hand to shake. 'Sir Ralph, what a pleasure it must be for you to come back to your old home! You'll find it vastly changed. But much improved. So warm now with the new central heating! When you've finished your appointment, come and find me and I'll show you round, then you can see the improvements for yourself. Jeremy, my love, will you show everyone to Cra . . . Mr Fitch's office?'

'Just in the process, dear girl.' He waddled off in front of them towards what Ralph remembered as the library. To look at him no one would have guessed how deeply he was suffering. Standing in the hall he'd seen ghosts from his childhood. The butler crossing the hall with his father's post on the silver salver. His nanny holding his hand and walking with him to the front door to take him for his walk. His mother, smelling of lavender, pulling on her gloves waiting to go to church with Father. Himself as a small boy holding her hymn book, dressed in his best which he hated. His heart bled at Venetia's words. Improvements indeed! Desecration would be nearer the mark. He was damned if this interloper was getting away with selling the church silver, if indeed that was what it was. Vulgar upstart, coming into his home and throwing his weight about. Damned if he'd let it happen. As he entered the library he stiffened his spine and prepared to meet the enemy.

His enemy was a slightly-built man of medium height, pale of face, looking to be in his middle to late sixties. The fierce, belligerent expression in his intense blue eyes matched well with the slightly sneering smile on his lips. His thick bushy hair was silver-white, his skin the smooth texture of a much younger man. He rose to his feet as they entered.

Jeremy introduced them. Craddock Fitch shook hands with them in turn, giving them an effusive welcome which didn't quite reach his eyes. 'Mayer, find chairs for my guests, please.'

Jeremy pulled chairs out and made a half circle with them in front of Mr Fitch's desk, and then stood to one side. Mr Fitch inquired if they would like coffee. They all three refused.

'Well, then, Charter-Plackett?' Mr Fitch looked across the library and saw Jeremy standing by the window. 'I'll call you up if I need you, Mayer.' Crestfallen, Jeremy quietly left the room. Ralph gritted his teeth. Peter pondered on the reasons for Mr Fitch's aggressiveness.

'Yes?' Mr Fitch looked at each of them in turn.

Jimbo nodded to Ralph, who cleared his throat. 'It has been brought to our attention that in the course of your alterations to this house, you have found certain articles of silver which, upon inspection, have proved to belong to the village church.'

'Have I?'

Ralph said an emphatic 'Yes.'

'And if I have, what then?'

'They belong to the church not to the house. We have concluded they were brought here secretly during the Second World War when England was threatened with invasion, namely June 1940. Obviously the intention was to return them to the church when hostilities ceased. In fact all three of the men we assume were concerned, including my father, died before the end of the war, so no attempt was made to recover the silver, because no one else knew where they had hidden it. It should be returned forthwith.'

'On whose authority?'

'The authority of all right-minded persons.'

'I bought this house, lock, stock and barrel. The roof in need of repair is mine, the grounds in need of attention are mine, the walls, the stables, the garden, anything and everything in it is mine. I learned when I had it surveyed that there was dry rot in the east wing, but I didn't say that bit isn't mine, I took it all as it was. Therefore the silver is mine and mine alone. Good morning, gentlemen.' He rose to his feet, a slight smile at one corner of his mouth. His eyes flicked from one to the other, assessing their reaction, but not really caring.

Peter quietly requested an opportunity to see what had been found.

'In deference to your clerical collar, yes, certainly you may. Best take your chance, I'm taking it up to town in the next few days, you won't be able to see it again. Charter-Plackett, I need a word. Do you wish to see my treasure?'

'No, I'll leave that to Sir Ralph and the rector,' Jimbo replied, not admitting he had already seen it. Mr Fitch flicked a switch on his intercom and asked Fenella to come. She led Ralph and Peter away, glancing back to wink at Jimbo while Mr Fitch answered his telephone.

Peter was deeply moved when he saw what Fenella brought out of the safe. He reverently cradled each piece in his hands one by one. 'Why, they're wonderful, just unbelievable. Worthy of a cathedral. So totally splendid. To think no one has been able to enjoy these for over fifty years. It's simply not right.'

Fenella, embarrassed by his obvious admiration for the pieces, observed, 'They are very beautiful aren't they? You must be very sorry they're being taken away.'

Ralph replied before Peter could answer. 'Not if I can damn well help it.' He glowered at Peter. 'If you won't put up a fight for these, then I shall. I don't remember any of this being in the church, but look at the engravings; this is church property and it's a crime to sell it off.' He watched Peter tenderly tracing the decoration on one of the large altar dishes. Gruffly Ralph said, 'Yes, certainly, this is one he isn't going to win.'

One by one the pieces of silver were carefully rewrapped and returned to the safe. Peter stood up and asked Ralph what he intended to do.

'I shall tell him that he has exactly three days to come to his senses and then I shall act. I shall begin by speaking to the son of a friend of mine. He's an investigative journalist and will be salivating, positively salivating, at the opportunity to dig up dirt about a big City name. Oh, yes, indeed. I shall give it all I've got.' He turned on his heel, and left the office.

Fenella looked alarmed. 'He's not going to challenge Mr Fitch, is he?'

'I rather think he is.'

'I'd stay here then, Rector.'

'I'd better go support him.'

Ralph had walked into Mr Fitch's office without knocking. Jimbo and he were leaning over some papers on his desk, comparing notes. Mr Fitch looked up when he stormed in. 'I beg your pardon, do you have something else to say?'

Ralph went to lean his hands on the desk. They confronted each other like two adversaries in a Roman arena. 'Indeed I do. If you take that silver and sell it, it will be blatant, absolutely blatant, theft and I shall make certain that a highly reputable broadsheet gets all the facts. For heavens sake, man, see sense. Don't make me do it. It's not in my nature, but I *will* act if you persist with the sale. Three clear days,' he held up three fingers, 'three days only, you have. If the silver is not back in the rector's possession by midnight on Thursday, first thing Friday morning I shall ring my contact.'

'I see. The church will pay me its market value, will it?'

Ralph snorted angrily and retorted, 'Don't think you can ride rough-shod over me. You've met your match in me, Mr Craddock Fitch. Heed what I say.'

He strode from the office, with Peter in his wake. Jimbo folded up the computer print-outs they'd been looking at and put them in an envelope. As Ralph left, Jimbo said, 'You'd be well advised to listen, he's no fool.'

'He's not coming here and flexing his moribund aristocratic muscle at me. Those days are gone, and gone for good, otherwise *he'd* be standing here in this library instead of *me*.'

Jimbo shook his head sorrowfully. 'Don't make the mistake of under-estimating him. He has connections in all the right places, believe me. Unfortunately for you the whole village will be behind him and that, believe it or not, is a power to be reckoned with. Make no mistake.' Jimbo turned to go. 'I'll study these at home. Let you have my opinion as soon as. Good morning.'

Peter and Ralph were waiting in Ralph's Mercedes for Jimbo to emerge. Ralph was gripping the steering wheel so tightly his knuckles were white. Peter was silent. Jimbo got into the rear seat and said after a moment, 'Thank you, Ralph, for being so forthright. It needed to be said.' After a pause he inquired, 'Do you really have a good contact in Fleet Street?'

'Of course. I'll finish him over this. If you have his ear, tell him so.'

'I've told him already.'

'Good. We'll have to hope he has the brains to do the right thing. Otherwise Fitch plc will be kaput.' He revved up the engine, crashed the gears, and they shot down the drive at top speed. Jimbo and Peter both wished they'd elected to walk home.

Jimbo, still pale around the gills after his nightmare drive back to the village, changed in the store room into his butcher's apron, bow tie and boater, grabbed a quick coffee from his customers' coffee machine, and took over behind the till.

For a Monday morning the Store was quite busy. There was a knot of people behind the cereal shelves arguing fiercely. A hold had been put on their shopping and they stood, wirebaskets on their arms, heads nodding, fingers wagging, voices lowered. Jimbo waited patiently; he knew he'd find out shortly what it was all about. They dispersed, finished collecting their groceries, and then came to the till.

Their spokeswoman plunged straight to the point. 'Now Mr Charter-Plackett, there's a tale going round the village that old Fitch up at the Big House has decided he's selling what's rightly ours. Is it true? We understand you've been up there today with the rector and Sir Ralph.'

Faced with such an outright question Jimbo had no alternative but to acknowledge the truth. 'How did you find out?'

'Well, one way and another we've all got relatives or neighbours who work up there. It doesn't take long for news to spread. My Barry was the joiner he asked to take down the panelling. My Barry bloody well knew what had been found, because he dragged the boxes out. What he didn't know was what the intentions were of that high and mighty City gent. 'Cept that's not what our Barry calls him.' She grinned and nudged the woman standing next to her.

'Well, yes, it is true. Sir Ralph has given him an ultimatum.'

'Ultimatum?'

'Yes, an ultimatum. It has all to be in the rector's hands by midnight Thursday or else.'

'Or else what?' a voice at the back of the crowd shouted.

'Or else Sir Ralph is telling the newspapers.'

'Serves him right. Stealing from the church. It's a wonder the heavens don't open and he gets struck by lightning. We all know what happened the last time someone stole from the church. Divine retribution, that's what.'

Jimbo was hesitant about blaming God. 'Steady, I say, steady, I don't think it works like that.'

'I may not go to church like you do, but I do know what's what. The rector, God love 'im, would find an excuse for the devil let alone that old Fitch plc, but we know. Oh, yes, we know what's right.'

'Remember!' said Barry's mother. 'Thursday night's the deadline. Pressure will be brought to bear! All agreed?' There was a general nodding of heads. 'How much is my shopping then, Mr Charter-Plackett? Ten pounds forty-two?' 'Ave you added that up right?' She peered angrily at her till receipt. 'Oh, yes, I'd forgotten about the chops.' As Barry's mother turned to leave she punched the air with her fist and said, 'Remember everybody! It's time for action!' She left the Store with her rallying cry echoing in their ears.

7

On the Wednesday morning, just as Linda was about to take her coffee break, an exact fifteen minutes which was not permitted under any circumstances to be shortened by the mistimed arrival of a customer for the post office, Venetia arrived in the Store.

She was shivering. 'Good morning, Venetia!' Jimbo raised his boater. Harriet, who'd been helping her mother in the mail order office, appeared in case Jimbo needed a helping hand in Linda's absence.

Having come to terms at last with Venetia's constant pursuit of any suitable male, including Jimbo, Harriet said cheerfully, 'Hello, Venetia, how's tricks?'

'How's tricks? Oh, golly, it's so beautifully warm in here. Can I stand by the radiator for a while?'

'You're welcome. What's more I'll bring you a coffee. It's freshly made.' Harriet busied herself at the coffee machine. 'Sugar? Milk? Cream?'

'Oh no, black please, no sugar. Got to think of my figure.'

'Well, your thoughtfulness certainly pays dividends.'

'Thanks Jimbo, how kind you are.'

Harriet handed the coffee to her and asked, 'Are we permitted to ask why you are so cold?'

'Something horrendous has happened to the central heating at Turnham House. The electrician says there's an essential part gone wrong called a gizmo or something, and they're in short supply and it could be a week before he gets the part. Jeremy's going spare. He's offered to drive anywhere, however far away, to get it, but the electrician says even the dealers have none in stock and it's to come from Germany. How we shall exist for a whole week without heating I don't know. That huge open fireplace in the hall is brilliant, but it only heats the hall and staircase, nowhere else. Added to which we had a complete blackout of the lights and power last night, so we were groping around with candles for nearly an hour. Crad . . . Mr Fitch is furious.'

She shivered as she drank her coffee. 'Oh! That's wonderful. Come to say the cook's had to go home with the 'flu, Jimbo. They can manage lunch, but Jeremy wants you to do something about dinner and pronto. I volunteered to come down to tell you, because the phones have been on the blink too. It's like a total shut-down. Fenella found the fax hadn't been on all night and she didn't realise it until just now, and she's lost a load of data off the computer. She's tearing her hair out by the handful. Believe you me, we were better off with pens and paper and a messenger boy on a bike.'

Harriet, knowing Jimbo as she did, suspected his complete disregard of Venetia's news meant he knew more than he was saying. She filled the silence by saying, 'Mr Fitch will be none too pleased.'

'No, he's not. In fact he's fuming. I've been trying to calm him down.' She fluffed her hair with her spare hand and adjusted her headband. 'He's leaving after lunch and says he wants everything in working order before he comes back on Thursday night or heads will roll.'

Jimbo said quickly. 'Is he taking the church silver with him?'

Momentarily Venetia looked guilty, rapidly changing her expression when she saw Jimbo scrutinising her face. 'Oh! I don't know, that's nothing to do with me. I'm not in the office.'

'You may not be in the office, but you do have his ear. Come on, it's vital I know. You owe me.'

She shuffled her feet a little, finished the last of the coffee and said reluctantly, 'He's taking it away on Friday when he goes back to London. That's privileged information.'

'Thanks. I'll make sure there's a replacement cook there by early afternoon. I've a few numbers I can ring. Will you excuse me?' He wandered off into the back.

Harriet served some customers and left Venetia keeping warm by the radiator. Several people stopped to have a word with her, and commiserated about the heating. Harriet had never heard them be so sympathetic to Venetia before. She thought she detected a hint of mockery in their voices.

'You never can tell with all these new-fangled machines, can you? Always going wrong just when there's a cold snap.'

'Fancy, having to come from Germany. Could be a fortnight, even. Well, I never. What bad luck.'

'Let's hope that electrician knows what he's talking about.'

When there was a lull and Harriet had a moment to spare, Venetia said she must be pleased that houses were going to be built on the spare land. 'Be a big increase in trade for you, won't it?'

'Well, I'm being very philosophical about it. It could all be rumour, you know. These things take so long and there's bound to be a lot of opposition.'

'I expect so. Well, I must be off, I've an executive trim class in half an hour. Do you really think it will take a week for the heating to come back on?'

'I've no idea, I really haven't. Come down to get warm any time won't you?'

Linda came back and Harriet went to find Jimbo. 'You were remarkably quiet when Venetia was telling us about the electricity cut. Do you know something I don't know?'

Jimbo took off his boater and stroked his few remaining strands of hair into place. 'Look, I could be completely wrong. It could all be coincidence, but I do know the village are planning a pressure campaign to force Fitch to give the silver back. They really mean business. So I think they've engineered it all deliberately.'

'Help! I didn't think they would dare go to such lengths. I mean, he's not a man to be trifled with is he?'

'No, and I've a feeling this is only the beginning.'

'It'll be effigies and pin sticking next.'

'Now Harriet, you're letting your imagination run away with you. Don't let's get ridiculous.' He placed his hands on her shoulders and kissed her soundly. 'Expectant mothers should be going home for lunch. Off you go.'

'Right then, I'll waddle off.'

Jimbo went up to the Big House in the early afternoon; he'd tried telephoning but couldn't get through, and he began to worry that his meticulous planning had gone awry. As he drove through the gates, he realised there was something fastened to each of the stone pillars either side of the drive. He braked rapidly, reversed out into the road again and saw two placards with thick red lettering on them. One said 'PUBLIC ENEMY NUMBER ONE', the other 'SNAKE IN THE GRASS'. He chuckled and then had a struggle with his conscience; after all he had a lot to lose. Should he take them down? But Jimbo decided that as Fitch had already left they would do no harm, and continued on his way up to the house.

But Mr Fitch hadn't left, he was standing outside the front door. There were several men with him, all in smart business suits. They were talking animatedly, with Mr Fitch the centre of it all. Jimbo got out and out of courtesy went to pass the time of day.

'Good afternoon, Charter-Plackett.'

'Good afternoon, just come to check my new cook's arrived and everything is shipshape.'

'Shipshape! Will anything be shipshape ever again? Damnation! The place is cursed.'

'Cursed?'

Mr Fitch almost exploding with annoyance, turned on his heel and disappeared inside the house. Jimbo raised his eyebrows questioningly at one of the young men.

'Wanted to leave straight after lunch but all his tyres are flat.' The young man had difficulty in restraining the smile which had crept to the corners of his mouth.

'Well, couldn't he borrow someone else's?'

'No one but him has a Rolls, and he doesn't want to travel in anything less. He's waiting for the odd job chappie to pump them up again with his foot pump. But it's taking a long time.'

'Ah! Right!' Jimbo nodded to them all and strode into the house. It was cold. Fenella was wearing her coat. 'Mr Charter-Pla . . .'

'Stop!'

'Jimbo, then, we're so cold. You can't repair boilers can you?'

'I have many, many valuable attributes, but repairing boilers is not one of them.'

'I bet you have! You'll have to tell me about them sometime! Have you come to see Mr Fitch? You'd better not have.'

'No, just come to check the kitchen's firing on all cylinders.'

'It isn't, there's a dispute about the new cook and they're all thinking of downing tools.'

'They'd better not.' He stormed through the green baize door into the kitchen. His staff were all clustered round the new cook and were in the process of voting on a decision.

'All those in favour then!' Using all his powers of persuasion he told them that as Mr Fitch was leaving, the only ones who would suffer from their downing tools were the trainees, so there was nothing to be gained. Added to which he wouldn't pay any one of them a single penny for hours not worked. They agreed not to strike. They were obviously doing it on purpose, but their faces were poker straight and none broke ranks and confessed it was all part of a campaign. He gave them one of his renowned pep talks, a combination of underlying threat mixed with morale-boosting statements about the valuable service they were giving, about image and confidence, about loyalty and pride, about the importance of the role each of them played, they weren't simply cogs in a machine et cetera. By the time he'd finished he seriously considered offering his services as guest lecturer at the house. He came out and saw Mr Fitch leave in his Rolls, his chauffeur speeding the car away in a flurry of scattered gravel. Oh God! The placards. He'd see the placards. Too late now.

By Thursday morning Peter had to admit to himself that he coveted the silver in Mr Fitch's safe. Each time he looked at the altar he could imagine how beautiful it would look on display there. He knew exactly where he would stand that huge candlestick, right there, no a little over to one side nearer the choir stalls, no would it . . . He stopped himself in his tracks. What was he doing? Expending energy on mere trivialities; it mattered not one jot how beautiful the church looked – well it did, but not to that extent. It was all very unedifying. What mattered most was the souls of his congregation. That was what should be at the forefront of his mind, not moaning about how to improve the appearance of the church for the greater glory of his ego. He felt ashamed of himself, and tried Caroline's patience by discussing the problem ceaselessly in the kitchen after breakfast. She took a much more commonsense approach.

'For heaven's sake don't torture yourself about it. The man is stealing. Full stop. He knows he is, we know he is, and it has to be stopped. When we get it back, *then* the decision can be taken as to whether or not it is sold or we keep it. The responsibility of keeping it safe is mind boggling, but there you are. Now, Alex is waiting for you to play football and Beth wants to play too, and she has a doll which needs mending, so please, darling, apply your mind to that and stop fretting.'

'What shall I do if he doesn't bring it back?'

'Report him to the police. At five minutes past midnight. Off you go, Sylvia and I have work to do and you're cluttering the place up with your moral dilemmas.'

The telephone rang in the Rectory at half past eight that night. Peter answered it.

'Good evening. Turnham Malpas Rectory. Peter Harris speaking.'

'Fitch. Craddock Fitch. Can you come to Turnham House?'

'Yes, I can.'

'Now?'

'Yes.'

'Thank you. Come straight in. I'll be in the library.'

On his way up the drive in the dark, Peter's way was barred by the estate Land Rover parked on the road. He got out. In the headlights he could see

Jeremy and two men, whom Peter recognised as village residents, struggling with what appeared to be a body hanging from a low branch of a tree growing about six feet from the edge of the drive.

One of the men touched his cap and grinned saying, 'Good evening, Rector. Just busy moving this. We'll be out of your way in a minute. Shan't be long.'

Jeremy, through tight lips, said, 'I'll get the damned fools who did this, and when I get my hands on 'em I'll throttle 'em.'

Peter peered at the body. It was dangling from a rope. Its head, topped by what appeared to be a mophead sprayed with silver paint, hung forward, the rope around the neck. A navy suit jacket covered the well stuffed rag body, and stabbed straight through where its heart would be were two thick, silver-coloured knitting needles. From its neck hung a placard with two words written on it: 'FITCH! THIEF!' A torch had been tied onto the branch so that the rag effigy was illuminated. It couldn't be missed by anyone going past. When they'd cut it down and taken the torch off the branch, they stuffed it in the Land Rover. The two men winked at Peter as they jumped in beside Jeremy, who sped off towards the house as fast as he could.

Mr Fitch was waiting in the library and offered Peter a drink, but he refused. Mr Fitch poured himself a whisky.

'Please, Rector, please sit down.' Mr Fitch sat in his desk chair. 'I suppose you saw my effigy?'

'I did.'

'Since Tuesday it has been mayhem here.'

'I did hear something about you having problems.'

'Indeed.' He paused to sip his whisky. 'I am unaccustomed to not getting my own way. But it would appear I am thwarted this time by a pack of country yokels not worth a ha'penny.' He snapped his fingers in a derisive gesture. 'If I sold the silver, the money I would get would be a drop in the ocean. That's not the point. It's the principle. What I buy is mine, or rather my company's.'

'You may snap your fingers at them, but to me they are my prime care. They are good, honest, hard-working people who instinctively know, without really knowing how, what is right. I owe them a lot. They have supported me through a very difficult time in my life, not saying anything but just being there, shoulder to shoulder like some invisible army. If you do what you intend, nothing will go right here. They'll see it doesn't.'

'I can bus people in.'

'Of course, there are ways round it. But sell what they feel is rightly theirs and somehow they will get their revenge. They will never accept you. Never.'

'You talk as if they are one body.'

'They are in a kind of a way. They and generations before them have lived here in this place. It is theirs. Not yours. Not mine. Theirs. We're here on sufferance till we've lived here fifty years and more. Imagine, if you can, the feeling of taking communion from a cup that has been used by one's ancestors for over two hundred years. Think of living in a cottage which was standing when the plague came. Worshipping in a church which has stood here for almost seven hundred years. What a sense of permanence. What a sense of history. What a sense of *belonging.* I feel deeply privileged to be allowed to be at the heart of these people.'

Mr Fitch swirled his whisky round his glass. He finished off the last drops and, resting his elbows on his desk, looked straight at Peter.

'What you're saying is if we are to keep going here, I've to kowtow to these yokels.'

'No, I am not saying that. I'm saying do what is right. If you kowtow, as you call it, it won't work. They are not fools and they'll know if they're being patronised.'

Mr Fitch pondered for a while, taking his time putting papers and files on his desk into neat straight lines. Peter watched his face and endeavoured to understand what he was thinking. Suddenly Mr Fitch appeared to make up his mind. He took some keys from his pocket. With a wry smile on his face he said, 'Then, my first step on this road to acceptance will be to return the church silver to its rightful place. Hopefully doing this will put an end to the chaos here. I don't mind admitting to you that effigy made me blanch when I saw it. Positively mediaeval!' Peter thought he saw him shudder.

Mr Fitch helped Peter stow the boxes in his estate car. He slammed down the door and turned to shake hands. 'I see you've got two safety seats in the back.'

'Yes, they're for my twins.'

'Lucky man. Goodnight.'

'Goodnight, and thank you.'

8

Dawn was just breaking when Malcolm the milkman brought his van to a standstill beside Jimmy's garden fence. 'Morning Mr Glover. You're up and about in good time. Not often I see you on the go so early nowadays.'

'No, well, I've got a project in 'and. Are yer wanting yer money?'

'If yer like, but it can wait till next week if yer busy.'

'I'll go inside and get it. I've turned over a new leaf since I 'ad that big win.'

'Are you still filling 'em in?'

'No, I'm not. I'm not greedy. 'Ang on.'

Malcolm waited while Jimmy went inside to get his money. Beside the fence was a big fourteen-pound hammer. Stacked neatly against the wall of the house were ready-made timber panels, which looked as though they would make a shed when put together.

After Jimmy had paid him, Malcolm couldn't resist asking what Jimmy's intentions were.

'Making a new chicken house.'

'But you've got one already.'

'I know I 'ave, but that's coming down and a new one, nearer the house, is going up.'

'I see. Why?'

'Wait and see.' Jimmy turned away and began work on the rough ground about twelve feet nearer the house than the old chicken run. Malcolm had to leave it at that, as Jimmy obviously had no intention of revealing what he had in mind.

Vera and Pat tolerated the hammering for most of the morning before coming out to protest.

Pat shouted across Vera's garden, 'Look, it's grand to see you working hard, but 'ow much longer is this banging going on for? My head's absolutely spinning.'

'And mine as well. What are yer doing, Jimmy?'

'You'll see, you'll see.'

'Making a new chicken run by the looks of it. What will yer do with the old one?'

'Knock it down.'

'Why?'

'Wait and see. Yer going to 'ave the surprise of your life shortly.'

'That'll be the day. Well, if yer won't tell us then, when this surprise appears I for one won't *be* surprised, I'll ignore it.'

'Do that then.'

'Winning that money 'as gone to your 'ead, Jimmy Glover, that's what.'

Flick Charter-Plackett stopped to have a word with him after lunch.

'Hello, Mr Glover. Will you sponsor me for Brownies? I've got my list here and a pen.' She held up a smart clipboard she'd purloined from Jimbo's office.

Jimmy leant on his fourteen-pound hammer, pushed his cap to the back of his head, and asked her what she would have to do for it.

'It's a sponsored silence. I've to promise not to say a word for a whole hour and then Brown Owl signs my sheet and I can collect the money.'

'You! Keep silent for one whole hour? You can't keep silent for one whole minute!'

'I can if I try. My Daddy gave me fifty pence for keeping quiet for one whole hour when we set off on our holidays. He said he needed peace and quiet to pull himself together after he'd struggled to organise us all. So Fergus and Finlay and me, we sat in the back of the car and never spoke for an hour. Mummy said it was like heaven. So I can do it.'

''Ow much 'as your Dad promised?'

'Well, he's promised five pence a minute, but that's because he thinks with all those girls there I won't manage it, but I shall. But you can give me one pence a minute if you like. That's what Mrs Wright next door has promised me.'

'If she's promised you one pence I'll give you two pence. 'Ave you asked Mrs Duckett?'

'I'm going there next, she wasn't in when I called before.'

'Put her name down and I'll give you two pence a minute for 'er and don't bother to ask 'er, right? And don't let on?'

Flick nodded sagely, 'Oh right, I understand. That's very thoughtful of you, Mr Glover.' After she'd carefully written in the names and amounts, Flick asked Jimmy what he was doing.

'Well now, Flick, it could be said that my moment has arrived. There comes a time in a man's life when he has to take steps and this is it for me.

I'm not telling you what I'm doing because it wouldn't be fair to expect you not to tell and I don't want anyone knowing. They've always thought of me as a daft useless old bugg— chap but I'm going to show 'em and not half.' He grinned at her, pulled one of her plaits in a friendly way and went back to work.

'I've never thought of you as a daft useless old what you said. I've always liked you, Mr Glover.'

'In that case then, we're friends for life.' He shook her hand and she left smiling.

By evening the entire village had grown weary of Jimmy's banging. Worse was to come, because before it got dark, he knocked down the old run with much gusto and then commenced on the fence. His chickens, objecting to their abrupt removal to new quarters, squabbled and squawked, adding to the general din.

No one except Georgie knew what he was up to and she refused to declare his secret. 'He told me the night he knew he'd won, and I've not told a soul, not even Bryn. It's Jimmy's secret and all will be revealed shortly. Now what can I get you?' Before the evening was over Georgie had made this declaration several times. Every customer who came in wanted to know; having put up with the din all day they felt justified in inquiring.

'Winning them pools 'as sent 'im crackers. That secretive he is.'

'He's always been secretive, it's nothing new. I remember when his wife died, what was 'er name? He spoke to nobody for months. Yer couldn't even say 'ow sorry yer were. 'E shut up like a clam.'

'How much money did he win, 'as he told you?'

'No, and not likely to, after I opposed him about his rabbit snaring.'

''Eard about these houses the council's building? Two hundred they say.'

'Two hundred? On that bit of land, never, they'll be like rabbit hutches.'

'I've heard they found out it's Sir Ralph's land and it's him building 'em.'

'Never! There's that many rumours flying about.'

'More houses, better chance of keeping the school open, more business for the Store and we need that, can't trip into Culworth every time yer need a packet of tea, could do us all good.'

'Well, I disagree. We don't want all them houses whosoever's building 'em. We got our own way about that church silver and we'll get our own way about this. Mark my words. With all our talk we still haven't found out what Jimmy Glover's doing. Whatever it is, he's either gone cracked or at last he's waking up to the twentieth century.'

*

It poured with rain the following day, so no one noticed Jimmy getting on the breakfast-time bus; they were all inside keeping dry.

Around five o'clock a bright red, brand new Vauxhall Cavalier rolled gently into the village. The driver signalled right to turn down Stocks Row in front of the weekenders' cottages, and then quickly signalled left and humped and bumped onto the bottom end of Jimmy's garden, now free of the fence and the chicken run.

It was Jimmy who got out of it. It was Jimmy who got out a handkerchief from his inside pocket and wiped his finger marks off the door. Though it was raining, it was Jimmy who strolled slowly round the car, relishing its colour and the complete and glorious newness of it. He got the key from the ignition and opened up the boot, but he had to close it quickly because of the rain wetting the inside of it. He got back in and, sitting in the driver's seat, he fiddled with the radio. Suddenly ferociously loud music hammered its way through the windows. Jimmy hurriedly twisted knobs and pressed buttons and the wipers began working furiously, the horn sounded, the lights went on and off until he got the noise under control. Before long, despite the rain, a small group of curious villagers collected. Georgie, tapped on the driver's window and signalled to him to wind it down.

'Beautiful, really beautiful. What a good choice.'

'Do yer think so? Isn't it great. I'm that pleased with it.'

'Since when did you learn to drive, Jimmy?' Vera asked.

'Learned years ago when I worked on Home Farm for a spell, and I've kept me licence up to date all these years.'

Pat said, 'We'd better warn everybody then if it's that long since yer drove! But Jimmy, what will yer use it for? It does seem an extravagance.' She trailed her fingers along its smooth glossy paintwork, enjoying the rich feel of it.

He got out of the car and locked the door. 'Central locking, yer notice. All mod cons.'

'Well?' asked Pat.

'I 'eard that one of the minicab drivers at Culworth Station had got finished, so I went there to see about it, and I've got miself 'is job. I start this week. This is an investment, this is.' He patted the car and then got out his handkerchief and wiped the bodywork in case he'd left any fingerprints.

'Well, I never. Jimmy Glover with a regular job. 'Ope you won't be coming 'ome from work at all hours and waking us up.'

'Yer never know.'

Saying that, he turned on his heel and walked into his house.

Pat swallowed hard. It was difficult not to be envious of such good luck. Ah well, egg and chips again tonight, and let Dean or Michelle grumble and they'd get the sharp edge of her tongue.

A week after starting work with the Culworth Cab Company Jimmy spent his only free evening in The Royal Oak. As he took his first frothing pint from Alan Crimble he said, ''Ow's that old banger of yours Alan? Still holding together is it?'

'Just about. Lady Luck doesn't come to us all yer know, Mr Glover. She's old, I know, but I love her. Living in this Godforsaken place, I 'ad to do something about my own transport. The last bus from Culworth gets here at six o'clock and what use is that to a young man with a sex life?'

Jimmy wiped the froth from his lips and said, 'Wouldn't know about sex life in Culworth. Didn't think they 'ad any.'

'Seeing as you're doing your taxi job now, I thought perhaps you'd know. That new night club, yer know in Deansgate, The Force . . .'

'That's a daft name and not 'alf.'

'Daft it might be, but it's great.'

'Anyways, last time I see'd your car, it struck me it needed servicing. Got to keep 'em well looked after, yer know.'

'Servicing? The money I get paid 'ere you couldn't afford to service a push bike.'

'Dangerous yer know, Alan, dangerous.' Jimmy took his pint to his favourite seat and settled down to wait for some company.

Pat Duckett came in. Jimmy watched her order her drink. Her shoulders were slumped and he noticed that the cheerful face she usually wore had been left at home.

'Hello, Jimmy.' Pat sat down on the settle opposite him and sipped her port and lemon.

'Need cheering up? Kids is it?'

'No, mi Dad. He's got his notice this morning. Job gone 'cos of council cuts and he has two months to get out of his house, goes with the job yer see. He's never saved any money so guess where he's coming?'

'I'm sorry, Pat.'

'Not as sorry as I am.' She dolefully took a sip of her drink and changed the subject. 'We've won over the church silver, haven't we? It was me found out, yer know.'

'Oh, right. Busybodying were yer?'

'No, just working up there, waitressing, the day they found it. Couldn't let 'im get away with that, could we? The old sod. Rich as hell and still wants to make more money. Couldn't 'elp but laugh about that dummy they hung up on that tree. 'Ope it frightened him to death. Did the trick, didn't it?'

'Do you know who did it?'

Pat looked him in the eye and said, 'No.'

'Yer lying, I can tell.'

'So?'

'You weren't the only one who brought pressure to bear.'

'Why, what did you do?'

'Just passing the bus stop when some of them students got off and asked me the way to Turnham House. All la di da they was. Plums in their mouths an' that. So I directed 'em down Royal Oak Road. I laughed all morning about that.'

'Jimmy! Yer never! That was a rotten trick, that was.'

'I know. It was the only thing I could think of to show my support.'

'Good for you.'

'Have they decided what to do with it?'

'Not that I know of, but then I'm not privy to what goes on at the church, am I?'

'No, yer not. I'll tell yer a tale, shall I? To cheer you up.'

'Go on then.'

'It's about mi job. I could work day and night seven days a week I could, yer know. The Cab Company's making money hand over fist. There's ten of us working from there, and the number of punters is amazing. All hours of the day and night.'

Pat leant forward and said they couldn't be respectable if they wanted a cab in the middle of the night. She said it hoping for some juicy story of night life in Culworth.

'There's lots o' folks needing taxis in the middle of the night. They come out of that night club, yer know that place in Deansgate, and want a lift home 'cos the buses 'ave stopped, or they come off trains in the middle of the night when they've been abroad. It's amazin' what goes on, or they've had too much to drink and 'ave to leave their cars and get a taxi 'ome. All sorts.'

'Bet you meet some funny customers, Jimmy.'

'Yer right there. Thursday night this chap got in, drunk as a lord he was, wanted to go to a house out near the race course. All of twenty miles. We were miles from anywhere, and he asks to get out for a minute 'cos he needed to 'ave a . . . well, relieve himself. He never came back. I waited and waited, then I went to see where he was. But he wasn't behind the bushes where I'd last seen 'im and I never saw him again.'

'What about yer money?'

'I didn't get it, but 'e did leave something behind.'

'What?'

'A set of false teeth on the back seat – and they weren't even clean!'

Pat shouted at him. 'Oh Jimmy, what a disgusting tale that is. Is them them that you've got in now?' She roared with laughter.

'No, they didn't fit!'

After the laughter had died down Pat asked him if he was making money at it.

'Oh yes, never made as much in mi life. Not a fortune, 'cos there's the running expenses of mi car to be deducted, but yes, I'm going to be a well-set-up young man shortly.'

'That's what I need, money. It sounds lovely having your own roof over your head but you've got the upkeep, painting it and that, and I've no money to spare for that. I don't know what I'm going to do, I really don't. Better get back to the kids. Thanks for making me laugh. 'Night.'

9

Ralph had made no effort to dispel the rumours which were rife in the village. He'd been approached several times by villagers, all hoping he would lead the protest against the council building the houses. All he'd said was 'I don't think the council will be building them', but hadn't enlightened them any further. He couldn't until he had resolved a problem. Namely persuading Muriel he was doing the right thing. She was still very unhappy about the whole affair. Ralph, sitting with her before the fire one late spring morning, was debating what to do about the impasse they had arrived at. Having been a bachelor for all his life until this last year he was unaccustomed to having his decisions queried, but because of his love for Muriel, he knew he would not have a moment's peace until she willingly came round to his point of view. To sweeten the pill, that was the problem.

'You know, Muriel, my dear, I've been thinking, you have a very good eye for things beautiful haven't you? Would it be an imposition if I asked you to co-operate with the architects and feed them some of your ideas?'

'I haven't got any ideas, Ralph. I don't want to have any ideas, truly I don't and I'm sorry to be so difficult but that's how I feel.' She avoided looking at him.

'What I thought was you could make sure they designed the outside of the houses, certainly the ones nearest Shepherd's Hill and Stocks Row, so that they would blend in with the old cottages already here. We don't want redbrick three-bedroom semis going up, do we? That would be appalling, and not at all what I have in mind.'

'If you hadn't thought of the idea in the first place, you wouldn't be appalled because there'd be nothing to be appalled about. I'm afraid the renowned Templeton charm is not going to work. My mind is quite set.'

Ralph sighed. Timid people could be so damned stubborn when they put their minds to it.

'If I called it Hipkin Close, would that help?'

'When Jimbo made Harriet so cross by starting the tearoom without consulting her first, he tried calling it "Harriet's Tearoom" to persuade her not to oppose it. It's a pity it had to close, isn't it? I did like it in there. Well, it didn't work with her and it won't work with me. Oh dear. I'm sorry, Ralph. You need my support and I should be giving it to you, not opposing you at every turn. I'm very sorry.'

'That's all right, my dear, you do have a right to your own opinions. What do you think to Neville Neal?' She paused for a moment before she answered. He waited, intrigued by the conflicting emotions in her face.

'As Church Treasurer he does an excellent job, but he's not quite a *gentleman*, is he?'

Ralph chuckled. 'I knew I could trust you to hit the nail on the head. However, I'll see if he has any advice on how to proceed with our ideas for Hipkin Gardens. That sounds better doesn't it, Hipkin Gardens, it will be a kind of memorial to your father, won't it? Your family were gardeners for generations so Gardens is ideal. It's much better than Hipkin Close. I'm going to ring Neville now to see if I can get to know anything, he always seems to know what the council is up to.'

'I'll make you some coffee, you can drink it while you talk. The business side is best left to you.'

Ralph was put through to Neville in his office and he began a long and fruitful conversation about planning permission. He became so involved in his discussion that he didn't realise that Muriel had been standing in the doorway listening. When he replaced the receiver he glanced up to find her glaring at him, her face scarlet and stormy and her eyes sparking angrily.

'Hipkin Gardens.'

'Hipkin Gardens?'

'Yes, Hipkin Gardens is *not* going to be built by a den of thieves. I won't have it.' She stamped her foot. Ralph stood up.

'Muriel, I assure you . . .'

'No, Ralph. I heard what you said. Oh yes I did! I don't want to hear any more about paying councillors and scratching people's backs for them to get you what you want. If it's to bear my name and my father's, it's to be done right.'

Ralph went to draw her into the room. He took her arm and said, 'Sit here my dear, I don't like you to be upset and angry, you're quite mistaken.'

'Mistaken? I'm not. I heard you saying "and how about if it was one hundred houses". I heard you, I did, I heard you, and what tricks you would get up to to get permission. I heard you! It will all be spoilt if we have to be underhand. I'm surprised at you and very, very disappointed. This behaviour is not at all in keeping with your position.' She flopped down into the chair Ralph offered her and then began trembling with distress. 'Oh dear, I'm so sorry, but I mean what I said.' She searched for a handkerchief but finally Ralph lent her his.

Ralph shook his head. Muriel was in tears.

'Muriel! Please!'

'All I came in for was to bring your coffee.' Tears trickled down her cheeks. Rather petulantly she cried, 'And I'm glad I did. I won't have it Ralph, I simply won't. I want it all to be lovely and great fun, and all it's going to be is nasty and horrid and small minded, and then there won't be any pleasure in doing good for the village at all. And no one will like us, and we shall have to leave, and that dreadful Mr Fitch will be in your place.' She dried her tears and said accusingly, 'Why *are* you talking about a hundred houses?'

'It was him talking about a hundred houses, and I went along with it to see how much I could learn about what to do.'

Muriel signalled her disbelief by lifting her chin and turning away her head. 'I can see which way the land lies, you're getting carried away with this idea.'

Ralph pulled a chair across the carpet and placed it in front of Muriel's. Taking her hand in his he said, 'I won't have this whole lovely idea spoiled for you, not on any account. I'd rather not go through with it than have you upset like this. I was only trying out ideas with Neville, about agreeing to one thing in order to get one's own way about another. You've quite misunderstood my conversation. You're right to be indignant. We're going to go about it the honourable way, I promise you that.' He smiled reassuringly at her.

Muriel smiled through her tears and said, 'I shall keep you to it, Ralph, I really shall. I won't be put off.'

'I know, dear. People like Neville need someone like you to remind them of the honourable way to do things. I promise you faithfully I shall do things the way you want them done, otherwise I couldn't live with myself. I love you, you see.'

Muriel kissed Ralph and said, 'Thank you for coming back to Turnham Malpas. The years ahead would have been very bleak without you.'

'Thank you for saying "yes". It makes everything I do so much more worthwhile. Let's go have lunch in The Royal Oak? They tell me Bryn has got a new home-brewed ale in, and I should like to try it.' He smiled pleadingly at her, trying to make amends.

Muriel took his hand and held it to her cheek. 'I always thought this Templeton charm business was a lot of tosh, but it isn't, is it? You've won me round. Yes, I'll come, but only on condition that you don't bring up the subject of the houses, I can't bear it. Please?'

'Cross my heart and hope to die.'

But they had no alternative. Three people came up to him in the dining room, promising their support when he decided to start a petition or demonstration or whatever it was he thought would be the best move. 'After all you helped us win the battle with that old Fitch, if we all stand together we'll stop the council too, won't we?'

Muriel blushed furiously and made a show of eating her lasagne so as to dissociate herself from the conversation. When they'd said their piece and left the dining room she muttered to Ralph, 'We shouldn't have come. I knew it, we shouldn't have. We'll have to leave the village. They won't let you build. They won't. Oh dear.'

Quietly Ralph said, 'My dear, please. They'll guess something's the matter if you cry.'

'Oh yes, they will, won't they? I shall pull myself together.'

'I shan't let bad blood occur. Believe me. I won't let it happen. You can rely on me.'

'Of course I can. Yes, of course.'

'Anyway it's not official yet, so everyone is jumping the gun.'

Muriel took a sip of her wine and said, 'When we've finished here I've to go to the Store for one or two things, and you're needing stamps, aren't you? You go on home, I shan't be long.'

'Another drink?'

'No, thank you. How is the ale?'

'Excellent. Bryn's a much better landlord than Mac and Betty ever were. Much more style and much more knowledgeable.'

Ralph went home and Muriel continued round the green to the Store. It was very quiet in there; besides someone at the post office counter she was the only customer. She wandered around the shelves choosing what she fancied. That was one of the lovely things about being married to Ralph; she didn't need to worry about every penny she spent. Though she wasn't foolish, of course, that wouldn't be right but . . . She was standing between the two racks of cards and stationery when she overheard the customer talking to Linda at the post office counter.

'And now, I want my pension and I'm collecting my neighbour's as well, she's signed whatever she has to sign, she told me. Bad leg she 'as and not 'alf. Come up like a balloon. She can't walk a step. Three second-class stamps as well, please. June's a right month for birthdays in our family. I dread it coming round. Talking of dread, 'ave you 'eard what I 'eard this morning?'

'Tell me.'

The speaker leant her elbow on the edge of the counter and said, 'I've heard it on good authority that it's Sir Ralph yer know, building the houses on that land when they pull the chapel down, and not the council at all. There's everyone thinking, no, certain, he's getting up a petition against it and all the time it's 'im 'imself. Greedy, that's what. 'As all that money and still he has to make more. These rich people are never satisfied. Yer've a bad cough Linda, and it's affected yer eyes as well, yer keep winking. Are you sure you should be at work?'

Muriel heard Linda whispering and then the speaker said loudly, 'Eavesdroppers never 'ear good of themselves.'

Muriel emerged from between the shelves and, keeping as calm as she could in the circumstances, said in a sharp tone, 'My husband isn't greedy. He may not be Lord of the Manor now, but he still has the interests of the village at heart. He wouldn't dream of doing anything to the detriment of the village, he loves it. He's not interested in making money. Please remember that.' She drew herself up, feeling not unlike a bantam squaring up for a fight.

'Beg yer pardon, I'm sure. But from where I'm standing that's what it looks like.'

'Well, it just isn't so.'

'Certainly made a change to you, Muriel Hipkin, being married to money. Wouldn't say boo to a goose before. Oh, no! Very shy and retiring yer were then. Different story now, I see. Well, you're not throwing your weight about with me. Anyway, time will tell who's right. But if he's making money out of it, I shall be at the front with a placard protesting!'

'There won't be any need for a protest. I shall see to that.'

The customer began backing off. 'Well, right then. Be seeing yer, Linda. Good afternoon, *Lady* Templeton.'

Muriel nearly decided to run home, but she'd promised Ralph the stamps so she would look silly if she left now. Linda looked very embarrassed when Muriel appeared at the grille.

'Ten first-class stamps please, Linda. Don't worry yourself, dear, I'm not going to bite your head off too. Some people can't stand change, that's what it is.'

'But Lady Templeton, is he really going to build these houses? Someone said they would be red brick with them nasty patio windows and that, and cost a fortune so village people couldn't buy them. They say it's all because he wants to make a lot of money. But Sir Ralph's not like that, is he?'

'Linda, not even my husband knows if it is going to be possible, so it's all speculation. But take it from me if they do get built they won't be for sale, they'll be to rent.'

'Oh, that would be lovely. My sister, the one who's just got married, had to move to the grotty end of Culworth 'cos she couldn't afford to buy. What a good idea.'

'Thank you, Linda, I'm glad you agree it's a good idea. How much do I owe? Can I pay for these cards here too?'

'Oh yes, I'll take for stationery but everything else at the other till please. Three pounds seventy-five, please. Oh, that's correct, good. I'm short of change.'

On her way home Muriel went into the church and knelt to pray. She prayed mostly for understanding about Ralph's plans. She prayed to be a good wife. She prayed that the village would understand what he was trying to do. There was no doubt about it, she'd have to support this idea of his. It was all to the good. She was sure now. When she'd finished she sat in the pew contemplating life and how lucky she was. She went home to tell him so.

'Are you busy, dear?'

'I shall be glad of a break. Come in and sit down.'

'Ralph, I have realised today how lucky I am. I've been in church having a word, and then I sat thinking about you and what you plan to do. I'd found myself saying in the Store that some people can't stand change. That used to be me, you know. I couldn't stand change. I've had to speak out in defence of you, I was so angry about what someone in the Store was saying. So I spoke up. It's not like me at all, is it?' Ralph shook his head. 'Then Linda said her sister had had to move away because she couldn't afford to buy a house in the village like she wanted to. So that's a possible family of children for the school and the church which we have now lost. We've got to stem the exodus, haven't we?'

'Yes.'

'So, I've been thinking, there isn't any suitable land anywhere else, is there? They certainly wouldn't allow building on farm land, would they?'

'No.'

'So, houses to rent within the village would be an excellent idea, and it's the only piece of land available so close. I know we shall cause a lot of trouble doing it, but in the end it will all be to the good. There!'

Ralph stood up and went to take hold of her hand.

'Muriel, my dear, you are wonderful. I'm delighted you see it my way.

You can keep your eagle eye on the planning. I'm not sure how it will work out, we'll have to see what the council think.'

'I don't want horrid council houses on it, Ralph!'

'But if it means houses to rent, then perhaps that will be the best way to go about it. We'll see, we'll see.' Ralph bent his head to kiss her cheek. He smiled down at her and said, 'Best day's work I ever did, coming back and marrying you. Do you know that?'

'Best day's work I did too. Let's get Pericles and walk round Hipkin Gardens, shall we, and do a bit of planning?'

'Lovely idea. Come along Pericles. Walkies! You're getting an extra outing today.' Pericles rose stiffly from his favourite position by the french windows, shook himself and wagged his tail.

'How old is Pericles now, Muriel?'

'Twelve.'

'Living on borrowed time, then.'

'Oh Ralph, don't say that in front of him, he might understand.'

'I know Pericles is clever, but he's not a philosopher.'

'No, you're right he isn't, and you do right to prepare me for him . . . well, going to glory.'

10

'Now look Harriet, if you wish I shall cancel this trip, and stay at home.'

'Under no circumstances, James Charter-Plackett, do you cancel! You can't let them down like that at the eleventh hour. I may be about to give birth but I still have a brain left. Our business would fold if you cancelled.'

'I'm sure the staff could do it without me.'

'And I'm sure they couldn't. Heavens above man, I've three weeks still to go. Three whole weeks. Now. Off you go. Mother's here, Caroline's just across the road and anyway I'm going out for the evening. You'll be back the day after tomorrow.'

'I know but . . . Where are you going tonight, then?'

'You've forgotten it's Caroline's Coffee and Gâteau Evening at the Rectory in aid of the refurbishment of the small church hall. Remember? You donated a gâteau?'

'Oh right, yes. I'd forgotten. A right hen party that's going to be. What about the children?'

'Mother's coming.'

He smoothed his hand across his chin and said, 'You will take care?'

'Of course. Get along man. I've checked the food, everything's there. Just the things to get out of the freezer and you're away.'

'You're brilliant. Thanks for all you do. When the baby gets here, I don't want to see you anywhere near the business for at least three months. I've got these new people organised, thank heavens there's a lot of unemployed, and we shall manage very nicely.'

'Don't, you're making me feel redundant.' Harriet kissed him, and pushed him out of the door. 'See you when you get back.'

'I'll ring.'

'Got your phone?'

'Yes!' Jimbo raced out of the house, leaving Harriet shaking her head at him.

She was looking forward to the coffee evening. It might be her last outing for months. Jimbo had a dread of leaving very young babies with babysitters, and she knew once it had arrived they'd have to entertain at home if they needed company. She'd caught him one day poring over a newspaper article about cot deaths. She'd been expecting Finlay at the time, and he'd looked up with tears in his eyes and said, 'I can hardly bear to read about this. God help us if we ever, ever, have this to face.' Harriet had stood beside him and cradled his head against her body. He'd put his arms round her and hugged her tightly and they'd said no more about it, but she knew he still carried the dread. So yes, Caroline, here I come.

Muriel arrived early at the coffee evening, as she always did at any function she attended.

'I know I'm the first one but I thought I might give you a hand. Here's my gâteau, it's Ralph's favourite. I hope I've not gone over the top with the lemon, he loves it really sharp but of course not everyone does, do they?'

'Come in Muriel. Come and put it on the dining table. It looks absolutely splendid. Sylvia and I have organised everything, there's nothing to do except look charming.'

'If there's nothing to do now, I'll stay behind afterwards and help clear up. Ralph's away visiting a friend at the moment so I shall be quite glad to stay. I'm surprised how lonely it feels being on my own. Before I married I never noticed being alone, but now I do. Doesn't the table look beautiful! Where did you get these gâteaux? They look marvellous.'

'Some are from friends, one I've made, this one Sylvia's made and Jimbo gave me the other one. I hope plenty of people turn up or I shall have a freezer full of cake, not that Peter would mind.'

'Is he here this evening?'

'No, he's playing squash at the club in Culworth. I've turfed him out for the evening. Time he got away from the parish and nappies for a while.'

The door bell rang again and Caroline excused herself while she went to answer it. Muriel heard her shout. 'Venetia! How lovely that you could come, and you've brought a gâteau, how kind, I didn't expect it you know, you're supposed to be here to eat them.'

'Thank you for inviting me, I really was thrilled. You're more than kind.'

'Not at all, I'm pleased you could make it. Come in the dining room.'

Venetia came in wearing a sizzlingly spicy orange trouser suit. Only Venetia, with her jet-black hair and well tanned skin, could have carried it off. Anyone else would have been obliterated by the powerful colour. Muriel almost wished she was wearing sunglasses.

'Hello, Venetia, how are you?'

'Very well, thank you, Lady Templeton. Is Sir Ralph here?'

'No, it's ladies only tonight, I'm afraid.'

'Pity, he's so charming and so kind.'

Caroline showed her to an armchair. 'Do sit down, Venetia, I'll put your gâteau here in the middle. It is perfectly splendid, you must be very gifted to be able to make this. I don't know how you manage to fit everything in, Jimbo says it's very busy up at the Big House.'

'Oh, I didn't make it. I was in Culworth at the sports shop getting some things we need for the leisure complex when I spotted that new cake shop that's opened opposite and I couldn't resist. Yes, we are busy. Very busy in fact. Jeremy is in his element in charge of the estate and things and I'm doing what I love, which is supervising the leisure activities. So, yes, it's busy. Bit different from when it was the health club! It's going to be busy every week until August. Then Jeremy and I are having a holiday.'

Suddenly everyone was arriving, among them Harriet. 'Had to come. Mother's sitting in for me. Hello, everybody.' She was greeted by a chorus of 'Hello, Harriet.'

'What have you done with Jimbo?' Venetia asked.

'He's in Bristol doing the VIP food at a big toy fair.'

Caroline came in from the kitchen carrying two coffee pots, which she put down beside the cups. She tapped a spoon loudly on the side of one of them. 'Right, ladies, I think we can begin. Please do come along and help yourselves, you'll be glad to hear we're not counting the calories tonight! Eat as much as you can! There's a dish on the gâteaux table and one where we're serving the coffee for your money. Muriel and Sylvia are in charge of the gâteaux and I'm serving coffee. Sheila Bissett, just back from her round the world trip, see how tanned she is, hardly recognised you Sheila, is in charge of the bring and buy. Enjoy!'

Muriel and Sylvia, stationed behind the table to serve the slices of gâteau, had a busy time. Muriel loved the delicate china plates and the silver cake forks and the delightful flowered napkins she folded and presented to each person as they took their plates. When she had a moment to spare between serving, she glanced round and thought how lovely the dining room looked. Caroline had put a crystal chandelier in place of the bulb dangling on the end of a piece of cable that Mr Furbank had had all those years. Lovely vases of flowers stood on any and every surface, and the carpet and the curtains had a slight oriental look which Muriel adored. If she'd married Mr Furbank, she'd have been stuck with a lifetime of dangling light bulbs. She blushed at her narrow escape. Well, not escape, because he'd never asked her and never would have done, but she had fancied him.

Georgie Fields came carrying her empty plate.

'More gâteau, Georgie?'

'Yes, the raspberry meringue this time, please, Lady Templeton.'

'Left Bryn in charge of the bar have you?'

'Yes. Couldn't miss this. The first elegant social "do" there's been since we got here.'

'Business doing well?'

'Oh yes. We were a bit apprehensive about moving out into the sticks as it were, we've always worked in towns before you see, but I must say it's been a complete success. Especially now with the dining room, that's really made us take off.' She placed a large piece of meringue in her mouth and, waving her cake fork at Sylvia, mumbled had she settled down to married life now?

'Yes, thank you, best day's work I ever did.'

'Wish I could get Alan married off. As a barman he's second to none, but at the moment he's sex mad. He can think of nothing else. I've told him, he'll find the right one eventually, but no, he's after anything in skirts. At thirty-two I expect he thinks it's time he got cracking.'

'You've known him a long time?'

'He's worked for us since he left school, he hasn't a family so it's good for him that he can live in. But I've told him, no girls on the premises, thank you. I won't have it.'

Pat Duckett overheard the conversation as she waited for Muriel to serve her a slice of the chocolate gâteau Venetia had brought.

'Nobody likes him, yer know,' she said. 'Good at his job but he's not liked.'

Georgie was upset. 'No one likes him? That's the first I've heard. Why ever not?'

'Slimy 'e is, slimy.' Muriel who agreed with Pat but didn't like to say so, muttered that 'perhaps that was a little unkind'.

'Unkind it might be, but it's the truth.' Pat thanked Muriel for the gâteau and, helping herself to another napkin, wandered off for what she hoped would be a worthwhile chat with Venetia.

Muriel did her best to pour oil on troubled waters. 'You'll have to excuse Pat, I'm afraid, she's very upset at the moment and doesn't know what she's saying.'

'Why?'

'Short of money and the children getting more expensive each year to feed and clothe, and now her father's coming to live with her, because he's just lost his job.'

'Oh dear, poor Pat. Yes, well, she does have problems, I suppose.'

'Yes, she does.' Muriel looked across the dining room to where she could see Pat talking to Venetia. They looked very intent.

'You see, my dad knows everything there is to know about gardening and then some. He's done it all his life. All he needs is a chance to prove it.'

'Well, I could ask Jeremy if he needs anyone.'

'He specialises in glasshouse work, but he can turn his 'and to anything actually.'

'You mean greenhouses?'

'Yes, he's been growing vines and peaches and figs and things all his working life. If it's under glass, you name it 'e grows it.'

'Look Pat, it's nothing to do with me, Jeremy's in charge of the estate, but I'll certainly have a word. I mean we never looked after the greenhouses when we owned it, and nothing's been done since Crad— Mr Fitch came, so yes, I do know they need attention. But then he's so forward looking. Cut your losses and start a new project, you know the kind of thing. He could quite easily say, pull the lot down, they're not worth the trouble. But I promise I'll see what I can do.'

'Thank you, yer've no idea what a help it would be if he got a job. I can't stand the thought of him round the house all day and nothing to do. I mean he was only nineteen when I was born so he's still got plenty of go in him. He's not ready for the scrap heap yet. More coffee? This one's on me.'

Harriet came to the table asking for another slice of raspberry meringue.

'I've no doubt I shall regret this around two o'clock this morning and will be lying in bed munching indigestion tablets, but there you are.'

Sylvia handed her the meringue and a fresh napkin, and was about to ask Harriet if the children were excited about the baby when the uproarious arrival of a crowd from Penny Fawcett put paid to any further conversation they might have liked to have.

It was quite late when Caroline's guests began to leave. Muriel stayed behind to help clear up.

'What a wonderfully successful evening, Caroline. How much money have we made?'

'Believe it or believe it not, I've counted up and it's a hundred and eighty-five pounds, seventy-five pence. Isn't that marvellous? The bring and buy stall just helped to top it up and we had far more people than I expected. I couldn't believe it when the minibus from Penny Fawcett turned up. I knew some of them intended coming, but a minibus full! There were so many they were sitting on each others' knees. Good thing the Sergeant didn't catch them!'

'Brilliant!' Harriet said. 'That's just a bit more than we needed to finish the refurbishment, isn't it? Now, I'm going to give a hand.'

'Oh no, you're not, you can be purely decorative, Harriet, and entertain us with dynamic conversation while we work. Muriel and I will clear up. There's not that much to do now. Pat did a lot for me before she left.' Caroline smiled at her as she bent over the dishwasher. 'Sit in my rocking chair and watch. I won't put this plate of yours in, Muriel, it might be the worse for wear if I do, we'll wash that in the sink.'

'By the way, Jimbo's asked Pat Duckett if she'd like some evening work waitressing when he has an outside catering job.' As she said this Harriet bent forward for a moment, and then continued. 'I know she would welcome the money and I'm sure she'd be relia— Gosh I've got the most incredible indigestion. I should never have eaten like I did. There's not enough room left any more for overeating. My insides can't cope. Hell, I don't know what can have made it so bad. Wow.'

'I've got some indigestion tablets, Harriet, would you like one?'

'Yes, please.' Caroline searched in a cupboard for them and eventually found the packet. Harriet took one gratefully. She sat quietly chewing the tablet and waiting for it to take effect.

'Would either of you like a drink before you go? Tea or something?' She turned to ask Harriet what she would like. 'Tea for you . . . Are you all right?'

'Things have improved I must say. It must be that meringue thing I had to finish with.'

Caroline said, 'Are you sure it's indigestion?'

'Yes. It must be, the tablet's eased it now. Where's Peter tonight?'

'Playing squash with an old college friend. He felt guilty, but I said it's a ladies' evening and we can manage perfectly well without you, so off you go.'

'It never ceases to amaze me that men think we can't cope without them. Jimbo was all hot under the collar before he left. You've got to go, I insist, I said . . . Oh dear, I've a nasty feeling it's not . . . indigestion.'

Caroline put her hand on Harriet's stomach and felt it harden as a contraction took hold. 'You're in labour.'

'Don't be ridiculous, Caroline, how can I be in labour, it simply isn't convenient at the moment with Jimbo away. I can't be, anyway it's three more weeks yet. I can't be. Can I?' She looked up at Caroline and as their eyes met they both acknowledged that she very likely was. 'Whatever will Jimbo say?'

'Have you a bag packed?'

'No. Didn't think I'd be needing it just yet. It's a false alarm. I'll go home and get to bed. Yes, that's it, I'm feeling odd because I've got overtired and I've got this blessed indigestion.'

Caroline suggested an ambulance might be more appropriate. 'Let's time two more contractions, and then we'll make our decision. Tell me when the next one starts. You watch the clock, Muriel.' Neither Caroline nor Harriet noticed the look on Muriel's face. If they had they would have got her a chair to sit on before she fell down.

Caroline saw a look of concentration come into Harriet's face. 'Now, Muriel.'

'It's ten past ten.'

'Right. Let's wait for the next one. Sit down, Muriel, it may be some time.'

They waited only eight minutes before the next contraction came.

'Shouldn't I be doing something, like boiling a kettle?' Her faint squeaky voice made Caroline look at her.

'Do you know what, I think it would be a good idea if you went across to Henderson's and got Sadie to pack a bag for Harriet. Could you do that now?'

'Of course, you don't need the kettle then?'

'If you like.' Muriel filled it, put it on the Aga and then quietly let herself out into the dark street. She scurried down Stocks Row and past The Royal Oak, where everyone appeared to be behaving quite normally, a fact which Muriel found difficult to understand in the circumstances.

She hammered on the front door of Henderson's and strained to hear Sadie coming down the hall. 'Come on, Sadie, come on.'

The door opened sharply. Sadie peered out into the dark. 'Heavens! Muriel! Is there a fire?'

'Fire? Oh no, it's Harriet. She's – she's gone into labour and it's very quick and Caroline said could you get her a bag ready for the hospital and she's thinking she will have to ring for the ambulance. Oh Sadie, I don't know anything about these things but it does seem to me that it's nearly here. Harriet is in such great pain, I don't know how she can bear it.'

'Oh my God, come in. Oh dear. I'm much too old for this kind of thing, I did tell her not to do it, but she never listens to me.' Sadie fluttered about the hall distractedly, still managing to look elegant despite her anxiety. 'Wait here, I'll run upstairs and see what I can find.'

Muriel waited on the hall chair, restless to be off, but at the same time wishing she didn't need to return to the Rectory. She couldn't leave Caroline to cope on her own, could she? She had to be brave and stick it out. Before Ralph came, life was so quiet and untroubled and now it seemed as though at every turn she was facing challenge. She heard Sadie opening and shutting drawers upstairs, then heard her collecting bottles and things in the bathroom. Then footsteps on the landing and Sadie came hurrying down, bag in hand.

'Give her my love and tell her I'll hold the fort till Jimbo gets back tomorrow. Oh God, I shall have to phone him on his mobile. He'll go mad. Tell her I'll stay here all night, OK?'

Muriel fled as fast as she could back to the Rectory hampered by the weight of the bag. Surely Harriet wouldn't need all this stuff? Anyone would think she was going in for a month.

Caroline opened the door. 'I've rung for the ambulance, it won't be long now.' Muriel handed her the bag and hesitatingly re-entered the kitchen. Harriet was standing up holding on to the edge of the kitchen table, her back bent, her whole body concentrating on managing the pain.

In a brief respite between the pains Harriet said, 'Terribly sorry about this. It's nearly here, you know.'

'I know it is.' They all three heard the ambulance draw up outside and Muriel fled to open the door.

The ambulance men came in to the kitchen and shook hands with Caroline as though they had all the time in the world.

'Well now, nice to see you back in harness again, Doctor. We've got here as quickly as we could. You were in good hands, Mrs Charter-Plackett, well known for being cool in a crisis is our Dr Harris.'

The telephone rang and Muriel went to answer it.

'The Rectory here.'

'Who's that?'

'Muriel Hipkin . . . oh, no, I mean Templeton. Oh dear.'

'Jimbo Charter-Plackett here. I've had a phone call about Harriet. Sadie gave a very incoherent message to one of my assistants, and I can't understand it. They said I'd to ring the Rectory.'

'Well Jimbo, Harriet can't come to the phone at the moment, because the ambulance has just arrived and she's going to hospital as quickly as possible because Caroline says the baby is nearly here.'

'Oh my God. Oh my God. Is she all right?'

'Yes, she's doing fine.'

'Oh my God, oh my God. What shall I do? I knew I shouldn't have left her. I did tell her. I don't believe it. It's so early.'

'She's made a kind of grand finale to the coffee evening.'

'Tell Harriet I love her and I'm coming home as soon as I've rearranged things for tomorrow.'

'Jimbo don't come home, go directly to the hospital.'

'Of course, of course, I'm not thinking straight. Thank Caroline for me, please.'

Muriel started to say, 'Drive carefully,' but the phone went dead so she replaced the receiver.

When she returned to the kitchen the ambulance men had wrapped Harriet in a blanket and were about to get her into the ambulance. 'Harriet, my dear, that was Jimbo. He sends his love and he's going directly to the hospital.'

Caroline followed them out of the door and laid Harriet's holdall on the floor of the ambulance. 'Good luck. It won't be long now. I'll ring in an hour and see how you are.' When Harriet had gone, Caroline went back into the Rectory to thank Muriel for her help and to make a cup of tea she'd promised when they were clearing up.

Muriel was sitting ashen-faced on a kitchen chair, her forearms resting in the table.

'I know I must look awful, I'm so sorry, but I'm not used to babies coming and it's upset me a great deal. I thought it was going to come here in the kitchen.'

'So did I. Thank heavens they got here quickly. I'm shattered. It's a long time since I did maternity.'

'I'm going home now to have a cup of camomile tea to steady my nerves. Thank you for a lovely evening, Caroline. I'm so glad it was such a success. Harriet will be all right, won't she?'

'Of course, don't worry. Babies do come quickly sometimes.'

11

Flick sat on the front pew swinging her legs, having a word with God. 'Thank you, God, for sending me a little sister. All this time I thought we were getting a boy. I really needed a girl. It's hard being the only female, you know, and I didn't think you understood. I've chosen a name for her. I think she looks as if she needs a dignified name. I'm Felicity really, you see, but I couldn't say it when I was little and it turned into Flick, so I've thought and thought and I think I'd like to call her Frances Charlotte Charter-Plackett. What do you think?'

She screwed up her eyes very tightly and waited for His reply. She hoped He was listening; after all, she was being naughty not going to school when Daddy thought she was there. But there are days when you can't do what you ought, and it's not every day a girl gets a new sister. 'It will have to begin with F, you see, or she'll think she doesn't belong to Finlay and Fergus and me, and I wouldn't want her to think she's adopted. She is beautiful, God, and I want to thank you for being so kind as to send me a pretty sister. I wouldn't have wanted an ugly one. But I do think you let Mummy leave it a bit late. It's not funny being born in an ambulance in the hospital car park. Whatever will she think when she grows up? She'll think we've been careless. When we get Mummy home tomorrow I shall tell her, Frances Charter-Plackett. It sounds very distinguished, don't you think?'

Flick heard footsteps, so she opened her eyes. It was Peter coming out of the choir vestry.

'Hello, Flick. Isn't it wonderful news about your new sister?'

'Hello, Mr Harris. Yes, but I wish you'd sent for me, I've been reading all about it, I could have helped.'

'Your sister was in the most tremendous hurry, I don't think Mrs Harris had time to think about sending for help.'

'She is a proper doctor, isn't she? You called her Mrs Harris then.'

'Well, yes, she is. I should have said Dr Harris in the circumstances, I know.'

'I'm so glad I've got a little sister. When you see her you'll think she's very beautiful, you know. Just as beautiful as your Beth.'

Willie came in through the church door, wearing his gardening clothes. 'Oh, there you are Flick, your dad's out of his mind. They've just rung from the school to say you never arrived. He's been out looking for you. He's gone back to the Store now, 'cos they're so busy this morning with everyone wanting to hear about your new baby.'

'I'd better go, then. He panics you know, Mummy says he does anyway. He does need me to look after him with her away. Bye bye.' Flick went out into the rain, her pigtails flapping as she ran.

Willie chuckled. 'A right old-fashioned little girl she is, and no mistake. Anyways, sir, I know it's raining but I'm going to make a start on extending that brick path by the . . .' He stopped speaking, halted by the sound of the most horrendous crash. He and Peter looked at each other, fear in their eyes. Without a word Peter picked up the skirts of his cassock and raced out through the door and down the path with Willie close behind, the rain lashing at them as they ran.

They found Flick lying misshapenly, face down in the middle of the road just past the lych gate, blood slowly seeping from her head onto the tarmac. The car which had run her down was slammed against the churchyard wall beyond the lych gate, with Alan Crimble still in the driver's seat, his head resting on the steering wheel. He too had blood seeping from his head, running in dribbles onto his knees. The silence was harrowing.

Willie went to turn Flick over. Peter shouted urgently, 'Don't move her. Get Caroline. Ring for an ambulance. Quick.' He knelt down in the road beside Flick and listened for her breathing. Shock. Yes, shock. Keep her warm. He unbuttoned his cassock and laid it over her. There were footsteps and it was Jimbo and then suddenly a crowd. Jimbo knelt on the road beside Flick. Deathly white, breathing as though he'd run in a race. His head almost touching the road, he looked into her face for signs of life. Almost afraid to touch her, he gently laid the back of his hand on her cheek. He pulled Peter's cassock more closely around her shoulders. Tucked it carefully around her small bare feet. He looked up at Peter. Inside themselves they both wept.

Peter went to attend to Alan. He sat motionless, crouched over the wheel. The windscreen had shattered and the crazed glass cast curious broken light on Alan's head. The blood still drip-dripping on to his trousers. Peter managed to force the car door open. He touched Alan's shoulder. Slowly his head came up. Peter saw a great gash on his forehead. Instinctively, he got a freshly laundered handkerchief from his trouser pocket and gave it to Alan to press to his head.

Peter helped him to get out of the car. Alan moved as though in a trance. He straightened up. He was dreadfully sick right there on the road. Peter turned away. He could see Caroline kneeling beside Flick. Jimbo was beside her, his hand on Caroline's shoulder. Waiting. Waiting.

'I can feel her pulse, Jimbo. All we can do is keep her warm until the ambulance arrives. They won't be long.'

Jimbo cleared his throat and tried to speak but the words wouldn't come. He gestured with his hands helplessly. Caroline patted his arm and smiled reassuringly. She stayed kneeling on the road beside Flick, stroking her hair and talking to her. The crowd, now much larger but still silent, stood watching Alan Crimble leaning against the church wall, handkerchief to his head, deathly white and panting.

Jimbo noticed him for the first time and in a flash galvanised himself into action. His voice, dry and choking, pushed its way out of his throat. 'I'll kill you for this.' In a moment he was across the road and his hands were around Alan's throat, squeezing, squeezing.

Peter grabbed Jimbo's wrists and forced his hands away from Alan's neck. Peter spoke firmly. 'This won't do Jimbo, go talk to Flick, she needs you. I'll take care of Alan.'

Alan found his voice; a small, thin piping voice begging for understanding.

'I never saw her, she came out of the gate and I'd hit her before I could do anything. I couldn't help it, it wasn't my fault she ran into the road without looking. I really couldn't help it. They can't blame me. They can't.'

'Compose yourself, Alan. Jimbo's very overwrought, you'll have to excuse him.'

'Is she . . . you know, is she dead?'

'No.'

'Thank God.'

'But she's badly hurt.'

Caroline left Jimbo to comfort Flick and went to speak to Alan. She lifted Peter's handkerchief from his forehead and examined the gash.

'You'll be needing stiches, Alan, but not to worry, it doesn't look too serious. How do you feel everywhere else?'

'All right I think, but I feel so cold.' He was trembling from head to foot.

Caroline looked at the silent crowd. They were standing completely still showing no emotion.

'Anyone a coat they could lend Alan? It's the shock, he's feeling cold.'

The question stirred them.

'So he should be.'

'Serves 'im right.'

'So?'

They began a kind of ugly murmuring which left to itself could have become explosive. Peter said in a loud voice, 'I have a blanket in my car, use that.' He gave Caroline the keys. She left him to face the crowd. His height gave him the advantage. Peter deliberately caught their eyes to stare them down. One by one they looked at him and then, outstared, glanced shamefacedly down.

'Flick will need all our prayers and love. And so will Alan, he didn't deliberately run her down, it was an accident.'

The sound of the ambulance siren could be heard as it came down the Culworth Road. The crew jumped out almost the moment it pulled up. Peter felt as though they had taken at least an hour to arrive, but when he checked his watch he found scarcely fifteen minutes had passed since he'd first heard the noise of the crash.

Caroline suggested Jimbo should go in the ambulance. He held her arm. 'Yes, yes, of course.' He pleaded with her for advice. 'Caroline, how am I going to tell Harriet?'

'Very, very gently, and with hope, Jimbo.'

The ambulance man nodded in the direction of Alan Crimble. 'We'll take this gentleman too, Dr Harris.'

'Of course. It looks like he only has that head wound, but he's in shock.'

He turned aside and said quietly to Caroline, 'You don't need me to tell you the little girl's in a bad way, Doctor.'

'I know, I know.'

'Very bad, actually.'

The driver stood waiting to close the ambulance doors. Alan, still wrapped in Peter's blanket, climbed unsteadily up the steps. Jimbo followed him in. The other ambulance man was inside attending to Flick, who lay on the stretcher silent and still, so contrary to the way she lived her life. The driver slammed the doors shut and strode round to the front to climb in the cab. He acknowledged Caroline's wave and then drove steadily out of the village. The crowd, left behind with no one to vent their anger on, drifted away in twos and threes, talking quietly.

Caroline pulled herself together to face the realities. 'I'm going to the Store, Peter, do you think we should close it for the rest of the day?'

'With both Harriet and Jimbo not there, I think there's no alternative.

I'll come with you.' Caroline saw Flick's blue flip-flops by the churchyard wall; rather strangely they were laid side by side, as if Flick had taken them off and put them neatly there to await her return. She carried them across to the Store, tears welling in her eyes. They looked so forlorn there in her hand, as though they felt of no use any more.

When they got into the Store, Sadie was behind the counter, tears pouring down her face. 'I'm not brave, I couldn't go out to see her.' She asked Caroline what she thought. 'What do you think? She isn't dead is she?'

'No, she isn't, but it is very serious. There are several bones broken. But I know the orthopaedic surgeon, Archie McKintyre, he's an outstanding man. If anyone can do anything for her, he will. He is quite brilliant. Very innovative.' Caroline put her arm round Sadie and hugged her tight.

'I'm being a damned old fool. For the boys' sakes I shall have to pull myself together.'

'What about closing the Store? You can't cope with everything and the boys will need your support, they can't be left alone.'

'How sensible. Linda write me a notice, "Shop closed temporarily, sorry for any inconvenience." If they complain they know what they can do. Tomorrow I shall get organised and bring in some help. Pray for her Peter, I'm sure your prayers will count for more than mine.'

Peter smiled gently. 'I don't believe that for one minute.'

Caroline held out Flick's flip-flops. 'I found these in the road.' Sadie cradled them against her face, and whispered, 'God help us all.'

At midday Caroline rang the hospital for news. She went to tell Peter in his study. 'They're taking her into theatre right now. Fractured skull, and several broken bones including both legs and her pelvis. But she's holding her own very well. She's a tough little girl, with lots of determination, if anyone can pull through she will.'

'Poor Harriet. At such a vulnerable time too. I think I'll be off to the hospital. God knows what you say to parents at this moment.'

'I know you'll find the right words, you always do.' She kissed him and went to hug her own two children, playing with water in the kitchen sink while Sylvia made the lunch.

That night, without Alan, Bryn and Georgie were short-handed in the bar. Of course they were extremely busy: all their regulars had come in wanting to know what had happened and to pass their own verdict on where the blame lay.

'Told Alan more than once he should have his car serviced. Right mess it was, yer know, Bryn. Wrecker's yard out Penny Fawcett way was the best place for it. That's where it will end up now, and not before time. You should've insisted.'

Bryn stroked his big moustache and replied, 'I'm not his keeper, only his employer.'

'Yer could have advised him.'

Bryn protested. 'He's a grown man and . . .'

'Grown man? He's a kid really. Irresponsible, that's what. Drives far too fast as we all know. See'd him once coming home from Culworth like a bat out of hell, however he made that sharp right hand turn by the signpost I'll never know. 'Nother time 'e scared the living daylights out of a friend of mine coming over that crossroads where the rector had his accident. Maniac behind a wheel, is Alan.'

'Police'll throw the book at him.' The speaker enumerated on his fingers the crimes of which he guessed Alan was guilty. 'Careless driving for a start. Driving without insurance. Driving without a road fund licence. No MOT. Tyres not up to snuff. Lights not working properly, and brakes not up to scratch, and that's *without* examining the car.'

Another regular pronounced in a loud voice, 'What's more I shan't want him serving me in 'ere of a night. Not a fella who can run a little girl down, and a lovely little girl she is too.'

Georgie, who'd kept silent until now, spoke up. 'Now look here, we all know that Flick ran out of the gate and into the road without looking, and Alan didn't see her because of the lych gate. She came straight out at him, he'd no time.'

'Even if he had had time to see her he couldn't have stopped because his brakes weren't good enough. If you'll take my advice you'll give him the order of the boot.'

'The order of what?'

'Give him his cards, finish him, sack him or whatever they call it nowadays. When will he be out of hospital?'

'Tomorrow, most likely.'

'Well, give him his notice tomorrow then.'

'I shall do nothing of the sort. Tell him that the day he comes out? That's not very Christian, is it? We've no cause to do that, he's a good worker, knows this business like the back of his hand. In any case Bryn and I employ whom we wish in our pub, it is our business after all.'

'It is, you're absolutely right and it's a free world. But if yer want yer takings to slump, you keep him.' Bryn quietly shook his head at Georgie, whose temper was beginning to boil up, and she let the matter go. The customers took their drinks to a table and left the two of them battling to keep everyone served.

*

It was two days after her operation before Flick regained consciousness. Harriet, shocked beyond endurance by the news of the accident, had been kept in hospital; she was taken in a wheelchair to the orthopaedic ward, where she sat in Flick's side ward watching and waiting. She couldn't bear seeing the tubes and the machines surrounding Flick. She couldn't tolerate the twenty-four-hour attention from the nurses, it seemed Flick was never left in peace. She almost begged them to leave her alone and let her go. Then she persuaded herself that while there was life there was hope. Jimbo, kept better informed than Harriet, didn't dare sound too encouraging.

They were both there when Flick opened her eyes. She gave the tiniest smile when she saw Jimbo and Harriet leaning over her.

'Darling, it's Mummy. Daddy's here too.'

'Frances, where's Frances?' Her eyes closed, and she drifted away again.

To cover his relief Jimbo said impatiently, 'What's she talking about? Who's Frances? Is it someone at school?'

'It's not anyone at school. I've never heard her mention Frances. I haven't the faintest idea. But Jimbo, she's coming round. She spoke, so that must be a good sign surely, Sister?'

'It certainly is, it certainly is. Still a long road to travel, but that's very positive.'

Jimbo became possessed with an idea. 'Sister, do you think it would be a good move if we brought the baby down from the maternity ward and let her see her? It might just trigger her into staying awake, mightn't it?'

'What a good idea. I'll phone Sister in maternity and ask how she feels about it. We could keep her here until Flick wakes again, couldn't we? The staff will be delighted. They'll all be in to see her.'

When Flick opened her eyes again, Jimbo lifted the baby from her cradle and held her where Flick could see her.

'Look darling, look who's come to see you. Flick, look Flick.'

He held the baby close to Flick's face and waited for her response.

Flick smiled, and in a tiny voice said, 'Hello, Frances,' and then drifted away again.

'Harriet, she wants to call the baby Frances, that's what it is, she wants to call her Frances. Well, we shall if it pleases her. Frances. I like that.'

'So do I. She's beginning to come round, isn't she, Sister?'

'It's encouraging anyway, I must say. Now you must both go and wait outside. Mr McKintyre is on his way.'

After the surgeon had examined Flick, he spoke with Jimbo and Harriet, waiting out in the corridor. 'Not out of the woods yet, but I must say the wee one's holding her own. A little fighter she is, yes, a little fighter. Early days, early days, but you'll be pleased to know the word "hope" has entered our vocabulary. Lovely wee bairn you've got there, Mrs Charter-Plackett. See you again.'

12

With the morning's post came a letter from Ralph's solicitor confirming his absolute right to the ownership of the spare land. 'At last we can go ahead, Muriel, my dear. Look, read this.' After she'd read it she asked, 'But Ralph, how did it all come about? Why should the spare land be yours again after all these years? Who made the mistake?'

'First things first. My great-great-great-grandfather Tristan Templeton, who lived at the end of the eighteenth century, was a racing man, and a gambler. Fortunately, he usually won so he didn't devastate the family fortunes. He had a rival, Geoffrey de Guillet, living in the old manor house in Little Derehams. All that's left of it are the walls of the old kitchen garden which the council have turned into the rose garden. You know which one I mean?'

Muriel nodded. 'Well, his rival threw out a challenge that he could beat my great-great-great-grandfather Tristan in any race he cared to suggest. They decided on a race starting at the stocks here in Turnham Malpas and finishing at the market cross in Culworth. The wager was that if Tristan won he would get the spare land as his prize, something he had always coveted. If Geoffrey de Guillet won he would get Tristan's prize racehorse. Well, Tristan Templeton won the race by three lengths. The deeds for the land were duly handed over. All the rest of the estate was in one large piece. The spare land he'd won was quite separate from it. When the council bought the estate in 1946 they intended using Home Farm and the surrounding woods and fields for teaching the orphan boys farming skills so they could earn a living when they left the home. All that didn't work out and the council sold off the estate except for that piece immediately surrounding the Big House and Sykes Wood.'

'Which is the land still belonging to the Big House?'

'Quite right. The council *assumed* the spare land belonged to them, but due to a slip-up in the original sales contract written in 1946 the land was not mentioned at all, but no one noticed that. I still have the deeds and this letter confirms officially that I have owned it all these years.'

'Well, isn't that amazing?'

'So now I can go ahead and see about building the houses.'

'I wouldn't wish to pry into your business affairs, Ralph, but how can you afford the money to build all these houses? Are you so well off?'

'No, my dear, are *we* so well off? We share everything.'

'Everything?'

'Yes. When we married I transferred half of everything I own to you.'

'To me? Was that what all those papers that I signed were about?'

'Yes, my dear.'

Muriel was aghast. 'But I didn't give anything to you! I still have my money, well my bit of money in my own bank account. When you said about being "truly married" I thought you meant . . . you know . . . making love.'

'I did, but I meant money and possessions too.'

Hands clasped together under her chin, Muriel contemplated what Ralph had said. 'What a wonderful gesture. What a completely wonderful thing to have done. You make me feel very humble, dear, very humble. I don't really deserve your generosity. I just do not. I was so confused at the time when I signed those papers I simply didn't realise. You must have thought me very ungrateful.'

'Well, now you know.'

'So in that case I own half the spare land?'

Ralph thought for a moment and saw he was in a tight corner. 'Because we've only just discovered the spare land is mine – ours, on paper nothing is official. But yes, in theory you do.'

'I see. I'll go make the lunch.' She left Ralph contemplating what would be churning around in her mind while she made it. After a few minutes Muriel popped her head round the door and said, 'So, if you shared everything equally with me when we married, I can have a say in what we do about building the houses?'

Ralph hesitated and then said, 'Yes, of course. But I would expect you would heed my advice.'

'I see.' Muriel returned to the kitchen to finish the lunch.

Part way through eating her lunch, Muriel said, 'But, Ralph, I still have my own bank account with my small savings in and with the money in it from selling my cottage. I shall go to the bank this afternoon and transfer it all into . . . What shall I transfer it into?'

'Don't do it.' With a twinkle in his eye he said, 'If I lose all our money on this house caper, we might need yours to live on.'

Muriel was shocked. 'You don't mean that, do you? There really isn't very much, you know.'

'No, I was teasing. But don't transfer it, I rather like the idea of being married to a woman with money. Anyway it helps you to keep your independence.'

'I shall have a flutter on the Stock Exchange. Yes, that's what I shall do.'

'You're getting very daring, my dear.'

'No doubt I shall change my mind as soon as I've done it, but I've decided I fancy the idea of living dangerously. Oh, I do wish there was good news about Flick. That poor dear little girl. She's taken a turn for the worse because of the anaesthetic, and her lungs are affected now. She was, I mean *is*, such a joy. Jimbo is a shadow of what he used to be.'

'Look, she's held on for a week, she's conscious and she's talking lucidly, so there must be hope. She's a tough little thing, you know, really tough. If anyone can pull through she can. I saw that Alan Crimble this morning. Like Jimbo, he's a shadow of what he used to be too.'

'Oh dear. What's that expression they use about ice cream? I know, he won't be flavour of the month, will he?'

'No, it could be very distressing for him. But she did run out of the shadow of the lych gate and into the road, apparently without looking. So it's not entirely his fault. The police took his car away. I doubt they'll find it roadworthy.'

'He'll be prosecuted then?'

'Without a doubt. I have letters to write, Muriel. The lunch was lovely. I'll study the *Financial Times* if you like, and we'll choose some shares.'

'Thank you, dear. When I've cleared up I'm going to the Store for a card to send to Flick.'

Harriet went in to say *au revoir* to Flick before she left the hospital with the baby. She thought perhaps there wasn't quite so much machinery around her now, but she still looked like something from outer space.

'Flick, darling, it's Mummy. Hello-o-o, anyone at ho-o-ome?' Flick stirred, opened her eyes and said, 'Are you going now?'

'Yes, darling, I am. Daddy or I will be here every day to see you. But I've got to go now. I wasn't supposed to be here all this time in the first place, so I've outstayed my welcome. And the boys are needing me, too. Look, nurse has brought Frances up for you to see to say bye bye.'

'Bye bye Frances. Isn't she beautiful, Mummy? So beautiful. Take care of them all, Frances, till I get back.' Harriet held the baby close to Flick's face and she kissed her. 'We belong together, Fran and me, you know. We're *sisters*.' Flick closed her eyes, twinkled her fingers at them both and went to sleep. Harriet stood watching her. How close they'd come to losing her. How very close. That first terrifying night Harriet had become obsessed with the idea that she'd been given Frances in exchange for Flick, and that Flick would die. But thank the Lord, here they both were, and Flick improving a little every day. She'd make a rota and get her mother and anyone she possibly could to come to spend time with Flick. The next few weeks were going to be horrendous, but they'd win through, oh yes. For a brief moment Harriet thought about Alan Crimble. Damn him and his stupid car. She didn't think she could ever speak to him again.

13

The problem of what to do about Alan was weighing heavily on the minds of Bryn and Georgie. Since Flick's accident things had been very uncomfortable for him. Despite Georgie's loyalty, Bryn and she were beginning to think that it would be better if they tactfully suggested Alan found another job.

There were some customers who refused point blank to be served by him; indeed some had walked out rather than have him pull their pints. The drop in takings was noticeable but not worrying. They dreaded the day his case would come up in court. It was very quiet in The Royal Oak this particular Saturday evening. The school parents were holding a Summer Barn Dance in the school hall, and there was the final whist drive of the summer season in the church hall. If their past experience was anything to go by, there would be a sudden influx of people shortly, all wanting to be served at the same time. Sure enough in they came, plus a group of young men holding a celebratory drink for a friend's twenty-first.

'Pint of bitter please, Bryn, what will you all have?' They sorted out what they wanted and while they waited for Bryn to serve them, they were laughing and jostling each other. One of them spotted Alan.

'Hallo, Alan. Still 'ere then? Thought you'd have been gone long since. When does yer case come up?'

Alan smiled his thin, ingratiating smile. 'Too soon for me to know that. I may not even get prosecuted.'

'They'll throw the book at yer, and it's only what you deserve.'

Georgie spoke up. 'It wasn't entirely Alan's fault, you know, Flick did run out without looking.'

'We know that, but he still deserves whatever he gets. That car was a heap and no one in their right mind should have been driving it. Just thank yer lucky stars, Alan, she's still alive.' The young man, a redhead, picked up his drink and made to move to a table. 'Yer deserve a horse whipping, but I reckon you'll most likely get the easy option and go to prison.'

Alan shrank back against the optics. 'Think so?'

'More than likely.' Alan's tormentor grinned at his obvious distress, raised his glass in salute and joined his friends.

The bar began to fill up, so Alan had to go round the tables clearing away the used glasses and wiping away spills.

'By Jove, Bryn, Alan isn't a patch on Sharon MacDonald, we all enjoyed her backside slipping between the tables as she cleared away the glasses. Always ready for a bit of slap and tickle was Sharon. He's a poor substitute is Alan. We can't enjoy a glimpse of his cleavage!'

'It was more than a glimpse with Sharon.'

'Good for trade she was, though. Alan puts us off, don't yer, Alan?' The speaker gripped his shoulder. 'Heaven alone knows what he gets up to in that cellar, down there in the chill cold air, attending the beer. Got some pin-ups down there, Alan, to warm you up? See'd you Thursday at The Force. Right little raver yer were with. All backside and big ti . . . teeth. She yer latest then?'

Alan withstood this barrage as best he could, but Bryn could feel trouble brewing. Customers had been awkward and truculent with him since the accident but tonight there was a different feel about the joking. From behind the bar Bryn called out, 'Alan, we need some more bitter lemons and tonics, please.'

'Rightio, governor.'

'He'll be saying that in prison, 'cept it'll be, "Certainly governor, yes sir, no sir, three bags full sir".' They laughed uproariously and began telling prison jokes.

Alan came back into the bar carrying the bottles Bryn had asked for. The twenty-first birthday crowd was getting noisier. One of them noticed Alan was back.

'You got any good jokes to tell us, Alan?'

The door swung open and in came Peter with the chairman of the school governors, his wife and Michael Palmer.

Peter called out, 'Good evening, everyone.' A chorus of 'Good evening, Rector,' came from the customers.

Peter took out his wallet and bought drinks for the four of them. They took them to the only spare table, and when they were satisfactorily seated Peter said, 'A toast to a very successful evening.' They echoed his words, and Michael said, 'And can I add a big thank you for all your support. I think it's been the best ever.'

Peter said, 'Most definitely.'

'I'm a great believer in school parents getting to know each other at social events. It all helps to pull them together as a team. I know of a village where . . .' The chairman of the governers looked set for a big speech. His wife, reading the signals, decided to escape. She interrupted with, 'Excuse me, while I go to the little room.' Peter stood up as she rose from the table. Standing up gave him a good view of what was happening to Alan. He could see him clearing away glasses at the table where his tormentors were seated, then saw him unbalanced by a savage kick at his ankle. Alan clutched at the table to recover himself. 'Oh, whoops, he's had one over the eight, he's been indulging down in that cellar. We all wondered what he got up to down there, and now we know.'

'Come on, Alan, we'll buy you a drink to top you up. Double whisky for Alan, please, Bryn!'

'My bar staff don't drink when on duty, sorry.'

'This one does.' Two of them grabbed Alan and pinned his arms behind his back. The red-haired assailant picked up someone's whisky and began trying to force it down Alan's throat.

Peter glanced across at Bryn. He saw him nod meaningfully at Georgie, who disappeared straight away, and then Bryn came out from behind the bar.

'This is getting out of hand, gentlemen, please. I won't have this.' Bryn spoke firmly.

'No, you won't, Alan is. Come on you demon driver, open yer mouth, that's it, that's it, that's the way, down the hatch.' The whisky was partly going down Alan's throat and partly running down his chin and splashing onto his shirt. Bryn stepped up and tried to pull one of the men away, but the others, enjoying the spectacle, dragged him off.

Peter walked purposefully towards Bryn, intending to give him moral support. The ugly situation was made worse by the fact that customers not directly involved were quite liking the idea of Alan getting some punishment. They all knew how long Flick had been in hospital and what a narrow escape she'd had, and they quite relished the thought that if the courts didn't punish him as he deserved, they certainly would.

Michael joined Peter and whispered, 'You grab the red-haired one, I'll get the other.'

Peter nodded. They both dived together, grabbing the two men from behind, and pulling their arms behind their backs. Neither of Alan's attackers had seen who'd pulled them away, all they knew was that the fun was at an end. As soon as Peter released his grip on his arms, the red-haired one spun himself round and without really looking at his victim swung his fist at Peter's jaw. Fortunately Peter's height lessened the impact, but even so he staggered.

Deathly silence. The customers froze. Georgie gasped. Bryn was rooted to the floor. Peter, determined to maintain control so his attacker wouldn't gain any satisfaction from what he'd done, stood steadily looking at his assailant.

One of the men pushed back his chair and stood up. 'Please, Rector, accept our apologies.'

'Apologies!' shouted Bryn. 'Going down on your knees and begging for mercy wouldn't be enough for what you've done tonight. The lot of you are banned. Banned, do you hear? Punching the rector! Causing mayhem in my bar! The courts will decide what happens to Alan, not a bunch of rabblerousers like you lot. And the court will decide what to do with you lot, too. Because when the police get here I shall tell them exactly what's happened. Then they'll throw the book at you.'

'We didn't mean any harm. Things got a bit out of hand.'

'Out of hand? I should say!'

'You shouldn't employ him in here.'

'Who I employ is my affair, not yours.'

'Well, if that's how you want it so be it, but we shan't want to drink in here.'

'I don't want you to drink here, and when the police . . .'

As though on cue the swing doors opened and in came the sergeant. He bent down to remove his bicycle clips and said, 'Now then, what have we here? My word, Rector, I could almost think someone had been giving you a good thumping.' The sergeant pretended to examine Peter's jaw. 'Now, who did that, I wonder? Ah, I see, don't need to look any further, you're the same lot I turned out of the Jug and Bottle in Penny Fawcett three weeks ago. Well, this time I'm definitely charging you.'

Peter started trying to speak in their defence, but the sergeant held up his hand and silenced him.

'No, Rector, I'm not listening to any excuses, sorry, but they need sorting. If I listen to you, sir . . .' Two of the men were trying to slip away. ''Ere you two, not another step, stay right where you are.' The sergeant pointed with the end of his pen. 'Right there. If I listen to you, sir, I shall be buying them a drink and tucking them up in their beds with a goodnight kiss before the night's out. No, sir, this is it. They've met their Waterloo.' His ballpoint pen wouldn't write, so he licked the end of it to make it work and began writing in his black notebook.

14

'Caroline, where are you?'

'In the nursery, Peter.'

He appeared in the doorway. 'I'm going to look a complete idiot in church this morning with this big bruise. It would be the very day we'll be using the altar silver for the first time and the church will be full. Is there anything I can do, do you think?'

Caroline traced her finger along his jawline and made him wince. 'Oh sorry, I didn't mean to hurt. It's swollen too, that ice we used last night didn't have the desired effect, did it? There won't be many rectors conducting matins this morning with a swollen jaw got in a pub brawl.'

'It wasn't a brawl, darling. Well, yes it was, but I wasn't part of it.' Alex flung his arms round Peter's legs and squeezed hard. 'No, no, Alex, this cassock's clean on, I don't want your sticky fingers on it, young man. Good boy. Well, what's the answer? It's no laughing matter.' Despite himself Peter had to laugh when he looked in the nursery mirror. Alex, whose vocabulary, though limited, was always spoken at the top of his voice, shouted, 'Dada poorly.' Beth looked on, thumb in mouth.

Caroline said, 'I hesitate to suggest this, but what about putting some makeup on to lessen the impact a bit?'

'Makeup? The congregation will have doubts about my sexual proclivities.'

Caroline grinned wickedly. 'I doubt it, with these two rampaging in the rectory pew! If I smooth moisturiser on I'll probably hurt you, so you do it and then put some powder on over the top.'

'No. I've decided, it's happened, everyone knows, so why worry. I'll go as I am.' He bent down to kiss her. She put her arms round his neck, laid her face against his good cheek, and whispered in his ear, 'Come to think of it though, you do wear a skirt!'

Peter playfully slapped her bottom and escaped from the nursery with

Caroline in pursuit. 'I'll see you later,' she shouted from half way down the stairs. The front door slammed and Caroline, laughing, captured Alex as he struggled down the stairs after his father.

'Nappy time you two, and then off to church.'

Mrs Peel, in the two years and a bit that Peter had been rector, had developed the music beyond her wildest dreams, Peter's educated interest and talent having inspired her to reach new heights. Caroline entered the church to find it filled with a haunting melody. No one chattered, they were all listening. The music set the mood wonderfully, and she felt grateful that Peter had such a wonderful atmosphere created for him before he began his part of the worship.

In between coping with the twins' energies and wishing for about the hundredth time that there was a crèche for the little ones, Caroline took time to admire the altar. The old silver gleamed in the special lights Willie had fitted. Willie had decided that if they were to have it all on display then display it they would, and he'd spent a long time trying first one combination and then another until he'd got the effect just right. Muriel and Ralph came in and sat in their front pew. She glanced along her pew just in front of the lectern and smiled at the two of them. Alex called out 'Mooey. Mooey,' and waved to Muriel.

'Shhhhh.' Caroline put her finger to her lips but Alex simply smiled. Then Mrs Peel began the processional hymn, and Beth settled herself for a sleep, as she always did when Peter came in. He claimed that the first time Beth stayed awake for his sermon he would know he'd finally reached the height of his preaching powers. Alex saw Peter and shouted, 'Dada, Dada.' Caroline's finger on his lips was far too late. She knew he made the congregation smile each time he said it, but privately she knew it upset Peter.

The service went beautifully and Caroline, despite the harassment of Alex wriggling about and trying to sing in all the wrong places, found it a deeply spiritual occasion. That was the lovely thing about Peter's services, so simple, so easy to understand his message, and yet so thought-provoking and moving. He stood on the altar steps waiting for the sidesmen to bring their individual collection plates to him. The collection plate came round and Alex put his twenty pence piece in and one for Beth, who was still asleep. Caroline put her envelope in and watched the sidesman take the plate to the other side of the aisle. He paused, for what seemed an eternity, and stood looking at Ralph, quite still, collection plate in hand. From where she sat Caroline could almost feel the sparks fly between the two of them. Then he deliberately moved to the next pew without passing the plate to him. Ralph, who had looked him straight in the eye when he'd hesitated with the plate, quietly put his collection back in his pocket. Muriel blushed to the roots of her hair, took out her handkerchief with a trembling hand and dabbed at her top lip and forehead. The entire congregation noticed what had happened, including Peter, whose face was like thunder.

Mrs Peel, watching in the organ mirror for when the collection plates arrived at the altar steps, stumbled with her notes and had to stop and begin the phrase again. Caroline suddenly found she could hardly see for the haze of embarrassment which had come down in front of her eyes. At that moment Alex slipped off the pew and fell head first with a resounding clatter onto the floor. His screams reverberated around the church. In her handbag Caroline found his dummy and, though she hated him sucking it in public, she rescued it from its plastic bag and popped it into his mouth. The howling stopped as though by magic, and Caroline busied herself rubbing his head and examining it for damage. She waited apprehensively to see what Peter would do.

The sidesmen came to stand before Peter, and waited for him to hold the huge silver dish ready to receive the collection. He looked down on them in silence. The congregation waited with bated breath. He replaced the dish on the altar and stepped forward down the steps. Looking straight at the sidesman who had so resolutely refused to do his duty by Ralph and Muriel, he reached out and took the plate from him. Then Peter went to Ralph and stood patiently waiting while he got his collection out again. Of course it had caught in his pocket and there was a moment when Ralph was struggling, Mrs Peel was running out of music because of the delay, and loud sucking noises could be heard from the Rectory pew.

Peter returned to the altar steps, put the collection plate on his dish, and then waited to receive the others. Loud mutterings could be heard all over the church.

Caroline was never more glad to reach the end of the service. Beth woke as Peter left the church. Caroline collected the two of them together and headed for the church porch to stand with Peter ready to shake hands with the congregation, but Peter was nowhere to be seen and she stood there by herself.

'So sorry, Dr Harris, whatever came over 'im?'

'What's it all about, do you know, Dr Harris?'

'Well, I never, what a to do. You all right then, little Alex, all right are yer? Rare old tumble you had there, and not half.'

'What with the rector's jaw and little Alex's head, good job you're a doctor, ain't it?'

'Your Beth's as good as gold in church, but little Alex is a right card.'

The speaker patted their heads. 'We'll have to start a crèche, what with your two and little Frances now, and there's them from Nightingale Farm, right brood they've got up there and no mistake. Four it is now, and not one of 'em at school yet. They can't keep four of 'em quiet in the pew, can theys?'

'He needs telling off, he does. Hope the rector gives it him good and proper.'

In the vestry the sidesman *was* getting it good and proper.

'No matter what your views are in this matter, Arthur, the church is not the place to air them.'

'He's no right to be making money out of the villagers. He's got plenty and he needs no more than what he's got, he's not that many years left and no one to inherit.'

'Sir Ralph's financial status has absolutely nothing to do with this matter. You deliberately prevented him from offering himself to God's service. This is what one is doing when one puts money in the offertory. Giving oneself as well as the money.'

'Well, you would see it like that, Rector. It's my opinion the church doesn't want his kind of money. They say he's building a hundred houses on there. What hope have we for a real village life with that landed on us?'

'So providing homes for villagers which they can afford is a nonsense is it?'

'Not a nonsense, Rector, a money-making deal that's what it is. He'll get planning permission, sell the land to the highest bidder and pocket the money. Money, money, money, that's all he thinks about. Next news we'll have yobbos and drugs and joy riding, it'll never be the same again.'

'That could be a danger, and whilst I appreciate your views, you have no right whatsoever to do what you did this morning. None. Absolutely none. I am deeply grieved, Arthur, deeply grieved. It leaves me feeling very sad.'

'I'm deeply grieved too.'

'I get the feeling that there's more to this. Is there something I don't know, or is it just the houses?'

Arthur paused for a moment and then said, 'As you say, just the houses.' He stopped again, thought for a few seconds, and then taking a deep breath said: 'I object to him sitting in his Lord of the Manor pew, with his Lord of the Manor look on his face, making money hand over fist by spoiling our village. As if he's got some kind of supreme right to do as he wishes because of what he was. I'm not the only one who thinks like that either. T'ain't Christian.'

'That's a matter between Sir Ralph and his God. I'm afraid an apology is needed.'

'To you?'

'To me. Oh yes! And best of all to Sir Ralph.'

Arthur shook his head. 'Oh no, not to him. But I will apologise to you, Rector. I'm sorry for what I did this morning and if it caused you grief then, yes, I'm very sorry. But I shall be one of the people who gets up a petition, see if I don't. I can't stand by and let it happen without a protest.'

'Thank you for your apology and it's accepted wholeheartedly. Friends again, Arthur?' Peter held out his hand. 'And next Sunday?'

'I'll take the collection at the back not the front, there'll be no repetition of this morning, Rector, that I promise.' Arthur looked up at Peter and smiled. He shook Peter's hand vigorously. 'You've a very persuasive way with you, Rector. That wife of yours must have a devil of a job getting her own way about things. You could charm a monkey out of a tree, you could. Glad we've got you here at St Thomas's, though. You're the best thing that's happened in a long time. I'll say good morning to you. See you next Sunday.' As he left the vestry he turned at the door, smiled and said, 'Will you sign my petition?'

'I'll think about it!'

Peter went out in search of Ralph, but he and Muriel had already left.

'My dear Muriel, sit down here in your favourite chair and I'll make you a cup of tea, I think that's just what you need.' He disappeared into the kitchen. Muriel didn't like him in there, it didn't feel to be a man's job making tea, but at the moment she was grateful. In church, to be rebuffed in church like that. In front of everybody. She felt so mortified. That was what made it feel so bad. He'd shown them up in front of everyone. How could that Arthur Prior do it to them? What business was it of his, anyway? She'd dread the collection being taken every Sunday from now on, wondering if he would do it again. People didn't care any more what they did or who they hurt, so long as they made their protest. She'd never dare show her face in church, not ever. How could she tell Ralph to abandon the idea of the houses, when he was so set on it?

He came in with the tray at that moment. 'I'll pour, you sit there and relax.' He sat with his hands resting on his knees, watching her and waiting for the tea to brew. 'Don't worry, my dear, it will all blow over. They'll all talk a lot and make a big fuss but we shall quietly get on with our project and they'll all come round, see if they don't. When they see how tastefully designed your houses are they'll love 'em.' She watched his elegant hands as they poured her tea, she never tired of watching them, so sensitive they were, really very artistic. When he placed her cup on the table beside her chair she said, 'Oh Ralph, I thought I was going to die.'

Muriel took a sip of her tea. 'What a humiliation. I could strangle that Arthur. What right has he to sit in judgement on us? Peter was very upset.'

'He'd every right to be.'

'I shall never go to St Thomas's ever again. We'll have to go to church in Culworth.'

'Generations of the Templeton family have worshipped in St Thomas's. I've no intention of allowing Arthur to stop *me*, the very last of them.'

'We're both assuming it's about the spare land. I expect that *was* it, wasn't it?'

Ralph emphatically agreed. 'Yes.'

'Maybe we should forget the whole thing and leave it as it has always been, a lovely piece of nature for us all to enjoy. If Arthur comes round here to apologise I shall run upstairs out of the way. Say I'm indisposed or something.'

'Living dangerously hasn't lasted long.' Ralph smiled and patted her shoulder.

'I'm not very consistent, am I?'

The bell rang, and they heard the door opening. Muriel looked petrified, but then she heard Peter's voice.

'Hello there, Peter here, may I come in?' He appeared in the sitting-room doorway.

Ralph stood up. 'Come in, come in.'

'Come to offer my apologies about this morning in church. Arthur has apologised to me but he won't come here and apologise to you, Ralph. It's all about the spare land. He claims you are going to sell it with planning permission for a hundred houses. Is this true?'

'I am still waiting for confirmation from the council that they agree the land is definitely mine. When I've got that in writing from their solicitors, I shall apply for permission to build houses for rent on it. How many I do not know, as yet. That's the story Peter.'

'I see. Well, thanks for telling me. You all right, Muriel? Don't worry, it won't happen again, he's promised.'

'Are *you* all right, after the fight in the bar last night?'

'Yes, apart from my colourful bruise. You see, that's what Arthur is worried about, masses of houses and bringing in what he considers are all the wrong influences like brawling, drugs, motorbikes and that kind of thing.'

'Well, we'll see, we'll see.' Ralph stood up and Peter took the hint.

'I'll be on my way then. See you soon. I'll let myself out.'

When Peter had closed the door, Ralph said, 'If we're not careful he will be persuading us not to go ahead. He doesn't like there to be dissension in the village, wants us all to live in harmony. Well, I won't be dissuaded from going ahead. My mind's made up.'

'Ralph, I couldn't bear it if Peter didn't like what we were doing.'

'Between the two of you, nothing controversial will ever get done. It's in the village interest for us to do what we said, believe me.'

'But if no one speaks to us . . .'

'They will, don't worry.'

Come Sunday evening Jimmy, taking Sunday as a day off that week, was ensconced in his favourite spot in the bar, with a willing audience of Pat and Vera, eager to hear any gossip going the rounds. None of them had been in church that morning, but they had heard about Arthur's rebellion.

Pat didn't take long to air her views when the subject came up. 'How he dared do that I'll never know. What an embarrassment for Sir Ralph, eh?'

'A lot of venom there, yer see.' Jimmy rather knowingly tapped the side of his nose.

Pat bent forward so that she could hear better. 'When you tap your nose, I *know* you've got a tale to tell. Go on then.'

'Yes, venom, stands to reason.'

'What stands to reason, what are yer talking about? Have they had a row before, then?'

'I can see you 'aven't 'eard. Here's Willie, he knows more than me – come and sit with us Sylvia, while 'e gets the drinks in.' Sylvia came across and greeted them all as she sat down. Vera shuffled further along the settle to make room for her. 'We're talking about Arthur and the collection plate this morning.'

'I know! I didn't know where to look. I thought the rector dealt with it wonderfully. Willie was furious. Opening up old wounds, he called it. Do you know what he meant, Jimmy?'

'I do, and that's a fact.'

Pat, fast losing her temper with all the secrecy, said, 'Will someone tell me what's going on please?'

Jimmy wanted to wait until Willie joined them.

'Well-l-l-l-l?' Pat said.

'Go on, Willie, you tell her about Arthur.'

Willie appeared to be weighing the matter up, and then he decided to speak. 'I'm amazed yer don't know. Arthur is a relative of Ralph's.'

Pat and Vera were scandalised. Pat was the first to recover. 'A relative of Sir Ralph's? Never! How can he be? On his father's side he's a Prior from down Shepherd's Hill, on his mother's side he's a Goddard, and his wife's a daughter of the old headmaster of the Grammar School in Culworth. 'Ow can 'e be a relative?'

Willie took a deep draught of his pint and began his story. 'Ralph's grandfather was a right well set up young man, handsome yer know. Sir Bernard, he was called. Well, he was an army officer and he fought in the Boer War. They do say . . .'

'How do you know all this?' Pat queried.

''Cos my grandma was a young woman at the time and she knew all about it. They do say that he was a right ladies' man. No one was safe if he took a fancy to 'em, from servant girls to high society. A right charmer he was and not half. Well, his parents persuaded him to get married, calm 'im down a bit they thought, put a stop to the scandal and that. He married just as the Boer War started, goes off after a few days' honeymoon to serve Queen and country in South Africa. Gets wounded, gets sent home. Right glamorous he looks with his arm in a sling and a walking stick 'cos of his bad leg. Goes back after a few months' recuperation, leaves Lady Templeton expecting, and what no one realised until later, he leaves Mrs Beattie Prior expecting too.'

Vera sat back amazed. 'No!! It all went on then just like it does now, it's no different is it?'

'Beattie Prior's husband was right set up, thinking that after ten years of being married he'd at last proved himself. Well, 'e 'ad dark hair, really dark hair, and she was dark like a Spaniard.'

'What's that got to do with it?' Pat asked.

'You'll see. One night there's this terrible thunderstorm, the night that big branch fell from the royal oak and they all thought it would die. That same night Beattie and Lady Templeton both 'ad their babies. The doctor attended at the Big House, and the old woman who acted as village midwife attended Beattie. They both had boys at dawn within an hour of each other. It was only when Prior saw the Templeton baby at its christening that his suspicions were really aroused. They had a big do yer see, 'im being the son and heir, and all the village was invited. So there's Beattie Prior standing there with 'er little lad in her arms and her husband beside her and up comes Lady Templeton with her little lad in *her* arms. Both babies were as fair as it's possible to be, with dark brown eyes like all the Templetons. So alike they could 'ave been twins! Arthur's grandad looked first at one and then at the other and so did Lady Templeton and snap! The terrible truth dawned.'

Drink forgotten, Pat said, 'What happened then?'

'Don't know. It was all hushed up. All I can say is that Beattie Prior and her husband suddenly moved into their farm down the bottom of

Shepherd's Hill. Up till then they'd been as poor as crows, 'im only a labourer on Home Farm. Sir Bernard and his wife 'ad another two boys after that first one. Anyway, First World War put a stop to it, 'cos Sir Bernard got killed and his son did too. Only just seventeen he was, lied about his age when he joined up.'

Pat shook her head. 'I don't believe a word of it, you've made it up. Arthur Prior a Templeton! That's a laugh.'

'I'm telling you the tale as my grandma told me, and she wasn't a liar.'

'So,' said Vera, 'Arthur is the son of that Beattie's baby?'

'That's right.'

'So,' said Pat, 'Arthur Prior is a kind of cousin to Sir Ralph?'

'I think that's what he'll be.'

'Does Sir Ralph know all this?'

'I don't know, no one mentions it any more.'

'Well, by heck, what a story. No wonder he's against Sir Ralph making more money. He's jealous, that's what. Maybe he thinks he ought to own the spare land. Maybe he thinks his eldest ought to inherit from Sir Ralph with him having no children. Maybe he even thinks he ought to be *Sir* Arthur.' She giggled at the thought. 'I wonder which one was born first? That could make a difference, could it?'

''Ere, wet yer whistle with another drink. My round.' The three women pushed their glasses towards Jimmy and while he got the drinks in they sat contemplating the implications of what they had just heard.

Sylvia asked Willie if he remembered both of them at school.

'Oh yes. Ralph as bright as it's possible to be, always leading, always ahead, always thinking up tricks to play and Arthur, good old Arthur sensibly plodding along. As kids we didn't know any of the history of course. It never dawned on us.'

'I tell you what Willie, maybe your Sylvia's married into the aristocracy!'

Sylvia laughed. 'Sir Willie! Surely not!'

'What d'yer mean?'

'I mean that maybe your dad was one of Sir Bernard's mistakes, yer never know, with 'im spreading it about so much!'

Willie took offence. 'That's enough, Pat, thank you, I'll have you know my grandmother was a Methodist, strict teetotal she was. Never a drop.'

'Can't say you've inherited her qualities! This building of the houses could be quite a story before the year's out, couldn't it? Wait till the papers get on to it!'

*

After the evening service Peter went home, changed from his cassock into a shirt and jeans, and went downstairs to spend time with Caroline. It being summer, they had left their evening meal until evensong was over and the children in bed. Caroline had pulled the dining table closer to the french windows to catch what small amount of breeze there was, and the two of them sat eating their supper together.

'Too hot for cooking tonight, hope you don't mind a salad.'

'Of course I don't mind. It's a prince of a salad and delicious. I've been thinking, my darling girl, it's time we had a Sunday morning crèche.'

'I had the very same thought myself, in fact someone mentioned it when I was shaking hands after the service. They said there's our two, there's baby Frances, and there's the four Nightingales, and that's just for starters. They can't possibly come with four of them, so, yes, something will have to be done. We'll need toys and things to keep them busy, a room and a rota for helpers.'

'I'll leave that to you, then. Although it's sweet of Alex to shout "Dada", it's not conducive to worship, is it? He must be distracting for other people besides me.'

'Yes, I'm sure he must be, but in the nicest way.'

'Yes, of course. Caroline, do you ever feel a little worried by Beth?'

'Worried? What about?'

'Well, she seems so quiet. She tags along behind Alex like a shadow. He's talking and making himself a nuisance, but Beth is so quiet. Those big blue eyes of hers take everything in but she doesn't talk and I mean! Going to sleep as soon as she sees me come in!'

'Are you saying you think she's retarded?'

'No, no, not at all, but there is something worrying me, and I'm not sure what.'

'You used the words "takes everything in" – you're right, she does. If I say I want something and it's within her reach, she goes straight to it and brings it to me. If I say it's bathtime she's half way up the stairs before you can say knife. If I've mislaid something she knows exactly where it is and takes me to it. She's not daft, believe me, just overshadowed by Alex.'

'I see. Well she is only nineteen months, so we'll give it a bit longer.'

'You watch, she'll surprise us all.'

Peter offered Caroline more potatoes. She shook her head. 'No, you finish them, I have enough. Peter, what do you think is behind that scene in church?'

'I'm convinced it isn't just the houses. You should have seen the look they gave each other, something goes very deep between the two of them. Arthur said he disliked Ralph's Lord of the Manor look, which I thought very scathing. No doubt, my darling girl will find out before she is much older.'

'No doubt she will.'

'I'm most concerned about these houses, though. Ralph is determined to go ahead with his plans, but I'm not too sure they could . . .'

'I think the whole matter depends on how many houses are built. Six or eight or even ten for renting would be ideal, but twenty or more would throw the whole village out of balance, and I would feel I should protest.'

'I don't know if we can get involved. I'd rather work from the sidelines to influence things. We certainly can't align ourselves with Arthur Prior's petition, nor with Ralph.'

'Why not?'

Peter, noting the challenging tone of Caroline's voice, searched for a diplomatic reply. 'Unfortunately, you and I have people from both persuasions under our care and we can't be seen to side with either, I have to do what's right by both of them.'

'I know.'

'You won't take sides will you?'

'I might.'

'Caroline!'

'I only said I might.'

'Look, we had all that trou . . . misunderstanding about Jimmy and his rabbit snares, please don't, darling, please don't begin another crusade.'

'Crusade? Well, really!'

'I mean it, Caroline, everything is going so well at the moment. The attendance figures are way up, all the things I've started are taking shape, and I don't want anything to mar it.'

Caroline left her chair and went to sit on his knee. 'Move round; that's it. It's ages since I sat on your knee. You and I promised we wouldn't trespass.'

'Yes, I know, but . . .' He couldn't go further because Caroline was kissing him.

'Peter, let's leave all this and go to bed.'

'You abandoned woman you, what will Sylvia think in the morning when she comes?'

' "Good on yer, Pete," she'll say!'

'You've watched too many Australian soap operas.'

'When do I get time to watch soap operas?'

'Never.'

'You lock up, I'll go up to bed.' Caroline trailed her fingers along his bruised jaw. 'Handsome man you are, did you know that? Handsome.' She got off his knee, kissed his cheek and ran up the stairs.

Peter decided he'd clear the table and stack the dishwasher. After he'd turned out the lights, checked the cats were in and the doors were locked, he followed her upstairs. Caroline was standing looking at herself in the mirror. The clothes she'd been wearing lay in a heap at her feet.

'Peter, I'm getting old. Look, everything I possess is beginning to sag.'

He kicked her clothes aside and stood behind her, locking his hands around her waist. She smelt of soap and toothpaste. She must have had a shower, for her skin was warm but at the same time slightly damp. Speaking to her reflection in the mirror Peter said, 'You look wonderful to me, and quite superbly tempting, Dr Harris. What's made you decide to take stock?'

He watched his own hands as they began to wander about her body, enjoying the feel of her smooth flesh. He bent to kiss the nape of her neck where her hair curled childlike against her skin, and he looked over her shoulder into the mirror to observe her reaction. She rested her body against his and taking his hand she held it to her breast, smoothing her fingers along the back of it, enjoying its strength, and twisting his wedding ring round and round. Then she took his hand to her mouth and gently kissed each of his fingers.

Peter turned her around and, with the same fingers she had kissed, began slowly tracing her profile from where her forehead began at her hairline, down her nose, her top lip, across her mouth and down her chin to her jaw. Then cradling her face in his hands, he caressed her mouth with long awakening kisses. He stopped, and looking deeply into her eyes said, 'You don't regret marrying me, do you, darling? I do realise it does put limitations sometimes on your reaction to things, doesn't it?'

'I don't regret one single minute of the time I've spent with you. It's not the easiest of occupations being a clergy wife, but the one particular member of that august body I've married makes all the limitations worthwhile. Mind you, I can't guarantee there will never come a time when I shan't put my foot down on some principle or another.' She grinned at him and said, 'I might even sign Arthur Prior's petition!'

He stopped kissing her and scrutinised her face. She laughed and so did he.

'Get thee to bed, woman of my heart.'

15

Pat placed herself next to Vera on the settle and put her orange juice down on the nearest beer mat. Vera inspected her glass and said 'Orange juice! Since when 'ave you, Pat Duckett, drunk orange juice? That's a turn-up for the book.'

'Mi dad's 'ere, isn't he? Staunch teetotal he is, Lord 'elp us. Went on the bottle when Mum died, straight down the slippery slope. Alcoholic he was and no mistake. Took himself in hand and hasn't touched a drop since. We shan't be seeing him in 'ere, believe me.'

Jimmy expressed himself as being disappointed. 'Fancied 'aving another chap to talk to, make a change from all you women.'

'Cheek. At least you get to know all the latest. That taxi job of yours takes up all yer time. There's only me and Vera to tell you anything. Isn't it hot tonight? Hardly slept a wink last night, tossing and turning, all the windows open and I was still too hot. Mind you, with our Michelle's bed in my room and her restless too, I didn't have much hope.'

'So, what is the latest then?'

'Well.' Pat took a long draught of her orange juice and pulled a face. 'I shan't last long on this game. It's only a token gesture to mi dad. Well, little Flick is doing fine. Been home two weeks now. Did yer see 'er this morning, sitting out in the sun watching your geese? Well, yer wouldn't 'cos yer were working, but she was. Two crutches she has, bless her heart. Jimbo, I call him that now, we're very close . . .'

'Close? You and Mr Charter-Plackett? That's rich!' Vera shook her head at this flight of fancy on her friend's part.

'Less of yer cheek, Vera Wright. I'm one of his most reliable staff. He's told me so. And now mi dad's come I shall be doing more work for him. So . . .'

Jimmy interrupted. 'You were telling us about little Flick.'

'Right, I was. Jimbo was saying she's so disappointed not to have got back to school in time for the start of term, but she's determined she'll be back before long. Mr Palmer says she can go mornings at first and see how she gets on. She goes for therapy in the afternoons. She adores that baby. And no wonder, that little Fran is beautiful. I could take 'er 'ome with me.'

'Yer'd soon change yer mind.'

Pat laughed. 'Yes, I expect I should! She 'asn't 'alf got some grit she 'as, that Flick. When yer think 'ow badly knocked about she was, and 'ere she is fighting to get back to school. Jimbo, as I call 'im now, is that anxious about 'er. But then so would I be if it was our Michelle.'

'I've been thinking, where's yer dad sleeping?'

Pat's face fell. 'With our Dean. He's none too pleased and I don't suppose mi dad is either, 'aving to share with a teenager.'

'Where yer working this week?' Vera asked, wondering if she might offer her services. Cleaning at the nursing home didn't bring in that much.

'We've a twenty-first dinner party at a big house far side of Culworth on Saturday, a fiftieth wedding anniversary lunch Sunday, and then Friday night Little Dereham's Cricket Club annual dinner. That'll be a right smashing do and not half. They're a right crowd. Then we've a special dinner up at the Big House for Craddock Fitch coming up soon. He's entertaining some of the local nobs. But I'm not helpin' with that.'

'Trying to ingratiate himself, is 'e?' Jimmy asked.

'Something like that. Doing overkill to make up for wanting to sell the silver.'

'What does yer dad do for a living then?' Jimmy asked.

'Up till now he's been in charge of the glasshouses at Bothring Park. Grapes, peaches, melons, you name it he grew 'em. I've asked Venetia if there's a job going up at the Big House, but I haven't heard anything positive.'

'Leastways he'll get your garden in order,' was Vera's heartfelt comment. 'My Don's sick of all them seeds from your weeds blowing into our garden, one body's work it is weeding.'

'If that's all yer've got to worry about I feel sorry for yer.'

Jimmy, seeing a row blowing up, offered to get the drinks in.

Pat spotted Willie coming in. 'Oh there's Willie, he's been in court today. Come on over Willie, and tell us 'ow yer went on,' she shouted.

After he'd settled himself in his usual chair he said, 'My Sylvia's babysitting tonight, the rector and Dr Harris have gone to a big dinner at the Deanery. So I shan't stay long, I'll go keep her company.'

'We know, we know, tell us 'ow yer went on at the court.'

'Well . . . them who stole the lead from the church roof got fined and community service. Ought to have been horsewhipped, stealing, but there you are. You might say I caught 'em too early, if they'd stolen more they'd have been fined more, might even have gone to prison.'

'No, really, is that all they got?'

'But . . .' said Willie, 'there's more.' He glanced round the bar. 'Guess whose case was before mine?'

'No idea. Whose was it?'

'Alan Crimble's.'

Pat nearly jumped from her seat. 'We haven't seen 'im serving tonight yet, 'e didn't get prison did he?'

'No. Asked a policeman I know from Culworth. "What did the last one get?" I says to 'im. "Not enough," he says.' Willie took another drink. Vera and Pat became impatient.

'Well, what did he get?'

'He got fined three hundred pounds, disqualified from driving for a year. He can pay the three hundred pounds off at so much a week. Car's a write-off of course, it was that before the accident anyways, we all knew that.'

'So are you saying, then, that Flick getting hurt like she did, didn't count?'

'Well, yer see for a start, there were no witnesses, were there? Middle of the morning, everyone in school, or out at work, and pouring with rain, yer know, nobody about, and she did run out from the gate without looking, she said so herself to the police, she told 'em when she was well enough to speak to 'em. Rector and I ran out *after* we'd 'eard the crash, so we didn't see it either. So it's all the legal things he copped for. No MOT, no insurance, no road fund licence and that.'

'Well, at least the roads will be safe for us to go out on for a year, that's something I suppose.' Pat suddenly put her head down and muttered, 'Don't look now, he's just come in.'

Jimmy shouted, 'Any chance of a lift, Alan? Mi battery's flat!'

Georgie's head came up and the pint glass she was filling overflowed. She served her customer, took the money, and came over to see Jimmy.

'That's enough Jimmy, he's been tried, got his punishment and now the matter is closed.'

'You might call it closed, Georgie, but I bet Harriet and Jimbo and little Flick don't call it closed. She's still struggling on crutches, but I notice Alan's walking OK. Looks to me like he's got off scot free in comparison.'

'Don't you think that perhaps Alan is feeling bad about all this? He doesn't exactly enjoy knocking down a child, you know. One day, Jimmy, it might be you who knocks down a child, and then see how you feel about it!' Georgie turned on her heel and marched back behind the bar. She left Jimmy still of the opinion that he was right.

Alan began serving. Bryn and Georgie were glad of his help, for the beautiful weather had brought out the crowds. Some customers had driven from as far as Culworth to sit out in the little courtyard and enjoy the summer's evening, or on the green or at the little tables Bryn had put outside the door. They encroached on the road a little but the sergeant turned a blind eye on hot summer nights. Bryn and Georgie and Alan were all kept busy serving, and the dining room was busy too; altogether the three of them were very pleased with the atmosphere and especially the frequent pinging of the till.

A young man came to the bar for six lagers. Alan gave him a tray, he paid for them and wandered off outside, balancing the tray carefully as he squeezed between the crowded tables. Jimmy watched him leaving and said, 'Isn't that chap a friend of them that punched the rector?'

'Can't be,' said Pat, 'they were banned.'

'I don't think he was 'ere that night. But I've definitely seem 'im in Culworth with 'em, boating on the river and causing a lot of annoyance with being daft. I recognise 'is funny haircut.'

Alan set off around the tables collecting the used glasses. He went to the bar with several and then Bryn said to him, 'There must be a lot outside, Alan, go take a look, we're running really short in here.'

It was the loud shouting which drew the attention of everyone inside the bar. Bryn looked at Georgie and then hastily pushed his way outside. The noise was becoming louder and louder and then they heard the crashing of chairs, and women screaming. Jimmy, Vera and Pat, being seated close to one of the exits, were the first of the concerted rush of customers to get outside to see what was happening. A whole group of lads had Alan on the ground and were kicking him. He was trying to protect his face and head with his hands, but they were kicking from all sides and he'd no chance of escape. Bryn muscled in, and with the help of some law-abiding customers they managed to pull Alan away, but then punches began flying and Bryn was unable to control the ensuing fight. Inside, Georgie had rung for the police, and those customers nervous of getting involved had spread out onto the green to avoid getting hurt.

Pat helped Alan inside. The cut he'd received in the accident was nothing to the condition his face was in after the kicking. Despite her anger at what Alan had done to Flick, she couldn't help feel sorry for him.

'Here, Georgie, you got a cloth or something? There's blood all over the place. Quick, be quick, it's running all down 'is shirt.' Georgie came with a tea cloth and between them they mopped his face. But he winced and protested so much at the pain they caused, they had to desist and leave him, slumped on a chair, holding the cloth to his face.

'Brandy, that's what he needs. Oh God, they're coming in 'ere now. Watch out.'

'Where is he, where is he?' Tables and chairs began crashing over, glasses and drink spilling all over the floor. The noise was almost more frightening than the fighting, and Pat wished the police would come pronto, but how many would it take to control this lot? The sergeant wouldn't be much good on his own.

Thankfully, the sound of a police siren pierced the air. Almost immediately the fighting stopped and there was a mass exodus of men. They struggled to reach the doors and get out before they got caught, but the doors were quickly secured and they were all confined in the bar. Two of the men headed for the gents', hoping to escape out of the lavatory window, but Georgie was standing in the passage waiting for them, brandishing a cricket bat.

'Oh, no, you don't! One step and I'll clobber you with this and I mean it.' She raised the cricket bat, ready to strike. They went forward with the intention of taking the bat from her, but the glint in her eye stopped them. 'You've done enough damage, and you're getting the book thrown at you. Get back in that bar.' She stepped forward holding the bat with both hands at shoulder level. Withering under her determined gaze, the two of them backed off. Georgie followed them, holding the bat at the ready.

Above the din she shouted, 'Officer! These two are the ringleaders, I've just stopped them trying to escape.' Everyone stopped what they were doing and looked at her. Petite and pretty with her fine delicate blonde hair, her eyes blazing in defence of Alan, the cricket bat held aloft, she made an arresting picture. Bryn came to take the bat from her, and as he did so her anger melted and she clutched Bryn's arm.

'Oh help, Bryn, I'm going to make a fool of myself. I'm going to be sick.' She disappeared behind the bar.

Before the police left, the senior officer had a word with Bryn.

'You'll have to look to your laurels, Mr Fields, this is twice in quick succession we've had to come to a brawl here, and this one is much more serious that the last. Better control, if you please. Or else next time your licence comes up for renewal it might be . . .' He drew his finger across his throat, making his meaning very clear.

Bryn grimly apologised. Losing his temper with the police would gain nothing. He was so angry with himself for not realising that the banned drinkers were actually on his premises. One of the men involved in the fighting volunteered to take Alan to casualty. Georgie saw him into the car, supplying him with a clean towel to hold to his face. 'Now take care Alan, get the hospital to ring us if there's any problems, won't you? Best of luck, love.' Alan nodded; he couldn't speak because his face was rapidly swelling.

The customers began trailing back inside to finish their drinks, but the overturned tables and chairs, the broken glass and spilled drinks made it impossible.

'This would never 'ave 'appened when Betty MacDonald was 'ere. She'd 'ave cracked their heads together, clasped 'em to 'er bosom and thrown 'em out,' Vera observed.

Pat laughed. 'Well, you should know Vera, she threw you out once.'

Vera laughed, wagged her finger at Pat and went home.

Alan came back from the hospital the following day. His nose was broken, he had several teeth missing at the front, two cuts which had needed stitches, and his whole face was badly swollen and bruised. In trying to protect his head, his hands had taken a lot of the punishment and they were bruised and swollen too, with three fingers broken. His back and chest were painful from bruising, making it difficult for him to move. After Georgie had got him to bed, she and Bryn held a council of war in their little office.

'I don't care what you say, Georgie, we can't have him serving in the bar for a long time, if ever again.'

Georgie pushed her hair back from her face and pleaded. 'What's he going to do if he doesn't work for us? You know full well he's not capable of standing on his own two feet, he needs us. We've looked after him for sixteen years, it'll be cruel to have to tell him he's to go. I could have killed those two last night.'

'I could see that. You looked full of fight.'

'I felt scared.'

'No matter how we feel about Alan, our customers don't want him here. In a big city he wasn't nearly so noticeable, but here his idiosyncrasies seem magnified. There is no way that we can sacrifice our livelihood to Alan. I know he's useless without us, but he's got to go, so you must make your mind up to it. The insurance will go mad when we send this claim in. Our premium will rocket, and we'll be working to pay the premiums instead of working to make a profit. We're in business, Georgie, we're not running a home for the inadequate.'

'Inadequate! That's unkind!'

'We were up till two this morning clearing up the mess, so I'm not in the mood for being magnanimous, believe me.'

Georgie put her arm through Bryn's. 'Can't I persuade you, not even one little teeny bit?' She smiled up at him, brushed a finger along his moustache and tweaked his cheek, but he didn't smile back.

'No, sorry, and at bottom you know the decision is right. I'll get in touch with that girl from Penny Fawcett who asked us for a job, and we'll give her an interview.'

'We can't turn him out till he's better and he's found somewhere else.'

'Of course not. I'm not that ruthless.'

16

Because of the Indian summer, Muriel was getting out of bed much earlier than usual to walk Pericles before the real heat of the day began. He was finding the hot weather almost unbearable and some days she felt real concern on his behalf. They walked slowly, in deference to his age, along Jacks Lane and down towards Shepherd's Hill. Pericles' nose began twitching and so did Muriel's. She was certain she could smell cooking, surely they weren't already working in the kitchens at the back of the Store? Seven o'clock? Surely not.

Pericles pulled on the lead, wanting a chance to investigate the smells.

'Pericles, all you think of nowadays is your stomach. You're getting very greedy.' As she crossed Shepherd's Hill, Muriel realised that something odd was afoot. She rounded the corner of the Methodist chapel, now boarded up prior to demolition, and gasped at what she saw. 'Oh, dear. No! Oh dear. Come! Heel, Pericles.'

Dotted here and there, on the grass between the trees, were parked ramshackle caravans, old converted buses and an assortment of motorised vehicles. There were dogs and children playing, some fires were burning, and the whole paraphernalia of permanent outdoor existence lay around. As she stood mesmerised by all the activity, two men came towards her each carrying large pickaxes. As they reached her they said: 'Morning, missus, nice day.'

'Yes, it is.' They passed her and went directly to the chapel, and began attacking the boarding nailed over the back door.

'That's private property, it was a chapel.'

'Not no more it ain't,' one of the men shouted, and continued his attack on the boarding. Two of the big dogs came rushing at Pericles. Muriel picked him up and the dogs began leaping at her to reach him. Pericles struggled with fright, and Muriel shouted. One of the men with a pickaxe bawled at the dogs, 'Give over.' But they didn't stop and he came across and hit them with the handle of his axe. They scurried away howling. 'Don't worry missus, they mean no harm. Let him off, he'll be all right.'

But Muriel hurried away. She crossed the green to give Pericles a chance to run about a little and then hurried back to Ralph.

'Ralph, Ralph are you up?' He was just coming downstairs. 'Oh, Ralph, there you are.'

'My dear, how did you get your dress so dirty? And . . .'

'Never mind about my dress, there are travellers camped on the spare land. Dozens of them with big dogs and they're breaking into the chapel. Oh Ralph, I was so frightened.'

Ralph put his arms around her and held her tightly. 'This *is* a pretty kettle of fish and no mistake. They didn't hurt you, did they?'

'Oh no, it was the dogs jumping up that dirtied my dress. What are we going to do Ralph?'

'When you say travellers, how many are you talking about?'

'There must be at least a dozen vehicles, possibly more, and there's loads of people and children and dogs, and there's all their things lying about. Everywhere is littered. Where on earth have they come from?'

'I don't know. I think I'll ring the police.'

'But the sergeant won't be able to do anything all by himself, there's so many of them.'

'We'll see. I'll ring him now. They must have moved in during the night, they weren't there at ten last night when we walked Pericles, were they?'

'Not a sign. I'll make your breakfast while you ring him.'

When the telephone rang, the sergeant was half way through his porridge, and he did enjoy it. He loved the rich dark swirls of black treacle contrasting with the bland flavour of the porridge as it passed over his taste buds. Now, with the phone ringing, it would be turning into a dark brown grey mush and he felt aggrieved.

As he listened to Sir Ralph telling him the bad news, he undid the top button of his pyjamas to give himself more air. He didn't relish this idea at all. Oh no. He'd need reinforcements, yes, definitely reinforcements.

'Certainly, Sir Ralph, I'll get onto it straight away.' Well, when I've finished my porridge that is, he thought. He sat down again, spooned the porridge into his mouth as fast as he could, drank his mug of tea down as quickly as possible, why did she always make it so hot? and raced into the bedroom to get dressed.

His wife called out. 'You'm can't go out on duty not shaved. Sir Ralph won't like that at all 'e won't, now will 'e? Only cause trouble you not being shaved, his lordship'll report you, he will, definite.'

He raced angrily into the bathroom and straight off cut his chin with his razor. This wasn't his day.

Sir Ralph was waiting for him. He got out his notebook. As soon as he saw the vehicles and the dogs he said, 'I recognise this lot. They've been camped on Arthur Prior's land for the last three weeks. In his back field down the old cart track. Wonder what made 'em move 'ere.'

Wryly Ralph said, 'I wonder.'

The sergeant looked at him. 'You thinking what I'm thinking, Sir Ralph?'

'Could be,' he answered. 'Well, what shall we do then?'

'First, they're in trouble for breaking and entering the chapel, and damaging trees what have a preservation order on 'em, look, they've chopped off them branches for their fire. I think we shall have to get Culworth to come, it's too big a job for one man this is. Two of these chaps have been up for grievous but they got off scot free, not enough evidence, but we knew they'd done it all right. Leave it to me, sir, best not get involved. You're the landowner now, I reckon.'

'I am, yes.'

'Right. I'll let you know.'

Close to the chapel a small crowd was watching events.

'Who is they, Sir Ralph?'

'Just travellers. They've broken into the chapel . . .'

'Oh no, the devils, what will they do next?'

'I sawed them in Arthur Prior's fields last week, made a right mess there, they have.'

'We shan't sleep safe in our beds. Better lock all the doors.'

'Yer right there. And windows. And keep yer cats in, case they run short of food.'

'Oh, don't be disgusting.'

'You mark my words.'

Malcolm the milkman stopped his van, and lifted a crate off the back.

'You're not selling 'em milk are yer Malcolm?'

'I've a living to earn, if they want milk and they pay me for it, milk they'll get. 'Scuse me, let me through.'

'Yer encouraging 'em, you are. Yer a traitor.'

'We want rid of 'em.'

'He can wait for his money this week, rotten little money grabber he is.'

Ralph stalked home. 'MURIEL! Where are you?'

'Here, dear. What's happening?'

'I'm going down to see Arthur Prior, he's at the bottom of this.'

'Why? Why has he done it?'

'You don't know? Of course you don't. I'll tell you the whole story about my dear cousin Arthur.' Ralph didn't make any bones about telling her. Her hand to her mouth she listened, horrified.

'So there you have it. Mainly revenge for past wrongs, I think,' Ralph concluded.

'Oh, Ralph, my dear, it's not your fault. You weren't even born and neither was he, and they did get a farm of their own, something they would never have been able to aspire to. Well, I never knew all this before. How long have you known?'

'My father told me when I started at the village school when I was four, he thought I should be forewarned in case anything was said. He found the right words to explain it and somehow I didn't find it dirty or nasty, because he told me so beautifully. No one at school ever mentioned it to me and I never did to Arthur, it didn't seem right somehow.'

'I should think not indeed.'

'So there you have it. I shall not give up. He can be as obstructive as he likes, I will still go ahead, because I know it is a good thing for the village and that's my concern, not Arthur Prior's hurt feelings or his jealousy.'

'That's what it is, isn't it, jealousy? He feels his father was as much a Templeton as any born with the name. He feels bitter inside.'

'It must have been a shock to him when I came back, after all those years away.'

'Of course, yes, they were invited to our evening wedding party and never came, said they already had an engagement elsewhere, so that explains it. I expect he's angry that you've been found to own land, when he thought all that side of the family wealth was over and done with. He's got two sons, hasn't he?'

'He has. Both sons work the farm with him. There is another aspect to this though.'

'What?'

'The farm belongs to them only so long as there is a Prior working the land and living on the farm. As soon as that stops, the farm comes to me or any person named Templeton alive at the time.'

'You mean they don't *own* it?'

'No, they pay a small rent each year to the family solicitor, something like twenty-five pounds. A kind of token. It's been twenty-five pounds all these years.'

'I see. That must be galling for Arthur. Very galling. Working hard and yet never his own. I expect he must have in his blood what you have in yours, a deep-seated satisfaction from owning land.'

'Yes, I think perhaps you could be right there.'

'Ralph, it seems odd they were given a farm so close to the village.'

'Well, at the time, being almost in Little Derehams was a long way away.'

'Yes, of course, it would be almost an hour's walk away, far enough I suppose. No one knew then that Turnham Malpas would become the centre of things, having the only church and the only school and the only Store, because they had their own then, didn't they? Actually, I'm beginning to feel quite sorry for Arthur.'

Ralph stood up and leant over her to kiss her cheek. 'You have a kind heart, my dear. A very kind heart, and I love you for it. Now I'm going to see Arthur to give him a piece of my mind. I'll teach him to meddle in my affairs. Who the devil does he think he is?'

Muriel ran after him down the garden path. 'Please, Ralph, don't be hasty, dear, come back in and we'll talk about it some more.'

'No, my dear, I'm going. Shan't be long.' She watched him back the Mercedes out of the garage and roar off down Pipe and Nook Lane, far faster than was safe. She ran through the house again and out of the front door signalling him to stop, but he raced past the front of the house ignoring her shouts.

He'd never been to Prior's farm in all his life. Delicacy forbade it. But there it was, 'Prior's Farm' painted on a smart swinging board at the entrance, He turned right and slowly made his way up the well-tended farm lane into the yard.

Even the best run farms usually have old equipment lying about, or hay scattered around the yard, but not here. Everywhere was immaculate. Except for the distant mooing of cows, it was almost impossible to imagine that a real live working farm was being run there. Every piece of woodwork was smartly painted, every door hung straight, beside each door were half barrels painted and filled with flowers. A sheepdog came good-naturedly up to him, wagging its tail. He bent to pat its head.

A curtain moved slightly; someone was watching them. He rang the door bell. No one answered, but Ralph heard footsteps approaching from behind.

'Yes, and what do you want? Come to view another of your properties, have you?'

Arthur Prior in corduroy trousers, matching cap and a plaid workman's shirt, stood legs apart, arms folded, awaiting a reply. The two men faced each other. Both stockily built, both white haired, both with the long aristocratic nose of the Templetons and each utterly determined to have his own way.

'No, I've come to see you.'

'Well I'm here, fire away.'

'I understand you have some travellers on your land.'

'Did have.'

'Right, did have. Was it you persuaded them to camp on the spare land during the night?'

'Now, as if I'd do a thing like that to you.'

'That's not an answer.'

'Maybe not, but it's all you're going to get.'

'Some kind of joke, is it?'

'What?'

'Persuading them to move?'

'Don't know nothing about it. Got up this morning and lo and behold they'd gone. Couldn't believe my eyes, I couldn't.'

'I bet.'

'Betting man are you, then?'

'Not specially.'

'I'll bet you a thousand pounds you won't get houses built on that land.'

'I wouldn't allow you to lay such a bet when I know I shall win.'

'You bloody well won't win.' Arthur stepped closer. He prodded Ralph's lapel with his strong brown finger. 'Not this time, Ralphie boy, not this time. You and your family have had it your own way round here for generations, but now it's my turn.'

'Houses to rent for country people is wrong, is it?'

'You making money hand over fist is what's wrong. You've enough money, what do you want more for? You'll get planning permission, then sell the land, pocket the money and with a smile on your face like a Cheshire cat you'll be off to some far distant shore with that new wife of yours to spend the proceeds, leaving us with the rabble to contend with.'

'What I do is my affair. I don't have to justify myself to you.'

'Don't you indeed! Arrogant, that's what you are, arrogant. Want me to touch my forelock to you, like in the old days. Not me nor one of my sons will *ever* kowtow to you, Ralph Templeton, ever. So off my land . . .'

'That's the rub, isn't it? It's not your land, that's why you're taking this stand. The arrangement wasn't of my making, you know, nor of yours.'

'My father offered your father the money for this farm and he refused, refused to sell. Said it wasn't his to sell, he only held it for his descendants, so we're in a bind, aren't we?'

'I'm sorry, but, yes, you are. At the same time, you're making a good living from it. However, I really came about the travellers. Obviously it *was* you got them to move. But don't think this will stop me, nothing will. I'm determined to have my own way about those houses, and I will. Nothing will stop me. Nothing.'

'And I shall dance on your grave, you'll see, making money out of that land will be the end of you and yours, mark my words.' Arthur shook his fist at Ralph. Ralph made a dismissive gesture and left fuming.

Muriel had spent the time he was away dodging from one pathetic occupation to another. Nothing she did was right, and worst of all she'd broken one of her mother's china ornaments whilst she was dusting. It was of a small boy sitting on a tuffet with a bowl of soapy bubbles on his knee and a clay pipe almost falling out of his hand because he'd fallen asleep. She'd often wondered if her mother would have preferred a boy like this one, with his dark curls and his stubborn chin, instead of her. The sound of Ralph's car pulling up outside made her jump.

She hurried to open the door.

'Oh! Ralph! Are you all right? I've been so worried.'

'It's him, I knew it, as soon as I saw those – those travellers, I guessed. He won't beat me you know, he won't beat me, I'm determined to build those houses. The more he protests the more determined I shall become.' He went to the whisky decanter and poured himself a double.

'Oh Ralph dear, you don't normally drink at this time in the morning, is it wise?'

'I don't know what is wise any more.' Ralph went to sit at his desk, he put the glass down and said, 'Ralphie, he called me, Ralphie! I could throttle him.'

'Ralph, that's not very kind.'

'I don't feel kind this morning. He's deliberately persuaded those – those – people to move on to my land. Purposely to cause me annoyance.'

'I'm sure it's quite by chance . . .'

'No, it's not, they were on his back field until last night, and this morning they have mysteriously moved onto mine.'

Not having witnessed Ralph in such a temper before, Muriel didn't know what to say next to calm him down. She flitted about the study wringing her hands. 'Ralph, dear, don't get too upset, I'm sure the police will sort it out eventually.'

'Oh eventually yes, months and months they'll take. It's the aggravation of it all I don't like. All we need is for the council to decide not to allow the application, and we shall be a laughing stock.'

'How can they refuse?'

'Because I agreed with you, and don't misunderstand me, you were absolutely right. I didn't let Neville Neal do his bit with the handouts to the appropriate councillors, so they'll get their revenge by refusing out of spite.'

'Well, what is to be, is to be. We shall just have to accept it.'

'The planning meeting is tonight, so we'll soon know. Neville said he'd give that councillor he is supposed to have in his pocket a ring after the meeting and find out what went on.'

'I didn't think you'd let Neville have anything more to do with it after I was so cross that day.'

'Oh, he's clinging on, he's wanting to invest in the project you see, tactfully suggested I might be overstretched and he could help. The cheek of the man!'

'Will you be overstretched?'

'We, my dear, we. You and I know that we only intend building at the most eight houses, but we've applied for twenty, on the basis that if we ask for more than we want, we might eventually be allowed the eight we intended, and honour will be satisfied on both sides. So if that is the case, yes, we can afford it.'

'Ralph! How ingenious!' She stood in front of his desk, her hands leaning on the top, and said quietly, 'Do you think it might be possible to persuade the travellers to go without having to get the police in and everything get nasty? I saw some of the children, they do look in need of help, they really do. I would hate the thought of any of them getting hurt.'

'What would you have in mind, my dear?'

'Well, if Arthur Prior managed to get them to move, they must have moved for a very good reason. Do you suppose he gave them money? I can't think of any other way they might move willingly, can you?'

'Muriel! Now it's your turn to be a genius. Of course, that's the way. They'd have to move off first, then I'd give them the money and then we'd get someone to tip piles of earth at the entrance to stop the vehicles re-entering. Yes, how clever of you, my dear.'

'There's more than one way of skinning a cat, as my mother used to say.'

'How right she was. How very right. We'd have to go about it very subtly. If we weren't careful they'd agree to a sum and then haggle to get more and then more, and keep putting off the move. Yes, you've hit the nail on the head.' Ralph spent the morning laying his plans.

When the local paper came out on Thursday, large headlines declared that the planning committee had refused permission for the twenty houses. There were many reasons given, among them that they feared houses would mean a severe encroachment on the green belt, and of course such a large number of houses would involve cutting down far too many trees, added to which the whole balance of the village would be upset and it might mean the overloading of the village school, et cetera, et cetera. There was a quote from Arthur Prior, saying how pleased he was that the houses would not be built, and that it was a victory for common sense. When the reporter had interviewed Ralph he had tried to aggravate him into being angry and saying more than he intended, but Ralph had simply said how disapppointed he was, and that he would be trying again for permission at the earliest possible moment. There was also a small paragraph mentioning that the travellers were intending wintering in their new quarters. He decided not to attend church that Sunday and he and Muriel went out for the day instead. So he wasn't there to hear his telephone ring several times that day, and it was important too.

17

Harriet had been awake with the baby since four am, so she was in no mood for the children playing up at breakfast time.

'If you two boys don't sit to the table by the time I've counted five I shall take steps.'

Flick was already seated, eating her cereal. 'I'm going to school this morning, coming home for my lunch.'

'Lovely darling, it's entirely up to you, you know that, but don't overdo things, will you? I'm counting! One, two, three, four . . . That's better. Now be quiet and eat. I've had a horrendous night with Fran and I'm in no mood for silly boys. Here you are. Jimbo! Never mind the post, please darling, sit down and eat.'

'Coming. God! I'm exhausted this morning. I'm sure Peter's added another mile to our run and not told me.'

'You exhausted? What were all the snores about then, around five o'clock?'

'Snores? I don't . . . I say look at this, an invite to dinner from old Fitch. Formal dress, two weeks on Friday. You know he asked me to cater for his special dinner party? Didn't realise we'd be included. Can't go. See to it, will you?'

'Can't go? Why not? Is that the night of the Freemasons' do? No, it's not, that's the following Friday. Finlay! Please! Butter your toast on your plate not on the tablecloth. Thank you. So we can go.'

'You know my rules.'

Harriet studied his reply for a moment. She knew his rules, but she'd been incarcerated with the family for four months now. With the baby, and with Flick needing so much care, she'd been absolutely nowhere at all. She needed, yes, desperately needed, to socialise.

'If I got Mother to . . .'

'She won't and I don't want to leave Fran.'

'Jimbo, at this particular moment in time I could leave Fran on the nearest available doorstep. I've had it where she's concerned.'

Flick shrieked. 'Don't say that, please. She doesn't mean it, does she Daddy?'

Fergus, impatient of his little sister creating such a crisis, said, 'For heaven's sake you know she doesn't. Don't be daft.'

Tears sprang to Flick's eyes. Jimbo patted her head and said, 'You know full well Mummy doesn't mean it. She's had a very bad night with Fran and she's worn out. You boys can get moving and clear your own dishes away for once. We've all got to pull together when Mummy's tired. I've got to get to the Store.'

He pushed his chair under the table and went to kiss Harriet. 'Love you, darling. Politically it wouldn't be good to refuse this invite, would it?'

'No.'

'Trouble is, if I go it would be like being on the rack, watching and not being able to jump in if things went wrong.' Neither of them had realised that Sadie had let herself in the house and was standing in the doorway waiting for a gap in the conversation.

'It's me. What's this invitation?'

Harriet explained.

'No problem there. I haven't received one, but then how can I? He doesn't know I exist. So you go and I shall hold the fort behind the scenes and make sure everything goes according to plan. What could be simpler?'

Harriet immediately felt better, till she remembered they'd then have no one to sit in.

'Ask Sylvia Biggs. She's used to looking after the Rectory twins, she'd be all right with Frances.'

'Of course. Wonderful mother, you are. So resourceful.'

'Yes, I am. I'm a wonderful mother-in-law too, am I not Jimbo?' He went to kiss her, then said, 'Look, all this kissing is not getting the Store open. I'm going.'

'So am I. Shan't be in this morning, Jimbo dear, got an appointment in Culworth with my hairdresser. My roots are showing. I insist upon a kiss from all my grandchildren. Come, children, kiss your grandmother, starting with the eldest.'

After they had dutifully kissed her the boys escaped without taking away their dishes, and Flick began painfully trying to do it for them.

Harriet protested. 'No Flick, leave that. You've quite enough to do just getting ready for school. I'll see to it all.' Flick limped away. Once she was out of hearing Sadie said, 'I do hope that limp isn't going to be permanent.'

'Mother! It's only four months since the accident, they're mightily impressed at the hospital. They think she's doing brilliantly and so do we. Thanks for saving the day about the dinner, I'm dying to go.'

'You would have all these children Harriet, one would have been quite sufficient considering the busy life you lead with the business. I told you so when Fergus was born, but oh no! Jimbo wanted a houseful because he'd known what it was like being an only one. But I can't see that you've suffered very much from being an only child.'

Frances' apologetic wail percolated into the kitchen. Sadie hastily picked up her bag. 'I'm going or I shall be late, I've got the first appointment. Bye!'

During the morning Jimbo learned they were not the only ones to get an invitation. Peter came in with some messages for him and mentioned that he and Caroline had been invited.

'Ah! Right. We have too. Harriet was thinking of asking Sylvia to sit in for us, Sadie can't because she's going to supervise for me while we play at being guests.'

'Not to worry. Willie is very good, he'll probably do it for us. The twins love him. We'll get something sorted. Is there a particular reason for this dinner, do you think?'

'I suspect he's wanting to make amends for the silver fiasco.'

'Yes, I expect so. I wonder if Ralph and Muriel have been invited? I don't suppose he'd want to go.'

'Look bad if he doesn't. Sheila Bissett and Ron have been invited. She's thrilled to bits. Been in this morning positively preening.'

'Actually she's not a bad sort you know.'

'That's magnanimous of you, considering the trouble she caused you.'

'We should have been honest in the first place. Must go, got lots to do. Bye Jimbo.' As Peter went to open the door to leave, Muriel came in. 'Good morning. God bless you, Muriel.'

She looked preoccupied. 'Oh, good morning Peter. Oh, dear. Oh, thank you.'

Jimbo came from behind the counter and pulled out a chair he kept for his customers' convenience.

'You look in need of a seat.'

Muriel looked puzzled. She glanced at the chair and promptly sat down rather heavily on it. 'Married life isn't all roses, is it Jimbo?'

'Oh dear!'

'Yes, oh dear. There's a lot of give and take, isn't there?'

'Oh yes. There is.'

'It's an invitation that came this morning. I say we should accept and Ralph, dear Ralph, says definitely no.'

'Is it for dinner at the Big House?'

'Oh! You've got one too?'

'Yes, and Peter, and Sheila Bissett.'

'Oh my word! Ralph says, you see, that under no circumstances can he face going up there again. He saw ghosts that day you all went to challenge Mr Fitch. He was very upset.'

'That's understandable.'

'But I do want to go. I can remember it you see, going in there when I was a little girl. His parents were lovely people. Out of the top drawer but so kindly. They never made you feel less than them. They never patronised.' She looked wistfully up at him. 'I would dearly love to go.'

'Getting quite a social butterfly, then?'

Muriel laughed. 'Remember your fortieth birthday dinner? I thought I would die of shyness that night. I expect if he did agree I'd be so scared on the night I wouldn't know what I was doing. I take up these challenges and then bitterly regret it.'

'Take some advice from a man with fourteen years experience of married life. Don't mention it when you go back home. Give the matter a complete rest. Behave as if it never happened. Be all sweetness and light. Tonight prepare him his favourite dinner, and then . . .' Jimbo cleared his throat. 'Well, the rest is up to you, but that's the moment to tell him how very much you want to go to the dinner. Catch him off his guard, if you see what I mean, when he's . . . well, when he's feeling mellow, as you might say.'

Muriel caught his eye and blushed. 'Jimbo!' She studied his idea for a moment and then said, 'I believe you could very well be right. I shall take your advice.'

'All part of the service. No charge! Did you come in to buy something?'

'Yes, but I can't remember what it was. I'll wander about a little and see if it comes back to me.'

From a sluggish start to the day business hotted up, and by lunchtime Jimbo was more than ready to leave the Store to his part-time assistant and go in the back for a quick bite to eat. He was sitting on his stool in the store room munching a pork pie which would be out of date by closing time, when he heard an excited voice shouting, 'Jimbo! Are you there?' It was Pat.

'In here, Pat, having lunch.'

'Can I come in?'

'Yes, come through.'

'Sorry about this, but I thought you'd like to hear my bit of good news. Mi dad's got the job up at the Big House.'

'Gardener, you mean?'

She nodded vigorously. 'First off he's to get the kitchen garden and the glasshouses in order, and then Jeremy says he'll see after that! You've no idea how pleased I am. Pay's good too. Dad wants our Dean to leave school and go work with him, but I'm not 'aving that and neither's Dean, he wants to stay on at school. Talk about relieved!'

'Relieved? I'm amazed!'

'Amazed? What for? What's happened?'

'Well, you've had a change of heart and no mistake.'

'Change of heart?'

'Yes. I thought Mr Fitch was public enemy number one as far as you were concerned.'

'Oh well, yes. I hadn't thought of it like that.'

'You certainly thought like that the night you and your Dean helped them with that effigy.'

'Effigy? Oh! you mean that dummy.' She scowled accusingly at him. ''Ow did you get to know it was me?'

Jimbo tapped the side of his nose with his forefinger and grinned. 'I have ways. Anyhow, you'll have to change your mind about him now, won't you? Now he's the saviour of the Duckett family.'

'I don't know about that. It's Jeremy's given him the job.'

'Believe me, Jeremy doesn't make a move without first consulting Mr Fitch, he has him on a very short lead. That's how the man works. I think you're all part and parcel of his new strategy to make amends for the silver débâcle.'

'Well, I don't care whether I am or not. If it gets Dad a job, that's what counts. Money talks.'

'Talking of money.' Jimbo reached into his desk and took out a clipboard crammed with papers. He flipped a few sheets over and then said, 'You OK for the Freemasons' dinner, and for a rugby annual dinner in Culworth, both on Fridays?'

'Yes, be glad to. Write the dates down for me and I'll put 'em in mi diary. You don't need me for the dinner up at the Big House then?'

'No, he's asked for waiters.'

'Pity! I'd have liked to be a fly on the wall! Who's going to be there?' Jimbo told her.

'Could be interesting, couldn't it? Sparks might fly, Sir Ralph going.'

'My mother-in-law will be in charge.'

'Whoever's working that night 'ad better watch it then. She's a tartar, she is. She misses nothing, she doesn't.'

'That's how it should be. We don't get asked again if things aren't absolutely perfect. It's people like you who help set the standard. You're good at your job, you know, Pat. Next time I have a small do I might give you a chance to show your mettle. Put you as senior waitress, see how you make out. With suitable remuneration, of course.'

'Really?'

'Oh yes. Reliable people, who know what they're doing and are willing to take responsibility, are few and far between, believe me.'

'Thank you Jimbo. Thank you very much.' Pat made to go and then came back in. 'You're right, I shouldn't let mi dad accept this job, should I?'

'Bleak economics dictate you should.'

'Yes, I really can't 'elp it, he's got to take it. Maddening though, isn't it, when money's your master.'

18

The night before the travellers were expected to move off his land, Ralph found he couldn't sleep. Muriel's restlessness was one reason, and the other was apprehension as to whether or not they would really move. The money was safely tucked under his pillow.

'Ralph, I'm going to make a cup of tea, I simply can't sleep. Would you like one, dear?'

'Yes, please, and then I'm getting up. The tension is killing me.'

'And me.' They sat side by side in bed drinking their tea. Muriel looked at her little china alarm clock. Five thirty. Another hour and they'd be off. When she'd finished her tea she placed her cup on her bedside table and slid down under the bedclothes for five more minutes before getting up.

It was the loud hammering on their door which awakened them both.

Muriel checked the time. It was seven o'clock. 'Ralph! it must be them. We fell asleep.'

Ralph leapt out of bed, flung on his trousers and a sweater and raced downstairs, the money carefully hidden out of sight in his trouser pocket.

'Right guv, we're on the road. Not too early for you, are we?'

'No, not at all. You've all moved off?'

'Yes. Like we said.'

'Right, I'll walk round and take a look, if you don't mind.'

'Don't trust us, eh?'

'Something like that.'

'Got the money?'

'I have. It's yours when I'm sure everyone has gone.'

He walked steadily round the green and on to the land. From the side of the Methodist chapel he could see right across to the beck. Not a vehicle in sight, but what a mess. Tins and dead fires, newspapers, old rusting scrap metal, bin bags swollen with rubbish, branches of trees, sawn down but not used. Litter over the whole area. Ralph didn't care, they'd moved off.

The man who'd hammered so loudly on the door waited.

'Well, guv, I'm right you see, they've all gone like we promised. Money, money, money.' He rubbed his thumb and forefinger together, anticipating the feel of the paper in his hand.

Ralph took it from his pocket and began to count it out.

'No need for that, I know you'll be true to your word. Thanks.' He folded the roll of bank notes and stuffed it into his back pocket. Ralph watched him climb into his old lorry beside a woman, two children and a big dog. He flung it into gear and rumbled away down Shepherd's Hill.

So, this was his land. The mess they'd left behind couldn't spoil his pleasure. He saw the trees, ancient, gnarled, undisturbed for centuries, unconcerned that they had lost some branches, for their powerful life force would overcome their loss of limbs. The beck babbled along the stones, not so deep as usual with the long hot summer they'd had. The willows providing welcome shade for the fishes still swimming along as they had done when he was a little boy. His father had brought him down here and they'd fished with a little net for minnows. What joy that had given him. Now it was all his, all his. Arthur Prior wasn't going to win. Ralph Templeton still owned this land and he'd get those houses built if it was the last thing he did. He shivered in the cold morning air and turned for home. Next, the telephone call that would bring the men and the lorries to clear the grass of the rubbish and then fill the entrance with soil carried away from the road works the other side of Culworth. He clenched his fist and punched the air. He'd win, see if he didn't.

He watched all morning while the men cleared up. Two lorry loads of rubbish, they collected. They found some more boards and replaced the ones the travellers had pulled down from the chapel. By lunchtime the whole site was clear, and by mid afternoon the soil had been tipped to secure the entrance.

Muriel was waiting for him when he got home. 'Are you all right, dear? I've been so worried about you.'

'I've only been watching, not doing anything, but I am tired.'

'I'll make a sandwich for you, you've had a long day. Sit down and rest. By the way Ralph, there's been a telephone call from a man called Colonel something or another, I couldn't catch his name, but he's chairman of the County Council and he says he thinks he went to school with you. He's ringing back in about an hour.'

'I wonder who that is?'

The telephone call came while Muriel was out with Pericles. When she returned Ralph flung his arms round her and danced her round the hall.

'Muriel, Muriel, that was Nobby Winterton-Clark on the phone, he rang us several times that Sunday when we went out for the day. He's been on holiday since then and just got back. Remembers me from prep school, we shared the same dorm and were in the cricket team together. He's heard about my intention of having houses to rent, realised who I must be, and he's weighing in on my side, by putting in some good spade work before the planning meeting this week. He wants to make sure my new application goes through. Delighted to be of service, very concerned about the drain of people from the villages hereabouts, and hopes my plans will bear fruit in other places too. Isn't that marvellous?'

'Oh, Ralph, how lovely, I'm so pleased.' Muriel clapped her hands with glee. 'We really will have Hipkin Gardens then?'

'Yes, fingers crossed we will. We'll go out for dinner tonight. Not the George, we'll try that new place, the other side of Penny Fawcett. I'll book the table right now. Everything's turning out right, isn't it?'

'Oh Ralph, I'm so pleased, you've just no idea. You see, the village will like what we're doing won't they? Just eight houses is absolutely right, isn't it?'

She wore her claret-coloured dress with the low neckline and swirling skirt, Ralph his newest suit, light grey with the finest white pin stripe. He looked so handsome, she was so proud of him. Her heart wept a little, wishing he had sons to follow on. He would have made a lovely father and his children would have been so good-looking. No more Templetons. No more at all. It was all very sad. Then it occurred to her there were Templetons of a kind, living and working on the land still. Templeton land. A germ of an idea came to her, but then they arrived at the hotel and Ralph was opening her door for her, and out of habit she braced herself for facing a new place. She took strength from the reassuring feel of Ralph's hand on her elbow guiding her up the steps. With him there there was nothing to fear, it wasn't like it used to be. Now she had Ralph to keep her safe.

Ralph dropped her off at the front door while he took the car round by Pipe and Nook Lane to put it away in the garage. How odd, Pericles always ran to greet her. She went to his basket in the kitchen. He lay quite still, his eyes glazed. 'Pericles? Are you all right, dear?' His breathing was unsteady and kind of ragged, his tail wagged very slightly, and he tried to lick her hand as she patted him and then there was a long shuddering sigh.

Muriel knelt down by his basket and laid her hand on his flank. There was only a very slight movement of his chest as he breathed, and then even that stopped.

'Oh Pericles, oh no, oh no!' Her tears dropped onto his head and she gently wiped them away. Her dear good friend, who'd been through thick and thin with her, troubles and joys, and now he was gone. His bright red collar, and his bright red lead. She'd loved them. They'd made him look so smart. Her hand hovered above his head for a moment and then she stroked him right from the tip of his nose to the root of his tail. Once, twice, three times. 'Goodbye Pericles. Goodbye.'

She heard Ralph's footsteps coming up the garden path.

'Muriel, I've been thinking . . . why, my dear, what's happened?' Muriel pointed mutely to the basket. Ralph looked at the old dog, lying as though he was still sleeping. He knelt down to lay his hand on Pericles' ribs. There was an unwelcome stillness. 'Oh, Muriel, I'm so sorry. Come here.' He helped her to stand up and Ralph folded her in his arms and hugged her closely to him. 'Never forget, my dear, he had the loveliest life and the loveliest mistress any dog has any right to expect. He wanted for nothing, and he's gone before life became too much of a burden, and for that we must be grateful.'

Muriel sobbed onto Ralph's new suit. 'I bought him because I needed someone to love and someone to love me. And he did, he did, he loved me. Now he's gone.'

'Will I make a good understudy?' Ralph held her away from his chest and smiled at her. She lifted her eyes and smiled back, 'Oh yes, you will, you will. No dog could match you, but it doesn't mean I shan't miss him at every turn.'

'Of course you will, my dear, and if you really want we could always . . . No, I'll save that for another day. Don't you think it was splendid that you were here when he went? He must have waited for you to come home and then let go. Tomorrow, I shall dig a deep, deep, hole at the end of the garden by the cherry tree, and we'll bury him there and then I shall go to the stonemason's and get a simple block of stone and we'll have whatever words you want engraved on it. That way he'll always be sleeping close at hand in your garden. Never far away.'

'Oh Ralph, what a lovely idea. Just "Pericles, a dear friend." Could we get a blanket and cover him, please?'

'Of course.'

It was Neville Neal who rang to tell Ralph that the planning committee had passed his application by a majority of one.

'How did you manage to persuade them to say yes? Not having taken my advice, I fully expected they'd all say "No" yet again.'

'Simply a very good idea they couldn't allow to be dismissed. And it is a good idea, and I'm very grateful for all the help you gave me. We can't wait to get going with the actual building now.'

'I did mention it before, Sir Ralph, but you didn't take me up on it, should you be in need of some capital, I would be more than interested to be of use in that sphere.'

'Thank you, but no. That won't be necessary.'

'I see, well, should circumstances change, then ring me any time, I shall be very willing to listen to any proposal.'

'Thank you again Neville, best wishes to you and Liz.' Ralph put down the receiver and shouted 'MURIEL!'

'Yes, I'm coming.' She appeared in the study doorway wearing a white nightgown. Her feet were bare, her hair brushed and hanging loose, and for a brief moment Ralph saw the girl he'd known all those years ago, the one he'd kissed over the little gate at the back of the churchyard; he on one side, she the other, the shy youthful gesture of two young things who'd thought they would never see each other ever again. The finality of their parting had lain like a stone in his heart for months.

'Muriel, my dear.' He held out his arms and she ran into them and he hugged her tightly. 'We've won, we've won, you and I, we've won.' He kissed her hard, and she kissed him back. 'My dear, that was Neville. The meeting's just finished and they've granted permission. Eight houses. Hipkin Gardens can go ahead.'

'Champagne! I'll get it.'

'Certainly not, I shall, that's my prerogative, Lady Templeton.'

They stood together in their sitting room and toasted the success of their venture. 'To the Templetons, long may they reign in Turnham Malpas!'

19

Jimbo had been asked to cater for twelve guests at Mr Fitch's dinner party. In the event on the night two people, friends of Mr Fitch, had telephoned to say their car had been involved in a multiple pile up on the Culworth bypass, and although not seriously hurt in any way, they were badly shaken and were returning home. So, gathered in the drawing room of Mr Fitch's private flat were Peter and Caroline, Muriel and Ralph, Harriet and Jimbo, Sir Ronald and Lady Bissett, and Craddock Fitch and someone called Oriana Duncan-Lewis whom he introduced, with a slight hesitation, as a family friend. She was a small, slender woman in her fifties, elegantly dressed; carefully made-up face, socially very assured, with an effusive manner which didn't quite ring true. Mr Fitch took her round introducing everybody.

'Delighted to meet you, Jimbo. Craddock has told me so much about you. You and your wonderful food. I'm looking forward to sampling it tonight. This must be your wife. You must be awfully proud of your husband, he's doing a wonderful job here. He's lucky to have someone like you to look after his domestic matters while he fights the battles out in the market place, isn't he? Behind every great man et cetera. You have children, Harriet, my dear?'

Harriet, seething at the implication that all she was fit for was giving birth and doing the washing up, replied through gritted teeth. 'Four.'

'Four? Then you'll be glad of the opportunity for an evening out, I'm sure. I expect you don't get many opportunities to socialise.' She swept on to Caroline.

'And you're . . .'

'Dr Caroline Harris.'

'You're a career woman, then.'

'You could say so. This is my husband, Peter Harris.' Oriana melted at the sight of Peter. From her five-feet-nothing height she looked up at him, with deep appreciation in her eyes. 'Considering how far out in the sticks this place is, there are some remarkably attractive people living here. First Jimbo and now you. Craddock, you didn't tell me how utterly delightful I should find your guests to be. And you, you must be Sir Ralph. Good evening, and good evening to you, Lady Templeton.' The two of them shook hands with her but from where Jimbo was standing he could see that neither Muriel nor Ralph relished the meeting. 'It must be terrible for you to come here and see this place when it was once your home, Ralph. You have my every sympathy.' She beamed understandingly at him, and patted his arm.

'It is a matter of indifference to me, in fact. I've created a whole new lifestyle for myself and my wife. and really wouldn't enjoy the burden of such a large property as this.' He curtly nodded his head to her and turned away to speak to Peter. Muriel was left to bear the brunt.

'I'm sure Craddock would be delighted to show you round.'

'That's most kind, but no thank you. Not when Ralph's not interested.'

They talked for five more minutes and then Mr Fitch asked everyone to go into dinner. The dining table was round, and beautifully set with crystal and china and a silver candelabra, in the centre a small flower arrangement in subtle shades of green and white. The wall lights threw an apricot glow over the table, enhancing its appeal and setting the crystal and silver twinkling. Muriel was fearful of being placed next to Mr Fitch, and in fact as senior lady guest that was exactly where she was led. A suave, well experienced host, Mr Fitch soon had everyone seated: Oriana on the other side of him, Jimbo next to her, with Caroline on his other side, then Ralph, then Harriet, then Sir Ronald, then Lady Bissett, and next to her Peter made the tenth person. Muriel was so pleased to have Peter on her other side, at least he would help to keep the conversation going. She sat back slightly so that Peter and Mr Fitch had an uninterrupted view of each other.

'Before we commence eating would you be so kind as to say Grace, Rector?'

Peter bowed his head and said, 'Ever mindful of your bounteous gifts to us, oh Lord, we thank you for the food we are about to eat. Amen.'

During the meal the conversation waxed and waned. Mr Fitch did his best to put Muriel at ease by asking her about village life before she and her parents had left all those years ago.

'Oh yes, Mr Fitch, every November there was this enormous bonfire up here. On Home Farm field. Ralph's father had the estate workers collecting the wood for it for weeks before. He always made sure he was at home for Guy Fawkes night. We always had a guy to burn, and potatoes in their jackets cooked in the big cooking range, and then when the children were going home they were each given a toffee apple. The grown-ups had cider and ale to drink and it all got very merry.' Her eyes were alight with the joy of recollecting those happy celebrations of so many years ago. Ralph watched her and was saddened by her memories. Mr Fitch encouraged her to reminisce; Jimbo could see his mind storing all this innocently given information.

'Then in the summer there was always the Village Fair. That took weeks to get ready for. That was held on Home Farm field too. Ralph's father paid for roundabouts for the children, we had coconut shies, and guess the weight of the fat lady, wrestling matches, though my mother would never let me watch those, there were cake stalls and craft stalls run by the ladies from the church. Tugs of war between teams from the Jug and Bottle in Penny Fawcett and our own Royal Oak. The Big House cook made lots of food for us to eat, the Morris dancers came from Penny Fawcett, and then in the early evening there was dancing to a band. They were good times. Of course we still have Stocks Day. Even during the war we always held Stocks Day.'

'Stocks Day?' Mr Fitch offered her more wine. 'What is this Stocks Day?'

Muriel rambled on with Mr Fitch listening intently. Jimbo's heart began to sink. He suddenly realised what was going on in the razor-sharp brain of Craddock Fitch. A takeover bid, no less.

'Of course, Jimbo here does a firework display for us now, don't you Jimbo?'

He nodded, and Mr Fitch said, 'Charter-Plackett! I'd no idea you were a pyrotechnic expert?'

Before he could answer Sheila Bissett interrupted. 'Oh yes, Mr Fitch, he's marvellous at it. When Sir Ralph and Lady Templeton married he did a wonderful finale with catherine wheels in the shape of their initials. It was brilliant, wasn't it, Sir Ralph?'

'Absolutely.'

'Are firework displays a hobby of yours, then?'

Jimbo agreed they were. Muriel remarked, 'And I'd forgotten the children from the school always did a PT display on the day of the Village Fair, and my husband's father always presented each of them with a small gift for being so clever. One year I got a mouth organ, I loved it, but the noise I made annoyed Mother and I had to put it away in a drawer. I have it somewhere. Yes, definitely somewhere. Small things mean so much to a child, don't they?' Muriel realised she was verging on the ridiculous in such sophisticated company. She blushed and fell silent.

Sheila Bissett filled the silence with, 'Wouldn't it be lovely if we had a Village Fair and a bonfire now? Don't you think so, Sir Ralph? You'll have to give it some thought, Mr Fitch. Don't you think, Sir Ralph?'

Ralph dabbed his mouth with his napkin and said, 'Ask Mr Fitch.'

So Sheila did.

'I had been thinking on those lines myself. Of course, I'd need someone to advise me on how to go about it, someone who remembers.' He looked questioningly at Muriel, eyebrows raised, face full of anticipation. She looked up and was about to nod her head in agreement when she caught Jimbo's eye. He quickly signalled a warning to her, and she glanced across the table at Ralph before replying. She had seen him angry before but never like this. It flashed through her mind how she'd persuaded him to come against his better judgement, and she saw clear as light the trap into which she'd fallen. Knives and forks were still. Jaws stopped. Wine untouched. Only Sheila Bissett moved; she was draining the last dregs of her wine. When she put down her glass she looked around the table.

'You'd be glad to help wouldn't you, Sir Ralph too? You both remember, don't you?'

Ralph put his napkin down beside his empty plate. In a voice full of barely controlled anger, he replied, 'I'm afraid Muriel and I will be too busy supervising the building of our houses in Hipkin Gardens to be free to act in any kind of an advisory capacity to anything at all. The houses will take priority over any other pettifogging concerns.'

Mr Fitch allowed a small smile to hover on his lips. 'How very disappointing. You've got permission to build then?'

'Yes, we have.'

'I'd be delighted to see your plans. I trained as an architect, a highly desirable qualification for the chairman of a major building company, is it not?' He smiled at Muriel inviting her approval, but she didn't look up. 'We don't want the village spoilt in any way, do we, Rector? You must have a specially close interest in these houses.'

Peter, anxious to defuse the overwrought atmosphere, assured Mr Fitch that Sir Ralph always had the interests of the village at heart and he was absolutely confident that the houses would be built in very good taste. Sheila, having got the bit between her teeth, wouldn't let the matter of the Fair and bonfire rest.

'How about it then, Mr Fitch? Can we look forward to a bonfire night this year? There's still time.'

'I think it would be absolutely perfect to have a Village Fair here and reinstate the bonfire night. Charter-Plackett, you have the kitchens and the staff, you would cater for it, wouldn't you? And I'd want a firework display to round off the evening.'

Jimbo, thinking on his feet, knew he'd no alternative but to agree and at the same time wondered how his relationship with Ralph would suffer. Before he could reply, Oriana gazing adoringly at Mr Fitch said, 'Oh, Craddock, could I be the one to light the bonfire?'

Muriel, without pausing for thought, said decisively, 'Oh no, I'm sorry, Ralph would have to do that, it's always a Templeton who lights the bonfire.'

It was only Ralph's innate good manners which prevented him from making a biting riposte to Muriel's announcement. Humiliation sat badly on his shoulders, and that was just how it felt. Total humiliation at the hands of this – this upstart. Under his eyebrows he shot an angry glance at Mr Fitch, and then said smoothly, 'I'm quite sure that Mrs Duncan-Lewis would make a much more decorative igniter of the bonfire than myself, and I shall gladly relinquish my time-honoured post to allow her to perform the ceremony.' He raised his glass in salute to her. Jimbo mentally applauded Ralph's adroit escape.

The situation was rescued by the waiters coming to clear away the dishes and serve the pudding. This provided a welcome break and the conversation broke up. Peter began discussing Trades Union business with Ron, Sheila leant across to speak to Caroline about the twins, and Ralph and Harriet began a discussion about the level of trade in the Store. Mr Fitch and Oriana discussed the best method for lighting bonfires, leaving Muriel and Jimbo talking about Flick and her two cats. When the pudding was cleared away Mr Fitch suggested sampling the cheeseboard, but his guests declined so they retired to the drawing room for coffee.

Sadie chose to bring it in, sensing that for the waiters, serving at table was one thing but serving people seated in armchairs and sofas would be too much of a challenge. Unruffled and looking elegant in a black tailored suit, she began pouring coffee. Only Sheila Bissett made a fuss. 'Sadie! how kind of you to be helping out. I didn't realise you were slaving away in the kitchen on our behalf.'

'All part of the Charter-Plackett service, Lady Bissett.' She served Oriana and then Mr Fitch. He looked up at her to say thank you, and stopped in his tracks.

'Why, you're . . .? Isn't it? It is. It's Sadie Chandler, isn't it?' Sadie put down the coffee pot, handed him the cream and then said, 'Well, yes I was Sadie Chandler but . . . oh! my word! You're not? No, you can't be. Yes, you are. Surely you're *Henry* Fitch. Aren't you?'

Mr Fitch stood up, put down his coffee cup, took her by the forearms and kissed her on both cheeks. 'You knew me as Henry, but I've used my other name for years.'

'Isn't this amazing. How long is it since . . .'

'I don't think we'll go into that. Let's say it's a long time since we met. How do you come to be here?'

'I have the honour to be Ji . . . Mr Charter-Plackett's mother-in-law.'

'My word! As they say, what a small world. I really can't believe we've met up again after all this time. What a coincidence. Oriana, may I introduce Sadie Chandler, of course that's not your name now, is it?'

'No, I'm Sadie Beauchamp now.'

'Introduce Sadie Beauchamp. We knew each other in our teens. Sadie this is Oriana Duncan-Lewis, a friend of the family.' Oriana shook hands with Sadie, in the manner of one unaccustomed to shaking hands with a minion. 'Charmed, I'm sure,' she murmured.

'I must finish serving coffee. I don't normally do this, but Jimbo wouldn't have enjoyed himself if he was fretting about the food, so I volunteered to step in.'

'We'll talk later, shall we? We mustn't bore my guests recalling past times. Would you join us?'

'Love to! What fun! I'll get myself a cup.'

Ralph's Mercedes roared down the drive just before midnight. Muriel sat miserably beside him, torn to shreds by remorse. If only she could put back the clock. Not just to seven o'clock that evening, but about three years. Then she would be living in her neat little Glebe Cottage, with her dear Pericles, with her dear little garden wearing its autumn clothes and absolutely no problems of any kind at all. She'd be sitting at the till in Harriet's tea room with nothing more challenging than handing out menus and taking money. She'd be lonely and life would be dull, but how blessedly unruffled compared with now. It wasn't that she regretted marrying Ralph, it was just that she knew she'd inadvertently roasted him on a spit tonight at the dinner. Not only roasted him but served him up, trussed, on a plate for Mr Fitch's consumption. She owed him a hugely enormous apology, but the right words wouldn't come. What was worse, Ralph wasn't even speaking to her.

She peeped at his profile as they surged through the gates. He looked grim. Yes, that best described him. Grim. Heaven alone knew how she would make amends. As they passed the church he spoke.

'My dear. Am I forgiven?'

Startled, Muriel said, 'Forgiven?'

'Yes. I have behaved like a complete boor this evening, all I can hope is that you will accept my apology.'

'Your apology! Ralph, it's myself who should be apologising. I let my tongue run away with me without a single thought for how you must have been feeling. I shall never forgive myself.'

He pulled up outside their garage, turned off the engine and switched on the courtesy light. He sat gripping the steering wheel. 'No, Muriel, you're not at fault. Not at all. You are so straightforward, you haven't a devious bone in your body, so you can't be blamed for becoming embroiled by a cunning swin . . . cunning specimen like Fitch. It was for me to have dealt with the situation much sooner than I did. My fault lay in allowing my pride to overcome my common sense. There is no way that I could possibly buy back and maintain a property of such a size as Turnham House. I wouldn't want to anyway, there wouldn't be any point. But it bites right into my innermost soul to see a monied upstart like Craddock Fitch lording it up there, in my father's house, where I grew up. I came close to walking out. But that would have been a betrayal of all my family have stood for. A betrayal of good breeding. Something Craddock Fitch, with all his money, will never have. I've sorted my feelings out now, and accepted the position.'

'Oh Ralph!' He put his arm along the back of her seat and bent his head to kiss her. Full of gratitude for the generosity of his spirit in not blaming her for what had happened, she turned to face him and as he kissed her she experienced an uncontrollable surge of passion. And Ralph rejoiced that his patient loving of her had at last reaped this rich reward for them both.

A few minutes later Peter and Caroline drove past up Pipe and Nook Lane to their garage. They both stared straight ahead, not wishing to embarrass the occupants of the Mercedes.

'Well, really! And illuminated too!'

'Caroline!'

'You're being stuffy again, Peter Harris. I keep telling you about it. Let's be glad they're all right with each other. I feared they would have a row to end all rows, because she really did put her foot in it.'

20

Sadie was late the following morning. There was a stack of mail orders to be attended to, and Jimbo was wanting to get them ready for the twelve o'clock post. If she didn't turn up soon he'd have to ask Harriet to come in to help. Then he remembered: of course it was Saturday and the children were at home. Damn and blast. Where was the woman?'

At a quarter to ten Sadie arrived. 'Don't look at me like that. You're privileged I work on Saturday mornings at all.'

'My God, Sadie, you look terrible.'

'Thank you. That's a very unkind and thoughtless remark to make.'

'You do, though. Hell's bells.'

'Lack of sleep. It was four o'clock before I got to bed.'

'Four o'clock?'

'Yes. Craddock and I sat up till half past three talking. I realise now I'm much too old for such juvenile capers.'

'May I ask how you come to know him?'

'We knew each other in our teens. In a fit of pique, I threw him over for Harriet's father. Had I had an old head on my young shoulders, I would have given her father the order of the boot and married Craddock instead.'

'Wow! He obviously isn't married now.'

'Oh, he was, but it's a long, very sad story. If I tell you, you mustn't tell anyone else, please? Promise?'

Jimbo drew a finger across his throat. 'Cut my throat and hope to die.'

'He told me that within three months of me finishing with him he met and married someone called Annette. He was just twenty and she was eighteen. They had four very happy years together and produced two sons. Apparently Henry, or rather, Craddock, felt that the two boys were his crowning achievement. He positively gloried in them. *Unfortunately*, dear Annette met this dashing army major and before you could say knife he resigned his commission and she hopped off to South America with him, where he became something big in polo. Consequently Craddock has not seen his boys since then. It's a continuous throbbing pain for him, and gets no better as the years go by. So he's thrown himself into his work. So now you know, Jimbo dear, and not a word to anyone. Busy, busy. Must get on. Coffee please. Black!'

He'd just returned from delivering Sadie's coffee when Pat Duckett came in. She wandered round the shelves putting a few items into her wire basket and frequently glancing at him. Eventually she came to the meat counter where he was topping up the display of joints of beef.

'Jimbo, could you give me some advice?'

'Of course, if I can. Willingly. Fire away.'

'This letter came through my door this morning. I 'aven't told Dad, but it's to do with him really, but I'm not going to say anything to 'im till I've decided what I want to do. Read it and see what you think.'

The letter was from Craddock Fitch, suggesting that Pat and her father go to live in the old Head Gardener's house at Turnham House, and her father could be in charge of the gardens on a permanent basis. He realised this would give her the problem of what to do with her cottage, but he would be more than willing to purchase it from her at its proper market value. Would she like to take time to consider the matter.

Jimbo folded up the letter when he'd read it and replaced it in the envelope.

'Well, what shall I do?'

'My word, Pat, it's a big decision and no mistake. First, does your dad want to be up there permanently?'

'Oh yes, he loves it. He's got all sorts of plans and he's itching to get cracking. Worked like a slave since he started and Jeremy's delighted with him. I 'ave 'eard the house has been done up something wonderful, all new fully-fitted kitchen and bathroom and that and painted throughout, and there's even a downstairs lav. Apparently it's 'ardly had anything done to it since Muriel's father left, so yer can imagine, Gawd 'elp us, it was a tip. Four bedrooms, there is. Imagine that. We'd all have one each. And Barry's mother says central heating too. Her Barry fitted the kitchen so she knows all about it. Bliss. Total bliss. Course we'd need new furniture. My stuff's rubbish. But then I'd have the money to buy it, wouldn't I? And there's Dad's redundancy money as well. It's bloomin' tempting, believe me.'

Jimmy Glover came to the counter to choose his meat for the weekend. 'You two plotting something, are yer?'

Pat shook her head. 'No, no, just 'aving a business consultation.'

'Spect it's about whether you're going to accept old Fitch's offer.'

'What offer?'

'That offer to buy your cottage. His typist was telling me about it last night when I took her to the station.'

'She'd no business discussing my private affairs with you, Jimmy Glover.'

'Great friends we are. She's bought this car and it's never been right since the day she got it, always in for something or another, and I've got to know her really well with keeping on giving her lifts. Any news I want to know about up there she tells me. It doesn't take much to egg her on to reveal all.'

'Well, honestly. What a cheek.'

'So you're taking it up, are yer?'

'Mind yer own business!'

'Yer'll be a traitor if yer take him up on 'is offer.'

'Traitor? Don't you call me a traitor, Jimmy Glover. You're rare an' glad to ferry people back and forth to Culworth Station in your taxi, I've noticed. You don't call that being a traitor, then?'

Jimbo intervened. 'In purely hard cash terms, it would be a good bargain for Pat. She could invest the money and have a nice little nest egg growing against the time when her father retired. Think about it over the weekend, Pat, and we'll have another talk on Monday. Yours truly would be glad to help with investments if you would like me to.'

Jimmy chose a pork chop and half a pound of braising steak. 'Tell yer what, yer'd need a bike. Kill yer, running up and down that drive to the school three times a day.'

Pat laughed. 'It'ud be worth it! Can yer imagine, a whole big beautiful house for us. If our Dean gets to university, I wouldn't mind 'is friends coming to a house like that. I couldn't ask 'em to my old cottage. Oh! no! Things are looking up for me, aren't they Jimbo?'

Jimbo studied her face before replying. He'd known her something like five years now, and he'd never seen her looking so joyous. Years had rolled from her face, the deep lines between her eyebrows and her downturned mouth were gone. Her dark eyes were sparkling bright and for the first time in a long while she looked her age. She deserved good luck. She'd earned it.

'They certainly are. And I'm glad. Must press on. Lots to do. Come in Monday after you've talked to the noble parent. We'll have another discussion.'

Pat gave him the thumbs-up sign and said to Jimmy, 'And you keep your trap shut about this. You've 'ad plenty of luck with your big win, this time it's my turn.' She spun on her heel and headed for the till.

Jimbo reflected that this was another move in Craddock Fitch's master plan. He hoped Ralph would be astute enough to accept what he couldn't change and still manage to maintain his place as the benevolent figurehead of the village.

Later that same day Ralph and Muriel were making the best of the autumn days by drinking their afternoon tea in the garden. The sun came round at just the right angle at this time of year and made a lovely pool of sunlight around four o'clock by their garden table and chairs.

'A biscuit, Ralph?'

'No, thank you dear, you have one though.'

'Yes, I will. Do you remember how Pericles used to love a corner of my biscuit?'

'Yes, or the whole biscuit given half a chance! Have you thought about getting a replacement for Peric . . .' They became aware of shouting out in the lane.

Muriel said, 'What's that? Who's shouting?'

'I don't know. I'll go take a look.' Muriel sat enjoying the sun and planning the end-of-season gardening jobs she would begin once her tea was finished. She closed her eyes and lifted her face to the sun. She could still hear shouting and a curious chanting noise and when Ralph didn't return, she went in search of him.

He was opening the front door when she entered the hall. Through the open door she could see banners. She called anxiously, 'What's happening, dear? What is it?'

Ralph stood four-square on the stone step. Facing him was Arthur Prior, holding a banner. Behind him was an assortment of villagers mostly holding banners, all of them chanting. The banners read:

'NO MORE HOUSES IN TURNHAM MALPAS'
'GREED! GREED! GREED!'
'WE SHALL APPEAL'
'OUT! OUT! OUT!'
'WE SHALL OVERCOME'

Beyond the crowd were the onlookers, some watching gleefully, others apprehensively. Ralph, so boiling with anger he could recognise no one but Arthur, thought, Well I've won, so it's all a waste of time. The fools. He waited for the shouting to stop and then, addressing Arthur, said quietly: 'Kindly remove yourself and your band of followers from outside my house.'

'Public road, can stand where we like.'

'You're causing a public nuisance.'

'Who says?'

'I do.'

'Oh, well,' Arthur said, 'in that case we'd better listen.' He turned to the crowd behind him and shouted, 'The Lord of the Manor has spoken, doff your caps everyone, *Sir* Ralph has spoken.' He took off his corduroy cap and stood humbly holding it in his hands, head inclined in submission.

Raising his head slightly and looking at Ralph somewhere at the level of his top waistcoat button, Arthur said, 'We're not going to let this go through. We intend to appeal.'

'Appeal all you like. What's done's done and you won't alter it. Eight houses for rent in a village this size is just right. Your sons won't need them but there are plenty of villagers who will.'

'And what about *your* sons? Will they be needing a house to rent?'

The crowd tittered. Ralph stared silently at Arthur. The demonstrators began tapping the ends of their banners on the ground, tauntingly keeping time with their chanting. Arthur waited on a reply.

'There's no more to say. The houses will be built and there's an end to the matter.'

Arthur raised his banner and shook it in time with the chant. 'GREED! GREED! GREED! MONEY! MONEY! MONEY!'

Some of the spectators joined the ranks of the protesters and swelled the shouting. Others, like Alan Crimble and Georgie, simply observed.

Georgie nudged Alan and whispered, 'There's going to be a fight!'

'No, not them, two old geysers like them's not going to fight.'

Alan stood on tiptoe and saw Ralph take a step forward. Arthur, mistaking his intentions, raised the banner in self defence. Ralph stepped back and stumbled against the edge of the stone step. The colour of his face changed instantly to a deathly grey, his hand went to his chest, and then he clawed at his throat as though trying to undo his collar to get more air. Beads of sweat appeared on his face and it went even more grey. The crowd fell silent. Muriel, who was still standing in the hall, and trembling from head to foot, didn't realise that Ralph was ill and it was only when he began to crumple to the ground that she let out a screech of terror. 'Ralph! Ralph!'

He fell partly on the road, partly on the stone step, his head missing the boot scraper by inches. Muriel rushed to his side, loosened his tie and undid the top button of his collar; she shook him and shouted his name over and over again, but he remained silent, his grey, grey face glistening with sweat. 'Do something, do something for him, please, please,' she pleaded. In a harsh whisper Alan said, 'God, Georgie, he's had a heart attack!'

'Do something! Alan! do something! Go on, you know what to do. That massage and breathing. Go on!'

'I can't, I'm scared.'

'Go on, it might be too late if you don't.'

Alan pushed his way through the crowd and shouted, 'Get an ambulance, go on, get an ambulance, someone get Dr Harris!' He roughly pushed Muriel out of the way and knelt down beside Ralph. He felt his neck where he knew the pulse would beat most strongly and, finding no pulse, began chest massage. One, two, three, four, five, then tilting back Ralph's head he pinched his nose and bent down to blow into his mouth. Then both hands to pump his chest. One two three four five. Then blow, blow, blow, blow, blow. Someone said 'There's no one in at the Rectory,' and Alan thought 'Hell's bells, it's up to me.' The only movement was him working on Ralph. The crowd was silent and afraid. Muriel stood on the step weeping uncontrollably. Georgie, inspired by Alan's competent manner, went to comfort Muriel.

In a shocked, quiet voice Arthur said, 'God help us, is he breathing?'

'Not yet.' Alan continued working on him. After one more try he stopped and checked his pulse. 'He's got going again.' A rustle of relief ran around the crowd, now swelled to twice its size with people who'd come out in surprise at the sudden silence and were standing on tiptoe at the back trying to see what had happened. Those who'd been demonstrating quietly put their banners out of sight.

Someone had brought out a blanket and Alan covered Ralph with it and stayed kneeling beside him, monitoring his pulse. Someone else brought a brandy for Muriel, and Arthur got a kitchen chair out of her house so she could sit down.

'I never meant this to happen, Muriel.' Arthur pleaded with her for forgiveness. She ignored him and kept her eyes on Ralph.

Alan, on his knees beside Ralph, waited desperately for the ambulance to arrive, constantly checking him, and worried sick that he shouldn't die, at least until the ambulance arrived. He'd never prayed in all his life, but he did at that moment. The ambulance came. His prayers had been answered, Ralph was still breathing.

Muriel went with Ralph in the ambulance and as soon as it had moved off with its light flashing, Alan felt a tremendous surge of relief and his legs went to jelly and he felt sick. Georgie flung her arms round his neck and kissed him in front of the whole crowd.

'Wonderful, Alan, you were wonderful! If it hadn't been for you he would have been a goner.'

'Thank goodness you were there, Alan!'

'Where did you learn what to do?'

Alan laughed shakily. 'Watched it on telly.'

'Brilliant. Brilliant. Drink on me tonight, Alan, see yer in there. Right?'

'Right! Thanks!'

'Poor Sir Ralph! Hope he'll be all right. What a thing to happen!'

'That Arthur Prior has a lot to answer for. Where is he?'

Arthur had gone home, ashamed and fearful at what his pigheadedness had caused. He'd left his car parked in the village and walked all the way. If Ralph died, he knew he'd never forgive himself.

That night Alan served in the bar again. Bryn had to put a stop to the number of drinks he was expected to consume. 'Can he accept the money and have it later? Do you mind? He's already had three drinks and he won't be able to stand soon,' Bryn suggested.

'Congratulations! Best day's work you've done in a long time.'

'You must be proud of him, Georgie. Really proud.'

'Oh we are. I knew he'd turn up trumps.' She kissed his cheek and gave him a hug. Alan blushed, unaccustomed to such adulation.

'I only did what I learned from the telly. Anyone could have done it. Watched "Casualty" and that. Just hope his ticker keeps going.'

One of the customers said, 'You're staying in the village, Alan, aren't you now?'

He grinned at Georgie. 'I hope so, but we'll see.'

Georgie agreed. 'Well, of course he is. I've always known what a good bloke he is, always. He's got to stay, hasn't he?'

'Certainly. How would you run this place without 'im?'

'Exactly!'

Standing at the bar was Linda from the Store. 'Gin and tonic, Alan, please, and get one for yourself.'

'Hello, we don't usually see you in here.'

'No, well, I had to come to see our hero, hadn't I?'

Alan blushed again. 'Don't know about that. I only did what anyone else would have done.'

'Well, I certainly couldn't have done it, could you Bryn?'

'No, not me.'

'Aren't you drinking with me, then?'

'Can I have the money instead? I've already had three, and that's more than enough when I'm working.'

'Yes, of course. Well, here's to you. Our hero of the hour.' Linda sipped her gin and then placed her glass down on the counter. She put the change Alan gave her in her purse and said, 'What's your night off this next week?'

'Monday.'

'I'll give my aerobics a miss then and buy you a drink.'

Alan straightened the knot in his tie, served another customer and then said, 'I'll take you up on that.'

'Pick you up then when I finish at the Store. Go into Culworth, you won't want to drink where you work.'

'No, that's right. I'll be ready.'

In the ambulance Ralph's heart had arrested for a second time, and the paramedics had to work hard to start him again. For twenty-four hours Muriel never left his side. On the second day Caroline took her home to take a bath and get clean clothes, but all the time she was intensely afraid that Ralph would slip away while she was in Turnham Malpas and he'd die alone. That was the one thing she couldn't bear, the thought that he might die alone.

When he'd been in hospital three days, wired to an unimaginable complexity of machinery, he opened his eyes and recognised her. 'Why, Muriel, you're still here.' His voice, shaky and soft, sounded not one jot like the voice to which she was accustomed. All his vigour had gone, there was no strength left for teasing or anything else.

'Of course I am, Ralph. Where would you be if it was I who was ill? Right beside me holding my hand. My dear.' She stood up, reaching round the wires, and kissed his forehead. 'I do love you, Ralph. You gave me such a scare.'

Ralph smiled gently and closed his eyes. After a few minutes he said, 'I can remember Alan, what was he doing?'

'Just helping you, dear. We were lucky he was there. He's sent you a card wishing you all the best. I've already written to him to thank him for what he did. When you're home we shall think of something we can do for him to show our gratitude.'

'I've forgotten what it was all about.'

'Well, never mind, you concentrate on getting well.'

Muriel held his hand to her cheek and sat watching him. How she loved him. Really loved him. Her life could be divided into two halves, the second half being the year and three-quarters she'd been married to

Ralph. More had happened to her in that time than in all the rest of her life put together. He made her feel so safe, and yet life was so exciting. She could face almost anything knowing she had him with her. What would she do if he . . . No, she wasn't going to think about that. Be positive, that's right, be positive.

'Drink of water, please.'

'I'll get the nurse.'

After the nurse had settled him again and checked the dials and adjusted the bedclothes, she said, 'There's a visitor just come, do you feel able to see him, Sir Ralph?'

Muriel said, 'Oh that'll be the rector. Yes, do ask him to come in.'

But it wasn't Peter; it was Arthur Prior. He stood hesitantly in the doorway, waiting.

Muriel jumped up, surprised and alarmed.

'I don't think you should come in, if you don't mind.'

'Yes, I know, but I . . .'

Muriel put her hands on his chest and tried to push him out. 'I don't want him having another attack, he's not really stable yet. You can see all the wires and things, he's very ill. Please, please go away.'

'Yes, but I want to say . . .'

'You're going ahead with the appeal, is that it?'

'That wasn't what I was going to say, all I'm wanting . . .'

'Just please go away, I don't want you here.' Muriel stamped her foot and became very agitated. Ralph weakly called out, 'What is it, Arthur?'

He stepped back into the room. 'I can't sleep for the worry. I've come to say I shan't be making an appeal. I genuinely thought you would sell to make money out of it, but Neville Neal tells me you really do intend to build and rent. That's all right by me. I wouldn't want to cause a man's d- I wouldn't want to cause trouble and I'm very sorry you're so ill.'

'Thank you, we'll talk another time when I'm feeling better.'

'You intend coming round then?' Arthur said smiling.

'Oh yes, I've everything to live for.' He painstakingly felt about on the counterpane for Muriel's hand and when he'd found it he held it tightly.

'Well, I'm glad you're still going to be around. Can't keep a good man down, can you?'

'No, that's right.'

'I'll be off then.' Arthur nodded to Muriel, hesitated, and then said, 'I want things to be all right between us.' He nodded to Ralph and left the room.

'I feel ashamed of stamping my foot and getting annoyed.'

'I quite like you in a temper, it suits you.'

'Ralph! Go to sleep! I'll stay with you and then while you sleep, I'll use your telephone and tell Caroline how much you've improved. You must have, if you're starting to tease.'

Some two weeks later, when Muriel popped home for some fresh clothes for Ralph, she checked the messages on the answerphone and found a call on it from the architect, asking to come to see them with the final plans for Hipkin Gardens. Muriel knew how pleased Ralph would be, but he wouldn't be able to be there, she'd have to put the architect off till Ralph was better. Yes, that's what she'd do, tell Ralph and then put him off. He needed to be there to walk round the site and crystallise their thoughts, yes and that would be weeks yet. Yes, she'd postpone his visit. Now Ralph was no longer connected to all the wires and pipes and could sit in a chair in his clothes he really did seem to be making progress, but he was by no means capable of dealing with business matters, not yet.

'When do you say he wants to come?'

'Next Wednesday.'

'And today's . . .'

'Friday.'

'Right. Don't put him off, we'll let him come.'

'Oh Ralph, I'm much braver than I was, but I really don't think I could talk to him, what if I get it all wrong, and you don't like it and he does the plans and then . . .'

'Don't worry, my dear, I shall be there, I'll deal with it.'

She jumped to her feet, her hands clasped under her chin. 'You're not coming home, Ralph, you're not ready yet, not by any means. You're teasing, aren't you, teasing?'

'Never been more serious. I've had enough of this place. I'm discharging myself.'

'You can't, I won't let you.'

Ralph chuckled. 'That temper of yours is getting the better of you, my dear.'

'I shall ring for a nurse. They'll make you see sense.'

'They can't keep me here against my will.'

'I can.'

'Not even you can, Muriel. I've made up my mind I'm going home. I want to sit in front of the fire, and eat scones and drink tea with my wife. Go to bed in a proper bed with my wife beside me holding my hand. There's no better tonic, believe me.'

'I shan't make any scones and I shan't hold your hand, so you might as well stay here.'

'Come here to me.' She went closer to his chair. 'Closer. That's it. Now give me a kiss. A lovely long lingering kiss, and *then* tell me I can't go home.' Ralph's arms around her shoulders and her arms tucked between his back and the cushions, they kissed one of those deep satisfying kisses which say so much more than words. 'Oh Ralph, yes, please come home!'

They were disturbed by a polite cough. Muriel straightened up to find Peter waiting in the doorway.

'Shall I come back later?' His eyes were twinkling. 'I can if you wish, I have got someone else to see.'

Muriel blushed, and held her hands to her hot cheeks. Ralph beckoned to Peter. 'Come in, you're just the man I want to see. My wife is insisting that I go home . . .'

'I am not, it was your idea. Really it was, it was Ralph's. He's going to discharge himself. He shouldn't, should he?'

Peter gravely considered her question. 'No, he shouldn't, but being at home is a marvellous pick-me-up, I must admit, and he would get every care wouldn't he?'

'Oh yes, of course he would, but I . . .'

Ralph interrupted decisively. 'It's settled then. Muriel, ring for the nurse. Peter, give me an hour, I've got to see the consultant and persuade him I'm doing the right thing, I've got to pack and pay my bills, and then could you drive me home, if you're going straight back?'

'Certainly. An hour then.'

Ralph, resting his hands on the arms of his chair, had heaved himself upright before Peter had left the room. 'Now Muriel . . .'

They talked that evening sitting in front of the fire, drinking tea and eating scones.

'I like to sit in the firelight, you know, it smoothes out all my wrinkles and I can imagine I'm young again. More tea, dear?'

'Yes, please, and another scone.' When Muriel had placed his scone on his plate and made sure his tea was to hand, he asked her to listen to what he had to say.

'I have something to talk to you about and then we shall never, never mention it again. Not ever mention it again. I spoke to the consultant, as you know, and to sum up what he said, if I sit in a chair and do nothing, and be pernickety about my diet, and turn myself into a doddery old fool, then I might last ten years. But, Muriel, I don't want to be a foolish old man. I would much rather have five years living a full life than ten years watching TV and doing the crossword to pass the time. I know it's a difficult decision to make and we've never talked about it because we didn't know we would have it to face, but I wondered how *you* felt about the situation?'

Muriel picked up her cup and drank some of her tea while she found the right words to say. Then she answered him.

'Well, I certainly don't want to be married to a doddery old man. I love you as you are and I'm sure you would get quite miserable with nothing to do, then we'd get on each other's nerves and it wouldn't be lovely any more. So I'll watch over you and get advice from Caroline if I get stuck, and we'll try to carry on as if nothing has happened.'

He took her hand and said, 'Thank you, my dear, for being so understanding. Let's hope we shall have many more wonderful years together. The doctors have told me that I shall need regular checkups and will have to watch my diet and my weight and take sensible exercise, and they've given me a list of the foods I need to avoid. I know it will cause you a problem having to make a new approach to your shopping and cooking, and I'm sorry.'

'There's no need to be sorry, I shall be only too glad to help. And we *shall* have many more wonderful years together. First we've got to see the architect, and then you'll have to supervise the plans and make sure they're not skimping on anything, and then we shall need a holiday before they start building and . . .'

'You're turning into a martinet!'

'Oh, I shall be, don't worry. Enjoy that scone, because I don't think you'll be allowed many of those after today.'

'Help! The woman's a tyrant!'

When she'd cleared away their tea things, Muriel went into the garden in the dark to put the remaining two scones on her bird table, because she hated 'second day' scones. She stood by the cherry tree pretending to be looking at Pericles' headstone. With her back to the house, so Ralph couldn't possibly see, she wept painful scalding tears.

21

Muriel had a list with her to remind herself of the things Ralph needed for his new regime. She was wandering round the shelves waiting for Jimbo to cut her two very lean lamb chops when Flick appeared with a friend.

'Hello, Lady Templeton.'

'Hello, Flick dear. I see you're managing very nicely without your sticks now. You must be pleased.'

'Yes, I am. The specialist says I've done extremely well, but he says it's only what he can expect from someone with as much guts as I've got.'

'Well, naturally.' Muriel smothered a smile. 'Who's this friend of yours?'

'This is Sebastian Prior from Prior's Farm. You must remember him? He's in my class at school and we both play the recorder too, don't we Sebastian? And we both share the same birthday. Isn't that odd?'

'It is indeed. Of course I remember you, Sebastian. My word, you have grown. When I played the piano in school you were quite the smallest boy in class. I can hardly recognise you.'

'I know, he's had a growing spell since he had his tonsils out, haven't you?'

Sebastian nodded. Muriel studied his face. So this was Arthur Prior's grandson. The same very fair hair, the same dark brown eyes. The nose wasn't quite right, but that might come with age. The germ of an idea which had come to Muriel just before Ralph's heart attack emerged again in her mind. This might be the trigger she needed.

'Are you spending the afternoon with Flick?'

'Yes, he is.'

'Ask Mummy if you and Sebastian could come to tea with me and Sir Ralph, would you, Flick? Would you like that, Sebastian?'

'Yes, he would, wouldn't you? I certainly would.' Sebastian nodded.

'Tell her I'll bring you both safely back.'

While Muriel waited for Flick to run home to ask her mother, she finished her shopping. She remembered she needed stamps for Ralph. Muriel felt a tug at her skirt. It was Flick and Sebastian back.

'Mummy says yes, it's all right.'

The two children helped her to carry her shopping home. She hadn't yet heard Sebastian speak; no doubt he would, given half a chance. The accident hadn't put a stop to Flick's chatter.

Muriel opened the front door and said, 'Ralph! Ralph! Where are you, dear?'

'Here.' His reply came from the study. She opened the door and said, 'I've brought two visitors for tea. One is Flick and the other is her friend from school, they share the same birthday, isn't that a coincidence? He's called Sebastian Prior. I thought you'd enjoy talking to them both. Flick is walking without her sticks now, isn't that wonderful? Come in, children.'

Sebastian stood quietly in the doorway looking at Ralph, who had stood up abruptly when Muriel had told him the name of Flick's friend. Flick rushed straight in. 'Hello, Sir Ralph, you're looking much better than you were. Come in, Sebastian, come on.'

'You talk to my husband while I get the kettle on. Do you both drink tea?'

Sebastian nodded. Flick said, 'Yes, we both do.'

When Muriel took the tea tray into the sitting room Ralph had already seated the children in there. He and Sebastian were talking about horses.

'You ride, then?'

'Oh yes, Sir Ralph, every weekend and in the holidays. My daddy rides too, when he's got time.'

'And your grandfather?'

'No, he's never learned.'

'I see. Do you ride sometimes, Flick?'

'No, but it would be a good idea.'

'Do you have your own pony, Sebastian?'

'No, I share with my sisters.'

'How many sisters have you got?'

'He's got four, haven't you? All older than him.'

'You've got cousins who ride though, haven't you?'

'No. My Auntie and Uncle haven't got any boys and girls.'

'I see.'

Muriel placed a small table beside each of the children, gave them napkins which they spread on their knees, and then served tea. Sebastian watched her pouring from the silver teapot with the coat of arms.

'Your teapot has letters on it. What do they say?'

Ralph explained. Sebastian brooded over the reply and then said, 'I see. Are you royal?'

'No, not royal at all, but a very old family, we go back about five hundred years.'

'I see. Silver teapots are very posh, aren't they?' Flick kicked his ankle and said, 'Shush.'

Ralph, feeling a little embarrassed by this conversation, said, 'Well, yes, I suppose they are.'

Muriel diverted Sebastian's curiosity by handing him a plate of chocolate biscuits.

'Thank you, Lady Templeton.' For some reason, Sebastian saying that drove home to Muriel the task she had set herself. It really was sad that this little boy was, in his own way, as much a Templeton as anyone alive, and yet he had no rights to silver teapots, nor titles, nor anything else. She patted his head as he took two of the biscuits. Flick took one and nibbled delicately. She was obviously enjoying being a grown-up.

Ralph and Flick and Sebastian chattered away together until Muriel finally had to say it was time they went or Flick's mummy would be wondering where they'd got to.

Ralph said, 'I could take Sebastian home.'

Flick jumped at the chance. 'In your Mercedes?'

'Yes.'

'Could I come too? It's only polite to take my guest home isn't it?'

'Oh yes. Muriel ring Harriet, please, my dear, and ask her if it would be convenient.'

It was and he did. Muriel stayed at home to clear up and left Ralph to take them himself.

When he got back he went straight to his study and stayed there until his evening meal was ready. Their dessert was pears poached in honey and lemon juice. When Ralph finished eating his, he laid down his spoon and said, 'Those pears were delicious, Muriel. The lamb chops were grilled to an absolute turn, and now all I need is my coffee and I shall be ready for anything.'

She poured his coffee for him, laying her hand over the sugar bowl as he reached for it. 'No! Ralph, remember!'

'Are you guilty of trying to organise me?'

'Well, you know you have to watch your weight, I'm only doing my wifely duty.'

'You were quite right to stop me putting sugar in my coffee, but I wasn't thinking of the sugar.'

Muriel looked down at her cup as she stirred in the sugar and said nothing.

'Well?' Ralph bent his head and tried to catch Muriel's eye.

'Only with the best of intentions. He's a very nice little boy, I knew him at school, you see, but of course I didn't know the rest of his story till you told me.'

'He is a very charming boy, when he gets a chance to speak! Have you noticed Flick limps quite badly?'

'Yes, but not nearly as badly as she did, she's improving all the time. He's got your colouring, well, till your hair went white.'

'Brown eyes and fair hair, you mean.'

'Yes. It's very distinctive. It does come out strongly in each generation, doesn't it? It must be an enduring link, musn't it?'

'What do you have in mind?'

'I have nothing in mind, Ralph, nothing at all.'

'Muriel!'

'No, really, I haven't anything specific in mind, truly I haven't, but I do feel something should be done.'

'I see. Give him or them money, you mean?'

'Oh no, indeed no, they'd be much too proud to take money, that wouldn't be right, something more significant needs to be done.'

'I don't really see why.'

'If you had descendants things would be different, but you haven't. So they are a branch of the family, aren't they, in a way.'

'Illegitimate.'

'Oh yes, but they can't be blamed for that. But it must be true or Sebastian wouldn't have the Templeton colouring. They'd just have been dismissed, so your grandfather knew – oh yes, he knew.'

'Yes. It's true all right. I'll think about it.'

'Did you meet anyone when you took him back.?'

'Arthur's son. Sebastian's father.'

'So what's Arthur's son like?'

'Tall, very tall, not like a Templeton, but the same colouring. Nice chap. Have you laid your plans for New York?'

'Are we going still? I thought perhaps you wouldn't, not after . . .'

'But yes, we are. We both said we'd carry on as usual and we shall. You can do your Christmas shopping on Fifth Avenue, how about that?'

'I should be terrified of getting lost in New York, you will look after me, won't you?'

'Of course. They'll be starting work on Hipkin Gardens while we're away. I know that's a long way off, but how about before the weather gets too inclement we have a little ceremony? You put in the first spade. What do you think?'

Muriel clapped her hands and said, 'Oh, what a lovely idea! We'll have reception here for everyone afterwards. Drinks and things to nibble, shall we? Whom shall we invite?'

They made a list. 'Add Arthur Prior and his wife to the list. See if they'll come.'

'Should we?'

'They can say no, can't they, if they don't want to come?'

'Oh dear, after the fuss they all made do you think *anyone* will accept?'

'Of course they will, they all love a chance for a chat and food. We'll have champagne, and you can cut the first sod with a silver spade.'

'Oh Ralph! We're not building the British Library or a museum or something. I think a brand new stainless steel one would be sufficient!'

22

'Muriel!'

'In the kitchen, Ralph.' She glanced up as he came in. 'You're going out, dear?'

'Yes, I'm off up to town for the day.'

'To town? Today?'

'Yes, just something I need to talk over with the solicitor.'

She looked at his face, but could detect nothing that would give her a clue to his intentions. 'You're not driving up and back in one day?'

'No, I thought I'd take the train. Leave the car at the station.'

'How about if I pack you a bag and you stay overnight? It does seem a long way to go, there and back in a day. It's already nine o'clock.'

Ralph stood undecided. Muriel watched him, puzzled by his secretiveness. He looked out of the window for a moment and then said, 'Yes, I will then. If you're quick I shall be able to catch the ten five.'

'I'll be quick.'

Instinctively, Muriel didn't inquire his intentions, and didn't ask to go with him. He'd been struggling with some dilemma ever since she'd brought little Sebastian home. Presumably he had come to some conclusions on which he needed legal advice. She waved him off, and then set about tidying up before going to the Rectory for morning coffee. While she tidied up she worried. What right had she to interfere? The Priors were Ralph's problem not hers, but somehow the situation did need clarifying. She went to Caroline's very preoccupied.

Ralph came back in time for lunch the following day.

'You must have left very early, dear?'

'Caught the nine ten. It's a rattling good train, that one.'

'I'm making sandwiches because I hadn't expected you back so soon.'

'That's fine.'

Though the central heating was perfectly adequate, Muriel had lit the fire in their dining room because the weather had turned really cold. After lunch they pulled their chairs close to the fire while they drank their coffee.

'I know it's lunchtime, but I think I'll have a brandy. Just one.'

He pulled a side table towards his chair and placed his coffee and his brandy on it. Muriel waited. Before long he would tell her what he'd been doing in London.

'I've been up to see my solicitor.'

'Yes, I know.'

'Yes, well I listened to what you had to say and I've made a decision. You're quite right, something needs doing, and I've come up with the answer.'

'I see.'

'It's perfectly in order for me to go ahead, so I am.'

'I see.'

'In a way it's going against an old steadfast arrangement, but I've got to do it.'

'I see.'

'When we shared everything when we married there was one thing we couldn't share, and that was Prior's Farm. That was under a completely separate arrangement and had to be kept in direct line because of its peculiar nature. So although I can ask you what you think, ultimately the decision is mine.'

'Ralph, I can't keep saying "I see" for much longer, because I don't see. What are you trying to tell me?'

'I've decided to . . . No, no, I was going to tell you the whole story, but frankly, Muriel, I think it would be a good idea if I didn't say anything until I get back home. You see, Arthur may not agree, and then I shall have to disappoint you by telling you it hasn't come off. Can you be patient with me a little longer?' Ralph smiled at her.

'Of course I can. I did want you to do something about straightening it out, but I didn't know what to suggest.'

'Well, what I've done I've done, let's hope he agrees. The solicitors were all for putting my ideas on to a pile of work needing attention. But I said no, I want it doing right now, not in ten years' time. This is a now decision, get your finger out and get it typed up, so I can come away with it in the morning. So they delivered it by messenger to the hotel this morning, about eight o'clock.'

'Are you going now?'

'No, it's market day, Arthur won't be back just yet.'

'How do you know?'

'Sebastian told me, he goes every week. So I'm going to lie down for a while and then set off and be back for dinner.'

'Very well, dear. Whatever it is you've done, I'm sure it will be right.'

'Let's hope so, this feud has got to be stopped. These old wounds fester for generations, and there won't be another generation after me so I've got to be the one to make the move.'

'I do hope he doesn't take umbrage and refuse to accept. He has got a wild temper, as we've seen.'

'I'll do my best.'

Ralph had changed from his city suit into his tweeds before he left. He felt more comfortable wearing them, and they seemed more appropriate to the moment. The lane was just as smart and the yard, now sporting tubs of winter flowering pansies, still as neat as before.

There was no one around, so Ralph rang the door bell. He heard heavy footsteps crossing the yard, and turned to see who was coming. It was Arthur.

Ralph changed his briefcase over to his left hand and held his right hand out to Arthur. 'Good afternoon, Arthur. Had a good day at the market?'

Arthur shook his hand. 'How did you know?'

'Your Sebastian told me you usually went.'

'Good opportunity for meeting other farmers and seeing if they're doing as badly as yourself. What have you come to see me about?'

'It might take some time. Shall we sit on the wall?'

'If you like, or we can go inside.'

'Somewhere where we won't be overheard?'

'No, the children are home from school, so the house is full. Come in the stable.' He led the way across the yard to the end stable, opened the door, and invited Ralph inside. On top of some bales of hay he found two strong wooden crates, which he turned upside-down and placed on the stone floor. He invited Ralph to 'take a pew.'

'I'm very sorry about that time when I wouldn't pass the collection plate to you. The rector told me off and not half. He's only a young man, but my word, he's got some kind of power, he has, he kind of sees right through you, and you've got to do what's right. I finished up apologising to him but I was too stubborn and angry at the time to apologise to you, but I am doing now.'

'That's all right, Arthur, your motives were honourable and that's what counts.'

'You're looking well now, bit thinner, but well. I come in here when I need to get away from them all, so I keep a bottle for private consumption, do you fancy a drop? Bryn's best, it is.'

'When I've finished what I've come to tell you, then yes, I'll be delighted.'

Ralph opened his briefcase and took out some papers. 'A lot of water's gone under the bridge since 1900. More than ninety years, and it's time things were put to rights. I've come to suggest . . .'

Arthur's face lit up. 'You don't mean you're going to suggest I buy the farm? Is that what you're going to say?'

'Well, not buy it exactly . . .'

'What then, what's your alternative? I've got the money all put by, just waiting for the day.'

'It is in my power to release you from this ridiculous peppercorn rent you pay, and I'm here to say there's no need to pay it any more.'

'Bloody hell, Ralph, I'm not poor. Twenty-five pounds a year isn't going to mean the difference between surviving or going under. What the hell!'

'Arthur!'

'Arthur nothing! If that's all you've come to tell me you can put yer papers away and skit. Whilst I pay that rent it's all legal; if I stop paying, then I'm under an obligation to you and I won't have it, absolutely not. I will *not* be under an obligation to *anyone* with the name of Templeton. My father was bitter to the end of his days about the way your family treated his mother and him. It wasn't his fault and it wasn't her fault, it was your grandfather's fault, but he never spoke to my father from the day he was born. Never acknowledged him, not once. He could pass him in the road and wouldn't even look at him. His own father! I'd have thought you'd have had more sense than to come here with a daft notion like you have. Go on, get off my land.' He sprang up from his crate and opened the bottom half of the stable door so Ralph could go. The horse in the stall whinnied its approval.

'You're too impulsive, Arthur. Be quiet and listen, we're getting too old for stupid misunderstandings, there've been enough of those in the past. You and I, between us, are putting a stop to the trouble. Sit down, and listen.'

'All right, then, all right.' He answered impatiently and still with half a mind to make Ralph leave, then on second thoughts he sat back down again and waited.

'Here are the deeds of the farm. Wallop Down Farm is its real name, did you know?'

'No! Wallop Down Farm? That's a daft name.'

'These deeds are yours and your children's. The farm is no longer owned by me nor any of my descendants. From today the farm is entirely yours and your children's, forever.'

The only sound in the stable was that of the horse gnawing the edge of the door. It stamped its feet and then whinnied joyously and then kicked the door. Ralph waited, observing the emotions flitting across Arthur's face; first anger, then delight, then anger again, then a strange kind of yearning. Arthur held the deeds in his hands, turning them over and over, relishing the feel of the strong thick parchment, and the sound of its crackling in his hands. His finger traced the lines of writing on the front as he looked across the yard to his house, and then back to the papers.

'I love this place. Love it, like I love nothing else. I love my boys and the grandchildren, but this,' – he thumped the door of the stall with his fist – 'this is me, it's in my bones. Each morning I open my eyes glad, no, *rejoicing* that I have fields in which I can walk, woods that are mine to tend, crops that are mine to harvest, animals that are mine to feed and care for. But there's always been that knowledge deep down that I was living a lie, because it wasn't really, truly, actually, mine. My pride tells me I should throw these' – he held up the deeds – 'back in your face and tell you I shan't accept favours from a Templeton, living or dead. But it's no good, I can't do that. If I die tomorrow I shall die a happy man now, and we can't ask more than that, can we?'

Ralph smiled and agreed. 'And now where's that drink we were going to have?'

Arthur stood up and, going behind the bales of hay, he brought out a bottle of Bryn's home-brewed ale and two glasses. He blew bits of hay out of the glasses and then poured them each a brimming glass.

The two men stood facing each other. Ralph proposed a toast. 'To Wallop Down Farm and the Priors!'

'To the Priors, and long may they reign at Wallop Down Farm!'

As Ralph was leaving, Arthur said, 'I've half a mind to change the name, do you know that? Daft name, but it has a ring to it and if that's its real name, why not?'

'Why not indeed?'

23

Ralph propped up the spade in the hall and called for Muriel. 'I've collected the spade, dear, come and have a practice. The inscription looks good.'

Muriel came from the kitchen, wiping her hands on her apron. 'Oh Ralph, doesn't it look lovely! I shall feel like the Queen.' Muriel held the handle with both hands and rested her foot on the spade. 'I declare . . .' She laughed and put the spade back against the wall. 'It's so shiny and new, and I love the words you've chosen. Hipkin Gardens, it does sound grand. My father would have been delighted if he knew.'

'Maybe the dead do know what the living are doing, so perhaps he does know.'

'Yes, maybe you're right. I'm well on with the nibbles and organising the table and the cutlery and things. I just need you to attend to the drinks side and I'm nearly ready. What's it like out?'

'Mild for the time of year, but most important, it's fine.'

'I do hope I don't let you down.'

'Of course you won't. You'll be just right. Memorised your speech?'

'For the twentieth time, yes. It's not long.'

'Doesn't need to be. I'm going for a rest after I've done the drinks. I'll lie on the bed and watch you getting ready.'

'That won't take long, I'm all clean on underneath. I've only got to take my dress off and put my new suit on. I've been thinking of buying trousers to wear on cold days in the winter. Would I look silly, do you think?'

'With your figure, Muriel, you'll look enchanting.'

'Thank you. You're so good for my self-esteem. I'd none before we married.'

'I've done you a good turn then?'

'Oh yes, indeed you have. I'm so pleased about Arthur and the farm. You did the right thing there.'

'It was your idea.'

'No it wasn't, it was yours.'

'You may not have suggested it, but you planted the seed.'

'Ralph, we must stop talking, I'm going to be late!'

'Muriel, you've never been late in your life!'

The sun came out as the crowd gathered to watch Muriel put in the first spade. Ralph had persuaded the builders to hang bunting around the trees, and they had improvised a small dais covered with a huge union jack for Muriel to stand on while she made her speech. There was quite a strong wind blowing and she was glad of the microphone; it was hateful to go to listen to a speech and then not be able to hear, and her voice wasn't strong. She felt incredibly nervous. There were far more people there than she had anticipated. Everyone had come round to Ralph's way of thinking and she was so grateful, if there'd been protesters there she would have been devastated. As it was she was having to summon up all her courage. Being on the sidelines fitted her personality better. She pulled the microphone down to her height and began her speech.

'Ladies and gentlemen. It gives me great pleasure on this wonderfully special day to plunge in the ceremonial spade, beautifully inscribed to commemorate this special occasion to which Ralph and I have looked forward for so long. As many of you will know, my father, and generations of my family before him, were head gardeners at the Big House. When the estate was sold we moved away and at the time I had no idea that I would ever come back here again. But life has come full circle and I'm standing here with Ralph my husband, whom I have to confess was a childhood sweetheart of mine' – the crowd cheered goodnaturedly at this – 'to inaugurate the start of the building of houses for the village. The two of us have planned and schemed and worried about the designs, because we so wanted the houses to be exactly right for country people to live in. A glazed porch over the back door for boots and the dog's water bowl, central heating, good-sized bedrooms, not rabbit hutches, two bathrooms so there's no queue in the mornings, and a good-sized garage because country people need cars nowadays, and if you haven't got one then you can always put the things you're saving for the scout jumble sale in there, and lovely pleasant gardens too. We shall be retaining most of the lovely trees which we all find so delightful, so Hipkin Gardens will be a lovely leafy place to live. We've already got three names on our list of people interested in renting, so hopefully they will all be occupied as they become ready. I do hope they will be a useful and pleasant addition to our village. I hereby declare the commencement of the building of Hipkin Gardens.'

Muriel stepped down from the dais and took hold of the spade. She grasped it tightly and, placing her foot on the top, pushed it firmly into the ground and removed the first sod.

Cheering and clapping broke out amongst the crowd and Muriel, having had her moment in the limelight, quietly stood back for Ralph to say a few words. He mentioned the opposition, but in a kindly and understanding way, and said how pleased he was that now everyone agreed that the eight houses would be of great benefit to the village. He caught Arthur's eye and smiled. A few of the crowd craned their necks to see who he was smiling at, and glanced at each other with knowing looks.

Finally, Peter said a prayer for the happiness and wellbeing of the people who would be living in the houses, and then Ralph asked everyone home for champagne.

Muriel and he led the way across the green to their house. She still missed Pericles running to greet her when she came home, but the press of all their friends and neighbours pouring up the lane behind them put him out of her mind.

For the first half an hour Muriel was frantically busy attending to everyone's needs. Ralph and Peter opened the champagne and Ralph proposed a toast 'To Hipkin Gardens!' They all clinked their glasses and drank the toast and then flocked to the dining room, where Muriel had laid out the food. There were people everywhere, in the sitting room, squeezed in the study, sitting on the stairs, and the hubbub was deafening.

Deep in conversation on the stairs were Venetia Mayer and Pat. Ralph offered to refill their glasses. 'Oh, yes please, Sir Ralph. Thank you very much.' Pat took a sip of her champagne and listened to Venetia chatting up her host.

'Thank you, Sir Ralph. What a lovely speech Lady Templeton gave. You've done the village a really good turn deciding to build these houses. It's just what's needed. Glad to see you looking so much better, you gave us all quite a turn when you had your heart attack, it's lovely to see you up and about. And looking so well. It certainly hasn't harmed your good looks. Still as handsome as ever!'

Ralph bowed in acknowledgement. Pat nudged Venetia. 'I don't know how you dare to speak to him like that.'

'Like what? I was only making him feel good. I read somewhere that you should try to make everyone you meet feel better for having spoken to you, so that's what I was doing.'

'Oh yes, sometimes you do go over the top with it though. Especially with one person I could mention.'

'Who's that?'

'Craddock Fitch.'

At the mention of his name Venetia jumped and knocked Pat's elbow, whereupon she spilled her champagne and it splashed on Venetia's suit.

'Oh, I'm so sorry, it hasn't spoiled it, has it?'

'No, I'll dab it off, it'll be all right.'

Pat watched her drying the splashes and, not to be put off by the incident, pressed home with her quest for some inside information.

'He seems to come to the Big House a lot.'

'Well, he's interested in making sure everyone is satisfied.'

'Is *he* satisfied?' Pat said with a knowing wink.

Venetia wriggled out of that by saying, 'Jeremy would be sacked and so would I if he wasn't satisfied with our work.'

Venetia grinned. Pat gave her a dig in the ribs and a wink. 'Yer can't do nothing in this village yer know, without us all finding out. I've written to Mr Fitch. Done it all official like. Told 'im we want to move into the house and Dad get the job permanent. Oh Venetia, yer've no idea how much I'm looking forward to it. A big house, all those bedrooms, and with our Dean studying so much it's just what he needs, his own room.'

'I'm quite envious of you, Pat. It's a lovely house. That view across Sykes Wood!'

'I know. I've looked round it with the kids and mi dad. Our Michelle's in 'er element. She's in charge of the gardening at the school, yer know. Green fingers, Mr Palmer says she has. So she's looking forward to 'elping Dad. And really it's you I've got to thank for putting in a good word for us.'

'That's all right, Pat. You can invite me to tea one day when you get settled.'

'Oh, right I will. Can't invite yer where I live now, but when we've moved I will, that's a date. Just going to find the bathroom.'

'With the new house, and working for Jimbo and the school, things are looking up for you, aren't they?'

Pat gave Venetia a thumbs-up and wandered off. She requested directions and Muriel pointed her the way. As she went up the stairs she heard voices. Rounding the bend she came upon Linda from the Store and Alan Crimble. They were standing close together on the landing. Alan was holding Linda's hand and she was straightening his hair. 'You should comb it over to this side, Alan, it looks more modern like that. Oh!' They hastily broke apart when they saw Pat.

'What are you two up to then? Canoodling, eh? Whatever next?'

Linda retorted, 'You mind your own business, Pat Duckett.'

Alan patted Linda's arm. 'Now, now, Linda.' He spoke to Pat. 'Linda and me's going out together.'

'Oh, my word. That's a turn-up for the book. What a surprise!'

Rather defiantly, Linda began to say, 'We've been going out since . . .'

'Since that day I saved Sir Ralph's life. That's when it started.'

'I thought how wonderful he was. Saving a life like that.' She gazed up at him adoringly.

'Well, he was wonderful. Certainly redeemed himself, and no mistake.'

'In fact, you can be the first to know.' Alan took hold of Linda's hand. 'We're getting engaged at Christmas.'

'Engaged! That's quick work, I must say. Still neither of yer's spring chickens. You must be thirty-seven or eight, Linda, if yer a day. Yer've worked in the Store since before I got married. You've seen some changes there, and not half. Remember old Mrs Thornton? Disgusting it was. No hygiene at all. And you, Alan, 'ow old are you?'

'Thirty-two.'

'Well then, there you are. Why waste time 'anging about. Get on with it, I say. Have yer planned where yer going to live?'

'We're thinking of asking to rent one of Sir Ralph's houses.'

'Good idea. Considering what you did for 'im, yer should be top of the list. Got to go, I'm dying.'

As Pat returned downstairs into the fray she found the Rectory twins sitting side by side on the bottom step. Alex had a piece of cake in his hand, and Beth a small bowl filled with crisps. She was feeding them to Alex, who was obediently eating them. In between she kept popping one into her own mouth.

'Well now, you two, can your Auntie Pat squeeze between you?' They both looked up. Beth shuffled along a little and made enough room for Pat to get by. She paused for a moment and watched them. Beth was dressed in a dark-pink flowered long-sleeved dress, with a white collar and cuffs. In her blonde curly hair Caroline had tied a matching ribbon. Her tights were dark-pink, and on her feet she had a pair of black patent leather shoes. Alex was dressed in red; red tartan shirt with a bow tie, matching tartan trousers and a smart plain red waistcoat. For once, his mop of reddish-blond hair was neatly combed and smoothed down. They both looked up at her and smiled.

Beth offered her a crisp. 'Cri'p, Aun'ie Pa'?'

'Oh, thank you, Beth. Talking, are yer now?'

Alex shouted. 'Yes!'

Caroline came rushing out of the dining room. 'Oh! Thank goodness they're there. I need eyes at the back of my head with these two. They're into everything.'

'Aren't they growing up? Beth's just given me a crisp. She called me Auntie Pat.'

'Really? She's just begun talking, actually. Peter's been quite worried about her. She's always let Alex do it all up until now. So pleased to hear about the house, Pat. You must be delighted. I haven't met your father, is he here?'

'No. Doesn't socialise much. And he's a teetotaller, so you won't be seeing him in The Royal Oak either. Soon as the paperwork's gone through we'll be moving in. Can't wait.'

'You deserve it, Pat.'

'Can I ask something? Will you and the rector be going to the Bonfire Party up at the Big House?'

'We've had an invite popped through the door, and I think probably we shall. It is awkward though, isn't it?' She nodded her head in the direction of Ralph, who was seeing someone off at the door.

'Exactly. I mean, I can't refuse in the circumstances. Do you know if Sir Ralph's going?'

'No idea. Haven't mentioned it. Bit tricky really.' Caroline smiled at her, scooped up the twins, one under each arm, because they'd begun to sprinkle crisps on Muriel's hall carpet, and went to find Peter. It was time they went; the twins had behaved well for quite long enough, and she could see problems arising shortly.

'Excuse me, darling, I think it's time we went home.' The twins began protesting, wriggling and shouting to get down. Peter took Beth from under Caroline's right arm and swung her up into the air. Alex shouted, 'Alex. Dada. Alex. Up.' He swung Beth up twice more and then put her down and picked up Alex. He swung him up into the air and Alex screamed his delight.

'Peter! We really must go!'

'Yes, we must. Before trouble starts. Right, Alex, that's enough. Off we go. Go find Auntie Moo and Uncle Ralph.' They found them by the front door saying goodbyes.

Sheila Bissett and Ron were just leaving. 'Thank you so much for inviting us, we have enjoyed ourselves, haven't we Ron? These houses can only be good for the village, I'm so pleased it's all going ahead. See you at the Bonfire Party!' She twinkled her fingers at Ralph and stepped out into the road. Ron shook hands with Muriel and Ralph and followed her across the green.

Caroline kissed Muriel and thanked her. 'Do hope the twins haven't made too much mess. They're just at that age. Sorry.'

Ralph said, 'Don't worry, they've behaved excellently for two such small people.' He patted their heads, but Beth reached up and pursed her lips. She wanted to give him a kiss. So he bent down and she kissed him. 'Bye, bye, Raff. Bye, bye, Moo.' She leapt off the threshold and landed on the stone step. Peter caught her hand before she ran into the road. The four of them waved and went up Church Lane to the Rectory.

Muriel and Ralph stayed by the door to say goodbye to all their guests.

'Thank you for coming.'

'Glad you enjoyed it.'

'Thanks for your help.'

'Thank you again, it's been lovely.'

'Mind how you drive after all that champagne!'

Arthur and his wife Celia were among the last to leave. Arthur shook Ralph's hand and said, 'Thanks, Ralph, for inviting us. I'm very pleased about the houses, it's a grand gesture which will revitalise the village.'

Ralph smiled. 'Thank you, I'm glad I've got your approval. Glad you've forgiven me! That grandson of yours, Sebastian, is a charming boy, you must be proud of him.'

Arthur acknowledged the compliment and said, 'We're proud of the girls too, aren't we Celia?' They stepped out into the road and waved goodbye.

Harriet kissed Ralph and Muriel and said, 'Glad you got your own way, it's a very good thing for the village. I knew they'd all come round in the end.'

Jimbo said, 'Got to dash, children home from school soon. Thanks for a lovely time. Come along, Harriet. We shall be late.'

Muriel fell into bed that night completely exhausted. She listened for Ralph bringing up her camomile tea. She needed something to calm her jangled nerves. Still, the whole event had been a complete success. She'd provided far too much food, but most of it she'd put in the freezer for another time. So many people had come to the ceremony. Thank goodness they'd all decided to approve. She couldn't bear disharmony, no, she really couldn't.

She could hear Ralph coming up the stairs. He laid the tray on her bedside table. 'Thank you for making it such a splendid day, Muriel. You were wonderful. Can a husband give his very best and only wife a thank-you gift?'

'Oh Ralph!' Muriel sat up. 'Have you bought me a present?' He sat on the edge of the bed.

'Yes, I have. It took a lot of choosing. I do hope you like it. I do know it's the right size.' From his dressing-gown pocket he took a small velvet box. Muriel almost snatched it from him. She'd never grown blasé about his gifts; she was still as she had been as a child, so grateful that someone thought enough about her to buy her a present.

She lifted the lid of the tiny box and inside, nestled in the black velvet, was the most beautiful diamond ring she had ever seen. It had a big central diamond and on either side a triangle of smaller diamonds. The stones glinted and sparkled in the light from her lamp.

'Oh Ralph, I love my engagement ring but this . . . why, it's wonderful. Just wonderful.' He put it on her finger and it fitted perfectly.

She kissed him and said, 'Thank you, dear, from the bottom of my heart. I'm so happy. I've got you, and everyone in the village likes what we're doing about the spare land, so everything in the garden is lovely. I couldn't be any happier. No, I really couldn't.'

24

But there was just one matter which was worrying Muriel, and she hadn't yet found the right words to introduce it to Ralph. Considering the blinding mistake she'd made when the problem first arose, it was more than likely she never would find the right words.

She decided to ask Jimbo's advice. No, she'd ask Caroline's advice; Jimbo was too involved. Yes, she'd ask Caroline for coffee, no she wouldn't, because she couldn't guarantee Ralph wouldn't be in. No, she'd go to the Rectory or perhaps catch Caroline in the Store or helping at the church with something. Yes, she'd ask her then. Because it was already 1 November and only four more days to go. He'd read the leaflet with his morning post, he must have seen the posters in the church hall and in the church porch, and yet he'd never said a word.

No, she wouldn't wait, she'd go round this morning. Caroline never minded visitors, though sometimes it was possible to catch her at the most inopportune moments. Alex and Beth had certainly changed the lifestyle in the Rectory. She remembered the day she had called round with some things for the white elephant stall, and there was water dripping through the kitchen ceiling because Alex had managed to turn the washbasin tap full on and it had overflowed, Beth had scribbled on some work Peter had ready to go to the printers, and Caroline had just found that Alex had come down the stairs with a crayon in his hand and drawn a line on the wallpaper all the way down.

Muriel called about eleven. Sylvia had taken the twins out for a walk in their pushchair, in the rather vain hope that they would both fall asleep for a while. Caroline was clearing up toys, and Peter was in his study.

'Is it Peter you've come to see?'

'No, it's you. Is it convenient?'

'It is. I'm just about to stop for coffee. Then when Sylvia comes back I shall take over and she can have hers. Come through into the kitchen.'

They chatted about this and that, and when the coffee was ready Caroline sat in her rocking chair and said, 'I'm all ears.' Muriel sat at the kitchen table because rocking chairs made her feel seasick.

'The Bonfire Party.'

'Oh yes. Are you going?'

'Well, that's just it. Normally Ralph and I discuss everything, but I made such a mess of it at the dinner party I daren't mention it, and he hasn't either. Are you going?'

'Apparently most of the village is waiting to hear what Ralph is doing.'

'Oh dear. I desperately want to go. I know it won't be the same as when I was a child, but it was the highlight of the year for me. The smell of the woodsmoke, the cold wind up on the field, the feel of the hot potato through my gloves, and the frizzling of the sparklers. I loved it all.'

'Well, Peter and I . . .' The doorbell rang. 'Excuse me, I'll go and answer that. Peter's writing his sermon, he won't want disturbing.'

Muriel could hear voices in the hall, and then Peter's study door opening. Caroline came back into the kitchen and said, 'That was Craddock Fitch for Peter. Peter and I are going. With it starting at six, we're taking the twins for an hour and then coming home.'

'I see.'

'Me being me, I think being honest is best. Quite simply, ask him if he's going. Straight out. If he definitely doesn't want to go, but if you decide you do, come in the car with us. We can squeeze you in, the only problem is I think the fireworks will frighten the children, they're a bit young for revelling in loud bangs, so we may come home early. It will be good fun, won't it? It will be quite like old times, really, for you.'

'I won't go if he won't, thank you all the same. No, I couldn't.' She gazed out of the kitchen window, deep in thought. She was being childish. She wouldn't mention it. She hadn't got Caroline's sound common sense. No, she'd leave it to Ralph.

They heard the study door open: Peter's voice boomed out across the hall. 'Caroline! have you a minute?'

'Excuse me, I won't be long.'

Muriel heard a shriek of delight from Caroline, a lot of laughter, and her saying, 'Unbelievable. Many, many thanks. Greatly appreciated. The village will be delighted. We can go straight ahead now. That's solved all our problems, believe me.'

What on earth were they talking about? The front door shut and Peter and Caroline came into the kitchen. Peter was waving a piece of paper in the air.

'Muriel! Believe it or believe it not, Craddock Fitch has just given us fifteen thousand pounds for the church central heating! Can you imagine that? Look, here it is.' He held the cheque for Muriel to see. In bold, confident writing were the words 'fifteen thousand pounds' and a flourishing signature; H. Craddock Fitch.

In a tone somewhat less than enthusiastic, Muriel said, 'How wonderful.' This cheque made matters even worse. Fifteen thousand pounds to buy himself the position of Lord of the Manor. That was Ralph's place. Yes, it was. He was the gentleman. Close to tears, she stood up, thanked Caroline for the coffee and her advice, and went home.

Peter and Caroline looked at each other.

Peter asked, 'Should I go after her?'

'No, leave it. She and Ralph need to get things straight between them. This cheque blessed well won't have helped, though. You can see his strategy, can't you? Paying for the heating, reintroducing the Bonfire Party, buying Pat's cottage. It's as plain as the nose on your face. An awful lot will depend on whether Ralph decides to go to the Party on Saturday.'

Muriel found she'd locked herself out, so she had to ring the bell.

'I'm so sorry, I forgot my key.'

'You're back early. I thought you would be gone for the morning. Caroline busy, is she?'

'Sylvia had the twins out in the pushchair, and Peter was writing his sermon, so we had the kitchen to ourselves.'

'You didn't stay long, though?'

'No, I didn't. Oh, you've had coffee.'

'Yes, I am capable of making my own you know, my dear. Well, sometimes.'

'I see. I'll just go and do some little jobs upstairs. I've the ironing to put away, and I want to get your suit out ready for the cleaners and . . .'

Ralph took her hand. 'Muriel, my dear. What is the matter? I can see you're upset. Tell me, please, and if I can put it right I shall. Nil desperandum.'

'I don't want to hurt *anyone* and most of all I don't want to hurt you. But I have done, or rather I *did* do. Now I can't mention it again.' Muriel paused for a moment and then continued. 'But I've got to.'

'Come in the sitting room and sit beside me and tell me everything. What are husbands for if not for solving problems?'

'But that's just it. You *are* the problem.'

'Me?' He struck an attitude of mock despair. 'Are you – are you wanting a divorce? So soon! So soon!'

'Ralph! How could you? I'm going to come straight out with it.' She took a deep breath and asked, 'Are we going to the party on Saturday up at the Big House?'

He let go of her hand. 'Ah!'

'Apparently the village is waiting to see what you are going to do.'

'Are they indeed?'

'Matters are even worse than that. You know he's buying Pat's cottage, and who can blame her? Well, now, this morning, he's been to the Rectory and given Peter the fifteen thousand pounds to pay for the church heating. Something we couldn't expect he could refuse, either. So now you know it all. And I'm sorry and I don't know what to do. And oh! Ralph I *do* want to go to the party, but if you say no then no it will be.'

Ralph stood up and went to the window looking out over the green.

'Has he, by Jove? Determined devil, isn't he? Just think. When my father went to war in 1939 he owned every cottage in this village. His ancestors gave the church the land it stands on, he owned the woods, the fields, the spare land, Prior's Farm, and his word was law round here. In the space of just fifty years all I own is this house, which I've had to buy, and now the spare land and by the middle of next year eight houses on it. Times change.' He stood lost in thought. Muriel sat watching, twisting her handkerchief round and round in her hands. Twice she nearly spoke, and twice she resisted the temptation.

When he did continue, his tone was so vehement he made her jump. 'I'm damned if that chap is going to get the better of me. Financially he very definitely has the edge, but where the people of this village are concerned, if I can keep faith with them, he won't win in the end. He might think he has, but he won't have. So yes, damn it, we shall go, and we shall damned well enjoy ourselves, or at least look as if we are. Make sure everyone knows.'

Muriel clapped her hands and rushed across the room to him. She took his hands in hers and kissed them both. 'Oh Ralph, what a good decision. How absolutely perfectly right. Don't worry, I'll make sure they all know. That Oriana Duncan-Lewis will spoil it for me, her lighting the bonfire, indeed! But I shall look the other way till she's done it.'

Ralph smiled indulgently. 'It won't alter anything, doing that.'

'No, it won't, but it will make *me* feel better! I really think I might need some extra bits and pieces for lunch. I'm off to the Store.' She set off with a glad heart; in fact she felt like standing in the middle of the green and shouting out her news to whoever cared to listen. She just hoped the Store would be full of people and then the news would spread like wildfire.

*

Sadie Beauchamp was at the till when she went in, and best of all there were plenty of customers about.

Sadie called out, 'Morning, Muriel. How's things?'

'Oh very good, thank you, Sadie. Yes, very good indeed.' In a loud voice she asked, 'Shall we be seeing you at the bonfire on Saturday?'

Barry's mother's head popped up over the top of the breakfast cereals. 'You going then, Lady Templeton?'

'Oh yes, indeed we are. My husband and I are really looking forward to it. Let's hope the weather's good.'

'Oh, well, that's all right then, we didn't want to miss all the fun.' She raised her voice and shouted, ''Ear that, everybody? Sir Ralph's going! I hear there's going to be a big buffet in the marquee! They've been putting it up this week.'

'Really?'

'Oh yes, Mr Charter-Plackett's catering so it's bound to be good.'

'And there's going to be toffee apples and presents for any children going.'

'And Mr Charter-Plackett's doing the fireworks, isn't he, Mrs Beauchamp?'

'Yes, he's up there now planning it all.'

'Hope he's got some o' them mighty big rockets. I love seeing them going up.'

'There's to be a Guy Fawkes. Specially made with fireworks in 'im.'

'No! Just 'ope it doesn't look like old Fitch! Not after the last time. Right put the lid on it, that would!'

'Who's lighting the bonfire, Mrs Beauchamp?'

'As I do not have the ear of Mr Fitch, I'm afraid I can't help you on that score.'

Barry's mother nudged her neighbour. 'Liar. We all know she knew him years ago, and they've been seen out together. Sat in the back of his Roller with the chauffeur strutting his stuff in the front.'

'No! Really?'

Barry's mother nudged her neighbour again and whispered, 'Bit of blooming good luck for her and not half, he's a right catch, with all that money. Bit of a cold fish, but so what? Wouldn't mind him myself.'

'Get on, what would your Vince say?'

'I wouldn't ask him!' They chortled together behind the cereals, but Muriel ignored them. If Barry's mother knew, then the whole village would know before long. Satisfied with her efforts she paid for her shopping and left. As she stepped out into Stocks Row, she found Sheila Bissett tying Pom to the post Jimbo had provided for dog owners.

'Good morning, Sheila.'

'Good morning, Muriel. I do miss seeing your Pericles out and about. I expect you miss him too.'

'Oh yes, I do. Good morning, Pom.' She bent down to stroke him. 'He does do well for his age, doesn't he?'

'Shall we be seeing you on Saturday? You and Sir Ralph?'

'Yes, you shall. We're really looking forward to it.'

'Oh good. It'll be a bit upsetting for you both, but time marches on, doesn't it? We all have to adapt.'

'Yes, we do. Let's hope it doesn't rain.'

'Let's hope so.'

25

In the dark of the early evening of Guy Fawkes Day, Pat Duckett, Dean and Michelle were standing outside the Head Gardener's house, savouring thoughts about moving in.

'Won't it be lovely, Mum? A whole big bedroom to myself. And one for you too.' Michelle gazed up at the blank windows, picturing herself sitting at one of them looking out over the gardens, wearing a beautiful white dress with an open book resting on her lap, like that lady she'd seen in that old film on the telly.

Dean kicked a lump of brick across the rough grass. 'I'll need a desk, Mum. With a chair and some bookshelves. I'll have to have a bike. Can't walk all that way to the school bus and back.'

'So will I, won't I, Mum?'

Pat nodded. 'We'll all three need bikes. And you'll need a new bed, Dean. That one of yours is going to the tip. We'll get you a lovely long one. Yer growing that fast, you'll be needing a chair at the end for yer feet with that old thing you've got now. Wonder if yer grandad still has his driving licence. Maybe we could even afford a car after a while. Then 'e could take us out for rides. Might even go on 'oliday.'

Michelle's eyes lit up. 'On holiday? Oh Mum, just think, on holiday!'

'We'll have to watch the pennies, mind. No silly spending. Perhaps we could rent a cottage by the sea. Yes, I'd fancy . . .' She heard footsteps in the dark. 'Who's there? Who is it?'

'Only me!' Through the gloom the three of them could see the outline of Grandad. He came to stand beside them. 'Come to see our new abode. By heck, kids, we've landed on our feet here, haven't we?' He gazed up at the front of the house. 'Chosen which bedroom you want? I'd like one big enough to have a comfortable chair in it with my own telly. Can't stand them daft programmes you kids watch.'

Michelle said her grandad could have the biggest one, then. 'Right thanks, that'll do nicely. Greenwood Stubbs, Head Gardener, accepts with pleasure. You and me, we'll turn this place round and not half, Michelle.' He gave her a friendly conspiratorial nudge. 'All it needs is dedication, and I've got plenty of that. Don't expect you'll be helping, will yer, Dean?'

'Might. If yer pay me.'

'Oh. Well, we'll need casual labour from time to time, so I'll put you at the top of my list.'

'Put Rhett on yer list as well, Grandad.'

'Rhett? Who's he when he's at home?'

'Rhett Wright from next door.'

'We'll put his name down as well then. With a moniker like that he needs all the help he can get. Will he work hard, though?'

'Do anything for money, will Rhett. Come on then.'

Pat asked, 'Shall we need net curtains, do you think?' But no one answered, they'd all set off to the bonfire.

She stood listening to the silence. Be lovely living up here. What with the bathroom, and the modern kitchen. A whole new start. Well, wherever you are Duggie, either down there or up yonder, at least now yer know the Ducketts are doing better than expected. Oh yes, much better than expected. Yes, this Christmas was looking good. She'd be off to the sales after, buying furniture and things. She ambled off, hampered by her fur boots and thick trousers. Pat pushed her scarf back from her face and, looking up at the clear starry sky, watched a rocket exploding. That was just how she felt. Explosive. Yes, exploding with joy.

Pat cut through the neglected kitchen garden, opened the door in the wall and stepped out onto the path. From where she stood she could see the crowds arriving for the Party. Old Fitch had erected floodlights so the whole of Home Farm field was illuminated. The marquee erected to one side was glowing softly, and people were going in and out carrying trays and boxes. The bonfire was enormous. You could have thought it was Coronation night or something. Perched right on top was the guy. She chuckled to herself. What a scream it had been, making that dummy of old Fitch. It was Dean's idea to spray a mophead for his hair. Looked a treat, it did. What a laugh they'd had, but it'd done the trick. If ever he found out she'd helped . . . Ruthless, he was. But no matter, he'd transformed her life. She went gleefully down the slope to join the throng.

Muriel and Ralph were walking to Home Farm field by cutting through the churchyard and using the little gate in the wall, which had been put there dozens of years ago so that the Templetons could walk to church from the Big House without having to go the roundabout way via the drive. The gate was stiff, and Ralph had to struggle with it to get it open.

Weeds had twined themselves around it and grass was growing in the hinges.

Muriel held the torch for him while he forced it open. 'We shouldn't really be using this, should we?'

'He won't know, will he? I don't expect anyone else remembers about this gate.'

'I do. It's a special gate for me. You stand that side and I'll stand this side and we'll kiss like we did when we thought we were leaving Turnham Malpas forever. I was twelve and you were fourteen. I can even remember the dress I was wearing.' They had their commemorative kiss, and then hand in hand in the dark they wended their way along the disused path towards the floodlit field. 'I'm determined to enjoy myself tonight, no matter what.'

Ralph squeezed her hand. 'So am I. I hear there's a beer tent as well as the marquee, so I shall visit that and get my money's worth out of him!'

'Well, as you're not driving, I expect you can. Do you know, I've never seen you worse for drink?'

'My dear, you never shall. Merry, perhaps, but never under the influence. Have you a key in case we lose each other?'

Muriel felt in her coat pocket. 'Yes, I have.' Her eyes alight with anticipation, she strode forward. Ralph looked at her face as they came within the arc of the floodlights. She looked not a day older than twelve. No one looking at her now could imagine for one moment the heights of passion he had released in her. He just hoped they had plenty more years left in which to enjoy their new-found delights, despite this dratted heart business. He felt a tug at his overcoat. Looking down he found little Beth standing beside him, her mouth pursed ready for a kiss. 'Raff! Ki'. Raff.' He bent down to receive her kiss. 'Now, Beth, where's your mummy? Muriel! just a moment dear, Beth's here and there's no one with her.'

'Oh dear. Oh dear. Caroline will be desperate. Beth, where's Mummy? Where is she?'

'Mummy gone.' She put her hand confidently in Muriel's. Ralph and Muriel anxiously scanned the growing crowd. Then Ralph shouted, 'That's Peter, over there. He looks frantic.' Ralph shouted and waved his arms and Peter, turning his head this way and that in his anxious search for Beth, suddenly caught sight of Ralph and came running across.

'Thank God!' He swung Beth up into his arms and hugged her. 'Daddy's been wondering where you were, Beth. I'm sorry, but you're going to have your reins on.' She began struggling when she saw him pull the reins out of his pocket. 'No. No.'

'Yes. Yes. Sorry.' He persevered with Beth as she twisted this way and that to stop him getting the reins on her. 'Caroline has Alex and I'm supposed to be in charge of Beth, I'm not doing a very good job, am I? There, young lady, that's you secure. Aren't we lucky having such a wonderful evening for the bonfire? It's all going to be perfectly splendid. I have never seen such a huge bonfire, have you?'

'No. But then he would want the biggest and the best!' Ralph commented. Peter looked sorrowfully at him and Ralph apologised. 'Sorry. He is trying hard, too hard perhaps. Come, Muriel, into the fray.'

Peter relayed a message to them. 'Mr Fitch has suggested we use the front hall for our drinks and buffet. He said if I saw you would I say you would be most welcome to join him, before the fire is lit. They're turning out the floodlights at a quarter past six and then lighting the bonfire. So you're invited right now.'

'Shall we go, my dear?'

'Oh yes, just to be polite, but then I want to be outside after that.'

'Of course. Lead the way, Peter.' Ralph found Beth's little hand stealing a grip on his, and she wanted Peter and him to swing her as they walked. Ralph had a lump in his throat.

The hall was brightly lit. The reception desk had been cleared of papers and telephones and a small buffet had been laid out. Behind the buffet stood Venetia, and by a small table beside the desk stood Jeremy, helping to serve drinks. Oriana, Sadie, and Mr Fitch were already there, and Caroline too, with Alex.

Venetia, looking tense, was serving Oriana with a plate of food. 'A couple of canapés too? So fattening all these things, aren't they, but so tempting. We've Jimbo to blame for that. He always caters so wonderfully you can't resist. Staying the night, are you?'

Oriana Duncan-Lewis pointedly ignored Venetia's question. 'That will be sufficient, thank you. I'll get myself a drink. Oh, there's champagne! Craddock knows how much I love champagne. He's such a dear, isn't he, and so thoughtful.'

Venetia, unsettled by Oriana's imperious manner and seething with jealousy, answered between gritted teeth. 'Very thoughtful, oh yes. Always so considerate.' Oriana's reply was a scathing look. She thanked Jeremy for the champagne he'd handed to her. Knowing that Venetia was watching, she caught Mr Fitch's eye and with a very possessive, intimate look silently toasted him.

He briskly acknowledged her salute and then went to welcome Ralph and Muriel. Shaking hands with them, he said, 'Please call me Craddock. It's ridiculous to be excessively formal nowadays. May I call you Ralph and Muriel?' The two of them agreed. Taking Muriel to the buffet, he asked her what she would like. 'I'll have a gin and tonic but nothing to eat, thank you, Craddock. I will take a jacket potato to eat by the bonfire, if you don't mind.'

'Not at all. Do exactly as you wish. You're my guest, so help yourself whenever you wish. I'm delighted that you've come. I'm here to stay, so we may as well get on with each other as best we can. I shall be having the Village Show here too. Is it possible I might be able to enlist your help with that?' He smiled at her.

Muriel replied, 'I should have to give it my consideration.'

'Please do. We can't let the village miss out just because we don't see eye to eye, can we?' He looked at his watch. 'It's almost time for lighting the bonfire. Where's Oriana?' He looked across the hall at her. She didn't reply because she was having an angry confrontation with Sadie.

'I've told you, I mean what I say!'

Sadie laughed. 'So, we go, just once, to the theatre to a première for which Craddock had been given two tickets. That hardly constitutes a major relationship.'

'Well, don't you get any bright ideas. He's mine and don't you forget it.'

'Yours?' Sadie laughed. 'Since when has anyone been able to claim Henry Craddock Fitch as their own?'

'As from now. Keep off!'

The two of them became aware that their raised voices were being overheard. Oriana looked highly embarrassed. Sadie merely looked amused. 'Craddock, I understand Oriana has a ball and chain attached to your ankle.' She pointedly studied his feet. 'I can't see it?' Oriana flushed dark red.

Mr Fitch snapped out his answer. 'You won't. There isn't one. I think, my dear Oriana, you've overstepped the mark.'

'Overstepped the mark? But you and I . . .'

Mr Fitch grimaced '. . . Are friends, that's all. Sadie is a lady who holds a special place in my esteem. I don't care to have her spoken to in such a manner.'

Oriana became not only indignant but very angry. In a low voice she said, 'How dare you treat me in such a cavalier fashion in front of your guests? How dare you?'

Sadie intervened. 'Steady, Oriana, it never does to throw a temper with Craddock. I did once, and lived to regret it.'

'I shall throw as many tempers as I like. Well, Craddock, you haven't answered my question.' Glass in hand she went towards him. He stared fixedly at her and asked, 'I've forgotten. What was the question?'

For the moment anger had got the better of her and she couldn't remember. Mr Fitch laughed. 'Come, come, do calm down. Storm in a teacup.'

His patronising tone angered her even more and, frustrated at not being able to better him verbally, she threw the contents of her glass straight in his face. In a very controlled way he withdrew his handkerchief from his top pocket and wiped his face dry. When he had dried himself to his satisfaction he opened his mouth to speak, but Oriana forestalled him by screeching, 'You can light your own damned bonfire,' and storming out, leaving the assembled company stunned into silence. Before they had recovered themselves she returned to pick up her bag, which Alex had found and was taking to show his mother. She snatched it from his hands and as she stormed out a second time she shouted over her shoulder, 'I just wish you were the guy on top!'

Alex cried, Beth cried in sympathy, Muriel went bright red and Craddock Fitch stood grey-faced and tight-lipped. Ralph gave a wry smile, remembering just in time to turn his back to the other guests so they couldn't see how amused he was. Venetia, delighted at the turn of events, silently toasted Oriana with champagne. Sadie drained her glass and said 'Well! That brought that little confrontation to a satisfactory conclusion!' She picked up her gloves and left.

Muriel, in a rather high squeaking voice, said, 'I think I'll go outside to see what's going on.' Others followed her lead and they trailed after her, leaving Ralph and Mr Fitch alone.

'Well, Ralph, after that exhibition of ill breeding I appear to have no one to light my bonfire. Would you do me the honour? It would look foolish for me to light my own.'

'Yes, I will.'

'Thank you. Let's go.'

As they went out of the front door and crossed the lawn to the field, Arthur Prior and his family were crossing it on their way to join the party. 'Good evening, Arthur. Have you met Craddock Fitch?'

'No, we haven't had the pleasure.'

'May I introduce my cousin and his family, Craddock?' While he was doing the introductions an idea occured to Ralph. 'Now Sebastian, how would it be if you helped me to light the bonfire? Mr Fitch wouldn't mind, would you?'

'Of course not. He isn't a grandson of yours, is he? No, he can't be, of course he can't.'

'Unfortunately no, he isn't, but he's the next best thing.' Ralph took Sebastian's hand in his and together they marched with Mr Fitch onto the

Home Farm field. At a signal from him the floodlights were turned out, someone played a fanfare on a trumpet, and Ralph and Sebastian stepped forward to ignite the biggest bonfire Sebastian and everyone else had ever seen.

With Sebastian's help Ralph held the flaming torch, and the two of them went steadily round the great pile of wood, lighting it in the eight evenly-spaced places where oil-soaked kindling had been placed. The crowd waited for the flames to take hold, and suddenly they did and roared up into the sky. A great cheer went up. The flames lit all their faces, good and bad, young and old, friendly and hostile, plain and beautiful, joyous and sad. From the loud-speaker system boisterous brass-band music blared forth, and then the music was stopped while a voice announced that the beer tent was open and the jacket potatoes would be brought round shortly.

Muriel had tears in her eyes. Her heart had nearly burst with pleasure when she saw Sebastian helping Ralph. She felt so proud of Ralph. So proud. Two Templetons lighting the fire. How fitting. Things did have a way of working out. She pulled her wool hat a little closer about her ears. She'd forgotten how sharply the wind blew straight across this open field. Her jacket potato held in her gloved hands, Muriel went to find Ralph.

Pat still hadn't found the rest of her family. She'd been looking for them before the bonfire had been lit and still hadn't made contact. She just hoped Michelle was OK. The girl was so confident, like as not she'd wandered off. Pat didn't like the skin of jacket potatoes, so she found a convenient bush and popped her skin behind there, content in the thought that a badger or a fox might be glad to eat it during the night.

'Caught in the act. What you up to?'

Pat jumped and spun round to see who it was.

'You stupid thing, Barry. Gave me the shock of mi life, you did.' Pat pressed her hand to her heart.

'Pleased with yer kitchen, are you? Put a lot of work into it, I have. I bet you'll be cooking some real nice meals in there, and I thought that bit of blank wall near the door yer could have a table and chairs. Nice warm kitchen to eat yer porridge in on a morning.'

'Well, there's one thing for certain, *you* won't be eating *your* porridge in there.'

'Aw! Pat! I'm cut to the quick. We could make a right go of it, you and me!'

He tried encircling her with his arms, but she gave him a hefty push on his chest. 'Daft thing you are. Get off with yer. You've been drinking!'

'I haven't! It's you, yer get my blood racing! Don't send me packing. We'll go for a drink in the beer tent and toast your good luck. Right?'

Why not? Pat argued to herself. 'Right, yer on.'

'Tuck yer arm in mine, don't want yer tumbling on this rough grass before you've even had a drink.' The first person they met was Venetia, wending her way back to the Big House. Venetia winked and gave Pat the thumbs-up. How embarrassing. Then she thought, who cares?

Peter and Caroline had got separated again. Beth was tired and fractious and obviously wasn't going to stay awake long enough to see the fireworks. 'Harriet! Have you seen my dear wife anywhere?'

Flick spoke before Harriet could reply. 'Wasn't Sebastian lucky to get chosen to light the bonfire, Mr Harris? I wish it had been me. Are you staying for the fireworks? I am. I'm having a lovely time, are you, Mr Harris?'

'I am indeed, Flick. I'm glad you're well enough to come tonight. Don't overtire yourself, will you?'

'Daddy says I'm almost A1 at Lloyd's now. So no, I'm not tired. Dr Harris is in the marquee, we've just left her there.'

Harriet laughed. 'When this daughter of mine allows me to get a word in, she's looking for you because Alex is tired and she's wanting to go home.'

'Right, I'll head for the marquee, then. Hope the rest of the evening goes well.' He waved and turned to go, but was stopped by Sheila Bissett. With her was a tall girl, a feminine edition of Ronald Bissett.

Sheila, bubbling with pride, introduced her daughter. 'Oh Rector, this is my daughter Bianca, you've never met, have you? She's come back home to live with us. Bianca, this is Peter Harris, our rector.' Bianca held out her hand to shake Peter's. He changed Beth over to his other arm and shook hands saying, 'Welcome to Turnham Malpas, Bianca. Nice to meet you. You've got a new job, then, somewhere close?'

'No, not yet. The bank where I worked was downgraded, someone had to go and it was a case of last in, first out. I've got various feelers out, so I'm hoping to get somewhere shortly. Mother tells me you have a very vigorous choir at the church. I'm a choral singer, sang Verdi's *Requiem* only last month. I should love the opportunity of singing in the church choir.'

Peter, never wishing to turn down an offer of help in the church, hesitated a moment before replying. It was all male, and the choir master intended it staying that way.

'I should have to speak with the choir master, he prefers an all male choir, and the St Thomas à Becket choir has been all male since time immemorial . . . so I'm afraid . . .'

'Surely you're not going to exclude me on the basis of sex?' Bianca's dark eyes began to spark. There was something about the way she hesitated before she said 'sex' which made Peter feel uncomfortable.

'Oh, no, no certainly not on that basis. I wouldn't like to be thought old-fashioned, but he is in charge not me, but I will have a word with him.'

'I have very good secretarial skills, so while I'm at a loose end perhaps I could do some work for you?'

Sheila decided to put a word in for Bianca. 'You'd be pleased for some help, wouldn't you, Peter? You've got excellent computer skills, haven't you, dear?' Bianca, not taking her eyes from Peter's face, nodded and smiled. Pressing the matter further, Sheila continued. 'You have a computer in your study, haven't you, Peter?'

'Good evening.' They hadn't heard Caroline approaching. She'd been listening to the conversation and had decided to interrupt. 'Sheila. Bianca.' She nodded her head in greeting. 'Nice to meet you. I'm Peter's wife, Caroline. I wonder if you would mind awfully if Peter and I took the children home? They're both very tired and I think they're going to have the screaming abdabs once the fireworks start. Perhaps you could discuss your contribution to the parish another day. I really am anxious to leave.'

Bianca surveyed Caroline. She noted the expensive suede jacket, the well cut trousers, the Jaeger scarf at her neck, the air of authority. Caroline observed Bianca's bleached hair, her strong features, and she recognised the hungry speculative look of a woman reaching thirty and still without a man of her own, and desperately wanting one.

Peter, a little surprised by Caroline's manner, agreed they needed to leave. 'I'll think about what you've suggested and let you know. Nice to have met you. Enjoy the rest of the evening, won't you? Goodnight.'

'Goodnight, Rector, 'night, Dr Harris.' Sheila and Bianca waved as the Rectory party left.

Out of their hearing Peter said, 'You were rather abrupt, darling.' By the light of Caroline's torch they crossed the field towards their car.

'Sheila Bissett and I will never get on. The woman thoroughly irritates me. If that Bianca wants to sing in the choir, it will take all your diplomatic talents, believe me, to achieve a result.'

'I know, but I couldn't say no straight out, could I?'

'You're too kind and I love you for it. I can't spot the car. Where did we leave it? Oh, there it is. Perhaps not, but be warned. Open the door quickly, darling, Alex is getting awfully heavy, I think he's already fallen asleep. Predatory females are the last thing an attractive rector needs.'

They drove home in silence. Peter pulled up outside the Rectory, switched off the engine, and turned to look at Caroline. 'My darling girl, you may well be right. I simply didn't notice. I don't need to say, do I, that I shall do everything in my power to keep the woman at arm's length?'

'Just watch your step. Occupational hazard, I'm afraid. Extraordinarily uncanny, how like her father she is in her looks. Come on, let's get the children to bed.'

By the time the firework display was over Jimbo was shattered. It had been a busy Saturday in the Store, and the organisation of the display had been more taxing than he had anticipated. Clearing up had to be left until Sunday, and he was glad. Rhett Wright and Dean Duckett were lined up to help clear away first thing Sunday. He wasn't too sure about Rhett. There seemed to be something odd about him. But if he did a good job then Jimbo decided he wouldn't complain. He collected Harriet and the baby, Flick, who was looking as shattered as he felt, and the two boys, and they went into the Big House to say their goodbyes and thank yous to Mr Fitch.

He was standing talking to Ralph, Muriel and Sadie. As soon as Mr Fitch saw Jimbo he broke off his conversation and went across to speak to him.

'Charter-Plackett! Brilliant display. Brilliant! Thank you very much indeed. Send your invoice in and it shall be paid immediately. Now, children, you've got your toffee apples I see?'

The children thanked him. He picked up a cardboard box. 'Look, I've some spare ones here in the box. Why not take an extra one home, each of you? Would you like that?'

The three children said in unison, 'Yes, please, Mr Fitch,' and helped themselves from the box he was holding.

'Clever husband you have, Harriet. When I heard what he'd done, left the bank and opted for a village shop, I thought, what a fool. But maybe he isn't as much of a fool as I thought! I'm quite taking to this country life.'

Harriet thanked him and, making her apologies, shepherded the children out. Frances was sleeping in her pram and Mr Fitch pulled back the blanket and took a peep at her. His face softened. He patted her arm, said, 'Goodnight, young lady,' and went back to Ralph and Muriel.

'Now, have the three of you time for a drink in my flat before you go?'

They followed him up the stairs and along the corridors to his flat. When he'd settled the two ladies with their drinks he handed Ralph his whisky, and as he did so Mr Fitch said, 'I've a proposition to make to you,

Ralph. I should like to own some land around here – myself that is, not my company. These houses you're going to build. Now you've got planning permission, I wondered if you might be interested in selling the remainder of the land to me. Just the rest of the field, not the land the houses will be on. What do you say? I'll give you above the market valuation.'

Ralph was so staggered by his unexpected proposal that for a moment he was speechless.

Muriel answered indignantly. 'Certainly not! I wouldn't agree. It's Ralph's. It's ours. I won't allow it.'

Mr Fitch looked at Muriel and said, 'It's a joint venture then, is it?'

'Oh yes, it is.'

'I can't tempt *you* with money then? Not even above-market valuation? Surely it will tempt you, just a teeny little bit?'

'No, it won't. Will it, Ralph?'

Having collected his wits, Ralph ignored Muriel's question and asked Mr Fitch what he proposed to do with it; if he knew what he wanted it for he might, just might, be tempted. Muriel fumed. Mr Fitch smiled a little and replied, 'My ideas are not for public scrutiny yet. Suffice to say I want it and I'm willing to pay well for it. Now what do you say?'

'On the face of it, the offer is very tempting. Selling you the land would help finance the building of the houses, but I would want a good price, believe me, oh yes, a very good price. One can't afford to turn down a good offer, can one? I could well be tempted. Oh yes! I certainly could. Most definitely.'

Mr Fitch laughed triumphantly and thumped his fist against the palm of his other hand. 'Ha! I knew you'd see common sense.'

Muriel began to tremble with anger. She kept a tight grip on herself; after her last exhibition in front of Mr Fitch she daren't take any risks with her temper. But wait till she got Ralph home.

Ralph asked, 'What do you want to use it for?'

'As I've already said, I'm not disclosing that for the moment.'

Sadie interrupted their discussion. 'You know full well what you want to do with it, Craddock, for heaven's sake stop playing the business magnate and be honest for once.'

Mr Fitch's lips tightened into a straight line. He sometimes felt Sadie had too much to say for herself.

Ralph pressed on with what he wished to say. 'The use to which my land is put is of paramount importance to me. If I'm not told what you will use it for I simply will not sell, no matter how much you offer. What's more, when I think about it, I couldn't trust you not to do something which would spoil the whole village, and this village of ours takes precedence over any get-rich-quick schemes you might care to come up with.' He calmly put down his glass and, slowly taking a cigar case from his pocket, nonchalantly selected one and then asked, 'Do you mind if I smoke?' The others shook their heads and watched him light it.

Mr Fitch, exasperated by his attitude, permitted his anger to break through his iron control. 'Hah! You country gentry think you own the world. I'm sorry, but it's laughable.'

'I do own the world. Round here, that is.'

'Well, I have to say I'm here to stay and I intend to buy up every cottage that becomes available, every piece of land I can. I love it around here, I really feel as though I've "come home".'

'Indeed! That's good! I'm glad you love it, I do too and no one can stop you buying up houses and land. But there's one thing you won't buy and that is their hearts. They're mine!' He stretched wide the fingers of his upturned right hand and then, tensing his fingers, slowly closed them as though encompassing the entire village in his grasp. He held up his clenched fist to Mr Fitch. 'Mine! You can't buy their love and loyalty, they have to be earned over the years. And think on this, most of them only came tonight because they knew *I'd* agreed to come.' Ralph refrained from smiling triumphantly. He stood up. 'Now, Muriel, you must be ready to leave, I know I am. Thank you, Craddock, for a lovely evening. Very generous of you. Very. Goodnight, Sadie.'

Mr Fitch stood up when Muriel rose to her feet. He shook her hand and said, 'Well, I'm sorry you won't sell, very sorry. Sleep on it. You might change your mind. I can always live in hope!' He smiled pleadingly at her and then offered to see them to the main door. Ralph refused his courtesy. 'No thanks, Craddock. I actually do know my way out.' As the door to the flat closed behind them they heard Sadie say 'Touché!' and burst into peals of laughter. Ralph took Muriel's hand in his and led her along the corridors and down the staircase into the hall. He opened the main door and they stood looking out at the winter sky, enjoying the now frosty air and watching the glowing remnants of the bonfire across the field. Ralph blew a cloud of cigar smoke into the air and followed it with his eyes as it disappeared.

'Oh Ralph! You were wonderful! I'm so proud of you. To my shame, for one dreadful minute I really thought you *were* going to sell it to him.'

'He won't give up easily. But Fitch is not getting it. That land is the only land I own. Arthur Prior owns more than me. The years ahead could be very interesting, I'm looking forward to the challenge.'

He closed the door behind them and by the light of Muriel's torch they went down the neglected path to the gate in the churchyard wall, down the church path, out of the lych gate past Willie Bigg's and the Rectory, and on to home.